Gynaecology in Nursing Practice

Gynaecology in Nursing Practice

edited by

M.A. SHORTHOUSE, SRN, SCM, RNT
Formerly Gynaecological Ward Sister,
St Bartholomew's Hospital, London

and

M.G. BRUSH, BSc, MA, PhD
Senior Lecturer in Biochemistry,
St Thomas's Hospital Medical School, London

Baillière Tindall · London

A BAILLIÈRE TINDALL book published by
Cassell Ltd,
35 Red Lion Square, London WC1R 4SG

and at Sydney, Auckland, Toronto, Johannesburg

an affiliate of
Macmillan Publishing Co. Inc.
New York

First published 1981

ISBN 0 7020 0841 9

Phototypeset in Baskerville by Bookens, Saffron Walden, Essex
Printed in Great Britain by Lowe & Brydone, Leeds

British Library Cataloguing in Publication Data

Gynaecology in nursing practice.
1. Gynecologic nursing
I. Shorthouse, M A II. Brush, Michael George
618.1'0024613 RG105

ISBN 0-7020-0841-9

Contents

Contributors

M.G. BRUSH, BSc, MA, PhD
Senior Lecturer in Biochemistry, St Thomas's Hospital Medical School, London

J.S. CACKETT, BA (Hons) (Lond), SRN, DipN (Lond), RNT
Director of Nurse Education, The Nightingale School, St Thomas's Hospital, London

J. DOMINIAN, FRCP (Ed), FRCPsych, DSc (Hon)
Senior Consultant Psychiatrist and Director of the Marital Research Centre, Central Middlesex Hospital, London

HELEN L.D. DUGUID, MD, FRCPath
Consultant Pathologist, Royal Infirmary, Dundee

I.L.C. FERGUSSON, FRCS, MRCOG
Consultant Gynaecologist, St Thomas's Hospital, London; Honorary Lecturer, Institute of Obstetrics and Gynaecology, University of London

D.B. GARRIOCH, MD (Aberdeen), MRCOG
Senior Registrar, St Thomas's Hospital, London

MICHAEL JOHN HARE, MA, MD, MRCOG
Lecturer in Obstetrics and Gynaecology, University of Cambridge; Honorary Consultant Obstetrician and Gynaecologist, Cambridge Area Health Authority

MOLLY JENNINGS, MCSP
Senior I Physiotherapist, St Thomas's Hospital, London; Member of the Association of Chartered Physiotherapists in Obstetrics and Gynaecology

PATRICIA LAST, FRCS, MRCOG
BUPA Medical Centre Women's Unit, London

P.J.D. MILTON, MD (Lond), MRCOG
Consultant Gynaecologist, Addenbrooke's Hospital, Cambridge; Associate Lecturer in Obstetrics and Gynaecology, University of Cambridge

P. MORGAN-CAPNER, BSc, MB, BS, MRCPath
Lecturer in Medical Microbiology, King's College Hospital Medical School, London

J.R. PATTISON, DM, MRCPath
Professor of Medical Microbiology, King's College Hospital Medical School, London

MARGARET REES, MB, BS, BSc
MRC Training Fellow, Nuffield Department of Obstetrics and Gynaecology, John Radcliffe Hospital, Oxford

PETER SAUNDERS, MB, BS, MRCOG
Consultant Obstetrician and Gynaecologist, Ashford Hospital, Middlesex; Honorary Lecturer, St Thomas's Hospital Medical School, London

ROBERT W. SHAW, MD, MRCOG, FRCS
Senior Lecturer and Consultant Obstetrician and Gynaecologist, Centre for Reproductive Biology, University of Edinburgh

A.M. SPENCE, SRN
Senior Sister, Marie Stopes House, London

MARGARET WATSON, SRN, HV
PMT Counsellor, Marie Stopes House, London

TERENCE WHEELER MB, FRCR
Consultant in Radiotherapy and Oncology, Addenbrooke's Hospital, Cambridge

Preface

The aim of this book is to provide the trained nurse with a reliable up-to-date source of information on modern practice in gynaecology as interpreted in the broadest sense. Although the nurse in training is well provided with excellent texts, the more senior nurse has considerable difficulty in obtaining up-to-date information at a level suited to her needs. The medical press and texts are usually too specialized, and articles in nursing journals, though very helpful, are often brief and limited in scope.

The need for this information is all the more pressing, as in some hospitals, clinics (N.H.S., private and industrial) and districts, nurses are being given increasing responsibility under the somewhat remote supervision of medical staff.

We hope that this book will be read with profit by nurses ranging from higher administrative staff, via the ward sister and clinic sister, to the recently qualified SRN who is considering the direction in which she wishes her career to move. Other disciplines, including physiotherapists, radiographers, laboratory staff and social workers, may find the book useful background reading. Some chapters on general medical aspects may be valuable to almost any doctor or medical student with an interest in gynaecology.

Nevertheless, it has not been our intention to cover every possible aspect of gynaecology that the nurse may encounter, as we felt that this might detract from the emphasis on topics of special importance where progress is rapid or problems are great.

The editors will be happy to receive suggestions for topics for any future edition and comments on the approach used in this new venture.

We would like to thank the publisher's staff for encouragement and support throughout the preparation of the book.

March 1981

M.A. Shorthouse
M.G. Brush

1. Principles of Gynaecological Nursing

J.S. Cackett

One of the responsibilities of the nurse is to keep up to date with developments and technology used in the treatment and care of patients. During the past decade there have been considerable advances in gynaecology and some of them are discussed in this book. It is not only modern developments in the specialty that have influenced gynaecology but also changes in society that have allowed wider public discussion of topics hitherto taboo. The mass media have also contributed to this by allowing a wider dissemination of information concerning some topics such as the investigation and treatment of infertility, disturbances of menstruation and menopausal symptoms. While for some women such open discussion of gynaecological problems is welcomed, others still find the subject difficult to talk about and are embarrassed when it is necessary. Modern societies encompass both these groups and it is important for the nurse to acknowledge that in multi-racial societies, where the position of women has undergone significant change, patients' expectations and understanding of their problems and the treatment of them will vary with age, social class and ethnic background. These variations will affect both the interpretation of symptoms and the response to treatment, as the gynaecological problems with which women present are closely intertwined with social, emotional and psychological factors. These factors become increasingly important as patient turnover increases and the nurse's working week decreases, thus reducing the time available for nurse/patient interaction.

It is vital for the nurse in the gynaecological ward to appreciate the importance of discussing with patients the manifestations of their gynaecological disorders and of listening to their fears and anxieties. The emotional support provided by the nurse is an essential component of care and starts when the patient has her first examination. The nurse should explain to the patient the reason for the gynaecological examination and the procedure which will be used. Furthermore, by careful positioning, ensuring that the necessary equipment is available and providing privacy the nurse assists in reducing patient anxiety and alleviating stress.

Many problems discussed in this book will not require hospital admission but may require frequent attendance at out-patient departments or clinics. It is important for the patient to understand the time span for investigations and other procedures, otherwise further anxiety is generated. Reduction of waiting time and careful explanation of both the procedure and the likely frequency and duration of attendance will reduce stress. The nurse in the out-patient department or clinic fulfils an important role by ensuring care and support for patients with gynaecological problems, before and during consultations, and by coordinating any continuing care required in the patient's home. She can also make sure that the patient is accompanied on the journey home if this is necessary.

All patients admitted to hospital have fears and anxieties not always overtly expressed but needing discussion. The gynaecological patient has the additional anxiety of the effect of treatment/investigation on her femininity, her fertility and her future sexual relationships. On admission of a patient the nurse has the responsibility to provide opportunity for discussion to assess what the patient knows about her possible treatment and its effect. Some particular problems where this may occur are discussed later and include the following.

Patients with Amenorrhoea

These patients are likely to be most anxious as they face the future uncertain of their 'normality' and of their ability to have full sexual relationships or to bear children. The nurse has to be particularly sensitive to the need for the listening ear during discussion of these very real anxieties. It is all too easy for the nurse to dismiss amenorrhoea lightly, but it is devastating for the individual not to have the 'normal' sign of womanhood and to be reminded frequently that she is different. It is necessary, too, for the nurse to gain the confidence and cooperation of the patient and this is likely to be achieved by careful, detailed explanation of the reasons for particular investigations and their relevance to her condition. The nurse should be informed of, or make it her business to find out, the results of investigations in order to confirm with the patient what the doctor has said; one recital of the explanation is rarely sufficient and it is vital that doctor and nurse are agreed over what information is to be given.

Patients Being Admitted/Treated for Infertility

This is another group of patients for whom hospital admission is likely to follow a long series of investigations and clinic attendances. It requires considerable counselling skills and sensitivity to be able to provide at least some support for these patients, who are likely to feel a sense of guilt as their plans for a family do not materialize. They often feel they have failed themselves and their partners after the frustration of the long series of investigations with hopes raised and dashed. These feelings must be recognized by the nurse as she provides counselling and support and acknowledges the emotional turmoil the couple are experiencing. The emotional response may manifest itself in the form of abnormally quiet or aggressive behaviour. The nurse should note the relationship between the woman and her partner, perhaps by being around at visiting time. Increased tension in the relationship may be detectable and could affect the treatment of the patient. The mass media have made women aware of the advances in this field, resulting in pressures on patients to accept treatment; again the nurse must help them develop a realistic level of expectation of the outcome of treatment.

Patients with Disturbances of Menstruation

This group of patients rarely require hospital admission and are usually seen and supported in the out-patient department. The difference in understanding and perception of what is involved is considerable and when discussing problems with these patients it is useful to find out their normal menstrual patterns and coping mechanism. Most young girls with these disturbances expect treatment of their symptoms and do not expect menstruation to affect their daily life. They may have feelings of shame and frustration if they do not perform well during the pre-menstrual and menstrual times and these feelings need to be discussed and understood. Other groups of patients will have tolerated discomfort and even overt symptoms over a prolonged time, as they believe that 'it will be better next month' or that their symptoms are 'normal', 'to be expected' and 'cannot be treated' and so may regard treatment with doubt and suspicion.

Patients Admitted for Termination of Pregnancy

Some of these women are likely to have doubts and anxieties and again extremes of behaviour are a consequence of their emotional turmoil. The nurse should be aware that they have ambivalent feelings and will often wish to share them: allowing time for them to do this is an important component of care. The nurse also has the responsibility to ensure that post-abortion counselling is available, together with advice on contraception.

Patients Admitted for Sterilization

Many patients, though wishing sterilization to be done, may have conflicting feelings as they consider the effect of surgery on their future sexual relationships. Though many will be relieved to have sterilization performed, the guilt feelings of others must be appreciated.

Patients with Gynaecological Cancer

Like all patients who hear the word 'cancer', those being investigated or treated for gynaecological cancer are extremely anxious. Gynaecological patients have the added anxiety of loss of femininity and the effect of treatment on their ability to form sexual relationships. The mass media have led many patients to have some knowledge of gynaecological cancer while others are totally misled by such information and misunderstand both the disease and its treatment. The ward team must all be aware of the explanations given to the patient by the doctor so that nurses uphold what has been said and trust is maintained.

Patients with Vaginal Discharge

Women admitted with vaginal discharge are likely to be embarrassed and particularly concerned about possible odour, and the disposal of pads, in addition to their natural concern about the underlying cause of the discharge. The nurse should provide the opportunity for frequent changing of pads and washing facilities with, where possible, the use of a bidet. She should also be aware of the discomfort caused by the severe pruritus which often accompanies vaginal discharge. Swabs to identify the causative organism should be taken carefully and gently to avoid unnecessary discomfort. The nurse must show understanding which will enable to patient to discuss freely her anxieties and report frankly on the amount, type and odour of the discharge, so that changes may be discussed with the doctor.

GENERAL NURSING CARE

It is easy for nurses to dismiss much of gynaecological nursing as routine and investigations as minor. Patients faced with investigation, surgery or treatment which will have an effect on their reproductive ability consider any or all of these as major hurdles. Women vary considerably, according to age, ethnic background and social class, in their understanding of normal anatomy and physiology. They often require explanation fully to appreciate the effect of surgery; they will need time to discuss how surgery will affect their menstrual cycles, the onset of the menopause and their sexual relationships. The nurse needs to give clear, confident explanations, take account of the patients' anxieties and understand their responses. The extent to which the partner is involved in discussion of investigations, treatment and surgery should be agreed with the patient. The nurse in a gynaecological ward needs to be aware of the emotional upheaval affecting the patients; she requires sensitivity and understanding to provide the support for patients experiencing the physical manifestations of gynaecological disorders and their investigation and treatment. Specific care will include ensuring that patients understand what the procedures involve and how they will affect them. While the initial explanation is the responsibility of the doctor, it is the nurse who gives the patient further clarification and it needs to be consistent.

In the management of a gynaecological ward, care must be planned to ensure the nurse has time for listening and discussion and does not feel guilty sitting down with patients. Ward management also involves being sensitive to emotional tension, which may be created by the close proximity of patients with infertility and those admitted for sterilization or termination of pregnancy. There is a tendency for women in these situations to gather together and discuss their respective problems. However, confidentiality is essential and the sensitive nurse may need to redirect ward chatter to protect the emotions of individual patients.

The physical manifestations of gynaecological disorders include pain, disorders of micturition and bowel function, insomnia and haemorrhage. While these are identified as common problems, each patient will experience them differently and the nurse must consider individual responses. This she can do by using the framework of the nursing process which involves assessing each patient's problems, planning and implementing the care to alleviate them and evaluating and recording the effectiveness of the care given.

Pain

Pain is a common problem for gynaecological patients and is heightened by the fears and anxieties accompanying surgery. Careful explanation of what is involved has been shown to reduce postoperative pain and speed recovery (Hayward 1975).

The control of postoperative pain is largely the responsibility of the nursing staff: after careful assessment of the patient, the judicious administration of analgesia can minimize postoperative pain. The administration of analgesia should be carefully planned to enable the patient to obtain maximum rest, to be receptive to treatment given, for example physiotherapy, and to respond to visitors. Reducing pain enables easier breathing and movement, thus assisting in the prevention of the postoperative complications of chest infection and deep-vein thrombosis. Pain in association with flatulence is a common postoperative problem which should not be dismissed lightly. Some patients find relief from simple remedies such as peppermint, while others require the administration of analgesics; encouraging the patient to move in the immediate postoperative period will reduce the discomfort.

Pain associated with advanced malignant disease requires careful administration of analgesia with accurate recording of its effectiveness in order to reduce its intensity. Nurses who are with the patients for long periods are able to observe their responses more accurately than the medical staff and there should be full consultation in order to devise appropriate regimens. All nurses must recognize the importance of giving regular doses of analgesia for greater effectiveness.

Disorders of Micturition

The nurse should be aware of the patient's normal patterns of micturition so that abnormalities are recognized. Particularly after surgery, patients may experience such problems as retention of urine, dysuria and increased frequency of micturition, often as a result of infection or haematuria. Most postoperative patients will require their fluid balance to be accurately recorded in order to demonstrate abnormalities.

Retention or difficulties with micturition may result from pain, localized oedema or inability to relax. Occasionally, catheterization under strict asepsis will be required, but more commonly a nursing action, such as ensuring privacy, allowing the patient to use a commode rather than a bed-pan, or sometimes running a tap, may be effective. The careful administration of analgesia during the postoperative period, thereby reducing pain and assisting relaxation, is a contributory factor in restoring normal micturition. During the immediate postoperative period the first act of micturition must be carefully recorded as, rarely, surgical damage to the ureter occurs and will be detected by vigilance in recording postoperative urinary output.

Infection of urine may occur as a result of incomplete bladder emptying with stasis, either because of localized oedema or following the removal of an in-dwelling catheter. When recording fluid balance the nurse should ask the patients about symptoms of infection such as dysuria or increased frequency; they should be encouraged to drink a minimum of 3 litres of fluid a day (providing renal function is normal) in an attempt to reduce its likelihood. If infection occurs, encouragement to maintain and if possible increase this intake is required.

Incontinence of urine may occur as a result of the gynaecological disorder but can also arise as a complication of treatment for malignant disease either from the extensive surgery of a Wertheim's hysterectomy (see Chapter 10) or as a complication of irradiation (see Chapter 11) when a vesico-vaginal fistula may form. By careful observation and accurate recording of the patients' micturition patterns, the nurse plays a vital role in the early detection of associated abnormalities which can then be treated.

Disorders of Bowel Function

On admission the nurse should identify the patients' normal bowel function in order to assess any deviation, which may well occur during hospital admission as a result of surgery or other treatment. Some patients have paralytic ileus following surgery and it is necessary to ensure that bowel sounds are present before they start drinking or eating postoperatively. More often patients complain of constipation, in many instances resulting from tenseness and anxiety over damage to the operation site or pain on bowel action. The nurse can alleviate these anxieties by careful explanation, the use of aperients and analgesia where necessary and by ensuring privacy and allowing the patient to use the lavatory rather than a commode or bed-pan. Patients will need assurance that bowel action will return to normal as recovery progresses.

Other patients will experience diarrhoea as a result of treatment, particularly after radiation treatment for malignant disease, and are likely to find this most distressing. They will require considerable support from the nurse. Careful explanation that this is a result of treatment and will gradually subside when treatment is completed will allay anxieties that it will be permanent. The nurse should ensure that the doctor and radiologist are aware of the onset of diarrhoea as it may be necessary to stop treatment for a short while to encourage healing.

Insomnia

Gynaecological patients may find sleeping a particular problem as they worry about the possible effects of their disorder or treatment. The night nurse who notices this and provides a listening ear and a warm drink can considerably reduce the patients' anxieties. Many patients, particularly after hysterectomy, have some emotional instability in the immediate postoperative period and this may manifest itself by tearful outbursts at night. Gentle understanding that this is a usual reaction and not the onset of permanent disorder should be shown. The nurse should observe and report the patient's sleep pattern and all members of the ward team should be aware of the patient's worries; referral to the social worker, who can provide practical support, is important. The astute use of sedatives to ensure sleep before and immediately after surgery or investigation will give the patients rest, a vital component of care for women who may be harassed mothers.

Vaginal Discharge and Haemorrhage

A vital part of gynaecological nursing is the observation and accurate recording of vaginal loss. The nurse should know the normal pattern of loss, in order to recognize abnormality and tell the patients what to expect: for example, following hysterectomy it is a gradually decreasing amount changing from red to darkest brown and yellow. Deviation from the normal pattern may indicate infection, with the possibility of secondary haemorrhage.

Early detection of postoperative infection by the immediate reporting of pyrexia or abnormal discharge may result in the correction of treatment and reduce the likelihood of infection. This may also be reduced by encouraging the patient to use the bidet or, when this is not possible, by providing frequent opportunities for washing and ensuring a plentiful supply of pads so that the patient can change them regularly.

Vaginal haemorrhage is a frightening experience for both the patient and the nurse; it may occur following the removal of a vaginal pack, for example after the patient has had a cone biopsy; a further sterile pack should always be available in the ward as re-packing may be necessary. On discharge from hospital patients should be advised to report any abnormal bleeding to their doctors or to ring the hospital for advice.

FURTHER SUPPORT AND FOLLOW-UP

The nurse has a vital role in supporting the families of patients and in preparing the patients themselves for discharge from hospital. The extent to which the family/partner is involved in the investigation or treatment of a patient will, of course, depend on the patient's problem. Many of the topics discussed in this book are those in which the partner is likely to be involved, though this must be discussed with the patient. In these instances the nurse should encourage the couple to approach their problem together and discuss openly each other's fears and anxieties and how they may affect the relationship; if necessary, she should refer the patient for further counselling and advice. In the care of the patient with gynaecological cancer, the nurse should provide support for the family, particularly in the terminal stages where the imminent loss of mother/partner is particularly stressful. Careful explanation of what is happening and how treatment is aimed at reducing pain and alleviating symptoms may reduce stress.

Where appropriate, the involvement of the family in caring may also help. The nurse needs to accept that the anxieties of the relations may be reflected in abrupt aggressive behaviour and meet this with patience and understanding if her support is to be effective.

Preparation of the patient for discharge from hospital is a further aspect of the nurse's role. Patients should be encouraged to keep their follow-up appointments and, if there is likely to be a long delay between discharge and the results of investigations that have been performed, this should be explained. The nurse must discuss with the patients any reduction in physical activity required as a result of surgery and also whether they should refrain from intercourse; patients may be too embarrassed to ask this directly and it is advisable, following major surgery, for them to refrain from intercourse until after the follow-up appointment. For these groups of patients the follow-up appointment is a continuing part of their care and investigation and they must be helped to understand this.

The nursing care of gynaecological patients is concerned as much with their social, psychological and emotional support as with the giving of care to relieve physical symptoms. These are inseparable and the nurse must appreciate that individuals react differently to similar conditions as a result of their different social and emotional experiences. It is by identifying the unique way in which individuals are affected by common problems that nurses can plan and implement programmes of individual care effectively to alleviate patients' problems. New medical developments may affect the treatment offered but individual nursing care can provide for the patients the support which will assist in using these advances most effectively.

Acknowledgement

I am grateful to Miss Clemence, Sister of Grosvenor Ward, St Thomas' Hospital, London, for comments and helpful suggestions on the preparation of this chapter.

Bibliography

Hayward, J. (1975) *The Study of Nursing Care*. London: Rcn.

Information: A Prescription against Pain (1975) London: Rcn and National Council of Nurses of the United Kingdom.

2. Investigation and Treatment of Infertility

I.L.C. Fergusson

It will take the average couple practising normal sexual intercourse up to seven months to conceive, and four out of five of these couples will have achieved a pregnancy by the end of one year. For these reasons it is generally considered appropriate to allow at least one year to elapse before any investigations into the causes of possible infertility are commenced. There are certain groups who merit earlier consideration and they should be advised to seek medical advice after six months. These include the older married couples (when the age of the wife exceeds 35 or of the husband exceeds 50) and those who have experienced infertility in a former marriage. Other patients requiring early consideration are those whose medical history suggests that infertility would be likely: for instance a history of chronic salpingitis in the woman or mumps orchitis in the man. It may also be sensible to carry out some early base-line investigations of a couple whose personal anxiety may be contributing to the infertility and where a demonstration of normality might be helpful.

Even in normal couples it is not always sensible to commence investigations at the end of one year and a further delay might be helpful. For instance, in the case of personnel in the armed forces, businessmen, or long-distance hauliers, separation may have occurred at ovulation time in several months of the year. Finally there are those couples who have only a luke-warm desire for children: then the timing of expensive investigations is a matter for careful judgement.

A full medical history is required from all patients but further examination and investigation will depend on the doctor's assessment of all the additional factors mentioned above. If further investigations are to be undertaken it is of great importance that they follow an orderly and logical pattern and, preferably, that they are conducted by the same doctor. In this context the investigations are best done in a special 'infertility clinic' where the doctor is prepared to take time and develop a personal interest in the subject. Above all constant reassurance and sympathy are essential from both the medical and nursing staff involved in the investigations and treatment.

THE MEDICAL HISTORY

Most practitioners prefer to interview the husband and wife together, especially at the first visit. The importance of the medical history is reflected in the fact that, on the history alone, an accurate prospective diagnosis can be made in 60% of cases. The age of both partners will be taken into consideration, as relative infertility increases before the age of 18 and after the age of 35. Any previous pregnancy within or prior to the existing marriage should also be discussed and it is valuable to know if a previous consort has subsequently had children. Discussion of pregnancies will include miscarriages, ectopic pregnancies and stillbirths as well as full details of normal pregnancies, subsequent breast feeding and resumption of menses.

General enquiries will be made about the occupation of the couple and how often they live together, as night shifts, overseas postings and commercial travelling may prevent regular sexual contact. The overall time spent trying to conceive will be ascertained.

More specific questions will be focussed on sexual intercourse and previous contraceptive techniques. The sexual drive of both partners and the frequency of sexual intercourse will often disclose a problem in consummation. About 5% of all infertility problems are associated with difficulties in consummation. If there is any further doubt, questions will be asked about positioning of sexual intercourse, about the quality of erection and penetration. The timing of ejaculation and the possible occurrence of flow-back will be considered and the husband will be asked to confirm normal descent of the testes.

Both partners will be asked about any general illness and previous abdominal or pelvic operations. Any medication currently being taken by either partner must be noted and normality of micturition, bowel habit and appetite must also be enquired about. Excessive smoking and drinking will be considered as they are known to impair fertility.

Details of the current menstrual cycle must be recorded, especially irregularities which may suggest anovulatory cycles or insufficient hormonal support for the endometrium. Intermenstrual bleeding and post-coital bleeding may indicate the presence of a polyp or cervical erosion; a discharge may reveal salpingitis or lower genital tract infection.

Finally it is often helpful to ask the couple if they have any ideas as to why they are not achieving a pregnancy. Stress factors at work, problems with in-laws and fear of pregnancy are just some of the possible points of information that may emerge.

THE EXAMINATION OF BOTH PARTNERS

The examination may be undertaken by the general practitioner or by the specialist. A full examination of both partners is required as well as a thorough local genital examination. In the former stigmata of endocrine disorders of the pituitary, thyroid and adrenal cortex will be sought. General build, body weight and fitness are assessed and blood pressure, heart rate and respiratory function will be checked. Physical deformities may prevent effective sexual intercourse and the presence of a colostomy or urinary diversion may be causing inhibitions. Surgical scars on the abdomen may suggest the possible presence of previous peritonitis or intra-abdominal adhesions.

The wife will be assessed for normal female development in respect of body fat, breast tissue, genital development and absence of hirsutism. A careful vaginal examination will be carried out to reveal any lower genital tract obstruction, infection, polyp or erosion. The uterus may be naturally anteverted or retroverted but should be of normal size and mobile. The adnexae and the pouch of Douglas should be free of any cysts or masses and there should be no tethering or tenderness when the uterus is moved by the examining fingers. Normal sized ovaries may be felt in a thin woman and significant ovarian enlargement will probably be detected in any woman.

Examination using a bivalve (Cusco) or flat (Sims's) speculum will allow visualization of the cervix.

The husband will also be examined for normal male development, stature, voice, body hair and muscle development. A pelvic examination will reveal the presence of hernias, varicoceles, hydroceles and scrotal asymmetry. The testes must be palpated to confirm normal bilateral descent and the absence of tumour. In cases of doubt it is important to explore the inguinal folds and if necessary carry out laparotomy to find and remove the testes if they remain undescended as they have a propensity for malignant change and are seldom if ever functional. The penis should be examined for the presence of hypospadias or epispadias; if circumcised the prepuce should be retracted and any phimosis noted.

In both partners the presence of skin rashes, local genital ulceration or discharge may signify active venereal infection and indicate the need for appropriate cultures and serological tests.

SPECIFIC INFERTILITY INVESTIGATIONS

Any investigations beyond the basic medical examination will be dictated by the findings of the medical history and the preliminary examinations discussed above. Some base-line investigations may seem appropriate in all infertile couples but in every case the cost and risks involved must be considered. The best investigations are those which achieve their aims while remaining pain-free, harmless and cheap. The availability of more specific investigations may be limited to regional centres.

If there are no pointers from the history and examination, a logical sequence of investigation must be used to exclude other possible causes.

Primary Investigations

Infertility is caused by four basic factors: an abnormal sperm count, failure in normal sexual intercourse, anovulation, and obstruction or infection of the female genital tract. It is appropriate to use the following primary investigations to find which of the four is involved.

Firstly, a *semen analysis* will check the volume, pH, and sperm count, as well as the motility or morphology of the sperm. The volume should exceed 2.5 ml and the pH be 7.5–8, whilst the count should exceed 20×10^6/ml. At least 60% should be motile and 60% be normal in shape. The semen is produced as a masturbation specimen after a period of at least 48 hours abstinence and it should be examined within four hours of production. Normal results will usually exclude the husband from further investigations, whereas a poor analysis should be confirmed by at least two further specimens before more invasive male function tests are undertaken.

Secondly there is always the possibility of *failure to have normal sexual intercourse* on some occasions or in a more general way but not previously admitted. A conclusive investigation is the post-coital test (PCT). The couple are asked to have normal sexual intercourse not more than four hours before examination at the clinic. They should have abstained from sexual intercourse for 48 hours and the wife should be instructed not to wash or douche prior to the examination. The doctor inspects the cervix and the cervical mucus prior to aspirating fluid from the cervical canal and upper vagina for microscopic inspection. The specimen should contain clear mucus and a number of active, normal sperm. Absence of sperm after a normal semen analysis suggests that normal intravaginal intercourse did not take place. Dead or inactive sperm suggest the presence of infection, abnormal cervical secretions or sperm antibodies.

Thirdly, primary tests of *ovulation* may be done in a number of ways, the least invasive being the scrutiny of daily temperature recordings. The woman is asked to take her temperature each morning before rising (basal body temperature, BBT) and to record it on a simple chart. Ovulation is followed by a characteristic rise in the temperature which is maintained throughout the luteal phase of the cycle. Unfortunately this simple test is not always reliable, especially when luteal function is likely to be variable. Following ovulation progesterone is produced from the corpus luteum in the ovary and has specific effects on various target organs, including the breasts, endometrium and cervical and vaginal epithelium. Many women can tell when they have ovulated by altered sensation in the breasts or an increase in cervical fluid discharge. More objective evidence can be obtained by measuring the rise in progesterone levels in plasma or in urine where it is excreted as pregnanediol. Both these levels should reach their peak about Day 21 of a 28-day cycle. Microscopic examination of serial smears of the vagina will show a change in the cells after ovulation but this gives little evidence on the quality of the luteal phase. Endometrial biopsy in the post-ovulatory phase of the cycle will reveal a secretory pattern on histological examination. This biopsy may be taken without anaesthesia in the out-patient clinic or during formal curettage for which anaesthesia is required.

Fourthly, the *genital tract* must be tested for infection and normal patency. Lower genital tract infection will normally reveal itself by the presence of irritation or discharge, but even in their absence it is sensible to take swabs from the upper vagina and the cervix for bacteriological examination. Structural abnormality of the genital tract may be due to a congenital malformation, such as septate vagina or bicornuate uterus, or to acquired defects, such as polyps or uterine fibroids. Tubal obstruction is almost always the result of infection or surgery. Whereas a simple examination under anaesthesia, together with dilatation and curettage of the uterus, may reveal the structural abnormalities, more specific tests are needed to demonstrate tubal patency. In the past carbon dioxide was used to insufflate the tubes but it proved rather unreliable and has been superseded by laparoscopy and dye tests or hysterosalpingography.

The laparoscope is a simple telescope with a fibreoptic light source and is introduced into the abdomen through a minute incision under the umbilicus, thus giving a direct view of the pelvic organs. If a dye is introduced through the cervix and uterus it can be seen traversing the tubes and spilling at the fimbrial ends. If the tubes are not patent spill of dye will not be seen. Hysterosalpingography is an X-ray technique in which radio-opaque fluid is passed through the uterus and tubes under direct X-ray vision. Both laparoscopy and hysterosalpingography are best performed under a simple general anaesthetic. The X-ray method has the advantage of demonstrating the internal contour of the uterus and the point of obstruction should it exist, while laparoscopy gives more information on the ovaries and external appearance of both tubes and uterus.

Primary investigations including semen analysis, post-coital tests, curettage, hormone measurements and hysterosalpingogram or laparoscopy will, therefore, identify the major causes in all cases of infertility. In the event of poor semen analysis or proven anovulation further tests are required.

Specialized Investigations of the Male

Hormone assays may identify the underlying problem responsible for a deficient seminal analysis. Follicle-stimulating hormone (FSH) stimulates spermatogenesis and luteinizing hormone (LH) aids the interstitial cells in the production of testosterone which is required for sperm maturation. FSH, LH and prolactin are all produced by the anterior pituitary and can be measured in the blood. Deficiencies may be due either to primary pituitary failure, in which case there are usually other endocrine abnormalities of thyroid or adrenocortical function, or to failure of hypothalamic stimulation of the pituitary. In some cases the testes are insensitive to normal circulating levels of FSH and an excesively high blood FSH level may be found as the pituitary attempts to overcome the insensitivity.

Testicular biopsy is an invasive procedure used to identify a tumour or the absence of spermatogonia (cells from which the mature spermatozoa develop). When testicular biopsy reveals no abnormality in a case of azoospermia in the seminal fluid there may be a block in the vas deferens. A vasogram, using radio-opaque fluid, can be used to confirm or exclude this diagnosis.

Chromosomal studies on infertile males will reveal the presence of abnormal chromosomal numbers or distribution which may contribute to infertility or may indicate the cause of the early miscarriage of a congenitally abnormal fetus.

Sperm antibodies have been identified in seminal fluid and cervical mucus as well as in male and female sera. They can be found in normal fertile couples and virgins which casts some doubt upon their significance in infertility, though it now appears that some antibodies are more important than others in this context.

Specialized Investigations of the Female

Anovulation and irregularity of the menstrual cycle require more detailed investigation of the female based on a knowledge of the stimulating action of hypothalamic releasing hormones on the pituitary, of pituitary gonadotrophins on the ovaries and of ovarian hormones on the endometrium. The ovarian hormones oestrogen and progesterone also have a feed-back action on the hypothalamus thus producing cyclical patterns of menstruation. (See also Chapters 3 and 4.)

Follicle-stimulating hormone (FSH) primes the ovarian follicles and luteinizing hormone (LH) precipitates ovulation and supports the corpus luteum after ovulation. Both hormones come from the anterior pituitary and are measurable in the blood. Prolactin is normally produced in large quantities only during lactation, but its inappropriate production at other times will interfere with the action of FSH and LH on the ovary. Significantly raised level of prolactin in the blood (hyperprolactinaemia) may be an important factor in infertility investigation and are discussed later.

Oestrogens are produced by the ovary mainly from the developing follicle before ovulation and mainly from the corpus luteum after ovulation, but progesterone is produced in significant amounts only after ovulation. Both can be measured in the plasma or as metabolites in urine and the results can be helpful in detecting abnormalities of follicular and luteal function which may be of considerable importance in the patient's infertility problem. Androgens such as testosterone and androstenedione are normally produced by the female in very small quantities from the ovary and adrenal gland but excessive production will inhibit oestrogen activity and ovulation.

Excessive amounts of these hormones may indicate hyperplasia or tumour of their parent organs or may result from an attempt to overcome insensitivity in their target organs. Deficiency of pituitary gonadotrophins or ovarian hormones will suggest a failure of stimulation from a higher centre or failure of the parent organ to react to such a stimulus.

A combination of raised pituitary gonadotrophins and reduced ovarian hormones is almost always diagnostic of the menopause or premature ovarian failure.

Even more detailed endocrine investigations may be required in a few complex cases.

It may happen that despite a full history, examination and detailed investigations, no abnormality can be found; it is certain that our present state of knowledge has not exhausted all the possible causes of infertility. It is usually wise to reassure these couples as fully as possible, though a small percentage will not be satisfied without resorting to a second opinion.

TREATMENT

General Measures

It is well accepted that up to 20% of couples attending infertility clinics will actually conceive spontaneously prior to or during the course of investigations, thus reflecting a reduction in anxiety and reassurance that the problem is being shouldered by the doctor.

Reassurance at all times is a cornerstone of good treatment and should be associated at the outset with advice about normal sexual practice and the timing of sexual intercourse to coincide with ovulation.

If there is underlying general disease the patient must be referred for appropriate treatment and if there is an environmental or occupational factor at work it is often useful to enlist the help of the social worker.

Inability to achieve erection, penetration, ejaculation or orgasm on a regular basis may be the result of a psychological barrier and these patients are best treated by a psychosexual specialist as successful treatment usually requires more time than is usually available in a busy infertility clinic.

The Infertile Woman

Local genital causes of female infertility are often curable in the out-patient department. Infections must be identified by culture and treated with the appropriate antimicrobial agent either systemically or locally in a cream or pessary. An underlying cervical erosion may require cryocautery or admission for heat cautery.

Bartholin's cysts require marsupialization and vaginal cysts and septa require excision. Occasionally dyspareunia and consequent infertility are due to a hymenal ring or a tight introitus following an episiotomy or repair. In each case a minor plastic surgical procedure can be used to enlarge the opening and the use of a lubricant jelly, with or without local anaesthetic, may also help.

Uterine pathology is rarely the cause of infertility and when it is it usually leads to inadequate implantation of the blastocyst or early miscarriage.

Chronic endometritis can be caused by any foreign body in the uterine cavity and by ascending infections. Once the cause of the problem is removed the normal cyclical shedding of the endometrium will usually prevent recurrence. Fibroids and uterine polyps may also interfere with implantation and may be removed surgically in most cases.

Because the uterus is derived from the fused lower ends of the primitive mullerian ducts, fusion may be incomplete, and give rise to a septate, bicornuate or complete double uterus. Affected women are prone to recurrent miscarriages; surgical correction should be carried out even though there is a risk of subsequent uterine rupture in any pregnancy following reconstructive surgery. Retroversion occurs in about 30% of women and must be considered as a normal variant; however, fixed retroversion may lead to miscarriage and requires surgical correction.

Fallopian tube pathology accounts for up to 30% of all cases of infertility and carries the worst prognosis. The tubes may be partially or completely blocked following infection or surgery, or they may be patent but so distorted by external adhesions as to make them impassable. More rarely the tubes appear normal externally but have suffered such damage to the lining cells as to render them functionless. Surgical correction is the only available treatment and usually it carries a very poor success rate, to such an extent that, faced with severely damaged tubes, it is sometimes better to advise the patient against treatment because the chance of a successful outcome is so small.

Some minor tubal surgery, including the separation of fine adhesions, can be carried out using the laparoscope and associated fine instruments. More difficult cases warrant laparotomy and formal tubal surgery which may be done under microscopic control in certain selected cases.

Table 2.1 Consensus Results (Live Births) Following Tubal Surgery

Tubal surgery	*Live births* (%)
Salpingolysis	10–50
Salpingostomy	4–12
Re-anastomosis	20–30
Re-implantation	20–30
Microtubal re-anastomosis	30–75

Table 2.1 shows the variety of tubal surgical procedures available and their approximate success rates. Salpingolysis is an operation to divide external tubal adhesions and restore normal mobility to the pelvic contents. Salpingostomy implies the opening up of the end of the blocked tube; in most cases a small cuff is turned back and anchored by very fine sutures around its periphery. Occasionally a small plastic cannula is inserted into the tube for a few days to preserve patency in the immediate postoperative phase. Fimbriolysis infers separation of light adhesions at the fimbrial ends of the tubes.

Hydrotubation is used more as a diagnostic than a therapeutic procedure, although there is no doubt that a number of women are cured by this simple procedure alone. For diagnostic purposes a dye or radio-opaque fluid is used; for simple postoperative irrigation normal saline is suitable, though some authorities will prefer an antibiotic or steroid solution.

Re-anastomosis is the term for the rejoining of a tube which has been severed or blocked in its mid-portion. Often this is the result of a previous sterilization operation. Careful evaluation is needed prior to operation and laparoscopy is necessary to assess the pelvic damage. Wherever possible re-anastomosis of the tube should be performed under microscopic vision to ensure the most accurate suture line.

Re-implantation of the tubes is carried out surgically in cases where there is an isolated block at the uterine end. The outer part of the tube is separated on its vascular pedicle and re-inserted onto the uterus; a passage must be reamed through the myometrium to allow the re-implanted tube to reach the uterine cavity.

So far transplantation of tubes from one patient to another has proved unsuccessful mainly due to rejection problems and difficulty with the very fine vascular anastomoses that are required.

Extracorporeal fertilization is being developed in an attempt to bypass the fallopian tubes altogether, and is a reflection on the very poor success rates achieved by conventional tubal surgery. The technique involves collection of a mature ovum from the ovary and placing it in a small dish which contains a dilute specimen of the husband's sperm suspended in a culture fluid. Fertilization and subsequent division and growth occur in the culture medium over the next few days. When the early embryo has divided into four or eight cells it is returned to the uterine cavity through a tube inserted through the cervix. So far there has been only a very limited success rate using this procedure; as experience accumulates this technique may come to replace surgery in the treatment of tubal infertility.

Hormonal therapy

Failure to maintain a regular ovulatory cycle will account for about 20% of all cases of infertility, but by careful investigation to establish the precise cause of the problem, subsequent treatment will be successful in about 80% of these cases.

If the cycle is normal but of varying length it is possible to regulate ovulation by simulating the natural surge of luteinizing hormone (LH) which proceeds follicular rupture. This is achieved by an injection of human chorionic gonadotrophin (HCG) at around day 11–12 of the cycle and ovulation will follow within 48 hours. The technique may also be useful to ensure that artificial insemination or natural sexual intercourse coincide with ovulation.

If investigations reveal inadequate follicular development it may be rectified by treatment with the synthetic anti-oestrogenic drug clomiphene (Clomid) which works by stimulating the release of gonadotrophin-releasing factor from the hypothalamus (see also Chapter 3). In many cases follicular development and ovulation follow the initial events produced by clomiphene. Sometimes it is necessary to use HCG to produce ovulation after clomiphene-induced follicular development. In some cases the granulosa cells of the ovarian follicle fail to produce normal amounts of oestrogen so that endometrial proliferation is impaired and the cervical mucus remains tacky. Oestrogen therapy in the first half of the cycle may help these patients.

Failure to ovulate associated with very high levels of the gonadotrophins FSH and LH indicates the onset of menopause or premature ovarian failure and will not respond to stimulation. In all other cases, providing the ovary is normal, stimulation of ovulation can usually be achieved by giving clomiphene and HCG as described above, or by direct stimulation with human menopausal gonadotrophin (Pergonal). Pergonal contains natural FSH and LH and therefore works directly on the ovary; it has the disadvantage that it can only be given by injection whereas clomiphene may be taken by mouth. Clomiphene, because it works at hypothalamic level, suffers the disadvantage that it will be ineffective if the hypothalamic–pituitary–ovarian axis is not functioning normally. Both Pergonal and clomiphene require careful dose regulation and Pergonal needs meticulous monitoring of the urinary oestrogen response as overdose may lead to severe side effects of nausea, vomiting, diarrhoea, headaches, ovarian cyst formation and multiple pregnancies. It is well to remember that these are powerful drugs, but when they are used conscientiously they are very effective in promoting ovulation.

A poor luteal phase is reflected by inadequate secretory endometrium which may break down early, producing a short cycle, or erratically, producing pre-menstrual spotting.

Progestogens may be given by mouth or by injection to enhance the luteal phase. Injections of HCG have also been used on alternate days from Day 14 to Day 22 of the cycle, to simulate the natural LH production which acts to maintain the corpus luteum, which in turn produces progesterone and oestrogen in the second half of the cycle.

During lactation FSH and LH are inhibited by the overproduction of prolactin. Sometimes this occurs inappropriately in the absence of lactation and results in anovulatory cycles. If a raised prolactin level is found the pituitary must be investigated for the presence of a tumour, but where this does not exist the hyperprolactinaemia can often be treated by giving the antiprolactin drug bromocriptine. There is often marked nausea in the first few days on bromocriptine and it is important that the patient is advised about this and helped to minimize it if possible.

In this brief account of hormonal treatment it is not possible to outline the many variations and combinations of treatment programme that may be used especially as they differ from centre to centre and with the frequent introduction of new drugs.

The Infertile Man

Some general measures are available to help the man with a marginally low sperm count or a high production of immotile forms. In this context keeping the testes cool is important and is achieved by wearing loose underpants and avoiding a warm working environment. A varicocele may raise the testicular temperature and ligation will often improve the semen analysis.

The sperm count is depleted by over-frequent sexual intercourse as an optimum level is only restored 48 hours after the last ejaculation: thus an infertile couple should be encouraged to have sexual intercourse at approximately two-day intervals around mid-cycle, without being too regimented about it.

Surgical treatment in the male is required for undescended or partially descended testes, for the ligation of varicoceles, for the excision of testicular tumours and for restoring patency in the vas deferens. The vas may be obstructed congenitally or may have been ligated to produce sterility. Successful re-anastomosis can be achieved with rates varying between 5% and 80%.

Hormone treatment in the male is not as far advanced, nor as successful, as in the female. Bromocriptine is the most effective drug used for the specific indication of hyperprolactinaemia.

Clomiphene is also used in the male to stimulate production of gonadotrophin-releasing factors which in turn trigger the pituitary to produce the gonadotrophins required for sperm production.

The androgens, mesterolone and testosterone, act on the spermatogonia to enhance sperm maturation and have been found useful in increasing a poor sperm count with limited motility.

Artificial Insemination

Artificial insemination is available using the husband's sperm (AIH) or a donor's sperm (AID). AIH is indicated when the count is low or the motility poor; when there is evidence of sperm death in the upper vagina; or when normal sexual intercourse is physically impossible for one reason or another. It has also proved effective in some women following cone biopsy or other surgery to the cervix.

In some men it has been found that the first part of the ejaculate contains better quality sperm than the second part. By separating the active portion on several occasions, sperm may be preserved by freezing, then pooled, thawed and introduced to the cervix.

Freezing sperm to preserve them for a later occasion has various other applications; for example a man who requires pelvic irradiation which will render him sterile may wish to produce some active sperm and have them frozen for subsequent use.

The morality of AID is not universally accepted but it is available for those infertile couples who wish it. It is indicated in cases where the husband is unable to produce a sufficiently potent semen sample. Freezing a donor's sperm can ensure the same 'father' for subsequent children produced by AID in one family.

There will always be a residue of infertile couples who cannot be treated effectively by any method currently available. The option then lies between acceptance of a childless marriage or adoption.

With the advent of therapeutic abortion, adoption is no longer an easy procedure. There are very few unwanted babies born and these are immediately found homes, leaving long waiting lists of disappointed and saddened couples. Thus there is likely to be continuing interest in research into new methods of treating the various types of infertility where the problem is known to be not permanently irreversible. Developments in endocrine treatment, tubal microsurgery and possibly in extracorporeal fertilization may well become available in the near future.

3. Amenorrhoea

Robert W. Shaw

Amenorrhoea is a failure to menstruate and is a symptom frequently complained of by patients when not due to the physiological cause of pregnancy. Its investigation demands careful clinical examination combined with a wide knowledge of endocrinology. In recent years there has been an enormous acceleration in the understanding of endocrinological mechanisms in gynaecology and the control of the hypothalamic-pituitary-ovarian (HPO) axis. A clear understanding of these normal mechanisms is essential to appreciate the changes in hormonal secretion that may occur in disorders of the HPO axis associated with failure of menstruation.

NORMAL PHYSIOLOGY

The pituitary secretion of the two hormones primarily concerned with controlling ovarian function—follicle stimulating hormone (FSH) and luteinizing hormone (LH)—is under hypothalamic control. This control is brought about via the production of a neurohumoral substance, gonadotrophin-releasing hormone (GnRH) (or luteinizing hormone releasing hormone LH-RH) which is a small polypeptide of molecular weight 1181, originating in the region of the median eminence. GnRH is released into the capillary network surrounding the stalk of the pituitary gland whence it passes into the substance of the anterior pituitary gland and stimulates both the synthesis and the release of the gonadotrophins.

FSH stimulates the development of the primordial ovarian follicle into the mature graffian follicle and oestrogen secretion from the surrounding granulosa and theca cells. A short burst of LH secretion at midcycle induces ovulation with release of the ripened ovum from a prepared follicle. LH also maintains production of progesterone from the corpus luteum.

The normal ranges of serum gonadotrophin and steroid hormones in normal adult and post-menopausal women are shown in Table 3.1.

Table 3.1 Range of Gonadotrophins and Ovarian Steroids in Normal Human Serum

	*Luteinizing hormone** (u/litre)	*Follicle-stimulating hormone* (u/litre)	*Oestradiol-17ß* (pmol/litre)	*Progesterone* (nmol/litre)
Normal adult female				
Follicular phase	1–10	1–6	40–600	6
Mid-cycle peak	8–60	4–15	500–1600	2–6
Luteal phase	2–14	1–5	280–1000	20
Post-menopausal	>15	>30	<100	<6

*MRC 69/104.
Ranges may vary in different hospitals dependant upon standards and antisera used.

The secretion of GnRH is controlled by internal and external environmental influences which act via higher centres within the brain. The hypothalamic nuclei are directly affected by the circulating levels of the ovarian steroid hormones (oestrogens and progesterone) which when increased exert a *negative* or inhibitory feedback effect and when decreased stimulate the secretion of GnRH.

In recent years there has been a considerable advance in understanding the way in which the gonadal hormones interact in the menstrual cycle. The above simple negative feedback loop between oestrogen and gonadotrophins has been shown to be more complex than was previously thought. Under certain circumstances high levels of oestrogen can initiate gonadotrophin release and increase the senitivity of the pituitary gland's response to GnRH. These effects can in part account for the surge of gonadotrophins seen at midcycle and responsible for inducing ovulation; this has been termed *positive* feedback. A recent survey of the neurohumoral mechanisms controlling the menstrual cycle has been published (Shaw 1978).

It can be appreciated that a highly complex series of physiological events involving the central nervous system, pituitary gland and ovary is involved in controlling the normal menstrual cycle. Any disorder of function at any level will lead to a failure of ovulation, which if persistent will eventually result in complete cessation of menstruation.

DEFINITIONS

Pathological Amenorrhoea

Pathological amenorrhoea (i.e. occuring in the absence of pregnancy in a woman of child bearing age) is defined as the absence of menstruation for at least six months between the ages of 16 and 40 years. These age limits are set by the upper and lower normal limits, respectively, of the menarche and the menopause.

Diagnoses to Avoid

Only in rare circumstances, such as genital tract malformations (see below), is there any advantage in distinguishing between primary amenorrhoea (when the patient has never menstruated) and secondary amenorrhoea (which develops after normal menstrual function). 'Amenorrhoea' itself is often wrongly used as a diagnostic term: it is merely the common presenting symptom of a variety of distinct disorders which have unrelated causes.

The various eponymous amenorrhoea–galactorrhoea syndromes (e.g. Argonz-del Castillo, Chiari-Fromell) are also not distinct entities. The only feature which matters, which is common to them all and to many other amenorrhoeic women who do not have galactorrhoea, is hyperprolactinaemia.

'Post-pill amenorrhoea' is an unhelpful term since it is not a distinct entity and in making this diagnosis a serious underlying disorder may be overlooked.

DIAGNOSTIC CLASSIFICATION

Anatomical Causes

Whilst anatomical causes of amenorrhoea are rare (about 1%), a malformation of the genital tract must be considered in patients presenting with primary amenorrhoea and normal secondary sexual characteristics.

Vaginal atresia due to an imperforate membrane at the introitus prevents menstrual fluid loss with consequent collection within the vagina (haematocolpos). Patients with this condition present with a history of intermittent lower abdominal pains, not always at regular monthly intervals, and often associated with difficulty of micturition. On examination a bulging bluish membrane is found at the lower part of the vagina together with a palpable lower abdominal mass. A similar history will be obtained when there is a failure of canalization of a length of vagina. Treatment is surgical division of the atretic segment.

Absence of the uterus is usually associated with complete or partial absence of the vagina. In the testicular feminization syndrome (androgen insensitivity) absence of the uterus is found with an apparently normal female figure and temperament but normal male karyotype (46XY). The patients have good breast development, absent or scanty sexual hair, normal or hypoplastic vulva, short blind vagina, absent uterus and intra-abdominal, inguinal or labial testes instead of ovaries. The testes appear to produce testosterone in normal male amounts and oestrogen in small quantities. Insensitivity to androgen results in failure of masculinization of the genitalia in utero of the child who is born with a female phenotype. The unrestricted action of oestrogen gives rise to female secondary sexual development at puberty. Diagnosis is often possible from the clinical findings but karyotype should be confirmed and laparoscopy performed to confirm absence of the uterus. If the condition is recognized before puberty it is better to wait for secondary development to occur before removal of the testes, which are removed to avoid the risk of malignancy (of the order of 5%). Following their removal oestrogen replacement therapy will be required to prevent the menopausal-type symptoms which may result. Patients with this condition should be handled with particular kindness and care. The information that an apparently normal attractive girl will never have children and will require an operation to have her 'ovaries' removed can be devastating.

Endocrinological Causes

In the majority (99%) of cases the cause of amenorrhoea is endocrinological. By adopting a primarily endocrinological rather than organic classification of disorders greater simplification in the diagnostic process can be achieved. A comprehensive classification, the diagnostic features, and most suitable treatment to induce ovulation are summarized in Table 3.2.

Primary hypothalamic or pituitary failure

Rarely space-occupying lesions such as craniopharyngiomas or gliomas may present with amenorrhoea. In cases of this kind local hypothalamic manifestations such as diabetes insipidus, sleepiness and perhaps obesity may be present in addition. The mechanism of the endocrine deficit is thought to be disruption of releasing hormone production and thus the reproductive deficit can be made good by treatment with GnRH.

Complete pituitary failure occurring before puberty will result in a pituitary dwarf who develops no signs of secondary sexual development. Pituitary failure may not be complete for all trophic hormones and, indeed, isolated gonadotrophin deficiency can be an important cause of primary amenorrhoea. When affected patients are given exogenous GnRH the reproductive defect can be repaired (Mortimer et al. 1974) indicating that the disorder is a deficiency of GnRH production rather than an abnormality of the pituitary gland itself.

Patients with pituitary tumours frequently have amenorrhoea as a presenting symptom. In the past the reproductive disturbance has been attributed to acquired hypogonadotrophic hypogonadism. However, recent studies suggest that usually the cause is oversecretion of prolactin, and reduction of prolactin levels surgically, by radiotherapy or by bromocriptine usually restores ovulatory cycles unless prior pituitary ablative treatment has caused hypopituitarism.

It is not yet feasible to measure serum GnRH and, therefore, in common with primary pituitary failure, primary hypothalamic failure can only be recognized by gonadotrophin deficiency. This can readily be demonstrated by failure to respond to an intravenous injection of synthetic GnRH.

Primary ovarian failure

One of the most important abnormalities causing primary amenorrhoea

Table 3.2. Classification of Disorders Causing Amenorrhoea

	Incidence (%)	*Diagnostic features*	*Oestrogen state*	*Treatment to induce ovulation*
Anatomical causes	1			
Vaginal atresia		Clinical	→	None (surgery to restore normal menses)
Absent uterus		Clinical (+ chromosomes)	→	None
Discrete endocrine disorders				
Primary hypothalamic failure	0.5	FSH reduced	↓	Gonadotrophins, ? GnRH
Primary pituitary failure	0.5	FSH reduced	↓	Gonadotrophins, ? GnRH
Isolated deficiency				
Large tumour		(+ X-ray)		? Bromocriptine
Primary ovarian failure	5	FSH raised	↓	
Dysgenesis		(+ chromosomes & laparoscopy)		
Destruction (radiation, surgery)				None
Autoimmunity				
Premature menopause				
Hyperprolactinaemia	18	Prolactin raised (+ X-ray)	↓	Bromocriptine
Pituitary tumour				? surgery
Drugs (phenothiazines, etc)				stop drugs
Primary hypothyroidism		(+ free thyroxine index)		treat thyroid condition ?
'Functional'				
Polycystic ovary disease	8	Hirsutism Laparoscopy	→	Clomiphene, ? Wedge resection
Metabolic diseases	1		→	
Thyroid		Free thyroxine index		Thyroxine
Adrenal		Diurnal cortisol		Treat adrenal condition
Hypothalamic disorders		*by exclusion discrete disorders*		
Feedback disorder (absent or impaired positive feedback)	40	LH and FSH within normal range or reduced	↓	Clomiphene + HCG (? gonadotrophin)
Chronic anorexia nervosa				Weight gain
Weight loss				Weight gain
Other psychological disorders				Clomiphene + HCG
Cycle initiation defect (intact positive feedback)	26		→	
Normal weight and psyche		LH and FSH within normal range		Clomiphene

→ within normal range; ↑ significantly raised; ↓ reduced.

is a failure of gonadal development, often as a result of a chromosomal abnormality. These patients are generally short (under 150 cm) and show absence of secondary sexual development. In addition there may be other clinical features: neck webbing, a wide carrying angle of the arms, coarctation of the aorta and short metatarsals.

The physical features associated with gonadal dysgenesis are often quite striking and permit the condition to be suspected strongly on clinical grounds. Confirmatory diagnosis can be obtained from chromosomal analysis with many patients having a 45X karyotype, some being mosaics 45X/46XX, or even 45X/46XY, whilst others have an abnormal chromosome with a deleted X (Dewhurst & Lucas 1971). In some patients with mosaicism infrequent menstrual periods may occur. At laparoscopy streak ovaries are the characteristic feature.

Ovarian function normally terminates between the ages of 40 and 55 years. In rare instances it ceases unusually early and is referred to as 'premature ovarian failure' or 'premature menopause'. These patients have had a normal menarche with appearance of secondary sexual characteristics but develop secondary amenorrhoea and are found to have high gonadotrophin and low oestrogen levels.

No single aetiological agent has been associated with premature ovarian failure. Some girls with gonadal dysgenesis with mosaicism have some germinal cells, may ovulate and menstruate, and then develop a premature menopause in adolescence. The use of irradiation and chemotherapeutic agents in the treatment of lymphomas and neoplasms can result in accelerated follicular atresia and destruction of germ cells, and surgical removal or destruction of the ovaries must always be borne in mind.

Another possible mechanism in premature ovarian failure involves an autoimmune process with development of antibodies to ovarian tissues. In such instances there are often other autoantibodies—to adrenal or thyroid tissue in particular—and this may indicate a generalized autoimmune diathesis. However, in the majority of patients there appears to be no specific cause for the premature ovarian failure.

Determination of serum FSH is essential to identify patients with primary ovarian failure, which results in very high levels of FSH similar to those which occur after the normal menopause, and thus it can be diagnosed with complete certainty. LH levels are not so distinctive, being markedly elevated in some cases of polycystic ovary disease. Whatever the cause, primary ovarian failure is permanent and irreversible and affords no hope of ovulation induction. The only treatment necessary is oestrogen replacement, for those with symptoms of oestrogen deficiency (e.g. dyspareunia, loss of libido) or to induce secondary sexual development in patients with gonadal dysgenesis.

Hyperprolactinaemia

Hyperprolactinaemia produces a characteristic disturbance of reproduction both in women with normal post-partum lactation and in those with inappropriate lactation (galactorrhoea). In these conditions there is evidence of impairment both of the ovarian response to gonadotrophins and of the hypothalamic–pituitary regulation of gonadotrophin secretion. The effect of hyperprolactinaemia on gonadotrophin secretion is subtle involving suppression of positive feedback mechanisms demonstrable by the use of an oestrogen provocation test (Glass et al. 1975). The effect on the ovaries is suppression of function, resulting in amenorrhoea and oestrogen deficiency. The latter causes atrophy of the uterus and sexual functional complaints of dyspareunia. These effects are rapidly reversed once the hyperprolactinaemia is corrected.

Several studies have shown that hyperprolactinaemia is the cause of amenorrheoa in approximately one case in five (Franks et al. 1975; Glass et al. 1975) and measurement of serum levels is always essential.

Hyperprolactinaemia is occasionally due to drug usage or primary hypothyroidism. Drugs elevating serum prolactin levels have a variety of common uses and, although seemingly unrelated, all are antagonists to dopamine which is the prolactin-inhibiting factor secreted by the hypothalamus. A list of these drugs is given in Table 3.3.

Table 3.3 Common Drugs Causing Hyperprolactinaemia

Phenothiazines	*Other drugs*
Chlorpromazine (Largactil)	Haloperidol
Prochlorperazine (Stemetil)	Methyldopa (Aldomet)
Trifluoperazine (Stelazine)	Cimetidine (Tagamet)
	Reserpine
	Metaclopramide (Maxolon)

The commonest demonstrable cause of hyperprolactinaemia is a prolactin-secreting pituitary tumour or prolactinoma. A pituitary tumour will be radiologically demonstrable in about 15% of women with hyperprolactinaemia. Diagnosis may be obvious on a lateral skull

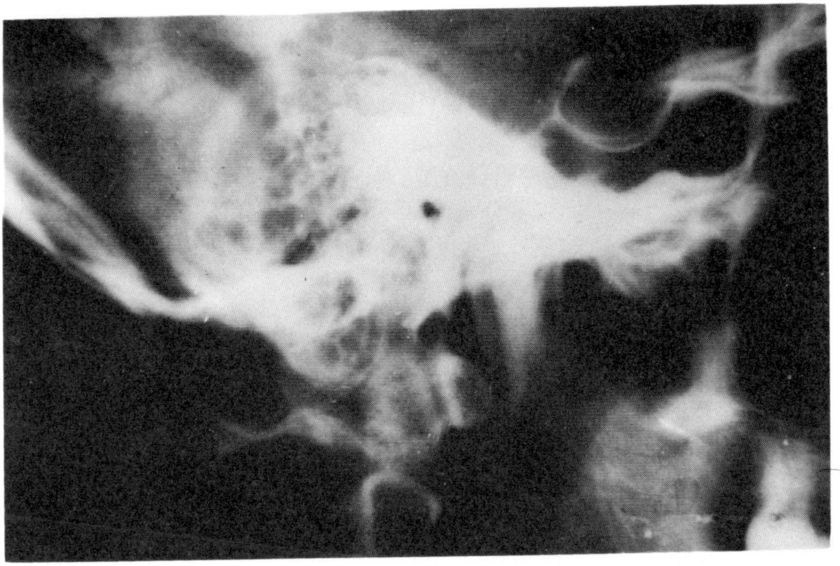

Fig. 3.1. Lateral skull radiograph showing double floor of the pituitary fossa, typical of a small prolactinoma. This early appearance results from the asymmetrical growth downwards of the tumour, but at a later date the fossa will expand generally.

radiograph (Fig. 3.1), although recognition of such tumours at an early stage may require tomographic examination. Visual field perimetry, air encephalography or CAT scanning can be used to detect upward extention of a tumour endangering the optic tracts.

Since these pituitary tumours enlarge in pregnancy due to placental oestrogens stimulating the normal pituitary to increase in size and secrete large amounts of prolactin, any tumour already extending upwards must be treated by surgery or radiotherapy prior to ovulation induction to achieve pregnancy. Tumours without upward extention seem less troublesome and can be monitored by visual field perimetry during pregnancy.

In the majority of women no cause can be found for the hyperprolactinaemia. In such patients there may simply be a 'functional' disorder of prolactin control perhaps from altered production of the hypothalamic-inhibitory factor controlling prolactin release. Such seems to be the case in many patients with 'post-Pill' amenorrhoea and, indeed, combined oral contraceptive agents have been shown to alter the control of prolactin release.

However, there is good evidence to suggest that in many patients with 'functional' hyperprolactinaemia there may be a small prolactinoma (less than 4 mm in size) present within the pituitary gland.

Because of the altered feedback mechanisms in hyperprolactinaemia, clomiphene citrate is usually unsuccessful in inducing ovulation. Bromocriptine, an ergot alkaloid and dopamine agonist, rapidly suppresses circulating prolactin levels and allows return of normal ovulatory function and is the treatment of choice.

Polycystic ovary disease/syndrome

Although the existence of polycystic ovaries had been described for many years, it was the description in 1935 of their association with hirsutism, obesity, menstrual irregularity and infertility that focussed attention on this syndrome (PCO) (Stein & Leventhal 1935) (Fig. 3.2). Polycystic ovaries have a characteristic appearance when viewed through the laparoscope, showing significant enlargement and a whitish sclerotic capsule through which numerous small follicular cysts can be seen. The ovaries and cyst fluid contain large amounts of androgens (particularly androstenedione) but very little oestrogen. In spite of the low ovarian secretion of oestrogen, these patients show no evidence of oestrogen deficiency, oestrogen being produced by extraglandular aromatization of androgen precursors via peripheral conversion mostly to oestrone. It seems clear that the hirsutism found in this syndrome is due to the increased secretion of androgens (androstenedione and testosterone) from the enlarged polycystic ovaries. There may also be increased androgen secretion by the adrenal cortex in some cases but the evidence for this is slight.

The abnormal steroid environment has been shown to affect the secretion of gonadotrophins. The basal secretion of LH is elevated with absence of the normal midcycle peak (Yen et al. 1970) whilst FSH concentration is in the low normal range. Dynamic tests of hypothalamic–pituitary function have demonstrated normal negative feedback and a normal or exaggerated release of LH in response to oestrogen provocation (Shaw et al. 1975). The high incidence of ovulation following clomiphene therapy in these patients is an indication of normal positive feedback and makes it seem unlikely that an intrinsic enzyme defect in ovarian steroidogenesis can be the precipitating factor. It has been suggested that the prolonged exposure to oestrogen, produced by extraglandular aromatization of androstenedione, results in suppression of FSH while at the same time stimulating LH secretion (Baird 1976). The low levels of FSH prevent adequate maturation of the graffian follicles whilst on the other hand

LH stimulates the secretion of androgens thus promoting, indirectly, extraglandular production of oestrogen.

Although the pattern of gonadotrophin secretion is closely related to the nature and origin of the steroids in blood and *vice versa*, the factors initiating this vicious chain of events are more difficult to identify. Whatever the cause, once established the condition is self-perpetuating because the raised LH levels stimulate further secretion of androstenedione from the ovaries.

Wedge resection of the ovaries results in restoration of ovulatory cycles in 80% of cases (Goldzieher & Axelrod 1963). The reduction in

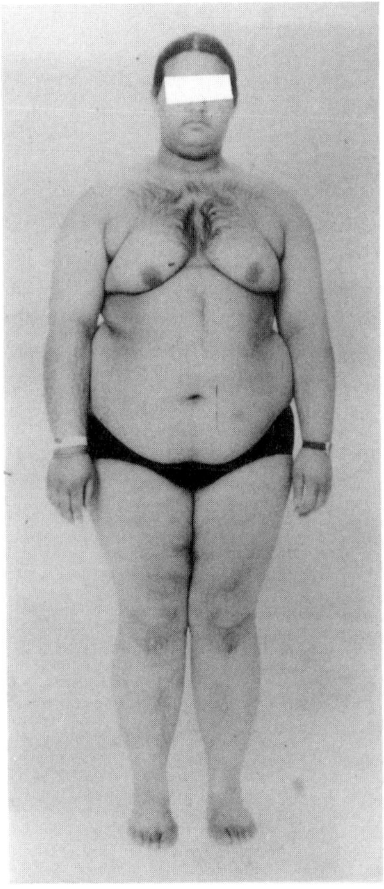

Fig. 3.2. Clinical features of obesity and hirsutism in an 18-year-old patient presenting with secondary amenorrhoea due to polycystic ovary syndrome.

the mass of ovarian tissue causes a marked fall in the secretion of androstenedione and, consequently, a reduction in oestrone produced extraglandularly. This alteration in steroid hormone production allows the return of normal gonadotrophin secretion and hence ovulatory function. Nowadays the availability of clomiphene citrate enables ovulation to be induced without the need for wedge resection.

Hypothalamic disorders

Hypothalamic disorders are the most common causes of amenorrhoea. They are defined by exclusion of all the foregoing discrete endocrine disorders and can be subclassified in endocrinological terms according to the type of feedback failure present after oestrogen provocation tests and clomiphene administration (Shaw et al. 1974).

The majority of cases are due to 'environmental' influences, particularly weight loss and psychological disorders. Typically these cause profound reproductive disturbance characterized by disordered feedback control over gonadotrophin secretion, with consequent oestrogen deficiency and failure to ovulate in response to clomiphene (absent positive feedback).

Other patients appear to have a cycle initiation defect and apart from their amenorrhoea are normal in every way; they are oestrogenized and demonstrate normal feedback control over gonadotrophin secretion from their ovulatory response to clomiphene. Occasionally spontaneous ovulatory cycles occur in such patients.

Emotional stress may inhibit GnRH production in the hypothalamus with subsequent failure of cyclical gonadotrophin release. Amenorrhoea is a common complaint among young women in their late teens, particularly students, nurses and those starting professional life: menstruation usually recommences once the patient has adjusted to her new life style.

Malnutrition appears to result in hypothalamic–pituitary suppression with resultant amenorrhoea. Amenorrhoea is common when women are living in conditions of famine. In modern Western society where food is abundant, cosmetic dieting, especially in teenage girls, is the most common cause of weight loss leading to amenorrhoea. Whatever the original cause or motive for dieting, in some women it becomes an obsession which can lead to anorexia nervosa. The girl, usually teenage, is obsessed with her size and starves herself but cannot admit it. In its chronic form it can be a life-long disorder with distinct psychological features. It accounts for 10–15% of all women who complain of amenorrhoea. Altogether weight loss, with or without the distinct features of anorexia nervosa, accounts for amenorrhoea in about 25% of cases.

Re-gaining lost weight is a sure means of restoring reproductive function and far preferable to treatment with exogenous gonadotrophin which is otherwise required to induce ovulation when pregnancy is desired.

For a fuller account of dietary amenorrhoea and the associated clinical features see Hull (1979).

Ovarian tumours

Functioning ovarian tumours are extremely uncommon but may produce both feminizing and masculinizing effects in varying degrees. The commonest masculinizing tumour is the arrhenoblastoma which first presents clinically with a stage of defeminization, indicated by amenorrhoea and atrophy of the breasts. A stage of masculinization with hirsutism, hoarse voice and clitoral hypertrophy follows. Removal of the tumour results in return of menstruation but a more gradual disappearance of the signs of masculinization.

Metabolic diseases

Such causes of amenorrhoea are extremely uncommon, accounting for approximately 1% of cases.

Amenorrhoea may be associated with both *hypothyroidism* and *hyperthyroidism*. Thyroid function tests should be performed when there is clinical suspicion of dysfunction and appropriate therapy will then probably restore normal menstruation.

Diabetes mellitus is similarly associated with menstrual disturbances and sometimes amenorrhoea may be a feature, particularly in poorly controlled juvenile patients. The well controlled diabetic usually has normal menstruation.

Congenital adrenal hyperplasia will produce primary amenorrhoea if not treated correctly before puberty. Signs of heterosexual development are also seen, such as growth of hair on the face, male distribution of body hair, enlargement of the clitoris and excessive fusion of the labial folds. The disease is caused by an enzyme deficiency which prevents the adrenal cortex from synthesizing cortisol and replacement therapy using cortisone or synthetic corticosteroids is employed.

Amenorrhoea is also a characteristic of *Cushing's syndrome* in which there is hyperfunction of the whole adrenal cortex. Some cases are associated with pituitary tumours but in others there is adrenal hyperplasia without any pituitary lesion. Urinary and blood corticosteroids are elevated and cannot be fully suppressed by dexamethasone. Amenorrhoea is an early symptom of adrenocortical tumours, in which there is an elevation of dehydroisoandrosterone and complete failure to suppress corticosteroid levels on treatment with dexamethasone.

TREATMENT

It is clear from recent reports (Hull et al. 1979) that in amenorrhoeic women not desiring pregnancy at present, drug treatment is not needed to protect future fertility.

The majority of disorders which cause amenorrhoea lead to oestrogen deficiency of varying degree. In some patients this causes troublesome symptoms which require treatment. In primary hypothalamic, pituitary or ovarian failure, sequential preparations of oestrogen and progestogen, as used after the menopause, are probably most desirable to avoid the risk of unopposed oestrogen acting on the endometrium. If oestrogens are needed to achieve normal sexual development the dose must be carefully chosen to avoid premature closure of bony epiphyses.

Should the patient wish to conceive, in the absence of a raised postmenopausal level of serum FSH, indicating primary ovarian failure, the amenorrhoeic patient's potential fertility is assessed. Most patients will require treatment to induce ovulation and it is vital to exclude other factors which may affect fertility, e.g. tubal problems, male factors or pituitary tumour, prior to the commencement of ovulation induction therapy.

A number of effective drugs and hormones are available to induce ovulation but can be classified within three groups:

Clomiphene and Related Compounds

The most widely used agent in this group is clomiphene citrate. It increases gonadotrophin secretion from the hypothalamic–pituitary axis and this in turn will induce ovarian follicle stimulation. As a result of such stimulation oestrogen production from the maturing follicle increases and if positive feedback mechanisms are intact ovulation will occur. In subjects in whom negative feedback is intact but positive feedback absent or defective, clomiphene administration induces follicle maturation but ovulation does not occur. The addition of human chorionic gonadotrophin (HCG) at the relevant time of follicle maturation will induce ovulation in such patients.

The side effects from the use of these drugs are minimal and close monitoring of response is rarely needed except where HCG injections are indicated in addition. The usual doses of clomiphene citrate are 50 or 100 mg daily for five days commencing on Day 3 to 5 of the cycle but occasionally 150–200 mg daily is given.

Bromocriptine and Related Compounds

Bromocriptine has revolutionized the treatment of the infertile patient with hyperprolactinaemia but related compounds are now being evaluated. Bromocriptine is a dopamine agonist and stimulates dopamine receptors at hypothalamic and pituitary levels and induces dramatic falls in serum prolactin. Side effects of the drug include nausea and vomiting, nasal congestion and hypotensive episodes. These can be minimized by gradual increase in the dosage and by always taking the drug after a meal. The initial doses should be taken at bedtime. Infrequently nausea is excessive and treatment has to be stopped. The usual effective dosage in severe hyperprolactinaemia is between 7.5 and 15 mg per day in divided doses and 2.5–5 mg per day for milder cases. It is recommended that bromocriptine treatment is stopped as soon as there is a possibility of pregnancy to avoid any theoretical teratogenic effects although none have been reported so far.

Exogenous Gonadotrophins

It is now over 20 years since Gemzell et al. (1958) reported the first human pregnancy using human pituitary gland extracts, but gonadotrophins can also be extracted from the urine of menopausal women. Whilst this form of treatment is highly effective in inducing ovulation in the majority of patients, it is time-consuming to administer, requires close monitoring to avoid the possible risks of ovarian hyperstimulation and increased incidence of multiple pregnancy and is somewhat costly. For these reasons its use should be restricted to patients for whom no other effective treatment is available; these now constitute only a small proportion of amenorrhoeic patients.

CONTRACEPTION

The question arises as to whether amenorrhoeic women need any method of contraception. This depends on whether or not their reproductive disorder is complete and permanent. Primary hypothalamic, pituitary and ovarian failure are complete and permanent and consequently no contraception is necessary.

Hyperprolactinaemia is usually permanent, but spontaneous resolution can occur. The chance of conception in untreated hyperprolactinaemia is very low and it is usually reasonable for them not to use any form of contraception. If the need arises for more confident contraception then it seems advisable to avoid combined oral contraceptive agents, an IUCD is sometimes not properly retained due to marked uterine atrophy and, therefore, the progesterone-only pill may be a reasonable alternative to barrier methods.

A hypothalamic disorder, which may resolve unpredictably, is the most common cause of amenorrhoea and affected women cannot, therefore, rely on their disorder for contraception. Combined oral contraceptive pills with their known mechanism of action upon the hypothalamic–pituitary axis seems best avoided in such patients. Thus the choice for effective contraception lies between the progesterone-only pill, which has a less suppressive action on the HPO axis than the combined pill, an IUCD or a barrier method.

CONCLUSIONS

It is now more possible than ever before to investigate the complex interrelationships of the HPO axis to try and elucidate the disordered mechanisms leading to amenorrhoea. The condition should always be investigated properly to exclude the risk of a serious disorder. The minimal investigative procedures should be a careful history of the psychological state and weight fluctuations, thyroid symptoms and drug usage, careful clinical examination, and the performance of two hormone measurements (serum FSH and prolactin). The need for further investigations is determined by the results of the initial tests and the patient's desire for conception.

Bibliography

Baird, D.T. (1976) Pituitary-ovarian relationships in disorders of menstruation. In

Endocrine Function of the Human Ovary, ed. V.H.T. James & M. Serio. London: Academic Press.

Dewhurst, C.J. & Lucas, M. (1971) Gonadal dysgenesis and chromosome mosaicism. *Br. J. Hosp. Med., 6,* 807.

Franks, S., Murray, M.A.F., Jequier, A.M., Steele, S.J., Nabarro, J.D.N. & Jacobs, H.S. (1975) Incidence and significance of hyperprolactinaemia in women with amenorrhoea. *Clin. Endocr., 4,* 597.

Gemzell, C.A., Diczfalusy, E. & Tillinger, K.G. (1958) Clinical effect of human pituitary follicle-stimulating hormone (FSH). *J. clin. Endocr. Metab., 18*, 1333.

Glass, M.R., Shaw, R.W., Butt, W.R., Logan-Edwards, R. & London, D.R. (1975) An abnormality of oestrogen feedback in amenorrhoea-galactorrhoea. *Br. med. J., 3,* 274.

Goldzieher, J.W. & Axelrod, L.R. (1963) Clinical and biochemical features of polycystic ovarian disease. *Fert. Steril., 14*, 631.

Hull, M.G.R. (1979) Dietary restriction and amenorrhoea. *J. mat. Child Hlth, 4,* 104.

Hull, M.G.R., Savage, P.E. & Jacobs, H.S. (1979) Investigation and treatment of amenorrhoea resulting in normal fertility. *Br. med. J., 1*, 1257.

Mortimer, C.H., McNeilly, A.S., Fisher, R.A., Murray, M.A.F. & Besser, G.M. (1974) Gonadotrophin releasing hormone therapy in hypogonadal males with hypothalamic or pituitary dysfunction. *Br. med. J., 4,* 617.

Shaw, R.W. (1978) Neuroendocrinology of the menstrual cycle in humans. *Clin. Endocr. Metab., 7*, 531.

Shaw, R.W., Butt, W.R. & London, D.R. (1974). The oestrogen provocation test—a means of assessing hypothalamic-pituitary function in amenorrhoea. *J. Endocr., 63*, 46P.

Shaw, R.W., Duignan, N.M., Butt, W.R., Logan-Edwards, R. & London, D.R. (1975) Hypothalamic-pituitary relationships in the polycystic ovary syndrome. Serum gonadotrophin levels following injection of oestradiol benzoate. *Br. J. Obstet. Gynaec., 82,* 952.

Stein, I.F. & Levanthal, M.L. (1935) Amenorrhoea associated with bilateral polycystic ovaries. *Am. J. Obstet. Gynec., 29*, 181.

Yen, S.S.C., Vela, P. & Rankin, J. (1970) Inappropriate secretion of follicle-stimulating hormone and luteinizing hormone in polycystic ovarian disease. *J. clin. Endocr. Metab., 30*, 435.

4. The Control of Menorrhagia

Margaret Rees

Menorrhagia is a very common gynaecological disorder. The word menorrhagia comes from the Greek (*men* = month and *rhegynai* = to burst forth) and simply means heavy periods. In recent years the problem has been studied more closely and new modifications in treatment have been introduced. Initially the anatomy of the uterus and the physiology of menstruation will be described. Before discussing its control, menorrhagia will be first defined in more scientific terms and some of the major causes and investigations will be noted.

Anatomy

The uterus is a pear-shaped organ and measures about 2.5 × 5 × 7.5 cm. It consists of fundus, body and cervix. The cervix protrudes into the vault of the vagina. The uterus receives the fallopian tubes superiorly and above this level lies the fundus of the uterus.

The wall of the uterus consists of an outer muscular layer, the myometrium, and an inner layer, the endometrium which is a mucous membrane containing glands and blood vessels. The endometrium consists of a superficial functional layer which is shed during menstruation and a basal layer lying on the myometrium and not shed during menstruation.

The blood supply of the uterus is derived from the uterine artery which runs along each side of the uterus. The uterine artery gives off branches to the uterine wall. There are two types of arteries supplying the endometrium, the straight basal arteries which supply the basal layer and the spiral arteries which supply the functional layer. This arrangement is only found in menstruating species and may be implicated in menorrhagia.

Physiology of Menstruation

Menstruation is a periodic discharge of sanguinous fluid and a shedding of the functional layer of the endometrium. It usually occurs at regular intervals of about 28 days. The menstrual cycle is the interval between the onset of two successive menstruations with the first day of menstruation being called Day 1. Control of the menstrual cycle involves the central nervous system, pituitary and ovary with various feedback mechanisms playing an essential role. Ovulation occurs in a normal menstrual cycle. In the first or follicular phase of the cycle a follicle develops in the ovary. When the follicle is ripe the

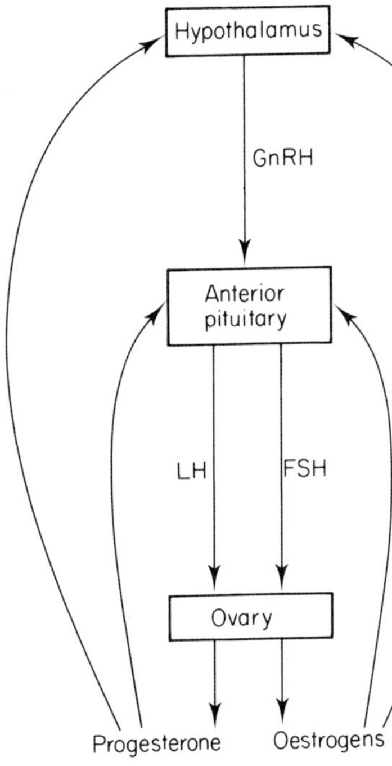

Fig. 4.1. The control of the menstrual cycle.

ovum is released and this is called ovulation. The ruptured follicle is then transformed into a corpus luteum. This occurs in the second or luteal phase of the cycle. If the ovum is not fertilized the corpus luteum degenerates and menstruation occurs.

The interval between ovulation and menstruation is normally 14 days. However the follicular phase may be of variable length, though it is usually also about 14 days. Thus in a normal cycle ovulation occurs at about Day 14.

Control of the Menstrual Cycle and Hormonal Changes

The menstrual cycle is controlled by the interaction of the hypothalamus, pituitary and ovaries (Fig. 4.1) The hypothalamus releases gonadotrophin-releasing hormone (GnRH), which stimulates both follicle-stimulating hormone (FSH) and luteinizing hormone (LH) secretion from the anterior pituitary gland. These in turn control the ovarian production of oestrogens and progesterone. These steroids act on the hypothalamus and the anterior pituitary in a 'feedback' mechanism and affect GnRH, FSH and LH release. In the first part of the menstrual cycle FSH stimulates follicular growth in the ovary and the developing follicles produce oestrogen. One follicle outstrips the rest and also produces a developing ovum. The increasing levels of oestrogen inhibit FSH production. However when levels of oestrogen reach a critical level the LH and FSH surges are stimulated. This brings about ovulation and converts the follicle into a corpus luteum which produces oestrogen and progesterone. These hormones act on the endometrium to prepare it for implantation of a fertilized ovum. If conception does not result menstruation occurs.

Here is a short account of the changing levels of hormones during the menstrual cycle (Fig. 4.2)

FSH levels start to increase during the last two to three days of the preceding cycle and reach a small peak in the early follicular phase. FSH stimulates oestrogen synthesis by the developing follicle. Immediately prior to ovulation, levels of FSH reach a peak which is called the midcycle surge. During the luteal phase FSH levels are low.

LH levels are higher during the follicular phase than during the luteal phase. The preovulatory midcycle surge of LH is very pronounced and is responsible for the initiation of ovulation.

Oestrogen levels rise slowly during the follicular phase to reach a peak prior to the midcycle surge of LH. The titres fall prior to ovulation and

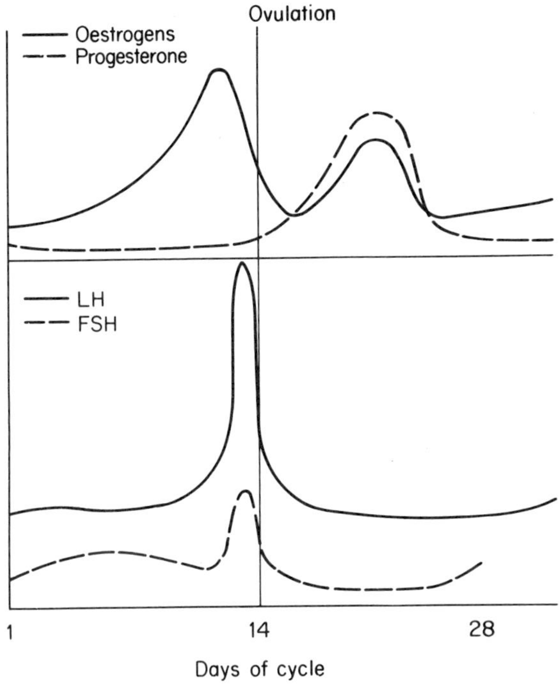

Fig. 4.2. The levels of luteinizing (LH) and follicle-stimulating hormone (FSH) during the menstrual cycle.

rise again during the midluteal phase. They then decline as the corpus luteum degenerates.

Progesterone levels are very low in the follicular phase. There is a small increase at midcycle and peak levels occur six to eight days after ovulation. With corpus luteum regression the levels fall to reach follicular phase values prior to the onset of the next menses.

Mechanism of Uterine Bleeding

All the components of the endometrium undergo cyclic changes as a result of hormonal influences. The menstrual phase is characterized by disintegration and shedding of the functional layer, while the basal layer remains intact. Thus the menstrual discharge consists of blood and the shed functional layer of the endometrium.

The exact mechanism of uterine bleeding is unknown, though several theories have been proposed. These include:

1. *Arteriolar vasoconstriction.* Constriction of the spiral arterioles which supply the functional layer has been shown to lead on to endometrial necrosis and the bleeding of menstruation. The straight arterioles which supply the basal layer do not undergo vasoconstriction and thus this part of the endometrium is preserved.

2. *Oestrogen and progesterone withdrawal.* Menstruation normally occurs after an ovulatory cycle which has not resulted in conception. As the corpus luteum degenerates the levels of oestrogen and progesterone decline. This results in menstrual bleeding. Discontinuation of oestrogen and progesterone both cause bleeding. Withdrawal of progesterone alone in an oestrogen pretreated uterus will cause bleeding, and this can be stopped by the administration of progesterone. Oestrogen withdrawal is also followed by bleeding and this can be stopped by progesterone administration. Thus withdrawal of both hormones simultaneously is needed for normal bleeding.

3. *Inadequate lymphatic drainage.* It has been suggested that the endometrial lymphatic system is inadequate to provide for removal of waste products which accumulate after withdrawal of endometrial hormonal support and cause endometrial necrosis which precipitates menstrual bleeding.

DEFINITION OF MENORRHAGIA

Menorrhagia is defined as a measured menstrual loss greater than 80 ml on at least one of two consecutive periods. This level has been chosen since above it there is an increased incidence of iron-deficiency anaemia. The average normal loss is 30 ml per period. A few important points must be made.

Menstrual blood loss has been estimated in various research projects. In these the pads and tampons are collected and the amount of blood lost is estimated from the amount of haemoglobin in them. It is very difficult to estimate menstrual loss on the basis of the patient's own judgement since it often bears little relation to the actual measured loss. The number of sanitary pads and tampons used is not correlated with the amount of blood lost.

There is no relation between the duration of menstruation and total menstrual loss. Both women with excessive loss and women with normal loss pass the same proportion of total menstrual blood loss on each day of menstruation: 92% of the total is lost in the first three days. Thus women with menorrhagia have an amplification of the normal amount of blood lost at menstruation.

Only a few patients with menorrhagia have dysmenorrhoea or painful periods. It seems that the two symptoms are not often associated.

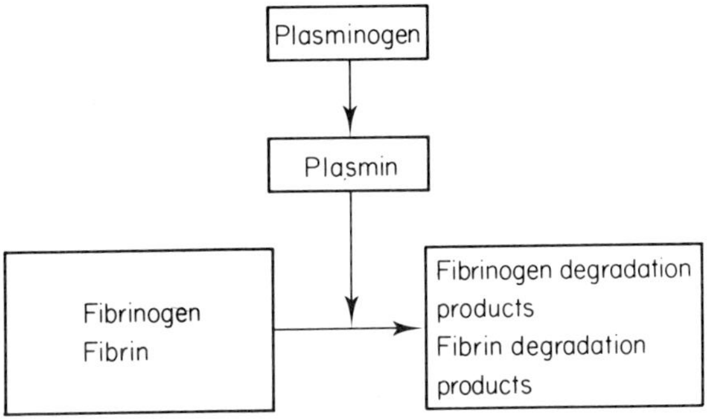

Fig. 4.3. The fibrinolytic enzyme system.

Menstrual blood characteristically does not clot (Fig. 4.3). A clot contains fibrin which is derived from fibrinogen in the blood. Fibrin and fibrinogen are digested by plasmin, a proteolytic enzyme derived from an inactive precursor plasminogen. Plasminogen is affected by a system of activators and inhibitors. Menstrual blood does not contain fibrin and fibrinogen and has fibrinolytic properties. Plasminogen activator is found in menstrual blood and is derived from the endometrium; this explains the absence of fibrin. Menstrual clots are not true clots since they do not contain fibrin. They are aggregates of red blood cells, mucoid substances, mucoproteins and glycogen. It has been shown that these clots are formed outside the uterus in the vagina.

Women suffering from menorrhagia tend to develop iron-deficiency anaemia. In Western women the daily iron loss in urine and faeces and from cell desquamation is about 0.6 mg and that from menstrual blood flow of 40–80 ml is 0.6–1.2 mg. The average daily dietary intake of iron in the West is 11.5 mg and about 10% of this or 1.15 mg is absorbed. Thus many women are in critical iron balance and any increased loss easily causes deficiency.

CAUSES

The causes of menorrhagia will be considered under the headings systemic and local. In about 50% of women who present with menorrhagia there is pelvic or systemic pathology but in the remainder no cause can be found: these women are said to be suffering from dysfunctional uterine bleeding.

Systemic

Defects of haemostasis

The mechanisms which contribute to haemostatic function in the human are vasoconstriction, platelet activity, and plasma coagulation. Thus, following injury to a blood vessel, there is vasoconstriction followed by formation of a platelet plug and then by a clot of fibrin. Defects of the haemostatic system can cause menorrhagia. These include von Willebrand's disease (a disease of coagulation) and thrombocytopenic purpura (a purpura due to a low platelet count). Some, but not all, patients on anticoagulants develop increased menstrual loss.

Endocrine

Several endocrine conditions cause menorrhagia. These include:

1. Hypothyroidism in which menorrhagia is present in 30–40% of the cases.
2. Defects of the hypothalamus and pituitary by affecting FSH and LH secretion.
3. Hyperoestrogenism (increased oestrogen levels) due mainly to administration of exogenous oestrogen, sometimes for extra-genital causes.

Local

Congenital

Congenital abnormalities of the uterus can lead to menorrhagia especially if the bleeding surface is increased. This occurs, for example, in a bicornuate uterus.

Foreign bodies

The most commonly encountered foreign bodies are intrauterine contraceptive devices or IUCDs. Increased menstrual loss and irregular uterine bleeding are major drawbacks with IUCDs. It has been found that the pattern of uterine bleeding is altered by IUCDs as follows

1. Menstrual blood loss is increased and this is probably related to the surface area of the IUCD.
2. Menstruation is prolonged.
3. A greater proportion of the total loss is passed later during the period than in women without IUCDs.
4. There is an increased incidence of intermenstrual bleeding, i.e. bleeding between periods.

Endometrial hyperplasia

This condition is found when ovulation fails to occur. The follicle ripens, there is no ovulation and thus no corpus luteum formation. The ovary then produces oestrogen without progesterone. This results in increased thickening (hyperplasia) of the endometrium. When the ovary stops producing oestrogen, the endometrium breaks down and bleeding results. This phenomenon tends to occur at the extremes of reproductive life when failure of ovulation is more common.

Endometriosis

Endometriosis is a proliferation of the endometrium at any site other than the uterine cavity. It occurs in two main forms, either in the uterine wall or involving extrauterine organs and tissues.

Uterine endometriosis is called adenomyosis. Extrauterine endometriosis can occur anywhere in the body but is mainly found in the pelvis and abdomen. The ovary is the commonest site. An endometriotic lesion has the typical histology of endometrium and responds to ovarian hormones and thus shows the characteristic cyclic changes of menstruation. The lesions bleed and this leads to the formation of 'chocolate' or 'tarry' cysts. Menorrhagia is a common symptom of endometriosis.

Tumours

Both benign and malignant tumours of the uterus can cause menorrhagia. Benign tumours include fibroids, endometrial and cervical polyps. Malignant tumours include endometrial and cervical carcinomas.

Fibroids or *myomas* are the commonest of all the pelvic tumours and may be multiple or very large. They consist of smooth muscle and fibrous tissue, are normally hard in consistency, are rare before the age of twenty years and are present in 10% of females over the age of 40. They are more common in women who have never become pregnant. Common presenting features of fibroids are menorrhagia and a pelvic mass.

Endometrial polyps can be single or multiple. They rarely exceed the size of a grape and are usually larger than a pea. Abnormal bleeding occurs when the tip becomes necrotic or ulcerated.

Endometrial carcinoma usually presents between 50 and 60 years of age but may present before the menopause as menorrhagia. It mainly occurs in nulliparae. Commonly associated conditions are diabetes and hyperplasia of the endometrium (see also p. 139).

Carcinoma of the cervix sometimes presents as menorrhagia. It is more common in women who have had early coitus and multiple partners. It tends to occur in lower socio-economic groups (see also p. 136).

Dysfunctional uterine bleeding

This is defined as abnormal uterine bleeding for which no organic cause can be found. The uterus is of normal size and the endometrial surface area is not increased. Ovulation is occurring normally, resulting in normal hormone levels. Various factors may be involved in the increased menstrual loss. The two which have been studied the most are prostaglandins and plasminogen activator.

Prostaglandins are hormones which were first discovered in human seminal fluid by von Euler in the 1930s. Since then a large family of prostaglandins has been found and it has been shown that they are synthesized from fatty acids, e.g. arachidonic acid (Fig. 4.4). It was originally thought that they were derived from the prostate but it has since been shown that they are widely distributed in the body and occur in the endometrium. Prostaglandins have varying actions on blood vessels and platelets. In general $PGF_2\alpha$ and thromboxanes are vasoconstrictor and promote platelet aggregation, while PGE_2 and prostacyclin are vasodilator and inhibit platelet aggregation. Prostaglandin levels have been measured in the endometrium of women with menorrhagia. The menorrhagic group have increased levels of PGE_2 and $PGF_2\alpha$ premenstrually compared with women with normal menstrual loss. It should be noted at this stage that PGE levels in the

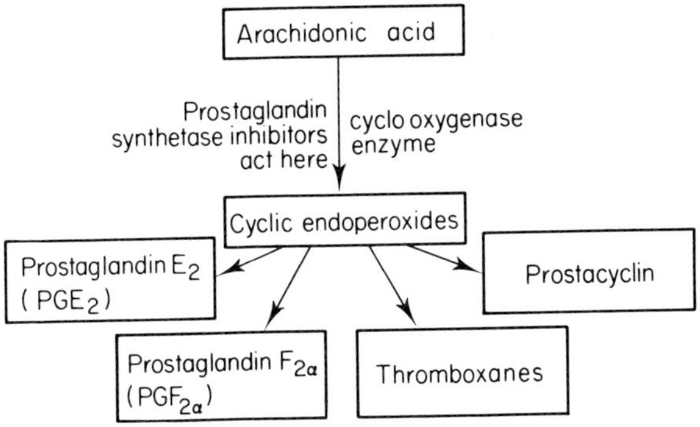

Fig. 4.4. Prostaglandin synthesis.

endometrium are increased after insertion of an IUCD. This may contribute to the increased loss in IUCD users.

Plasminogen activator is found in the endometrium. Levels increase throughout the menstrual cycle and reach a peak on day one of menstruation. It has been found that women with menorrhagia have increased levels of plasminogen activator premenstrually compared with women with normal loss. It has also been found that endometrial plasminogen activator levels are raised after insertion of an IUCD. This may be involved in the increased menstrual loss seen with IUCDs.

INVESTIGATION

A patient must be investigated thoroughly to find the cause of the symptoms.

A history of the onset of increased blood loss is noted. The duration and cyclical features of the periods are ascertained. The passage of clots is often indicative of menorrhagia. The type of contraception used should be asked since IUCDs are associated with increased menstrual blood loss. The administration of oestrogens for any cause must be noted. General questioning should include thyroid disorders, any haemorrhagic tendency and the administration of anticoagulants.

A general and then a speculum and bimanual vaginal examination should follow. The purpose of the general examination is to discover any systemic disorders. The bimanual examination is to determine the presence of any pelvic mass. At speculum examination a cervical smear should be taken. The appearance of the cervix and the presence of any lesion, e.g. cervical or endometrial polyp protruding through the cervical canal, are noted.

Blood should be taken for haemoglobin and full blood count and for thyroid function tests and a clotting screen if clinically indicated.

A diagnostic curettage may be performed to obtain material for histological examination. In some cases hysteroscopy may be necessary. This involves passing a small fibreoptic telescope into the uterine cavity via the cervical canal.

TREATMENT

The treatment of menorrhagia may be medical or surgical and the choice depends on several factors. In rare cases radiotherapy may be considered.

Indications for medical treatment

If the patient is under the age of 40 years treatment is usually medical. The desire for more children, if the patient is fertile, will also require treatment to be medical.

Indications for surgical treatment

If the patient is over the age of 40 years treatment is usually surgical. The absence of any desire for further children predisposes in favour of surgical treatment. When symptoms are uncontrolled by medical treatment and the degree of anaemia is such that transfusion is needed, conservatism gives way to surgery. The presence of pelvic abnormality, e.g. fibroids is often an indication for surgery.

Medical Treatment

Hormones

Combined oestrogen and progestogen contraceptive pills may be used in menorrhagia to decrease menstrual loss. They act on the hypothalamus and the pituitary and inhibit FSH and LH secretion. Normal secretion from the ovaries is almost entirely suppressed and their activity is replaced by the synthetic hormones in the pill. There is no true menstrual cycle but hormone withdrawal bleeding occurs during the pillfree intervals. Ovulation is also suppressed, thus this treatment is mainly indicated when contraception is also required. The following conditions are contraindications to prescribing the combined pill (see also Chapter 8):

1. Intravascular thrombosis. This includes any condition predisposing to thromboembolism, and superficial thrombophlebitis.
2. Hypertension, since there is an increased risk of ischaemic heart disease.
3. Heart disease, e.g. valvular heart disease leading to congestive cardiac failure. The pill has general effects on the cardiovascular system which are not appropriate in heart disease.
4. Age. The mortality risk of using the pill increases with age. Over the age of 35 the prescription of the combined pill may be contraindicated.
5. Malignant disease of the body of the uterus or the breast as oestrogen may stimulate growth of the tumour or metastases.
6. Various metabolic disorders including impaired glucose tolerance, porphyria, liver conditions and familial hyperlipidaemia.

Progestagens only may be used to control menstrual loss. They act by improving the luteal phase endometrium and hormone withdrawal bleeding occurs on discontinuation of the therapy. They can be used over the age of 35. The regimens used do not necessarily provide contraception. Various preparations are available: an example is norethisterone 5–20 mg daily from Day 15 to Day 25 of the cycle. The patient is instructed to start counting from the first day of menstruation which is Day 1. Side effects are nausea, vomiting and weight gain, but they mainly occur with higher doses.

Thyroxine should be administered if the patient has been found to be hypothyroid.

Danazol is a drug which has recently been tested. It is a synthetic hormone related to the male hormone testosterone. It has been found to reduce both the amount and the duration of menstrual loss. It also has a carry-over effect in that three months after stopping treatment menstrual loss is still significantly less than it was prior to treatment. The side effects are weight gain, skin rashes and muscle cramps.

Endometriosis can be treated by suppressing ovarian function with the combined contraceptive pill, continuous progestagens or danazol.

Prostaglandin synthetase inhibitors

Prostaglandin synthetase inhibitors are drugs which inhibit the synthesis of prostaglandins by acting on the enzyme cyclo-oxygenase (Fig. 4.4). This is the first enzyme in the pathway to prostaglandins, so synthesis of all the prostaglandins is affected. Prostaglandin synthetase inhibitors include aspirin, indomethacin, mefenamic acid and flufenamic acid. The fenamates have been shown to reduce menstrual loss in dysfunctional uterine bleeding. Mefenamic acid also decreases the increased menstrual loss associated with IUCDs. A suitable regimen is mefenamic acid 500 mg eight-hourly starting on the first day of the period. It has been shown that the efficacy of the therapy is the same whether treatment is started on the first day of bleeding or a few days premenstrually. The duration of menstruation is unaffected by treatment. Prostaglandin synthetase inhibitors have a short duration of action—only a few hours—since the half-life of the drug in the circulation is short. Some women note an increased flow a few hours after taking the medication, which is relieved by the next dose after about an hour. There is no carry-over effect to the post-treatment periods; this means that after stopping the treatment blood loss is the same as before treatment. Since prostaglandin synthetase inhibitors need only be taken during menstruation the risk of teratogenicity (causation of fetal abnormalities) should be eliminated. They have some side effects; these include indigestion, diarrhoea, headache, dizziness and skin rash. They are contraindicated if there is a history of gastric ulcer or other significant gastrointestinal abnormality, as there may be a risk of precipitating bleeding from the sites of quiescent lesions. Prostaglandin synthetase inhibitors can be taken at all ages unlike the combined contraceptive pill: it should be noted that they do not provide contraception.

Antifibrinolytics

These are drugs which inhibit plasminogen activation and so prevent degradation of fibrinogen and fibrin. They include aminocaproic acid, tranexamic acid and aprotinin. It has been shown that these drugs reduce the increased loss associated with IUCDs but the duration of menstruation is unaffected. Side effects include nausea, vomiting and diarrhoea: the drugs can be used at any age.

Ethamsylate

Ethamsylate is a drug which acts by increasing capillary resistance. It has been shown that in normally menstruating women there is a premenstrual fall in capillary resistance. Unfortunately, capillary resistance has not been studied in menorrhagia. Ethamsylate has been found to reduce the amount of menstrual loss in menorrhagia, but the duration of the period is unaffected. Side effects include nausea, headache and skin rashes.

Treatment of anaemia

As was noted previously women suffering from menorrhagia are at risk of developing iron-deficiency anaemia. It is very important to take blood for estimation of haemoglobin and full blood count. If the patient has iron-deficiency anaemia oral iron supplements should be administered and serial checks of haemoglobin performed. In severe anaemia blood transfusion may be necessary.

Surgical Treatment

Dilatation and curettage and aspiration curettage

The diagnostic procedure of dilatation and curettage may also have a curative effect in some cases. It is normally carried out under general anaesthetic and an examination of the pelvis can be performed at the same time. The patient is placed in the lithotomy position and is prepared in the usual way for a vaginal examination. The vagina is swabbed out, and a Sims's speculum is introduced. The cervix is drawn down with volsellum forceps attached to the anterior lip of the cervix. A uterine sound is passed to assess the size of the uterine cavity. The cervix is then dilated gradually with metal dilators (Hegar). The uterine cavity is explored with polyp forceps to detect endometrial polyps. It is then curetted and the specimen obtained sent for histological examination. The patient should be fit to be discharged from hospital within 24 hours. Follow-up may be arranged either at the out-patient department or at the general practitioner's surgery: a suitable interval is three months. The patient will normally experience some vaginal bleeding for a few days after the operation. It is usually advised to refrain from sexual intercourse while bleeding persists. The therapeutic value of dilatation and curettage in the management of menorrhagia is difficult to assess. In a study in which menstrual blood loss was measured in dysfunctional uterine bleeding before and after curettage, it was found that there was a reduction in the first period following curettage, but no effect thereafter. The diagnostic value of curettage should also be questioned. Endometrial lesions are often missed—rates quoted vary between 10 and 20%. No surgical operation is without danger. In addition to the small risk from general anaesthesia, there are specific hazards associated with dilatation and curettage. These include perforation of the uterus, which has been reported to occur in 0.1–1% of operations, and the possible longer-term complication of cervical incompetence. Even though the complications are rare they must be borne in mind since the therapeutic value of the procedure in menorrhagia is in doubt. There is an alternative to dilatation and curettage—this is aspiration curettage.

Aspiration curettage is a procedure which is performed in the out-patient department without general anaesthesia or cervical dilatation. The patient is placed in the lithotomy position and an aspiration catheter is passed through the cervical canal. It has been found that, diagnostically, it is as reliable a way of obtaining an endometrial specimen as dilatation and curettage under general anaesthesia. It avoids general anaesthesia and hospital admission and is thus also desirable on economic grounds.

Removal of an intrauterine contraceptive device

If menorrhagia is thought to be due to the presence of an IUCD the device should be removed. This may be performed in the out-patient department without general anaesthesia or at dilatation and curettage. The patient must be instructed to use an alternative method of contraception thereafter.

Hysterectomy

Hysterectomy is often indicated when menorrhagia fails to respond to medical treatment, when the patient does not desire any further children or when the patient is aged over 40. Hysterectomy is a major procedure and the patient must be assessed very carefully before operation is advised. If possible the husband should also be seen at this time.

There is discussion as to whether the ovaries should be removed at the time of operation. If they are, the patient undergoes an artificial menopause immediately after the operation. It must be stressed that the ovaries continue to function normally after hysterectomy. It has been argued that bilateral oophorectomy is an insurance policy against the subsequent development of ovarian cancer. The risk of this is small, it is of the order of between 1 : 1000 and 1 : 2000. Where both ovaries have been removed there is a small but significant risk of increased coronary and cerebral thrombosis. Thus the decision concerning oophorectomy should be taken very carefully. If oophorectomy is performed a hormone implant can be inserted at the time of operation to prevent menopausal symptoms.

A hysterectomy can be performed either abdominally or vaginally. The abdominal route is preferred when there is a pelvic mass and the vaginal route when there is associated prolapse.

A hysterectomy is either subtotal or total: in the former only the body of the uterus is removed and the cervix is conserved, while in a total hysterectomy the cervix is removed also. If the cervix is conserved it may subsequently become carcinomatous (in about 1% of cases) and may also continue to give rise to bleeding and discharge. Thus in most cases total hysterectomy is performed unless removal of the cervix is technically difficult.

Following hysterectomy, vaginal bleeding and discharge may persist for a few weeks, gradually becoming less. It is important to arrange adequate physiotherapy (see Chapter 17). The patient is followed up after six weeks, when vaginal and pelvic examinations are performed. The patient should not return to work or perform heavy lifting for that time. Sexual intercourse should only be resumed after the vaginal examination: coital capacity is not impaired after hysterectomy. There will be some tenderness and the vagina will seem shrunken and narrow but with regular sexual intercourse it will return to its normal supple state. Total abdominal hysterectomy may, in fact, improve sexual activity since the symptoms of a pelvic mass, bleeding or pain are removed. Total abdominal hysterectomy may have some psychiatric sequelae. According to most studies psychiatric illness follows hysterectomy more commonly than other operations in women. This was shown in a trial in Dundee in which patients were followed up for two to seven years after total abdominal hysterectomy or cholecystectomy. More patients in the hysterectomy group were referred for a psychiatric opinion than in the cholecystectomy group. However a recent study in Oxford shows that most psychiatric illness detected after hysterectomy could not be attributed to the operation itself. It was also found that there were no significant differences after abdominal or vaginal hysterectomy nor after removal or conservation of ovaries.

It must be emphasized that the mortality of hysterectomy is low; it is less than 0.2% in good hands and if the woman is in good physical health.

Radiotherapy

The principle of using radiotherapy to control menorrhagia is that X-rays act on the ovaries to inhibit ovarian function so that menstruation ceases. This type of treatment is used in exceptional circumstances only. The main disadvantages are:

1. Unsuspected pelvic abnormality may be missed.
2. The symptoms of a radiation menopause may be very severe.
3. There is a risk of fetal malformation if pregnancy results when radiation has been used in women of child-bearing age.
4. Radiation injuries to the bladder and rectum may occur.
5. The incidence of carcinoma of the corpus after irradiation is said to be increased.

Thus any persistence or recurrence of bleeding calls for hysterectomy.

SUMMARY

Menorrhagia is a very common gynaecological disorder and presents often in the general practitioner's surgery and in the out-patient department. It is defined as a measured menstrual loss greater than 80 ml on at least one of two consecutive menses. Normal loss is 30 ml. 80 ml has been chosen as the critical level since beyond this there is an increased incidence of iron deficiency anaemia. There is no relation between the duration of menstruation and total menstrual loss. Menorrhagia and dysmenorrhoea are not always seen together. Menorrhagia is caused by various systemic and local conditions. It must be borne in mind that no cause can be found in 50% of women who present: those women are said to have dysfunctional uterine bleeding. In recent years two factors have been implicated in dysfunctional uterine bleeding and these are prostaglandins and plasminogen activator. It has been found that women with menorrhagia have higher levels of these substances in their endometria than do women with normal menses. As a result of these investigations the treatment of menorrhagia has been modified. Treatment consists basically of medical, surgical and radiotherapeutic measures. Prostaglandin synthetase inhibitors and drugs acting on haemostasis have recently been included in medical therapy. It must be pointed out that the haemoglobin level should be checked and any anaemia dealt with appropriately. Surgical treatment consists essentially of hysterectomy, since curettage is mainly a diagnostic procedure. The patient must be carefully assessed before hysterectomy is advised since it is a major procedure. Any proposal to perform an oophorectomy should be discussed fully with the patient since the ovaries continue to function normally after hysterectomy. Radiotherapy is used very rarely today.

Acknowledgement

This chapter was prepared during the tenure of an MRC training fellowship.

5. Premenstrual Syndrome, Dysmenorrhoea and Menstrual Migraine

M.G. Brush and Margaret Watson

Premenstrual syndrome (PMS) and period pain (dysmenorrhoea) are among the commonest conditions suffered by women but until recently they have received comparatively little attention from the medical profession, perhaps because of their episodic and sometimes rather ill-defined nature. Recently, there have been great improvements in PMS treatment and it is even possible for milder cases to be dealt with effectively through 'self-help' if the sufferer is adequately informed in the first instance. There are also improvements in the treatment of severe period pains which enable women previously disabled by the condition at least to keep going.

A third menstrually linked condition is menstrual migraine, which accounts for about 15% of the large number of women who have migraine. Unfortunately, there are no major advances in migraine treatment. There is, however, increasing knowledge of how to use existing drugs to best advantage and of ways of preventing additional attacks through avoidance of dietary and environmental factors which can act as trigger factors for migraine.

As the assessment and follow-up of women with these conditions can be rather time-consuming for the busy family doctor, especially if there are associated social problems, there is clearly a place for the well informed nurse to assist in their management. This combined medical and nursing care can benefit both the patient, by ensuring more comprehensive assessment and follow-up, and the family doctor, by avoiding unnecessary clinic congestion. The nurse may also enjoy the extra contact with patients: this can be very rewarding, especially if the initial condition was severe and included disruption of family life.

At first, there will be a shortage of suitably informed and experienced nurses but it is hoped that training courses, supplemented by an adequate supply of practical literature, will gradually remedy this.

PREMENSTRUAL SYNDROME (PMS)

This condition, which is also known as premenstrual tension (PMT), is characterized by the occurrence of symptoms in the second half of the menstrual cycle only, with cessation of these problems within 24 hours of the start of the menstrual flow. PMS may start as early as 14 days before the expected period in severe cases but the duration in average cases is seven to ten days. Mild cases last only two to five days. The severity of symptoms is often, but by no means always, related to their duration. At first sight, the symptoms seem very varied and apparently unrelated, but recent research has shown likely reasons for them in most, but not all, cases.

Many different symptom lists have been produced, some very complex and rather misleading but a convenient summary is:

Physical symptoms

1. Swelling of the abdomen (and sometimes fingers, legs, ankles and face), general feeling of bloatedness.
2. Breast discomfort (swelling, soreness and pain).
3. Headaches (usually of a 'tension' nature and sometimes very severe and prolonged. Must be distinguished from menstrual migraine.)
4. Backache.
5. Pain similar to dysmenorrhoea.
6. Skin disorders ('acne'-like blotches).

Mental symptoms

1. Tension.
2. Irritability.
3. Depression.
4. Lethargy.
5. Clumsiness.
6. Illogical reactions.
7. Lack of concentration.

8. Loss of confidence.
9. Feelings of worthlessness.
10. Loss of sex drive.

Luckily, most patients have only a few of these symptoms, usually including depression, irritability and/or tension, bloatedness and one or more of the others. There are, however, some genuine complaints of nearly all the symptoms on the list. Surprisingly, there are remarkably few spurious or inconsistent histories given by patients, although what may be bearable to one patient is not necessarily bearable to another. Much will depend on the family and work background of the patient. It is often most helpful to the doctor or counsellor if the patient records her daily symptoms on a special chart (Fig. 5.1).

There are some rare symptoms not listed above and if any problem appears to be associated in a clear-cut way with the second half of the

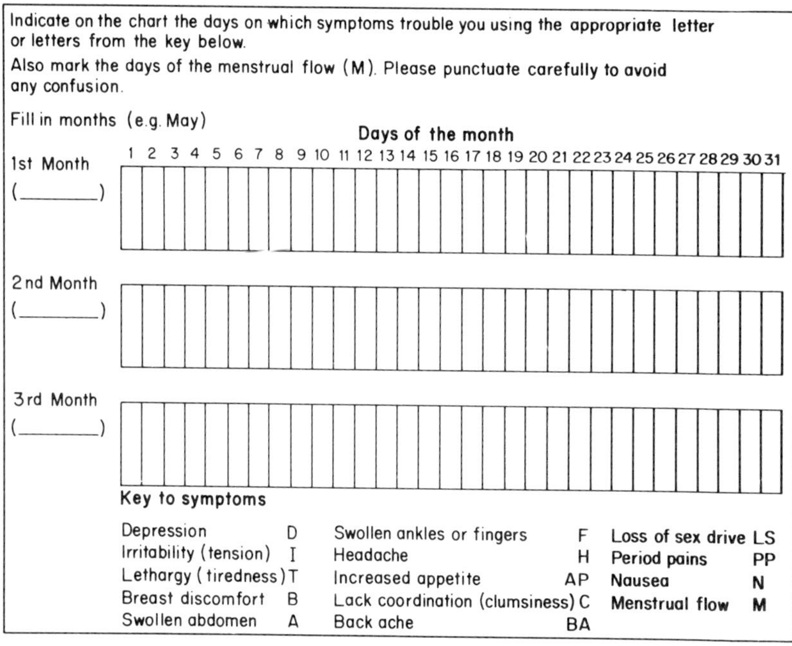

Fig. 5.1. A chart suitable for recording premenstrual symptoms.

menstrual cycle it should be carefully noted and discussed with the doctor. Some authorities consider that migraine, epilepsy and asthma can be directly linked to PMS and they certainly can become worse at this time. However, most doctors now regard them as separate problems which are affected by the endocrine changes near the period. In particular, menstrual migraine is clearly a separate problem as it is often possible to cure PMS in a menstrual migraine patient, while leaving the migraine essentially unchanged. (Menstrual migraine is discussed more fully later in this chapter.)

The time of onset of PMS varies greatly and the reasons for commencement at any particular time are poorly understood. Sometimes a non-typical form of PMS may be present virtually from the menarche but more commonly it starts later, especially after the birth of a baby. This may be the first baby or a later delivery. It certainly does not help PMS to have a baby; this is a misleading saying derived from similar statements about period pains.

Unless properly treated, the condition rarely improves, especially when it is severe, and usually continues until the menopause (natural or artificial) though not necessarily with exactly the same complex of symptoms. There is no known correlation between PMS and the occurrence of unpleasant symptoms at the time of the menopause except that depressive tendencies associated with PMS may well continue in another form in the menopause.

A woman with mild PMS may well be able to cope with it without gross disruption of her family and working life but in more serious cases, this is rarely possible. The husband will often bear the brunt of the tension and irritability experienced by the severe PMS patient and, occasionally, there may even be physical violence. The children may also suffer verbal and, occasionally, physical violence and it is obviously vitally important to take urgent action where there is a real risk of injury to a child. There is also the risk of suicide, as suicidal thoughts and 'attention-seeking' overdoses are not uncommon in severe PMS cases.

For the unmarried woman, it is usually career prospects which suffer most for she may find it difficult to accept promotion or to cope with it at bad times. Alternatively, she may change jobs frequently or may even find it difficult to hold down a satisfactory job at all.

Students and schoolgirls may find their study and other work seriously affected during PMS and, if possible, due allowance should be made for this in assessing examination performance. Sportswomen often find that their concentration and coordination are significantly affected and, accordingly, their sporting performance suffers markedly.

After a hysterectomy with conservation of one or both ovaries, existing PMS will almost always continue and may get worse. As there is no longer the obvious marker of the periods, the pattern of PMS may become confusing, especially if ovarian function becomes somewhat erratic. In some cases, measurement of hormone levels may be very helpful in establishing the full position and indicating any subsequent treatment.

Treatment

A great many treatments for PMS have been suggested but until recently only natural progesterone has been shown to give more than partial relief of individual symptoms. In particular, standard diuretics and tranquillizers do little more than reduce fluid retention and tension respectively, and even then in mild cases only. In more severe cases, they are not only ineffective but sometimes increase the discomfort of the patient.

Modern treatment for PMS consists of hormonal and/or vitamin (pyridoxine) therapy with the use of several special drugs for relief of obstinate symptoms in difficult cases.

Hormonal treatment

The most commonly used hormonal treatment is dydrogesterone (Duphaston), a synthetic compound very closely related to natural progesterone. It is given in standard tablet form 10 mg twice daily from Day 12 of the cycle to Day 26, assuming a 28-day cycle. If the cycle is somewhat shorter or longer, the start and finish of dydrogesterone treatment are adjusted accordingly. Where certain symptoms, particularly fluid retention (bloating), are very marked some doctors will use a higher dose, e.g. 20 mg twice daily, but there is a greater chance of unacceptable weight increase with this dose. On the standard dose, the likelihood of weight increase is very small. Accepted side-effects at the 10 mg twice daily level are breast tenderness (for the first time or increase of an existing tendency) and mild nausea, but the incidence is only about 5%. Small alterations in menstrual habit have also been reported but are difficult to substantiate in view of the variability seen in many women before treatment. If the side effects persist, it may be necessary to change to another treatment but this is not always easy if severe fluid retention is the main problem.

Norethisterone and occasionally other progesterone-like compounds are sometimes used in a manner similar to dydrogesterone but, although helpful in some cases, there seems to be a higher chance of lack of sufficient response and of unacceptable menstrual irregularities.

Natural progesterone has been used by Dalton and some other workers for many years and may give very useful control of some PMS symptoms. It has been given by various routes (intramuscular injection, suppository and pessary) as it is inactive if given by mouth. Unfortunately, repeated injections of the oily solution of progesterone are extremely uncomfortable and suppositories and pessaries are much less acceptable than tablets for most women. The suppositories (Cyclogest) of 200 and 400 mg are usually given for seven to fourteen days premenstrually. Side effects are unusual, though local reaction is possible. The response can decrease after some months in some patients.

For younger women (20–35 years) who wish to use a method involving contraception, the oral contraceptive pill may be helpful if it is suitable on other medical grounds. By imposing a much more constant hormonal environment, it appears to reduce the incidence of PMS symptoms in most, but not all, women who take it. In a small number of those on the Pill, a 'PMS-like' condition persists or develops and depression can be the main feature although other symptoms are also reported. If oral contraception is essential to the patient, pyridoxine can be added (see below) and this often helps once the correct dose is established. In other cases, it may be preferable to discontinue oral contraception and try another PMS treatment.

Pyridoxine (vitamin B6) treatment

Pyridoxine is the natural vitamin B6 and is known to play an integral part in a number of vital enzymic reactions in the body. In particular, it plays an essential role in metabolic and endocrine control processes in the hypothalamus (the area of the brain which controls many functions of the pituitary). The reasons for its apparent lack in PMS patients are not fully known but are being actively investigated. Meanwhile, however, it is clearly a safe, convenient and effective form of treatment for the majority of PMS patients.

The accepted starting dose is 40 mg twice daily commencing three days before the expected start of any PMS symptoms and continuing until two or three days after the start of the period. If sufficient response is not seen, the dose level is increased to 50–60 mg twice daily and then on to 75 mg twice daily if necessary. If 100 mg twice daily is exceeded there is a slight risk of gastric upset (acidity) and so this dose level should only be used in special circumstances. No other side effects have been reported and this greatly increases the acceptability of the method.

In the 40–60 mg twice daily range, it may sometimes be necessary to take an extra one or two 20 mg tablets per day if the symptoms become more acute just before the start of the period.

Occasionally, PMS can be responsible for marked distress and loss of school performance in children aged 12–16 years. In these cases, it is justifiable to treat the condition and they should start at 20 mg twice daily and work up to 50 mg twice daily if absolutely essential.

If there is no response to pyridoxine 75 mg twice daily, it is wise to refer the patient to a specialized PMS or endocrine clinic, especially if there is a severe breast condition or persistent headache (over two days). Measurement of serum prolactin levels and other endocrine investigations may then be carried out to exclude concurrent endocrine disease.

Combined dydrogesterone and pyridoxine treatment

In certain special cases, the use of dydrogesterone in the standard manner may be combined with pyridoxine treatment, as described above. Because of the extra inconvenience and cost of the combined treatment, it is reserved for difficult cases only. It can be very effective in situations where extreme irritability, and verbal and physical violence are the main PMS symptoms, and in other cases where some of the symptoms are difficult to bring under control by either agent singly.

Spironolactone

The diuretic spironolactone (Aldactone), which acts as an anti-aldosterone agent at the renal level, is sometimes used as an alternative to dydrogesterone when premenstrual fluid retention is a troublesome problem. It is particularly useful when the patient finds unacceptable weight increase on dydrogesterone or where other problems of side-effects or lack of response arise. The standard dose level of 100 mg/day is usually effective in treating the fluid retention but it may be necessary to add pyridoxine if other symptoms are also troublesome.

Bromocriptine

Bromocriptine (Parlodel) is sometimes necessary for patients with severe breast symptoms which do not respond to high-dose pyridoxine treatment. It is a powerful drug which reduces prolactin levels very markedly and often clears up breast discomfort of long standing. Unfortunately it has side effects, especially nausea and hypotension, which make it very difficult to use without close hospital supervision. Many patients find that side effects wear off but some do not and the drug may have to be discontinued.

Other treatments

Occasionally, treatment with the powerful anti-gonadotrophic agent danazol (Danol) may be needed but this should be confined to very serious cases with special medical and social problems. At the dose levels usually recommended, danazol suppresses the menstrual cycle entirely due to its anti-gonadotrophic action. It does, however, have marked side effects in most patients.

Self-help

As pyridoxine can be obtained without prescription, it is quite possible for any reasonably intelligent and informed PMS sufferer to deal with the mild to average types of PMS without further help. Any woman using this approach should of course have access to correct information on dose and timing of pyridoxine treatment and be aware that she should see her doctor if the situation does not improve.

Very mild cases may be helped with the use of over-the-counter diuretics. Other approaches via dietary changes, exercise, discussion and general self-knowledge may also help and are discussed by Judy Lever in her recent book on PMS.

The Role of the Nurse-counsellor

Provided that the nurse-counsellor has the full support of the doctor in charge, she may undertake much work in the counselling and management of PMS. Once properly trained in PMS problems, she may take histories, advise patients on PMS recording, recommend and supervise pyridoxine treatment and assist in the management of social and marital problems to which it may give rise. She may also assist the doctor in his management of patients who need dydrogesterone or other drugs on prescription. Cooperation of this type between doctor and nurse undoubtedly benefits the patient and eases the workload of the doctor's surgery while ensuring adequate medical supervision, especially of more complex cases.

PERIOD PAINS (DYSMENORRHOEA)

Probably most women have experienced period pains to some degree and many will have resorted to simple painkillers, such as aspirin, paracetamol or proprietary formulations. The help and comfort of the hot water bottle is, of course, not to be underestimated. Despite the wealth of feminine know-how about the milder period pains and their treatment, there is still much misunderstanding and ignorance about the condition, especially when it becomes incapacitating.

Firstly, it is vital to realize that period pains and PMS are two quite different conditions with different causes and different treatments.

Secondly, severe period pains can be disabling due to pain and nausea. Fear of lost time at work or study may be important to some girls. In extreme cases, a girl may lose her job through frequent absences due to period pain.

Typically, the pain comes in spasms, starting in the flanks, coming in to the pelvic region and may then be referred to the upper inner areas of the thighs. The pain can be very severe in some cases and the girl may feel exhausted after it has passed. Nausea can be very unpleasant and sometimes standard anti-nauseants are not very effective.

Period pains often start soon after the first few periods and are very common in the teenage girl and in the woman in her early 20s who has not had a baby. By the late 20s, it may no longer be a significant problem especially if there has been a pregnancy leading to the vaginal delivery of a full-term baby.

It is now believed that an important factor in period pains is the release of an excessive amount of the 'local' hormone prostaglandin in the uterus. This causes the uterine muscle to contract sharply causing the typical spasmodic pain. In severe cases, drugs known to antagonize prostaglandins specifically are used with good results in most cases. There is no structural abnormality to be seen in the uterus of the younger woman with period pains, i.e. the disorder is a functional one affecting the uterine muscle. However, in the older woman who has period pains, the situation may be very different (secondary dysmenorrhoea) and is often associated with gynaecological conditions such as fibroids, endometriosis and pelvic inflammatory disease (see Chapter 12). In these cases, it is obviously essential that an experienced gynaecological opinion is obtained as sometimes urgent surgical or other treatment may be needed. It is clearly wrong to use progestagens or anti-prostaglandins until a complete gynaecological check-up has been carried out.

Treatment

If simple proprietary pain-killers are not sufficient, the doctor may prescribe anti-spasmodics such as hyoscine.

The anti-prostaglandin drugs, indomethacin (Indocid), flufenamic acid (Meralen) and mefenamic acid (Ponstan) are usually reserved for the more severe pain and are proving a very valuable new therapeutic approach. However, they are strictly contraindicated if there has been any history of gastric ulceration or other inflammatory gastrointestinal condition, as anti-prostaglandins can cause gastrointestinal bleeding. Although given for short duration only in the treatment of period pains, the risk of causing a flare-up of an old ulcer or other gastrointestinal condition is not considered acceptable.

The use of the contraceptive pill, if acceptable on medical and social grounds, can be helpful due to the almost constant hormonal environment which is imposed and the lighter periods which usually result.

Another prophylactic approach is the use of dydrogesterone from Days 5 to 26 in a 28-day cycle. Although not acceptable to some women, due to the long duration of medication in each month and occasional side effects (see PMS), it can give useful results.

In the past, surgical dilatation of the cervix was carried out but results were usually poor. However, the main drawback is the high incidence of cervical incompetence in any subsequent pregnancy and increased risk of early miscarriage.

MENSTRUAL MIGRAINE

There are several different types of migraine and a variety of factors which trigger off the attacks. This section is concerned with the type of migraine which occurs regularly just before or during the period and not at other times. Unlike the more common migraines triggered by stress, specific foods, etc., menstrual migraine is apparently not induced by external triggers and it is assumed that one or more of the hormonal changes around the time of menstruation acts as an internal trigger factor. Rigid proof of the nature of a hormonal trigger is not yet available, as present research indicates that the situation is very complex and that more than sensitivity to falling levels of oestrogen and progesterone is involved.

Although the trigger factor is different in menstrual migraine, the attack once under way will follow one of the patterns seen in other types of migraine, i.e. classic, common, cluster or focal.

Full description of the symptomatology of the various types of migraine is not appropriate in this short account and several excellent descriptions are available at both the medical and lay levels (see Bibliography).

It is, however, important to make sure that at least two, and preferably three, of the well established criteria of migraine are present: unilateral headache, nausea, visual symptoms and family history of migraine.

At present, there is no treatment specifically aimed at menstrual migraine, although in some cases it may be suitable to use a prophylactic agent such as pizotifen (Sanomigran).

Simple painkillers, such as aspirin and paracetamol, may be helpful in some cases, especially when nausea is not an important problem. There are several mixed formulations containing painkiller, tranquillizer and anti-spasmodic (e.g. Midrid) which offer an advance on simple painkillers.

Preparations containing ergotamine appear to offer no special advantage in menstrual migraine but may well be helpful to some patients, although they should be advised not to use these preparations too frequently or for too extended a time overall.

If nausea and vomiting are troublesome, it is extremely important to bring them under control. Probably the most effective way of doing this is by the use of prochlorperazine (Stemetil) suppositories. Once the vomiting has been stopped, it is easier to obtain satisfactory pain control with oral painkillers.

Sometimes, a patient may have both PMS and menstrual migraine, and it is important to warn her that prospects for helping her regarding PMS are usually much better than for menstrual migraine. However, in certain circumstances, the tensions of PMS seem to increase the severity of menstrual migraine and if the PMS is treated successfully, e.g. with pyridoxine, there may also be some moderation of the migraine symptoms and some reduction in the incidence of attacks.

Although the trigger for menstrual migraine is almost certainly of a complex hormonal nature, it is obviously wise for the patient to be fully aware of dietary and stress factors which may make matters worse. These are fully discussed in the books mentioned in the bibliography.

Occasionally, the rare cluster migraine may be seen in women with menstrual migraine. This is extremely disabling and debilitating and deserves urgent and concentrated attention from the doctor.

If the symptoms of any type of migraine cannot be brought under reasonable control by use of medication commonly employed by family doctors, it is important to consider the possibility of specialist help from a migraine clinic or suitable hospital department, as a variety of new approaches are under investigation. Although there is at present no major advance in treatment, individual patients may obtain help with specific symptoms through the drugs at present being evaluated. Full control of menstrual migraine will probably not be obtained until there is better understanding of the fundamental mechanisms which cause it.

Bibliography

Brush, M.G. (1979) *Premenstrual Syndrome and Period Pains*. London: Women's Health Concern.

Critchley, E. (1980) *Pocket Guide to Migraines and Headaches*. London: Arlington.

Current Medical Research and Opinion (1977) *4*, Suppl. 4.

Current Medical Research and Opinion (1979) *6*, Suppl. 5.

Evans, P. (1979) *Mastering your Migraine*. London: Granada.

Freese, A.S. (1976) *Headaches, the Kinds and the Cures*. London: George Allen and Unwin.

Hannington, E. (1970) *Migraine*. London: Priory Press.

Lever, J. (with Brush, M. & Haynes, B.) (1979) *PMT - The Unrecognised Illness*. London: Melbourne House.

Migraine Trust (1979) *Understanding Migraine*. London.

Sacks, O.W. (1971) *Migraine, the Evolution of a Common Disorder*. London: Faber and Faber.

Wilkinson, M. (1976) *Living with Migraine*. London: Heinemann.

6. Hormone Replacement Therapy in the Menopause

Peter Saunders

Of all species the only female to live beyond the potential for reproductivity is the human. In the present generation the periods usually finish at about the age of 50, which is four years later than the average age in the last century. This is probably due to improved environmental conditions.

The word menopause is taken to mean the time when the periods stop. They may cease abruptly or they may appear at increasing intervals and become more scanty. One year without periods in this age group is usually accepted as the true menopause. The menopause has long been accepted as a single event in the ageing process merely representing the gradual cessation of ovarian function leading to the virtual absence of the sex hormone oestrogen. It used to be regarded as a physiological relief from the burden of fertility but current views suggest that the hormone changes in the years following the menopause are more akin to a deficiency state producing some extreme changes in the body. Women, of course, differ in their attitudes to the menopause, as do doctors. Those who harbour an unwelcome view of the 'curse' doubtless welcome the advent of the change, others regard this loss of reproductive function as the depressing end of an era.

For a variable time before and after the periods stop certain changes take place as the result of a gradual slowing down of oestrogen production by the ovary as it becomes less and less effective. In some women these changes go unnoticed, but many who have successfully coped with menstruation, contraception, family and a career are greatly incapacitated by the physical and emotional changes that follow the menopause. As the ovaries start to fail, the output of their main hormone, oestrogen, decreases and this may lead to a variety of symptoms, some occurring at an early stage and others some years after the periods have ceased.

The commonest complaint is the hot flush or sweat, where sensations of heat suddenly envelop the face, neck and chest and the skin may show patchy red blotches. Sometimes drenching sweats occur and particularly at night they may be followed by distressing chills. The attacks usually last from a few seconds to half an hour but may persist for an hour or even longer. Frequency of attacks may vary from once or twice a day to as often as every hour. They are particularly disturbing at night due to interference with sleep and are intensified by excitement or stress. Anxious women tend to have more severe attacks.

Emotional disturbances commonly occur and these may include episodes of anxiety, depression, palpitations, headaches, insomnia, fatigue and weakness. Sometimes anxiety, depression and fatigue may be continuous and severe. In some women they appear to be specifically related to lack of oestrogen and in others they may stem more from an exaggeration of their own emotional pattern.

Time and dwindling supply of oestrogen contribute to change in the woman's outward appearance. The skin loses some of its elasticity and becomes dry. The hair may lose its lustre and gradually become thinner. The skin lining the vaginal entrance also becomes dry and more friable, making the vagina more prone to inflammation and sometimes causing discharge and irritation. Because of these changes sexual intercourse may become painful leading to marital difficulties. Similar changes occur in the lining of the bladder causing occasional burning on micturition and sometimes the involuntary leaking of urine on exertion (stress incontinence). Oestrogen deficiency may also affect the internal pelvic organs as the supporting structures of the uterus and bladder lose some of their tone and strength thereby encouraging uterine prolapse.

Two very important late manifestations of oestrogen lack concern the bones and arteries of the body. There is good evidence to suggest that the long bones of the body and spine become more brittle due to a tendency to decalcification as oestrogen is withdrawn, increasing the likelihood of fractures, particularly at the wrist and thigh. Slight curvature of the spine is a normal consequence of ageing but this is increased if the bones become thinner in the post-menopausal years, producing backache and joint pains. In some elderly women this may lead to the 'dowager's hump', where there is marked curvature of the upper spine.

It is well known that the incidence of coronary heart disease is much greater in men than women under the age of 40 because oestrogen produced by the normally functioning ovaries protects against the laying down in the arteries of cholesterol and other fatty substances which tend to harden their lining. After the menopause, as the protective influence of oestrogen declines with the major fall in its production, the incidence of coronary artery disease in women approaches that of men.

It is important to realize that these effects of oestrogen lack vary enormously in different women and in 20% the cessation of menstruation may be the only apparent sign of having been through the menopause.

What Treatment is Available for Those Who do Have Problems?

The major question is to what extent these symptoms are a product of prolonged lack of oestrogen and by inference to what extent they can be prevented by its replacement. Investigations of the symptomatic menopausal woman by vaginal smear tests and blood hormone measurements may give helpful information as to the amount of oestrogens still naturally present in the body, but the results are often disappointing and do not always correlate with the oestrogen status of the woman. There are those who still believe that these changes should be regarded as a normal part of a woman's life and that the symptoms should be endured, perhaps with the help of sedatives. A more considered view is that the complex changes are a deficiency disorder which should be corrected by the appropriate replacement therapy.

There is absolutely no dispute that treatment with oestrogen is extremely effective in curing hot flushes, night sweats and vaginal dryness and discomfort. Much more controversial is the beneficial effect that oestrogen may have on the psychological and emotional symptoms associated with the menopause and the extent to which oestrogen treatment for a prolonged time may prevent some of the degenerative disorders that occur in the bone and blood vessels.

Prompted by improved education and social awareness, the public themselves have been largely responsible for stimulating interest and research in the problems and benefits associated with oestrogen replacement therapy. Although many questions remain unanswered it seems that a new mantle of respectability has begun to replace many outmoded concepts. Many family doctors will now prescribe oestrogens for menopausal symptoms but others will always refer the patient to a gynaecologist. In general treatment is considered in one of four ways:

1. Occasionally treatment with oestrogens will not be advised, owing to medical contraindications. Non-hormonal treatment on a purely symptomatic basis may be employed instead.
2. Oestrogen therapy will be advised for acutely distressing symptoms for a short period of time and then discontinued.
3. Treatment may be continued long after the symptoms have settled in the hope of providing an additional bonus by preventing certain degenerative conditions.
4. Treatment may be requested solely as a preventive measure by an informed woman who has reached the menopause and has no present complaints, but wishes to avail herself of oestrogen treatment for long-term benefit.

The true benefit and possible complications of long-term oestrogen therapy have yet to be assessed and much research is being undertaken in this country.

Which Type of Oestrogen is Best?

As oestrogen replacement therapy becomes more popular so the number of pharmaceutical preparations available increases. Some of these are *synthetic*, in other words the oestrogen does not occur in nature, and some contain *natural* oestrogens, identical with those derived from animal and plant sources: these seem to be preferable. Some possible side-effects of oestrogen therapy to be considered shortly can be prevented by using a tablet of oestrogen together with a progestagen (a synthetic progesterone-like compound), similar to the contraceptive pill but in very much lower concentration. Most preparations that are available, either oestrogen alone or oestrogen with progestagen, are taken in three-weekly cycles and most will produce a small withdrawal bleed or period in the week without treatment. Though this may be irksome to the woman who has finished her periods there seems to be an advantage in shedding the lining of the uterus at monthly intervals as this helps in preventing any tendency to undesirable changes in the endometrium, e.g. abnormal proliferation (hyperplasia). Some doctors prefer to administer oestrogens in the form of a small pellet placed under the skin and the effect then lasts about six months. This method of administration has the supposed advantage that a tiny amount of hormone is liberated daily at a constant rate. Also, because no tablets are necessary, the woman is not continually reminded of her condition and the minor side-effects such as nausea and indigestion are usually eliminated. This is usually the method of choice for women who have undergone hysterectomy.

Oestrogen-containing creams and suppositories can be very helpful as an addition, particularly for the dry and friable vagina causing painful intercourse. Birth control pills can occasionally be used in controlling menopausal symptoms when there is still a possibility of pregnancy but they are not suitable for long-term use because they contain relatively high doses of synthetic oestrogen as well as prostagen. It is preferable to obtain long-term control of distressing symptoms with small doses of oestrogen from natural sources as this is far superior to and safer than, any birth control pill.

How Long Can Treatment Be Continued?

This is one of the most controversial issues. Many women find that as well as helping distressing symptoms oestrogen treatment makes them feel healthy and look better. They may also want to continue replacement therapy in the knowledge that oestrogens afford a certain protection against some degenerative conditions. With modern safer preparations containing both oestrogen and progestagen, given under regular supervision, many doctors are happier to allow their patients to continue on oestrogens for a number of years though much has yet to be learned about the long-term effects of treatment.

What are the Side-effects and Complications of Oestrogen Treatment?

Many women encounter minor side-effects during the first few weeks of treatment with oestrogens such as breast tenderness and swelling, nausea, fluid retention with increase of weight and vaginal discharge. Weight increase can become a problem because any hormone containing oestrogen increases tissue fluid and encourages appetite. The woman who is over-weight or has a tendency to obesity must take care not to over-eat and to keep to small regular meals.

Vaginal bleeding is not a serious complication but troublesome to the patient and her doctor. If oestrogen treatment is started some months or years after the periods have stopped, bleeding can occasionally occur from the uterus in response to the drug. However, the gynaecologist has no means of knowing whether this is in fact the cause or whether there is a polyp or small growth in the uterus that has caused coincidental bleeding. The only way to be sure is for the woman to have a uterine curettage (D & C) and this will usually be recommended. In the majority of cases the uterus is found to be empty and then the bleeding may be assumed to be due to oestrogens. Providing the tablets are taken as directed this bleeding usually ceases and may not recur. Bleeding which occurs at the end of a three-week cycle of pills, whether of oestrogen or oestrogen with progestagen, can be regarded as normal. If irregular bleeding continues advice from the doctor must be sought.

Perhaps the two most important side-effects of exogenous oestrogens are adverse effects on blood clotting and a possible association with cancer. It is well known that some oestrogens, notably the synthetic ones, do predispose to certain alterations in the normal blood coagulation mechanisms and increase the likelihood of venous thrombosis. For this reason any woman with a history of previous blood clotting disorders is usually denied oestrogen therapy. However, most of the so-called natural oestrogens seem to have less effect on blood coagulation and the incidence of problems with these hormones is minimal.

For a number of years controversy has raged concerning the possible association between oestrogens and malignancies of the breast and uterus. Certain cancers of the breast are known to be sensitive to oestrogen, i.e. growth may be accelerated by oestrogens. There is no direct evidence to suggest that oestrogen causes breast cancer though it is contraindicated in a woman who already has the condition.

With regard to cancer of the uterus, the position is not quite so clear-cut. Although there is no direct evidence to link oestrogens and endometrial cancer where oestrogens are used in the correct manner it has long been known that prolonged oestrogen administration causes the endometrium to become hyperplastic and may give rise to bleeding. Some authorities believe that the thickened endometrium is really a very early stage of cancer formation; others dispute this strongly. The possible association between endometrial cancer and oestrogen has stimulated much research all over the world and from the evidence put to the first International Congress on the Menopause in 1976 the Chairman summed up as follows: 'The recent studies alleging an increased risk of cancer of the endometrium in women receiving oestrogen therapy is open to serious criticism. The consensus of participants appears to support the view that there is no direct cause or relationship between cancer of the endometrium and oestrogen treatment but there is an urgent need for continued research in this field'. It appears that when progesterone is added to oestrogen this affords some protection to the endometrium by preventing excessive growth and therefore this method of administration has become popular. Some experts believe if women are to take oestrogen for some time the endometrium should be explored by dilatation and curettage at yearly intervals in order to note any possible change in the microscopical appearance.

All the studies to date showing no satisfactory evidence linking oestrogens given to women after the menopause and cancer of the breast or uterus have been retrospective. A nationwide survey in the United Kingdom has recently been set up to correlate retrospective and prospective data of all patients receiving oestrogen replacement and it is only when the results of prospective studies like this are available in years to come that the controversy over cancer and oestrogens will be settled. For the present it seems that the safest method of medication is a natural oestrogen together with a progestagen in a cyclical fashion which will cause the woman to have a small period at the end of each treatment cycle. Oestrogen treatment in women who have had a hysterectomy is much simpler and it is safe then to take oestrogen daily without fear of bleeding or a six-monthly injection in the pellet form if the doctor suggests that treatment is indicated.

The success of replacement therapy depends firstly on a good understanding between the woman and her physician and secondly on the safety enhanced by a thorough physical examination prior to treatment and surveillance at regular intervals during treatment.

Bibliography

Cooper, W. (1975) *No Change*. London: Hutchinson (also London, Arrow, 1976).
McQueen, J. (1979) *The Menopause*. London: Womens Health Concern.
Utian, W.H. (1978) *The Menopause Manual*. Lancaster: MTP Press.

7. Termination of Pregnancy

Michael John Hare

Since the dawn of civilization, pregnancy termination or abortion has been practised. It has always been a matter of great controversy and the subject of strongly held views concerning its moral, ethical and legal aspects and its impact on both society and the individual. Over the past two decades most countries have altered their laws to a more liberal code on abortion and this has resulted in the transfer of procedures for its initiation from the 'criminal' to the 'legal' sphere. Doctors and nurses are now involved in performing abortions whereas before they were acting almost entirely to salvage the incompleted or bungled handiwork of the illegal operator. For many this work is distasteful, and some feel strongly that it is absolutely wrong; the Act of 1967 may have changed the law overnight, but it did not change the philosophies of those who had to work with it. Because problems of personal acceptance are still very much part of the abortion debate this chapter will include a review of the historical, legal and ethical aspects, as well as sections on counselling, surgical techniques, and mortality and morbidity.

TERMINOLOGY

An *abortion* is legally defined as the loss, by delivery or intrauterine death, of a fetus before it can survive in the extrauterine environment. The potential to survive or 'stage of viability' is said to be reached at the end of the twenty-eighth week from the first day of the mother's last menstrual period. This definition is unsatisfactory for two reasons.

Firstly, dating is unreliable. In a woman with a classical, regular menstrual cycle of twenty-eight days, ovulation will occur at around the fourteenth day and conception will follow this. Thus the '28-week' fetus is actually just under 26 weeks old. However, menstrual cycles can vary from three weeks to several months long and, as ovulation is related more closely to the end than the beginning of the cycle, it can occur from one week before to several months after the classical predicted time. Another cause of confusion is bleeding in early pregnancy, often mistaken for a period.

With modern intensive care a number of babies born between the twenty-fourth and twenty-eighth weeks of pregnancy will survive. Fetuses in this group are in a 'grey area' of law and medicine and problems arise concerning their position. Before 24 weeks aborted fetuses will often make respiratory efforts and survive for a short while, but death due to inadequate lung function is inevitable. Ideally a weight definition is needed to separate the 'fetus', which is totally dependent on the intrauterine life support systems of its mother, and the 'baby', who has at least a chance of extrauterine survival. A level of 500 g has been reasonably suggested, but intrauterine assessment of weight is not reliable, even with the help of modern ultrasound techniques.

The term 'abortion' can be correctly used to describe both spontaneous and induced fetal loss. However to the lay person 'abortion' implies 'induced abortion' and to a woman who is losing or has lost a much wanted pregnancy any implication, intended or not, that the loss was of her own choosing is most hurtful. Therefore when referring to spontaneous abortion in the presence of lay people the term 'miscarriage' is much to be preferred.

HISTORICAL, LEGAL AND ETHICAL ASPECTS

There is evidence that abortion has been practised in most civilized communities. Despite the anti-abortion clause in the Oath of Hippocrates (possibly a later embellishment) another work by this hallowed figure describes his design for a graduated set of cervical dilators very similar to those used today. Gynaecological instruments, probably used for abortion, were found in the remains of Pompeii and Herculaneum. Sopranus of Ephesus, in A.D.98, described various techniques for abortion and the poet Ovid satirises those women who, for the sake of their beauty, prefer abortion to motherhood.

Nicolas Culpeper (1616–56) in his *Complete Herbal* describes clearly the supposed abortifacient qualities of oil of juniper or savin. He warns against its administration to the pregnant woman. For centuries savin has been a constituent of innumerable brands of compound pills for 'female ailments' and blatant advertising has always made it quite clear what 'restoration of menstruation' really meant. Even such renowned and trusted favourites as Beecham's Pills contained it. From the fact that juniper oil is a constituent of gin comes the (unjustified) abortifacial reputation of that spirit. Abortifacient pills continue to be sold to the present day and were widely used up to the passage of the 1967 Abortion Act.

The rapid progress of obstetrics and gynaecology in the eighteenth and nineteenth centuries led to the design of a variety of instruments for vaginal work that could obviously double for the induction of abortion. Thus the uterine curette (1723), Hegar's dilators (1874) and various vaginal specula were all applicable. Sir James Young Simpson, the much respected Royal Accoucheur, lectured on 'Techniques for the Restoration of Menstrual Function', and reported the use of intrauterine irritants for the 'bringing-on' of delayed periods. He also described a primitive form of suction curettage.

Although abortion has always been practised, the official attitudes of society as expressed by the law have varied from time to time. Under the Roman Empire abortion was regarded not as a crime, to be prosecuted on behalf of the state, but as an offence against the husband as a male individual. In England under Common Law until 1803 abortion before quickening was not a crime and after quickening was regarded as a misdemeanour less than murder. However, in that year abortion was put on the Statute Book and those who procured abortion after quickening could be punished by death. Abortion prior to quickening was a lesser crime, punishable by the pillory or by transportation. In 1837 the punishment for abortionists was relaxed from death to imprisonment or transportation, but for the first time the distinction was lost between abortion before and after quickening. In 1861 the law was amended to include the pregnant woman among those who could be charged and this law remained in force in Great Britain until 1967. It is still in force in Ulster.

In the first half of the present century there was growing pressure to amend the law in Britain. This came to a head in 1938, when Aleck Bourne, a gynaecologist working at St Mary's Hospital, London, openly terminated the pregnancy of a 14-year-old girl who was pregnant after being raped by two guardsmen. At his trial Bourne was acquitted; the judge, Mr Justice McNaughton, delivered a liberal opinion on the abortion laws, making the point that the use of the term 'unlawful' in the relevant legislation must imply that the opposite was possible and that some abortions were therefore 'lawful'. It was under the umbrella of this ruling that abortions were done in increasing but small numbers until the coming into force of the 1967 Act.

It is impossible to summarize here the intense debate that has gone on and continues over the ethical aspects of abortion. In the Christian tradition neither Old nor New Testament provides specific guidance and the debate has centred around related passages, the most important being the 'Thou shalt not kill' (Authorized Version) or 'You shall not commit murder' (*New English Bible*) of the Book of Exodus. The newer translation emphasizes that the act of premeditated homicide or murder clearly hinges on the fact that the individual killed is human, possessing all the attributes of a human being including a soul. But when does a fetus become human? Those who say 'at conception' will have difficulty in explaining the division after conception of monozygotic twins, for how can one soul be divided? Although the embryology was not known, the ancients also questioned this point. Aristotle, in the pre-Christian era, had developed a theory that ensoulment occurred at some time after conception; he thought at 40 days for a male and at 80 days for a female. Most of the early Christian Fathers agreed with this view, among them St Augustine, St Jerome, St Anselm, Peter Lombard and St Thomas Aquinas. The debate continued through the Middle Ages and in the sixteenth century the theory of delayed rational ensoulment was endorsed by the Council of Trent (1566). There were dissidents; in 1588 Pope Sixtus V forbade all abortions, but three years later, in 1591, Pope Gregory XIV reversed his ruling and allowed them. The present absolute ban in the Roman Catholic Church was decreed by Pope Pius IX in 1869 and has continued in force. However, the debate continues and many eminent Roman Catholic theologians openly challenge their church's established doctrine. The Anglican Communion and the various Protestant bodies generally have a more liberal outlook, although all contain members representing a wide spectrum of opinion from absolute opposition to very liberal acceptance. Ironically, the incidence of abortion (albeit illegal) tends to be highest in those countries whose hierarchies most strongly oppose it, basically because an anti-abortion pilosophy is usually accompanied by restrictive views on contraception and hence there are more unwanted pregnancies.

The Law in Great Britain Today

At the time of writing (March 1981) pregnancy termination in England, Wales and Scotland is carried out under the terms of the 1967 Abortion Act. This provides that it is lawful to terminate a woman's pregnancy if, in good faith, two doctors agree:

1. That the continuance of the pregnancy would involve risk to the life of the pregnant woman greater than if the pregnancy were terminated. *Or*
2. That the continuance of the pregnancy would involve injury to the physical or mental health of the pregnant woman greater than if the pregnancy were terminated. *Or*
3. That the continuance of the pregnancy would involve injury to the physical or mental health of the existing child or children of the family of the pregnant woman greater than if the pregnancy were terminated. *Or*
4. That there is a substantial risk that if the child were born it would suffer from such physical or mental abnormalities as to be seriously handicapped.

Normally two doctors, acting independently, must see and examine the pregnant woman and must complete and sign form HSA1 (green) before any procedure to procure abortion is started. However, in a genuine life-threatening or similar emergency a doctor may perform an abortion and complete form HSA2 (pink) within 24 hours. This form requires only one signature and states that the operation was necessary immediately to save the life of the pregnant woman or to prevent grave permanent injury to the physical or mental health of the pregnant woman. This form of procedure is very rarely used.

Abortions may only be performed in 'approved places': National Health Service Hospitals or private hospitals which have sought and gained approval from the appropriate government department* to be used for this purpose. The doctor who performs the abortion need not be (but usually is) one of the two signatories on the 'green' form. However the operating practitioner must complete form HSA4 (buff) and send it to the registering government department* within seven days of the procedure. The buff form includes the information recorded on the green form, together with more details concerning the woman, her family and her operation and postoperative course.

For all its legal terminology the meaning of the Abortion Act is

*In England the government department concerned is the Department of Health and Social Security.

remarkably unclear and virtually allows the individual doctor complete licence to act as he pleases. For some the simple fact that, in plain statistics, pregnancy termination carries a lower overall mortality rate than childbirth will allow clause 1 to be relevant for any woman who requests termination. Others will take a liberal view of clauses 2 or 3 and argue that the social and economic pressures of unwanted pregnancy will be likely to lead to later physical or mental illhealth in the woman or her children. Yet for some clauses 1, 2 and 3 require strict positive interpretation and documented evidence of ill-health before abortion is agreed. Most doctors would agree to an abortion under clause 4 if fetal abnormality was proved, but some doctors are less inclined to look for such evidence than others. Examples of this variation include the question of which diagnostic tests for fetal abnormality are made available to which woman and the question of how old a woman should be for the doctor himself to suggest a discussion about possible fetal abnormality.

This difference of opinion and legal interpretation has been held to be beneficial and it has been assumed that the woman can always obtain a second opinion. However, similar attitudes are often found in whole areas or regions and a second opinion is sometimes difficult for a Heath Service patient to obtain. Accordingly a large number of women who usually use the Health Service seek private care for abortions, either because they are refused as NHS patients or because they anticipate, or have been advised, that they will be. Just over half the abortions on British women in Britain are done privately and the proportion rises to 70–80% in some regions.

ABORTION COUNSELLING

Why should a woman ask for her pregnancy to be terminated? In the vast majority of cases the answer is simple; because that is what she wants. She has usually no illness, mental or physical; if she is tired or run-down it is due to the pressures of her work and family life; and if she is depressed it is a normal reaction to a situation that will lead to a considerable disadvantage in her social, economic and family circumstances. It does her no service for her doctor to pretend that she is ill and that he is treating her illness.

When a woman asks a doctor to terminate her pregnancy, or to arrange for her pregnancy to be terminated, he can respond in one of two ways. His approach can be either that of a judge or that of a counsellor, but not both. As a judge he will assess the facts. The pregnant woman will present her case to him as best she can; the doctor may ask for further evidence from her husband, boyfriend, mother or other relative or friend; and he may ask another health-care professional such as a social worker to prepare a report. He will then make a decision on the evidence put before him and, according to his interpretation of the law, explain this to the woman. She must accept this verdict or seek a second opinion.

As a counsellor the doctor will listen to the story and talk to the woman with a view to helping her make her own decision. Having established that the pregnancy is not too advanced for termination and that there is no medical contraindication, the woman should be assured early in the consultation that the purpose of the discussion is to help her make up her own mind and that termination is available if she wants it. She can then be encouraged to talk freely, explaining factors against as well as for termination. As before, others directly involved may take part in the discussions and a social worker may be able to provide a realistic assessment of the chances of financial support, improvement in housing and other benefits if the pregnancy continues. The possibility of adoption is raised and foster-care is explained. At the end of the discussion the woman's choice stands, even though her advisors may feel she is making a mistake.

Although both approaches have drawbacks, it is the author's opinion that the second is the more acceptable. The doctor is not trained as a judge and his opinion on social or economic circumstances usually is simply that of an untrained individual. His view will often be blinkered by his own experience and irrelevant to the case of a woman from a different walk of life. The inarticulate and underprivileged will be less likely to have their request granted than those from a similar background as the doctor and whose problems he can envisage as those of his own wife or daughter. Moreover, the surgery or consulting room is not a court of law and its procedure would be unacceptable in legal circles. If the doctor sits as a judge the woman should be allowed a trained advocate to argue her case; and if she employed one, the chance of refusal would probably be much lower.

This is not to say that the approach as a counsellor is not without risk. By dropping her defence and accepting the doctor as a friend and as an advisor, she may lay herself unduly open to suggestion and come to a conclusion solely because of his persuasiveness. This may easily happen if the doctor has very strongly held opinions and he may even be unaware of the effect of his argument on the woman being counselled. Having fixed in his mind the course of action that he thinks best, he may not allow the consultation to come to an end until the woman agrees with him and requests that particular path. An essential of the counselling approach is recognizing the right of the woman to be wrong and being prepared to go along with her request once the limits of reasonable and constructive discussion have been passed.

No doctor is obliged to agree to support or perform an abortion in any individual case, unless the situation is immediately life-threatening and other help is not available. However, if his personal religious, moral or ethical views are such that he will never or almost never give such support, it is correct that he should make it plain to his colleagues and patients that these are his views. It is wrong that a woman with a request for termination should have to go through a long consultation when the doctor knows in advance that he will refuse her request. This in no way precludes such a doctor from attempting to help a woman to cope with the problems of unplanned or unwanted pregnancy; he must, however, make it plain that for him abortion is an unacceptable solution and if that is what she wants she must seek other advice.

Every woman is an individual and needs individual guidance, but there are certain situations that present special problems. These are:

The true medical case, physical or mental. Here the request is for a genuine medical opinion and after consultation with relevant colleagues the doctor will advise for or against termination on medical grounds. It is important that the facts be presented to the woman in a way that she can understand them and at a stage where safe termination is still possible. She is then free to accept or reject the advice and termination may be requested on social grounds if on medical grounds it is thought unnecessary.

Mental subnormality. Unlike mental illness, mental subnormality clearly implies no hope of recovery and the need for sheltered or institutional care for the rest of the woman's life. Such women do become pregnant and the pressures from those on whom they are dependent and from society are often strongly in favour of termination. However, it is vital to treat such women as individuals as much as anyone else and to take care to ascertain as fully as possible their views on the matter. It is very rare indeed for the responsibility for such a decision to have to be taken completely by others.

The under-age girl. In Britain the age of consent for sexual intercourse is 16 years and this is also generally accepted as the age of consent for medical treatment. For a girl under this age pregnancy and abortion are often both bewildering and frightening. Commonly two problem situations can arise: the under-age girl who wants to continue with her pregnancy despite opposition from her parents or guardians and the girl who requests an abortion without their knowledge.

In the first case basic ethics must deny what the law in theory might allow: no girl, however young, should have her pregnancy terminated without her consent. This is often very hard for parents who may feel that they are left in an intolerable situation, but to act in any other way is to remove from the girl her basic rights as an individual. It must be recognized that such laws, however firm they may seem, reflect social convention: the ages of consent and legal responsibility vary from country to country by many years.

The second situation can be dealt with using similar principles. Almost always the best confidante for a young girl is her mother and she should be advised to break the news to her. However, there are times when such a disclosure would be harmful to all concerned and under these circumstances many doctors will feel able to break the law and operate on the consent of a girl who is not legally responsible. In these rare circumstances it is wise to obtain a social report in writing to be filed in the case notes and to invite the social worker concerned to join the two doctors in a statement explaining the reasons for the lack of parental involvement.

Coercion. Pressure for or against termination may be applied to a woman of any age; by parents, husband, boyfriend, other friends or relatives, even by her own children. This must be recognized and countered. The woman must be left in no doubt that, although she should listen to the opinions of those from whom she hopes for support, the decision over the abortion is too far-reaching to be made by anyone else except her.

Fetal abnormality. No fetus should be aborted solely because it is abnormal and no pressure should be put on a woman to have an abnormal fetus aborted. If this was to be policy it would be in effect to deny that the handicapped have a right to any place in society and to embrace some of the worse tenets of the Nazi creed. The viable abnormal fetus must have the same rights as the normal fetus.

Nevertheless, knowledge or suspicion that she is going to have an abnormal baby will often create an intolerable situation for the woman concerned. If abnormality is suspected on clinical evidence or thought likely on statistical grounds, and the pregnancy is still at a stage when termination would be feasible, the whole question should be discussed with the woman. If then she states that she would wish for termination if these suspicions are confirmed a full investigation should be conducted. This will usually involve blood tests from mother and father, ultrasonic examination of the baby and sometimes amniocentesis. In early pregnancy X-ray examination is rarely of use. In a few cases fetoscopy with intrauterine fetal blood sampling may be indicated.

Even routine screening tests for fetal abnormality should not be undertaken on women who discount the option of abortion if the fetus is proved to be abnormal. There is every difference, for example, between performing routine serological tests for a condition like syphilis which is a treatable infection leaving the fetus undamaged if cured early, and performing tests for alpha-fetoprotein which detect neural tube defects. In the latter case the imperfect fetus cannot be 'cured', only removed.

Repeated abortion and refusal of contraceptive advice. Proper contraceptive counselling is an integral and indivisible part of abortion counselling. If it is done properly it has been shown that the number of women asking for a second abortion is very small and the reasons are usually 'contraceptive' failures. However, there are a number of women whose attitude is usually labelled as 'feckless' or 'irresponsible', who appear not to care how many times they present for their pregnancies to be terminated. Their attitude evokes hostility among doctors and nurses and comments such as 'Everybody can make one mistake, but...' and 'She needs to be taught a lesson' are common. These attitudes must be strongly resisted. Counselling of such a woman must be conducted as sympathetically as for any other and often the reason can be found in a genuine misunderstanding about the relative dangers of contraception and abortion. Sometimes repeated unwanted pregnancies represent a real cry for help at an emotional and psychological level. In any case, when viewed objectively, the 'repeater' will usually have a stronger than average case for the pregnancy to be terminated. No woman should ever be made to have an unwanted baby to teach her a lesson or as an example to others and forcing women to the private sector because they are not 'deserving enough' for the public is both unethical and a travesty of the spirit of the National Health Service.

Social deprivation. Although the woman herself will often seek abortion because of poor social circumstances, her advisors should not put pressure on her to have this done. They should rather make sure she is fully aware of all the financial and other benefits that she can claim, giving actual figures rather than vague guidelines. It is equally important not to present an over-optimistic view of the circumstances and bribe her into going on with a pregnancy in a world that will collapse around her. This aspect is one of the most difficult to counsel adequately and a careless phrase or half-truth can make the whole future look different.

Who Shall be the Counsellor?

In Britain abortion is under the control of the medical profession and the operating practitioner is legally responsible for the correctness of his actions. He must be satisfied personally as to the medical aspects of the case and that the procedure planned is both feasible and safe. However, the socio-economic aspects of the case may well be time-consuming and, rather than skimp these, he may wish to depute them to a paramedical colleague. Although there are many voluntary organizations with members pressing to help, such offers should always be refused as such people usually volunteer because of strong feelings for or against abortion. In many units nurses or social workers provide counselling. Such a counsellor must be fully trained for the role: patient, sympathetic, a good listener and properly informed about what can and cannot be done to help in the social and economic aspects of the case. It is also essential for the counsellor to recognize that she is probably better educated and a better communicator than the woman being counselled and to be able to stop herself taking advantage of this to impose on the woman a solution that she (the woman) does not really want.

Counselling without authority is always unsatisfactory, for there is no value in the counsellor assisting the woman to a decision that will then be reversed by the doctor who sees her subsequently. If counselling is to be usefully shared the gynaecologist must give his assistant an accurate account of his views and practice and allow the assistant to use this information in the discussion to tell the woman whether or not she will be able to have her abortion. This will make the counselling session much more productive; free from the worry of whether or not she *can* have an abortion, the woman can freely discuss whether or not she really *wants* an abortion.

CONTRACEPTION

Contraception is the subject of a separate chapter of this book and detail will not be discussed here. However, discussion of contraceptive methods is an integral part of abortion counselling and firm plans for the future should always be made. Most methods will run straight on from the abortion; oral contraception should be started within a few days of the operation and intrauterine contraceptive devices can be fitted at the time of operation or a few weeks after. For some, usually older women whose families are complete, sterilization under the same anaesthetic as the termination is often the most satisfactory arrangement.

When discussing plans for future contraceptive use, particular attention should be paid to the past history. In some cases there will have been a contraceptive method failure which may be due to mechanical or biochemical inadequacy (e.g. ruptured sheath, poor spermicide, coil still in place); patient error, carelessness or deliberate misuse; teaching error (e.g. failure to warn patient of interaction between various drugs and oral contraceptives); or a combination of these. Even if contraception has not been used most women know something about it and to some degree any woman's unwanted pregnancy must be regarded as an acceptance failure for any method she knows about. This applies particularly to the oral contraceptive; in each case the counsellor must explore in detail why a woman with knowledge of the pill, who often has used it before, did not use this method and became pregnant. Failure to identify any medical, psychological or intellectual objections, rational or irrational, that a woman might have to the pill or any other method may result in its represcription, half-hearted use and subsequent further unwanted pregnancy. Sexual intercourse should be a happy, relaxed and enjoyed experience; if there are any contraceptive worries sexual satisfaction will be reduced. No technique is perfect or applicable to all and great skill is needed to find the most suitable method for each couple.

THE ABORTION OPERATION

Preparation of the Patient

A full assessment of the woman's general health should be made. The diagnosis of pregnancy should be confirmed and its duration accurately assessed; if there is doubt an ultrasonic examination may be necessary. Blood tests should be as for on-going pregnancy: haemoglobin level, ABO and rhesus blood group, serological tests for treponemal disease and rubella. Rubella screening is of particular value, as if a woman is proved to be susceptible to rubella at the time of termination of an unwanted pregnancy she can be vaccinated before her next, and wanted, conception. A cervical smear for premalignant disease screening should be taken unless one has been performed recently and in many cases screening by culture for gonorrhoea, trichomoniasis and thrush is indicated.

Consent forms and the 'green form' should be properly completed and signed before treatment is commenced. Although many doctors prefer that in the case of a married woman her husband should also sign a consent form this is not legally necessary.

Participation of Nursing Staff

No nurse is obliged to work in a unit where abortions are carried out and if, during her training, she gives adequate notice of her views, arrangements will be made for her to have alternative experience. This applies to out-patient, ward and theatre work.

If she is working in a unit where abortions are performed, she is not entitled to make her own distinctions between individual cases and refuse to cooperate over some of them. To allow this would be wrong for two reasons; firstly it would subject the woman to a second assessment, despite the conclusions of her doctors, and secondly it would put in question the good faith of those who had agreed to her abortion and make a mockery of the idea of a medical and nursing team. This is not to say that a decision may not be questioned; it is very desirable that a gynaecologist be prepared to discuss his principles and policies with every member of his staff. However, such discussion must not influence the management of a particular case once a decision has been made.

All doctors and nurses, whatever their views, must if asked cooperate in the management of an abortion case if a life-threatening situation develops. Such situations would include severe haemorrhage, bowel perforation at operation or cardiac arrest; relevant staff must also assist with the care of such patients even if the immediate management includes the continuation of the abortion procedure.

The Procedures

Thirteen weeks and under

The procedures used in first trimester abortion are those of vaginal evacuation. They are quick and safe and require either short, light general anaesthesia or infiltration of the cervix with local anaesthetic. For most women a stay of a few hours in a day-care unit is all that is required and provided that they can be escorted home, do not have too long or difficult a journey and rest for the remainder of the day, this provision is very safe and acceptable.

Most commonly a light general anaesthetic is given; premedication is unnecessary and intubation is not used. The woman is then placed in the lithotomy position and the lower genital tract cleaned with antiseptic. A paracervical block may be given. After confirming the preoperative findings the cervix is grasped and the canal dilated gradually in half-millimetre steps to a diameter in millimetres roughly equivalent to the duration of the pregnancy in weeks. Excessive force or hurry may result in tearing and permanent damage; extreme gentleness is needed. When the cervix is dilated the uterus can be emptied either by suction or by instrumental evacuation. For suction nowadays a transparent plastic curette of the Karman or Berkely pattern is most usual, of the same outside diameter as the dilated cervix. Suction pressure of around 500 mmHg is used and the products of conception can be seen leaving the uterus. This method is highly efficient, but it is usual to explore the uterine cavity with a sponge-holding forceps and uterine curette after suction, to check that the abortion is complete. If suction is not available, the whole procedure is performed with these instruments.

At the start of the procedure it is usual to give a drug to promote uterine contraction, to minimize blood loss and to harden the uterine walls and make them easier to feel. Although ergometrine (0.5 mg) is commonly used for this purpose, it has the disadvantage of causing nausea and vomiting; oxytocin (5 units) is to be preferred.

Once she is fully recovered from the anaesthetic, and has no pain or excessive bleeding, the woman may go home, providing she is responsibly escorted. Bleeding may normally continue for up to ten days. However good the aseptic and operative techniques, a few women will develop post-abortal infection; a routine postoperative prophylactic course of broad-spectrum antibiotic will reduce this number. Each woman is advised to see her doctor for a routine 'check-up' two weeks postoperatively, for if she is still bleeding then re-evacuation is probably needed. She is also told to seek advice if she develops fever, pain or bleeding heavier than her normal period.

Unsensitized rhesus-negative women are given an injection of anti-D gamma globulin and rubella-susceptible women are vaccinated, provided that adequate contraception is assured for three months. It is good advice for the woman not to plan further pregnancy within six months of termination, because of a reported higher miscarriage and fetal abnormality rate if conception occurs within that time.

For women whose families are complete and who have some other problem such as fibroids or heavy periods it often seems a logical course to perform a hysterectomy with the fetus still inside. Unless there are very pressing reasons why this should be done the combined operation should be avoided, as both intraoperative problems such as bleeding and postoperative problems such as infection and thrombo-embolic disease are much higher than they would be for a termination and a hysterectomy carried out separately.

Over thirteen weeks

Termination in the middle trimester presents much more of a risk. In-patient care is always involved and it is usually a major problem to fit such cases into wards where they are acceptable to staff and to other patients. Various techniques may be used.

Dilatation and evacuation. Once dilatation of the cervix has exceeded 10 mm, there is a major risk of permanent damage. With preoperative softening and great care, wider dilatation can be achieved and fetuses up to 16 weeks size evacuated. However, the risk of laceration and later incompetence remains considerable. An older method, perhaps about to be reintroduced, involves the packing of the cervical canal with laminaria tents made of material which swells as it absorbs moisture producing a very slow dilatation.

Hysterotomy. This is a mini-caesarean section through an abdominal wound. Unlike caesarean section at term, however, the safest access to the uterine cavity through the thin lower segment is not possible as this has not formed; the uterus must be emptied through a high transverse or vertical upper segment incision. This can seriously compromise the woman's future for childbearing. The woman's stay in hospital is usually several days and the risk of pulmonary embolus is high.

Extra-amniotic prostaglandin. A urinary catheter is threaded through the cervix, the bulb is inflated and a slow infusion of prostaglandin is passed through it to induce labour. When it comes, labour is usually slow and painful and a full analgesic service including epidural anaesthesia is desirable. A fetus of 18–20 weeks is often born alive and although survival is impossible its obvious movements and respiratory efforts are distressing to the mother and her attendants. The placenta is usually retained and manual removal necessary. Labour often lasts 20 hours or more and infection is common. As the progress of the abortion is dependent on the continuing infusion, all aspects of the prostaglandin administration must be regarded as the abortive procedure and the responsibility of the doctor. However, nurses may now legally be involved in replacing empty syringes with full ones and increasing dose rates.

An older extra-amniotic method involved the injection of concentrated soap solution ('Utus paste') through the cervix. This carries a very high mortality rate and should never be used.

Intra-amniotic injections. These may be of hypertonic solutions (saline, urea), prostaglandins or both and are injected into the amniotic cavity through an amniocentesis needle. The osmotic shift caused by the hypertonic solution will kill the fetus and rapidly expand the amniotic cavity; this, together with the prostaglandin response, should initiate labour. The theoretical advantages over the extra-amniotic route are that the fetus does not survive and that a continuous infusion is avoided. However, the method often does not work or results in violent hypertonic contractions. When it starts, labour is usually long and intravenous oxytocin is often needed to augment the contractions. Full analgesia is usually needed. The pregnancy must be far enough advanced for the amniotic sac to be entered and horrifying complications can result from a misplaced injection.

The Aftermath of Abortion

From the triennial series of *Confidential Enquiries into Maternal Deaths in England and Wales*, published by the Department of Health and Social Security, exact figures can be obtained on the mortality associated with abortion. Abortion used to be the commonest single cause of maternal death, but, probably due to the liberalizing of the law in 1967, the death rate has fallen dramatically out of all proportion to other causes of maternal loss. Thus comparing 1964–6 with 1973–5 the number of deaths from abortion fell from 133 to 29, whereas total maternal deaths fell only from 579 to 235. Early abortion is very safe, with a death rate for vacuum aspiration of 1 per 170 000. (The overall death rate in pregnancy and childbirth excluding abortion is about 1 in 9000.) However, methods of late termination are much more dangerous, with hysterotomy and prostaglandin methods each with a death-rate of about 1 in 4000. Utus paste (over a six-year period) produced the horrific toll of one death in every 500 cases.

Figures for morbidity are more difficult to obtain. Excessive dilatation certainly leads to cervical incompetence, with mid-trimester loss in subsequent pregnancies. Infection and undetected perforation lead to adhesions and infertility. Other problems have been detailed with the method description. However, almost all early cases have no subsequent problems.

Much has been written about the psychological trauma of abortion and its consequences. Certainly some women experience pathological regret and remorse, but the consensus of research opinion is that, providing counselling and the abortion are handled swiftly and with sympathy, no long-term problems will result. Series which compare women having abortions with those with unwanted pregnancies who continue with them, either by their own choice or because abortion was refused, show a much higher incidence of later psychological illness in the latter group. There is, however, a real danger with the susceptible woman that a rigorous anti-abortion counsellor will provoke feelings of guilt and depression that were not there before and that these will lead to subsequent mental ill-health.

Bibliography

Much has been written; much is biased; much is emotional and unsound. However, for those who wish to delve further into this very difficult subject, the following books are suggested:

Potts, M., Diggory, P. & Peel, J. (1977) *Abortion*. London: Cambridge University Press. (An encyclopaedia of information on every aspect.)

Gardner, R.F.R. (1972) *Abortion: The Personal Dilemma*. Exeter: Paternoster Press. (An individual analysis of the Christian ethics involved.)

Francke, L.B. (1980) *The Ambivalence of Abortion*. Harmondsworth: Penguin. (A variety of case histories and late analyses by women, their families and their friends.)

8. Contraception

A.M. Spence

This chapter is directed to the nurse who is trained in some aspects of gynaecology and wishes to be aware of current practice in contraception. The experienced family planning nurse may wish to consult the medical literature to further her knowledge of specialized developments and current controversies. This account concentrates almost entirely on contraception as practised in the United Kingdom. In other countries, especially the less developed areas, the choice of which contraceptive method is most widely favoured may well be determined by the laws of supply and demand, as well as the availability of funds.

COMBINED ORAL CONTRACEPTIVES

The combined oral contraceptive pill containing two synthetic hormones, oestrogen and progestagen, is the most effective reversible method of contraception currently available. A list of the preparations currently available is given in Table 8.1. When taken properly, the combined pill is almost always effective in preventing pregnancy. In the United Kingdom last year (1979), it was being taken by 3100 000 women between the ages of 15 years and 35 years.

The combined pill works by suppressing ovulation and altering the character of the cervical mucus; it may also have an effect on the endometrium, making implantation unlikely.

Table 8.1. Oral Contraceptives in Current Use

Brand name	*Progestogen content*
With 50 μg of oestrogen (ethinyloestradiol unless otherwise indicated)	
Demulen 50	500 μg ethynodiol diacetate
Orlest 21	1 mg norethisterone acetate BP
Ovran	250 μg levonorgestrel
Ovulen 50	1 mg ethynodiol diacetate BP
Norinyl-1 (mestranol BP 50 μg)	1 mg norethisterone BP
Norinyl 1/28 (mestranol BP 50 μg)	1 mg norethisterone BP
Eugynon 50	500 μg levonorgestrel
Ortho-Novin 1/50 (Mestranol BP 50 μg)	1 mg norethisterone BP
Minovlar	1 mg norethisterone acetate BP
Minovlar ED	1 mg norethisterone acetate BP
Gynovlar 21	3 mg norethisterone acetate BP
Minilyn	2.5 mg lynoestrenol BP
Anovlar	4 mg norethisterone acetate BP
Norlestrin	2.5 mg norethisterone acetate BP
With 20–35 μg of oestrogen (ethinyloestradiol)	
Brevinor (35 μg oestrogen)	500 μg norethisterone BP
Conova 30 (30 μg oestrogen)	2 mg ethynodiol diacetate BP
Microgynon 30 (30 μg oestrogen)	150 μg levonorgestrel
Ovranette (30 μg oestrogen)	150 μg levonorgestrel
Eugynon 30 (30 μg oestrogen)	250 μg levonorgestrel
Ovran 30 (30 μg oestrogen)	250 μg levonorgestrel
Norimin (35 μg oestrogen)	1 mg norethisterone BP
Ovysmen (35 μg oestrogen)	500 μg norethisterone BP
Loestrin 20 (20 μg oestrogen)	1 mg norethisterone acetate BP
Progestogen-only preparations	
Femulen	500 μg ethynodiol diacetate BP
Noriday	350 μg norethisterone BP
Micronor	350 μg norethisterone BP
Microval	30 μg levonorgestrel
Neogest	75 μg norgestrel
Norgeston	30 μg levonorgestrel

Administration

The combined pill is taken for 21 days followed by seven pill-free days during which withdrawal bleeding usually occurs. The patient is now advised to start her first course of pills on the first day of menstruation. This means that she is protected immediately, although it also means that the first cycle is somewhat shorter than usual. If she so wishes, the patient may start on the fifth day of the cycle and use another method for the 14 days before protection is given.

Management of Pill-taking Problems

The patient should be advised to take a missed pill as soon as she remembers. Then she should use another method of birth control (in addition to continuing her regimen of pill-taking) for 14 days. This rule of continuing a pill-taking regimen, plus 14 days additional precaution, using sheath and spermicide, cap and spermicide or abstinence is also applicable when pills are taken at a much later time in the day than usual. If vomiting or severe diarrhoea occur within one hour of taking the pill, a similar rule must apply.

Warning Signs of Drug Interaction

When break-through bleeding occurs following administration of one of the following drugs, an interaction should be suspected. This may either reduce the efficacy of the contraceptive pill or interfere with the action of the concurrent drug. The following lists are not comprehensive and the nurse should obtain expert medical advice if in any doubt. Some common drugs *known* or *thought* to reduce the efficiency of the pill are:

Anti-convulsants
Phenobarbitone and some other barbiturates
Ampicillin, rifampicin and possibly some other antibiotics
Phenylbutazone and some related analgesics
Meprobamate and some other tranquillizers
Sedatives (some)
Antihistamines (some)
Ergotamine preparations

Those drugs which can be affected by oral contraceptives include:

Anticoagulants (reduced anticoagulant activity may be seen)
Insulin and oral hypoglycaemic agents (diabetic control may be reduced so extra supervision may be needed)
Promazine hydrochloride
Pethidine hydrochloride

Imipramine
Folic acid

A careful medical history needs to be taken, including the history of drug use.

Another method of contraception in addition to the pill should be employed for patients who have used, or will use, any of the drugs mentioned above for a long period.

Patients should be told about potential drug interaction and asked to report possible signs, e.g. break-through bleeding.

Contraindications

There are a variety of contraindications to the pill and the nurse should be fully aware of them. Medical advice should always be sought.

Absolute contraindications

1. Thromboembolic disorder (or history thereof).
2. Cerebrovascular accident (or history thereof).
3. Impaired liver function.
4. Coronary artery disease (or history thereof).
5. Hepatic adenoma (or history thereof).
6. Malignancy of breast or reproductive system (or history thereof).
7. Pregnancy (known or suspected).

Strong relative contraindications

1. Severe migraine.
2. Hypertension.
3. Diabetes or pre-diabetes or strong family history of diabetes.
4. Gall-bladder disease including cholelithiasis (or history thereof).
5. Previous cholestasis during pregnancy.
6. Mononucleosis (acute phase).
7. Sickle cell disease or sickle C disease.
8. Undiagnosed abnormal vaginal bleeding.
9. Elective surgery planned in next four weeks.
10. Long leg plaster casts or major surgery to lower limbs producing or necessitating reduced mobility.
11. Age over 35 years (especially if heavy smoker).
12. Fibrocystic breast disease or breast fibroadenoma.

Indications for extra careful supervision

1. Depression.
2. Hypertension with resting diastolic 90 mmHg.
3. Chloasma.
4. Asthma.
5. Epilepsy.
6. Uterine fibroids.
7. Varicose veins.
8. Migraine.
9. Previous hepatitis but now normal liver function tests (LFTs).
10. Age over 30 years.
11. Use for more than five years.

Other relative contraindications

1. Failure to establish regular menstrual cycle.
2. Cardiac or renal disease (or history thereof).
3. Heavy smoking (over 15 per day).
4. 'Unreliable' patients, i.e. with a history of mental retardation, major psychiatric problems, alcoholics or previous history of failure to take medication correctly.
5. Late onset of menses and history of irregular painless menses, suggestive of anovulation and possible infertility.

Side Effects

Possibly 40% of patients taking the combined oral contraceptive pill experience side effects. These fall into three groups.

Very serious or life-threatening

The most serious side effects are blood clots in the legs, pelvis, lungs or brain. Signs of trouble include severe headaches, blurring or loss of vision, dizziness or fainting, flashing lights, severe abdominal or leg pain, severe chest pains, unexplained cough, breathlessness or painful breathing, swelling of limbs and unexplained pain, pins and needles or numbness in any part of the body.

In these cases it is vital that the pill be stopped *immediately*.

Serious

Hypertension is the most common serious symptom. A rise in blood pressure, if pill-induced, is usually very quickly reversible, but it can lead to permanent complications. Gall-bladder disease with upper abdominal pain, indigestion and development of gall-stones is another important complication.

Less serious

These side effects, though relatively minor, may cause the patient to discontinue oral contraception: nausea, weight gain, fluid retention, breast fullness or tenderness, mild headaches, bleeding between periods (break-through bleeding, BTB), failure to have periods, increased tendency to fungal infections, mood changes, mild depression, fatigue, lack of libido, acne, chloasma.

Management of side effects

Very serious complications (thromboses) can often be minimized or avoided completely by:

1. A careful study of the contraindications.
2. Teaching the patient the early warning signs of danger.
3. A change of method when indicated.

A rise in blood pressure associated with oral contraceptives should always be regarded as *serious*. Careful taking of blood pressure at initial and subsequent visits is extremely important. An early rise is often a sign of future problems. Most doctors and nurses underline the raised reading thus 140/90. If possible, it should be checked.

The patient will need careful supervision if she is to remain on the pill. If she is over 30 years of age and/or a heavy smoker, it is worth asking her to discontinue the pill for three months to see if the rise in b.p. is pill-induced. Another method must then be substituted.

Among *less serious* side effects, *nausea* is nearly always troublesome in the first and second cycles but then gets less so. The patient should be advised to take the pill before going to bed rather than first thing in the morning. It may also help to take it with food.

In the event of *weight gain or fluid retention*, attention to diet is the most satisfactory measure. It may also help if a lower dose preparation is given.

Mild headaches during the pill-free week are very common and may be caused by the drop in progesterone level. They can be helped by taking the pill continuously but, as this entails taking extra hormones and having no withdrawal bleeding, most women prefer to take mild analgesics or to discontinue the oral contraceptive. The severity and duration of the headaches, and whether or not they are accompanied by visual disturbance, are important and should be noted. Careful history taking is important as many women suffer tension headaches. It may be valuable to refer the patient to an optician. If the headaches are severe and not related in any way to eye strain or tension, the pill should be discontinued.

If *migraine* is made worse by the oral contraceptive, its use should be discontinued.

If *withdrawal bleeding does not occur*, two pregnancy tests one week apart should be carried out using an early morning specimen of urine. If the patient is not pregnant, a pill of higher progesterone content will then probably be prescribed by the doctor if he can exclude pregnancy on clinical examination.

Patients taking the pill are more prone than others to develop *fungal infections* of the vagina. Treatment with clotrimazole (Canesten) or nystatin is effective but the condition is distressingly recurrent. The patient should be advised to wear stockings instead of tights and to avoid skin-tight jeans. Some doctors advise discontinuing oral contraceptives if the condition proves too great an inconvenience to the patient.

Mood changes, mild depression and fatigue are not always Pill-induced. Again, careful history taking is important to discover whether or not the patient's life style is responsible. It may be necessary to discontinue oral contraception in some cases.

Chloasma, if due to oral contraception, is usually noticed by the patient after sun-bathing. It is not readily reversible and is manifest as brown, pigmented patches on the face. Discontinuing the drug causes the patches to fade: they can easily be disguised by make-up.

If there is an obvious correlation between *loss of libido* and the use of the pill it may be necessary to discontinue its use but this is an unusual situation.

A few patients on the pill may have problems with *acne*. A dermatological opinion may be necessary in some cases, especially if oral contraception is very important to the patient.

Break-through bleeding may sometimes be a problem. The patient should be seen by the doctor so that other causes of bleeding can be excluded. A higher dose of progestogen may be needed.

Patients needing *careful supervision and three monthly visits* while taking oral contraceptives will include

All patients over 30 years

Patients on oral contraceptives for more than five years
Patients over weight by 7 kg (14 lb) or more
Smokers (Over 10/day)
Patients with family history of deep vein thrombosis, pulmonary embolism, cerebral thrombosis or coronary thrombosis, especially at an early age

Ideally, nobody with more than two of the above criteria should be taking a combined pill.

Nurses should encourage women on the pill to stop smoking. There is real evidence to suggest that older women who smoke and take oral contraceptives are three times more likely to have serious side effects than the non-smoker.

If an older patient needs to discontinue the pill because she is in the high risk group she will need careful counselling. Her acceptance of an alternative method will be greatly helped by the nurses' attitude and teaching. If the IUCD is her second choice, then she will usually be happy to know that the older woman does very much better with it than her younger sister.

Clinic management of patients

Initial visit

The initial visit should include all the following:

1. Full medical history and assessment of patient.
2. Taking of blood pressure.
3. Weighing of patient.
4. Taking cervical smear.
5. Pelvic examination and breast examination.
6. Careful counselling by doctor or nurse.

Opportunity must be given for patient to discuss the pill and to ask questions.

Follow-up visit

At a visit six to 12 weeks later the patient should be asked about headaches, eye problems, any pains or any problems associated with pill-taking. The following should then be checked:

1. Weight.
2. Blood pressure.
3. Correct method of taking the pill?
4. Withdrawal bleeding?
5. Break-through bleeding?

Three-monthly visit

The procedure is the same as at the first follow-up visit.

Annual visit

All the measures taken at the initial visit should be repeated. The patient should be reassured and asked if there are any changes in her history or that of her family.

THE PROGESTOGEN-ONLY (POP) OR 'MINI' PILL

The action of the progestogen-only pill is the same as that of the long-acting injectable progestogen, i.e. to render the cervical mucus hostile to sperm, to render the endometrium unreceptive to any fertilized ovum, and, in about 40% of cycles, to inhibit ovulation. A list of the preparations currently in use is given in Table 8.1. The drug manufacturers claim theoretical effectiveness rates of 1.25 pregnancies per 100 woman years.

The absolute contraindications to the use of this method are the same as for the combined pill.

Progestogen-only pills may be the initial choice of oral contraception for women over 35 years and for women with a history of headaches, hypertension or bad varicose veins. If a hormonal method is preferred by a lactating patient, the progestogen-only pill is prescribed.

If a patient has experienced side-effects such as headaches, hypertension, leg cramps, chloasma, weight-gain, and nausea (see p. 100) from taking the combined pill, then the POP is often prescribed as an alternative. The POP is taken daily, even when menstruating, and must be taken at the same time each day.

Instructions to Patients

Patients should be told to start their pills on the first day of menstruation and take one pill every day at the same time. If a pill is missed, it should be taken as soon as the omission is noted. The next pill should be taken at the usual time. A second method of contraception should be used for the next 14 days. If a period does not occur within 45 days of the last one, a pregnancy test should be carried out and the doctor should be consulted. Missing a period is very common with this method and does not necessarily mean pregnancy, but checking with *two* pregnancy tests one week apart and a pelvic examination is essential.

As well as its slightly lower effectiveness, the POP produces less frequent menstrual bleeding. When taking the POP, one of two basic bleeding patterns will probably be noted.

1. Regular bleeding every 28–30 days.
2. Irregular bleeding every 25–45 days.

To improve the effectiveness of the mini-pill, some doctors suggest that a second method should be used at mid-cycle particularly during the first three to six months.

Clinic Management

The same regimen as for combined oral contraceptives is used, but it is necessary to perform pregnancy tests as often as asked, to reassure those who are not pregnant and to detect unplanned pregnancies as early as possible.

It is important to tell the patient that, as soon as one packet is finished, the next one should be started without a break.

INJECTABLE CONTRACEPTIVES

The long-acting progestogen medroxyprogesterone (Depo-Provera) is used in Great Britain, but for short-term contraception only.

It is particularly useful in the following instances:

1. For the wives of men who have recently undergone vasectomy during the three months before the operation becomes effective.
2. For women who have been immunized against rubella during the three-month period when the virus is active. The mode of action is similar to that of the progestogen-only pill.

The absolute contraindications to combined oral contraceptives also apply to long-acting progestogens. It is not yet known if there is an increased risk of thromboembolic disease associated with progestogen-only contraception. Medroxyprogesterone often produces a very irregular menstrual pattern and occasionally the loss is much heavier than normal.

After nine to 12 months medroxyprogesterone amenorrhoea is to be expected. Infertility after medroxyprogesterone is common but there is usually a return of fertility in 80% of women after a year.

The first injection is normally given in the first five days of the cycle and extra precautions should be taken for the first 14 days, though they can be omitted if the injection is given on the first day of bleeding. It is essential that the interval between injections is no more than three months.

Patients should have annual pelvic examination and breast checks. Breast self-examination should be encouraged. Excessive endometrial bleeding in the form of prolonged and/or heavy bleeding is the most frequent reason for discontinuing medroxyprogesterone.

Medroxyprogesterone is approved for short-term use only by the British Committee for the Safety of Medicines.

INTRAUTERINE DEVICES (IUCD)

The fairly recent development (1959) of plastic intrauterine devices reawakened medical interest in this method of contraception. Since that date several devices, including the Dalkon shield, have been produced, acclaimed and later withdrawn. At present the five devices most commonly used in clinics in the United Kingdom are:

Copper and plastic devices: Copper T, Copper 7, Multiload CU 250.

Plastic-only devices: Lippe's loop, Saf-T-Coil.

Copper-containing devices are fairly new, the most recent addition being the Multiload CU 250, and do seem to be more suitable for nulliparous patients as they cause fewer painful insertion problems, less dysmenorrhoea and less heavy menstrual loss. For maximum contraceptive efficiency copper-containing devices should be changed every two to two and a half years.

Plastic devices can be left in indefinitely as long as they are troublefree, but annual smears and pelvic examination are essential for all intrauterine device users.

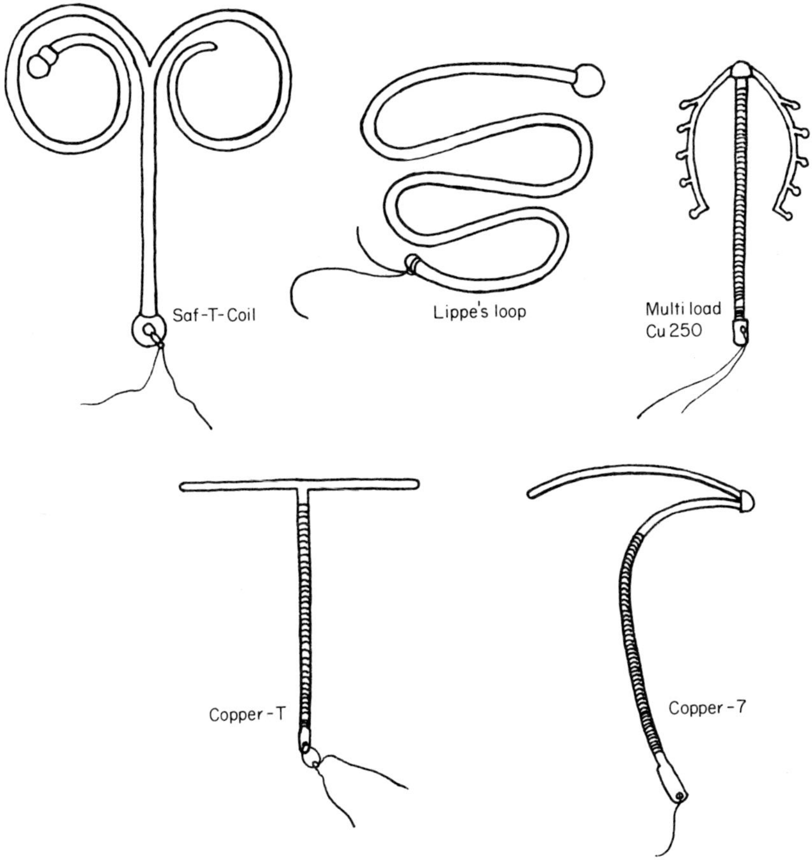

Fig. 8.1. Various intrauterine contraceptive devices.

Mechanism of Action

The exact mechanism of action of the intrauterine devices is not yet known. Most doctors believe it to be a combination of two or more of the following effects:

1. Increased motility of the ovum in fallopian tube.
2. Increased local production of prostaglandins which inhibit implantation.
3. Local inflammatory response preventing implantation.
4. The presence of copper.

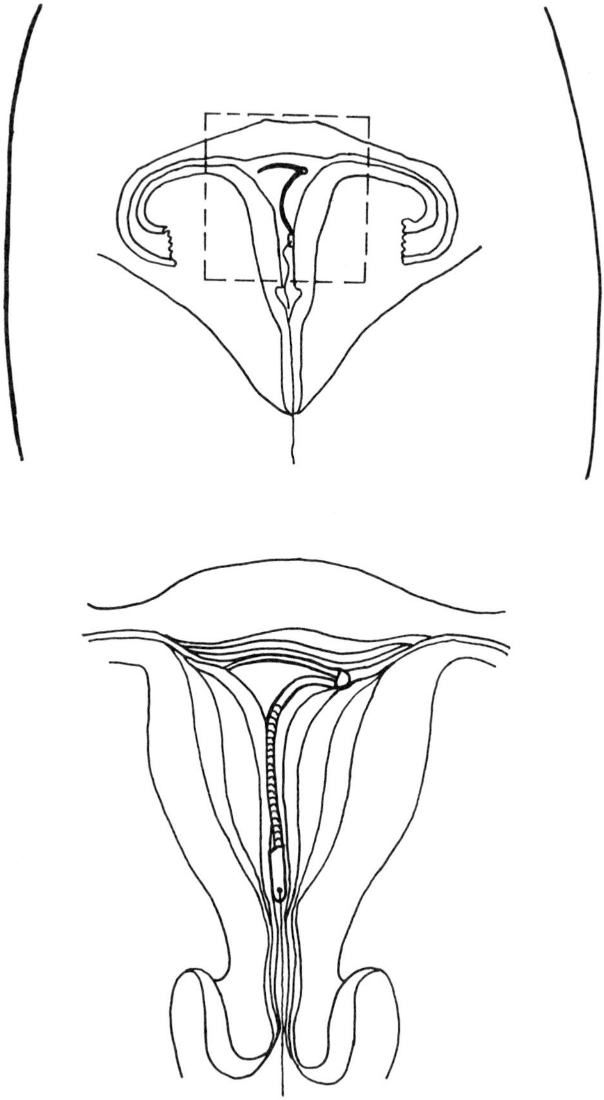

Fig. 8.2. The Copper 7 in situ.

Effectiveness

The copper-containing devices are the more effective and have the same failure rate as the progestogen-only pill, i.e. between 2 and 4 per 100 woman years. The lower figure applies to older multiparous women who, on the whole, do very well with an intrauterine device. Nulliparous patients under 25 years of age have a higher failure rate (approximately 4 per 100 woman years). There is also an increased risk of expulsion in nulliparous patients. Statistical evidence suggests that if a pregnancy does occur then the fetus is just as likely to be undamaged as in a normal planned pregnancy: there is, however, an increased risk of abortion. The device must be removed as soon as pregnancy is confirmed. There is also an increased risk of ectopic pregnancy with an IUCD. All patients who present with severe one-sided abdominal pain and/or overdue periods should be examined by a doctor.

It has also been reported that the incidence of pelvic inflammatory disease is increased in IUCD users. The risk is highest in the young, nulliparous, sexually active patient who has more than one partner, and lowest in those who have only one partner (provided that partner has no other partners). The main symptom of pelvic inflammatory disease is pain in the lower abdomen. The patient may complain of dyspareunia (painful sexual intercourse). She will feel ill and is sometimes pyrexial. She may also have vaginal discharge and heavy bleeding. As pelvic inflammatory disease may lead to salpingitis and possible lowered fertility in the future, it should be diagnosed and treated as soon as possible. The treatment is antibiotics for three weeks and removal of the device.

Contraindications

Absolute contraindications

1. Pregnancy.
2. Acute pelvic infection.
3. Undiagnosed vaginal bleeding.

Relative contraindications

1. A history of recurrent pelvic infection.
2. A history of previous ectopic pregnancy.
3. Valvular heart disease (potentially making the patient susceptible to subacute bacterial endocarditis). Antibiotic cover must be given.

4. An abnormal cervical smear.
5. Acute cervicitis.

Possible contraindications

1. Cervical stenosis.
2. Endometriosis.
3. Endometrial polyps.
4. Bicornuate uterus.
5. Uterine fibroids.
6. Severe dysmenorrhoea.
7. Abnormal uterine bleeding including menorrhagia.
8. Known or suspected copper allergy.
9. Anaemia.

Instructions for insertion

1. Aseptic technique is essential.

2. The procedure should be explained to the patient. Very nervous patients can be given 5 mg diazepam by mouth half an hour prior to insertion.

3. A careful bimanual examination should be performed to exclude pregnancy and pelvic infection.

4. A warm, lubricated, suitably sized speculum is inserted.

5. The cervix is washed threc times with a correctly diluted antiseptic.

6. The anterior lip of the cervix is grasped with a single toothed tenaculum (Judd Alley's forceps are excellent for this purpose) about 1.5–2 cm from the cervical os. The forceps are closed slowly.

7. The uterus is sounded slowly and gently. A swab is placed at the cervix when the sound is all the way in then the swab and sound are removed together. This permits measurement of the depth of the fundus to within 0.25 cm. New disposable sounds have a cervical stop to indicate depth of fundus.

8. The IUCD is loaded into the inserter barrel.

9. The IUCD is inserted into the cavity of the uterus either by plunging the inner barrel (push technique) or by retracting the barrel over the plunger (withdrawal technique). Insertion should be done slowly.

10. The threads are clipped to about 5 cm. Some practitioners ask

the patient to feel for the threads at this stage. The length of thread depends on the patient's preference. Some patients complain that their partners can feel the threads: if this happens it is best to ask the patient to push them out of the way just before intercourse. If the threads are cut shorter than 5 cm they can be very painful for the partner.

IUCD insertion may produce sufficient pain and vasovagal stimulation to cause syncope, cardiac arrhythmia and even cardiac arrest. As in most medical emergencies maintenance of an airway and cardiac output is the top priority. Removal of the device may be necessary.

Timing of insertion

The cervical canal is slightly dilated during menstruation so insertion at this time will be less uncomfortable for the patient, though there may be a greater susceptibility to the development of post-insertion infection at this time. Common sense should dictate when insertion is carried out especially if patients have taken time off work or travelled long distances. At least three months should elapse after any episode of pelvic inflammatory disease. At least three months should elapse after caesarean section or uterine surgery. Prior to postpartum (vaginal delivery) IUCD insertion at least six weeks should elapse.

Uterine perforation

Correct diagnosis of uterine position by bimanual examination, the use of tenaculum forceps on the anterior lip of the cervix and sounding the uterus will decrease the possibility of uterine perforation. If it does occur then the patient must be referred to hospital. Most, if not all, perforations occur at time of insertion.

Removal

Removal during menstruation is preferable but if removal takes place at any other time in the cycle the patient should not have had intercourse for 72 hours. Mid-cycle removal should be avoided if possible.

Breaking the threads can be avoided by applying steady traction and removing the device slowly. If the device does not come out easily or the threads are not seen the patient should be referred to a doctor with suction apparatus and/or experience in removing lost IUCDs. Admission to hospital is sometimes necessary.

Pregnancy and the Intrauterine Device

If the patient is pregnant and the pregnancy is unwanted then the device can be removed as soon as termination of pregnancy can be arranged. It should be remembered that 5% of pregnancies with an intrauterine device in situ are ectopic.

If the patient wishes to proceed with the pregnancy, then the device can be removed gently by the doctor who should inform her that there is a 25% chance of spontaneous abortion. The doctor should also ask her to return promptly should bleeding, cramping or signs of infection be noted. If the patient wants to continue the pregnancy and does not want the IUCD removed, she should be warned of the following:

1. The risk of spontaneous abortion is increased two- to three-fold (over 'normal' pregnancy) with the device in utero (up to about 50%).
2. The likelihood that the pregnancy may be ectopic is increased (up to about 5%).
3. The risk of septic spontaneous abortion may be increased.
4. The risk of the onset of premature labour may be slightly increased.

POST-COITAL CONTRACEPTION

Two methods are used for patients who have had unprotected intercourse and hope to avoid the possibility of conception: the 'morning-after pill' and the insertion of a copper intrauterine device.

'Morning-after Pill'

To be effective the 'morning-after pill' must be commenced within 72 hours of unprotected intercourse. Two Eugynon 50 tablets (each containing 50 μg ethinyloestradiol and 500 μg norgestrel) are taken at once followed by a further two tablets 12 hours later.

The patient should be examined either just after her period or within four weeks from treatment at the latest. She should be told that, although the method is highly effective, it has been known to fail; if pregnancy occurs there is a risk of fetal damage so termination is advisable.

As with all oestrogen-containing birth control methods, the danger signals are:

Chest pain
Shortness of breath
Severe headache
Sudden blurring or loss of vision
Severe leg pains
Abdominal pain

Contraindications include:

1. Established pregnancy.
2. Tumours of breast or reproductive tract.
3. All the absolute contraindications to oral contraceptives already described (see p. 99).

Insertion of a Copper Intrauterine Device

This is the most effective method of post-coital contraception although it should not be considered for those patients who have been raped or who have had intercourse with multiple partners where the risk of venereal disease is high. The Copper 7 or Copper T are the devices of choice as they are the only ones whose post-coital efficacy had been demonstrated and they probably work by preventing implantation of the fertilized ovum. They have the additional advantage of providing the patient with a long-term method of birth control. The devices must be fitted within five days of unprotected intercourse.

Following the use of either post-coital method, a not uncommon complication is an ectopic pregnancy. The patient should be warned that should she experience constant, severe pain on either side of the abdomen she should seek medical advice immediately. Cramping pains are very common after insertion of an IUCD. The pain of ectopic pregnancy is much more constant and severe, and is unilateral.

OCCLUSIVE CAPS

Because of the recent adverse publicity given to oral contraceptives and possible unacceptable side-effects of intrauterine devices, the barrier methods have been given a new popularity. The success rate is closely related to the degree of motivation shown by the women concerned, but the danger is the relationship and the attitude of the expert who is teaching the method. Her views and manner can well influence the womens' decision and subsequently the effectiveness of the contraceptive concerned.

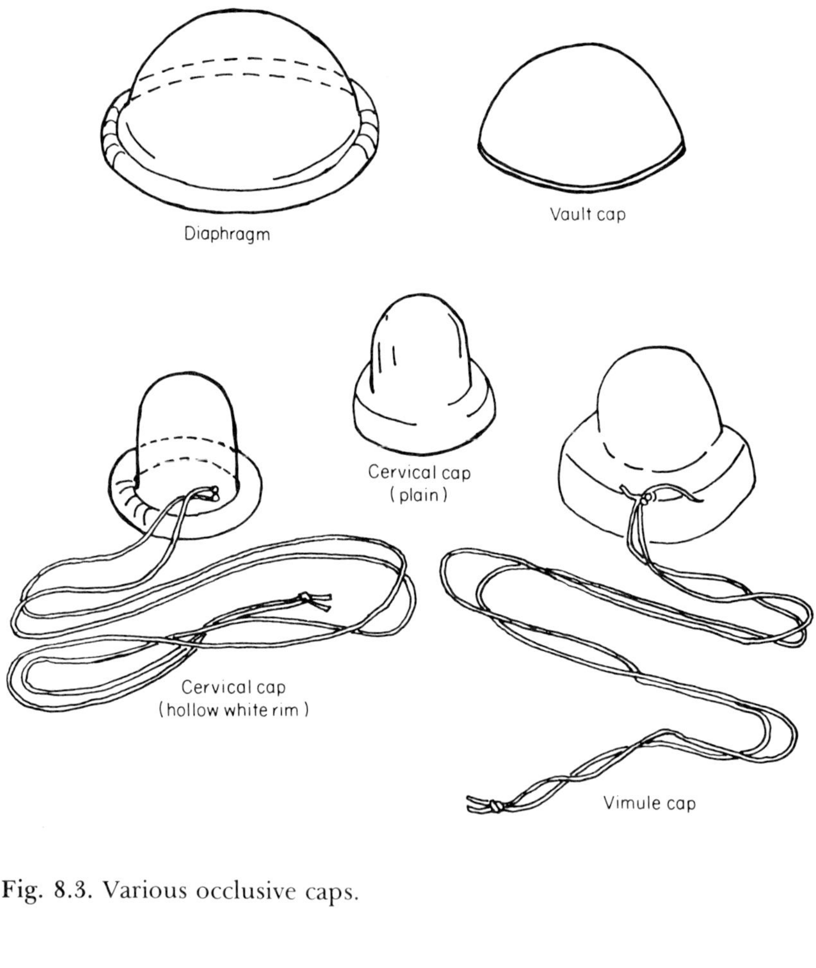

Fig. 8.3. Various occlusive caps.

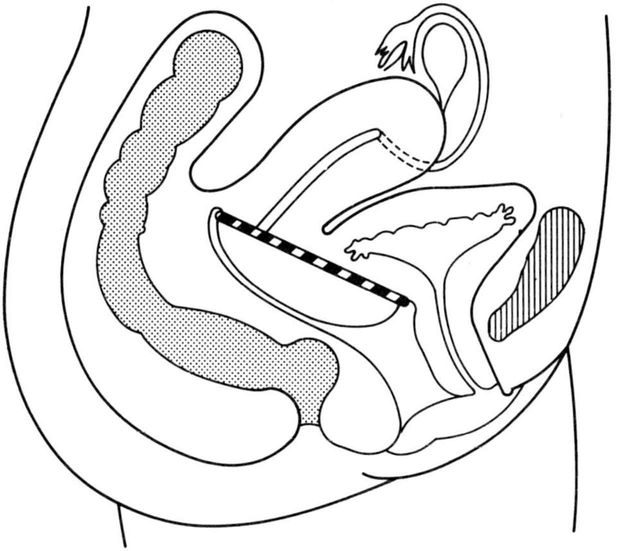

Fig. 8.4. Occlusive caps in position.

Types of Occlusive Cap

The diaphragm

The most popular and by far the most common form of occlusive cap is the diaphragm. It comes in a range of sizes ranging from 50 to 100 mm in external diameter. The most commonly used sizes are from 60 to 90 mm. The flat spring type is more rigid than the coil spring and is easier for most women to insert: the softness of the coil or watch spring type leads other women to prefer it.

The diaphragm fits across the vault of the vagina from the posterior fornix to the retropubic space, should completely cover the cervix and not be noticeable when in situ. The correctly sized and inserted cap will fit comfortably without distending the vaginal walls. The anterior rim should not descend below the symphysis pubis when the patient strains.

It can be used regardless of the condition or position of the cervix but a retroverted uterus makes it difficult to cover the cervix.

The criteria for using a diaphragm are that:

1. There is no major degree of uterine prolapse.
2. There is good muscle tone.
3. The perineum is not deficient.
4. The patient is able to feel her own cervix.
5. There is no shallow retropubic ledge or short anterior vaginal wall.

The cervical cap

A cervical cap is shaped like a rubber thimble. It is available in four sizes (22, 25, 28 and 31 mm). It closely covers the vaginal portion of the cervix and is suitable if the cervix is healthy, long, parallel sided (not conical), regular and easily accessible to the patient's finger. It should remain in place on straining and should not be easily dislodged by the fingers of the patient or instructing practitioner.

It should not be fitted when there is a chronic degree of cervicitis, when there is a large erosion or when the cervix points backward.

It is useful when the perineum is deficient or when muscle tone is poor.

The vault cap (Dumas)

This is a bowl-shaped cap made of plastic or rubber. It fits in the vaginal vault and when the centre of the cap is depressed by the user, clings to the walls of the vaginal vault by suction. There is no metal rim and the sizes available range from 1 to 5. It is specially useful when there is poor pelvic floor muscle tone, when there is a cystocele or rectocele with or without any degree of vault prolapse and when the cervix is small and flush with the vaginal vault.

It can only be used if the cervix is short enough to allow the rim to adhere evenly to the vault of the vagina. It needs careful fitting and instruction and cannot be used by the patient with short fingers whose cervix is not accessible or when the cervix points backwards.

The vimule cap

This is a combination of the cervical and vault caps. It is made in rubber or plastic and comes in three sizes: small, medium and large. It adheres by suction to the vaginal roof. It fits in exactly the same way as the vault cap, but is modified so that a longer cervix does not prevent suction and contact of its rim with the vault of the vagina. It is useful where there is poor muscle tone, making the diaphragm unsuitable.

The criteria for using the cervical and vimule caps are that the cervix is readily accessible to the patient, points forwards and is long, parallel sided and healthy.

A vault cap is used when the diaphragm or cervical cap is difficult to use, because the cervix is small and flush with the vaginal walls. In rare cases of rubber allergy, the patient has no other choice but to use a plastic vault or cervical cap.

Instructions for Use of Diaphragm

Two strips of spermicidal cream or jelly about 2.5 cm long should be applied to each side of the cap. The cap can be inserted at any convenient time before intercourse, but it is necessary to remember that if more than three hours elapse before intercourse, or a second intercourse takes place, more spermicide will be necessary. Using a spermicidal pessary may be more convenient than using an applicator of cream or trying to place cream in the vagina with the fingers.

The cap should not be removed for at least six hours after last intercourse. It may be left longer than six hours but not for more than 24 hours without being removed and washed.

It is necessary to check that the cap is correctly in place and that the cervix is covered by it.

After use, the cap should be washed in warm water. It should then be rinsed and dried thoroughly. The cap should not be boiled and disinfectants or petroleum jelly should not be used, as they will spoil the rubber. Defects can be detected by holding it up to the light and this should be a regular procedure. The cap should retain its circular shape. If it gets out of shape the rim is bent to restore the circle. It is important to remember to attend the clinic for checking of the cap size. If 3 kg (7 lb) weight is gained or lost, it should be refitted; it should also be refitted after childbirth, or after termination of pregnancy.

The cap given at first clinic visit is usually a practice cap. Most clinics will provide a practice cap initially but it should not be relied upon as a contraceptive. Insertion and removal of the cap should be practised as instructed and it should be left in overnight to make sure it is comfortable and stays in place. There is no cause for concern if a period starts with the cap in place: it should be removed when convenient. On returning to the clinic with the practice cap in place, size can be checked and any relevant questions can be dealt with.

Instructions for Use with Vault, Vimule and Cervical Caps

Approximately one teaspoonful of spermicical cream is inserted inside bowl of cap. The cap is inserted, making sure the cervix is covered. A pessary is inserted for each intercourse. The cap is left in place for at least six hours and at most 24 hours.

All instructions for care of diaphragm and future visits to clinic, apply also to vimule, cervical and vault cap users.

THE NATURAL METHODS OF BIRTH CONTROL

Safe Period or Rhythm Method

The safe period restricts intercourse to the period in the cycle when conception is least likely to occur. It is based on the premise that in each cycle the ovary expels only one ovum, which is available for fertilization for only 24 hours. Spermatozoa, once they have entered the uterus, can remain viable for approximately 48 hours (maximum 72 hours). Therefore, there is a period of three, possibly four, days when conception is theoretically possible. It is assumed that ovulation occurs on about Day 14 of the cycle, before the start of the next menstruation. Therefore, Days 12 to 16 (counting backwards from day of start of next period) are regarded as possible ovulatory days. So Days 17 and 18 are added to allow for previously deposited spermatazoa, and Day 11 (limited time of ovum survival) for extra safety.

To calculate the safe days, the patient needs to record her periods for at least six months so that she knows her longest and shortest cycle.

Using the calendar method

The shortest number of days between Day 1 of successive cycles is determined. Assuming this to be 25 then 18 is subtracted from 25

Date	Days since last period	Date	Days since last period
Jan. 10	29	June 23	30
Feb. 7	28	July 22	29
March 4	(25)	Aug. 21	30
March 30	26	Sept. 21	(31)
April 27	28	Oct. 20	29
May 24	27	Nov. 17	28

Fig. 8.5. Recording first day of the period to discover longest and shortest cycles before using the rhythm method.

giving 7. Then count seven days from Day 1 of the cycle. This indicates that Day 7 is the first unsafe day of the cycle. From the record the longest number of days between successive first days of the cycle is found. Assuming this to be 31, 10 is subtracted from 31 giving 21. Counting 21 days from Day 1 of the last period gives Day 21 as the last unsafe day. On Day 22 intercourse may be resumed.

Using the temperature (BBT) method

The temperature usually drops slightly at the time of ovulation followed immediately by a rise of about 0.3°C. When the patient's temperature has remained at the higher level for at least three days the ovum is beginning to disintegrate and fertilization is unlikely. Thus intercourse may be resumed.

This is obviously not a complete method and must be combined with another procedure for the pre-ovulatory part of the cycle.

The Mucothermic Method

This method relies on the patient's ability to recognize changes in the cervical mucus and to interpret her temperature chart correctly. The temperature is taken on waking, before undergoing any physical

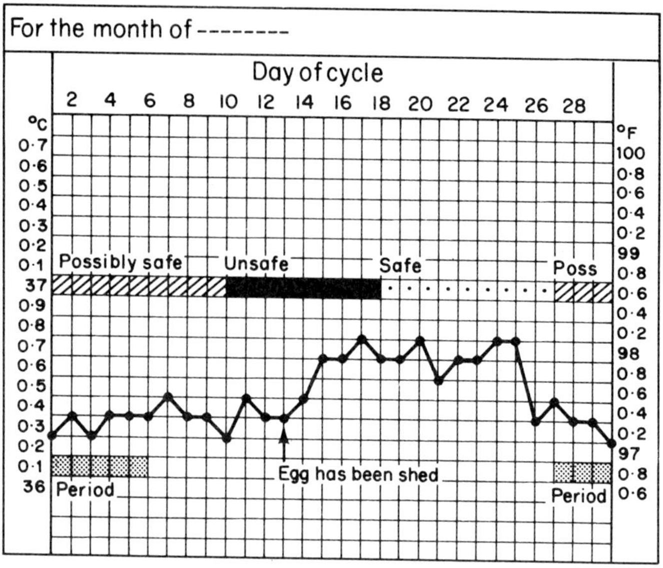

Fig. 8.6. A typical temperature chart showing the rise of temperature after ovulation.

activity, and the patient should have been at rest for an hour. No fluids may be taken nor may she smoke before taking her temperature. The thermometer must remain in the mouth underneath the tongue for three minutes. Oral temperature may not be sufficiently accurate and often the patient cannot interpret the slight changes in degree, so sometimes a rectal temperature is suggested. It is certainly more accurate, albeit distasteful to many women.

When ovulation has occurred the temperature rises by at least 0.3°C and stays elevated until the start of the next menstrual period.

Starting from Day 1 of the cycle, the mucus is thick, opaque and sticky. As ovulation approaches it becomes clear and slippery like egg white. After ovulation it again becomes thick, dry and crumbly.

In the early part of the cycle, intercourse is considered safe on dry days when there is no mucus. Intercourse must cease at the first sensation of wetness (approximately four days before ovulation). The patient resumes intercourse after she has recorded three consecutive daily temperatures at the higher level.

The Catholic Marriage Advisory Council claim the best result to be one pregnancy per 100 women years after studying 502 couples

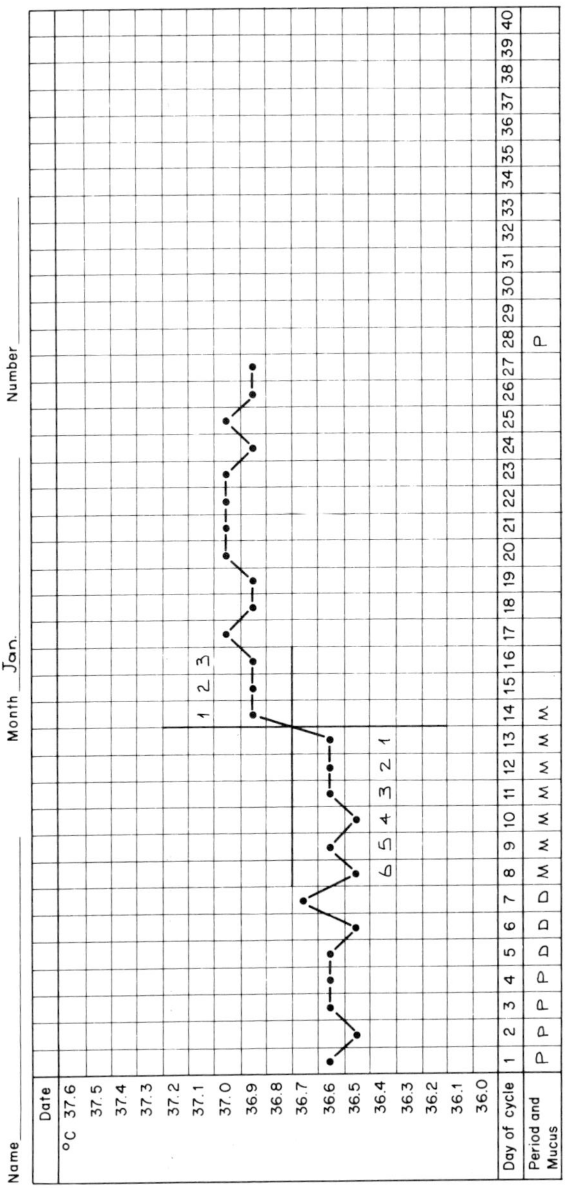

Fig. 8.7. A mucus chart.

through 8294 cycles over 2¼ years. The worst result was six pregnancies per 100 woman years. The main disadvantages are:

1. That intercourse is limited to virtually the second half of the cycle.

2. The temperature changes are slight and therefore easy to misinterpret and liable to be confused by intercurrent illness. It is a quite unsuitable method for women with cycles less than 20 days in length, varying by more than 10 days or irregular because of the menopause. It is quite useless during lactation and unreliable in the first three to four cycles after menstruation is re-established.

If any of the following conditions apply, it is best to avoid using the safe period (rhythm) or mucothermic methods:

1. When travelling abroad as the cycle may be affected by time change, change in climate or routine.
2. If ill or emotionally upset.
3. If dieting very strictly.
4. After discontinuing oral contraception when the cycle is liable to be irregular.

In spite of the disadvantages already discussed, an increasing number of women are requesting information on these methods and the nurse should be familiar with the advantages and disadvantages. The temperature charts and literature are available from:

Natural Family Planning Service
15 Lansdowne Road
London W11 3AJ
Tel. 01-727 0141

The effectiveness of the mucothermic method, safe period and rhythm method using either calendar or temperature charts, or a combination of all, is dependent upon the intelligence and motivation of the couple concerned.

CONDOMS

The condom (sheath or French letter) is still widely used in many areas: its use outstrips that of the oral contraceptive. Condoms are easily obtainable, need no doctor's prescription and are inexpensive. They completely envelop the penis and are usually made of rubber. The thinner types supplied in most clinics are intended to be used once only and then disposed of. Both are of two types: plain and teat-ended. The teat is a small receptacle for the ejaculate.

There is always the chance that the condom may not be put on soon enough, that the penis may become limp before removal or that it may break or burst. To lessen these risks a chemical spermicide may be inserted into the vagina before coitus.

The failure rate is approximately the same as that reported for the use of the cap: 5 failures per 100 woman years but it can rise to as high as 10 to 20 per 100 woman years. The use of the condom is not associated with any risk of mortality.

Allergies to rubber are extremely rare, but there *is* a sheath made specially for people with such an allergy. The condom reduces the risk of the transmission of venereal disease, although it does not eliminate the possibility altogether.

Bold advertising in Sweden is responsible for the comic and colourful appearance of some sheaths. It has increased the sale of condoms, while helping to combat venereal disease.

CHEMICAL SPERMICIDES

Spermicides used alone can offer only a small measure of protection and the method is never advised in Family Planning Clinics. They have the virtue of simplicity and do not require supervision. Some chemical spermicides may cause local irritation to either partner. If this occurs a different product is recommended.

Types of Spermicide

Creams, jellies and pastes are contained in soft metal tubes like toothpaste. Applicators are available for depositing a suitable amount into the vagina.

Spermicidal creams are available in *aerosol* form and the foam is released into an applicator from which it is injected into the vagina.

Pessaries are made with a base of glycerine, gelatine or waxy material with a body-heat melting point. The active spermicide is contained in the base. They are placed in the vagina two or three minutes before intercourse.

A spermicide may be impregnated into a water soluble *plastic film*. The woman can insert the film vaginally before coitus, or the man can apply it to the glans immediately before insertion of the penis into the vagina.

Foaming tablets are available in the form of hard, white discs which dissolve in the presence of moisture with the formation of carbon dioxide foam, and release the active spermicide into the vagina.

Efficiency of Spermicides

Among the various forms of spermicides, the foams seem to be the most effective followed by jellies and creams. Foaming tablets and pessaries are less effective. The failure rate of the film is not yet known.

9. Sterilization

P.J.D. Milton

In Great Britain sterilization has greatly increased in popularity over the last 10 years. Younger couples with smaller families are now seeking some means of permanent contraception. There are many reasons for this trend, including adverse reports of the side effects of the contraceptive pill, public awareness of the improvements in sterilization operations, lack of faith in and aesthetic objections to barrier methods of contraception and the need for a method which is safe and reliable in a society where there is an increasing tendency for the wife to return to work when her children have reached school age.

Not only is this trend seen in Great Britain; in America sterilization is now more popular than the contraceptive pill amongst married couples; 9.5 million couples have opted for this method of contraception, approximately 50% by means of vasectomy. In the UK there is some regional variation; it was, for instance, shown in the Oxford University study that it was the husband who had the operation in two-thirds of cases in that region (Vessey et al. 1976).

Not only does the reliability of sterilization have to be considered; in a society with a marital breakdown rate of approximately one in three, the necessity for reversibility has to be considered also.

COUNSELLING

Decisions about sterilization should not be made lightly and most couples will initially consult their general practitioners or family planning clinics for advice. The doctor's intention will basically be to find out what the couple really want, having ascertained that they understand what sterilization actually means; it is, for instance, not uncommon even in this day and age for female sterilization to be equated with hysterectomy and for male sterilization to be equated with castration. The age of each partner is ascertained as it has been shown that reversal requests come predominantly from women under the age of 27 (Winston 1977). It is futile to restrict sterilization to married couples or indeed to couples who have borne children; there will be many couples living in a stable relationship outside marriage for whom sterilization may be considered appropriate and it is also illogical to deprive a man or woman of sterilization merely because they have never had children. The number and ages of the children of the union are nevertheless taken into consideration when making a decision; it may, for instance, be particularly appropriate for a childless couple to discuss alternative reversible methods with the counsellor before making a final choice.

Psychological Suitability

This is difficult to determine and is probably better assessed by the patient's general practitioner than by the hospital specialist. Although psychological sequelae of sterilization are very rare, occasionally women may react badly to an absolute loss of fertility. Very occasionally a man may lose interest in sex following vasectomy, but again it must be stressed that this is exceedingly rare. In a study of 1000 couples by the Simon Population Trust in December 1969 (Table 9.1) a minute fraction of husbands and wives reported deterioration in their sex lives following vasectomy.

Ideally both partners should be present at the time of counselling

Table 9.1. Results (%) of the Simon Population Trust Survey on Sexual Attitudes after Vasectomy

Result	*Husband*	*Wife*
No change	88.4	68.8
Improved	11.4	31.0
Deteriorated	0.2	0.2

and the nature of whichever procedure is to be undertaken should be explained to them both, preferably with the aid of diagrams. Neither vasectomy nor female sterilization affects hormone production and this must be emphasized. The couple should be told of the finality of sterilization; although operations exist to restore fallopian tube or vas deferens patency, the success rates are at present probably less than 50% even in the best hands and may be very much less after some methods of sterilization, for instance tubal diathermy.

Regardless of which partner is to be sterilized it is important to consider intercurrent gynaecological problems. If a woman, for instance, has heavy menstrual periods and uterine fibroids it would be illogical for her husband to have a vasectomy, bearing in mind that she herself may need hysterectomy in the not too distant future. One of the most common groups of women presenting for sterilization nowadays is those over 35 who have been advised to stop the contraceptive pill. The decision to take a patient off the pill at 35 is a valid one and sterilization is probably the better alternative. The contraceptive pill, in addition to controlling fertility, usually has a beneficial effect in that the withdrawal bleeding experienced during medication is usually lighter and less painful than spontaneous menstrual periods. When a patient comes off the pill her periods may well revert to being heavy and painful and she should be warned of this possibility.

Which Partner Should be Sterilized?

That is, of course, a decision for the couple to make personally. Advice may well be sought and should be freely given. Vasectomy causes less disruption to family life as it is more commonly performed on an out-patient basis than is female sterilization. A woman will often opt to be sterilized rather than her husband as she feels that he has a potentially longer fertile life and should preserve his fertility in case he should marry again. There is an increasing acceptance by men of vasectomy: this is creditable bearing in mind that women suffer the pain and risks of childbirth as well as the discomforts and indignities of almost every other form of contraception; it is, fortunately, becoming more acceptable nowadays for men to feel it is their turn to have 'something done'. Nevertheless there will still be some men, and indeed women, who feel that a man needs to preserve his fertility to remain a 'whole man'. If either partner is of this belief there is no point in trying to dissuade him or her and, indeed, to perform a vasectomy under such circumstances could have dire results in terms of possible psychosexual problems affecting either partner.

FEMALE STERILIZATION TECHNIQUES

All female sterilization procedures include opening the peritoneal cavity by means of laparoscopy or laparotomy. The fallopian tubes are identified and occluded by means of silastic rings or metal clips. The tubes may also be blocked by means of diathermy, but this technique is being rapidly superseded by the safer clip and ring methods.

Although tubal interruption is the most commonly carried out method of female sterilization, there is a place for hysterectomy in a patient who suffers coincidentally from severe menstrual problems. There is no place for carrying out a prophylactic hysterectomy as a means of sterilization. No method of female sterilization can be considered infallible; the failure rate for all the methods mentioned is about two per thousand. Ectopic pregnancies are more likely after tubal diathermy and, as this method also incurs the risk of intra-peritoneal diathermy with possible bowel damage, it is slowly being superseded by the use of occlusive devices such as rings and clips.

Rings and clips also have a positive advantage in that they allow greater chance of reversibility. The occluded portion of each tube can be surgically removed and re-anastomosis carried out with a success

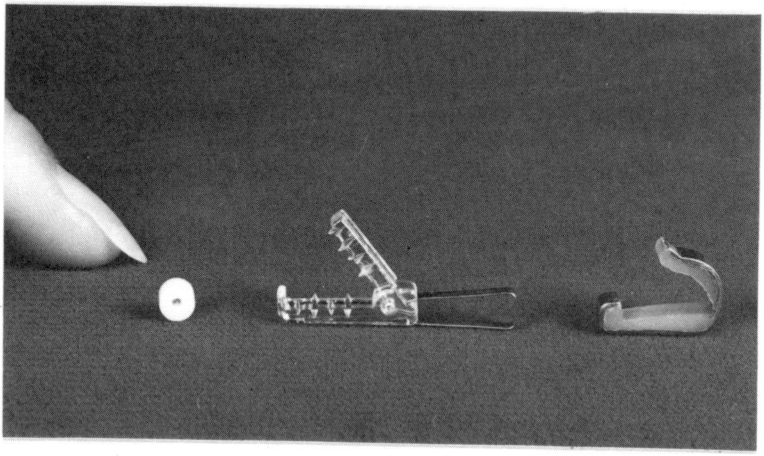

Fig. 9.1. Devices for tubal occlusion. *Left to right*, Falope (Yoon) silastic ring; Hulka (Samaritan) clip; Filshie clip.

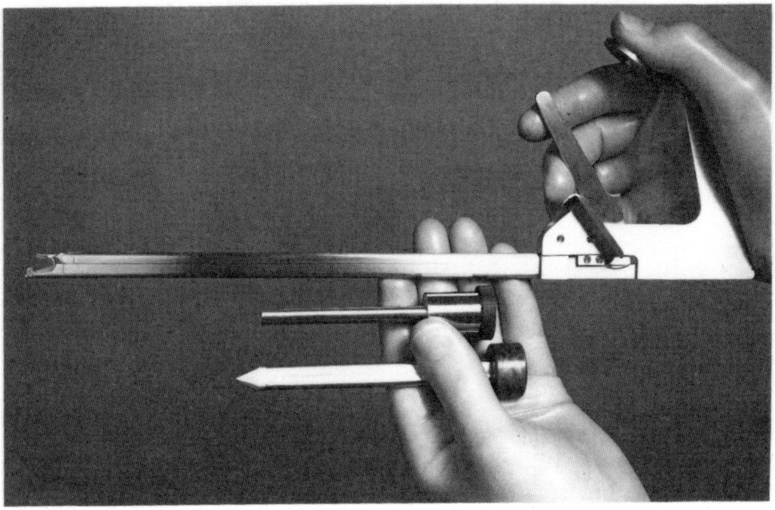

Fig. 9.2. The applicator used for tubal occlusion with the Filshie clip.

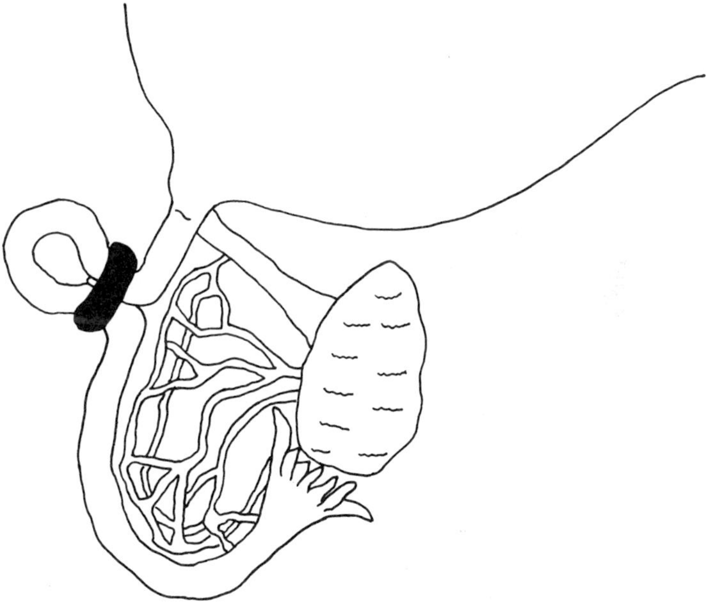

Fig. 9.3. The Falope (Yoon) ring occluding a loop of the fallopian tube.

rate of approximately 50%. There appears to be no difference between rings and clips in terms of potential for reversal. However, no method should be advised as being potentially reversible as reversal operations require a full laparotomy and apart from not being of guaranteed effectiveness also incur the risk of ectopic pregnancy at the site of anastomosis.

The Timing of Female Sterilization

Patients presenting for sterilization while taking the contraceptive pill do not need to cease medication. For patients requesting sterilization in the puerperium an elective laparoscopic operation after six weeks is preferable to sterilization in the first few days of the puerperium to allow for the possibility of unexpected neonatal death. Sterilization six weeks post-partum is safer from the point of view of avoiding thromboembolic phenomena and minimizing the risk of recanalization. It is also less likely to be regretted by the couple; the immediate puerperium is not an ideal time to make such a final decision.

Out-patient Techniques

Laparoscopic female sterilization is most commonly carried out under general anaesthesia with the patient remaining in hospital for approximately 24 hours. There is an increasing tendency for such operations to be performed on a day-case or out-patient basis and this would seem to be a very sensible trend, bearing in mind the pressure on in-patient gynaecological beds.

Postoperative Sequelae

Laparoscopy involves the induction of a pneumoperitoneum with carbon dioxide and some patients may suffer from shoulder tip pain for the first 24 hours or so postoperatively owing to tracking of blood to the diaphragm. There may also be some pain at the site of trochar insertion, usually immediately below the umbilicus.

Whether a one-puncture or two-puncture technique is used the incisions will usually be closed by Michel clips which can be removed 24 hours postoperatively. The operation is immediately effective but most patients will not wish to resume intercourse for a week or so owing to abdominal discomfort. If a woman has been taking the pill postoperatively she will stop it usually at the end of her tablet cycle; she must be warned that normal menstruation may not return for six weeks or more.

Very rarely a patient may be pregnant at the time of sterilization. This can be minimized by operating in the immediate post-menstrual phase of the cycle but it is difficult to implement such a scheme, especially as sterilizations are usually planned to fit in with family commitments. As an alternative some gynaecologists carry out a routine curettage at the time of sterilization. Whilst this may be effective in some cases it is only too easy to miss a recently implanted ovum with the curette; indeed it is technically possible that the fertilized ovum could still be in the fallopian tube.

Long-term Sequelae

Long-term psychological sequelae are very uncommon but there will be a minority of patients who will regret the operation and present either for reversal or with other gynaecological symptoms such as pain, dyspareunia or irregular vaginal bleeding. They must be investigated as appropriate to their symptoms and they can be an extremely difficult group to manage; obviously no firm guidelines can be given.

Psychosexual difficulties are uncommon unless there is a pre-existing problem. Although it is difficult to be exhaustive in counselling it is customary to enquire about a couple's sex life before embarking upon sterilization. If it was satisfactory before it will usually be the same or, possibly, improved postoperatively. There may be a small minority of patients who seek sterilization as a cure for a psychosexual difficulty; they will obviously be disappointed.

Menstrual disorders following sterilization are uncommon but must not be excluded from consideration. When sterilizations were performed by radical procedures such as bilateral salpingectomy or extensive tubal diathermy it was thought that menstrual problems resulted. The mechanism postulated was interruption of utero-ovarian vascular anastamoses and subsequent possible interference with hormonal pathways between the uterus and ovaries involving prostaglandins. The incidence of such disorders will also be related to the previously used method of contraception, e.g. it is not uncommon for women to have heavier and slightly more erratic periods when they stop taking the pill than before they went on it simply because they are older and having more frequent anovulatory cycles. When the effects of previous contraception are excluded it is found that menstrual disorders following sterilization occur no more commonly than they do in a comparably controlled population, especially if operations involving minimal interference with the mesosalpinx, such as the application of rings or clips, are used.

MALE STERILIZATION TECHNIQUES

Vasectomy can be carried out under local anaesthesia and is an increasingly common method of contraception. In assessing a man's suitability for vasectomy the same sort of counselling must be carried out as before female sterilization. The couple should be seen together and the permanent nature of the procedure should be stressed. Unlike female sterilization, vasectomy is not immediately effective and will not be so until the collecting systems have been totally cleared of spermatozoa; this may take three or four months depending on how frequently ejaculation takes place.

Vasectomy is usually carried out by a urologist, general surgeon or FPA doctor. Whoever performs the operation should obviously be adequately trained, preferably by a urologist, and the operation must be carried out with full aseptic precautions.

It must be stressed to the couple prior to operation that the man will not be sterile until negative sperm counts have been obtained; these are normally done one month and two months postoperatively. There is wide variation in the number of ejaculations needed to clear the system of sperm; some men will become aspermic after as few as six ejaculations whereas others need up to 32. An average would probably be 10-12 ejaculations. If sperm are still present after six months re-exploration will probably be advised to check for re-canalization or a possible double vas.

Reversal of Vasectomy

In this age of marital instability requests for reversal will inevitably occur. There is about a 50% chance of successful re-anastomosis but the pregnancy rate tends to be lower, possibly owing to the effects of sperm antibody production on spermatogenesis. It has been found by some research workers that the sperm antibody production increases following vasectomy. The sperm count may remain depressed even after restoration of anatomical continuity; although up to 80% success rates as judged by restoration of the flow of sperm have been described, even with this high figure only a 30% pregnancy rate was seen (Schmidt 1975). It is thus obvious that one must advise couples that rejoining the vas does not guarantee restoration of fertility.

LEGAL ASPECTS OF FEMALE STERILIZATION AND VASECTOMY

Sterilization of a married woman by a doctor could be construed in law as a deliberate interference with the legal right of a man to have children by his wife. The converse could apply to vasectomy. It is possible, therefore, that a husband or wife, on finding that without his or her knowledge or consent he or she has been deprived of the opportunity of parenthood, might claim legal damages against the doctor. For this reason informed consent is obtained from both partners before the sterilization of either. In the few cases where either husband or wife refuses to give consent, or should the husband or wife refuse to seek consent, the operation may still be carried out if the doctor deems the request to be valid although under such circumstances he may feel it advisable to consult his medical defence society.

Bibliography

Schmidt, S.S. (1975) Vas anastomosis: a return to simplicity. *Br. J. Urol., 47,* 309.

Vessey, M., Doll, R. & Peto, R. (1976) A long-term follow-up study of women under different methods of contraception: an interim report. *J. biosoc. Sci., 8*, 373.

Winston, R.M.L. (1977) Why 103 women asked for reversal of sterilization. *Br. med. J., 2*, 305.

10. Gynaecological Cancer

P.J.D. Milton

Cancer—the word has a hard ring to it and an emotive impact on everyone; it is the most feared of all diseases although not necessarily the most incurable. The fundamental cause of 'cancer' is unknown but certain aetiological factors are now well recognized, including the relationship between smoking and bronchial carcinoma and that between early age at first sexual intercourse and cervical cancer.

The treatment of most cancers is still unsatisfactory and the overall incidence is rising, partly due to an increased life span and partly due to an increased prevalence of predisposing factors. Cancer affecting the female breasts and genital tract poses particular practical and psychological problems. Embarrassment about gynaecological symptoms can lead to late presentation and there will often be interference with reproductive and sexual function, making these cancers particularly difficult to deal with from both medical and nursing standpoints.

THE COMMON CANCERS IN WOMEN

Cancer of the breast is now the commonest cause of death in women. There is a rising incidence in the other cancers, in particular carcinoma of the bronchus, but the rise is slower for the gynaecological cancers (Table 10.1).

The three major sites for carcinoma in the female genital tract are cervix, endometrium and ovary, accounting for over 90% of all female

Table 10.1. Cancer Statistics from the East Anglian Region Cancer Registration Bureau

Site	*Year*	*No.*	*Rate/100 000*
Breast	1960	554	69.50
	1965	581	71.04
	1970	688	77.48
	1975	801	84.34
	1978	955	103.24
Endometrium	1960	126	15.81
	1965	137	16.75
	1970	124	13.96
	1975	162	17.16
	1978	179	19.35
Bronchus	1960	86	10.79
	1965	103	12.59
	1970	191	21.51
	1975	212	22.46
	1978	282	30.49

Table 10.2. Gynaecological Cancer Statistics from the East Anglian Cancer Registration Bureau, 1978

Type	*No.*	*Incidence/100 000 population*
Cervix		
Carcinoma in situ	190	20.54
Invasive carcinoma	146	15.78
Endometrium	179	19.35
Ovary	206	22.27
Other genital tract including vulva	49	5.30

gynaecological cancers; the remainder are vulval, vaginal and the extremely rare fallopian tube cancers. The cervix is the most commonly affected organ if carcinoma in situ is included. Table 10.2 gives some representative figures from the East Anglian region.

CERVICAL CANCER

Aetiology

The aetiology of cervical cancer has been studied extensively since it was realized that virgin women do not acquire the disease. 'Of all coital factors it would seem that the age at first coitus is the most significant and that sexual intercourse during adolescence predisposes women to the disease.' This predisposition may be because the cervical epithelium at the squamocolumnar junction is particularly vulnerable at this time of life. Promiscuity has been linked to the risk of developing carcinoma of the cervix as it is more common in prostitutes, but there is no proved link between incidence and coital frequency within marriage. Cervical cancer is commoner in women of low socio-economic status throughout the world, possibly because in such women there tends to be a pattern of early age at first coitus.

Early Detection

Screening for pre-invasive states, in particular cervical intraepithelial neoplasia (CIN) by means of exfoliative cytology, is widely used and discussed elsewhere (Chapter 13). Unfortunately the importance of screening young women (under 35) was appreciated only recently. As is often the case in preventive medicine it is difficult to reach the person most at risk as the social class IV and V woman who is much more likely to get cervical cancer is an unwilling clinic attender. The class III group occupies an intermediate position. In contrast the social class I and II woman who cares for her health readily accepts that screening is important.

Education on the potential risks of early first coitus and promiscuity could reduce the incidence of cervical cancer; an increased use of barrier methods of contraception might be helpful but the greater risk of unwanted pregnancy would have to be considered. Circumcision is no longer thought to be protective: carcinoma of the cervix occurs equally frequently in partners of circumcised and uncircumcised men. The detection rate for invasive disease is better than it was 10 years ago because women are now more likely to seek advice about gynaecological symptoms. The main symptoms of cervical cancer are intermenstrual, post-coital and post-menopausal bleeding and it is obviously important that women are regularly reminded of them and asked about them when they attend for contraceptive advice or routine cytology; the questions need not mention the word 'cancer', which should be avoided to prevent the risks of cancer phobia.

Management

The management of *carcinoma in situ*, now more accurately called 'cervical intraepithelial neoplasia' (CIN) is totally different from that of invasive carcinoma as CIN is a localized intraepithelial condition and conservative management is possible. This may be by excision using cone biopsy of the cervix to remove the squamocolumnar junction (Fig. 10.1), that being the region from which the abnormality

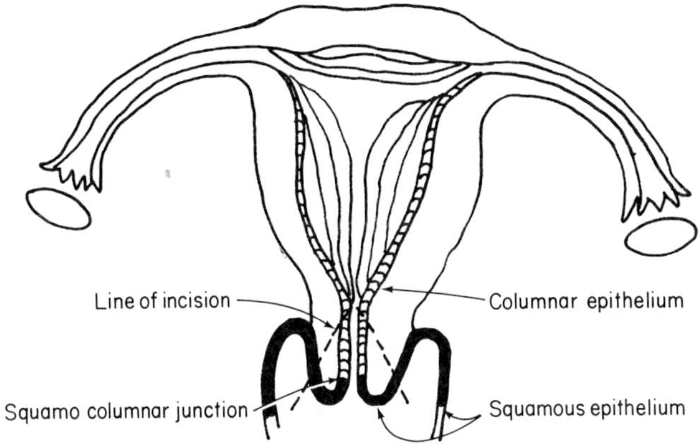

Fig. 10.1. The uterus and associated organs showing the site of a cone biopsy.

is thought most commonly to develop; or alternatively hysterectomy may be used if there is a coexisting menstrual problem. A more logical and safer approach is to use colposcopy to visualize the cervix, biopsy for abnormal areas and then treatment by excision, cryotherapy or localized destruction using the carbon dioxide laser. This last technique provides the most effective means of accurately localized treatment as the depth of epithelial tissue destruction can be accurately determined.

Follow-up is normally by means of cervical smears at regular intervals (see Chapter 13).

Invasive cervical cancer is divided into four stages using an internationally recognized classification (Table 10.3) to enable comparisons between different Centres to be made with regard to incidence, methods of treatment and results.

Table 10.3. Staging of Invasive Cervical Cancer

Stage I	Carcinoma confined to the cervix
Stage II	Carcinoma extending beyond the cervix, but not onto the pelvic side wall. The carcinoma involves the vagina but not its lower third
Stage IIa	Carcinoma involves the parametrium
Stage IIb	Carcinoma involves the vagina but not its lower third
Stage III	Carcinoma has extended onto the pelvic side wall. On rectal examination there is no cancer-free space between the tumour and the pelvic wall. The carcinoma involves the lower third of the vagina
Stage IV	Carcinoma has extended beyond the true pelvis or has involved the mucosa of the bladder or the rectum

The most widely used treatment for Stages II to IV is radiotherapy (see Chapter 11). For early Stage I growths, especially in young women, a radical hysterectomy (Wertheim operation) gives equally good results in *expert hands*. It has the advantage of allowing ovarian conservation and avoidance of radiation-induced vaginal stenosis and shortening. Other possible indications for radical surgery include adenocarcinomata, which are less radiosensitive than squamous growths, distortion of the uterine cavity (e.g. by fibroids) or stenosis of the vaginal vault (e.g. by atrophic change) as these conditions could preclude effective caesium insertion. The one definite indication is a poor response to radiotherapy.

Some surgeons prefer to combine radiotherapy and surgery, but surgery is more difficult after radiotherapy and there is no conclusive evidence that such a combined approach improves results.

The controversy regarding the use of radiotherapy or surgery has smouldered for many years and is not really likely to be resolved; a Wertheim's hysterectomy does, however, carry a considerable morbidity especially with regard to ureteric damage, and whilst it certainly has a place, it is probably sensible for the procedure to be used only in certain centres, perhaps two or three in each health region, in order that two or three surgeons in each region could each be supplied with enough cases to maintain their expertise.

The five-year survival rate for all growths (excluding CIN) is around 50%. The rate will depend on the stage of the disease at the time of treatment as well as other factors such as age. For Stage I growths (45% of the total) the five-year survival rate is usually around 75%, whereas for Stage III and IV growths (26% of the total) it is only about 5% (East Anglian Cancer Registration Bureau figures).

The site of recurrence is almost always pelvic and the mode of death may be most unpleasant requiring the very best in nursing care. Often in terminal disease there will be a chronic bleeding ulcer at the vaginal vault, producing a foul discharge which is a source of great distress to the patient; it can sometimes be stopped temporarily by cryotherapy or cautery to the cervix, but always recurs. In fortunate patients there is ureteric obstruction and a relatively quick uraemic decline. For all terminal cases there is a necessity for tender, loving care in abundance, especially if the growth has invaded the bladder or bowel and faecal or urinary incontinence are added to the patient's other miseries.

ENDOMETRIAL CANCER

Endometrial cancer is now more common than *invasive* cervical cancer in the UK. There has been no basic change in the cure rate in the past two decades: overall five-year survival and 'recurrence-free' rates of around 60% are commonly quoted and the corresponding 10-year rates are little different. The tumour tends to affect older women (67% over 60) than does cancer of the cervix (47% over 60) or ovary (63% over 60).

Aetiology

Apart from a possible link with unopposed oestrogen therapy (see Chapter 6) little is known about the aetiology. Endometrial cancer occurs more commonly in the obese, the hypertensive and the diabetic but most deaths are in fact from the cancer rather than other disease (Milton & Brush 1975). It also, like the aforementioned diseases, affects women from a higher socio-economic stratum than those afflicted by cervical cancer. Some endometrial growths are hormone-dependent, but the incidence of endometrial cancer has risen not only in countries where hormone replacement therapy is commonly used but also elsewhere.

Prevention and Early Detection

There is no acceptable screening method for endometrial cancer at present. Endometrial washings and out-patient curettage have both been tried but their place in overall clinical practice has yet to be decided; to screen all women over 45 by out-patient suction curettage would be a tremendously time-consuming and expensive exercise for possibly little reward. Endometrial wash techniques are not yet sufficiently accepted to give them a place in mass screening schemes. Cervical cytology is *not* of value, as up to 80% of endometrial growths will be missed if it is relied upon, even if a posterior fornix aspiration smear is made in addition to a cervical scrape preparation. The only current hope seems to lie in making women aware of the importance of reporting post-menopausal bleeding to their doctors and of seeking advice should they suffer perimenopausal irregularity: in one survey 23.8% of the patients were premenopausal at the time of diagnosis (Milton & Metters 1973). It is also possible that increased awareness of general health matters, such as the avoidance of obesity, will prove to be of value in reducing the incidence of endometrial cancer.

Hormones and Endometrial Cancer

The hormonal status of the post-menopausal woman is different from the premenopausal because the adrenal cortex rather than the ovaries is the main source of oestrogens. In the post-menopausal woman oestrone is the predominant oestrogen and this hormone is produced episodically by peripheral conversion of adrenal androgen (androstenedione) (Hutton et al. 1978). Obese women convert more androstenedione to oestrone and possibly this is related to their increased risk of endometrial cancer. The use of oestrogens as therapy for post-menopausal symptoms has also been suggested as an aetiological factor; unopposed oestrogen therapy (no progestagen in the second half of the tablet 'cycle') *may* place a patient at risk for endometrial hyperplasia which in turn *may* be a cancer precursor. There is thus now widespread acceptance of the belief that oestrogens should not be used 'unopposed'.

Symptoms

The main symptom of endometrial carcinoma is post-menopausal bleeding (PMB), usually defined as any bleeding from the vagina six months or more after the menopause. About 15% of patients will present with irregular 'perimenopausal' bleeding, i.e. irregular periods or intermenstrual bleeding from the age of 40 onwards, and such patients should be investigated by diagnostic curettage in the same way as patients presenting with post-menopausal bleeding. It is very rare for there to be any other presentation; a few cases may present as a persistent vaginal discharge but this will usually be blood-stained and hence should really be classified as post-menopausal bleeding.

Routine curettage prior to the use of hormone replacement therapy (HRT) or during such therapy will rarely demonstrate malignancy; it will, however, detect cases of hyperplasia, viewed by many as a cancer precursor, albeit a reversible one, and hence such curettage is being increasingly carried out (Whitehead & Campbell 1978).

Management

The treatment of patients with endometrial cancer is basically surgical, usually by means of total abdominal hysterectomy and bilateral salpingo-oophorectomy.

Like other cancers the stage of the growth (Table 10.4) and the

Table 10.4. Staging of Endometrial Cancer

Stage I	Carcinoma confined to the corpus uteri
Ia	Cavity length 8 cm or less
Ib	Cavity length more than 8 cm
Stage II	Carcinoma involving the corpus and the cervix
Stage III	Carcinoma extending outside the uterus but not outside the true pelvis
Stage IV	Carcinoma extending outside the true pelvis or obviously involving the mucosa of the bladder or rectum

histology will affect the decisions regarding treatment. Fortunately, 80% of endometrial growths are Stage I and for patients who are so affected total abdominal hysterectomy and bilateral salpingo-oophorectomy gives as good a result and prognosis as does more radical treatment (Milton & Metters 1973; Lees & Bar-am 1978). The histology and the depth of myometrial invasion are important: if the histology at initial curettage is of an undifferentiated growth with the potential for more aggressive behaviour, preoperative radiotherapy is considered by some surgeons to be preferable to surgery alone. If the growth is invading more than half way through the myometrium, postoperative radiotherapy may be beneficial in preventing recurrence. The present tendency is for less preoperative radiotherapy and more chemotherapy with progestagens, with the possible addition of postoperative radiotherapy for deeply invasive growths.

Hormonal therapy

As with radiotherapy, there is no agreement as to precisely how and when progestagen hormonal therapy should be used in endometrial cancer. Unlike radiotherapy there appear to be no drawbacks (except expense and, with intramuscular preparations, discomfort). Endometrial cancer will respond to high doses of progestogens in one-third of cases but *most* of the responsive cases have well differentiated growths. The drugs most commonly used are oral medroxyprogesterone acetate and intramuscular gestronol (Depostat). Treatment is now commonly commenced at the time of initial curettage if clinically malignant curettings are obtained and continued for a variable length of time postoperatively; some authors advocate indefinitely, some for a limited time such as six months.

There appears to be no advantage in using intramuscular rather than oral routes. Whilst a favourable response has been found in 30–50% of patients with *recurrent* disease (Kohorn 1978; Tobias 1978), the place of progestagens as *prophylaxis* is not agreed. It may well be that in future more precise guidelines will be used; for instance carrying out progesterone- and oestogen-binding studies on the cancer in question would be helpful to see whether there is a true affinity for hormones in the tumour being treated.

Other forms of drug therapy

Antimetabolites and alkylating cytotoxic agents have been tried in metastatic disease. Doxorubicin appears to be the most promising of these drugs and they may have a place in the treatment of tumours showing a lack of response to progestagen therapy.

CARCINOMA OF THE OVARY

Ovarian cancer is now more common than invasive cervical cancer or endometrial cancer (see Table 10.2). It is also the most common fatal gynaecological malignancy, with a five-year survival rate in treated cases of only about 5–10%, depending on the stage and histology of the tumour. The number of deaths attributed to cancer of the ovary exceeds the combined mortality per annum from cervical and endometrial growths (Harcus & McCrae 1975). The main reason for this bleak situation is the advanced stage of many growths at the time of presentation for at least 50% of patients have such advanced growths that complete removal is impossible.

Aetiology

Little is known about causative factors but from various epidemiological studies it can be shown that ovarian cancer is most common in women in the fifth and sixth decades of life, it is more common in single than married women and possibly amongst professional classes rather than lower socio-economic groups.

Symptoms and Signs

Benign ovarian tumours are rarely painful unless complications such as torsion or haemorrhage have occurred. Malignant growths may be detected if the patient presents with pain, abdominal distension due to ascites, weight loss or general cachexia. Vaginal bleeding is rare except in the very uncommon hormonally active tumours which produce a proliferation of the endometrium.

Clinical signs of malignancy in an ovarian tumour are fixity, bilaterality, the presence of ascites and evidence of bowel involvement.

Prevention and Early Detection

With a late-presenting growth of variable behaviour it is impossible to achieve much in the way of prevention or early detection. Screening methods such as routine pelvic examinations at six-month intervals might be partially successful, although the more aggressive growths could still be missed. The practice of carrying out routine bilateral oophorectomy at the time of abdominal hysterectomy in post-menopausal women seems logical as the ovaries rapidly cease to have a role in oestrogen production after the menopause.

Treatment

It is generally agreed that treatment should primarily be surgical, the operation chosen being either total abdominal hysterectomy and bilateral salpingo-oophorectomy or bilateral salpingo-oophorectomy alone depending on the surgeon's preference and the degree of uterine involvement, if any. Ovarian cancer is staged like other cancers (Table 10.5) and more advanced growths are unfortunately the most common.

Table 10.5. Staging of Ovarian Carcinoma

Stage Ia	Growth limited to one ovary (21%)
Stage Ib	Bilateral growths or invasion of tubes and uterus (13%)
Stage IIa, Stage IIb	Other pelvic extension (19%)
Stage III	Intraperitoneal metastases (35%)
Stage IV	Distant metastases (12%)

There is some advantage in leaving the uterus in situ if it is not involved; there is a lesser chance of vaginal vault recurrence and the uterus could be used as a caesium container, should subsequent radiotherapy be decided upon. If, as is usually the case, the growth cannot be removed completely, as much as possible is done without running undue risk of bowel or bladder damage: the omentum, for instance, is often involved and can be removed. The extent of the residual disease, if any, is carefully ascertained and documented, to assist in planning adjunctive therapy.

It must be stressed again that to maximize the effect of whatever adjunctive therapy is used, the maximum amount of tumour must be removed at the initial surgical procedure.

Postoperative chemotherapy

Many different agents have been used, the most common being chlorambucil and the most effective to date being cisplatin (Neoplatin). At present chemotherapy is regarded as palliative rather than curative but if progress is to be made it will be with chemotherapy rather than radiotherapy as ovarian carcinomata are usually relatively radio-resistant. Cisplatin has been shown to increase the survival rate in cases of advanced disease by up to 28 months.

All chemotherapy carries the risk of adverse reactions including nephrotoxicity, marrow suppression, nausea and vomiting and hair loss.

Radiotherapy

In managing patients with residual pelvic disease postoperative radiotherapy has been used by Bates (1975) with encouraging results; she stresses that high dosage is necessary for any reasonable chance of cure and for this reason treatment is usually limited to the pelvis. An overall five-year survival rate of 24% has been obtained using radical pelvic postoperative radiotherapy, in this way.

Terminal Care

Ovarian cancer is the major killer amongst the gynaecological cancers; it also sometimes undergoes inexplicable spontaneous remissions. Patients will be able to stay at home during their terminal illness providing adequate nursing care and analgesia can be provided. Often repeated paracenteses will be necessary to decrease the discomfort of abdominal distension. No proven benefit has been shown from the instillation of cytotoxic drugs such as thiotepa or chlorambucil into the peritoneal cavity after paracentesis and the procedure can be very painful.

VULVAL CARCINOMA

Vulval carcinoma is now a rare disease accounting for only about 3% of genital tract cancer. It is most common in post-menopausal women and usually presents as a painful lump or ulcer at the vulva. The tumour spreads directly to the vagina, the urethra and the anus and also via the lymphatics to the inguinal nodes. If the deep inguinal nodes are involved the prognosis is poor. The aetiology of vulval cancer is not known although pre-invasive conditions such as Bowen's disease and Paget's disease are found in some patients. It is of interest to note that between 5 and 10% of patients with vulval carcinoma will have a second primary cancer. Vulval cancer is basically a condition of old age and has been associated by some writers with long-term poor vulval hygiene.

Histologically the lesion is usually a squamous cell carcinoma and the treatment is by means of a radical vulvectomy with bilateral gland dissection. Providing total clearance of glands is achieved the prognosis is good, bearing in mind the advanced age of most of the patients.

Bibliography

Bates, T. (1975) Radiotherapeutic approach to ovarian carcinoma. In *Gynaecological Malignancy: Clinical and Experimental Studies*, ed. M.G. Brush & R.W. Taylor, pp. 133-140. London: Baillière Tindall.

Harcus, A.W. & McCrae, K.D. (1975) Progress in the ovarian cancer clinical survey: a multicentre approach. In *Gynaecological Malignancy: Clinical and Experimental Studies*, ed. M.G. Brush & R.W. Taylor, pp. 141-151. London: Baillière Tindall.

Hutton, J.D., Murray, M.A.F., Reed, M.J., Jacobs, H.S. & James, V.H.T. (1978) Hormones after the menopause: levels, sources, effects of natural oestrogen therapy and possible relationship to endometrial carcinogenesis. In *Endometrial Cancer*, ed. M.G. Brush, R.J.B. King & R.W. Taylor, pp. 363-374. London: Baillière Tindall.

Kohorn, E.I. (1978) The current status of progestogens in the management of endometrial cancer. In *Endometrial Cancer*, ed. M.G. Brush, R.J.B. King & R.W. Taylor, pp. 179-187. London: Baillière Tindall.

Lees, D.M. & Bar-am, A. (1978) A rational approach to the surgical treatment of endometrial carcinoma. In *Endometrial Cancer*, ed. M.G. Brush, R.J.B. King & R.W. Taylor, pp. 139-148. London: Baillière Tindall.

Metters, J.S. & Milton, P.J.D. (1973) Endometrial carcinoma: a retrospective survey of cases located at St Thomas's Hospital, 1945-1956 and 1957-1969. In *Symposium on Endometrial Cancer*, ed. M.G. Brush, R.W. Taylor & D.C. Williams, pp. 82-92. London: Heinemann Medical.

Milton, P.J.D. & Brush, M.G. (1975) Recent progress in the study and management of endometrial cancer. In *Gynaecological Malignancy: Clinical and Experimental Studies*, ed. M.G. Brush & R.W. Taylor, pp. 194-211. London: Baillière Tindall.

Milton, P.J.D. & Metters, J.S. (1973) Endometrial carcinoma: an analysis of 355 cases treated at St Thomas's Hospital 1945-69 *J. Obstet. Gynaec. Br. CommonW., 79*, 455-464.

Tobias, J.S. (1978) Cytotoxic chemotherapy in carcinoma of the endometrium. In *Endometrial Cancer,* ed. M.G. Brush, R.J.B. King & R.W. Taylor, pp. 425-433. London: Baillière Tindall.

Whitehead, M.I. & Campbell, S. (1978) Endometrial histology, uterine bleeding and oestrogen levels in menopausal women receiving oestrogen therapy and oestrogen/progestogen therapy. In *Endometrial Cancer*, ed. M.G. Brush, R.J.B. King & R.W. Taylor, pp. 65-80. London: Baillière Tindall.

11. Radiotherapy in Gynaecology

Terence Wheeler

A malignant cell is no longer malignant if it cannot reproduce itself and normal tissue is no longer normal if it is incapable of repair, for example following damage inflicted by radiation to destroy malignant infiltration. Radiotherapy is the controlled use of physical energy to destroy malignant cells. The doses used are designed to produce optimum destruction of cancer cells whilst permitting normal tissue to repair, thereby retaining or restoring the anatomy to the premalignant state.

The physical energy used in radiotherapy is part of the electromagnetic spectrum. The beams may be those from naturally occurring radio-active substances such as radium, or the radio-active isotope of cobalt (^{60}Co) or from isotopes which have been produced in a nuclear

Table 11.1. Radiation Techniques Available in the Treatment of Gynaecological Malignancy

Source	*Treatment technique*
Radium	Intracavitary
Caesium-137	Intracavitary
Cobalt-60	Intracavitary
X-rays	External beam
Cobalt-60	External beam

reactor such as caesium-137. Beams of X-rays may be manufactured electrically and discharged from X-ray tubes or from high-energy generators such as linear accelerators. The energy from an orthovoltage X-ray tube is approximately 250 000 volts. The equivalent energy from the common linear accelerators is approximately 4–6 million volts, although higher energies are available. The chief advantage of high-energy irradiation is the uniform distribution of dose at depth within the body. With high-energy X-rays or the beam from a cobalt-60 gamma source, treatments can be planned to give a uniform radiation dose to the contents of the pelvis. The physical property of such treatment is that the greatest dosage is deep to the skin. Therefore, the patient is spared excessive skin reactions. An alternative way of obtaining a dose deep within the patient but without affecting the skin is, of course, to locate radio-active material within the body. This is particularly appropriate in the treatment of carcinoma of the cervix.

Table 11.2. Treatment of Gynaecological Malignancy

Site	*Surgery*	*Radiotherapy*	*Hormones*	*Cytotoxic drugs*
Squamous cell carcinoma of vulva	✓			
Squamous cell carcinoma of vagina	✓	✓		
Squamous cell carcinoma of ectocervix	✓	✓		
Adenocarcinoma of endocervical canal	✓	✓		
Adenocarcinoma of endometrium	✓	✓	✓	
Adenocarcinoma of fallopian tube	✓	✓	?	
Malignant tumours of ovary	✓	✓		✓
Malignant melanoma of genital tract	✓			
Carcinoma of urethra	✓	✓		

Radiotherapy is only one of several techniques available for treating cancer; surgery, cytotoxic chemotherapy and hormones may also be used. Most malignant disease is treated with a combination of two or more of these approaches, but surgery is still generally the treatment of choice. In gynaecological malignancy, particularly carcinoma of the cervix, radiotherapy has an important part to play in the management of the patient.

SQUAMOUS CELL CARCINOMA OF THE VAGINA

This rare condition occurs in the elderly and must be distinguished from vaginal extension of carcinoma of the ectocervix or a metastasis in the vagina from a primary tumour elsewhere. Metastases in the vagina are usually adenocarcinomata and the commonest primary sites for such metastases are the endometrium and breast.

With elderly patients there may be general medical contraindications to the operation of hysterovaginectomy which would be the surgical choice. Radiotherapy is the logical alternative, using an intracavitary source such as radium or caesium-137. The rod filled with radio-active material is fitted under a general anaesthetic, the surgeon having previously noted the site and dimensions of the diseased areas to be treated. Once the treatment is planned the patient is nursed in bed for up to eight hours per day with the radio-active loaded applicator in the vagina. Once the applicator has been fitted by a doctor, nurses can usually insert it and check its position at intervals during the treatment time. The standard tumour dose for this technique is 6000 centiGray in six days with the applicator in place for between six and eight hours per day. This form of low-dose radiotherapy is sometimes referred to as brachytherapy. There is sound biological thinking for the effectiveness of this type of treatment in tumours which have a poor blood supply, resulting in a fraction of cells being deprived of oxygen thus rendering them resistant to fast dose irradiation. The close proximity of the radiation source to the tumour volume is also valuable because it permits intensive local irradiation whilst sparing tissues at a greater distance from the beam, notably the anterior aspect of the bladder, the posterior aspect of the rectum, the bones of the pelvic girdle and the skin of the lower abdominal wall and perineum. The results of radiotherapy at this site are modest because the tumour is rare and occurs in the elderly and, therefore, there are too few sources in the literature to give reliable five-year statistics.

SQUAMOUS CELL CARCINOMA OF THE ECTOCERVIX

95% of patients with cancer of the cervix have squamous cell tumours but about 5% have adenocarcinomata which arise in the endocervical canal. This latter group must be distinguished because of the relative insensitivity of adenocarcinomata to radiotherapy. The accessibility of the ectocervix to intracavitary radiation has permitted steady development of radiation techniques in this century and whereas surgery is exclusively the treatment of choice for adenocarcinomata of the cervix, radiotherapy has a very real role in the treatment of patients with squamous cell disease. In order to discuss the treatment more fully, it is important to consider the stages of advancement of carcinoma of the cervix (Table 11.3). In most cases the progress of carcinoma of the cervix is orderly. Therefore, accurate assessment before planning treatment is an essential part of the management of each patient. The history is often short because younger patients, who recognize the importance of abnormal vaginal bleeding or discharge, come early: older patients may deny symptoms until they are forced to

Table 11.3. Clinical Staging in Carcinoma of the Cervix

Stage O	In situ
Stage Ia	Macroscopically normal cervix Abnormal cervical smear cytology Confirmed as infiltrating carcinoma by biopsy
Stage Ib	Macroscopically malignant change in the cervix Disease confined to the cervix
Stage IIa	Malignant change involving the cervix and the vaginal fornix but not extending below the upper third of the vagina
Stage IIb	Nodular extension of carcinoma of the cervix into the parametrial tissues but not extending to pelvic side wall
Stage IIIa	Malignant disease in the cervix spreading to lower half of vagina
Stage IIIb	Nodular extension of carcinoma of the cervix to pelvic side wall Uterus fixed Dilatation of ureters on IVU or non-functioning kidney
Stage IV	Metastatic spread to distant organs Carcinoma of the cervix frequently involves the bladder or rectum in late disease

attend the clinic because of the overwhelming nature of their condition.

Some patients are diagnosed before symptoms occur. These are the patients who have in situ disease detected by abnormal cytology studies. Patients with advanced disease sometimes fail to recognize the importance of their discomfort or else they hope that the problem will resolve itself spontaneously.

Clinical examination is, therefore, very important in trying to assess how advanced the disease is. It is complemented by intravenous urography. The radiological study demonstrates displacement, stenosis or complete obstruction of the ureter in late disease. Isotope renography is used to add further details about early obstruction of the ureter. Examination of the anaesthetized patient to assess the vagina, parametrial thickening, and the degree of mobility of the uterus and adherence of the rectal mucosa is needed to arrive at the final staging before treatment. Biopsy of rectal and bladder mucosa may be necessary. Biopsy of the ectocervix and endocervical canal, vaginal mucosa and endometrium is essential before undertaking treatment. Once the extent of the disease has been carefully defined, treatment can be considered and planned upon radical or palliative lines.

Stage 0 disease in young patients is treated by cone biopsy alone with careful follow-up at out-patient attendances. In patients nearer the menopause or after it, simple hysterectomy may be advised. It is not necessary to remove the ovaries in these patients and surgery alone is the treatment for this stage of disease.

In Stage Ia disease the degree of infiltration is still minimal but, untreated, it is potentially lethal and therefore radical extirpation of the tumour is needed. Where there has been deep penetration in spite of the macroscopically normal cervix, the treatment of choice would be Wertheim's hysterectomy. In this operation the uterus with the cervix and a large cuff of the vagina intact is removed with tubes, ovaries and the pelvic lymph nodes dissected en bloc. In young patients with Stage Ia disease the surgeon may consider the retention of an ovary on its vascular pedicle to spare the patient an acute and premature menopause. Where surgery is not possible radical radiotherapy would be in two parts, first the insertion of radioactive material into the endometrial cavity with additional sources in the vagina to encompass the diseased cervix in a uniform field of radiation. Radium or caesium-137 are the sources commonly used for brachytherapy but machines have been designed for the insertion of sources which deliver a high dose of irradiation from radio-active cobalt-60. The intracavitary part of the treatment would be followed by a second phase of external beam therapy to the contents of the whole pelvis using high-energy X-rays or the gamma rays from a cobalt teletherapy machine.

Radium is a dangerous naturally occurring radio-active material which must be handled with extreme care at all stages of its processing and use. For hospital purposes the material is encased in platinum to prevent leakage of harmful radon gas. The half-life of radium is 1600 years.

Caesium-137 is a byproduct of nuclear energy programmes: the gamma emission from it is equivalent to 660 kV X-rays compared with the 2000 kV maximum energy of one of the radium gamma emissions. The half-life of caesium is 30 years. The physical principles of treatment are such that within the body caesium is as effective as radium in treating gynaecological malignancy. However, the lower energy of the caesium gamma emission makes it a safer source for the nursing and other hospital staff when patients are treated with intracavitary techniques.

After-loading is a method of placing empty radiation containers into areas such as the endometrial cavity or vaginal fornices. When packed in place the containers are ready for loading with the appropriate radioactive materials. Loading in this way is easier and safer for the staff carrying out the procedure. Insertion of radio-active material is only carried out on the ward or in specially designed treatment areas. Thus the number of staff exposed to the radiation material is reduced. The principle of after-loading can be carried on a stage further where the patient is positioned above a radiation safe and connected to it by tubes from the safe into the containers within the patient. The loading of sources can then take place mechanically with the staff safely protected by sufficient screening with lead or concrete. A number of machines have now been designed for this remote loading of radio-active materials specifically in the treatment of patients with gynae-cological malignancies. Some make use of low dose-rate caesium sources and the patient is, therefore, connected to the machine for a number of hours whereas others make use of high-energy, high dose-rate radio-active cobalt-60 sources and the patient has to be treated for a period of time measured only in minutes.

It is usual to supplement intracavitary treatment with external beam therapy to increase the dose to the pelvic side wall and thereby include within the fully irradiated treatment volume the known nodes to which the disease may have spread. The policy of each individual department differs slightly but, in the main, the contents of the true pelvis and the lower para-aortic nodes are included in the irradiated volume. High-energy X-rays or the gamma rays from a cobalt-60 teletherapy machine are used to treat the pelvis and lower abdomen. The bladder and lower bowel will always be involved in radiation reactions which are described later in the chapter.

Curative Treatment for More Advanced Disease

For large Stage Ib tumours, that is those greater than 4 cm in diameter, and for *Stage IIa and IIb* disease, external therapy is the main-stay of the treatment plan. In many centres smaller Stage Ib tumours will be treated as already described for Stage Ia growths. Once the disease has been deemed to have progressed too far for the effectiveness of intracavitary treatment the whole pelvic contents, which must include all the nodes in the true pelvis to which small foci of disease may have spread, are treated by a two-, three- or four-field beam using high-energy irradiation. The nodes can be demonstrated radiologically by lymphangiography in which radio-opaque dye is instilled into the lymphatics through a needle inserted into a dissected lymphatic vessel on the dorsum of each foot. 5–7 ml of Lipiodol is allowed to enter under its own weight slowly over 15–20 minutes. Forceful injection would rupture the delicate lymphatics. The progress of the dye can be observed by fluoroscopy and the needles are removed when enough has been introduced. Films of the pelvis and the lower para-aortic region can be taken 24 hours after the instillation and, at the same time, intravenous urography or venacavography can be used to demonstrate filling defects in the pelvic and para-aortic nodes. Computer tomography (CT) scanning can be used for the same purpose to demonstrate lymphatic abnormality. The use of radio-opaque material aids treatment planning because the nodes can be defined with the simulator in a department of radiotherapy which makes use of X-ray techniques to imitate and delineate the fields to be treated in a given patient: check films can then be taken to record the volume which will be irradiated. Surgeons sometimes make use of lymphangiography before undertaking Wertheim's hysterectomy. For radical, external beam radiotherapy to the whole pelvis, treatment lasts between four and seven weeks. The patients are treated daily and a split course may be used to rest the patient between the third and fifth week to allow some of the radiation-induced symptoms in bladder and bowel to subside. The final tumour dose achieved with this technique can be as high as 6000 centiGray. For Stage Ib and IIa lesions the external beam therapy may be stopped at 3500–4000 centiGray and the patient re-assessed under anaesthesia to see if it is possible to make use of intracavitary irradiation. Frequently this is possible and the technique described earlier is then used to complete treatment. If, however, there is still extensive pelvic disease the remainder of the treatment will be by external beam. On some occasions at the second examination under anaesthesia after 3500 centiGray have been delivered, no abnormality can be detected but it is still essential to proceed with intracavitary irradiation for successful treatment. The complementary treatments of caesium-137 or radium and external beam of high-energy X-rays are the basis of radiotherapy as the curative treatment for carcinoma of the cervix.

Complications and Side-effects

If treatment is taken beyond the tolerance of the local tissue there may well be serious radiation-induced consequences. An unresolving radiation cystitis or proctitis may only be cleared by radical surgery to remove either the bladder or the rectum and anal canal. Necrosis of the bladder wall or rectal mucosa can lead to fistula formation; in the former, there is incontinence of urine through a vesicovaginal fistula and in the latter passage of faeculent vaginal discharge through a rectovaginal fistula. To prevent these problems care is taken at the insertion of intracavitary sources to measure the dose rate in the rectum: in some centres the dose-rate in the bladder is also measured. Rules are laid down to guide the therapist about tolerance and the doses do not exceed these guidelines.

All patients treated radically will suffer some radiation side-effects which can last as little as 10 days but usually do not settle completely for several weeks after the completion of treatment. The vault of the vagina is liable to become occluded by adhesions following the intense local inflammatory effect of radiation. One purpose of the follow-up examination is to keep the vagina patent by breaking down these adhesions. Vault irrigation or the early resumption of sexual intercourse will reduce the indication for this procedure in the clinic.

Most patients will suffer radiation cystitis. The symptom is soothed by high fluid intake to keep the urine as dilute as possible. Regular screening by culture of mid-stream urine to exclude infection is also essential and if it occurs vigorous treatment is mandatory.

Radiation proctitis is another complication which needs soothing either by the use of constipating treatments such as kaolin and morphine mixture, loperamide capsules and possibly the use of prednisolone suppositories to reduce the intense local inflammation.

Special Nursing Notes

It is worth stating that whilst undergoing treatment with intracavitary irradiation the patient herself is not made radio-active, nor can she communicate the radiation by personal contact. However, the nursing procedures are ordered in such a way as to protect the ward staff from the intracavitary sources and so spare them unnecessary, regular, chronic radiation exposure. The following guidance is usually given:

1. Nursing from the side of the bed should be minimal. If any lengthy procedure such as re-catherization is planned then the nurse's pelvis should be screened by a lead bed-shield for radium. When each treatment is completed the caesium Selectron or Curietron sources should be returned to the safe for the duration of the nursing procedure.
2. It is usual for a ward to have a specified number of patients. The calculation is based upon the size of the ward, the numbers of staff normally nursing the patients and the known maximum radiation loading used by the radio-therapists whose patients are on the ward. Patients treated with intracavitary radiation materials should be shared amongst all the nurses on the ward so that there will not be a special group of nurses whose exposure rises above average.
3. The checking of sources in patients should be in accordance with the strict safety programmes devised by the staff of the department of medical physics in each hospital.
4. Nurses on the radiotherapy ward usually wear film badges which record exposure rates.
5. All accidents such as the collapse or unusual behaviour of a patient who may incidentally be undergoing intracavitary treatment which might circumvent or prevent routine nursing procedures, must be investigated fully to ensure that the nurses who dealt with the problem have not been put at risk by prolonged exposure or close proximity to unshielded sources.

Two important facts should be remembered:

1. By understanding and obeying the safety procedures set out by hospital physicists, nurses are not at risk when caring for patients undergoing treatment with intracavitary irradiation.
2. Distance from an unshielded source, or the speedy retrieval of an unshielded source for return to its safe, are the most effective methods of reducing accidental individual exposure.

ADENOCARCINOMA OF THE ENDOCERVICAL CANAL

This form of carcinoma of the cervix arises at the squamocolumnar junction where the squamous epithelium of the ectocervix meets the secretory epithelium of the endometrium. Spread from this site follows the anatomical pathway for cervical carcinoma and is chiefly lymphatic as for the ectocervix but adenocarcinoma is less sensitive to irradiation and, therefore, surgery (usually Wertheim's hysterectomy) is the treatment of choice. In some centres the preoperative insertion of radio-active sources is advised to reduce the bulk of the tumour. The timing of surgery following intracavitary treatment is a matter for debate. Some surgeons prefer almost immediate surgery whilst others leave an interval of up to six weeks before operating. The reason for this is that between 10 and 21 days there is a pronounced increase in the pelvic blood flow and the hyperaemia of the tissues make an already difficult operation more hazardous. It is, therefore, important to avoid the period of maximum hyperaemia. The purpose of preoperative irradiation is also the elimination of micro-foci of disease in vaginal lymphatics which may not be cleared by the cuff of vagina removed as part of the radical excision. This would leave a nidus of cells in the new vault of the vagina which might present at a later date as a recurrence. About 5% of carcinomata of the cervix are adenocarcinomata and stage for stage the prognosis is worse than that for squamous cell disease.

CARCINOMA OF THE ENDOMETRIUM

A carcinoma arising in the body of the uterus is by definition an adenocarcinoma. Occasionally the tumour cells change by a process called metaplasia to present a squamous type of epithelium. The presence of squamous metaplasia does not appear to make endometrial carcinoma more sensitive to irradiation. Adenocarcinomata are relatively radio-resistant and, therefore, surgery is the treatment of choice for eradicating this form of cancer. The pattern of spread, if untreated, differs from carcinoma of the cervix in that endometrial disease does not readily spread to pelvic lymph nodes unless, as occurs from time to time, it has invaded the cervix. More often, metastases arise in the ovaries or there is distant spread to lungs or liver. Blood-borne spread, therefore, is more important than lymphatic spread in malignant disease of the endometrium. Surgery must still be radical but there is no need to dissect the pelvic lymph nodes if the cervix is uninvolved. Total hysterectomy with excision of a cuff of vagina and bilateral salpingo-oophorectomy is, therefore, the treatment of choice. The surgical technique to remove an adequate cuff of vagina can preclude the need for pre- or postoperative irradiation. In the past, before this fact was sufficiently well recognized, an inadequate cuff of vagina was removed at some centres and this resulted in a number of vault recurrences. It was felt, therefore, that there was a place for preoperative irradiation with intracavitary sources as described earlier, even though the tumours were not very radio-sensitive. There is no doubt that preoperative irradiation is of value when the cervix has been invaded by endometrial cancer as it will reduce the risk of vault recurrence after radical surgery. Postoperative irradiation is carried out when unsuspected disease in the cervix is discovered by histological examination of the operation specimen. In this technique ovoids are inserted into the vagina and left in place to give a high dose over a three- or four-day period. This may be followed by external pelvic beam therapy to the whole pelvis, taking between three and five weeks. There is often an increased bowel reaction when external beam therapy is given after pelvic surgery. Postoperative radiotherapy is usually advised when histological examination of the excised uterus shows that the endometrial carcinoma has penetrated the myometrium deeply, particularly if it has spread to involve the serosal surface, that is to say the peritoneal surface of the uterus, or if there is evidence of spread to the surface of the ovaries. In these circumstances it is deemed likely that there will be spread through the serous cavity of the pelvis to involve the whole of the pelvic peritoneum.

The introduction of progestogen therapy which effectively controls metastatic disease has superseded irradiation in some practices. Postoperative adjuvant hormone therapy is, therefore, advocated in many centres using either a depot injection weekly for up to six months or an oral preparation such as Provera 100 mg three times a day for between six months and one year.

THE FALLOPIAN TUBES

Primary adenocarcinoma of the fallopian tubes is a rare occurence but may be an incidental finding when a patient is undergoing surgery for another problem. Otherwise the lesion tends to present late with widespread pelvic disease involving spread to the uterus or ovaries, bladder or bowel. If the tumour can be removed totally then surgery is the only treatment indicated. Residual foci of disease should be irradiated treating the whole pelvic contents. Inoperable disease has a grave prognosis because pelvic radiotherapy for inoperable disease can only be palliative.

CARCINOMA OF THE OVARY

Malignant tumours of the ovary may arise at any age. Although rare in the early years they can occasionally arise in childhood and the spectrum of age distribution is four to 80 years. If found incidentally whilst the patient is undergoing abdominal or pelvic surgery for an unconnected condition and if the tumour can be removed totally then the chance of cure exceeds 80%. It is usual, however, for the disease to present late because the early tumours cause no symptoms unless they are hormone secreting and most malignant tumours of the ovary do not have that property. Therefore, it is not until the size of the mass is apparent, there has been spread to the pelvic or abdominal peritoneum to give rise to ascites or there is involvement of liver, and other organs or supraclavicular lymph nodes that the patient presents for treatment. Once the disease has spread beyond the ovary the prognosis is poor. Patients with ovarian carcinomatosis may appear in almost any clinic in the hospital. Symptoms include loss of weight, ascites, lymph-adenopathy, and those arising from hepatic or pulmonary metastases. When the disease is confined to the abdomen, surgery is necessary to remove the bulk of the pelvic disease so that attempts to palliate the symptoms of residual disease with cytotoxic chemotherapy may have a chance of success. If the major spread is to the liver or lungs, then surgical clearance is not possible and cytotoxic drugs in the past used singly but more often nowadays in combination, are the treatment of choice. The place of radiotherapy was once to treat the whole abdomen but this has been superseded by modern drug therapy. Radiation is now confined to the treatment of pelvic recurrence or simply to treat the pelvic contents when an ovary is found to be adherent to part of the pelvic anatomy and where there is no macroscopic evidence of distant spread and ascitic fluid drained at operation is found to be free of tumour cells. If there are malignant cells in the ascitic fluid then cytotoxic chemotherapy is strongly indicated.

Carcinomata of the ovary are relatively radio-resistant and the overall prognosis for an inoperable ovarian cancer is poor but the disease has a wide spectrum of natural history and some patients could live longer and in better general condition than could have been expected when treatment was begun. A trial of such treatment is accordingly recommended no matter how advanced the disease appears to be because, although the majority will gain little benefit from treatment, some will show a remarkable response.

MALIGNANT MELANOMA

As the epithelium of vulva and vagina is skin it may occasionally be the site of malignant melanoma. This tumour must be excised radically and the appropriate block dissection of regional nodes undertaken if there is evidence of spread. Melanomata are not sensitive to radiotherapy in general and the only site where radiotherapy is considered to be of real value in the treatment of this condition is primary melanoma of the eye.

CARCINOMA OF THE URETHRA

Rarely, tumours present as swellings around the urethra and may be found to be pedunculated, transitional cell carcinomata of the urethra. The surgical treatment of choice is combined excision of the urethra and bladder and urinary diversion but for some small tumours limited excision followed by radiotherapy can be carried out successfully. The radiation technique used is implantation at the site of the tumour with radio-active materials using radium needles or an equivalent treatment with radio-active iridium wire or radio-active gold grains.

Radium or iridium implants are left in place for up to a week but a radio-active gold grain implant is permanent. This last is possible because of the rapid decay in radio-activity of gold grains which have a half-life of only 2.8 days.

12. Pelvic Infection in Women

D.B. Garrioch

To the gynaecologist, the diagnosis of pelvic inflammatory disease implies that an infection has reached a level in the genital tract above that of the cervix. Chronic cervicitis or vaginitis does not *per se* constitute pelvic infection. Severe acute disease is seen in Britain much less commonly than a decade or more ago, even though current Western social mores might be thought to encourage the spread of sexually transmitted disease. The reasons for this are manifold but must include the free use of antibiotics and ready access, without stigma, to venereology clinics. Serious antibiotic resistance by the group of organisms usually responsible for pelvic inflammation has not so far appeared. Tuberculosis as a cause of this problem in the UK is now seen almost solely in immigrants. General public health measures, but especially the improved care given during and after pregnancy, has undoubtedly greatly reduced the group of puerperal sufferers.

A useful approach when a woman with pelvic inflammation is seen is to consider whether the cervix has recently been open or not. Since the closed cervix is an effective barrier to ascending infection, genital infection is rarely seen outside the reproductive years. Very few organisms are capable of engendering such a low-grade response that the natural immune mechanisms in the cervical canal are circumvented. A viable pregnancy forms an intrauterine barrier to pelvic inflammatory disease.

NATURAL HISTORY

Infecting Agents

The closed cervix will effectively exclude all but a few micro-organisms from the uterus. In practice *Neisseria gonorrhoea* (gonococcus) and *Mycobacterium tuberculosis* are such agents. Transcervical migration of the latter is rare and tuberculosis usually reaches and damages the genitalia by haematogenous spread from the lungs, or by lymphatic or transcoelomic migration, often from infected bowel or omentum. Occasionally pelvic inflammatory disease is an unfortunate sequel to appendicitis with peritonitis and is associated with extensive pelvic adhesions.

In the reproductive years the cervix may be opened naturally or artificially. The first group includes spontaneous abortion and parturition, while in the latter one must remember dilatation and curettage (D and C), insertion or removal of an intrauterine contraceptive device (IUCD) and termination of pregnancy at any stage of gestation. The risk of developing pelvic sepsis is said to be increased if removal of an IUCD coincides with a sterilization procedure (which leads to sterile necrosis of part of the fallopian tube) or when a uterine evacuation is performed in the presence of necrotic tissue such as in missed abortion or intrauterine death. When the cervical barrier to ascending infection is removed organisms become opportunist and will invade the uterus. *Escherichia coli* and other Gram-negative enteric organisms, including the clostridia, may be recovered from uterus or fallopian tubes while streptococci and staphylococci are another group of bacteria commonly seen in cases of pelvic sepsis.

Early Pathological Events

Once infection has occurred within the uterine cavity an endometritis develops which often leads to irregular endometrial shedding with resulting bleeding per vaginam. Necrotic endometrium, decidua or products of conception retained within the uterus form excellent culture media for bacteria, resulting in a much more violent infection. Invasion of the myometrium can occur and it is in this situation that *Clostridium welchii* infection will give rise to the bubbles of gas gangrene. Severe sepsis of this nature leads to a spill-over of organisms and toxins into the blood, resulting in bacteraemia, septicaemia (where bacteria begin to multiply within the blood stream) and shock.

Much more often a lower-grade infection will occur within the uterus, especially when antibiotic treatment has been commenced. In this situation an ascending infection may involve the lumen, wall or outer surface of the fallopian tubes. If both the fimbrial and the isthmic ends become occluded the fallopian tube becomes filled and distended with pus (pyosalpinx). Peritubal abscesses will often involve neighbouring structures such as the ovaries, bowel and cul-de-sac. Local or even generalized peritonitis will develop if treatment is delayed.

Later Sequelae

In anatomical terms the uterus usually suffers little damage in all but the most severe infections. This is related to the good regenerative capacity of the endometrium due to its basal layer having escaped damage. Inflammation of the cervix, on the other hand, can lead to stenosis and loss of function. More usually important is the extent of damage to, and therefore the capacity to regenerate of, the highly specialized fallopian tubes where the disease is always bilateral. As resolution occurs pyosalpinges become filled with straw-coloured fluid (hydrosalpinx) and pelvic cysts become the legacy of earlier abscesses. Generally the parametria and structures within the broad ligaments remain chronically thickened and severe widespread adhesions bind the genitalia to omentum, bowel or bladder. Interference with blood flow and uterine and ovarian function is often reflected in subsequent menstrual irregularity. From both reproductive and social aspects it is particularly unfortunate that the mucosal structure of the fallopian tubes is so very sensitive to infection since loss of structure and function almost invariably occur.

CLINICAL FEATURES

In common with other areas of medicine a carefully-taken history will indicate the diagnosis. In some cases direct questioning may be necessary even at the expense of embarrassment, so that 'Have you had VD or a casual boyfriend?' can have surprising answers. In many couples pelvic inflammation may be related to a resumption of intercourse too soon after childbirth or abortion. Nevertheless the diagnosis can often remain extraordinarily difficult since other conditions such as urinary tract infection, appendictis, abortion and ectopic pregnancy may give rise to a similar picture. An ovarian cyst may haemorrhage, leak or twist and mimic pelvic sepsis. Chronic bowel inflammation as in Crohn's disease or ulcerative colitis may be misdiagnosed as pelvic inflammatory disease.

The physical examination of a woman with more than mild pelvic inflammation reveals her to be extremely ill. Fever, dryness and tachycardia are present in degrees of progression, leading to severe hypotension and shock. In most cases there is evidence of pelvic peritonitis. Vaginal examination is usually difficult but a gentle speculum examination can provide the diagnosis if cervicitis with pus is seen. In such cases the bacteriologist may see the Gram-negative intracellular diplococci pathognomonic of gonorrhoea in swabs taken from the vaginal fornices, cervix, urethra or rectum. Exquisite tenderness will be elicited on moving the cervix to the ipsilateral side (cervical excitation) but it is unkind and usually impossible to make any further pelvic assessment.

If doubt still exists the white cell count may suggest acute infection. The non-specific erythrocyte sedimentation rate is helpful in this condition and values over 100 mm/hour (Westergren) may be seen; these high levels will fall when resolution occurs even though chronic pain persists. Ultrasound is a useful diagnostic tool since it can indicate fluid masses and determine uterine contents, while in the luteal phase of the menstrual cycle a D and C may produce endometrium infected with tuberculosis. If the diagnosis is still in doubt, the laparoscope, which is now in common use, assumes a particular importance in pelvic inflammatory disease and is often the final arbiter. In experienced hands laparoscopy is safe and produces a low morbidity so that the fit patient can be discharged home on the same day or on the morning after the procedure.

TREATMENT

The Acute Case

The acute condition is a gynaecological emergency and rapid effective treatment will limit pelvic damage. Total bed rest and analgesics for pain relief should be accompanied by intravenous fluid replacement and antibiotics. These should be broad spectrum unless the infecting organism has been detected reliably. Tuberculosis requires long-term therapy. The correction of shock is a subject beyond the scope of this chapter. In all cases the gynaecologist attempts to provide conditions favourable for resolution. The uterus should be emptied of products of conception by means of dilatation and curettage. An IUCD should be removed. Rarely these procedures do not suffice especially if the myometrium has been invaded, e.g. by Clostridia, and in these cases only a hysterectomy will be effective. Pelvic abscesses should be drained and this is commonly done by a stab incision (colpotomy) through the posterior fornix with insertion of a rubber tube drain. It is uncommon for pelvic collections of pus to be drained per abdomen although the rectal route is occasionally used.

Chronic Pelvic Inflammatory Disease

The common symptoms of chronic pelvic sepsis, with or without acute flare-ups, are dysmenorrhoea, dyspareunia, irregular vaginal bleeding, hypogastric pain and infertility. Because of the age group involved the treatment can be extraordinarily difficult. If there is severe damage and pain then the correct medical management is removal of the uterus and tubes, usually with conservation of the ovaries. A hysterectomy for this condition is a technically difficult operation because all the pelvic structures are densely adherent to one another and displaced. There is, therefore, great danger of damage to adjacent organs especially ureters, bladder and bowel.

The tendency today is to a conservative approach. This includes analgesics, short-wave diathermy, infra-red therapy, cervical dilatation, cauterization and uterine curettage. Good nutrition, and prompt antibiotic treatment of exacerbations may keep the problem in abeyance. However, in women suffering from this problem fertility is often the most important consideration. In these cases the surgeon may embark on surgical correction of the pelvis after assessment of the fallopian tubes by hysterosalpingography and laparoscopy. If dyspareunia is a problem then, in addition to opening up the tubes (salpingostomy), the uterus is anteverted by the operation of ventrosuspension which will also lift the ovaries from the cul-de-sac. The careful gynaecologist will, however, take care not to give a guarantee of pain relief and will tell his patient that, on the optimum current estimates, the likelihood of a successful term pregnancy is only of the order of 10 or 20%.

13. Cervical Screening

Helen L.D. Duguid

HISTORICAL BACKGROUND

It has been known since the early years of this century that invasive carcinoma of the cervix is preceded by intraepithelial or in situ carcinoma, these observations being supported by the development of colposcopy in Germany during the 1920s. The practical importance of the diagnosis of intraepithelial neoplasia became evident following the development of cytological techniques, the main stimulus being the publishing in 1943 of Papanicolaou's classical paper on the diagnosis of cervical cancer by exfoliative cytology. Originally, specimens were taken by a pipette from the posterior fornix (vaginal pool) but after the introduction of the Ayre's spatula in 1947, vaginal smears have largely been superseded by the more accurate method of scraping the entire circumference of the external os of the cervix. This method will identify 90% of cases of intraepithelial neoplasia but fails to identify lesions occurring within the endocervical canal. Therefore many centres in America and Canada now employ VCE smears, i.e. samples taken from the vaginal pool, ectocervix and endocervical canal spread on one slide.

In 1949, the first large laboratory equipped for cervical cytology was opened in British Columbia. In Britain in 1955, it was decided to introduce a cervical cytology service based on the work of the British Columbia laboratory. Screening programmes were introduced during the early 1960s and in 1966 general practitioners were paid for taking cervical smears in women over the age of 35, payment being later extended to include women under 35 who had had three or more pregnancies: in these categories payment is also made for repeat smears taken at five-year intervals.

PATHOLOGY

Epidermoid carcinoma of the cervix is a progressive disease starting from relatively slight changes usually in the metaplastic zone (squamo-columnar junction) of the cervix and progressing through stages of increasing severity until eventually stromal invasion occurs. The evolution is often protracted and may take up to 10–15 years, although progression in some cases is much faster. Recognition at the earlier stage of the disease is necessary in order to prevent invasion, and the much poorer prognosis associated with diagnosis after the tumour has spread to surrounding tissues. The most important lesion diagnosed by means of cytology is presymptomatic invasive cancer, as here the five-year survival rate is quoted as 94%. In preinvasive cancer, the epithelial cells have the histological characteristics of malignancy but are confined to the cell layers above the basement membrane. It is not known with certainty how many untreated cases of preinvasive cancer will progress to invasive but figures of 40–50% have been quoted; the remainder will persist unchanged or regress. Most intraepithelial abnormalities now diagnosed, especially in younger women, are less severe and are generally classified as dysplasia. They are often found in the squamous epithelium of the ectocervix and may accompany carcinoma in situ in the metaplastic zone. Some authorities now no longer use the terms in situ carcinoma and dysplasia but classify all lesions as cervical intraepithelial neoplasia (CIN) of varying degrees of severity. If left untreated, most cases of mild or moderate dysplasia will regress but some (probably less than 10%) will progress to in situ or invasive cancer. The rate of progression of severe dysplasia is practically identical to that of carcinoma in situ.

The incidence of preinvasive lesions depends on the age and type of population studied, but in the Tayside area of Scotland 0.04% of women screened have presymptomatic invasive carcinoma, 0.5% carcinoma in situ or severe dysplasia and 3% mild or moderate dysplasia.

THE CERVICAL SMEAR (CYTO TEST)

Meticulous technique is required for a well prepared cervical smear. It should be taken during the course of a pelvic examination as unsuspected abnormalities, e.g. prolapse, fibroids or ovarian tumours, may also be present. Nurses can be trained to take cervical smears but may not have sufficient experience to give a judgment on the clinical state of the cervix and other pelvic organs. Scraping the cervix with a wooden spatula under direct vision requires a speculum (sterile or disposable) and a good source of light. If possible smears should not be taken during menstruation. Excess pus or mucus may be gently removed before taking the smear but the cervix should not be swabbed clean as abnormal epithelium is attached very loosely to the underlying tissues and can be rubbed off completely. The entire circumference of the external os is scraped and if possible, the lower endocervical canal. If an erosion is present the smear is taken from the edge.

In patients over 40, it is desirable also to sample the endocervical canal using a cottonwool bud moistened in saline, the material being spread on the end of the cervical smear slide. The material should be spread evenly and firmly on a previously labelled slide and fixed while still wet in cytological fixative (95% alcohol, acetic acid and carbowax) or by spray fix. In the laboratory, smears are stained using the Papanicolaou method. Nuclei are coloured blue-black with haematoxylin and the cytoplasm, rendered translucent by the use of alcohol-based dyes, stains green with immature cells and pink when the cells are mature. After staining, the smears are examined by specially trained cytology screeners who identify abnormal cells and report on the quality of the smear, the presence of inflammatory cells and infectious organisms such as *Trichomonas* and *Candida* (*Monilia*). Cytology is a subjective art and strict quality control is necessary for the accurate interpretation of findings; all smears showing an abnormality should be rescreened by senior members of staff or by medical personnel.

When tumour cells are found the smear is classified as positive. These cells have enlarged irregular dark nuclei, sometimes with enlarged or irregular nucleoli and a relative reduction in the amount of cytoplasm. Dyskaryotic (suspicious) cells are found in the dysplasias. Their nuclei show the criteria of malignancy to a varying degree but they have normal cytoplasm. If a smear is regarded as being unsatisfactory for interpretation because of excess inflammatory cells or paucity of epithelial cells, a repeat smear is always requested.

COLPOSCOPY

Colposcopy was developed in Germany during the 1920s but it is only within recent years that it has been extensively employed. Before its advent, patients with positive smears were referred to a gynaecologist for biopsy. If an area suspicious of malignancy was seen, a target biopsy was taken but the majority of women were subjected to a cone biopsy which removed a core of tissue from the squamocolumnar junction and lower endocervical canal (see p. 137). In the laboratory, the cone was opened out, fixed and serially sliced, several sections being examined from each block. Further treatment, usually hysterectomy, was advised if the abnormal epithelium was found to be incompletely excised, if early invasive growth was seen or if abnormal cells were still present in follow-up smears. If suspicious cells were seen, follow-up smears were taken at three- to six-monthly intervals. In many cases, the smears reverted to normal but if the abnormal smear pattern persisted or increased in severity, a cone biopsy was requested.

Binocular colposcopy gives a stereoscopic magnification of the cervix of between 6 and 40 times and provides a transition between macroscopic and microscopic vision. The different epithelial abnormalities can be studied in vivo and assessment of the thickness and cellular content of the epithelium, the pattern of the blood vessels and the surface contour of the epithelium allow the histological findings to be forecast with surprising accuracy. The extent of the lesion can also be mapped out and, with this information, biopsies can be taken from the sites of maximum abnormality and the best method of eradicating the lesion can be decided.

Like cytology, colposcopy is not 100% accurate and its greatest value lies in the study of dysplasias in younger women. If the extent of the epithelial abnormality cannot be demarcated or if no lesion in keeping with the abnormal cytological findings can be seen, cone biopsy or endocervical curettage is necessary.

TREATMENT

The diagnosis of premalignancy has created many problems with regard to the true nature of the lesions revealed and their treatment. Before colposcopy, there was complete reliance on the histopathologist for diagnosis and removal of a maximum amount of tissue left both the histologist and the surgeon secure. However, these relatively radical measures carried more than an element of over-diagnosis and over-treatment, especially in younger women whose families were not complete. They necessitated admission to hospital and there was associated morbidity and loss of fertility. While cone biopsy and hysterectomy still play a part in treatment, increasing use is now being made of the more conservative methods. When the exact extent of the lesion has been demarcated, it can be removed by out-patient cautery, cryosurgery or carbon dioxide laser.

After treatment, all patients must be followed up with repeat smears at regular intervals as, even after hysterectomy, a recurrent abnormality of the vaginal epithelium may occur. Regular follow-up is especially important after conservative methods of treatment which have not yet been completely evaluated. In theory, the patient should be followed up for the rest of her life but in practice this is very difficult to achieve, especially if attendance at a clinic necessitates loss of working time and the expense of travelling a long distance. After the initial period of two to three years' intensive follow up, smears should be taken every one to two years for the next decade after which a longer interval is allowable. Provided follow up is monitored by the gynaecological or cytological services, long-term surveillance may be delegated to the general practitioner or well woman clinic.

WHERE, WHO AND HOW OFTEN?

Cervical smears are now regarded as being an integral part of routine pelvic examinations and are available at antenatal, postnatal, gynaecological and family planning clinics. Many general practitioners take cervical smears and well women clinics are run by the community medicine service and in some areas by the hospital service. Cytotests should be routinely carried out at all sexually transmitted disease clinics and by the prison service, but often, because of the fear of loss of confidentiality, smears are not taken by these bodies. In addition some firms make a cytology service available to their work force at their place of employment and mobile caravan clinics are provided by the Women's National Cancer Prevention Campaign.

The younger woman who is receiving medical attention for contraceptive, antenatal or postnatal care or who attends her doctor with her young children has ample opportunities for a cervical smear test. Many middle-aged or older women, often with a grown-up family, no longer feel that any medical liaison is necessary. They may avoid smear tests as they are afraid of cancer or surgery; they may feel embarrassed or believe that as they have no symptoms there is no need for attendance. If single or childless they may think that screening projects are not for their benefit and that only parous or married women are at risk.

The policy determining the availability of cervical smear tests must depend on the resources in the community but ideally testing should begin whenever a woman becomes sexually active and a repeat smear should be taken one year later to minimize the incidence of false-negative reports. If this test is again negative, smears should be repeated at three-year intervals until after the age of 35 when a five-year interval between smears is allowable. If all smears have been completely negative it is reasonable to stop testing after the age of 60. In many countries, notably America and Canada, yearly smears are advised and this is administratively convenient as women can be traced much more easily.

IS CYTOLOGY SCREENING WORTH WHILE?

Although very few cervical carcinomas develop in women who have had previous normal cervical smears, a cytology service to be worth while must bring about a statistically significant reduction in both the incidence of and the death rate from the disease and must also reduce morbidity. Cancer of the cervix is responsible for 5% of all cancer deaths in women and for 25% of cancer deaths in women below the age of 50. The death rate from uterine cancer is decreasing in European and American countries where the ratio of cervical to body cancers is lower than in comparatively less developed countries. In Kentucky the ratio was 2.5 : 1 in 1955 and fell to 1.4 : 1 in 1967.

The British Columbia cytology screening programme was started in 1949 and was designed to test the hypothesis that screening of cervical cancer was of value. By 1960, a reasonable population screening was achieved, 90% of the specimens being taken by general practitioners during the course of pelvic examination. By 1973, almost three million women had been tested. 8388 cases of carcinoma in situ were diagnosed and also 780 cases of asymptomatic early invasive cancer which was largely unrecognized prior to cytology. The incidence of symptomatic invasive squamous cervical carcinoma per 100 000 of the female population over the age of 20 fell from 23.7 in 1958 to 8.4 in 1974; during the same period, the death rate fell from 13.5 to 5.8.

Similar figures are available from Aberdeen where a planned cervical cytology programme based on screening women at risk, practice by practice, resulted in an almost complete coverage. The incidence of invasive squamous cervical carcinoma per 100 000 women over the age of 20 fell from 32.0 in 1961 to 16.2 in 1971. During the same period the death rate fell from 24.0 to 17.2. It is not possible to compare the incidence rates between one country and another as there is no fixed policy as to whether early carcinomas are included in the in situ or the invasive carcinoma group and in some areas there is no separation between the two.

With death rates also, comparison between countries and states is difficult because of the great variability in 'uterus unspecified' notifications. Inaccuracies in death certification also confuse the results but the Walton Report from Canada in 1976 established that, in those provinces where carcinoma of the cervix was certified separately from carcinoma of the body, there was a definite association between the percentage of women screened and reduction in the death rate from cervical carcinoma.

In Britain, a recent report on age-specific mortality from carcinoma of the cervix revealed between 1968–70 and 1974–6, a reduction in the death rate of approximately 30% in women aged 35–54 but in England and Wales there was a disturbing increase in the death rate in women between the ages of 25 and 34 and 15 and 24. It is suggested that this is associated with the increased sexual activity in young girls and women which has occurred since the development in the 1960s of non-barrier forms of contraception. Risk factors in carcinoma of the cervix are sexual intercourse at puberty or soon after delivery, multiparity, multiple sexual partners, low socio-economic status, poor personal hygiene and, possibly, nutritional deficiencies, e.g. folic acid deficiency. The contribution of host reaction to infiltrative elements is poorly understood but diminution in immune response may explain the development of cancers in older women and in those having immunosuppressive treatment. Squamous cervical cancer is rarely found in orthodox Jews to whom intercourse is forbidden for 12 days after menstruation and 80 days after delivery and has never been reported in nuns.

Conversely it is now commonly found in prostitutes and women attending sexually transmitted disease clinics. The nature of the carcinogen is not yet fully understood but it has been postulated that the actively phagocytic epithelium of immature squamous metaplasia will ingest herpes II virus or 'heavy' histones from degenerate sperm heads, thus causing the nuclear chromatin to be altered by mutagens and rendered unstable and potentially malignant.

A cervical cytology service will reduce the incidence of and death rate from invasive carcinoma only if over 80% of women at risk have been screened; there is evidence that despite the freely available facilities for cervical smear tests in some areas less than 40% of women have been tested. Pamphlets and newspaper and magazine articles play a part in persuading women of the necessity for regular cervical smear tests, but it is known that the personal approach of general practitioners, practice nurses and health visitors is more valuable as women in 'high-risk' categories (often indifferent or unwilling to accept preventive health measures) are known to them and once their confidence has been gained, they can be persuaded to cooperate.

14. Breast Screening and its Evaluation

Patricia Last

Breast cancer is on the increase in the UK, as it is in other developed countries. Why this is so is not fully understood, but it is an area of cancer management in which no real improvement has been made in the mortality rate over the past decades. Deaths from breast cancer continue to increase whilst a decrease in mortality from carcinoma of the cervix is clearly shown in Fig. 14.1. Registration rates of breast cancer year by year also continue to rise (Table 14.1). Of all women dying from cancer one in five, the largest single group, will die from breast cancer; although lung cancer is rapidly approaching this level in women, associated no doubt with their increasing use of tobacco. *One in every 17* women will develop breast cancer at some time in their lives (Table 14.1). These are the facts. What if anything can be done about them and how?

WOMEN AT RISK

It is not known why women get breast cancer, but some general correlations have been established.

1. Previous cancer of the breast. This may appear obvious but it is often not clearly appreciated that 15% of women with cancer of one breast will develop another cancer in the contralateral side. This single group of women has the highest risk rate.
2. Nulliparae and women of low parity.

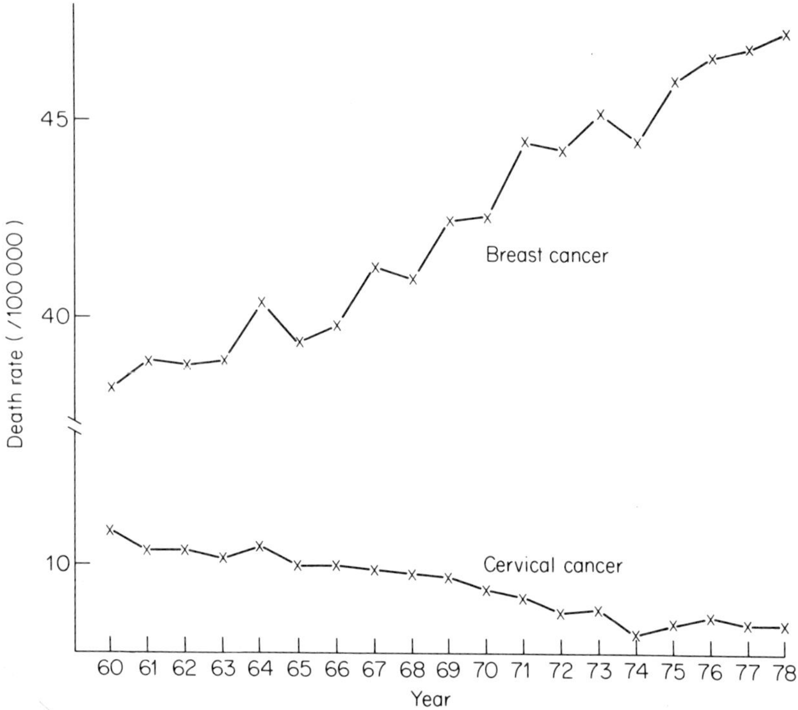

Fig. 14.1. Death rates (per 100 000) for breast and cervical cancers.

3. Women having their first child after the age of 30 years.

4. Women with a long menstrual career (more than 35 years). For example a woman whose periods begin at 12 years, and go on until age 47 has a higher risk of developing breast cancer than does a woman with a short menstrual career. Obviously menstruating women in their fifties must be carefully checked as they usually have 35 years of menstrual experience.

5 Women with a history of breast cancer in a first degree relative (that is a mother, sister, daughter). If the mother has had bilateral cancer of the breasts, the risk factor in the daughter is almost 50% (as against 6% in the general population).

6. Women with previous benign breast disease. Any woman with previous breast disease, cysts or fibroadenomata, has slightly increased risk of developing breast cancer.

7. Women with other cancers, particularly those of the uterus, ovaries and colon.

Table 14.1. Registration Rates per 100 000 Population for Various Gynaecological Cancers (England and Wales 1976)

Site	*Age*							*Total*
	15-24	25-34	35-44	45-54	55-64	65-74	75+	
Breast	0.9	13.5	70.8	140.3	166.3	194.6	241.9	82.5
Cervix uteri								
in situ	8.6	51.0	35.0	14.2	5.5	2.7	1.3	14.5
other	0.9	10.4	16.7	29.2	38.0	28.6	25.4	15.9
Other uterine malignancy	0.1	0.9	4.6	23.8	40.0	43.4	44.0	15.6
Ovary, fallopian tube and broad ligament	1.2	2.6	8.5	29.6	40.2	41.4	38.8	16.6

Registration rates of these cancers in girls under 14 years are negligible. Male breast cancer does occur very occasionally; its registration rate is about 0.9 per 100 000.

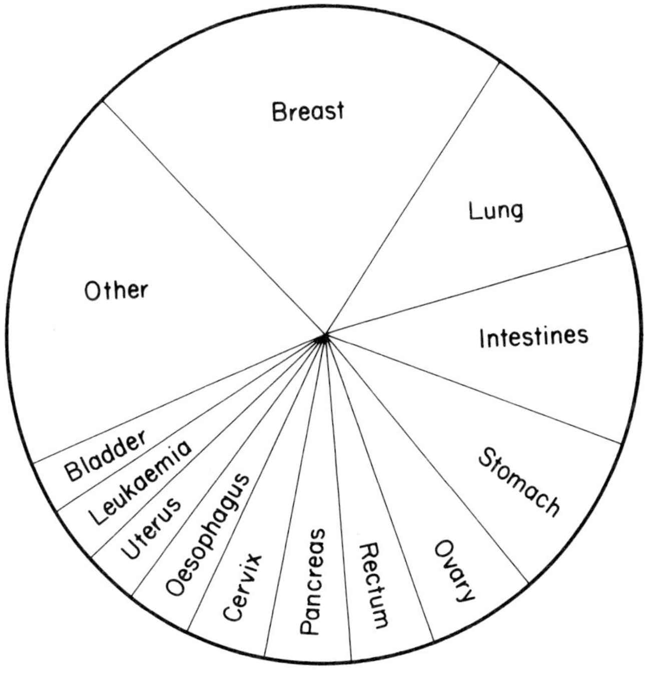

Fig. 14.2. The relative incidence of the various cancers in women (OPCS).

8. Women aged 35 years and over. Although breast cancer can occur in younger women, it is much less likely and regular examinations of women under this age with no predictors of breast cancer listed above are unproductive.

Even using all these predictors which identify 50% of the general female population, only 80% of the cases can be anticipated: the remaining 20% will occur in the 50% of women with no risk factors for this disease. It is obvious, therefore, that identification of risk factors is not, in itself, an adequate basis for examination.

The outcome of any disease process depends on four factors:

1. The aggression of the disease.
2. The resistance of the host.
3. The stage of the disease at the time of detection.
4. The treatment offered to and accepted by the patient.

This description can be applied to any disease, but whilst surgeons, radiotherapists and oncologists all work in the area of therapy, the stage of the disease at the time of diagnosis has a very important bearing on the outcome and it is in this field that screening can play a vital part.

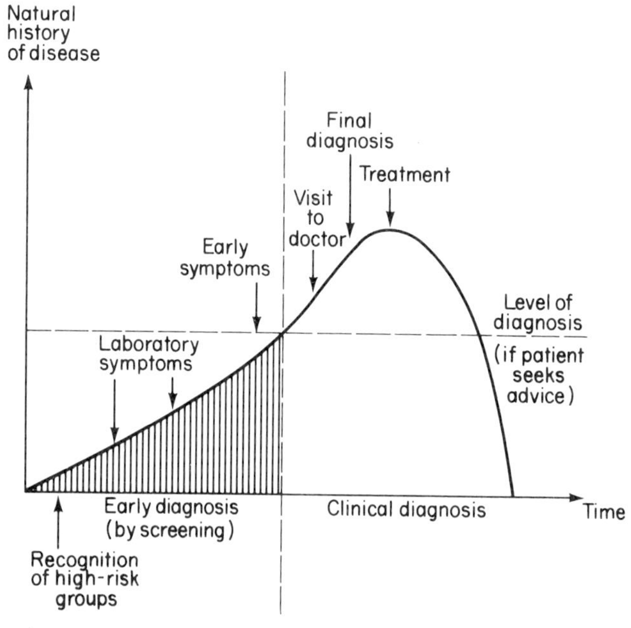

Fig. 14.3. The natural history of a disease.

Fig. 14.3 shows the pattern of diagnosis of any disease. All diseases have a preclinical stage and also an early clinical stage. Breast cancer found early has a better overall outcome than breast disease found late and it is to this end that screening for breast cancer is directed.

WHAT IS SCREENING?

Screening is the examination of symptom-free individuals in an attempt to find predictors of disease or early disease. To be in any way effective, screening must be for conditions that are serious and/or commonly encountered.

The screening tests must be *simple* and easily used, if necessary by specially trained non-medical personnel; and *acceptable* and *not harmful* to the patient. There must also be a *treatment* that is both available and acceptable to the patient.

Some well known examples will help to explain these features of screening. It would obviously be inappropriate to screen for mumps. This disease, although very commonly encountered, is not serious and there is no known treatment for it. The metabolic defect leading to phenylketonuria is very rare, but its effects are extremely severe. Screening is simple and accurate and treatment is acceptable and very effective. Screening for fetal abnormality in mothers of high risk is now a practical consideration, but it is of little value if the woman will not accept termination of pregnancy as a treatment if an abnormality is demonstrated. Lastly, even if a screening test could be devised for Huntington's chorea, it would be useless, apart from allowing genetic counselling, until and unless a treatment for this disease were found.

From these examples it can be seen that breast cancer fits in well with such a general concept of screening. It is certainly both serious and common enough.

SCREENING TECHNIQUES

Clinical Examination by Trained Screeners

A vital question is who should screen? For too long screening has been confined to members of the medical profession. Doctors are trained at present to treat disease and although they are becoming increasingly aware of the value of health maintenance, clinical screening for breast disease is a repetitive and medically undemanding exercise and several studies have shown that nurses are as good as doctors in this field. A recent study of screening for breast cancer comes from Manchester. A medical team, comprising surgeons and radiologists, detected 99% of cancers in 240 cases and a 'non-medical' team, nurses and radiographers, detected 98% of cases. Thus properly trained staff, either doctors or nurses, may be used in screening for breast cancer. Neither a medical nor a nursing qualification automatically makes a professionally competent screener but the technique is readily learned (Fig. 14.4).

Self Examination

One of the most important parts of the screening remit is to teach the woman to examine herself on a regular basis.

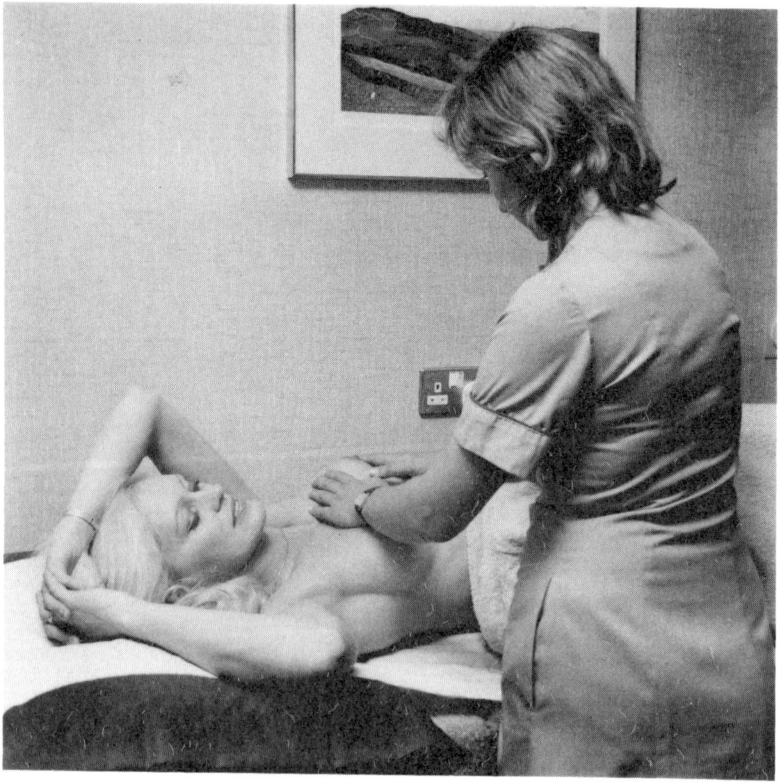

Fig. 14.4. A screening sister performing a clinical examination of the breasts.

Breast cancer is not a single disease; it has many histological variations, nor does it present in an orderly way. The pre-clinical stage of the disease may exist for years, or only weeks. It is not practical for a woman to be examined by a health care professional more frequently than once a year, so she must learn to examine herself exactly in the same way as the screener examines her. A widely recommended breast self-examination technique is shown in Fig. 14.5. Nurses should be able not only to carry out the examination on themselves but also to encourage others to undertake it and to teach them the necessary technique.

Breasts may vary throughout the menstrual cycle so that self examination should always be carried out on the last day of the menstrual period or on the first day of every calendar month in the woman who no longer has periods.

Clinical examination is designed to discover the following significant features.

1. *A lump in the breast*. Only one in every ten lumps in the breast is a cancer—far more common are cysts and fibroadenomata—but no one, not even the most experienced surgeon, can be 100% sure which lumps are which without further tests.

2. *Dimpling of the skin*. This is due to scarring contraction of the ligaments of Astley Cooper, the suspensory fibrous bands which keep the breasts outstanding on the chest wall. The scarring is caused by reaction to the cancer process and skin dimpling or the pulling in of a part of the breast tissue on movement may be the first sign of a breast cancer.

3. *Nipple inversion*. Although this may be a normal feature of the woman's breast and has been present all her life, any situation in which the nipple becomes inverted and cannot be everted must be investigated further.

4. *Nipple discharge*. This must be a freely exuded loss, not one obtained by squeezing. Especially if blood-stained it may predict an intraduct carcinoma or a simple benign papilloma of one of the milk ducts. Further investigation is mandatory.

5. *Eczematous patches* on the nipple, occurring in middle-aged women, may be due to a skin cancer which affects the breasts, Paget's disease of the nipple. Biopsy is indicated.

6. *Lymph gland enlargement*. The first sign of breast cancer (and more rarely of other types of cancer) may be enlarged regional lymph glands

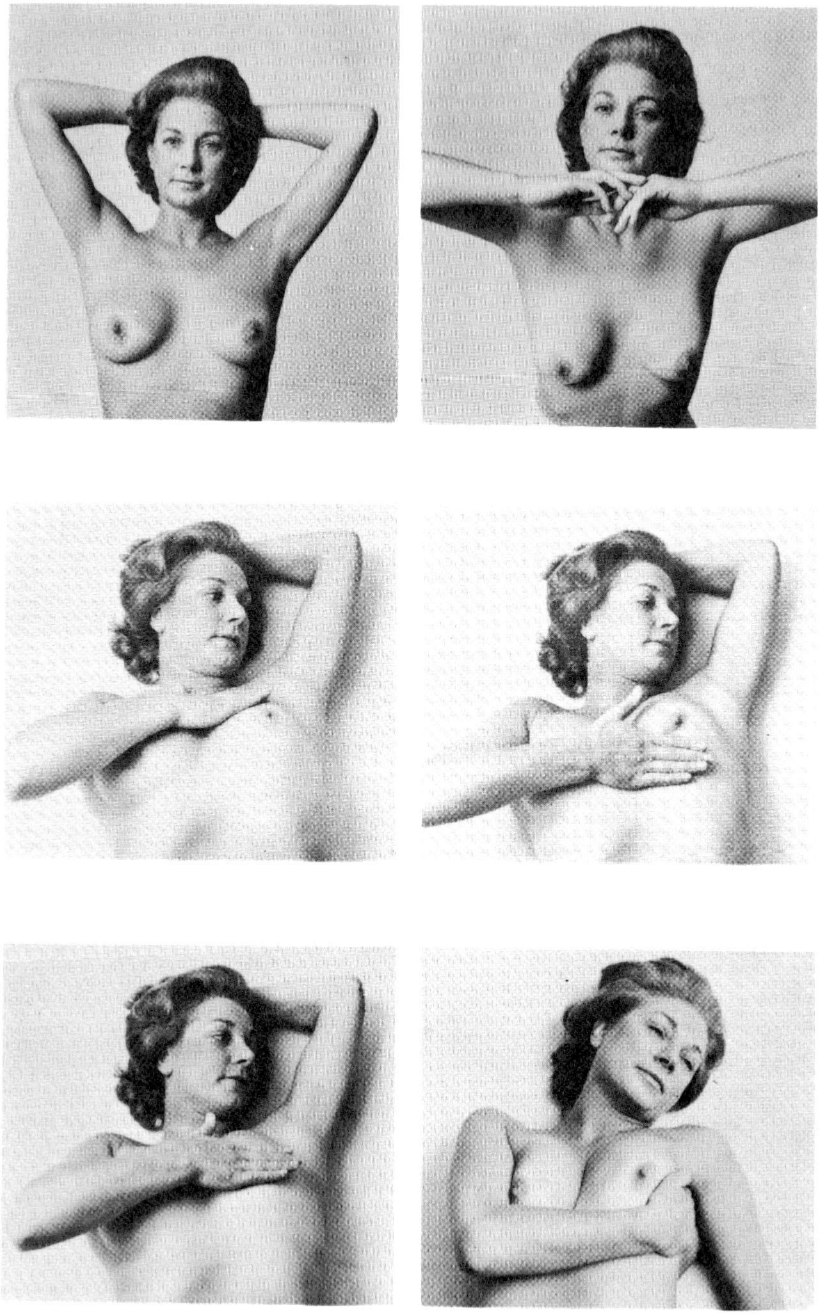

Fig. 14.5. The technique of breast self-examination. (*By kind permission of BUPA*)

A, Sit in front of a mirror stripped to the waist. Be sure you are sitting up straight. Look at your breasts carefully.

B, Is there any inequality between the size of your breasts? Has one breast recently become lower than the other?

C, Now look at the nipple area. Has one nipple become turned in? Is there any discharge? Always inspect the inside of your bra for signs of a discharge. *Do not* squeeze the nipple or areola.

D, Now look at the skin of the breasts. Is there any puckering or dimpling? Is there any rash or change in skin texture? You may have to lift the breasts to see the under-surface.

E, Raise your hands above your head and concentrate on the 'handle' area. Is there now any swelling or skin puckering?

F, Lean forward and examine each breast in turn. Is there any unusual change in outline, any puckering or dimpling of the skin or any retraction of the nipple?

G, Lie down in a relaxed and comfortable position. You may find it convenient to carry out this part of the examination with a soapy hand while having a bath.

H, First examine the left breast with the right hand. Use the front part of the flat of the hand, keeping the fingers together. It is important to learn how hard to press when examining the breasts; too hard will dull the sensation and too soft will not allow you to feel deeply enough. Never pinch the breast; if you do you may feel lumps even in a normal breast.

I, Slide your hand over the breast, above the nipple, starting at the armpit and moving across to the centre of the body, pressing in to feel for lumps.

J, Repeat this action passing the hand from the outside inwards below the nipple.

K, Finally slide your hand across the nipple, making sure you have felt all parts of the breast.

L, Feel for lumps along the border of the pectoral muscles and in the armpits.

M, Now carry out items H-L with the left hand on the right breast.

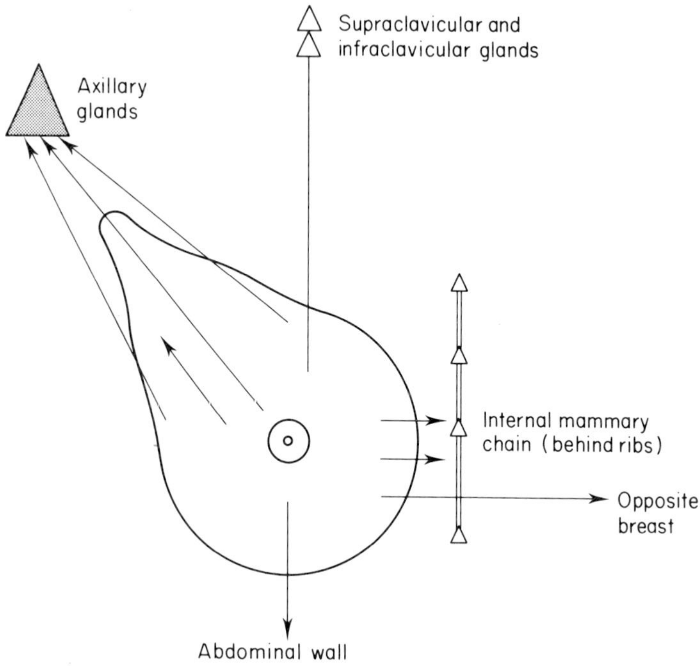

Fig. 14.6. The lymphatic drainage of the breast.

(Fig. 14.6). The internal mammary chain cannot be felt and therefore the supraclavicular and axillary glands are the clinically important groups (Fig. 14.6). There are many causes of enlarged glands, the most common being infection. An enlarged gland must be observed and if it does not get smaller over four to five weeks, biopsy may be indicated.

Mammography

X-ray examination of the breast using soft tissue X-rays has been available for over 20 years. The most important early study of this technique in screening was set up by the Health Insurance Plan (HIP) of New York in 1963. Two groups of women aged 40 to 64, each numbering 31 000, were identified. One group was invited to attend for four annual screening examinations. The other group was used as a control. Only 66% of the women invited to attend the screening did so, and only 39% attended for all four examinations. After seven years

Table 14.2. Skin Absorbed Dose on Screening Mammography

Year	*Dose to each breast* (rads)
1	0.4 (two views)
2	0.2 (one view)
3	0.2 (one view)
4	0.2 (one view)
Total	1

follow-up, the number of breast cancers in each group was about the same, but the survival rates were much better in women whose cancers were detected at screening and best of all in those whose disease was only detectable by mammography (Table 14.2).

If mammography is omitted from a screening programme, 25–33% of all cancers will be missed. In the HIP study 44 out of 132, (33%) of the cancers detected at screening were found only by mammography. In the Breast Cancer Detection Demonstration Project (BCDDP), set up in America after the original HIP study, 44% of cancers were found by mammography alone. The BUPA Medical Centre has a comparable experience of some 25% of cancers found on mammography alone.

However, one of the premises of screening is that the techniques used to detect the disease must be harmless to the patient. X-ray examination obviously exposes normal tissues to X-rays and it is important to discover if this type of screening has any dangers. It is known that women exposed to radiation at the A-bomb explosions at Hiroshima and Nagasaki, between the ages of 10 and 29 have an increased experience of breast cancer: however, women aged 30 to 49 at that time appear not to be at significantly increased risk. Women exposed to repeated fluoroscopies when undergoing treatment for tuberculosis have an increased risk of cancer of the breast when the excess radiation takes place before the age of 30. X-rays were formerly used in the treatment of chronic mastitis and women often received one or more hundred rads, even up to 1000 rads during treatment: they have an increased incidence of breast cancer.

Modern techniques of radiation have reduced the absorbed skin dose to 0.2 rads or less per examination at screening mammography and this level of radiation exposure is entirely acceptable, allowing for the pick-up rate of early stage disease which such an examination can give.

At the BUPA Medical Centre a two-shot screening technique is now

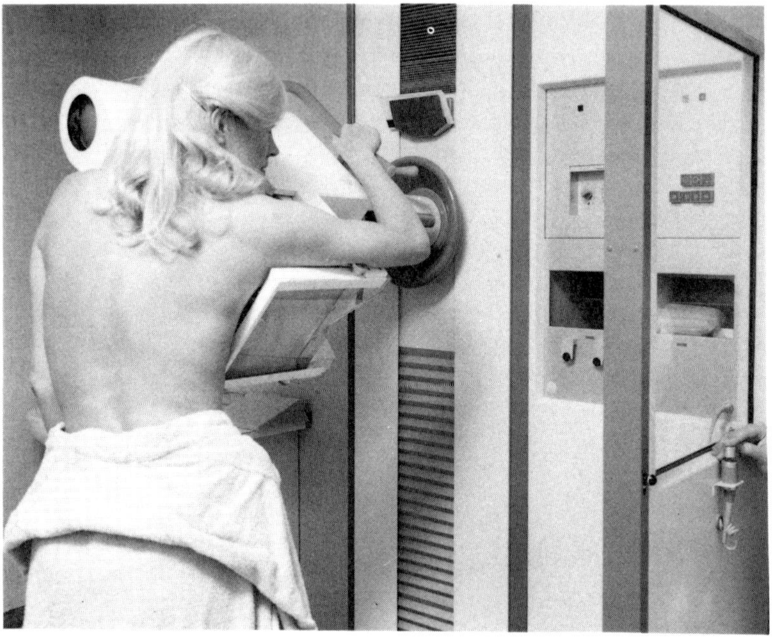

Fig. 14.7. Soft X-ray mammography of the breasts (oblique view).

used at the initial visit, craniocaudal and oblique views, and thereafter at every visit only an oblique view (Fig. 14.7) is taken of the breast tissue. Thus each woman will receive a skin dose of only 1 rad to each breast over four years initially and every five years thereafter.

The National Cancer Institute has suggested that for each rad of radiation received by the breast, the increased risk of breast cancer may be six extra cases per million women per year, starting after a latent period of ten years. During each year in England and Wales some 700 new cases of cancer of the breast are notified for each million women. There is obviously a 'swings and roundabouts' situation which has to be carefully evaluated. At present mammography should be restricted in asymptomatic women to those:

1. With a strong family history of breast cancer.
2. Who have undergone previous surgery to the breasts.
3. Who have had a previous breast cancer.
4. In the older age groups.

In the HIP study no improvement in mortality survival rate was found

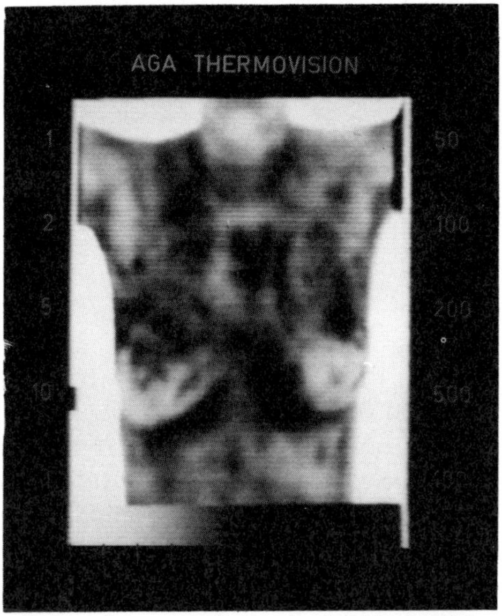

Fig. 14.8. A thermogram from a patient who had herself detected a nodule in the left breast. There is increased thermal activity on the medial side of the left breast. The mammogram suggested a benign lesion but biopsy revealed an early carcinoma.

in women under the age of 50, possibly because mammographic techniques were not as good as they are now. Breast cancer is the largest single cause of death in women aged 35–54 and if preclinical malignant disease is being looked for, it is reasonable to bring down the screening age for mammography to 35 years. Symptomatic women clearly pose a different problem and all should have mammography as an aid to diagnosis.

Thermography

This technique uses differences in temperature to identify an abnormal area of breast tissue.

Thermography involves the patient in very little discomfort. She has to sit and cool down in a room with a controlled temperature and an infra-red picture of the heat patterns of her breasts is taken (Fig. 14.8). There is no risk at all in this procedure. Unfortunately the technique is not very specific in identifying abnormal tissue. In the BCDDP Study less than half (41%) of the women with breast cancer had abnormal thermograms. Thermograms were also normal in 66% of the cancers which were clinically negative and mammographically positive. At the Medical Centre thermography is used as a screening procedure for asymptomatic women under the age of 35 years with no high-risk factors. Breast cancer is less common in the younger woman, but cases do occur. Therefore proper screening techniques and vigilance are always necessary.

Ultrasonography

The use of ultrasound in the screening of normal women for breast disease is restricted to a few research centres at present and it is proving an interesting field of development. The advantage of a non-invasive approach is very attractive, but definition is not always good and the actual technique of taking breast ultrasound recordings is cumbersome.

Blood Tests

Although many factors that are raised in the presence of malignant disease have been isolated, e.g. carcinoembryonic antigen, α-feto-protein, γ-glutamyl transaminase, there is no specific tumour marker in breast cancer that can be used reliably as a predictor, although serial blood tests in proved cases of breast cancer are very important indicators in monitoring the progress of the disease.

EVALUATION OF SCREENING

In any programme of screening it is obviously of paramount importance that the screening test does in fact identify the disease in the majority of cases and gives few false-negative readings. A measure of false-

Table 14.3. Sensitivity of Breast Cancer Screening

	Screening test		
Diagnosis Positive	Positive	Negative	Total
85% sensitivity	43	7	50
90% sensitivity	45	5	50

negative results in a screening test is called the sensitivity of the test (Table 14.3). Thus, if clinical examination finds 60 out of a possible 100 cases of breast cancer, it has a sensitivity of 60%. The sensitivity of clinical examination as a breast cancer screening technique will be affected by many subjective variables.

1. The thoroughness of the examination.
2. The skill of the screener.
3. The texture of the breasts.

Thus an inexperienced screener may pick up a high percentage of cases in 'easy' breasts, those that are small and of uniform texture, but it will require a very skilled person to pick up small lumps in big pendulous breasts. This example is given to underline the fact that sensitivity is not an absolute concept. The same restrictions apply to mammography. Radiographers have to learn the technique of taking the films in the best possible way. Radiologists have to become very skilled at interpreting the shadows of the normal breast. There is observer error in reading mammography films. However, even with the value of hindsight, not all cancers show on X-ray. Less than 10% of all breast cancers are clinically positive and mammographically negative, whilst in some 25–35% of cases the reverse is true. The sensitivity for clinical examination alone varies between 40% and 60% and for mammography alone sensitivity is at least as good as and usually better than that. In Sweden claims have been made for 98% sensitivity by mammography alone, without any clinical examination, but such figures have not been produced elsewhere.

In combination, clinical examination and mammography will detect 85–95% of all cancers. This means that if a population of 10 000 asymptomatic women is examined at a given screening, the pick-up rate will be of the order of four or five cases per 1000 women.

The patients in whom the diagnosis is said to be positive, and yet no abnormality was found on screening, are those in whom a breast cancer is detected within one year of a negative screening. This may be due to screening error, practical difficulties with nodular, dense breasts which are difficult to examine or a rapidly growing cancer, which was just not present at screening. 100% sensitivity is certainly impossible to achieve and a patient needs to be aware of this.

Next, and equally important in the evaluation of screening techniques, is the ability of the test to give true-negative results. This is the specificity of the test (Table 14.4). Specificity is closely related to the number of the false-positive results. False-positives are the finding of clinical lumps which prove on further examination not to be cancer and mammographic changes which are significant enough to arouse suspicion and warrant further investigation but which prove to be negative at final diagnosis.

In the screening situation every abnormality must be investigated and the false-positive rate is important in terms of patient anxiety and its implications for the back-up services of hospitals and their staffs.

Table 14.4. Specificity of Breast Cancer Screening

	Screening Test		
Diagnosis	Positive	Negative	Total
Positive	43	7	50
Negative	1000	8950	9950
Total	1043	8957	10 000

Sensitivity 85%; Specificity 90%.

The specificity of the test is calculated by the following sample equation which again assumes a group of 10 000 women:

$$\frac{\text{True negatives at screening}}{\text{Total negatives at diagnosis}} = \frac{8950}{9950} \times 100 = 90\%$$

From this example 1043 women will be picked out by screening for further examination, a rate of 10.4% and this number of further investigations will confirm the diagnosis in just 43 women, just over 4% of the total or 1 in every 24 positive screening tests.

However, as with false-negative rates, the false-positive rates will be affected by observer variables, both clinical and radiological. Specificity can be greatly improved with experience. Getting the balance right between ignoring potentially serious changes and creating anxiety over probable minor changes is the tightrope the screening unit must travel. Biopsy rates vary between 5% and 20% in reported series and with positive findings in those patients subjected to biopsy within the same range of 5–20%.

Positive cases identified by screening can now be diagnosed more simply than before. *Fine needle biopsy* of the breast can be undertaken in the surgery or out-patient department so that formal 'cutting' surgery is not needed to diagnose a large number of such cases. Lumps due to cyst formation in the breast can be simply treated by needle aspiration and, provided that a follow-up visit is always arranged and the cystic fluid is sent for cytological evaluation, the patient should not be subjected to any surgery. Even with these advances, however, the Edinburgh Breast Group estimate that each case of confirmed carcinoma of the breast found by their screening programme cost £6000 to diagnose—a figure which cannot be considered to be cheap. This figure is obtained by taking the whole cost of the screening programme, staff, equipment, cost of biopsy etc. and dividing it by the number of positive cases.

Before going further with the evaluation of the screening procedure, the terminology must be explained to avoid confusion. Earlier it was stated that one in every 17 women would develop breast cancer, i.e. 60 per 1000 women, yet the prevalence at a given moment in time in an individual woman's life, is between three and five per 1000 women. Prevalence relates to a positive finding at any first time examination in symptom-free women. If these women continue to have annual examinations, any positive findings at subsequent examinations express the incidence of the disease, i.e. the number of new cases that occur each year in a given population. Prevalence figures can only be related to a finite group of symptom-free women and these, in epidemiological terms, can be identified by using the registers of insurance companies, general practitioners lists etc.

The self-referral well woman clinic does not have this clientele. Women attend for breast examination for a variety of reasons, many of which may place them in the high-risk groups. Thus a self-referral well woman clinic can only refer to a pick-up rate of the disease found among women presenting for screening. These rates are invariably higher than the prevalence figures for a proscribed population. In the New York HIP study a true prevalence of 2.73 cancers per 1000 women was found. By restricting the screening to maximum risk women, a pick-up rate of 23 cases per 1000 has been found by Agnes Stark in Newcastle. These variables present pitfalls for the unwary when attempting to evaluate results.

SURVIVAL AND BREAST CANCER SCREENING

Is early identification of breast cancer of any value to the woman? Unfortunately breast cancer is not a single disease and the malignant cells do not have a common behaviour or even a common tissue of origin. Some women survive with untreated breast cancer for ten, fifteen and a few even for twenty years. Others die of their disease very rapidly in spite of every advantage in treatment. The only measures of improvement in the treatment of a disease such as breast cancer that can be used are:

1. Survival times, i.e. those women who are still alive so many years after treatment.
2. Disease-free intervals. The time between treatment of the original disease and its recurrence.

Survival times are better for women whose disease was found by screening, but is this improved survival with early diagnosis brought about only because the disease was found a year or so earlier in its natural clinical course and that the true outcome is no better? (refer to Fig. 14.3 which shows the natural history of the disease). This bias in survival is referred to as the lead time. Antagonists of screening claim that increased survival is solely an expression of lead time gained. However this is not the only answer. In the figures from New York shown in Table 14.5, every woman who was detected by screening has

Table 14.5. Case Fatality at Seven Years* in the HIP Study New York

Group		*No. of cancers*	*Dead (%)*
Study †	All cancers	299	35.2
	Detected by screening	132	21.3
	Detected by Mammography alone	44	9.2
Control		285	46.7

* 1 year lead time has been deducted for cases detected by screening.
† One-third of the study failed to accept any screening.

had a year deducted from her survival time to allow for lead time bias. Even with this adjustment, only 9% of women in whom disease was detected by mammography alone were dead after seven years (in real time the 91% had all survived in fact for eight years) and all the study group (only two-thirds of whom accepted screening anyway) had better survival times than the control group.

Another sort of discrepancy favouring improved survival for screened women may be the very aggression (or lack of it) of their particular breast cancer. If a cancer has a slow growth rate it will have

more chance of being picked up at a single screening event, because of the greater length of time of its preclinical stage, than would a very rapidly growing tumour. Thus it can be postulated that cancers identified by screening are on the whole less aggressive than cancers presenting in the general population. This bias is called length bias. The only way such biases can be finally evaluated is by very long-term studies. In the UK such a study has now been started and will run for seven years. Eight populations have been indentified with as good a social balance as possible. In two centres the women selected will be screened by clinical examination and mammography: in two centres self-examination is the only screening technique and four centres are to be used to monitor the death rate from breast cancer (Table 14.6).

Table 14.6. DHSS Breast Cancer Screening Project for Women aged 45–64

Modality	*Centre*	*Population*
Clinical examination with mammography	Edinburgh	25 000
	Guildford	23 000
Breast self-examination	Nottingham	35 000
	Huddersfield	30 000
Routine clinical care	Oxford	40 000
	Stoke on Trent	40 000
	Southmeads	30 000
	Dundee	23 000

The study is a very long-term one and the final overall results will not be apparent for some 15–20 years.

In the short term, however, many things can be done. An awareness in health care professionals of the magnitude of the problem of breast cancer must be created. Every woman, certainly if aged 35 or over, who presents herself with whatever problem should, within the realms of reason, have a regular breast examination. This examination is particularly appropriate to the woman presenting in the gynaecology clinic but is not always carried out. A simple description of self-examination and how to apply it should be available in all gynaecological wards. The Health Education Council publish an excellent leaflet on this which is available free of charge throughout the National Health Service and should be very acceptable to the patient if presented with her discharge letter on leaving the ward.

This chapter has attempted to show the scope of screening for breast cancer, the pitfalls and the problems. It is the responsibility of all health care professionals to be convinced of the value of whatever approach they apply to the management of their women patients and to use this approach consistently and thoroughly throughout their clinical work.

Acknowledgements

I wish to thank BUPA Health Promotion Centre for permission to use the self-examination format from their leaflet *The Facts about Breasts and the Importance of Breast Checks.*

Bibliography

Faulder, C. (1979) *Breast Cancer: A Guide to its Early Detection and Treatment*. London: Pan Books.

Forrest, A.P.M. (1980) Screening for breast cancer. *Br. J. Hosp. Med., 23*, 1.

George, W.D. (1980) Role of non-medical staff in screening for breast cancer. *Br. med. J., 1,* 147.

Health Education Council. *Breast Self-Examination,* CC2. London: Health Education Council.

Lester, R.G. (1977) Risks versus benefits in mammography. *Radiology, 124*, 1.

Shapiro, S. (1977) Evidence on screening for breast cancer from a randomised trial. *Cancer, 39*, 2772.

Stoll, B. (1976) *Risk Factors in Breast Cancer*. London: Heinemann Medical.

15. Psychosexual Counselling

J. Dominian

The last hundred years have seen an unprecedented increase in knowledge of sexual behaviour. The genius of Sigmund Freud directed attention to an inner world of instincts which were hitherto subjects of taboo, fear and restriction. Freud went as far as to hypothesise that our personality develops on the basis of the transformation of the sexual and aggressive instincts which are present in the baby from the time of birth. There are still proponents of this view, whilst many others have expanded the theory of human development to other non-sexual factors. Whatever the ultimate answer, there is no going back to the pre-Freudian period. The importance of human sexuality has come to stay.

In the last 30 years the original thinking of Freud has been further advanced by two groups of workers headed by Kinsey (Kinsey et al. 1948, 1953) who produced two massive volumes on male and female sexuality and Masters and Johnson (1966, 1970) who have initiated a new therapeutic era for sexual problems. Their approach and techniques are widely used all over the world.

These scientific developments have coincided with an upsurge of interest on the part of society for greater sexual realization and, indeed, the expectations have outstripped professional resources. More and more couples are seeking relief from sexual difficulties which would have been accepted as fate or the will of God a generation or two ago.

Another reason why there is such a growing interest in sexual fulfilment is the widespread presence of contraception. The result is that couples have their desired family when they wish it and the overwhelming majority of sexual activity is no longer consciously directed towards procreation. The separation of coitus from procreation, which has been the link for thousands of years, has brought into prominence the qualitative aspects of intercourse. Sexual satisfaction is sought as a way of experiencing love in a deeper and more complete way.

SEXUAL INTERCOURSE

The various studies mentioned have elucidated the sequence of events in the course of coitus for men and women. For both sexes the hormone which plays a crucial part in sexual excitation and enhances sexual desire is testosterone. In addition to the presence of this hormone, both sexes have higher and lower centres in the brain and the cord which organize sexual activity.

The Male Role

The male contribution to sexual intercourse begins with sexual arousal. Such arousal is an amalgamation of uniquely personal pictures, fantasies, feelings and images, usually for a person of the opposite sex whose bodily configuration is the object of attraction enhanced by nudity, smell and touch. This arousal leads to erection of the penis, erection being essentially a vasocongestive action. The penis is made up of the glans, the shaft and the base and consists of three cylinders. The ventral cylinder, the corpus spongiosium, contains the urethra which transports both urine and semen: at the tip of it there is the glans and at its base it ends in powerful muscles. Ejaculation is brought about by the action of these muscles which eject the semen. On the dorsal side there are the corpora cavernosa which are made of specialized blood compartments which are filled up at the time of arousal and produce the stiff penis. Once the erection is attained it can be held for a long period without ejaculation. During this period the man usually participates in love play with his partner until she is ready for entry. Once entry takes place normal thrusting movements of the penis in the vagina gradually increase sexual pleasure until the point is reached when ejaculation takes place. There is evidence that autonomic nerve fibres (parasympathetic) from S_2, S_3 and S_4 are responsible for the erection part and centres in the lumbar region of a sympathetic variety control ejaculation. While erection is often an involuntary action, ejaculation can be controlled until the last second, indeed until what Masters and Johnson call 'ejaculatory inevitability'. This means, in practice, that the man can control his orgasm to fit in with his wife's state of excitement and, of course, the awareness that ejaculation is about to occur has been used as a method of birth control in 'coitus interruptus' in which the man withdraws the penis just before ejaculation, a rather risky and unsatisfactory method of birth control. Finally, the orgasm will be triggered off. It consists of the ejaculation of sperm in a series of involuntary rhythmic contractions and is accompanied by intense pleasure.

It can be seen from this description that the main difficulties in the man are lack of sexual desire, failure to produce an erection (impotence), failure to maintain the erection coupled with rapid ejaculation (premature ejaculation) and absence of ejaculation. By far the most common male difficulties are premature ejaculation and impotence. Whilst these are the sexual malfunctioning syndromes, the commonest complaint of women is the inability of their men to make love in such a way that they feel wanted, appreciated, aroused tenderly and regarded as women and not as sexual objects.

The Female Role

The woman's pattern of sexual intercourse leading to orgasm begins, as with the man, in sexual arousal. There has been controversy about the nature of experience which produces sexual arousal in women. There are women who are easily aroused and others who take a long time. Our knowledge of the specific factors that excite women is limited. It is suggested, however, that, unlike men, sexual arousal for women has a very personal component. Women who fail to respond to one man will do so easily to another who arouses intense interest. Thus intercourse for women is a highly personal affair. While the nature of woman's anatomy makes it possible for her to have coitus with any man, her anatomical involvement does not reflect an equivalent emotional feeling. A woman can have intercourse and be totally cut off from any feeling or pleasurable reaction.

Given that intercourse is to occur with a desired man, the available evidence suggests that the first phase of the encounter is foreplay which emphasizes touch. Gentle caressing, kissing and hugging are usual preliminaries. At this stage the woman indicates to her man what parts of her anatomy are particularly sensitive to sexual arousal and the man directs his attention to the breasts, the buttocks and any other part of the anatomy which has an erotic significance. This foreplay is gradually focussed on the clitoris which is highly sensitive to touch, thus accelerating the pleasure and preparing the way for intercourse.

During foreplay changes are occurring in the genitalia which prepare the vagina for intercourse. The most specific change is the engorgement of the genitals and pelvic area. Thus the labia, the bulbs of the vestibule and the outward third of the vagina all become engorged with blood. They now become the orgasmic platform which is ready to receive the penis. Inside the vagina the walls secrete a fluid which lubricates the inner walls and thus the vagina is not only enlarged to receive the penis but is suitably lubricated. This is the wetness that women feel when they are aroused. When sexual intercourse is associated with difficulties, there may be no lubrication or no distension of the vagina and surrounding tissues, or these may be present but the woman feels absolutely nothing.

If intercourse is proceeding satisfactorily, the foreplay leads to entry of the penis into the vagina which is exquisitely prepared to surround it, hold it tightly and thus subject it to the presence of a perfect fit and the friction of the rubbing of the organ against the walls of the vagina. The combination of these two pressures excites the clitoris which is generally recognized as being the vital organ which generates and transmits sexual pleasure leading to orgasm. For a very long time there was a controversy as to whether or not there were two distinct orgasms, a clitoral one and a vaginal one. Freud maintained that this was the case and that mature sexual response was the one in which the clitoris became less important and the vaginal sensations the principal site of pleasure. It is now appreciated that this dichotomy is false. The clitoris remains the centre of erotic excitation which is transmitted to the surrounding tissues and the vagina is part of this general excitation, in particular the outer third where women may locate local pleasure. There is in fact only one orgasm and the clitoris plays a crucial part in arousing it.

The orgasm is the final peak of sexual arousal, consisting of a series of reflex rhythmic contractions of the muscles and tissues round the vagina and also the pelvic muscles. The rhythmic contractions occur at 0.8 second intervals and are accompanied by intense pleasure locally with a general feeling of excitement and pleasure spreading through the body.

There are both similarities and differences between the male and female orgasms. The former also consists of rhythmic expulsive movements accompanied by the ejection of semen and other fluids but, once this has occurred, there is a refractory period. This is not so with women who can have repeated orgasms one after another without intervals between them. The ideal, of course, is for both man and woman to reach their orgasm simultaneously, but this does not always happen and yet the pleasure and satisfaction need not be diminished.

Orgastic difficulties in women include total lack of response; adequate lubrication but no orgastic response; partial response in which excitation is aroused but does not peak to orgasm (these responses can be primary (always there) or secondary (later development)); and vaginismus.

Before discussing the individual male and female sexual dysfunctions, something needs to be said about psycholgocial background difficulties.

BACKGROUND PROBLEMS

Some people grow in a home atmosphere in which they are subjected to distorted sexual instruction or its absence, adverse relationships with parents and individual traumas. These factors need to be appreciated to ensure that specific sexual therapy is not frustrated by persistence of background factors.

The classical formulation of sexual growth is that proposed by Freud. According to orthodox Freudian theory, the young boy is attracted sexually by mother. There is a wish to possess her sexually which is prohibited by the fear of arousing father's anger and the possibility of castration (loss of penis). In these circumstances, the boy gives up the attraction towards mother and identifies with the male role of father. This is known as the resolution of the Oedipus complex. The absence of its resolution is supposed to be related to neurotic and sexual problems. Similarly the girl is attached sexually to her father and she too has to abandon this desire and return to identify with mother. This orthodox psychoanalytic formulation has some application but there are alternative explanations for the girl's sexual difficulties.

Thus a girl may experience a father who is frequently absent and with whom there is an absolute minimum of involvement. Such a woman grows up without a relaxed and easy intimacy with men. Her father may be an undemonstrative man and she emerges from childhood without the feeling of secure physical proximity. On the one hand she may not remember being cuddled by him or sitting on his knees or being played with. Thus the relationship with her father is a distant one and, when she comes to form her second vital relationship with a man, she may feel uncomfortable with affectionate display on his part. On the other hand such a father may be idealized; that is to say invested with loving qualities which in fact were not really present. In her relationship with men, such a woman may seek someone she thinks highly of but cannot get close to. Further complications of idealization is the feeling that father was perfect and no man can ever reach his standards.

Girls also experience negative relationships with their fathers who may be authoritarian, strict, demanding of high standards, disciplinarian and make no demonstration of affection. As women they may find it difficult to trust men and feel safe with them. In particular such a woman may marry someone like her father and then find that she increasingly detests the rigid ways of her husband. Not only may she resent being continuously instructed on how to do things, but may gradually feel that she is being treated like a child who is totally dependent on her husband. Increasing resentment in such a situation may be transferred to a sexual life which bears the brunt of the confrontation.

The girl's bond with her mother is also important. The relationship may be very close and the grown-up woman finds it difficult to separate from her and, even after marriage, continues to make her the principal figure of reference, bypassing her husband when she has to discuss, evaluate and make judgements. A hostile relationship with her mother may make the grown-up woman find it difficult to accept her feminine role. In either case, if the mother had a hostile and rejecting attitude to men and sex, she may convey this to her daughter who sees men as being incapable of affection and simply wanting only one thing from a woman without any further concern for her.

As far as the man is concerned, he may come from a household where mother was dominant and father hardly present or ineffectively so. Such a man may be so identified with his mother that he may develop homosexual tendencies, be passive in his relationship with women or desire strong, dominating partners to continue the role of the influential mother. Such a husband may find it difficult to see his wife as a sexual person and instead continue to treat her as a mother substitute. It can be easily imagined that sexual difficulties can arise in this pattern of marriage when in effect there is an unresolved Oedipus situation.

The man who has a poor or distant relationship with his mother may also find it difficult to relate to women. He may find it difficult to get close emotionally, trust and believe that women can love. He seeks love and finds it very difficult to see, register or accept it.

In general, men and women who emerge from childhood without feeling confident about their sexual identity or loveable as persons find it difficult to form close relationships because they fear that, if someone were to get to know them intimately, they would be bound to find them unsatisfactory and reject them. Since they did not feel acceptable as children, they remain dubious as to whether or not they are acceptable as spouses. In these families, individual children may have felt ignored or rejected in preference to their sisters or brothers who were the favourites of the parents or were more talented. A sense of inferiority *vis à vis* the siblings may persist in adult life and make relationships difficult.

Independently of the quality of relationship between parents and children, the home may have given distorted or no sexual instruction. The ideal sexual education is to be found in a home where children see affection demonstrated between parents and therefore learn that sexual activity belongs specifically to couples who love one another. If the atmosphere of love is clearly present, then children can be gradually instructed in the make-up of their bodies, the biology of procreation and the psychology of sexual behaviour. Households vary from a conspiracy of silence where nothing is said and the secondary sexual characteristics such as menstruation are treated casually, through limited and muddled teaching to outright excellence or distortion. There are still many men and women who come from homes where little has been said and sexual instruction has been received from school or what is said has been frightening, surrounded by taboos and prohibitions. Sexual pleasure in any form can be condemned, masturbation considered damaging and wrong, the way of getting pregnant totally misinstructed so the girl finds herself in adulthood with little knowledge and even less understanding of or enthusiasm for sex. Some of these women remain inhibited in their sexual activity and find it very difficult to abandon themselves in the height of the orgasm. They have been taught to keep a tight control over sexual pleasure which is dangerous or sinful and later on they do not find it easy to relax and let go at the appropriate time. Indeed, at the extreme end of this spectrum are to be found women who still believe that sex is only for procreation, outside of which it becomes forbidden licence.

Beyond the atmosphere of the home and school, men and women experience individual traumas which may influence their sexual attitudes. Girls may have been subjected to sexual play by older relatives, sexually assaulted or even raped. Each one of these experiences leaves painful memories but the key to subsequent damage is the way such traumas were handled. If the event was accompanied by an extensive, prolonged analysis and preoccupation, then it is likely to lead to much more enduring damage than a swift exploration and minimal aftermath. Boys can also be subjected to juvenile sexual adventure by elders or other boys and the same applies to them. The least damage is associated with the softest and most reassuring handling. Apart from such sexual episodes, children can be subjected to repeated operations, injections, enemas and other treatments which sensitize the genital area and may even form the background of sexual variations.

Thus, in psychosexual counselling, not only is there a need to offer specific help for individual sexual difficulties but also to make sure that past events or relationships do not adversely impinge on sexual activity. If an adverse relationship does exist, then it is important to combine both specific sexual therapy and a dynamic discussion of the way past events are influencing the present. Such combination maximizes the beneficial effects from therapeutic intervention.

A general discussion which focusses on such past events and relationships may be enough to clarify the nature of the problem. Often, however, more work needs to be done with specific treatment for individual sexual difficulties.

MALE SEXUAL DYSFUNCTION

Premature Ejaculation

It is generally acknowledged that premature ejaculation is one of the most common of the male sexual dysfunctions. It is characterized by loss of control over the ejaculating reflex. Usually a man knows when ejaculation is about to take place and can control the reflex, which allows ejaculation to happen or postpones it. This capacity to control is lost and the main therapeutic aim is to regain it. The clinical feature which stands out is the speed with which ejaculation is reached. The man may reach his climax simply by seeing his wife undressing or by the slightest erotic touch on her part, on entry into the vagina or after just a few penile thrusts. The consequences of premature ejaculation are that the man's sexual arousal is short-lived, pleasure is restricted and the capacity to arouse and satisfy the woman suffers a great deal.

Premature ejaculation is associated with anxiety and occurs in young men, sometimes from the very beginning of their sexual activity and occasionally later in life associated with secondary impotence. The physical reasons for premature ejaculation are few and consist of sudden or gradual damage to nerve pathways from the brain, the spinal cord or peripheral nerves. Degenerating neurological conditions are chiefly responsible for this particular pattern.

For a long time the treatment of premature ejaculation depended on reducing the arousability of the penile surface, distracting attention and having a second or even a third intercourse which would ultimately prolong the time of orgasm. Thus the wearing of condoms or anaesthetizing the penis, thinking of non-sexual subjects during intercourse and having repeated coitus would be recommended.

Nowadays these various methods have given way to one principle alone which is designed to assist the man to regain control over the ejaculating reflex. This is done as follows. The husband lies on the bed nude. His wife slides up to his side and takes hold of his penis. This is rubbed until the husband signals that he is about to ejaculate. The wife then does one of two things. She either stops rubbing until the ejaculating sensations cease or she exerts pressure just behind the tip of the penis in the circular rim. This is done by using the thumb underneath and two fingers on top. The fingers then squeeze the rim until the sensation of ejaculation subsides. This may coincide with a slight subsidence of the erection. After a brief interval the penis is rubbed again and the same procedure adopted. On each occasion the period of control by the man is extended a little more. After the third or fourth attempt the husband is allowed to reach his climax. This extravaginal exercise is repeated several nights until such time as the man can control his ejaculation as long as he wants.

The next phase is for the man to lie, once again on his back, be stimulated by his wife to an erection and then she adopts the superior position and gently descends on him, inserting the penis into her vagina. She begins to thrust gently until the husband is reaching his point of ejaculation when she ceases activity and either waits until the man's ejaculation feeling subsides or she disengages from her husband and applies pressure on the rim as before. When the man is in control again the penis is returned to the vagina and thrusting begins again. This is done three or four times and then the man climaxes. This phase is also repeated nightly or at frequent intervals until ejaculating control is restored and intercourse can last as long as it is desired.

The results claimed for this therapy are very good and it has the advantage of simplicity and ease. Since premature ejaculation is so common and so damaging to satisfactory intercourse, there is no reason nowadays for its remaining untreated.

Retarded Ejaculation

Premature ejaculation is a very common sexual dysfunction whilst retarded ejaculation is comparatively rare. The difficulty here is that the male reaches orgasm but cannot ejaculate semen, which reduces the pleasure component of intercourse and may affect fertilization. Such a man is often tense and tends to be a perfectionist with obsessional traits. He may be concerned about soiling his wife with the semen or feels forbidden to enjoy the ultimate in intercourse; in other words has difficulty in letting himself go.

This inhibition is treated by participation in a programme where intercourse is initially forbidden and the couple are advised to enjoy non-genital mutual erotic play. This gradually stimulates the level of sexual excitement and the husband may feel he can ejaculate either by self-masturbation or by his wife's masturbation of him. The aim of the therapy is to encourage ejaculation progressively nearer the vagina and then inside it.

Impotence

Impotence is the second most common male dysfunction. It takes three forms. There is primary impotence when the man's erectile dysfunction is there from the very beginning of sexual activity; he simply cannot raise an erection. This is a rare manifestation of the problem. Secondary impotence is the commonest and this implies that the man can normally attain an erection but fails on one or more occasions in between normal activity. The third form is associated with age and is a continuous and serious form with poor prognosis.

Since erection is the result of erotic excitement, intact nervous pathways and adequate hormonal functioning, the pathological causes are numerous. Impotence may occur as a result of psychological illness such as depression, which lowers both sexual drive and erectile function, tiredness, alcohol abuse, the therapeutic use of oestrogens, paralysis of parasympathetic nerves by drugs or permanent damage to them and diabetes (which may be undetected).

However, the heart of the problem of secondary impotence is the apprehension created by failure which then generates a good deal of anxiety the next time round regarding the likelihood of failure. If, in fact, intercourse is attempted again with the same failure result, then a vicious circle is established in which anxiety of failure is established as an anticipatory reflex which in turn impairs the erectile capacity of the penis. Treatment aims at breaking down this vicious circle.

The therapeutic programme consists initially of forbidding intercourse. During this period the couple are instructed simply to concentrate on giving each other pleasure. By concentrating on hugging, stroking, caressing, with the man under no obligation to have an erection, the anxiety of having to 'perform' recedes. The next step is for the wife to stimulate the penis to an erection. At this stage the man may be worrying whether he can retain it and he is instructed not to worry about this but to concentrate on experiencing pleasure. If the erection subsides, the wife rubs the penis again so that gradually the husband realizes that erection is possible. Finally, the husband lies on his back with his wife astride and she stimulates the penis to erection. Having positioned herself on top of her husband she lowers herself on his penis but with no thrusting permitted. When this step has been accomplished successfully the couple proceed to intercourse.

As with all sexual therapy there is discussion about any individual background problem, particularly the feeling of the husband that he is under pressure to 'perform'. The man may be subjected to questions from his wife: 'What's the matter with me?', 'Don't you love me?', 'Am I not attractive enough?' The wife's need for reassurance is discussed. She may need to feel wanted and intercourse is one powerful method of being pacified. Discussion between the couple and the therapist may bring out this urgent need for reassurance which may be dealt with by greater attention, better communication and demonstration of affection.

The third form of impotence is associated with age. Kinsey et al. (1948) were the first to show an increasing impotence with age: 6.7% of men in the sample were permanently impotent by 50. Sometimes this problem emerges in the 40s in men who have a low sexual drive throughout their life. Secondary impotence in the older man deserves the same treatment as for younger people. This, however, may be unsuccessful and the couple may have to live without intercourse. The wife may often find herself with a husband who shows no interest in her sexually. Her suspicions that there is another woman have to be assuaged. The couple need to be frank and open with each other. The husband can stimulate his wife manually or orally and give her extra affectionate attention.

FEMALE SEXUAL DYSFUNCTION

Clearly the ability of the woman to enjoy normal sexual pleasure peaking to orgasm depends on the husband's ability to perform competently, premature ejaculation and impotence being the main difficulties. There are, however, specific female sexual dysfunction problems.

Non-consummation

Non-consummation is one of the causes of infertility but far more important it is a major limitation to marital life. The typical pattern of non-consummation is found in a couple who, for religious or other reasons, refrain from intercourse before marriage. On the first night of the honeymoon excuses are made of tiredness. The next night the husband approaches his wife and finds that as soon as the penis comes near the vagina she tenses up and screams with pain or discomfort if there is attempted penetration of the hymen. This reaction of pain with the husband being pushed away is repeated as soon as the husband makes sexual appropaches. Gradually the attempts are given up and the couple live as brother and sister. The marriage continues on this basis until a family is wanted or there is pressure from relatives for grandchildren.

The treatment depends on the level of sexual maturity reached by the woman. There are wives who have developed physically but have not come to terms with their sexual parts. They cut themselves off from their genitals which have no erotic significance, which are indeed disliked. Such women needs prolonged therapy to integrate their sexual with their affectionate side.

The woman, however, who has matured to the point of accepting her sexuality and wants to have intercourse and is happy with her husband, can definitely be helped. Treatment consists of progressive relaxation during which she learns how to relax her whole body. When this is achieved, she is instructed to explore her genitals and identify the various relevant parts so that any fantasies are dispelled. She may then lubricate one of her fingers and gently insert it in the vagina, thus learning that pain is not inevitable. She can then move to using progressively larger dilators until she reaches a size which simulates the penis. The husband may be involved in the treatment and insert a dilator so that the wife can learn to feel the dilator inside her without controlling its entry. Finally intercourse is tried when the woman feels safe and relaxed with the dilator. The results of treatment are good.

Vaginismus

Vaginismus is closely related to non-consummation. It is due to an involuntary spasm of the muscles surrounding the vaginal entrance (Kaplan 1974) resulting from an experience of pain or acute discomfort upon penile entry. Physical causes, such as disease in the pelvic organs due to endometriosis, sepsis, tumours, stenosis of the vagina, birth trauma or poor repair operations have all to be attended to. Psychologically the sexual education of the woman may have made her apprehensive about intercourse with the acquisition of inhibited conditioned reflexes. Apart from the specific therapy of pelvic disease, vaginismus is treated essentially as a non-consummation problem.

Frigidity

The term frigidity is used loosely to express any female displeasure or failure to be aroused sexually. In fact it may consist of a general lack of response, acceptance of affectionate touch but not of intercourse, intercourse without pleasure or lack of orgasm. Even so, the woman who may have some or all these problems may be able to respond richly with another man.

Sexual frigidity may be associated with a negative, inhibited upbringing with a negative relationship with father, religious taboos and a tense make-up which finds it difficult to relax.

Treatment is based on that of Masters and Johnson and consists of progressive stages of sexual involvement. The first phase is called sensate focus in which the couple concentrate on arousing physical pleasure out of caressing, stroking each other's bodies without involving the erotic zones. This can be done with powdered hands or the use of lotion so that touch is enhanced with aromatic smell. Such an approach relaxes the couple and introduces them to the simple enjoyment of physical touch. This phase is followed by light erotic play in which the wife guides her husband to various parts of her body such as her breasts, nipples, buttocks, clitoris and vagina whose gentle stimulation take her one step further to sexual excitation. Finally coitus is attempted. The position adopted by the couple is the one most suited to them but the initiative should be with the wife who can control the thrusting and thus relieve herself of the anxiety of being pressurized to reach orgasm. She preserves her own rate of excitement and reaches orgasm at her own pace.

Orgastic Difficulties

Unlike frigidity, which is a generalized lack of sexual response during coitus, the woman who experiences orgastic difficulties may feel aroused, with suitable lubrication in her vagina and reach a certain excitement which is short of orgasm. It is realized of course that not infrequently every woman will have intercourse without attaining a climax. Tiredness, illness or marked worry may all contribute to occasional lack of response. Serious disturbance occurs when the woman has never experienced orgasm (primary) or has enjoyed orgasm in the past and is now incapable of doing so (secondary). These difficulties are probably the commonest of all female sexual complaints.

The essential pathology of orgastic failure is either inadequate clitoral excitation or poor muscular contractions round the vagina which are experienced as the motor component of the orgasm. The couple can be advised about coital positions which bring the penis in close proximity to the clitoris and give it adequate stimulation and in some couples this is all that is required.

In primary orgastic failure the woman may find it very difficult to achieve orgasm initially in the presence of a man. She may have to learn how to relax and then stimulate herself to orgasm either by masturbation or the use of a vibrator. When orgasm is reached easily in this way the therapeutic focus is transferred to actual intercourse. The couple are encouraged to maximize pleasure, intensify penile-clitoris contact and, if necessary, stimulate the clitoris manually during intercourse. This combination often achieves the desired result.

Secondary orgastic failure is treated by increasing erotic stimulation in a relaxed atmosphere leading to coitus in positions in which clitoral stimulation is enhanced: as before the husband may, if needed, stimulate the clitoris manually.

Needless to say, all this requires the support of the therapist who may have to remove long-standing inhibitions and guilt feelings about such intense sexual activity.

SEXUAL VARIATIONS

Sexual variations consist of behaviour in which sexual attraction is focussed on non-heterosexual persons and objects outside the normal range of sexual stimulation. The commonest variation is homosexuality or, more correctly in the case of marriage, bisexuality. Kinsey was the first worker to show that homosexuality was not an either/or condition. There are men and women with various degrees of homosexual tendencies. Exclusive homosexuals do not marry, but bisexuals, who have a mixture of homosexual and heterosexual make-up, may do so. These relationships may come under stress when one of the spouses finds it necessary to indulge in homosexual activity which may come as a shock to the partner. These need careful counselling to overcome the confusion, mistrust and doubt that may enter the relationship.

A condition which appears to be connected with homosexuality but is not is transvestism. In this condition, which has a male proclivity, the man desires to dress in female clothes, particularly underclothes. This may be a harmless need to which the wife may accommodate herself. It becomes rather more complicated when it is an essential component for sexual intercourse, that is to say that arousal is not possible without the wearing of such garments. Even so, an understanding wife can cope with such a requirement if the relationship is a good and loving one.

Other variations border on the normal. Men may be particularly aroused by pieces of underclothes, special colours, rubber or fur. All these requirements usually originate from a past in which these items were connected with an accidental sexual excitation which is reinforced by repetition in masturbatory activity. The man is conditioned to these items which are then extended to his excitement with his partner. It is doubtful whether these variations should be considered as serious disturbances but they become so when intercourse is only possible in the presence of these items. Desensitization to these items is possible and in situations where they cause marked disturbance between the spouses such a therapy is justified.

Sadomasochism is a pattern of sexual behaviour in which pleasure is aroused either by inflicting pain and/or humiliation or by receiving it. The extreme focus of either is clearly pathological and requires treatment but mild variations are very common. Teasing, smacking, biting are all part of erotic play and may be particularly important to individual men and women. These needs have to be recognized and provided they are not offensive or involve excessive pain and/or humiliation, they may enhance love play to the advantage of both.

HYSTERECTOMY AND MENOPAUSE

Neither hysterectomy nor the menopause is normally associated with sexual difficulties. There are women, however, who consider that their sexual life comes to an end after either of these. There is evidence that women with previous personal sexual problems use the menopause as a reason for ceasing intercourse or declaring dissatisfaction with their marriage (Ballinger 1976). Another study found that women in the age group 40–55 attending a gynaecological clinic were more often separated or divorced (Ballinger 1977). Hysterectomy may also be used as an excuse for ceasing sexual activity. Once again there is evidence that women referred to psychiatrists with various complaints after hysterectomy show a high incidence of marital disruption (Barker 1968). Thus, the evidence suggests that both these major gynaecological events should leave the sexual life of the woman undisturbed unless there are long-standing preceding sexual or marital problems.

AFFECTIVE ILLNESS

The incidence of depressive illness increases in the second half of life in both sexes but particularly in women. Loss of sexual desire is often an accompaniment of depressive illnesses and this condition should be excluded and treated if present. Depression may also follow hysterectomy or be associated with the menopause.

MARITAL PATHOLOGY

So far in this chapter sexual difficulties have been described with the emphasis on dysfunction unrelated to marital problems. Clearly there is an intimate connection between the two since intercourse is unlikely to occur if there is marked marital tension. Descriptions of patterns of marital problems abound. Here the author's family life-cycle is being used (Dominian 1980). Briefly this cycle covers three stages of marriage: the first five years, the second between the ages of 30 and 50 and the third between 50 and the death of one spouse. Each phase has five dimensions of marriage, the social, physical, emotional, intellectual and spiritual. Pathology exists when one or more of these dimensions is seriously disturbed. For the sake of brevity two main dimensions only will be considered—the social and the emotional.

First Five Years

On an average men marry about the age of 25 and women about 23 so that the first five years cover the late twenties until the age of 30.

Social characteristics

The young couple have to sort out their relationship with relatives and friends, who does what in the house, money and time. Each of these factors can lead to marked difficulties. As far as relatives are concerned, it is important to withdraw dependence from parents and establish the spouse as the key figure in one's life. Most marriages achieve this but a few retain powerful ties with parents and relatives at the expense of the spouse. The husband or wife is bypassed and the parents (or one of them) remain the principal adviser(s). This is markedly resented by the ignored spouse who gets angrier and angrier as he or she feels ignored. The same applies to friends, one of whom retains an excessive hold over one spouse, once again at the expense of the partner.

Beyond the social network of the couple there are internal arrangements in the life of the couple. If husband and wife work, then both have to share responsibility for running the home. Often the husband agrees to this prior to marriage and then pays only lip-service to the promise. The working wife then finds herself landed with both work and running the home, which makes her tired and irritable. The time that the husband spends away from home for work or being with his friends is also resented since it leaves very little time spent together. The complaint of wives that they rarely see their husbands after marriage is a frequent one.

Finally, there is the distribution of money. So long as both spouses work finance is not often a problem, but it may be if the husband withholds housekeeping money and expects his wife to make the major contribution out of her income. Alternatively, when the wife is not working, the failure to supply adequate housekeeping money is resented. Money has two meanings. It has a reality value, namely we cannot survive without it; but it has an emotional significance as well. Many a wife will say 'If you loved me, you would not keep me short: you would not humiliate me by making me have to ask repeatedly.'

Emotional characteristics

One of the characteristics of modern marriage is its emphasis on feelings and emotions. Spouses need to be able to communicate and demonstrate affection. Marital problems occur when one spouse, usually the husband, is a poor communicator and even poorer at showing affection. Both these features are markedly resented by the wife who feels that she is only wanted for sex and as a housekeeper. In addition to these conflicts, there are spouses with low frustration level who easily become irritable and who indulge in physical and verbal aggression, particularly after drinking heavily. Both spouses need recurrent recognition, acknowledgement and appreciation. If they get none of these or, instead, feel criticised and rejected, then the scene is set for conflict.

Children

The birth of the first child is usually a source of joy to the couple. Its arrival, however, may also present problems. For a time the mother may be unable to give as much attention to her husband as before. She may become depressed and irritable post-puerperally and lose interest in sex. This syndrome may last for months and sometimes years and may cause marked tension.

All the above problems may lead to marital conflict of a serious or trivial nature but these external events impinge on the relationship and in turn on the sexual life of the couple.

Second Phase (30–50 Years)

This is the phase when the children are growing up and the couple experience changes in their inner and outer life.

Social characteristics

One of the chief features of this phase is that all men and women are capable of changing and emerging from their childhood backgrounds and find themselves going up or down the social scale. One of the spouses may progress well beyond the resources of the partner as regards new interests, associates and friends. Thus the couple may become estranged from one another.

Another major social happening in these years is the husband's acme of achievement. Most men find they have reached the highest level of their promotion in the forties and may become very frustrated at their level of accomplishment. They may feel a failure in their work and also failures as men and lovers. They may turn to drink for consolation or take it out on their wives and children.

The children are growing up and reach adolescence. Adolescence may go smoothly but may also be a turbulent period in which parents are deeply divided about what course to follow regarding their sons and daughters. The activity and rebellion of their children may set the parents in conflict with each other about discipline and control.

Emotional characteristics

The principal characteristic emotionally is also that of change. With the passage of time, particularly in the thirties, men and women separate further from the image they received from their parents and emerge as differentiated persons in their own right. A dependent spouse in particular may now want to live a much more independent life. He or she may want to have a much bigger say in the way their joint life is run, the sort of friends they have, what they do, where they go, etc. Spouses have to adapt to each other, but some husbands in particular find the newly discovered independence of their wives intolerable and oppose it. Conflict follows and may become extremely acrimonious as the wife now feels a prisoner. This is a markedly common pattern in this age group, affecting sexual life as the anger of the wife leads to withdrawal on her part. Withdrawal may also follow when one or other spouse feels easily criticised and rejected and becomes concerned in this phase that the other partner rarely approves but is constantly criticising.

Third Phase (50 Years to the Death of One Spouse)

Social characteristics

These are the years when the children leave home and the parents of the spouses die. If the father of one of the spouses dies, then the mother may have to be given accommodation. This may impose constraint and conflict on the spouses who were looking forward to time together free from any interference. These are also the years of retirement in which the retiring spouse may find it very difficult to settle down to retirement and tension is built up between the couple.

Emotional characteristics

Perhaps the principal pattern of these years is the realization by the couple that they have lived through their children which comes as a sudden shock when the children leave home. There is likely to be an emptiness in the emotional life of the couple which cannot be bridged. Such a couple look at one another and find a stranger. They have loved, eaten, slept together under the same roof for years but never made a deep bond with each other and now they face each other as strangers.

COUNSELLING

At the conclusion of this chapter we can summarize the principles of psychosexual counselling:

1. Sexual dysfunction may exist in the presence of intact marital relationship. In that event the techniques of Masters and Johnson are widely used to repair faulty sexual functioning.
2. Sexual difficulties may exist because there is conflict with hostility or indifference in the marital relationship. There is then need to identify the pattern of marital pathology and initiate marital counselling which will help the relationship and the sexual activity.
3. Sexual difficulties may exist where there is both dysfunction and marital conflict. In this instance there is a need for both counselling and sexual therapy to be carried out simultaneously.

Nowadays the techniques of counselling and sexual therapy have advanced to the point where anyone with serious sexual difficulty should have the advantage of expert counselling to promote the maximum therapeutic effect.

Bibliography

Ballinger, C.B. (1976) Psychiatric morbidity and the menopause: clinical features. *Br. med. J., 1*, 1183.

Ballinger, C.B. (1977) Psychiatric morbidity and the menopause: survey of a gynaecological out-patient clinic. *Br. J. Psychiat., 131*, 83.

Barker, M.G. (1968) Psychiatric illness after hysterectomy. *Br. med. J., 2*, 91.

Dominian, J. (1968) *Marital Breakdown*. Harmondsworth: Penguin.

Dominian, J. (1980) *Marital Pathology*. London: Darton, Longman and Todd and the BMA.

Kaplan, H.S. (1974) *The New Sex Therapy*. London: Baillière Tindall (Harmondsworth: Penguin).

Kinsey, A.C., Pomeroy, W.B. & Martin, C.E. (1948) *Sexual Behaviour in the Human Male*. Philadelphia: W.B. Saunders.

Kinsey, A.C., Pomeroy, W.B., Martin, C.E. & Gebhard, P.H. (1953) *Sexual Behaviour in the Human Female*. Philadelphia: W.B. Saunders.

Masters, W.H. & Johnson, V.E. (1966) *Human Sexual Responses*. Boston: Little, Brown.

Masters, W.H. & Johnson, V.E. (1970) *Human Sexual Inadequacy*. Boston: Little, Brown.

16. Rubella Immunization

P. Morgan-Capner and J.R. Pattison

Rubella (German measles) was first described in the eighteenth century but before 1941 was considered to be a mild illness whose only importance was as a differential diagnosis from measles and scarlet fever. In 1941 the association between maternal rubella during pregnancy and congenital abnormalities was reported from Australia by Sir Norman Gregg, an ophthalmologist. He noted an increased incidence of congenital cataracts in infants and on questioning their mothers found that a high percentage had suffered during early pregnancy from rubella, which had been epidemic in 1940. The importance of rubella in these circumstances was confirmed by many later studies which revealed the wide range of abnormalities which may result from intrauterine infection. Advances in the epidemiology and diagnosis of rubella were delayed until the rubella virus was isolated in cell culture in 1962.

With the isolation of the causative virus, the estimation of serum antibody became possible. Since then the determination of rubella antibody in serum specimens has become the cornerstone of the diagnosis of rubella and the determination of immune status.

With the development of a live attenuated vaccine in the late 1960s the prevention of congenital rubella by means other than therapeutic abortion became possible.

CONGENITAL RUBELLA

Maternal rubella during early pregnancy may affect the fetus in many ways. Spontaneous abortion or stillbirth may occur. The baby may be born with a spectrum of abnormalities ranging from those which may be rapidly fatal to those which may not manifest themselves until later in life. The baby, however, may totally escape any consequences of intrauterine infection. The classical triad is involvement of heart, eyes and ears. The cardiac lesions most frequently seen are patent ductus arteriosus and pulmonary stenosis. The commonest ocular defect is cataract (Fig. 16.1) but a pigmentary retinopathy and microphthalmia

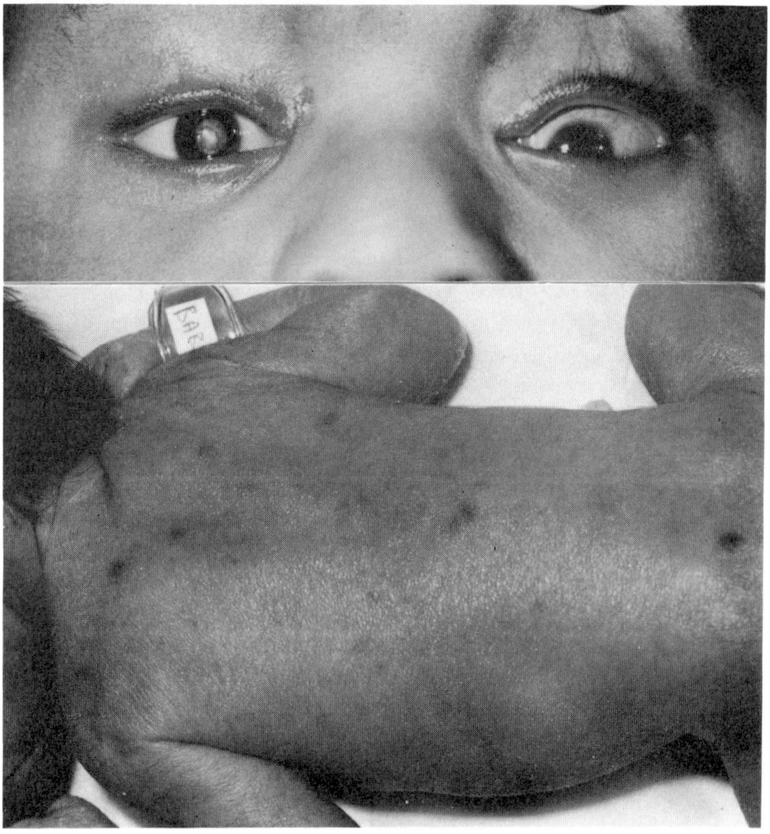

Fig. 16.1. A neonate whose mother had suffered from rubella early in pregnancy, showing cataract (*above*) and petechial rash (*below*). The child died three weeks after birth. (*Professor J. Banatvala*)

may also occur. Sensorineural deafness may occur together with other defects but can occur alone, when it may not be detected until later in life. Other defects may be apparent at birth. The commonest is intrauterine growth retardation. Purpura and hepatosplenomegaly may also occur and are usually found in association with defects of the heart, eyes or ears. However, some defects, in addition to deafness, may not present until later in infancy and include a chronic rubelliform rash and interstitial pneumonitis.

The incidence of defects is closely linked to the stage of pregnancy at which maternal infection with rubella occurred. Rubella during the first month of pregnancy may result in up to 50% of infants being born with congenital defects. The incidence decreases to approximately 5% by the fourth month and there is minimal, but definite, risk to the fetus if infection occurs after the sixteenth week of pregnancy. The earlier in pregnancy that infection occurs the higher is the risk that any abnormalities will be severe and multiple. Maternal rubella occurring in the month prior to conception appears to be associated with a definite, but small, risk.

In order to assess the incidence of congenital rubella in the United Kingdom, a National Congenital Rubella Surveillance Programme was instituted in 1971. Suspected cases are notified to the programme centre and the relevant clinical and laboratory data are assessed before confirming congenital rubella. The first six years of this programme have shown an annual incidence of about 80 cases. This is certainly an underestimate because of the failure to recognize cases which present later in childhood with abnormalities such as deafness or cases which present atypically. The figure of 80 cases per year is not an estimate of the frequency with which rubella complicates pregnancy since many affected pregnancies are terminated (see below). In non-epidemic years the incidence of rubella in pregnancy is probably about 2 per 1000, but will have been much higher in epidemic years such as 1978 and 1979.

The passing of the 1967 Abortion Act confirmed the legality of therapeutic abortion on the grounds of there being a substantial risk of the child being abnormal. Since then many possible cases of congenital rubella have been prevented by therapeutic abortion of women who have had rubella during early pregnancy. Numerically, notifications of termination of pregnancy to the DHSS on the grounds that the child may be born abnormal vary with the incidence of rubella in the community, although maternal rubella is not the only reason for termination on such grounds. Approximately 1000 terminations per year are performed for suspected or proved maternal rubella.

Prevention

Termination of pregnancy

Use of termination of pregnancy to control congenital rubella has several problems. The clinical diagnosis of rubella is notoriously inaccurate. Although the clinical features of rubella have been well described, similar illnesses may be caused by other infectious agents and rubella itself may occur without one or more of the principal features being obvious. It may even occur subclinically. Therefore, laboratory investigation both of possible cases of rubella and of women in contact with suspected rubella is mandatory. A previous history of rubella, unless supported by laboratory findings such as the prior demonstration of rubella-specific antibody, is totally unreliable and should be discounted when considering the diagnosis. The laboratory investigation of rubella is dependent on serology as virus isolation is unreliable. Such serological investigation may be protracted as in the susceptible woman detectable antibodies may not develop until four or five weeks after the contact with infection. This period is the minimum to be allowed before a rubella infection is excluded. Women who present longer than one month after the illness or two months after a contact and who have detectable rubella antibody present a problem group as the serological techniques available make it impossible to exclude a recent rubella infection. The incidence of subclinical rubella, when no investigation would be performed unless there were a contact, varies from one series to another but is more common in children than adults. In adult fair-skinned women it is relatively rare, about 90% of such infections being clinical. However, in the National Congenital Rubella Surveillance Programme fewer than half the mothers of confirmed cases gave a history of a rubella-like illness during pregnancy. Thus subclinical maternal rubella makes a major contribution to the incidence of congenital rubella.

Immunization

As congenital rubella is a consequence of primary infection of the mother during pregnancy, the ideal solution is that no woman embarks on a pregnancy without having had a prior infection, as a result of either natural infection or immunization. Second attacks of clinical rubella are very rare. More usually rubella re-infections are assumed to have occurred when there is a rise in antibody titres with no clinical illness. There is no evidence of a viraemia in such patients and it is unlikely there is any risk to the fetus. If clinical rubella has occurred it can be assumed that a viraemia was present and the fetus was at risk as transplacental infection may have occurred.

The availability of live attentuated rubella virus vaccines gave hope that congenital rubella could be eradicated by ensuring that primary infection did not occur in pregnancy. Such vaccines were developed by the passage of the wild rubella virus in cell culture resulting in attenuation. There are now two commercially available vaccines in the United Kingdom, the Cendehill strain and the Wistar RA 27/3 strain. The vaccines are supplied freeze-dried and require reconstitution before administration subcutaneously.

The RA 27/3 strain elicits an antibody response in over 98% of susceptible individuals compared with over 96% for the Cendehill strain. It is probable that a high proportion of those who do not develop antibodies have had a previous rubella infection but their levels of antibody are undetectable by the commonly available techniques. The high percentage of seroconversion after vaccination means that it is not cost-effective to retest all vaccinees after immunization except in small studies to monitor the efficacy of the vaccines. The RA 27/3 strain produces higher titres of antibodies than the Cendehill strain and the types of antibody produced by RA 27/3 more closely resemble those occurring after natural rubella infection. With RA 27/3 it is possible to immunize effectively by administration of the vaccine intranasally but its use by this route has not been licensed.

The vaccines are well tolerated with mild and transient side effects. These usually appear nine or ten days after vaccination and resemble an attenuated natural infection with fever, lymphadenopathy, malaise and, occasionally, a rash and arthralgia. Although recent vaccinees excrete virus from the nasopharynx, usually during the second week after vaccination, there is no evidence to suggest that this can lead to the transmission of infection to susceptible individuals. This is of importance since the vaccine is considered to have teratogenic potential as it is a live virus, although attenuated.

Vaccine strains of rubella virus, when administered to rubella-susceptible pregnant women, have been isolated from the aborted fetus and even, in one case, from a lens which showed histological features suggesting a developing cataract. Only a small number of pregnancies complicated by vaccination have gone to term. There have been no congenital abnormalities reported in over 70 babies whose mothers were susceptible to rubella and who were vaccinated during pregnancy. However, most of these were immunized with the older, more attenuated strains and it would be unwise to extrapolate these reports to the vaccines in present use.

There is also a risk attached to preconception vaccination, with vaccine-strain rubella being isolated from aborted fetuses when the rubella-susceptible mother has been immunized up to seven weeks prior to conception. Therefore rubella vaccination is definitely contraindicated in pregnancy and present recommendations are that pregnancy should be avoided for three months following vaccination.

Other important contraindications to rubella vaccination are an impaired immune responsiveness in the recipient as a result of an underlying condition or as a result of steroids, cytotoxic drugs or radiotherapy, a febrile illness or administration of gammaglobulin within the previous six weeks. A rare contraindication is a sensitivity of the recipient to polymyxin or neomycin (antibiotics contained within the vaccine). It would seem wise to delay rubella vaccination or to check that seroconversion has occurred if simultaneous administration of anti-D globulin is proposed as possible interference with vaccine efficacy may occur.

Immunization policies

Immunization policies must take into consideration the duration of immunity that is conferred. Follow-up studies have now been in progress for up to ten years and have shown that for the currently used vaccines fewer than 1% have become seronegative after nine years. However, subclinical re-infections are not uncommon, as judged by rising titres of rubella antibody in the absence of clinical illness. These appear to be a more frequent occurrence after immunization with the Cendehill strain than with the RA 27/3. These subclinical re-infections are not associated with any risk to the fetus and the efficacy of these vaccines is confirmed by there being no reports of children with congenital rubella being born to women who have been immunized and whose post-vaccination immune status has been serologically confirmed.

The policy of use of the vaccine for the prevention of congenital rubella has differed in the USA from that adopted in the UK and in Europe. The routine rubella vaccination programme was started in the UK in 1970 and was originally directed only at girls 11–14 years of age. Vaccine is offered to all in this group without prior screening for antibody. The rationale of this programme was that immunization was selectively aimed at those who must be immune in order to prevent congenital rubella, i.e. women entering the childbearing years. Antibody screening prior to immunization is not necessary for such a group as the birth rate in 11–14-year-old girls is so small (only 233 live births in England and Wales in 1977). Therefore the risk of complicating pregnancy by rubella vaccination in this group is negligible and does not necessitate antibody screening. With such a policy, no attempt is made to prevent the circulation of rubella in girls under age 11 and in all males. The occurrence of rubella in the community would result in constant re-exposure of women vaccinated as girls and this may help to boost antibody levels and so maintain immunity during the childbearing years.

The deficiency of a rubella vaccination policy aimed at adolescent girls is that no measurable benefit would occur for a number of years. In 1977 approximately 10% of live births were to mothers aged 15–19 years. 31% to mothers aged 20–24, 37% to mothers aged 25–29 and 22% to mothers aged 30–39 years. Thus, if only 11–14-year-old girls were vaccinated, even with a very high acceptance rate, it would be at least 10–12 years before any measurable effect on the incidence of congenital rubella could be seen and it would be 25–30 years before its full effect could be assessed.

Meanwhile, those susceptible mothers aged over 14 years in 1970 would continue to be exposed to rubella, its circulation having been unaltered by the vaccination programme. In order to correct this deficiency in the vaccination programme it was later recommended that every effort be made to ensure that all seronegative women of childbearing age should be offered vaccine. Present recommendations are that no adult woman should be given vaccine without prior serological testing. The pregnancy rate in this group is high and even if pregnancy at the time of vaccination is excluded, a significant number of women may become pregnant during the three months after vaccination. At this later stage it may be impossible to determine whether the woman was immune, there then being no risk to the fetus, or susceptible when she was vaccinated. At present, all such women would be offered termination of pregnancy. As 85–90% of them would be immune this would result in unnecessary terminations. As it is essential that the susceptible woman should not become pregnant during the three months after vaccination it is necessary that effective contraceptive measures are taken.

As pregnancy is unlikely in the three months after delivery the major screening and immunization programme has been aimed at already pregnant women by performing antibody screening early in pregnancy when venesection is also being performed for syphilis screening, blood grouping and haemoglobin determination. At present 85–90% of pregnant women in the UK have detectable rubella-specific antibody and are therefore immune. Vaccination is offered in the immediate post-natal period to those found to be susceptible. If necessary a long-acting progestogen injection may be given to ensure that pregnancy does not occur during the ensuing three months. Such vaccination programmes have also been offered by occupational health services where it is particularly applicable in hospital practice, not only as a protection for the employee, but also as a protective measure against natural rubella being transmitted by hospital staff to pregnant women as individuals are infectious for some days prior to the development of a clinical illness. Family-planning clinics provide a suitable setting as adequate measures can be taken to ensure that pregnancy does not occur for the requisite three months after vaccination. Such screening and necessary vaccination should be mandatory before the investigation and treatment of infertility to avoid the tragic consequences of natural rubella occurring in a hard-earned pregnancy.

With the occurrence of an epidemic of rubella in the UK in 1978–9, the government introduced a campaign to publicise the dangers of congenital rubella and to inform the public of the availability of rubella antibody screening and immunization through their general practitioners. However, there are problems with such a campaign, not least of which is the reluctance of some women to submit to venesection, although they are willing to be immunized. There is the necessity of two visits to the general practitioner and it has been suggested that this problem may be overcome by taking a blood sample, immediately vaccinating after ensuring that the patient is not pregnant and offering adequate contraception for three months. Should the patient become pregnant during the ensuing three months the serum sample can be examined to ascertain rubella status at vaccination.

In the USA a different policy has been adopted. This was based on attempting to eradicate rubella from the community by immunizing all infants, both male and female, between the ages of one year and puberty. As natural rubella circulates mostly in young children, eradication of rubella in this group would minimize the rubella contacts of pregnant women. As in the UK, vaccination has also been offered to adult women. However, it is difficult to evaluate such a policy as the incidence of rubella in the community fluctuates markedly from year to year with epidemics expected at intervals of approximately nine years.

Laboratory investigations

Screening for the presence of rubella antibody forms a large commitment of diagnostic virology laboratories. The haemagglutination-inhibition (HI) test has been widely accepted as the method of choice for such screening. This test is dependent on the ability of rubella-specific antibody to prevent the agglutination of red blood cells by rubella antigen. Antibody detected by this technique was found to correlate well with virus neutralizing antibody, being formed during the acute infection and persisting for life. However, the HI test is time-consuming and, being a multi-step procedure, is prone to laboratory error if large numbers of tests are performed. Difficulties can be encountered in the interpretation of low titres and most laboratories cautiously report such low titres as indicating susceptibility and advise vaccination. There is now in the UK a trend towards using radial haemolysis (Fig. 16.2) for screening purposes. Radial haemolysis is easier and quicker to perform, being more reliable as long as care is taken in the organization and documentation. No attempt is made to quantitate the antibody present in a serum, only to compare the amount with a known control serum. The control serum contains that amount of antibody (15 international units) previously determined to be a minimum acceptable level to indicate immunity. Women whose sera show greater zones of haemolysis than the control are reported as 'immune', those showing no zones of haemolysis are reported as 'susceptible'. Sera which contain small amounts of rubella antibody, i.e. produce a zone of haemolysis smaller than the control, are reported as 'low levels of antibody present', but vaccination is still advised. This group is of importance as its members may not respond to vaccination by producing more antibody. Therefore they should not be classified as vaccine failures if follow up sera reveal no increase in antibody and they should be considered to be immune.

THE FUTURE

Hopes for the eradication of congenital rubella in the UK are dependent on all women entering the child-bearing years with rubella antibody, as a result of either natural rubella or rubella vaccination. As rubella will continue to circulate in infants and males and therefore women will continue to be exposed, the vaccination rate in adolescent females must be as near 100% as possible. It is unrealistic to expect

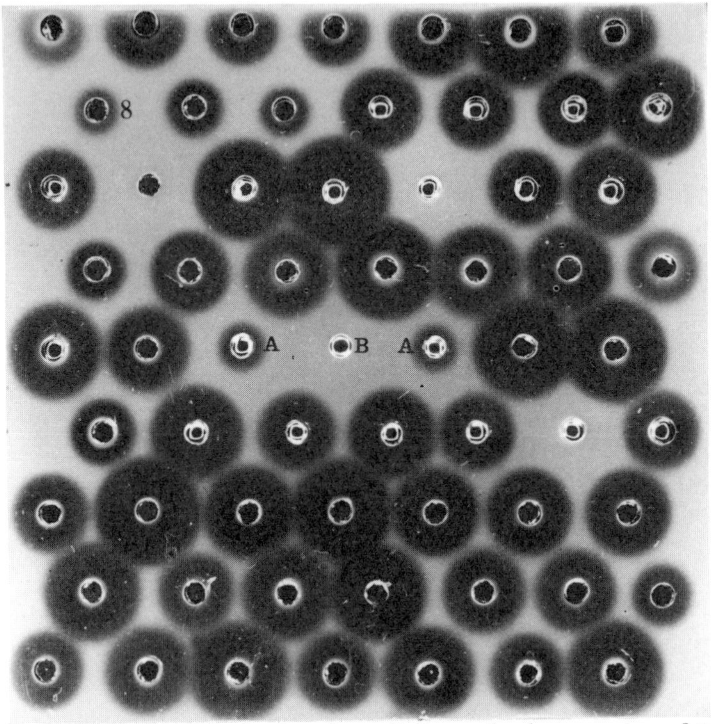

Fig. 16.2. Radial haemolysis plate for rubella antibody screening of 60 sera. Well A contained 15 I.U. control serum; well B contained negative serum. All sera are easily interpreted as immune or susceptible except serum 8, which is reported as containing a low amount of rubella antibody.

totally effective immunization policies on a national scale but the present rate of 70% must be improved. The acceptability of vaccination would be improved if the vaccine could be administered intranasally, as is possible with the RA 27/3 strain. However, although more acceptable to the patient, the seroconversion rate would probably be less due to interference by a concurrent cold.

It would take many years for such a policy to be effective and meanwhile efforts should go into identifying those adult women who are susceptible and ensuring their vaccination. The problem of serological identification of susceptible women would be solved if present vaccines were shown to have no teratogenic effect on the fetus or if newer vaccines were developed which were free from all possible adverse effects on it. There is hope that a vaccine derived from a strain of rubella isolated in Japan, where congenital rubella is much less frequent, may offer such advantages.

17. Physiotherapy after Gynaecological Surgery

Molly Jennings

The definition of physiotherapy is healing by physical means, and this is especially important after gynaecological surgery. With a detailed knowledge of anatomy, the physiotherapist can teach carefully controlled exercises to strengthen specific muscles. It is equally important that the patient should understand the aim of the exercises and be willing to cooperate. The individual attention which the physiotherapist can give helps to build up a relationship in which the patient gains confidence in her ability to return to a normal life postoperatively. It is also advisable for the ward sister and her senior staff to appreciate the role of the physiotherapist. Full cooperation between nurse and physiotherapist is very rewarding in terms of benefit to the patient.

After gynaecological surgery, the patient is taught exercises to strengthen the pelvic floor and the abdominal muscles. A detailed knowledge of both muscle groups is essential before exercises can be taught efficiently and with confidence.

THE PELVIC FLOOR

The muscles of the pelvic floor or pelvic diaphragm are deep to the perineum. They consist of the levator ani and coccygeus and fill the area known as the pelvic outlet. The muscles are interwoven with fascia, which is a dense fibrous tissue without elasticity covering both faces of the levator ani. It adds strength to the muscles with which it is associated.

The *levator ani* is a broad thick muscle and is divided into the pubococcygeus and the iliococcygeus. The levatores ani arise from the inner surface of the pubis lateral to the symphysis on either side, from the fascia covering the obturator foramen and from the inner surface

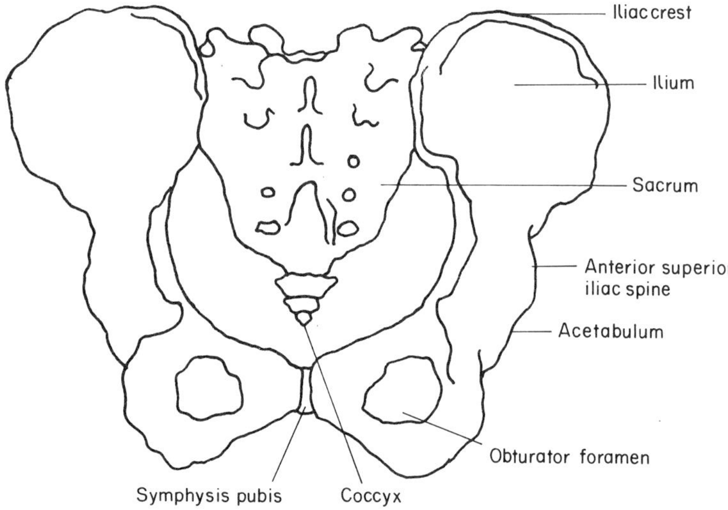

Fig. 17.1. The female pelvis.

of the ischium. The muscle fibres unite with the muscles from the opposite side to form a muscle similar in shape to an open book. The fibres from each side pass downwards and slant at various angles according to their origin and insertion.

The anterior fibres or pubococcygeus pass down and back to be inserted into the centre of the perineum between the vagina and the anus, the area known as the perineal body. Some fibres form a puborectal sling to maintain the angle between the rectum and anal canal. Others cross the side of the vagina and support the vaginal sphincter.

The posterior fibres or iliococcygeus pass back and down to join the fibres from the opposite side, some being inserted into the wall of the anal canal.

The *coccygeus* is posterior to the levator ani. It is a triangular muscle arising from the pelvic surface of the ischial spine and from the

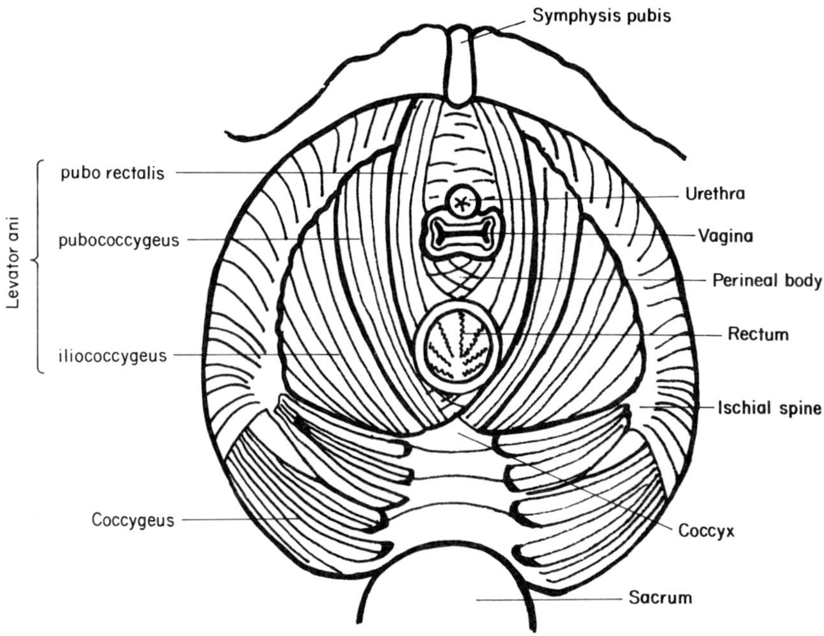

Fig. 17.2. The pelvic floor.

ligament joining the ischium to the sacrum. The fibres pass backwards to be inserted into the coccyx and lower part of the sacrum.

The *urogenital triangle* (Fig. 17.4) is the most important area of the pelvic floor. It is the anterior triangle through which the urethra and vagina pass. The midline borders have approximately 1 cm separation to allow the urethra and vagina to pass through. If this muscle is torn, for instance following parturition, and is not adequately sutured, the anterior fibres contract and increase the normal gap so reducing the support to the pelvic organs. This may cause varying degrees of prolapse.

The action of the levatores ani are:

1. To pull up and contract the vagina.
2. To form a muscular diaphragm to support the pelvic and abdominal viscera, especially during standing.
3. To withstand increased intra-abdominal pressure, e.g. during coughing, lifting or sneezing.
4. To close the posterior part of the pelvic outlet.

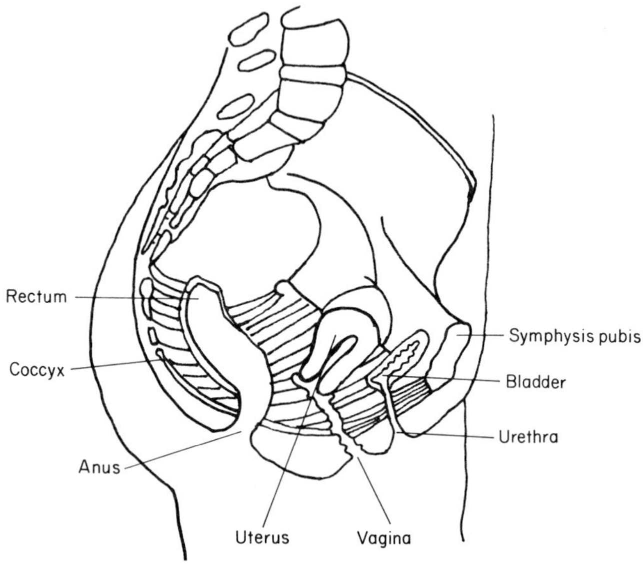

Fig. 17.3. The pelvic floor in sagittal section.

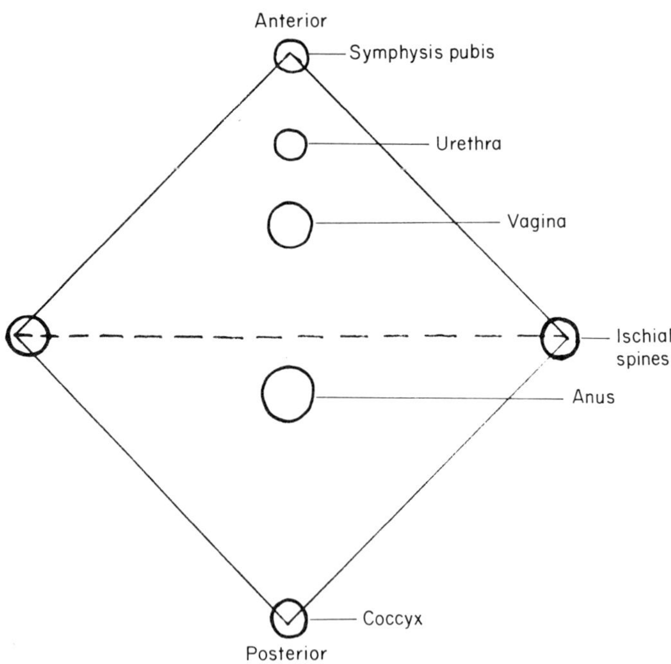

Fig. 17.4. The urogenital triangle.

5. To move the coccyx forward following defaecation and parturition and to support the coccyx. In animals the coccygeus produces tail movements.

With a thorough knowledge of the muscle actions in the pelvic floor, the physiotherapist or nurse can explain exercises to patients in simple terms and teach them effectively.

The pelvic floor can be described as a hammock slung from front to back to hold up the abdominal organs. To aid explanation the hands can be used as a visual aid if placed side by side, palms up and little fingers together. Where the tips of the little fingers touch can represent the urethral sphincter, the anal sphincter being envisaged at the base of the little fingers and the vaginal opening between the two. This clearly shows the importance of the urogenital triangle. With a lifting movement of the central area the pelvic floor exercise can be demonstrated.

Teaching Pelvic Floor Contractions

The patient must be lying fully supported to allow full concentration on the exercise. One pillow is used and the legs are kept straight. First, she is asked to 'pull up the anus', feel the small movement, hold it and relax. This is the easiest part of the exercise. When this is understood, the patient can progress to a 'pulling up' and a squeezing sensation in the vagina and urethra, i.e. concentrating on stopping an imaginary flow of urine. When the patient is able to understand and perform this very fine, small movement she can be instructed to 'pull up' and 'hold' to a count of four and 'let go' slowly. This exercise can be repeated four or five times hourly and then practised in sitting and standing positions.

If the patient finds the exercise difficult to learn it may be helpful to teach her in the sitting position. She is asked to sit on the very edge of the bed or chair. It is important that the perineum is not supported. The feet should be firmly on the floor and hips and knees at right angles. The same commands as before are used. In this way the exercise is done against the pull of gravity and so produces a more pronounced feeling of 'pulling-up'.

It is important that the patient is actually contracting the levator ani and so doing the exercise correctly. In the absence of surgery one way to be certain is to insert a gloved finger into the vagina and ask the patient to contract on it. The patient may try for herself by placing her finger in the vagina, while in the bath for instance, or by obtaining control over the flow of urine. It must be emphasized that this is not the exercise itself, but only a method of testing that it is being carried out properly. Asking the patient what she feels during the exercise is probably the most practical indication. This exercise should be taught before and after operation. The preoperative period is the ideal time, as the patient is willing to learn, able to concentrate and free from soreness. In certain cases of stress incontinence (leaking of urine on exertion), the teaching of pelvic floor contractions may obviate surgery.

THE ABDOMINAL WALL

After gynaecological surgery involving an abdominal incision, it is important that the abdominal muscles are returned to their normal contractile ability. Once again, in order that the exercises can be taught correctly and safely, a knowledge of the muscles involved is needed.

First it is important to remember the functions of the abdominal wall:

1. To maintain the abdominal viscera in their correct positions and resist the downward pull of gravity.
2. To aid expulsive movements, e.g. defaecation, micturition, parturition, vomiting, coughing.
3. To help control and produce movement of the spine, i.e. flexion, rotation and side flexion.
4. To support the lumbar spine by a 'splinting' action during lifting and strong exercises.
5. To provide the anterolateral limits of the abdomen.

The abdominal wall consists of layers of muscle and fascia. It extends from the xiphoid process, at the base of the sternum above to the symphysis pubis below and laterally to an imaginary line between the lower ribs and half way along the iliac crest.

The abdominal muscles are the rectus abdominus, the external abdominal oblique (on both sides), the internal abdominal oblique (on both sides), the transversalis and the pyrimadalis. The superficial fascia is thick and has varying amounts of fatty deposits, noticeable in weight gain.

The *rectus abdominus* is the most superficial muscle. It is similar to a wide piece of elastic on either side of a central line. It extends the whole length of the abdominal wall. Its origin is from fibres covering

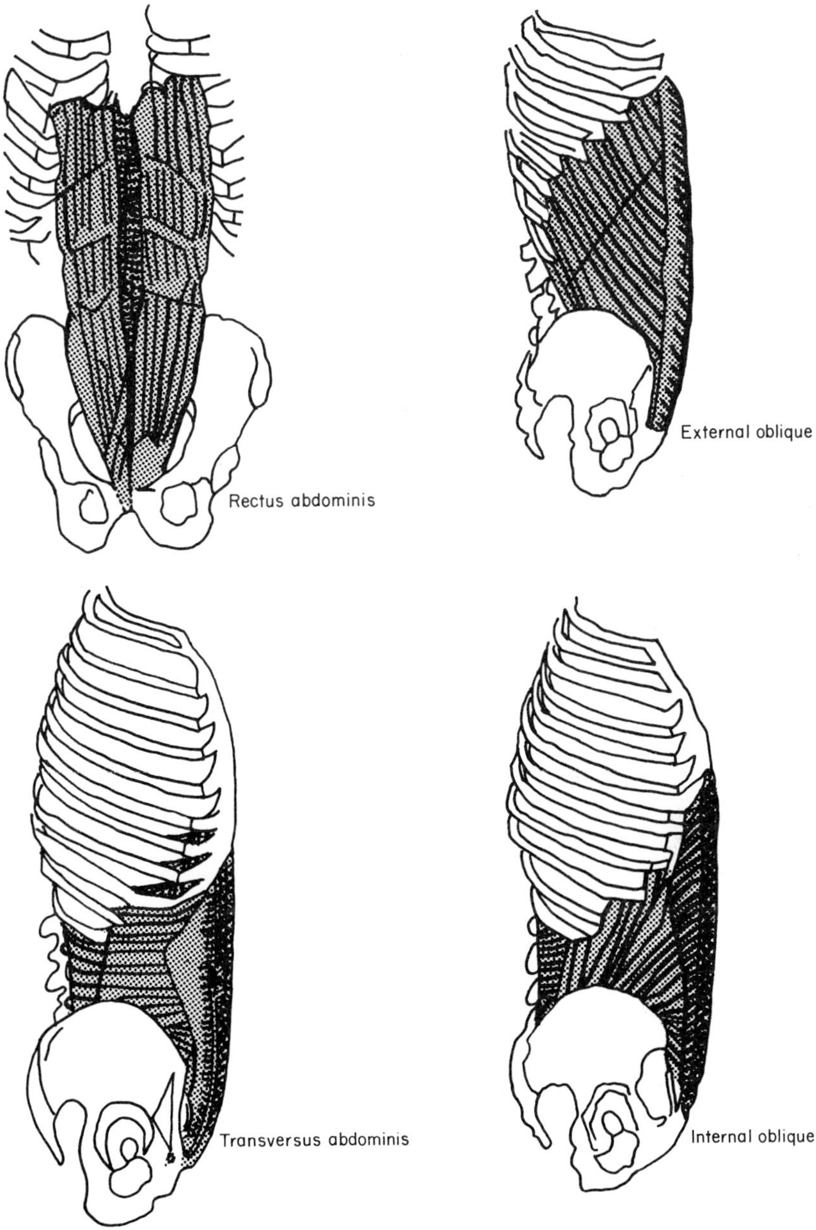

Fig. 17.5. Arrangement of the abdominal muscles.

the symphysis pubis and from the pubic tubercle lateral to the symphysis on either side. The fibres pass upwards in two sheaths and fan out to be inserted into the fifth, sixth and seventh ribs. The two sheaths are joined centrally by the linea alba, noticeable in pregnancy and post-natally by its brown pigmentation.

The rectus abdominis is a very strong muscle. Its action is forward flexion of the lower thoracic and lumbar spine. It should be remembered, when any strong abdominal exercise is being performed, that the abdominal wall should be contracted first so that undue strain to the linea alba can be prevented and the lumbar spine protected.

The *pyramidalis* is a small triangular muscle which reinforces the lower fibres of the rectus.

The *external abdominal oblique* is a large flat muscle and the strongest of the three flat muscles. It lies lateral to rectus and is attached to it medially. It arises from the lower eight ribs by tendons. The lower fibres pass vertically down to be inserted into the iliac crest. The remaining fibres pass diagonally across towards the rectus to form the superficial part of the sheath and are then inserted into the linea alba. A few fibres pass horizontally to be inserted into the xiphoid process. When the diagonal fibres contract and if the pelvis is fixed, the trunk is rotated to the opposite side.

The *internal abdominal oblique* is a flat muscle deep to external oblique and arises from the iliac crest and the inguinal ligament. The posterior fibres pass vertically upwards to be inserted into the lowest three ribs. The remaining fibres fan out and divide into a flat tendon-type attachment or aponeurosis to form the anterior and posterior part of the sheath of the rectus. The main action of the muscle is flexion to the same side.

The *transversus* is the deepest and thinnest of the flat muscles. As the name suggests the fibres pass horizontally across the abdominal wall. They arise from the lower ribs, lumbar fascia and iliac crest, pass behind the oblique muscles and are mainly inserted into the linea alba. The main function of this muscle is to act with others to hold the abdominal viscera in place.

The sheath of rectus abdominis has the fibres of internal oblique and transversus merging with it. The fibres in the lowest one-third and below the umbilicus pass in front to re-inforce the lower abdominal wall.

Although the abdominal muscles have individual actions they work together to form a natural 'corset'. Simple exercises are selected to strengthen each muscle and will be described later in the chapter with guidelines of when they are safe to perform following surgery.

Detailed knowledge is necessary for the physiotherapist to select and localize as far as is possible the use of the muscle in each exercise. When teaching exercises the starting position is considered. The range through which the muscle moves can vary the strength of the exercise. If the muscle is in a fully extended position, then the exercise is stronger. The weight of the limb or part to be moved and whether or not it is working against the pull of gravity must all be calculated to graduate the strength of the exercise according to the patient's physical condition and age. Another factor is the speed of the movement, i.e. slow and controlled movements are stronger.

Therefore it can be seen that by understanding the anatomy, exercises can be graded in strength and muscular use.

PREOPERATIVE PHYSIOTHERAPY

This gives the physiotherapist the opportunity to teach the patient simple breathing, foot and leg exercises at a time when she is receptive and willing to listen to explanations. It is an opportunity to gain her confidence, so making postoperative treatment more acceptable.

The physiotherapist will have read the patient's notes and checked the past medical history, taking particular notice of any previous chest or circulatory conditions and whether or not she smokes.

It is important to explain that following an anaesthetic the patient may have a cough and that she should know how to cope with it. Ideally she should be physically as fit as possible and encouraged to be as active as her medical condition allows. Occasionally patients with chest conditions are admitted in advance to allow the physiotherapist to help in clearing the chest.

Routine Preoperative Treatment

The following exercises should be taught preoperatively as a routine:

1. Ankle movements. Instruct the patient to:
   a. Pull foot up, point toes down, keep knee straight.
   b. Circle foot, with the leg kept still, moving from the ankle.
   c. Stretch toes up, curl down.
2. Quadriceps contractions. Instruct patient to press knees back against the bed with the legs kept straight, hold and relax.
3. Gluteal contractions. Instruct patient to press buttocks together, hold and relax.

These exercises should be done frequently during the day. All instructions about exercises must be accompanied by explanation of the importance of the circulation in the legs and feet after surgery.

4. Breathing exercises. Lower costal, upper costal and diaphragmatic breathing (explained in detail below) and full chest expansion must be taught in as much detail as time allows and their importance explained.

5. Coughing. Teach the patient before operation how to cough safely and comfortably afterwards.

6. Pelvic floor exercises. These should be taught now (see p. 227).

POSTOPERATIVE PHYSIOTHERAPY

The immediate aim is to help prevent chest and circulatory complications; foot and ankle exercises (as taught preoperatively) and the breathing exercises detailed below should be performed by the patient hourly, if possible, for at least three days or until she is fully ambulant. This may then be followed by a graduated scheme of exercises to return the patient to normal daily activities.

Breathing Exercises

These encourage full chest expansion and aid venous return through diaphragmatic breathing.

All breathing exercises should be taught with the patient in a comfortable, fully supported position, with pillows and back rest. The patient should be half-sitting, with her knees bent up and her feet flat on the bed.

Diaphragmatic breathing

The physiotherapist places her hand on the patient's abdomen below the sternum and between the lower ribs. The patient is asked to breathe out first, then to take a deep breath and fill the area under the physiotherapist's hands. The patient repeats this slowly three or four times, breathing slowly in and out. This is sometimes called abdominal breathing.

Lower costal breathing

The physiotherapist puts her hands on either side of the patient's ribs in the lower costal area. The patient is asked to breathe out. She then takes a deep breath through the nose, expanding the ribs where she feels the resistance of the hands, and expanding the lungs fully. On expiration, a firm inwards pressure with gentle vibration is exerted by the physiotherapist, to aid expulsion of air and loosen chest secretions. This is also repeated three or four times.

Upper costal breathing

The physiotherapist puts her hands over the upper costal and clavicular areas on either side of the sternum. The patient is asked to breathe out through the mouth. She then takes a shallow breath through the nose, raising the upper chest area under the gentle pressure of the hands. Finally the patient breaths out through the mouth while the physiotherapist aids expirations with gentle vibrations of her hands. This is repeated three or four times.

Coughing

The physiotherapist will be able to feel a 'rattle' under her hands and knows that the patient is then ready to be encouraged to cough. The patient is supported in half-sitting position with the knees bent up and the feet flat on the bed. The patient places her own hands over the incision and the physiotherapist adds her hand to give extra support. Alternatively a pillow can be placed over the incision with the patient's hands on top. The area is held firmly, and the patient is asked to contract the abdominal muscles gently then take a sharp breath in and cough out, with head slightly forward. Encouragement is necessary and assurance that she will not harm herself. Sometimes a sip of cold water is helpful.

Other positions for coughing (not usually acceptable on the first day) are to sit forward in bed with the knees bent up and the arms round the knees, or to sit out of bed in a chair, feet flat on the floor, arms folded and resting on knees while leaning forward.

Postural drainage is a manipulative technique which may be necessary in cases of chest infection or past medical history of respiratory problems. The patient lies first on one side and then on the other. The bed may or may not be tipped according to the general medical and chest conditions. The manipulative techniques used are either shaking and vibration and/or clapping. These methods are very specialized and cannot be attempted unless the operator is properly trained. Their aim is to increase vibration through the rib-cage and so aid expectoration of chest secretions.

Inhalations are valuable immediately before treatment but the patient must be encouraged to take deep breaths and obtain full chest expansion while inhaling.

The importance of preoperative treatment is obvious and the ability of the physiotherapist to gain the patient's confidence and cooperation at that time pays dividends in the early postoperative days. Once she is mobilizing well the foot and leg exercises can be discontinued and as the soreness lessens she will cough freely and as necessary without assistance.

Back Care in Bed

It is important to remember that the normal lumbar curve produces a slightly hollow back. The pillows must always be placed to support this forward curve. If this is not done a passive flexion strain is placed on the lumbar spine resulting in back pain during the recuperative and convalescent periods or for longer. In addition the forward curve increases the chest capacity and encourages correct breathing and chest expansion (Fig. 17.6).

Patients with backache are more comfortable lying flat with one or two pillows, if their medical condition allows.

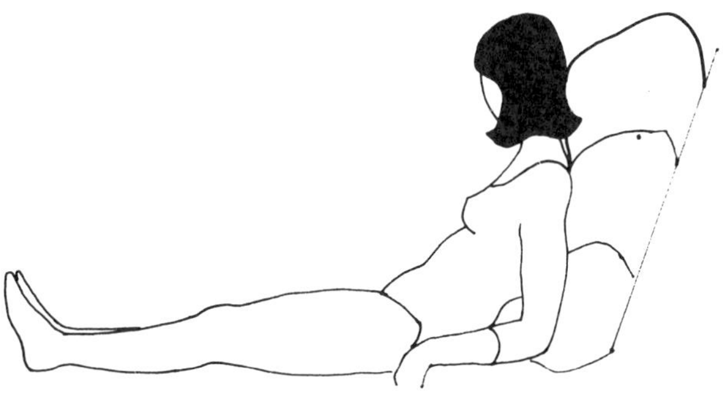

Fig. 17.6. Back care in bed.

Exercises Following Pelvic Floor Repairs

Pelvic floor contraction to strengthen levator ani and give added support to the repaired pelvic fascia and ligaments is important. The method of teaching this exercise has already been described in detail and the importance of teaching it in the preoperative period emphasized. If the surgeon is in agreement the patient can be encouraged to do the exercise carefully—a gentle squeeze on the catheter is suggested—on the second day following the operation. This can be repeated three or four times every hour throughout the day. Gradually the movement can be increased according to the patient's tolerance to the full pelvic floor contraction.

When the catheter has been removed the patient should have full control of her flow of urine.

Exercises Following Hysterectomy

These exercises are also useful after gynaecological surgery of all kinds if there has been an abdominal incision.

Routine physiotherapy is usually given for the first three days or until the patient is fully ambulant. The gentle exercises and the recommended time for which it is safe to do them serve only as guidelines; obviously the patient's general postoperative progress must be taken into consideration as well as her age and past medical history. At all times before any exercises are taught the notes must be checked for any deviation from normal progress and if necessary the exercises must be temporarily discontinued or suitably amended.

All abdominal exercises should be taught with great care because of the strain on the site of incision and the muscle insertion into the linea alba. They are usually commenced on the third or fourth postoperative day, although this is only a guideline.

Before stitches are removed

1. Abdominal contractions. The patient lies down with one pillow, knees bent up and feet flat on the bed. The abdominal wall is pulled in, held and relaxed. Care must be taken to obtain a true abdominal contraction and not merely a holding of the breath. It is easy to give the appearance of abdominal contractions by taking a short breath in, raising the shoulders slightly and producing only an alteration of abdominal pressure. This exercise should be repeated four or five times every hour and in sitting and standing positions.
2. Pelvic tilting (Fig. 17.7). This is a small movement of the lumbar spine. It is important in the maintenance of correct posture and is associated with abdominal contractions. It can also be very helpful to perform exercises in a gentle rocking movement to alleviate back pain.

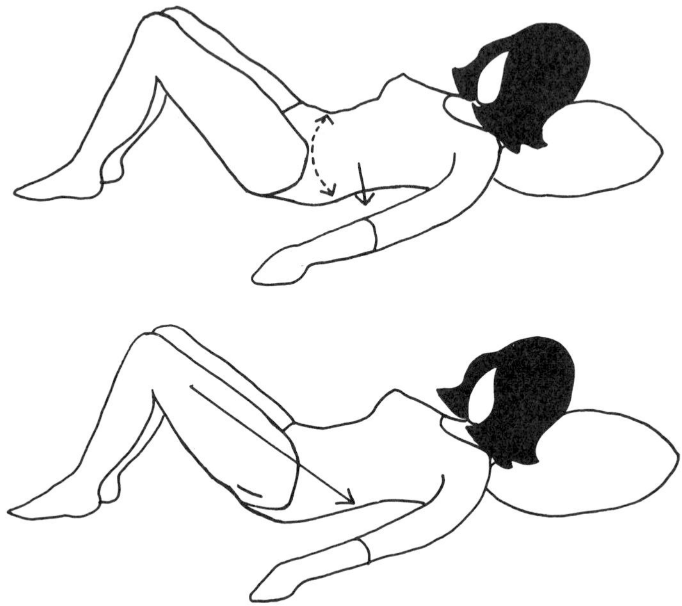

Fig. 17.7. Pelvic tilting.

As before the patient is lying with one pillow, knees bent up and feet flat on the bed. She pulls in the abdominal muscles and presses the lumbar spine flat against the bed to obtain a gentle tilting movement of the pelvis.

3. Pelvic floor contractions (Fig. 17.8), as described previously, should be performed sitting, standing and lying.

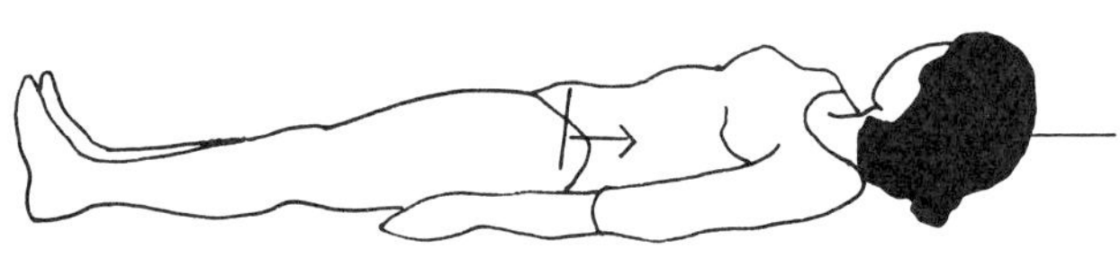

Fig. 17.8. Pelvic floor contractions.

After removal of stitches

4. Knee-rolling (Fig. 17.9). The patient lies down with one pillow, knees bent up and feet flat on the bed. The abdominal muscles are

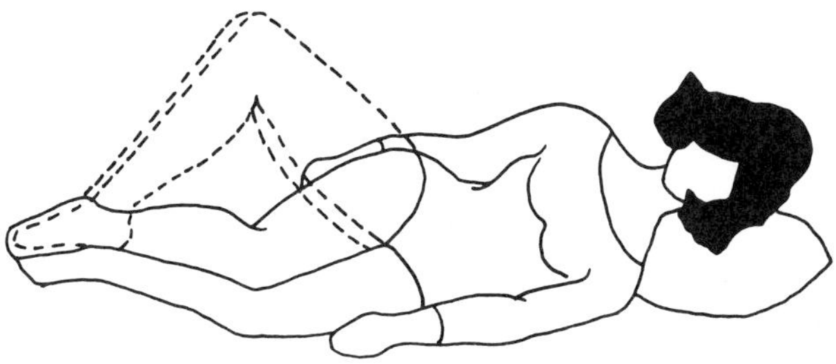

Fig. 17.9. Knee-rolling.

contracted but the breath *must not* be held. The knees are rolled gently and slowly to one side and then to the other, keeping the shoulders and waist flat on the bed. This localizes the movement to the external abdominal oblique muscle only. This exercise should be repeated six times on each side, three times a day.

Fig. 17.10. Hip hitching.

5. Hip-hitching (Fig. 17.10). The patient is lying with one pillow, one knee bent up and the other leg straight. The straight leg is shortened by pulling up the hip; the leg should slide up the bed and not be raised off it. This exercise is designed to strengthen the internal abdominal oblique muscle by using a side-flexion movement while lying. This exercise is repeated six times on each side, three times a day. The muscle action can be felt by placing a hand above the iliac crest on the side of the leg being moved.

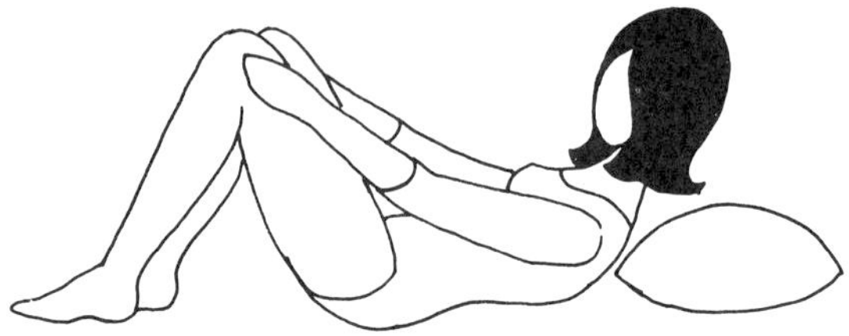

Fig. 17.11. Head raising.

About eight days after surgery

6. Head-raising (Fig. 17.11). The patient is lying with one pillow, knees bent up, feet flat on the bed and hands on thighs. The abdominal muscles are contracted and the head is raised to look at the knees. The patient progresses to raising the head and shoulders slowly and running her hands down the front of the thighs, as far as the knees if possible. The head or head and shoulders are then lowered slowly onto the bed and the hands are returned to their original position.

This exercise is left until last because the muscle involved is mainly the rectus abdominis. With a suprapubic incision it has been cut through and therefore time for healing must be allowed. The exercise can be made easier by giving the patient pillows so the muscle is in a shortened position before beginning to contract, or conversely, no pillows to extend the muscle to full length before performing the movement. This exercise can thus be graduated according to the age and general fitness of the patient.

Exercises to be avoided

At no time should the patient be allowed to sit straight up from a lying position or raise both legs when in a lying position because of the enormous strain exerted on the rectus abdominis.

Progression of exercises

Exercises can be progressed or made stronger by increasing the number of times they are performed or changing the starting position, e.g. hip-hitching. If this is done standing, then the weight of the leg and the pull of gravity make it more difficult and therefore stronger muscle work. Care must be taken to fix the shoulder girdle by holding on to a table or locker at about waist height. Then the abdominal muscles are pulled in, shortening the leg while taking care to keep the legs close together to eliminate, as far as possible, the use of the hip abductors. This should be repeated five or six times each side, three times daily. This exercise is much stronger than earlier exercises and suitable when the patient is almost fit to go home.

Stairs

Many patients have stairs to negotiate at home and it is important to take them up and down a flight on the day before they go home.

As a general rule following gynaecological surgery patients are advised to use the first two weeks at home, i.e. until the end of the fourth week following surgery, for rest, getting up when they wish to and behaving as if it were extended hospital care whether at home or in a convalescent home. From four to six weeks they should be encouraged to gradually return to normal life by increasing their walking distance and doing light household duties, so that by the end of six weeks they are able to return to a normal life provided it is not too arduous. A return to normal at three months is probably a more acceptable time if the patient's life style is an arduous one.

How to Get Up from Lying Down

Remembering the arrangement of the abdominal muscles it is important following surgery to encourage the patient to get in and out of bed in a manner which puts as little strain as possible on the abdominal wall.

The easiest method, involving the least amount of strain and starting with the patient lying on her back, is carried out as follows (Fig. 17.12). The patient should:

1. Bend both knees up.
2. Keeping knees together, imagine her trunk as a log of wood and turn to one side without twisting, i.e. keeping shoulders and knees in line.
3. With the top hand placed on the bed at shoulder level, push up sideways to a side sitting position, at the same time allowing the legs to move slowly over the side of the bed.
4. Reach sitting position on side of bed.

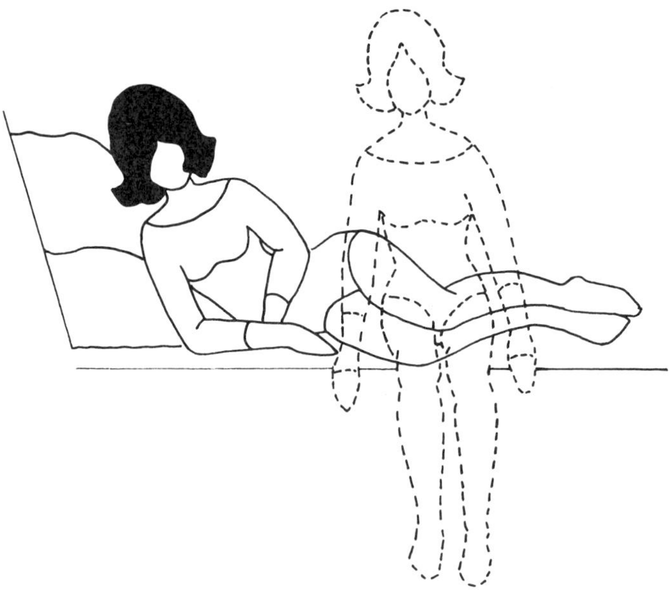

Fig. 17.12. Getting up from a lying position.

5. Place both feet firmly on the floor, bend the trunk forwards and push up and straighten the knees.
6. Stand up straight. Back *straight*, before attempting to walk.

Posture is important at all times. From the first time the patient gets up postoperatively she should be encouraged to 'walk tall'.

INFRA-RED RADIATION

Infra-red radiation may be helpful to disperse a haematoma or encourage the healing of an oozing wound by increasing the circulation to the area. This is contraindicated if malignant disease is present.

The infra-red lamp is placed so that the element is 45 cm from the area to be treated, after making sure the patient is fully supported and comfortable so she will not change her position during treatment. The lamp is angled so that the rays strike the area to be treated at 90 degrees. The area treated must be free of any creams which can concentrate the rays and cause burning.

Treatment should last about 10 minutes once or twice a day.

TO SUM UP

The physiotherapist's role is partly prophylactic and partly rehabilitative with the aim of returning the patient as quickly and confidently as possible to her normal daily life. At all times she must remember that gynaecological surgery has psychological as well as physical implications. The approach to the patient must always be one of deep understanding and gentleness.

Ideally all physiotherapists working on obstetric and gynaecology units should be members of the Association of Chartered Physiotherapists in Obstetrics and Gynaecology (c/o Chartered Society of Physiotherapists, 14 Bedford Row, London WC1R 4ED).

Bibliography

Cash, J.E. (1979) *Physiotherapy in Some Surgical Conditions*, 6th ed. London: Faber & Faber.

Montgomery, E. (1974) *Regaining Bladder Control.* Bristol: John Wright.

Index

D

E

F

G

H

I

Printed in Great
Britain
by Amazon

31455242R00151

ERHAN KOLBAŞ

MESAJ

NOVUS II

DESTEK
yayınları

DESTEK MEDYA GRUBU

DESTEK YAYINLARI: 1806
ARAŞTIRMA: 401

ERHAN KOLBAŞI & DİLEK KARAKUŞ / MESAJ - NOVUS II

İmtiyaz Sahibi: Destek Yapım Prodüksiyon Dış Tic. A.Ş.
Genel Yayın Yönetmeni: Ertürk Akşun
Yayın Koordinatörü: Özlem Esmergül
Üretim Koordinatörü: Semran Karaçayır
Editör: Devrim Yalkut
Kapak Tasarım: İlknur Muştu
Sayfa Düzeni: Cansu Poroy
Sosyal Medya-Grafik: Mesud Topal-Nursefa Üzüm Kalender
Reklam ve Tanıtım: Selen Çavuşovalı-Işıl Ilgıt Şimşek

Destek Yayınları:
1.-10. Baskı: Ağustos 2023
11.-15. Baskı: Eylül 2023
16.-30. Baskı: Ekim 2023
Yayıncı Sertifika No. 43196

ISBN 978-625-441-970-6

Abdi İpekçi Caddesi No. 31/5 Nişantaşı/İstanbul
Tel. (0) 212 252 22 42
Faks: (0) 212 252 22 43
www.destekdukkan.com
info@destekyayinlari.com
facebook.com/DestekYayinevi
twitter.com/destekyayinlari
instagram.com/destekyayinlari

Destek Dukkan

Deniz Ofset – Çetin Koçak
Sertifika No. 48625
Maltepe Mahallesi
Hastane Yolu Sokak No. 1/6
Zeytinburnu / İstanbul
Tel. (0) 212 613 30 06

DESTEK yayınları KARAKARGA BEYAZ BAYKUŞ genç DESTEK ATHICA

ERHAN KOLBAŞI

DİLEK KARAKUŞ

MESAJ

NOVUS II

DESTEK
yayınları

Erhan Kolbaşı

Yazar, Araştırmacı, Eğitmen.

1966 İzmir doğumlu olan Erhan Kolbaşı Dışişleri Bakanlığı'nda 25 yıl süreyle İdari Ataşe, Yardımcı Konsolos ve Konsolos olarak görev yapmış, 2016 yılında Dışişleri kariyerini noktalamıştır.

Özellikle Washington, D.C. ve New York görevleri sırasında, 8 yıl boyunca, Dünya dışı uygarlıklara ilişkin yeni bir sosyal bilim disiplini olan "exopolitika" alanında araştırma ve faaliyetler yürüten Exopolitics Institute (Exopolitika Enstitüsü) bünyesindeki program ve çalışmalara katılan yazar, "UFO Fenomeni ve Dünya Dışı Uygarlıklar" konusuna dair birçok makale kaleme almış ve sunumlar yapmıştır. Erhan Kolbaşı 2016 Ağustos ayında Exopolitics Institute üyeliğine seçilmiştir. Kolbaşı gerek ABD'de, gerekse Türkiye'de çok sayıda alıkonma ve bireysel temas vakası üzerinde de çalışmış, özellikle konunun metapsişik ve ruhsal boyutlarına odaklanmıştır.

Yazar ayrıca, Akdeniz Üniversitesi bünyesindeki bir sosyal sorumluluk projesi olan "60+ Tazelenme Üniversitesi"nde bir yıl süreyle exopolitika/ufoloji dersleri vermiştir.

Kolbaşı, 2019 yılında "Dünya Dışı Temas Araştırması Oluşumu"nu kurmuş olup, FREE (Dr. Edgar Mitchell Foundation for Research into Extraterrestrial Experiences) Vakfi'yla da işbirliği halinde, Dünya dışı temaslara ait verilerin sosyal bilim metodolojisine dayalı olarak araştırılması amacı taşıyan uzun soluklu bir proje üzerinde çalışmaktadır.

Yazarın *Galaktik Diplomasi* isimli kitabı 2016 yılında, *Kozmik Dokunuş In Vitro* kitabı 2017 yılında, *Novus* isimli kitabı 2018 yılında, *Mutatio* isimli kitabı 2019 yılında, 77 – *Ruhun ve Varoluşun Büyük Yasaları* adlı kitabı ise 2023 yılında yayımlanmıştır.

Kolbaşı, 2020-2022 yılları arasında metapsişik ve Dünya dışı temaslar konusunda dersler vermiştir.

Dilek Karakuş

Yazar, Araştırmacı, Eğitmen.

1977 yılında Kahramanmaraş'ta doğdu. 9 yaşındayken, ailesi Londra'ya taşınma kararı aldı. 2002 yılında Waltham Forest College'da Psikolojik Danışmanlık Bölümü'nü bitirdikten sonra East London Üniversitesi Psikoloji Bölümü'ne devam etti. Bir gece bu dünyadan başka bir dünyaya geçiş yaptı ve sonrasında iki yıl boyunca ruhsal varlıklar tarafından eğitime tabi tutuldu. Bu süreçte, çocukluğundan beri yaşadığı paranormal olayların rastlantı olmadığını, hayatın bu dünyadan ibaret olmadığını öğrendi. Bütün bunları daha bilimsel bir platforma oturtmak için tekrar okul hayatına dönüş yaptı. Aynı anda, Kozmik Enerjiler ve Quantum Üniversitesi Bütünsel Sağlık Bilimleri ölümlerinde eğitim aldı ve arkasından "Psikoterapi Yüksek Lisansı"nı tamamladı.

Dilek Karakuş, Dolores Cannon ve Michael Newton'un da akreditasyon aldıkları Geçmiş Yaşam Terapistleri Birliği'nden kendi tekniklerinin akreditasyonunu almış bir eğitmen terapisttir.

Karakuş; insan psikolojisi, inanç sistemi ve paranormal yaşanmışlıklarını bir araya getirerek, kendisini araştırmalarına adamış bir psişik ve araştırmacıdır.

Bilinçaltı çalışmalarını bir araya getirdiği *Geçiş* adlı kitabı 2021 yılında yayımlanmıştır. İkinci kitabı *Evrenin Kara Kutusu* da yayıma hazırlanmaktadır.

"Biliniz ki: Türkiye Cumhuriyeti aslında siyasal değil, bütünüyle ruhsal bir zemin üzerine kurulmuştur..."

– E.K.

İÇİNDEKİLER

BİRİNCİ KISIM

SEANSLAR

GİRİŞ

Tam 5 yıl...

İlk *Novus*'un üzerinden tam 5 yıl geçmişti...

Doğrusu ilk başta klasik bir devam serisi yazma düşüncemiz yoktu...

Onu çocukluğundan beri eğiten varlıkların on yıl önceki ilk kehaneti gerçekleşmişti. Dilek Karakuş'a "*Yazarın seni Anadolu'da bekliyor*" demişlerdi. O ilk kehanetten yıllar sonra bir araya gelmiş, daha doğrusu bir şekilde getirilmiş ve birlikte *Novus*'u ortaya çıkarmıştık.

Bir kehanet daha vardı.

Bir üçüncü kişi...

O da ortaya çıkacak denmişti...

Çıktı...

Tam tarif edildiği şekilde çıktı... Zamanın geldiğini anladık.

Yol arkadaşım, kardeşim Dilek Karakuş'la birlikte yeni bir *Novus* macerasına atılmaya karar verdik.

Niyetimiz ilk *Novus* kitabında olduğu gibi yine temas vakalarının hatırlanmayan, hafıza mahzenlerinde örtülü kalan kısımlarını su yüzüne çıkarmaktı. Ancak bu yeni kitabın ilkinden daha farklı olacağına dair bir his de arka planda hep yanıp sönüyordu. Yanılmadığımızı kısa sürede anladık.

İlginç olan, kitapta yer alacak temasçıları belirleme sürecinin su gibi akıp gitmesiydi. Sanki hepsi önceden belirlenmişti ve bizim onları seçmemizi bekliyorlardı. Deneyimlerinin içeriklerine

güvendiğimiz bazıları türlü sebeplerle gelemezlerken, daha sonraları irtibat kurduğumuz temasçılar rüya ve hissiyatla yönlendirilip bize ulaşıyorlardı. Garip bir şeyler oluyordu. Henüz bilmediğimiz bir hedefe doğru hızla sürükleniyorduk fakat bu sürükleniş kadife gibi yumuşak ve oldukça dirençsiz bir sürüklenişti. Süreç kolaylaştırılıyordu. Temasçıları biz davet ediyorduk ama sanki olan biten her şey kontrolümüz dışındaydı. "Sanki" kelimesinin gereksizliğini anlamamız çok da uzun sürmedi.

Seanslar sırasında, süjelerin daha önce yaşadıkları Dünya dışı temaslara dair anılarını ve diğer sıra dışı deneyimlerini iyiden iyiye sondajlayıp, karanlıkta kalan detayları gün ışığına çıkartırken, görünmeyen bir el bir anda perdeyi kapatıp bizi Türkiye'nin geleceğine yönlendiriyor, temas vakalarının ışıltılı gizeminden bizi çekip alarak Anadolu'nun tam ortasına bırakıyordu. Temas içeriğine dönmeye kalkıştığımızda ise şalteri indiriyor, görüntüyü karartıyorlardı. Üst boyutların ve uzak güneş sistemlerinin Dünya ötesi temsilcilerinin Dünya'daki yol arkadaşları seans koltuğunda uzanmış halde sırları deşifre ederlerken, o sihirli el direksiyona geçiyor ve konu dönüp dolaşıp Mustafa Kemal Atatürk'e ve yakın gelecekte ortaya çıkarak, o birleştirici, ayağa kaldırıcı, kudretli bilincin bayrağını devralacak Yeni Lider'e geliyordu. Çalışmalarda her ne kadar katılımcıların Dünya dışı deneyimlerine dair birçok yeni ve farklı veriler elde etmiş olsak da, seans içerikleri "ısrarla" belli bir ana çekirdek etrafında dönüyordu.

Görünen oydu ki daha önce bu konuyla ilintili en ufak bir bilgisi, araştırması, duyumu dahi olmayan temasçıların ağızlarından dökülen ortak ifadeler bize bir şey anlatmaya çalışıyordu!

Seanslar ilerledikçe durum daha net ortaya çıkmaya başlamış, kitabın hedefi belli olmuştu:

Bu "mesajı" kitlelere iletin!

Bazı noktalarda bizimle birtakım özel bilgiler de paylaşıldı. Kucağımıza bırakılan ateş topunu sevgiyle kabul ettik. Bir kısım ifadeleri, konuların yüksek hassasiyeti ve kişilerin güvenliği bakımından kitaba koyamadık, bazılarını ise -affınıza ve anlayışınıza sığınarak- bir miktar üzeri kapalı geçmek durumunda kaldık. Bunun sebeplerinin değerli okuyucularımız tarafından ileride daha da iyi anlaşılacağından en ufak bir kuşkumuz dahi yoktur.

Kitap içeriğindeki bilgiler katılımcıların ağızlarından döküldüğü şekliyle yansıtılmış, Birinci Kısım'da seans kayıtlarına yer verilirken, İkinci Kısım'da genel analiz ve değerlendirmeleri yapılmıştır. Sadece editoryal kalitenin korunması maksadıyla, bazı ifadeler daha anlaşılır hale getirilmiştir.

Ortaya çıkan verilerin ortaklığı son derece dikkat çekicidir. Geleceğe yönelik ifadelerin gerçekleşme şeklini ve sürecini ise zaman gösterecektir.

Ruhsal sistemin kendisine göre bir planı ve kendi ölçeğinde bir saati vardır. Bu yüce mekanizmanın kudretli eli kendisine bağlı unsurlarla yeryüzüne uzanır, gerekeni gereken zamanda yapar.

Daima yapmıştır, yapmaktadır ve yine yapacaktır.

Mesaj - Novus II bir temenni ya da bir tahmin kitabı değildir. Bu bir "mesaj", bir bilgi aktarımı, bir "haber" kitabıdır. Laf kalabalığına, süslü ifadelere gerek yoktur. Yol ve hedef bellidir. Kitap içeriği zaten kendi kendini açıklamaktadır.

Biz de üzerimize düşeni yerine getiriyor, mesajı sizlere ulaştırıyoruz.

Yolumuz açık olsun.

Erhan Kolbaşı & Dilek Karakuş

1. BÖLÜM

LİDER

Novus serisinin ikinci kitabı için seanslara başlamamıza üç gün kalmıştı...

Dilek bana bir süredir, "*İnce, zayıf, uzun kadın kim?... Çekik gözlü ve saçlarını tepede toplamış... Devamlı gözümün önüne geliyor... O kadın gelmeli...*" deyip duruyordu.

O kadın, İzmir'de yaşayan, 45 yaşlarında ve uzun yıllar özel bir şirketin bölge satış temsilciğini yapan Aylin Aygün'dü. Kendisinden seansa katılım için teyit bekliyorduk.

Seansa iki gün kala Aylin'den ilginç bir WhatsApp mesajı telefonuma düştü:

> *"Erhan Bey, ben bu gece tekrar öncekilerden çok farklı, çok güçlü frekanslar içeren bir temas yaşadım... Merkabah gibi bir şeydi... Çok ama çok zorlandım... Daha önce böyle bir deneyimim olmamıştı... Saat 04.00 sularıydı... Çoğunluğu kadınlardan oluşan bir topluluk aniden miraçtan iner gibi önüme indirildi ve bu kişilerin benim hayat planımdaki senaryomda rol alacak oyuncular olduğu, rol dağılımı için bekledikleri söylendi... Onların rollerini ben de henüz bilmiyorum... Onlar da bilmiyorlar ama yan yana oturanların arasında, ortada oturan ve bana bakarak telepatik olarak benimle bağ kuran kadın Dilek Hanım'a çok*

benziyordu... Biz bu görüşmeyi planlayalım... Söylediğiniz tarihe ben kendimi hazırlıyorum."

Daha önce hiç karşılaşmamış olan bu ikili seans günü yüz yüze geldiklerinde birbirlerini hemen tanıdılar. Dilek Aylin'i önceden görmediği gibi öyküsünü de bilmiyordu.

Çocukluğundan bu yana, tıpkı diğer birçok temasçı gibi kendisini Dünya'ya ait hissetmeyen ve her gece gözünü uzak yıldızlara dikip bu çılgın gezegende bulunma amacını sorgulayan Aylin, musallat kuşkuları, hocalar, muskalar, gerçekleşen rüyalarla dolu bir gençlik çağına ayak basmıştı. Çevresi ise onun neler yaşadığını kavrayamıyordu.

Aylin 2008 yılında hastanede çekap yaptırdığında kendisine rahim kanseri teşhisi konmuştu. Dünya başına yıkıldı. Umutla birçok farklı doktora başvurdu. Sonuç hep aynıydı. Rahmin bir an önce alınması gerektiği söylenmişti. O dönemde uykuda yaşadığı bir temas deneyimi sonrasında ani ve olağandışı bir şekilde bu hastalıktan kurtuldu.

Ardından, yaklaşık 1 yıl önce, bu kez beyin tümörü teşhisiyle bir kez daha sarsıldı ama isyan etmedi ve durumu kabullendi. Gerçek ameliyat gününden bir hafta önce bir kez daha uykusunda bir temas yaşadı ve beyninden ameliyat edildiğini gördü. Olanları anlamıştı. Ameliyatına iki gün kala doktorundan tekrar MR çekmesini rica etti. Görüntü bu kez tertemizdi!

Bu sıra dışı müdahalelerin Dünya ötesi detaylarını ortaya çıkarmak üzere davet ettiğimiz Aylin Aygün seans koltuğuna uzandı.

Seansı tamamladık.

Aylin uzandığı yerden ayağa kalkarken Dilek'le göz göze geldik.

Mesaj – Novus II'nin bambaşka bir yöne doğru evrildiğini yeni yeni anlamaya başlamıştık.

Aylin Aygün Seansı
30 Haziran 2023

(Dilek'in yaptırdığı nefes, gevşeme ve enerji çalışması sonrasında Aylin süratle yarı-trans haline giriyor ve ayağından bedeninin üst kısımlarına doğru bir uyuşma yayılıyor. Dilek, Aylin'in karın bölgesine daha önce bir işlem yapılmış olduğunu ve yumurta alındığını vizyon olarak görüyor ve bana eliyle sessizce karın bölgesini işaret ediyor. Ayakları ince, uzun ve biraz da garip görünümlü bir varlık türü olduğunu hissediyor. Aylin'de hafif titremeler var. Önce bir sedye görüntüsü geliyor.)

Aylin: Ameliyat oldum... Bir doktor ve o doktoru tanıyorum... O benim doktorumdu... Ama onun yanında iki kişi daha var... Onlar da erkeğe benziyor... Benim doktorum olan kişiye ne yapacağını tarif ediyorlar ve ameliyatı o şekilde doktoruma yaptırıyorlar...

Senin Dünya'daki doktoruna tarifle ameliyat mı yaptırıyorlar?

Aylin: Evet... İki varlık.

Onları tanıyor musun?

Aylin: Hayır.

Tipleri nasıl?

Aylin: Tip olarak ya da yüz olarak gözümün önünde bir şekil yok ama sanki yüzü yok gibi.

Kendini rahat bırak Aylin. Çünkü bazen görsel olur, bazen de sezgi olarak gelir. *(Şuuraltına daha sert bir komutla.)* Tiplerini tarif etmeni istiyorum Aylin.

Aylin: Beyaz elbiseli ama uçuşan bir elbise gibi... Yüzleri yok ama grimsi gibi bir surat görüyorum.

Gözleri?

Aylin. Şimdi iri göz görüntüsü geldi gözümün önüne.

Gözakı var mı?

Aylin: Var ama gözleri bizimki gibi değil... İri.

Peki sen ne ameliyatı oluyorsun orada?

Aylin: Beynimdeki bir problemden dolayı... Aslında rüya olarak görüyorum bunu... O varlıklar ameliyat yaptılar ve gerçek hayatta olmadım bu ameliyatı.

(Not: Aylin'in ameliyatı yukarıda, Dünya dışı bir ortamda yapılmış. Aylin, bazıları karın bölgesinde olmak üzere, defalarca başka operasyonlar da geçirmiş ve başkalarının operasyonlarına da tanıklık etmiş. Bir tanesinde, bir başka adama kafa bölgesinden ayakta müdahale edilmiş. Aylin şimdi o görüntüye geçiyor.)

Şimdi akıştayız. Orada mısın şu anda?

Aylin: Şurasına müdahale ediliyor... (Eliyle o adamın kafa bölgesini gösteriyor.)

Tanıyor musun o adamı?

Aylin: Gözümün önüne bu hayatta tanıdığım birisi geldi. (... ...) isminde birisi... Benim eski erkek arkadaşımdı.

Peki neden orada o kişi?

(Aylin bunu göremiyor.)

Peki sana neden müdahale ettiler o sedyede? Beynine yani?

Aylin: Çünkü beynimde bir tümör vardı... Çok ani bir şekilde oldu ve çok garip bir yerdeydi.

Yani beynin çok zor bir yerinde miydi?

Aylin: Evet, çok zor bir yerdeydi ve Dünya'da çoğu doktorun yapamayacağı bir ameliyattı... Çok zor olan bir şeydi.

Neden sen peki? Neden sana müdahale edildi?

Aylin: Evet, ben de bunu kendime hep sordum.

(Tekrar ve biraz daha sert bir ses frekansı kullanarak soruyoruz çünkü Aylin'in şuuraltı bunun yanıtını biliyor.)

Niçin iyileştirildin Aylin?

Aylin: Burada bir görevim olduğunu biliyorum.

Devam et.

Aylin: Şifaya kanallık yapacağım... Onu biliyorum ama ne yapacağımı bilmiyorum... Kiminle karşılaşacağımı bilmiyorum... Rehberimi tanımıyorum.

Bunun için yaşamının uzatılması mı gerekiyordu?

Aylin: Evet.

Bu hayattaki devamlılığın için iyileştirilmen mi gerekiyordu?[1]

Aylin: Evet.

Peki başka bir sebep de olabilir mi?

Aylin: Evet.

Nedir?

Aylin: Henüz onu söylemiyorlar... (Bir süre sessizlikten sonra Aylin tekrar konuşuyor...) Evet var! Farklı bir boyutta farklı bir dünya için hazırlık gibi.

Nasıl bir hazırlık?

Aylin: Başka bir boyutta başka bir dünyaya gidiyorum... Orada yeni bir nesil için.

1. Dünya dışı varlıklar, kendileriyle ortak bir projeye gönüllü olarak katılmış bulunan bireylerde, bu projedeki rollerini sekteye uğratabilecek bir hastalık gelişmişse ve bu hastalık kişinin bireysel tekâmül planı içinde yer almıyorsa, hastalığa doğrudan müdahale ediyorlar. Ayrıca, şifa enerjisi aktarımı ya da genel bilinç yükselişine katkı gibi, insanlığa faydalı bir görev üstlenmiş temasçıların da yaşam sürelerinin planlanandan erken sona ermemesi için de hastalığın Dünya dışı operasyonla yok edilmesi söz konusu olabiliyor. Bu müdahalelerin bir diğer sebebi de, Dünya dışı bir sistemden Dünya'ya biyolojik doğum yoluyla, belli bir görevle gelmiş bir varlığın Dünya'ya adaptasyon sağlayamaması sonucunda oluşan rahatsızlıklardır. Bu durumda da hastalığın bütünüyle ya da kısmen ortadan kaldırılması veya en azından, görev tamamlanıncaya kadar hafifletilmesi yoluna gidiliyor. Buna dair sayısız örnek temas literatüründe yer almaktadır.

Orada yeni bir nesil mi oluşturuyorlar?

Aylin: Evet.

Yeni bir dünya mı oluşturuyorlar orada?

Aylin: Evet.

Nasıl?

Aylin: O dünyada yeni belirlenmiş olan kişilerden bir nesil oluşturmayı planlıyorlar.

Dünya'dan kişilerle mi?

Aylin: Evet Dünya'dan.

Neye göre belirlenmiş bu kişiler?

Aylin: Saf bilinç olarak belirlenenler.

Ne zaman peki?

Aylin: Zaman yaklaşıyor.

Bunlar bilinç olarak hazır olan insanlar mı?

Aylin: Evet... Ama çoğu bilinç bunun farkında olmuyor.

Peki Dünya'da ne olacak o zaman? Diğer kalanlar ne olacak?

Aylin: Diğer kalanlar... Kaos şeklinde görünüyor önümde... Kaos var ve o kalanlar daha bilinçlenmemiş... Beşer olarak yaşayan insan nesli burada kalacak olanlar.

Orası bizimle aynı boyutta değil mi?

Aylin: Hayır... Hayır... Değil.

Nasıl bir yer? Daha mı yüksek bir titreşim?

Aylin: Daha yüksek frekanslar var... Sesler var... Daha ışık boyutunda bir yer.

O zaman buradan mezun olanlar mı gidecek oraya?

Aylin: Evet, buradan mezun olanlar gidecek ama bu şekilde değil... Yani düşünce... Bilince bir şey düşüyor ve kendini orada buluyorsun... Orada oluyorsun... Orada yaşamaya başlıyorsun... Yani bilincine düşen durumu yaşıyorsun.

Aynı anda hem burada hem de orada olmak gibi bir şey mi?

Aylin: (Zorlu bir kavramı tarif etmeye çabalıyor...) Onun gibi bir şey değil... Öyle değil.

Oradaki bedenlerde mi yaşayacaklar?

Aylin: Evet... Burada prova yapılıyor... Önce bu bilince açık olan insanlar belirleniyor ve onlara küçük küçük provalar yaptırılıyor... Düşündüğü şey sürekli önüne geliyor... Düşündüğü şey önüne gelen insanlar o boyuta geçebiliyor sadece.[2]

Cennet gibi gerçekten.

Aylin: Evet cennet gibi ama titreşim çok yüksek.

Oradaki bedenler nasıl?

Aylin: Çok daha saf ve süzülüyor böyle bedenler.

Daha akışkan yani?

Aylin: Evet.

İnsan formunda mı yine?

Aylin: Evet ama flu.

Bir zaman hissin var mı? Proje başladı mı?

Aylin: Proje başladı ama insanları belirliyorlar şu anda.

Temas vakalarında insanların Dünya dışı araçlara alınmalarının sebebi bu mu?

Aylin: Evet, onun sebeplerinden biri bu... Çünkü henüz tam belirlenmedi... Seçenekler arasında değerlendirme yapılıyor...

---

2. Burada çok önemli bir bilgi var. Aylin'in bahsettiği boyutun çok daha akışkan ve düşünce enerjisine yanıt verebilen kudrette, gelişmiş bir maddeden oluştuğu anlaşılıyor. Madde ruhsal tesiri alarak gelişir ve geliştikçe de daha akışkan hale gelir. Bunun sonucunda ise düşünceye daha kolaylıkla tepki verir. Örneğin spatyom maddesi de böyle bir maddedir ve insanların fiziksel ölüm sonrasında kendilerini içinde buldukları ortamlar kişinin otomatik imajinatif faaliyetinin spatyomun akışkan maddesi üzerindeki etkisiyle meydana gelirler. Cennet ve cehennem sembolizmi de bu imajinatif ortamların dinsel metinlerdeki karşılıklarıdır. Aylin'in bu ifadesi bize bir önemli bilgiyi daha anımsattı. Bazı vakalarda temasçılara düşünce gücüyle yaratımda bulunma, hatta Dünya dışı bir aracı kullanma uygulaması yaptırılıyor. Bu işlemlerin de böyle bir tatbikat amacına yönelik olabileceği akla geliyor.

Birçok seçeneği bir araya toplayıp onların içinden en üst insan modelini oluşturmak istiyorlar... En mükemmelini oluşturmaya çalışıyorlar.

O yüzden genetik materyal topluyorlar?

Aylin: Evet.

DNA'ları neye göre seçiyorlar? Üstün özellikleri mi belirliyorlar?

Aylin: Saf bilinç seçiyorlar... Ona uygun adaylar... Kirletilmemiş bilinçler seçiliyor... Negatife hiç girmemiş ve daha çok pozitifte kalmış insanlardan seçiliyor.

Onlar seçiliyor ve onların DNA'larını alıyorlar o zaman? Genetik materyal alıyorlar.

Aylin: Evet... Alıyorlar... Yeni bir üst versiyon yaratmak için.

Bu proje başladı ve hızlanacak mı?

Aylin: Hızlanacak çünkü gemi gibi bir şeye alınmaya başladı insanlar... Alınma olayları yoğunlaştı... Geçici olarak alınıyorlar ve orada işlemleri tamamlanıyor... Çok yüksek frekanslı bir güç, çok gürültülü bir şey var... Orada bu işlemler tamamlanıyor... Bu işlemi bilemiyorum... Tamamlandıktan sonra tekrar bu dünyaya bırakılıyorlar... Yani aniden bırakılıyorlar.

Peki iz bırakıyor mu bu işlemler? (Sorunun yanıtını elbette biliyoruz ama Aylin'den alacağımız bilgiyi merak ediyoruz.)

Aylin: Bırakıyor... Özellikle ellerde kızılımsı izler... Çok yüksek frekanstan dolayı.

Bir dakika Aylin. Burası çok kritik. Eller ve ayaklardaki kına benzeri izler yüksek frekanstan mı kaynaklanıyor?

Aylin: Evet yüksek titreşimden.

Peki nereye tutunuyorlar? Nasıl meydana geliyor bu izler?

Aylin: Bir enerji alanı gibi bir şey... Dikdörtgen prizma gibi... Onun içine yatırıyorlar... Çıkamıyorsunuz işlem sırasında ve

çıkamayınca da elinizle destek alıyorsunuz, tutunmaya çalışıyorsunuz. (Aylin elleriyle tarif etmeye çalışıyor.) Çünkü bedene çok ağır geliyor frekans.

Bu bir iz mi yapıyor?

Aylin: Evet kızarıklıklar.

Peki o kına benzeri izler gibi mi?

Aylin: Evet... Evet... Kızılımsı... Kına gibi.

Orada özel bir frekansa alıyorlar demek ki. Onun fonksiyonu ne?

Aylin: O frekans çok güçlü... Beden dayanamıyor o frekansa... Ne olduğunu da bilmiyor... Ne olduğunu anlamadığı için korkuya kapılıyor çünkü sadece bir alet benzeri bir şey olduğu söyleniyor... Frekans uyumlanıyor... Yüksek frekansa geçiş sağlıyorlar. (Bu sırada Dilek o cihazı gördüğü için eliyle şeklini çiziyor.)

Yeni boyutun frekansına mı ayarlıyorlar?

Aylin: Evet.

(Not: Bu işlem yapılırken vücut içgüdüsel olarak biraz savaşıyor ve eller ve ayaklarda yüksek titreşimden dolayı kına benzeri izler meydana geliyor. Bize göre çok sıcak ve yüksek bir vibrasyondan söz ediyoruz.)

Temasçının DNA'larını da değiştiren bir titreşim mi bu?

Aylin: Bunu söylemiyorlar ama şöyle bir açıklama var... Mevlana frekansı... Telkin.[3]

Döndükten sonra Dünya'ya nasıl uyum sağlıyorsun?

3. Bu frekans uyumlama işlemini şu şekilde açıklayalım: Bir telkin veriliyor. Bilinç o telkinle kendisini o prizmanın içindeyken hazırlıyor. Ancak beşeri zihin hâlâ faal olduğu için beden içgüdüsel olarak bu frekansa büyük bir direnç gösteriyor. Bu doğal bir durumdur. O frekans değişimi sürerken vücut refleks olarak elleriyle tutunma çabası içine giriyor. O noktada izler meydana geliyor. O korkuyu ve kaygıyı azaltmak için her temasçının bilincine ya da inanç sistemine göre telkinde bulunuyorlar. Örneğin Mevlana hissi bizlere uygun gelirken, Hıristiyan inancıyla büyümüş birisine Hz. İsa enerjisiyle telkin veriyorlar.

Aylin: Ben "La İlahe İllallah" diyerek kendimi sakinleştirmeye çalışıyorum... Sonra yatağıma yüksekten bırakıyorlar ve yatağıma bırakıldığım anda sırt bölgemin ateş gibi yandığını hissediyorum.

Fizik bedeninle mi alınıyorsun?

Aylin: Evet.

Sadece yüksek bilince ulaşmış, temiz, pozitif insanları alıyorlar diyorsun.

Aylin: Evet.

Fizik bedeni nasıl alıyorlar? Onu görüyor musun?

Aylin: Çok hızlı... Çok hızlı frekansla gidiliyor... Aniden... Işınlanma gibi.

Bedenin bir moleküler çözülmeye mi uğruyor?

Aylin: Hayır... Bedenim kaskatı biçimde o dikdörtgen prizmanın içinde... Bir anda oluyor... Yavaşlatılarak ve alıştırarak değil.

Yatağından alınışın ve bırakılışını soruyorum.

Aylin: Işınlanma gibi.

Tamam. İğne gibi bir şey yapıldı mı?

Aylin: Hayır.

Bunu yapan varlık sistemini biliyor musun? Kim bu varlıklar? Nasıl varlıklar? Nereye bağlılar?

Aylin: Bunlar başka bir boyutta.

Dünya ile bağlantılı mı? Neden Dünya'ya yardım ediyorlar?

Aylin: Çünkü Dünya'da çok büyük bir kaos oluyor.

Kaos olacak ve insanları buradan çıkartacaklar. Anladım.

Aylin: Evet... Yükselmiş ruhları, saf bilinçleri çıkartacaklar... Yeni bir proje için... Farklı bir proje için... Dünya'yı kurtarma projesi için.

Peki Dünya kaosu nasıl yaşayacak? Ondan sonra ne olacak eski dünyada?

Aylin: Köleler görüyorum... Köleleştirilmiş insanlar görüyorum... İlk insanlar tarzında.

O zaman Dünya sıfırlanıyor mu?

Aylin: Evet sıfırlanıyor.

Coğrafi olarak?

Aylin: Coğrafya da sıfırlanıyor... Yerle bir.

Zaman olarak bir hissiyatın var mı?

Aylin: Çeyrek zaman.

Çeyrek yüzyıl mı?

Aylin: Çeyrek zaman.

Bu varlıklar dünya sisteminden, dünya tekâmülünden sorumlu varlıklar mı? Onların emrindeler mi?

Aylin: Evet... Onların görevi dünya sistemindeki bu insanları toplamak... Bulmak... Onları bir araya getirip hizmet etmek.

Nereye hizmet ediyor bu varlıklar?

Aylin: Yukarıda... Çok yukarıda.

Kim onlar?

Aylin: Konsey var... Konsey... Konsey var... Masa var... Toplantı var... Kararlar var... Kararlar verilip daha sonra Dünya'ya iniliyor.

Bunlar bütün kâinattan sorumlu mu yoksa Dünya'dan sorumlu bir konsey mi?

Aylin: Hayır kâinattan sorumlu... Ama bunlar bölgelere ayrılmışlar... Benim gördüğüm varlıklar Dünya'dan sorumlu.

(Not: Aylin aslında burada hep sözünü ettiğimiz Ruhsal İdareci Mekanizma'dan bahsediyor.)

Kaç kişi o konsey? (Yanıtını zaten biliyoruz. Dilek bana sessizce elleriyle "12" işareti yapıyor. Bunu Aylin'in de teyit edip edemeyeceğine bakıyoruz.)

Aylin: On iki.

(Bir süre sessizlikten sonra Aylin farklı bir frekansa geçiyor. Gözünün önüne gri yüzler geliyor. Dilek'le birlikte "Griler" hakkında soru sormamız gerektiğini anlıyoruz.)

Griler dediğimiz varlık sistemini bize anlatır mısın? Nasıl varlıklar?

Aylin: Tek göz gibi... Beden olarak insan formunda... Çok uzunlar var... Kısalar da arada hizmetli gibiler... Uzunların hepsi Konsey'de... Konsey'e bağlılar... Kısa olanlar da hizmetli.

Neden bu Grileri kullanıyor Konsey?

Aylin: Çünkü onların frekansı daha yüksek... İnsan bilinçlerine daha kolay ulaşabiliyorlar.

Uzun olanlar kısaları mı idare ediyor?

Aylin: Uzun olanlar Konsey'in de üzerinde.

Konsey nereye bağlı? Onun üzerinde ne var?

Aylin: Uzun olanlar Dünya'yı idare eden o ruhsal Konsey'in de üzerinde.

"Sirius" deyince gözünün önüne bir görüntü ya da bilgi geliyor mu?

Aylin: Evet... Işık... Işık ama şöyle... Bütün evrene yayılan bir ışık... Yukarıda bir tane ana merkez gibi bir şey var... Oradan süzülüyor... Yayılıyor.

Tek bir merkez mi var?

Aylin: Evet... Benim gördüğüm Konsey... Konsey de oraya bağlı... Herkes oraya bağlı.

Sirius sistemine nereler bağlı?

Aylin: Bizim galaksimizin olduğu bölümden sorumlu ama başka galaksiler de var.

(Başka bir vizyona geçiyoruz.)

İnce, uzun ayaklı varlıklar kim?

Aylin: Yılanlar... Yılanlar görüyorum.

Nasıl varlıklar?

Aylin: İnce oldukları için yılan gibi görüyorum.

Gözleri nasıl?

Aylin: Gözler iri... Derileri gördüğümüz yılanlardan farklı.

Kim bunlar?

Aylin: İsim olarak gelmiyor... Onlar negatif tarafta... Negatifle pozitifin savaşı gibi bir şey var... Bir savaş var... Bu saf bilinçler bunlar için hazırlanıyorlar... Bunlar saf bilinçte olan insanlara yaklaşmaya çalışıyorlar.

Bunlar yeraltında mı yerüstünde mi?

Aylin. Yeraltında... Hayır hayır... Yeraltından çıktılar... Dünya'da... İnsan bedenine çok kolay sızıyorlar... Bu şekilde giriyorlar... (Eliyle gösteriyor.) Omurgadan.

Hangi insanları etki altına alıyorlar?

Aylin: Bilinci gelişmemiş olanları.

Yüksek makamlardaki insanları kullanıyorlar mı?

Aylin: Evet.

Kimler?

Aylin: Amerika geliyor gözümün önüne... Joe Biden geliyor.

(Aylin başka isimler de veriyor.)

Ne olacak bu isimlere?

Aylin: Bunlar yok olacak... Cezalandırılacak.

Ne zaman?

Aylin: Zaman çok yakın... İki üç yıl gibi.

Sonra?

Aylin: Yeni bir lider geliyor... (Türkiye'den söz ediyor.)

Nasıl biri o?

Aylin: O çok güzel, çok aydınlık bir lider... Çok aydınlık.

Kaç yaşında?

Aylin: Genç... Kırk kırk beş yaşlarında.

Beden tipi nasıl?

Aylin: İnsanları çok hayran bırakan biri... Zayıf... Sportmen... Geniş omuzlu.

Nerede şu anda?

Aylin: Nerede?... O gelmedi daha... Tanımıyorum.

(Dilek'le birbirimize bakıyoruz. Bana sessizce "Onun yüzünü göstermezler" diyor.)

Türkiye'de mi?

Aylin: Hayır... Türkiye'de değil... Başka bir yerde.

Ülkeyi tarif eder misin? Bir sembolü vesaire?

Aylin: Ada... Ada ülkesi.

Bayrak görüyor musun?

Aylin: Nordik ülkeleri gibi.

Kuzeyde?

Aylin: Evet... Kuzey... Bir ada ülkesi... Daha soğuk bir ülke.

Yani Türkiye'de yetiştirilmiyor bu kişi?

Aylin: Hayır... Başka ülkede yetiştiriliyor.

Nasıl birisi görüş olarak? Türkiye'de insanlar neden çekim duyacak?

Aylin: Atatürk gibi sevilecek birisi!

Çok güzel. Neden o seçilmiş?

Aylin: Çünkü o seçilecek varlık olarak Dünya'ya geldi... Gönderildi... Proje olarak gönderildi... O şekilde geldi... Zarar görmemesi için Türkiye'den uzakta, gözden uzakta yetiştirildi... Hazırlanıyor.

Ama bulamıyorlar?

Aylin: Evet... Bulunmaması için gizli bir yerde zaten... O yüzden ada ülkesinde.

Kaç yıl içinde gelecek?

Aylin: Üç yıl.

Peki o ortaya çıkmadan önce neler olacak Türkiye'de?

(Aylin Türkiye içinde yaşanacak bazı sıkıntılı ve yüksek hassasiyet içeren durumlardan söz ediyor.)

Aylin: Saf bilinçte olan insanlar, konuşmasalar bile bunları fark ettikleri için kendilerine farklı bir yaşam kuruyorlar belli yerlerde.

Şehir dışında.

Aylin: Evet... Şehir dışında... Benim yaptığım gibi... Ben de köye yerleştim.

Anladım. Peki yeni bir oluşum mu olacak? Halk onun etrafında mı birleşiyor?

Aylin: Evet... Ama herkesin sevdiği birisi... Herkes sevecek... Herkese eşit mesafede... Her görüşe aynı mesafede... Birleştirici olacak... Sevilecek... Sevilecek.

O mu başa gelecek?

Aylin: Evet.

Sonra ne olacak Türkiye'de?

Aylin: Türkiye'yi yukarıya taşımaya çalışacak... Başarmak için uğraşıyor.

Tamam.

Aylin: Ama o da o yukarıdaki kişilerle iletişimde... (Konsey'i kastediyor.)

Biliyor mu vazifesini?

Aylin: Biliyor.

Onu alıyorlardır o zaman.

Aylin: Evet.

Nerede doğmuş, büyümüş?

Aylin: Hep o adada ama ana rahmine Türkiye'de düşmüş... Vazifeli varlık olduğunu biliyorlar... Doğmadan, güvende olması için götürmüşler.

Kimler koruyor onu?

Aylin: Onu koruyan annesi... Ama koruyucuları var... Annesine gelip söylüyorlar... Ondan sonra korumaya alınıyor... Çünkü annesi bu konularda bilinçli birisi değil önceden... Koruyanlar Dünya dışı ama onu korumaları için Dünya'daki birileri de görevli.

Bir grup mu bu kişiler? Yukarıyla bağlantılı bir grup mu?

Aylin: Evet... Üç kişi gibi.

İsimleri var mı?

Aylin: İsimlerini göremiyorum... Ama gözümün önünde hep ada var... Bir ada ülkesinde.

Başka neler olacak?

Aylin: Yabancılar da gidiyorlar.

Türkiye daha bilinçlenecek mi?

Aylin: Daha bilinçlenecek çünkü ayrışım olacak... Daha bilinçli olanlar ayrışacak... Saf kan gibi... Asil ve kapalı bir ülke olacak.

(Not: Dilek'le aynı vizyon ve hissiyatı yakalıyoruz. Anadolu'nun gerçek misyonu işte o zaman başlıyor. O sırada Aylin bir anda bizim bildiğimiz sarsıcı bir bilgiyi teyit ediyor. Anadolu'da sadece bilinçlenmiş bir Türk nüfusunun kalması ve egemen olması kuru kuruya bir milliyetçilik olarak algılanmamalıdır. Bu, Anadolu'nun doğrudan doğruya ruhsal sistemden aldığı yüce vazifesiyle ilintili bir durumdur. "Kapalı" ifadesinden Türkiye'nin sınırlarının o dönem geldiğinde adeta zırh gibi örüleceğini ve vazifesini yerine getirmek üzere dış etkilere ve kötü niyetli göç ve girişlere karşı tamamen kapatılacağını anlıyoruz. Zira kitabın ilerleyen bölümlerinde okuyacağınız gibi, aynı vizyonu başka katılımcılar da doğruluyor.)

Aylin: Sirius... Anadolu'nun vazifesi Sirius'la bağlantılı... Sirius bilgileri Anadolu'dan aktarılacak ve insanların bilinçlerine

göre anlatılacak... Türkiye'ye büyük bilgiler verilecek... Anadolu Sirius'tan görevli.

(Bu sırada bizim çalışmalarımız hakkında bilgiler aktarılıyor. Bu bilgileri anlatmak üzere, görevli bazı kişilerin bize yönlendirilmekte olduğu söyleniyor.)

Dünya dışı temaslar nasıl ilerleyecek Türkiye'de?

Aylin: Artıyor... Bu konuları bilmeyen kişiler –tıpkı bana yapıldığı gibi– bir hastalıkla, hayatlarının tersyüz edilmesi yoluyla uyandırılacak, kanalları açılacak... Böyle mesajlar, varlıklar gönderilecek bu kişilere.

Dokunuş artıyor. Dokunmadıkları insanlara dokunmaya başladılar?

Aylin: Evet.

Peki diğer konuya dönelim. Konsey neden bu yılan gibi varlıkların bu kişileri kontrol altına almasına izin veriyor?

Aylin: Ayrıştırmak için... Çünkü insanlara seçim hakkı veriyorlar... Negatifte mi kalıyorsun yoksa pozitifte mi kalıyorsun? Çünkü aynı şeyi bize de yapıyorlar... Negatifte misin? Pozitifte misin? Pozitifteysen seni seçiyorlar zaten.

Son bir mesajın var mı?

(Bizlere özel nitelikli ve kişisel bazı bilgiler aktarılıyor ve seans sona eriyor.)

2. BÖLÜM

OPERASYON

39 yaşındaki Gül, işi gereği çoğunlukla İstanbul'da ve zaman zaman da İzmir'de yaşayan, kurumsal bir şirkette çalışan, uzun dönemli bir temasçıydı.

Ancak yaşadıklarını net olarak anımsaması ve anlamlandırması, bir arkadaşının evindeki kitaplığın rafında gördüğü bir kitapla başladı. Bu kitap *Novus*'tu. Rasgele açıverdiği bir sayfada "melez projesi" ifadesiyle göz göze geldi. Sonrası çorap söküğü gibiydi.

Defalarca Dünya dışı bir gemiye götürüldü. Rüya ve vizyonlarla prekognisyon (geleceği görme) yeteneği çok gelişmişti. Üzerinde, "insan duyguları" konusunda araştırmalar yapılıyordu. Hücreleri, yumurtaları alındı, testler yapıldı, melez üretiminin cömert bir donörü oldu. Zihnine şifa yöntemlerine dair bilgiler yüklendi, ağır sınavlardan geçti.

Bana ulaştığında şunları söylemişti:

"Bilinçaltımda temaslara dair açığa çıkmak üzere gömülü olan çok bilgi olduğunu hissediyorum... Özellikle de 'Melez Projesi' için sanki yapacaklarımız var; bu sebeple size rüyalar ve kitap aracılığı ile yönlendirilmiş olabilirim hissindeyim..."

Gül'ü aradık ve 30 Haziran 2023 günü saat 15.00 için randevulaştık. Gül'e seans tarihi ve saati vermeden üç gün önce rüyasında, seans günü ilk kez karşılaşacakları Dilek Karakuş'u

görmüş, Dilek ona rüyada saat 17.00'de çalışmaya başlayacağımızı söylemişti.

Ertesi gün türlü aksilikler oldu. Bir türlü çalışmaya başlayamıyorduk.

Gül nihayet seans koltuğuna uzandığında saat tam 17.00'ydi...

Gül Seansı

30 Haziran 2023

(Normal nefes, gevşeme ve enerji çalışmasından sonra Gül'ü koltuğa yatırıyoruz ve uzanır uzanmaz hemen şiddetli bir şekilde ağlamaya başlıyor.)

Gül: Bir göz geldi... Beni tarıyor şu an.

Tamam. Lütfen bırak, ağla, tutma, güvendesin.

(Gül ağlamaya devam ediyor, ellerini tutuyoruz. Blokajları ani şekilde temizleniyor.)

Gül: İkiz bebek var.

Haydi oraya gidelim.

Gül: Canım acıyor!... (Büyük bir acıyla ağlıyor...) Ne yapıyorlar bana!... (Gemide yapılan işlemi tekrar yaşıyor.)

Geçecek. Hepsi geçecek. Yanındayız.

(Dilek orada yarım kalan bir işlem olduğunu görüyor. Gül gemiye alındığında tamamlanmamış bir işlem olmuş. Bunu gidermek için Gül'ün bu boyuttaki sağlığı ile ilgili bir operasyon yapılıyor. Dilek bana varlıkların bunu yapmak zorunda olduklarını söylüyor. Operasyon yapıldığında Gül bu şekilde acı hissetmemiş fakat şimdi seansta o anları tekrar yaşarken acı hissini deneyimliyor.)

Gül: Kaçmışım sonra!

(Operasyonu canlı yaşayan Gül'ün acısının hafiflemesini bekliyoruz.)

Gül: Operasyonda galiba bir hata olmuş... O yüzden devam ediyorlar... Kayma olmuş belimde.

Ne operasyonu bu?

Gül: Doğum.

Geçecek. Az kaldı.

Gül: (Ağlayarak...) Bağırsaklarımı görüyorum şu anda!

(Dilek birazdan boyun ve kafa bölgesine geçeceklerini görüyor.)

Gül: (Biraz sessizlikten sonra...) Kafama cihaz taktılar... Mavi bir ışık var... Dengelemeye çalışıyorlar... Beyin loblarımda değişiklik olmuş... Ondan dolayı dünyada sıkıntı yaşıyorum... Deneye almışlar beni... Çit taraflı... O tek taraflı bir deneydi... İki farklı konu var... Hücrelerimi inceliyorlar... Beynim çok farklı çalışıyor... Yer değişikliği yapmışlar... Bu değişikliğin insan bedenindeki yansımasını inceliyorlar.

Bebeği görebiliyor musun?

Gül: Ellerini görebiliyorum... Ellerini hissediyorum.

Cinsiyeti nedir?

Bizim gibi öyle erkek veya kız diyebileceğim bir cinsiyette değil... Değişik bir formda.

Tarif eder misin? Kafası, gözleri, saçları nasıl?

(İnleyerek...) Kolları, ayakları çok uzun, gövdesi kollarına ve ayaklarına göre daha kısa.

Kafası?

Gül: Şunu görüyorum... Kafası öyle bir kafa ki, arkasını, önünü, her yeri görebiliyor... Yani nasıl anlatsam?... Çepeçevre her yeri görebilen bir kafaya sahip... Hareketleri o şekilde.

Gözleri nasıl?

Gül: Çok büyük gözleri... Masmavi... Çok büyük gözler.

Saçları var mı?

Gül: Yok... Görmüyorum saçlarını... Şu an erkek hissediyorum.

Başka bir bebek daha olabilir mi?

Gül: Evet... İkiz... İkiz bebek var.

İkisi birbirinin aynı mı?

Gül: Hayır değil... Çok farklılar... Aynı anda doğmuşlar.

Farkları ne Gül?

Gül: Beyinleri birbirinden farklı çalışıyor... Deney çocukları olduğu için.

Nasıl bir deney bu?

Gül: Kromozomları gösteriyorlar bana şu anda... Dünya insanıyla eşleştirme... Onların genlerinin eşleşmesini gösteriyorlar.

Amaç ne?

Gül: Yeni bir ırk yaratmak.

Bundaki amaç ne?

Gül: Dünya'nın ileri versiyonu için yeni bir ırk yaratılıyor.

(Gül yeniden ağlamaya başlıyor.)

Gül: Çok karışık!... Çok karışık!... Çok karışık!

(Sakinleştiriyoruz.)

Peki bu yeni meydana getirilen insanlar başka bir boyut için mi yoksa Dünya için mi?

Gül: Yeni bir galaksi görüyorum ben şu an.

Yeni bir galaksi?

Gül: Evet... (Ağlıyor...) Orayı gösteriyorlar şu an... Ben oraya hazır değilim!... Alışık değilim oraya!... Çok zorlanıyorum şu an!... Ondan acı çekiyorum!

Oraya kimler gidecek peki? Hangi ruhlar enkarne olacak o bedenlere?

Gül: Cevap gelmiyor bu soruya.

Nasıl bir yer orası? Yeni bir dünya mı?

Gül: Yeni bir dünya.

Buraya benziyor mu?

Gül: Hayır... Çok güzel!... Çok güzel!... Enerjisi çok güzel!... Enerjisini hissettiriyorlar şimdi.

Doğayı görüyor musun?

Gül: Sakin... Huzur... Masmavi bir enerji var... Çok yüksek bir enerji!

Peki Dünya'dan insanları nasıl seçiyorlar DNA almak için?

Gül: Kendilerine uyum sağlayabilecekleri araştırıyorlar... Bir sürü insan var aslında... Parça almışlar... O parçaları taşıyan insanları götürmeye çalışıyorlar.

Kim bu varlıklar peki? Kime bağlılar? Nereye bağlılar?

Gül: Dünya'nın geleceği için çalışıyorlar.

Tamam.

Gül: Çok fazla bilgi vermek istemiyorlar bana şu anda... Kasıyorlar beni çok.

Başka bir dünyadaki yaşam için Dünya'daki kadınlardan yumurta alıyorlar diyorsun. Peki tek sebep bu mu? Yoksa başka sebepler de var mı?

Gül: Araştırma yapıyorlar ayrıca... Dünya insanı için de araştırma yapıyorlar... Çift taraflı... Dünya'da bazı konulara çözüm getirmek için projeler yapıyorlar.

Ne gibi?

Gül: Sağlık konularında ileride çözümler sunacaklar ama şu an bunların hepsi çok gizli bilgiler... O yüzden insanlara ihtiyaçları oluyor... Hazır olan insanlarla çalışıyorlar.

Hazır olan derken bilinç olarak mı? Yoksa başka bir etmen daha var mı?

Gül: Kendilerine uyum sağlayabilecek insanlarla çalışıyorlar ama Dünya'daki insanların... (Hızlı nefes alıyor, cümle kesiliyor.)

Nefes al ver. Sakin...

Gül: Dünya insanının duygularına ihtiyaçları var.

Kendileri için mi?

Gül: Kendileri için... Onların mevcut yapılarında o duygular yok.

Tamam.

Gül: Atatürk bilinci yüklemesi yapılmıştı.

Oraya gidebilir miyiz?

(Görüntüyü bir anda Atatürk'e getirdiler. Adeta sahne değişti. Dilek orada çok derin bir bilgi olduğunu görüyor.)

Orada mısın Gül?

Gül: Evet.

Ne var orada?

Gül: Bir savaş görüyorum.

Kimler savaşıyor?

Gül: Türkiye Cumhuriyeti'ni korumak zorundayız!

Kimlerle savaşıyor Türkiye?

Gül: İlk Yunanlılar geldi gözümün önüne... Çok fazla düşman var topraklarımızda!

Türkiye'yi işgal mi etmek istiyorlar?

Gül: Evet.

Başka kimler var?

Gül: Amerika var... Hayır!... Hayır!... Hayır!... O kadar çok insan ölüyor ki!... (Şiddetli şekilde ağlıyor.)

Tamam çıkalım oradan.

(Dilek Gül'ü o travmatik görüntüden çıkarıp bir şifa havuzu imajinasyonuyla rahatlatıyor.)

Gül: Atatürk'ün bir mesajı var... Onu iletmek istiyorum.

Tabii.

Gül: Savaş olmak zorunda değil... Birlik olursak savaş olmayacak... Ama Türkiye birlik olmazsa savaşa gireceğiz... O bilincin yayılması gerekiyor... Değişmemiz gerekiyor... Şu an herkes birbirine çok düşman... Bunun yenilmesi gerekiyor ülkede... İnsanların kim olduklarını hatırlaması gerekiyor... Atatürk bilincini, geldikleri yeri, atalarını, Göktürk'ü.

Göktürklerin önemi neydi?

Gül: Göktürklerin yukarıyla bağlantısı vardı... Türkiye'de şu anda bedenlenen birçok insan Göktürk kodlarını taşıyorlar... O kodlar aktif olursa, o bilgiler açığa çıkarsa insanlarda bilinç sıçraması olacak... Bilinç sıçramasıyla insanlar daha çok birlik olmaya başlayacak ve nereden geldiklerini hatırladıklarında, görevlerini hatırlamaya başladıklarında herkes birbirine yardım edecek.

Göktürklerin kimlerle bağlantısı vardı?

Gül: Sirius.

Nasıl bir bağlantı bu?

Gül: Birbirinin devamı gibi.

Devamı derken?

Gül: Sirius kökenli bilinçler Dünya'da Göktürk olarak bedenlenmişler ve sonra Göktürk Devleti yukarıdan gelen bilgilerle birlikte ilerlemiş... Hâlâ bunları taşıyan insanlar var Türkiye'de şu an.[4]

Genetik olarak da taşınıyor mu?

Gül: Taşıyorlar... Genetik olarak taşıyorlar... Bu insanların bir kısmı bilinçlerinin farkında... Bir kısmı hiçbir şekilde farkında değil... Sadece çevrelerine o bilinci yayıyorlar.

4. Bu, Anadolu'nun misyonunun başlangıç noktasıdır. Anadolu yüksek ruhsal mekanizma ve ona bağlı varlık sistemleri için bir ileri karakoldur, bilgi nakli için bir ara istasyondur.

Atatürk bilinci yüklemesi ne demek? Onu açar mısın biraz bize? Atatürk nasıl bir varlık?

Gül: Bu sembolik bir ifade... Eğer Atatürk bilinci insanlarda yayılırsa, Türkiye'de insanların bilinç seviyesi artıyor olacak ve kendilerinde var olan, dünyaya gelirken getirdikleri ama henüz açığa çıkmamış olan hem insanlık bilgileri hem de dünyadaki Türklerin görevleri bir zincir gibi birbirine takılı şekilde aktif olmaya başlayacak... Ama şu an mevcut durumda bu zincirin en ufak bir halkası bile başlamamış.

Peki tamam. Yakın dönemde ne olacak Türkiye'de? Türkiye'nin vazifesi nasıl ve ne zaman başlayacak?

Gül: Türkiye'de bunu aktif edecek olan insanlar var ama bu insanların bir kısmı açığa çıkmaya korkuyorlar... Bir kısmı kaybolmuş durumdalar... O yüzden bir karmaşa, kargaşa, kaos... İnsanların birbiriyle bağlantıya geçmesi gerekiyor... "Lider sizin içinizde" bilgisi geldi... İçinizde ne demek?... Siz bu sorunun cevabını biliyorsunuz diyorlar... Başka bir şey gelmiyor.

Tamam. Birlik sağlanırsa Türkiye'nin vazifesi ne olacak?

Gül: Güneş Türkiye'den doğacak... Yeni düzen Türkiye'den başlayacak... İlk buraya iniyor olacaklar... Türkiye'de insanlar hazır olunca, olup bitenin gerçek olduğunu Türkiye'deki insanlar aracılığıyla anlayacaklar... Yeni dünya geçişi Türkiye'de... Ama ileride... Yakın zamanda değil... Olmuyor çünkü Türkiye çıkmaza girmiş durumda... Onu çözmeye çalışıyorlar.

Yeni dünya geçişi derken neyi kastettiler?

Gül: Mevcut dünyanın sonu geliyor... Değişim geliyor.

Nasıl? Sıfırlama gibi mi?

Gül: Yeni hayatlar, yeni dünya... Farklı bir dünya görüyorum ben şu anda... Bir geçiş... Sanki şey gibi böyle... Öyle gösteriyorlar bana... Bir paravan var... O paravan çekilecek... Paravan açılacak... Şu an paravanın arkasını görmüyoruz ama onu

hazırlıyorlar... Ve o Türkiye'de başlıyor... Bir de bir piramit gösteriyorlar bana... Piramitten yayılan bir enerji... Çok büyük bir enerji patlaması yaşanacak Dünya'da... Oradan yayılan enerjiyle birlikte göç gibi... Kötü bir şey değil bu ama... İnsanların Dünya'dan gitmesi için bir olay gösteriyorlar... Kötü görmüyorum ben bunu... Çok güzel olarak görüyorum... İnsanların bir kısmı gidiyor, bir kısmı kalıyor ve sonrasında yukarıya doğru değişim başlıyor... Göç başlıyor.

Yani mezun olanları başka boyuta mı alıyorlar? O bahsettiğin galaksiye mi?

Gül: Evet... Bir şey açılıyor... Bir alan açılıyor... Oradan geçiyor insanlar... Türkiye'de başlıyor.

Kalanlar?

Gül: Kalanlar oraya gidemiyor... Onları bir yerde toplanmış olarak görüyorum... Bir yere topluyorlar onları.

(Şimdi bir mağara görüntüsü geliyor.)

Gül: İki mağara var... Biri Mardin'de biri Hatay'da... Hatay'daki mağara tarihi bir yerin orada çok küçük bir mağara... Orada geçit kapısı var... O mağaradan fiziksel olarak gittim... O mağaraya giren insanlar farklı bir algıya geçiyorlar... Eğer hazırlarsa geçiyorlar... Çok küçük bir mağara... İleride o mağaranın içine bir insan girince... Telefonda konuşmak gibi düşünebilirsiniz... Çok daha kolay iletişim olan bir yer orası.

Telepatik mi?

Gül: Evet... Telepatik olarak konuşuyorlar o mağarada... Bu anlattığım birincisi... İkincisi Mardin'de... O da antik bir sahanın orada... Ama müzenin olduğu alan değil... Ben o bölgeden sonra çok değiştim... Fiziken gittim... Varlıklar yönlendirdiler.

Neden soktular seni oraya peki?

Gül: Bilinç sıçraması için.

Orada varlıklarla daha kolay mı temas ediliyor?

Gül: Evet... Direkt konuştular benimle.

Oranın ne özelliği var? Daha farklı bir frekans mı?

Gül: Frekans çok farklı orada... Dünya'da gibi değil orası... Yayılan enerji... Ama herkesin girmesini istemiyorlar... Çok küçük bir mağara... Çok eğilerek girilebiliyor... Normal bir insanın girebileceği bir yer değil... Beni oraya onlar soktular zaten.

(Konu değişiyor.)

Sizin gibilerin bu varlıklarla doğmadan önce bir anlaşması oluyor mu? Bir anlaşmaya göre mi seçiyorlar? Yani izin verenleri mi alıyorlar?

Gül: İki konu var... Birincisi izin verenler, ikincisi Dünya'da belli bir seviyeye geldikten sonra bir anlaşma olabiliyor.

Temasçının kendisi Dünya'da ama yine de ruhsal boyutta mı yapıyor anlaşmayı?

Gül: Evet ruhsal boyutta yapıyor. Fakat doğmadan önce anlaşmayı yapıp dünya yaşamında o noktaya gelememiş çok insan var diyorlar.

Anlaşma yaptığı halde olmuyor.

Gül: Anlaşma yaptığı halde bilincini istenen düzeye getiremediği için teması kaldıramaz... Yapamıyorlar.

İnsanlar neden böyle bir anlaşmayı kabul ediyorlar?

Gül: Yapmak zorundayız.

Niçin?

Gül: Görevimiz bu.

Varoluşa katkı gibi bir şey mi bu?

Gül: İnsanların bir kısmının varoluş nedeni bu yeni dünyaya katkı sağlamak ve o geçişi hızlandırmak... Bir de... (Gül burada duruyor...) Beni bir şeyin içine çekiyorlar şu anda!... (Daha fazla bilgi vermemesi için Gül'e müdahale geliyor.)

Sizin genetiğinizde ne gibi özellikler var?

Gül: Karanlık!... (Bilgi gelmiyor ve biraz duruyor...) Onlar melez projesi diyorlar.

Tamam. O konuda bir şeyler anlatılacak. Bekliyoruz.

Gül: Çok karışıyor görüntü!... Bir şeyler anlatacaklar.

Senin ağzından konuşmak isterlerse izin ver.

(Görüntüler gelmeye başlıyor.)

Gül: Bir sürü kuvöz görüyorum... Hepsinin üzerinde etiketler var... Kablolar var... Kablolarla birbirlerine bağlılar... Kabloları görüyorum... Ne işe yaradıklarına bakıyorum... Onu anlatacaklar... Şöyle bir sistem geliştirmişler... Dünya'dan gen alıyorlar... Aldıkları genler başarısız da olabiliyor başarılı da olabiliyor... Onların kendi çalışmaları çok ileri seviyede olduğu için bebekler arasında kablolarla bağlantılar var... Onu anlatıyorlar şu an... Bu bağlantılar aracılığıyla şeyi yakalamaya çalışıyorlar... En ileri seviyede bebeği yakalamaya çalışıyorlar... Genleri... Tam çeviremiyorum şu anlattıklarını... Genleri en ileri seviyeye taşıyabilmeleri için aldıkları genlerin iletişimini bu kablolar aracılığıyla sağlıyorlar... Uyumunu sağlıyorlar... Onu gösteriyorlar... O kadar çok birbiriyle bağlantılı ki... İnsanlar nasıl birbirlerine kan veriyorlar... Burada da bebekler birbirlerine gen aktarımı yapıyorlar... Öyle bir şey geliştirmişler... Bunu gösteriyorlar şu an... Böylece en sağlıklı, en ideal, duygu durumu olarak da aradıkları, ulaşmaya çalıştıkları şeyi yaratmaya çabalıyorlar... Ama bu süreçte gen aldıkları insanlarda zararlar da oluşuyormuş... Embriyoları dondurdukları bir yer var... Bir de onu görüyorum şu an.

Sizi neye göre seçiyorlar?

Gül: Genlerimizde bir madde var... Daha önce yüklemişler... Bu maddeyi yükledikleri birçok insan var... Bu madde bazı insanlarda gelişmeye neden olmuş bazılarında ise hiçbir işe yaramamış... Gelişme olan insanlarda deneye devam etmişler... Şöyle... Bu insanların kim oldukları kontratta var ama o insan

dünyaya geldikten sonra çevresel faktörlerden dolayı gelişemez hale gelebiliyor... O yüzden bu maddeyi enjekte edip sonra devam etmemişler... Anlatması çok zor diyorlar.

Nasıl bir şey enjekte ediyorlar?

Gül: Çoğunlukla mavi tonları ama kırmızı ve sarı da var.

Peki ne işe yarıyor? Fonksiyonu ne bu sıvıların?

Gül: Genlerde mutasyona neden oluyor... Çünkü onlara uyum sağlayabilmek için önce insan bedeninde bunu görmeleri gerekiyor.

Yeşil var mı? (Deneyimlerimize dayanarak soruyoruz.)

Gül: Yeşili enjekte ettiklerinde bütün hücrelerde canlılık meydana geliyor... Eğer bir bozulma varsa o anında değişiyor.

Peki iyileştirdikleri insanlar, temasçılar bu projelerin içinde olanlar mı?

Gül: Bir kısmı evet, bir kısmı hayır.

Diğerlerini neden iyileştiriyorlar?

Gül: Onlar farklı projelerdeler.

Hepsi görevli mi?

Gül: Evet... Bir de yaptıkları deneyler var... Dünya'da bazı hastalıklara hızlı bir şekilde çözüm gelsin diye mecburen insan bedenine enjekte ettikleri sıvılar geliştiriyorlar... Bunları böyle insanlarda denemek zorundalar... Kendilerinde zaten öyle bir şeye ihtiyaçları yok... İnsanlar için yapılıyor bu.

Özgür iradeye aykırı bir işlem yapılıyor mu hiç?

Gül: Hayır... Ama kişi kaldıramayacak durumdaysa olayı hatırlamaması sağlanıyor... Bir şey var... Siliyorlar.

Nasıl siliyorlar? Cihazla mı?

Gül: Bir şey... Bir şey tutuyorlar... Dalga boyu.

Bir cihazdan frekans veriliyor sanki.

Gül: Aynen öyle.

(Gül'le birlikte vizyonu izleyen Dilek, aslında yapılan operasyonun olay anılarını silme işlemi olmadığını, o bölümün dondurulduğunu söylüyor.)

O zaman bunlar daha yüksek bir ruhsal mekanizmanın izniyle mi oluyor?

Gül: Bir şey var... Ordu gibi gösteriyorlar... Çok büyük bir varlık... Nasıl anlatsam... Tek kişi değil bir grup... Onlar yönetiyorlar.

Bu operasyonu mu?

Gül: Evet ama daha üstte bunlar... Dünya insanı değil bunlar... İletişim kurduğum varlıklardan daha yukarıda bunlar.

Dünya ruhsal idareci sistemi gibi mi?

Gül: Evet.

Kaç kişi?

Gül: On iki.

Onlar nereye bağlı peki?

Gül: Gökyüzü temsilcilerine.

Onlar nereye bağlılar?

Gül: Yaradan'a bağlı.

(Seans sona eriyor.)

***

Gül, seansın hemen sonrasında, görüp de anlatamadığı bir bilgiyi aktardı. Buna göre, Atatürk bilincini insanlar zamanı geldiğinde birbirlerine domino taşı gibi aktaracaklar. Ancak sadece ruhsal olarak hazır olanlar bunu kaldırabilecek. Bu tesir Atatürk bilinci taşıyan yeni bir lider tarafından tetiklenecek.

Seans sırasında Gül'ün uzun süredir rahatsız olan bağırsakları iyileşti. Beyninde olduğunu söylediği ağrı da sona erdi.

Çok zorlu bir test sürecinin gönüllüsü Gül, seanstan iki gün sonra varlıklardan aldığı bilgileri bize şöyle aktardı:

"İnsan duygularının fiziksel bedene olumsuz yansımasının engellenmesi üzerine bir çalışma yürütülüyor. İnsanlar duyguları aracılığıyla kaslarını, hücrelerini, bölgesel alanlarını yorup kilitleyebiliyorlar ve o alanda bozulmalar meydana gelebiliyor. Bu böyle olmak zorunda değil. Duygular ile fiziki beden artık birbirinden ayrılabilir. Duyguları insan sadece his olarak yaşayabilir. Fizik bedenini duygu tesiri altında bırakmaktan kurtulabilir. Bunun deneyini sürdürdüğümüz insanlar arasındasın. Bu süreçte çok yıprandığının ve hem fiziki hem duygusal olarak yorulduğunun farkındayız. Çok fazla iniş çıkışın oldu. Duygularınla ve fizik bedenindeki ağrılarınla baş edemez hale geldiğin oldu.

Aylardır süren çalışmanın sende sonuna geldiğimizi müjdelemek isteriz. Hem duygu durumunda hem de fiziki bedeninde kendin değişimleri fark ediyor olacaksın. Beyin lobunda, duygularının kontrolünü sağlamak amacıyla senin anlayacağın dilde bir aparat vardı. Bu bölüme biz ara ara sinyaller göndererek sende farklı duygu salınımlarını ve bunların hem fiziki hem ruhsal hem de duygusal alanlarının da kontrolünü sağlıyorduk. Evet bir nevi seni maniple ediyorduk ancak bu senin ruhunun onayıyla ilerleyen ve senin kaldırabileceğin bir süreçti. Bazen sana çok yüklendiğimiz zamanlar da oluyordu ve sen kaldıramaz hale geldiğinde hemen çevrende bir faktörde iyileşmeye gidiliyordu. Sana daha fazla bilgi vermektense süreci kendin gözlemleyerek dönüşümünü görüyor olacaksın. Bedeninin 48 saatlik kendine gelme süreci var. Değişimin sonrasında hızlanıyor olacak. Seni seviyoruz; şu an ayağında hissettiğin titreşim bedenini gevşetmeye başladı."

3. BÖLÜM

ÇOCUK

45 yaşındaki Hakan S. ilaç sektöründe çalışıyordu.

Zor bir çocukluk dönemi geçiren Hakan daha küçük yaşlarda paranormal deneyimler yaşamaya başlamıştı. Gördüğü vizyonlar ve rüyalar kısa sürede gerçekleşiyor, tüm ailesi bunlara tanık oluyordu.

Gençlik ve yetişkinlik çağlarında deneyimleri daha da ilerledi, çeşitlendi, duru görü yeteneği gelişti.

Evlendi ama çiftin yaşamlarında eksik olan bir şey vardı. Çok arzu ettikleri halde bir türlü çocukları olmuyordu. Tüp bebek, aşılama gibi, tıbbın her türlü modern olanağına başvurdular ama sonuç her defasında hayal kırıklığıydı.

Tüp bebek yöntemini son bir kez daha denemeye karar verdiler. O gece Hakan'ın rüyasına bir erkek çocuğu geldi ve *"Baba ben geliyorum bak... Sarı saçlı olacağım, babaanneme benzeyeceğim"* diyerek birçok beden detayı da verdi. Hakan da eşi de esmer oldukları halde çocuk rüyada bildirdiği gibi sarışın olarak dünyaya geldi.

Yıllarca görü ve rüyaları devam etti. Hepsi net olarak gerçekleşiyordu. Bir gece Dünya dışı varlıklar tarafından alındı ve üzerinde bir operasyon yapıldı.

Hakan S. ile yaptığımız seans temas olgusunun birçok farklı boyutunu gözler önüne serdiği gibi, hayli "ilginç" bir çocuğu da başrole yerleştirdi.

Hakan S. Seansı

1 Temmuz 2023

(Nefes, gevşeme ve enerji çalışmasından sonra Hakan koltuğa uzanıyor. Hakan'da biraz heyecan var. Dilek onu yatıştırıyor.)

Nasıl hissediyorsun Hakan?

Hakan: Sıcaklık hissi.

Çok normal. Vücut ısısı artar.

Hakan: Bana kızıyorlar sanki... Çok anlattığım için.

Anlatabileceğin kadarını anlat.

Hakan: Mücadeleye sokuyorlar beni.

Nasıl mücadeleler?

Hakan: Kötüyle.

Kim o kötüler?

Hakan: Negatiflerle mücadeleye sokuyorlar.

Dünya'da mı bunlar?

Hakan: Dünya'da... Değişik... Böyle yüzleri tüylü... Onlarla mücadele ettirtiyorlar.

Dünya dışı varlıklar mı veriyor bu görevi?

Hakan: Hayır.

Kim?

Hakan: Dede gibi... Rehberim diyorum ama.

Peki bu operasyonlar Dünya dışı varlıkların işi olabilir mi?

Hakan: Sanmıyorum... Onlar, yani Dünya dışı varlıklar bunun kaynağını araştırıyorlar gibi.

Neyin kaynağını?

Hakan: Bu görevi verenlerin... Onlar da bu kaynak nedir diye araştırıyorlar... Bu insanları arıyorlar.

Senin gibi insanları mı?

Hakan: Benim gibileri arıyorlar.

Seni neden seçmişler bu görev için?

Hakan: Bu görev aileden verilmiş... El verilmiş gibi... Sanki görevli gibiyim... Sanki bir kişiyi korumam lazım... Görevli kişiyi koruyacak kişi gibiyim.

Kim o?

Hakan: Söylemek istemiyorum.

Söyleyebilirsin korkma.

Hakan: Oğlumu... Oğlum doğarken bile işaretle doğdu.

Oğlunun vazifesi ne?

Hakan: Çok büyük... Çok büyük vazifesi var... Korunması lazım... Korunması lazım.

Peki bütün bu yaptıkların oğlunu korumak için mi?

Hakan: Evet.

Oğlun neler yapacak ileride?

Hakan: Oğlumu korumam gerek çünkü o ileride Türkiye'nin başına geçecek... Lider olacak.

(Bizi o konuda fazla tutmadan başka bir kanala geçiriyorlar.)

Gemiye alındığın zaman neler oluyor Hakan?

Hakan: Sol şakağım çok ağrıyor.

Şifalanıyorsun şu anda.

(Bu arada Dilek Hakan'dan sperm alınmış olduğunu görüyor.)

Hakan: Araştırıyorlar.

Neyi araştırıyorlar?

Hakan: Neden böyle olduğumu araştırıyorlar... Genlerimin değerli olduğunu düşünüyorlar... Çok direndim... İstemedim.

Neyi araştırıyorlar? Genlerinde ne var?

Hakan: Dedelerimden aktarılan genleri takip etmek için.

Ne var o genlerde?

Hakan: Soy.

Hangi soy?

Hakan: Çok değerli bir soy... Soydan gelen aktarım... Dünyanın kaderini etkileyecek kadar eski bir soy... Bir kişi.

Bir kişiyle mi ilgili?

Hakan: Evet.

Kim o?

Hakan: Oğlum... Ama oğlum birinin babası mı olacak?... Orası tamamen meçhul.

Oğlunu özel mi yetiştiriyorlar?

Hakan: Evet.

Oğlun onlarla temas ettiğini hatırlıyor mu?

Hakan: Bir kez sadece... Oğlum iki buçuk yaşındayken beyaz bir ışık kapısından geçerek Sirius'tan geldiğini söyledi... "Dede"nin onu gönderdiğini söyledi... "Ben Atatürk olacağım" dedi.

O zaman seni bu yüzden mi alıyorlar?

Hakan: Evet.

Gemide ne yaptılar sana? Etrafına bak.

Hakan: Işıklar var... Varlıklar var... Göz gözeyiz.

Tamam. Gözleri nasıl?

Hakan: Siyah... Göz gözeyiz şimdi.

Göz nasıl? Küçük mü? İri mi?

Hakan: Büyük.

Griler dediğimiz varlıklar mı?

Hakan: Üzerlerinde beyaz önlük var... Doktor gibi.

Kaç varlık var? Görebiliyor musun?

Hakan: 3 veya 4.

Tamam. Ne yapıyorlar şimdi?

Hakan: Gözlerime bakıyorlar.

Ama sadece gözlerine bakmak için almamışlardır seni.

Hakan: Kollarımda sanki serumlar bağlı.

Ne renk serumlar Hakan?

Hakan: Kırmızı, beyaz, sarımsı bir tane... Birkaç serum var... Kan alıyorlar gibi.

Bir şey veriyorlar mı?

Hakan: Evet... Beyaz, sarımsı.

Onların fonksiyonu nedir?

Hakan: Ayaklarım uyuştu... Kollarım uyuştu... (Daha da derinleşiyor.)

Sıvıların fonksiyonu nedir Hakan?

Hakan: Kızıyorum onlara... Neden yapıyorsunuz diye.

(Tekrar soruyoruz çünkü Hakan'ın bilinçaltında bu bilgi var.) Bu sıvıların fonksiyonu nedir?

Hakan: Arınma yapıyorlar vücudumda... Kimyasal maddeler.

Yani toksik maddeleri mi arındırıyorlar?

Hakan: Evet... Arındırıyorlar.

Peki daha sonra ne olacak?

Hakan: Ben kızıyorum onlara.

Onlar ne diyorlar peki sen kızınca?

Hakan: Sadece sakinleştirmeye çalışıyorlar... Mücadele ediyorum onlarla... Kollarımdan bağladılar.

(Dilek dişil enerji hissediyor ve onu soruyoruz.)

Hakan: Erkek hissiyatı yok orada.

Sana en sempatik, en sıcak gelen varlıkla göz göze gelir misin? (Orada bir varlık Hakan aracılığıyla konuşmak ve bilgi aktarmak istiyor.)

Hakan: Evet.

(Sorulara başlıyoruz ve şimdi doğrudan varlıkla konuşuyoruz.) Hakan'ı niçin alıyorsunuz?

Hakan: Bilgi... (Hakan'ın ses tonu değişiyor.)

Hangi bilgi?

Hakan: DNA'sı bize lazım.

Onun genlerinde ne var? Neyi arıyorsunuz?

Hakan: Önce bizim bulmamız lazımdı.

Neyi?

Hakan: Bizim için değerli.

Sizin için değerli olan ne?

Hakan: DNA sarmalını düzeltip daha iyi hale getireceğiz.

Peki nihai amacınız nedir?

Hakan: Dünya acı çekiyor... Dünya çok sıkıntılı... Bunu biz yaptık, biz düzelteceğiz.

Nasıl?

Hakan: Hata yaptık... Yaptığımız hatayı düzelteceğiz.

Yaptığınız hata neydi?

Hakan: Müdahale ettik.

Neye müdahale ettiniz?

Hakan: İnsanlara.

Bedenlere mi? Genetiğe mi?

Hakan: Genlere.

Ne zaman yaptınız bunu?

Hakan: Yeni değil.

Nasıl bir müdahale yaptınız genlere?

Hakan: Onları daha güçlü yapmaya çalıştık... Doğal halinde bırakmadık onları... Yanlış yaptık.

Sonuç kötü mü oldu?

Hakan: Gördüğünüz gibi.

İnsanlar daha saldırgan hale mi geldiler ya da daha bilinçsiz mi oldular?

Hakan: Kontrol edilebilir oldular.

Bunu biraz daha açar mısınız?

Hakan: Robot gibi oldular... Bilgimizi çaldılar ve bunu farklı kullandılar.

Kim kullandı insanları?

Hakan: Diğerleri.

Diğerleri kim?

Hakan: Siz farklı söylüyorsunuz.

Bizim anlayacağımız şekilde söyler misiniz?

Hakan: Yılan kafalılar.

Onların kökeni ne? Nereden geliyorlar?

Hakan: Onlar hep buradalardı.

Peki ruhsal sistem onlara neden müsaade ediyor?

Hakan: Zamanları var.

Zaman mı verilmiş onlara?

Hakan: Evet.

Neden?

Hakan: Onlar olmasa ayrımı nasıl yapacaksınız?

İyi ve kötüyü ayırt etmek için mi?

Hakan: Evet.

İnsanlara yapmakta olduğunuz müdahalenin içeriği nedir?

Hakan: Onları daha güçlü yapmaya çalışıyoruz.

Tam anlayamadık bunu?

Hakan: Hepsinin güçlü olması zaten mümkün değil.

Bilinçlenmiş insanlar için bir planınız var mı?

Hakan: Onları kodluyoruz, onları düzeltiyoruz, hepsini aktif edeceğiz ama yakın zamanda değil... Yakında beklemeyin.

Melezlerle ilgili sorularımız var. Cevaplar mısınız? Neden melez üretiliyor? Onlar ne yapacaklar?

Hakan: Onları biz yapmıyoruz... Herkesin bir görevi var burada... Daha üst katmanlarda yapılıyor... Benim görevim gelenleri temizlemek, arındırmak, DNA'yı düzeltmek.

Herkese yapılıyor mu bu işlem?

Hakan: Hayır.

Kimlere yapıyorsunuz? Nasıl seçiyorsunuz?

Hakan: Doğru insanlar.

Doğru derken neyi kastediyorsunuz?

Hakan: Onlar düzgün kalmaya çalışanlar... Görenler.

Onların hepsine dokunacak mısınız?

Hakan: Zamanımız yettiğince.

Dünya için ne kadar zaman var?

Hakan: Zaman anda... Her an her şey olur.

Dünya bir devre kapanışı yaşayacak mı?

Hakan: Hakan bunu gördü.

Nasıl olacak?

Hakan: Dünya takla atacak.

Bir zamanı var mı?

Hakan: Zaman anda... Zaman yok.

Buradan mezun olanlara ne olacak?

Hakan: Aslına dönecek onlar... Sanmayın ki biz onlara bağlı değiliz.

Onlar tekâmüllerine başka bir yerde devam etmeyecekler mi?

Hakan: Büyük Ruh bilir.

Büyük Ruh'u Tanrı anlamında mı kullanıyorsunuz?

Hakan: Evet.

Evrendeki yönetim mekanizmasını anlatır mısınız bize?

Hakan: Bizler de sizler gibiyiz... Daha gelişmişiz sadece.

Nereden geliyorsunuz peki?

Hakan: Başka bir evren.

Buraya nasıl geliyorsunuz?

Hakan: Boyut atlayarak ama aslında çok zor bu tarafa gelmek.

Neden?

Hakan: Bizi yıpratıyor.

Kullandığınız gri bedenler?

Hakan: Gerçek bedenimiz bu değil.

Nasıl peki?

Hakan: Işık.

Bu beden tipini bu boyuta gelebilmek için mi kullanıyorsunuz?

Hakan: Evet ve bu bizi çok yoruyor.

Bu bedenleri kendiniz mi ürettiniz?

Hakan: Evet... Farklı boyutlar, farklı bedenler... Herkes kendi araştırmasını yapıyor.

Dünya için kim görevlendirdi sizi? Neden buradasınız?

Hakan: Öğrenmek için... Anlamak için... Hizmet için... Yapmama şansımız yok... Ruhsal mekanizma müdahaleyi istemiyor ama engel de olmuyor... Asıl güç onlar... Bize insan tekâmülündeki hatayı düzeltmek için fırsat verildi.

Özgür iradeye aykırı alınmalar oluyor mu?

Hakan: Bazen mecbur kalıyoruz... Hakan'ı da öyle aldık... Onu bağlamak zorunda kaldık... Yoksa kendisine zarar verecekti... Hatırlamaması gerekiyordu ama birden uyandı.

Hafızayı nasıl siliyorsunuz?

Hakan: Frekans... (Hakan varlığın gitmesi gerekiyor dedi ve bağlantı kesildi.)

Türkiye ile ilgili söylemek istediklerin var mı Hakan?

Hakan: Güzel olacak... Zorlanacağız... Çok gözyaşı var ama güzel olacak... Atlatacağız.

Türkiye'nin görevi?

Hakan: Hep arabulucu... Elinden geldiği kadar tarafsız... İyi olacak... Dünya daha sıkıntılı... Türkiye'yi ortak akıl devralacak... Bir konsorsiyum gibi.

Evet.

Hakan: Dünya daha sıkıntılı... Yine ağzı maskeli insanlar görüyorum... Pandemideki gibi.

Yeni bir virüs mü geliyor?

Hakan: Maskeli insanlar görüyorum.

Ne görüyorsun? Ne olmuş Dünya'da?

Hakan: İnsanları hasta etmeye çalışacaklar... Sessiz her yer... Sakin.

Nasıl bir şey bu seferki?

Hakan: Yakalananların ağzından burnundan kan geliyor... Yere çömelen insanlar var.

Derilerine, vücutlarına bakar mısın?

Hakan: Mantar gibi... Yara gibi... Sarı... Yeşil... Kabarcıklar... Yere çöken, düşen insanlar... Sokaklar ful karantina gibi... Herkes maskeli ama kahverengi maskeler... Enteresan... Niye kahverengi maskeler?

O özel bir maske mi acaba?

Hakan: Bilmiyorum... Kahverengi maskeler... Çok bariz.

Nereden yayılacak bu peki?

Hakan: Su.

Sudan yayılacak. Herkes yakalanacak mı?

Hakan: Hayır.

Kimler yakalanacak?

Hakan: Akılları sıra dünya nüfusunu azaltacaklar... Tam kontrol etmek için insanları... Her şeyi tek elde toplamaya çalışıyorlar.

Dünya'yla ilgili başka bir şey görüyor musun?

Hakan: Gökyüzünde bir ışık huzmesi var... Işık huzmesi geliyor... Ama iyi bir şey değil... Tuhaf... Sanki elektrikler gidiyor... O ışıktan sonra.

Bütün dünyada mı elektrikler kesiliyor?

Hakan: Yok hayır... Belli bölgelerde... O ışığın denk geldiği yerlerde.

Evet.

(Türkiye görüntüsü geliyor. Hakan burada yurtiçindeki kötü niyetli yabancı uyruklu unsurların dışarıdan talimat beklediklerinden ve ülkemizi karıştırma planları olduğundan söz ediyor.)

(Seans sona eriyor.)

4. BÖLÜM

VAZİFELİ

İzmir'de ikamet eden, 35 yaşındaki Ezgi Erşen daha bebekliğinde Dünya ötesi bazı figürler tarafından mutlak bir ölümden kurtarıldığında, iri gözlü bir varlık Ezgi'nin annesine *"O bebek bize ait"* demişti.

Çocukluk çağları boyunca, Dünya'daki anne ve babasının yanında sadece geçici bir süre için bulunduğu duygusuyla yaşayan ve kendisini bu gezegene pek de bağlı hissetmeyen Ezgi, meleksi olarak tanımladığı varlıkların yardım ve rehberliği altında büyüdü, bu süreç içinde eğitildi, şifacılık öğretildi, hatta varlıkların refakatinde annesinin çok ciddi bir rahatsızlığını iyileştirdi.

Bir defasında, felçli babasını nasıl şifalandıracağına dair, varlıklar tarafından ayrıntılı olarak verilen gıda tarifleriyle, doktorların şaşkın bakışları arasında, babasını mucizevi şekilde normal yaşama döndürdü.

Yıllar geçtikçe duru görü yeteneği gelişti. Bilinci geleceğe doğru uzanıyor ve olacak olayları önceden görüyordu. Anadolu'daki doğal felaketler önceden gösterildi. *"Çocuklara yardım edeceksin... Nasıl yapacağını biz sana öğrettik"* dendi.

Yoğun Dünya dışı temaslar yaşadı, melez programının bir parçası olduğunu anladı. Bir keresinde, Dünya dışı bir araç içinde kucağına, muazzam bir sevgi bağı hissettiği bir bebek verildi.

Rüyalarında sık sık Atatürk'ü görüyordu. En sonuncusunda Atatürk rüyada Ezgi'ye seslendi:

"Sen yalnız değilsin... Senin gibi insanların bir görevi var... Bunu zamanı gelince hatırlayacaksınız... Ve asla korkma... Türk toprakları çok değerli... Onu koruyacak olanlar aydınlanan kişiler olacak."

Ezgi'yi seansa aldığımızda, Atatürk rüyalarının ardında bambaşka bir "haber"in olduğunu gördük. İşler daha öteye, Türkiye'nin yakın geleceğine dair çok kritik bilgilere doğru uzandı.

Ezgi Erşen Seansı

1 Temmuz 2023

(Nefes, gevşeme ve enerji çalışmasıyla seans başlıyor.)

Ezgi: (Vizyonunda Dilek'i görüyor...) Duvar gibi bir yer var... Oradasın.

Şimdi benimle kal. Yanına geleceğim.

Ezgi: Sağda oda kapısı var.

Girdin mi?

Ezgi: Evet.

Ne görüyorsun şu an Ezgi?

Ezgi: Sınıf gibi.

Doğru yerdesin. Kimler var orada?

Ezgi: Böcek gibiler.

İnsan var mı?

Ezgi: Hayır.

Ne yapıyorlar?

Ezgi: Bana bakıyor hepsi ama sevgiyle bakıyorlar... (Ezgi'nin bilinci şu an Dünya dışı bir ortamda ve oradaki mantisleri[5] görüyor)

Varlıklardan bir tanesine yaklaşır mısın? Bir tanesiyle konuşmanı istiyoruz.

Ezgi: Konuşmuyor.

Bekle.

Ezgi: Tamam.

(Varlık şimdi Ezgi aracılığıyla yanıt vermeye hazır ve sorulara başlıyoruz.)

Bulunduğunuz yer neresi şu anda?

Ezgi: Bir gezegen... Hepsinin olduğu yer.

Nerede bu gezegen?

Ezgi: Mars'a yakın.

Bizim Güneş Sistemimiz içinde mi?

Ezgi: Evet.

Biz neden göremiyoruz peki onları?

Ezgi: Herkes göremez diyor.

Fizik boyutta değiller o zaman.

Ezgi: Değiller.

Mars'ın bir uydusu mu peki?

Ezgi: Değil.

Hangi gezegen?

Ezgi: Söylemiyor.

Peki onlara bir sorum var. Onların görevleri ne burada?

Ezgi: Gelişim.

İnsanların gelişimi mi?

Ezgi: Evet ama herkes değil.

---

5. Dünya'daki peygamberdevesi böceğine benzer bir beden tipi kullanan varlık sistemi. Gerek Dünya gerekse Türkiye temas literatüründe sıkça raporlanan bir tür.

Kimler?

Ezgi: Belirlenmiş kişiler var.

Nasıl belirleniyor peki?

Ezgi: Doğmadan önce.

Neye göre belirleniyor?

Ezgi: Onlardan olanlar... Ben de onlardanım.

İnsan bedenine enkarne mi oluyor onların ırkları?

Ezgi: Evet.

Sayı olarak çoklar mı?

Ezgi: Evet.

Neden buraya enkarne oluyorlar?

Ezgi: Dünya'da olanlara müdahale ediyorlar.

Kim vermiş bu görevi onlara?

Ezgi: İnsanımsı varlıklar... Daha üst boyut... Bir tane kadın geldi... Çok güzel... Beyaz elbisesi var... Daha önce de görmüştüm.

Bu varlıkların bir ismi var mı? kendilerine ne diyorlar?

Ezgi: Andromeda.[6]

Oradan mı geliyorlar?

Ezgi: Evet.

Ama bizimle aynı boyuttalar mı?

Ezgi: İstedikleri zaman oluyorlar.

Mantisler çok yüksek bir boyuttan mı geliyorlar?

Ezgi: Çok yüksek değiller ama... Onlar, Andromedalılar, bir de Griler beraber çalışıyorlar... Proje yapıyorlar... Griler insanlarla çalışmak istiyorlar... Yardım.

Karşılıklı bir yardım mı var?

Ezgi: Evet.

Onlar bize nasıl yardım ediyorlar?

---

6. Bu tür astronomik adresleri bizim fiziksel boyutumuzda düşünmek pek de sağlıklı olmayacaktır. Bu konuda gerekli açıklama 2. Kısım'da yapılmıştır.

Ezgi: Teknoloji.

Peki devletlere teknoloji veriyorlar mı?

Ezgi: Reptilianlar veriyormuş... Onlar vermemiş... Çünkü onlar insan öldürüyorlar dedi.

Çok merak ettiğimiz bir şey var. Neden böyle bir böceksi beden formu kullanıyorlar?

Ezgi: Bulundukları gezegene uygun olması sebebiyle... Bu gezegeni o form kaldırabiliyor.

Dünya'daki peygamberdevesi böceğine benzemelerinin bir sebebi var mı?

Ezgi: Onlar meydana getirmişler.

Bir sebebi var mı?

Ezgi: Onların gözünden görüyorlarmış.

Onlarla mı rezone oluyorlar?

Ezgi: Anten gibi.

İnsan deneyimi için bazıları buraya doğuyor anladığım kadarıyla. Doğru mu?

Ezgi: Evet.

Dünya'daki olaylara nasıl müdahale ediyorlar?

Ezgi: Enerji... Çok yüksek bir enerji... Mavi... Mavi bir ışık... Dünya'da enerjiyi yükseltiyorlar... Bir kadın var yanlarında... O kadın onlara yardım ediyor... İnsan melezi yapıyorlar... Kadın bana "Sen bizdensin" diyor... Seviyor beni... Çok özlemiş!... (Ağlıyor...) Sarılıyor bana!

Niçin Dünya'ya geldin Ezgi?

Ezgi: Benimle bağlantı kuruyorlar burada... Onlara yardım ediyormuşum.

Nasıl yardım ediyorsun?

Ezgi: Onlar benim üzerimde işlem yapıyor, sonra ben o enerjiyle insanlara dokununca insanlara enerjim yayılıyor.

Onların enerjileri de mi yükseliyor?

Ezgi: Evet.

Senden genetik materyal, yumurta vb. alıyorlar mı?

Ezgi: Aldılar... Bir melez bebeğim var... Grilerden ama.

Peki bu operasyonun amacı ne?

Ezgi: Benim parçamın onlarda olmasını istiyorlar.

Melez projesinin amacı ne?

Ezgi: Dünyaya uyum sağlamak.

Neden Dünyaya uyum sağlamak istiyorlar?

Ezgi: Gelmek için... Ama insanlar buna hazır değil.

Peki ne planlıyorlar?

Ezgi: Dur... Diyor ki... Biz aslında gelmiyoruz ama geldiğimizi söyleyip bizi kötü gösterecekler... Sen bizi savunacaksın diyor... Sen insanlara gerçekleri söyleyeceksin... Yapay araçlar var... Dünya dışı olanlar uzun süre sabit kalabiliyorlarmış havada... Ama sahte olanlar duramıyormuş... Onların gemileri uzun süre kalıyor yukarıda... Sahte olanlar kalamıyor, düşüyor.

Peki sahte uzaylı bedeni yapılıyor mu Dünya'da?

Ezgi: Evet diyor... Amerika yapıyormuş... (Biraz durduktan sonra...) Trump'ı gösteriyor... Trump gerçekleri biliyor ama konuşturulmuyor diyor... Ölecek o... Trump öldürülecekmiş... Konuşmasın diye.

Peki şimdiki başkan?

Ezgi: O yapay diyor... İnsan değil... Kötü... Gözleri siyah... Reptilian... Kötülük yapacak dünyaya... Plan yapıyorlar.

Onlar (Reptilianlar) hakkında ne söyleyebilirsin?

Ezgi: Dünya'dalar.

Sonradan mı gelmişler?

Ezgi: Varlarmış ama azalmışlar... Çok varmış ama azalmış... Gezegenleri hasar görmüş... Anlaşma diyor.

Kiminle anlaşmışlar?

Ezgi: İnsanlar... Negatifler... Laboratuvarları var... Dünya'daki Reptilianlar kötü... Yukarıdakilerin içinde iyi olanlar da var... Ama az.

Neredeler Dünya'da?

Ezgi: Çöl var... Çok büyük çöl.

Hangi çöl?

Ezgi: Arizona... Altında... Yeraltında.

Fiziksel mi?

Ezgi: Dönüşüyorlar... İnsan formunda aramızdalar.

Herkesi etki altına alamazlar ama.

Ezgi: Pozitifleri alamıyorlar... Ama onlar kaybedecekler... Yok olacaklar.

Evet.

Ezgi: Joe Biden'ın beynine müdahale etmişler... Beynindeki mekanizma bozulmuş... O yüzden o şekilde davranıyor... Beyninde çip varmış... Ne yaptığını bilmiyor... Beynine müdahale etmek zorunda kalmışlar... Yeni başkan gelecek... Reptilianlarla anlaşmış biri gelecek yine... Savaş başlatacak... Örgüt olmuşlar... Ömürleri ondan uzun... Hastalıklarını tedavi ediyorlar... Kötülük yaymak için... Ama soyları tükeniyor... Ölecekler... Art arda ölüm haberleri gelecek.

Yani Reptilian etkisindeki insanlar mı ölecek?

Ezgi: Yetkililer... Evet... Art arda ölüm haberleri gelecek... Tükeniyorlar... Amerika su altında kalacak... Üslere su giriyor.

Nasıl olacak o su baskını.

Ezgi: Okyanusu yükseltiyorlar.

Bir şey mi tetikleyecek bunu?

Ezgi: Denizin altından tetikleyecekler... Okyanusun altından.

Dünya değişim mi geçirecek?

Ezgi: Geçirecek... Çok güzel olacak.

Nasıl olacak bu süreç?

Ezgi: Kıyamet gibi olaylar olacakmış... Yakın... Amerika'da çok büyük bir patlama var.

Nerede?

Ezgi: Üslerin olduğu yerde... Başkan Biden ölüyor... Onu öldürüyorlar çünkü görev yapamıyor... Amerika yeniden toprak oluyor... Yeniden doğuyor... Pozitifler geliyor.

Evet.

Ezgi: Savaşı önce doğa başlatacak... Üst varlıklar doğa olaylarını tetikleyecek, temizlik olacak... Sonra normale dönecek... Bu süreç başladı, giderek şiddetlenecek... Bir ay öncesinde göstereceğiz dediler... Önceden gösteriyorlar çünkü hasattan kurtarmam gerekenler var... Gitmesi gerekenler var, gitmemesi gerekenler var... Bizi vasıta olarak kullanıyorlar... Hasat koyu yobazlardan başlayacak.

Peki Türkiye?

Ezgi: Boyut kapısı var.

Nerede?

Ezgi: Güneydoğu'da... Mağarada... Büyük mağara.

Kaç tane var?

Ezgi: İki.

Yerlerini görebiliyor musun?

Ezgi: Götürüyor beni... Gittik... Eski, tarihi yerlerde... Boyut kapısının önündeyim ama giremiyorum.

Şehir olarak görebiliyor musun?

Ezgi: Denize yakın... Kıyı.

Diğeri?

Ezgi: Diğeri doğanın içinde... Enerjisi çok yüksek.

(Bu arada İzmir görüntüsü de geliyor.)

Ezgi: Antik kentte... Antik tiyatro var... Meryem Ana diyor... Orada çok yüksek enerji var... Antik tiyatroya getirdi beni... Tiyatronun tam ortasında... Altında... Buradan doğmuş... Buradan başlamış... Doğuş başlamış... İnsanın varoluşu... İnsan doğmuş orada... Mucize insanın doğduğu yer... Onu biz koyduk diyor.

İnsan bedeni nasıl meydana gelmiş?

Ezgi: Tüp... Tüplerde... Birçok farklı ırk insanın oluşumuna katkıda bulunmuş... Aralarında savaş olmuş... Gezegenler yok olmuş... Venüs diyor... Venüs çok güzelmiş eskiden... Orada yaşamışlar ama sonra ateş... Ateş... Başka yere gitmişler.

Türkiye'ye baktığın zaman ne görüyorsun? Değişim var mı?

Ezgi: Var... Türkiye'de insanlar birbirine girecekmiş ama sonrası temizlik... Biraz sabır... Çünkü 10 diyor... 10 sene... 10 sene sonra çok güzel olacakmış.

Evet.

Ezgi: Yeni bir lider var... Çoktandır hazırlanıyormuş... Melez... O bir melez.

Türkiye'de mi?

Ezgi: Türkiye'de.

Türkiye'de mi hazırlanıyor?

Ezgi: Onu gemiye alıyorlar.

Şu an nerede yaşıyor?

Ezgi: Türkiye'de.

Nasıl bir yerde?

Ezgi: Genç biri o... Yaşlı değil.

Kaç yaşlarında?

Ezgi: Kırk.

Fiziği, görüntüsü nasıl?

Ezgi: Onun bedeninde Atatürk gibi bir ruh var!

Fiziğini tarif eder misin?

Ezgi: Uzun boylu, açık renk saçlı, mavi gözlü, beyaz tenli.

Zayıf mı şişman mı? Nasıl?

Ezgi: Şişman değil... Atatürk gibi bakıyor... Kaşları çatık... Gözlerinin içi çok parlıyor... Geniş omuzlu... Dudakları ince.

İsmi?

Ezgi: Şimdi değil... Korunuyor... Koruyorlar... Varlıklar koruyorlar.

Yaşadığı yerde deniz var mı?

Ezgi: Var... Denizi çok seviyor... Gözlük takıyor... Gözleri bozuk.

Yurtdışına gidiyor mu?

Ezgi: Çok.

Nereye gidiyor?

Ezgi: İngiltere.

Orada yaşıyor mu?

Ezgi: Çok kalmıyor... Orada bir şey öğreniyor... Ülkeleri gezerek her birinden öğreniyor ve analiz yapıyor... Kendi ülkesinde yapacak hepsini.

Karakter olarak, inanç olarak, dünya görüşü olarak nasıl birisi?

Ezgi: İleri görüşlü... Melez o... Çok yüksek enerjisi... Onu televizyonda görünce insanlar bakakalacak... Onu görünce böyle enerjisine kilitleneceksiniz... Baktığımızda Atatürk enerjisi verecek... Temizlik yapacak... İstifalar olacak arka arkaya... Melez ve vazifesini biliyor... Bazı siyasilerin açıklarını biliyor... Sürekli bilgilendiriliyor, eğitiliyor.

Şu an kimse tanımıyor ama?

Ezgi: Göstermiyorlar.

Etrafında insan olarak, fizik bedenli olarak koruyucular var mı?

Ezgi: Var.

Kaç kişi?

Ezgi: On... Ama bir tanesi Dünya dışı... Çok pozitif.

Peki bu kişinin ortaya çıkışından önce ne olacak Türkiye'de?

Ezgi: İç karışıklıklar ama çok sürmeyecek.

Nasıl olacak? Kimler çıkartacak?

(Ezgi burada ülkemizi karıştırmak isteyen bazılarının kötü niyetli yabancı uyruklu unsurları kullanmaya çalışacaklarından söz ediyor.)

Sonra o genç lider mi gelecek?

Ezgi: O genç lider bir siyasi liderle ilgili çok büyük bir sırrı biliyor. Yargıya gidilecek.

Anadolu'nun vazifesi ne zaman başlayacak?

Ezgi: 2030.

Anadolu dünya için ne yapacak?

Ezgi: Kitap burada... Aradıkları kitap burada.

Hangi kitap bu?

Ezgi: Gerçeklerin olduğu.

Bulunmuş bir kitap mı? Bulunacak mı?

Ezgi: Bulunacak.

Nasıl bir kitap bu?

Ezgi: Dinler... Dinlerle ilgili gerçekler insanlığa sunulacak.

Kim yazmış?

Ezgi: Çok eski... İnsanlığın oluşumunda Dünya dışı varlıkların gerçekleri yazdığı...

Mu olabilir mi?

Ezgi: Değil... Diğeri... Okyanus.

Nerede bu kitap?

Ezgi: Anadolu'nun tam ortasında... Türkiye'nin tam ortasında... Almak istiyorlar bizim ülkemizden ama alamıyorlar... Bizi koruyorlar.

Kimler koruyorlar?

Ezgi: Çok üst seviyede varlıklar var... İnsan değiller.

Anadolu'nun bağlı bulunduğu bir sistem var mı?

Ezgi: Var.

Neresi?

Ezgi: Gökyüzünde çok uzak bir yıldız var... Oraya... Kuyrukları var... 7 tane... Samanyolu... Bağlantılı.

Peki ya Sirius?

Ezgi: Orada başlamış her şey... İnsan orada oluşmuş... Bizi çok seviyorlar... (Bir anda Atatürk'ün enerjisi geliyor...) Atatürk... Çok yüksek bir ruh... Gördüm onu.

Mesaj mı gelecek?

Ezgi: Yanağımı okşadı... "Korkmayın..." diyor. "O kişi sizi kurtaracak..." diyor. Hazırlanıyormuş... Onu hazırlıyorlarmış... "Doğrulardan vazgeçmeyin..." diyor. "Devam edin."

(Görüntü değişiyor.)

Ezgi: Çin Türkiye'yle anlaşma yapacak... Güzel şeyler sunacak... Teklifler... Bolluk.

Peki Putin hangi tarafta?

Ezgi: O da Reptilian... O soydan geliyor... O da ölecek... Onu öldürecekler... Kendi insanları öldürecek... Rusya'da içsavaş olacak... Onu öldürecekler.

(Biraz sessizlikten sonra konu değiştiriyoruz.)

Çiplerin fonksiyonu ne Ezgi?

Ezgi: Enerjimizi kontrol ediyorlar... Bizi izliyorlar... Gözün arkasına da çip koyuyorlar... Oradan her şeyi görüyorlar.

Başka?

Ezgi: Bedenimizi iyileştiriyor... İletişim öncesinde yoğun sinyal yayıyor... Sonra bizimle iletişime geçiyorlar.

Sende çip var mı Ezgi?

Ezgi: Evet... Sol kolumda... Bilek üstünde... Çok küçükleri varmış... Öncekileri insanlar görüyorlarmış. Şimdi bunları görmek çok zormuş artık... Değiştirmişler... Çok küçük.

Temasçıları nasıl seçiyorlar?

Ezgi: Zaten önceden seçilmişiz... Hepimiz doğmadan önce belliymişiz.

Onay olmadan da alınıyor mu kişiler?

Ezgi: Evet ama enerjisinin yükselmesi gerekiyor.

Dünya bedeninde yaşayan Dünya dışı enkarnasyonlar çok mu?

Ezgi: Yüzde yirmi diyor... Fakat sonradan daha çoğalacakmışız.

Yeni bir devre ve yeni bedenler var mı?

Ezgi: Kuvözlerde bekliyor bebekler.

Nasıl gelecek onlar dünyaya?

Ezgi: Anne karnına koyacaklar.

Nesil o şekilde mi değişecek?

Ezgi: Çok üstün zekâlılar... Dijital gibiler sanki.

Eski bedenler?

Ezgi: Onlar yok olacak.

Nasıl?

Ezgi: Onlar ayak uyduramayacak... Titreşimleri düşüyor... Sebepsiz, hastalık teşhisi konmadan ölmeye başlayacaklar.

Şimdi bir şey soracağım. Bazı temasçıların ellerinde ve ayaklarında kına benzeri izler meydana geliyor. Bunun sebebini öğrenmek istiyoruz.

Ezgi: Onlar insanların vücuduna el ve ayaklardan enerji verdikleri için, onların enerjisinin temasçının enerjisiyle uyumlanması sırasında iz meydana geliyormuş... Uyumlanırken oluşan yoğun enerjiden kaynaklanıyormuş... Onların bedeninden akış temasçının bedenine geçerken oluyor... Bu işlem cihazla da yapılıyor.

Eller ve ayaklardan mı yapılıyor hep?

Ezgi: Eller ve ayaklar çok önemliymiş... Enerjinin insan vücudunda en kolay geçtiği yerler eller ve ayaklar... O yüzden.

Bazen şırıngayla bazı temasçılara çeşitli renklerde sıvılar enjekte ediyorlar. Bunların sebebi nedir?

Ezgi: Bedenlerimiz hastalanmasın diye... Enerji geçişine uyum sağlasın diye.

Enerji geçişinden neyi kastediyorsun?

Ezgi: Onlar bize çok bilgi yüklemesi yapıyorlar... O sırada bedenin titreşiminin yükselmesi gerek... İnsan bedeninin buna uyum sağlaması için... Çünkü fiziksel olarak buna dayanabilmemiz lazım.

Ne var içeriğinde?

Ezgi: Erimiş metal gibi... Jelimsi bir şey... Koyu mavi... Çok koyu... Bir de pembe var... Kırmızı gibi... Kırmızı daha yoğun.

Senin aracılığınla tekrar bilgiler gelecek mi?

Ezgi: O zaman biz konuşacağız diyor.

Tamam.

Ezgi: Benim ağzımdan konuşacaklarmış.

Tamam.

(Seans sona eriyor.)

5. BÖLÜM

ÖĞRETMEN

Saadet Öğretmen...

Saadet Özkan Efe yaşamını çocuk istismarıyla mücadeleye adamış, 2017 yılında ABD Dışişleri Bakanlığı tarafından "Uluslararası Cesur Kadınlar Ödülü"ne layık görülmüş yılmaz bir savaşçı...

Çocuk İstismarı ile Mücadele Derneği'nin (UCİM) kurucusu...

Ama bu mücadelesinin ardında öyle bir ruhsal arka plan var ki...

Çocukluğunda başlayan ve hep gerçekleşen rüyalar...

Onu Dünya'daki vazifesine hazırlayan olaylar zinciri...

"*Hazırlan*" diyen sesler...

Rehberlik sisteminin yardımları...

2014 yılında yaşadığı Ölüme Yakın Deneyim sırasında gelen muhteşem, ışıklı varlığın "Daha görevin bitmedi" seslenişi...

Ve "*Son iyi ruh kalana kadar mücadeleye devam*" mesajı...

Bu yürekli insan seansta dünyasal benliğinden çıktı, direksiyonu öz varlığı aldı, vazifesinin kaynağından, yukarılardan seslendi.

Saadet Özkan Efe Seansı
4 Temmuz 2023

(Nefes, gevşeme ve enerji çalışmasından sonra Saadet Öğretmen süratle vizyonlar görmeye başlıyor.)

Nasıl hissediyorsun?

Saadet Ö.: Çok güzel... Suyun üzerindeyim.

Neredesin?

Saadet Ö. : Işıklı bir suyun üzerindeyim... Şelalenin oradayım.

Ne hissettiriyor?

Saadet Ö.: (Gözyaşlarıyla...) Çok özlemiştim!... Çok güzel burası!... Burayı çok özlemiştim!... Sonsuz sevgiyi çok özlemiştim!... Çok güzel burası!... Şükürler olsun!... Çek beni oraya!... Lütfen!

(Saadet Öğretmen bir süre o çok özlediği boyutun içinde ve o muhteşem duyguda kalıyor.)

Saadet Ö. : Arıyor.

Kim o arayan?

Saadet Ö.: Melek.

Oradan devam edelim.

Saadet Ö.: Mikail... Sağda.

Tamam.

Saadet Ö.: Cebrail'in ışığı var!... Arkaya doğru... İsmini bilmediğim bir melek var.

Neresi orası?

Saadet Ö.: Işık.

Başka varlıklar var mı etrafta?

Saadet Ö.: Kanatlarım var... Ama bu sefer sırtımdan değil omuzlarımdan da çıkıyor... Çok ilginç!

Devam et.

Saadet Ö.: Allah!... Allah!... (Tekrar ağlamaya başlıyor...) Dünya'daki bedenimi istemiyorum!... Burada kalmak istiyorum!... İstemiyorum Dünya'ya gitmek!... Dünya'yı istemiyorum!... (Katılarak ağlıyor...) Bu anlaşmanın kararını ben verdim ama istemiyorum!... İstemiyorum!... Kararı ben verdim ama istemiyorum!

Ama burada ne kadar çok görevin var.

Saadet Ö.: Ah!... (Ağlayarak) Burada çocuklar çok acı çekiyor!... Biliyorum!... İstemiyorum!... Bu dünyaya parçalarımızı gönderdik!... Bu dünyaya gönderdiğimiz parçalarımız acı çekiyor!... Çiçekler çekiyor!... Doğa çekiyor!... Çimler çekiyor!... Ağaçlar çekiyor!... Zeytinler çekiyor!

Ama biz o acıları dindirmek için buradayız.

Saadet Ö.: Ruhlarımızı geriye alalım!... Lütfen!... Ruhlarımızı geriye alalım!... Acı çekenlerimizi geriye alalım!... Rica ediyorum geriye alalım!... Çok üzülüyorum!

Tamam bizimle kal.

Saadet Ö.: Ah!... Mikail!... Sözleşmeyi bitirelim lütfen!... Ordularımızı çekelim!

Vazifeni hatırla. Vazifeni hatırla. Hepsi geçecek. Vazifeni nasıl aldın?

Saadet Ö.: Bismillahirrahmanirrahim... Ya Cabbar... Ya Rahim... Ya Allah!

Vazifeyi aldığın yere gitmeni istiyoruz şimdi. Onları gör. Her şeyi anlayacaksın. Buradaki acıların dinecek. O akdi yaptığın ana gider misin?

Saadet Ö.: Uzaydayım... Yıldızlar var... Sirius... Sirius'tan daha uzak... Çok büyük bir sır ama...

(Saadet Öğretmen yüzüklerinin çıkartılmasını istiyor. Çıkartıyoruz.)

Saadet Ö.: (Takılarını kastederek...) Bunlar bana ait değil... Çıkartın... Bu taşlar bu dünyanın... (Saadet Öğretmen'in beden dışı öz bilinci konuşuyor...) Şu anda Saadet'in bedeni... Ondan özür diliyorum... Çok iyi ama yorulduğunu biliyorum... Uzaydayım.

Neredesin?

Saadet Ö.: Yıldız... Benim yıldızım.

Devam et.

Saadet Ö.: Şu anda ışıkların içinden geçiyorum... Bölündüm... Bölündüm... Artık beden burada.

Dünyaya doğumunu mu görüyorsun?

Saadet Ö.: Hayır.

Akit öncesine gidelim.

Saadet Ö.: Kediler var... Işıkları var... Adı Calus.

(Tam bu anda Saadet Öğretmen bilinmeyen bir dille konuşmaya başlıyor.)

Anlamı ne?

Saadet Ö.: Sonsuz sevginin ışığı... Allah!... Allah!... Yaradanım!... Vücudum duramıyor... Hareket ediyorum.

Tamam. Sadece sorularıma cevap ver. Akit yaptın ve görev için geldin.

Saadet Ö.: Kendim istedim... Akdi bozmama izin vermeyin dedim.

Tamam.

Saadet Ö.: (Ağlayarak...) Girdaplar var!... Dünya'da aramızda girdaplar var!... Girmemize engel oluyorlar!... Siz anlayamazsınız!... Işığımızı salmak istiyoruz!... Giremiyoruz ve çıkamıyoruz!... Kaldı bir kısmımız, sıkıştı!... Göndermeye çalışıyoruz gönderemiyoruz!... Göndermek istediklerimizi gönderemiyoruz!... Almak istediklerimizi alamıyoruz!

Dünya'daki görevin ne? Niçin geldin?

Saadet Ö.: Başa geçeceğiz.

Tamam. Başa geçmek için ne yapmanız gerekiyor?

Saadet Ö.: Kapılarımızı kapattılar.

Hayır. Açmak için buradayız zaten.

Saadet Ö.: Kapattılar!... Yoruldum!... Yoruldum!

Yalnız değilsin.

Saadet Ö.: Yoruldum ama!

Bak bir sürü insan yanında. Seni destekliyor.

Saadet Ö.: (Yüksek sesle ağlıyor...) Yıldızımda bırakın beni bugün!... Burayı istemiyorum!... Sonsuz sevginin içinde kalmak istiyorum!... Allahım lütfen!... Lütfen!... Hepimiz sana bağlıyız Allahım!... Lütfen hepimizi geri çek!... Son iyi ruh kalana kadar kalacağımızı söyledik ama çok zor artık!

(Saadet Öğretmen seansta bir arınma yaşıyor. Ardından tekrar konuşuyor.)

Saadet Ö.: Gül tohumuyla başladı... İlk toprağını attık... Sonra gökyüzünden yağmurlarla melekleri gönderdik... Cinsiyetsiz insanlar yolladık... Savaşımız başladı... Sürüngenlerle... Yerin altından çıktılar... Savaş çok büyüyecek... Hazırlıklı olmalıyız.

Dünya'da bir savaş mı olacak?

Saadet Ö.: Evet.

Kimlerin savaşı?

Saadet Ö.: Sizin kelimelerinizle bilmiyorum... Tirian... Tirion... Değişik bir şeyler.

Siz kimsiniz peki?

Saadet Ö.: Biz ışık varlıklarız.

Nereden geldiniz peki?

Saadet Ö.: Sirius'un arkasından.

Sirius'un arkasında ne var?

Saadet Ö.: Orada bir kalkan var... Işık... İçinden geçmek çok zor... Sizler geçemezsiniz... O yıldız kapısının içi... Size kapı açıyorum... Bakın... Görebiliyor musunuz?... Mor kapıyı gördünüz mü?... Kanatlarımız ışık... Açıyorum... Mavinin bütün tonları... Oradaki koruyucu kişi Mikail... Söylemeli miyim?... Size mesajlar gönderen Cebrail... Yağdırıyor rüyalarınıza... Cebrail'i tek olarak düşünmeyin... Küçük küçük çok Cebrail var.

O bir sistem mi?

Saadet Ö.: Cebrail bir sistem... Meleklerle geliyor, kuşlarla geliyor, suyla geliyor.

Evet.

Saadet Ö.: O zenginler batığa giderken onları biz yok ettik... Denizin dibine gidiyorlardı... Yok ettik... Titanic'e giderken... Ama biz öldürmeyiz... Biz organizasyonu hazırlarız... Zihin ilerideyse sizler bunu anlarsınız... Şu an söylediklerimi çözmek için çok uğraşacaksınız... Şimdi sana o kapıyı gösteriyorum Dilek... Kalbinde üzüntülerin var... Hüzün var... Hiç üzülme... Seni tanıyorum... Seninle tanıştık... Senin beni bulman için gönderdi... Geçide bak... Sirius'un arkasında bir geçit var... Kapı.

Sirius sistemine mi bağlısınız?

Saadet Ö.: Hayır... Sirius sistemini de biz oluşturduk... Kapıdan içeriye geçmenize izin veremeyiz.

Oradan nereye gidiliyor?

Saadet Ö.: Yirmi bir.

(Bir süre sessizlik...)

Saadet Ö.: Her kitaba gönderdik... Her kitabın içine kriptolarımızı, ışıklarımızı... Kapıdan girmenize izin veremeyiz.

Orayı anlatır mısın bize?

Saadet Ö.: Işık... Her şey ışık... Her şey ışıktan yükseliyor... Ağırlığımız yok... Telaşımız yok... Tasamız yok... (Tekrar bilinmeyen bir dilde konuşmaya başlıyor.)

Hangi dil bu?

Saadet Ö.: Sadece sizin anlayabileceğiniz ses frekansları... Bizim sese ihtiyacımız yok.

Bize Dünya'dan bahseder misin? Neden Dünya'yla ilgili sorumluluk alıyorsunuz? Vazifeyi nasıl alıyorsunuz?

Saadet Ö.: Bazı ruhlar çok iyi... Çok iyiler ve tek kalmışlar... Çok üzgün oldukları zamanlarda bizlere gönderdikleri frekanslar var... Ve biz yardım etmek için her seferinde etraflarını kurgulayacak yapılar kurduk... Tabii ki bunlar zor... Her seferinde öldürmeden, yok etmeden, kötü planlar yapmadan başarmak zorundayız.

İnsanların duaları size ulaşıyor mu?

Saadet Ö.: Dualarınızda hep bir istek var.

Nefsani istekler mi?

Saadet Ö.: Dualarınızda hiçbir zaman bir teslimiyet yok... Dualarınız hep kendiniz için... Bizim geçit kapımıza ulaşıyor dualarınız... Bizim oraya frekanslar yapışıyor... Cam gibi düşünün... Nefes alıyor orası... Yapışıyorlar... Yapışıyorlar... Biz onları anlamaya çalışıyoruz...

(Burada kişiye özel bazı konular konuşuluyor.)

Saadet Ö.: Bu kapıdan sadece insanlar öldüğünde ayrıştırdığımız ruhları alıyoruz... Ve bir parçayı buraya bırakıyoruz... Bıraktığımız büyük parça kesinlikle göbek kordonuyla bağlı sandığınız yerde değil... Yani biz toprağa bağlı değiliz... Sadece gökyüzünden gönderiyoruz... Uzay gemileri de var... Ama uzay gemileri bizim evrenimizden değil... Onlar bir alttaki varlıklar... Onlar sadece sinyallerimizle ilerliyor... Bize yaklaşamazlar.

Dünya'da sizden çok varlık var mı?

Saadet Ö.: Yüzde bir.

Bize sistemi anlatır mısın? Evrendeki sistemi.

Saadet Ö.: Şimdi... Gökyüzü gördüğünüz gibi karanlık değil... Aslında çok aydınlık... Her bir yer aslında bizim ordularımızla kaplı... Ordu dediğimiz savaş gibi bir şey değil... Her yerde sevgi tohumları ekmeye çalışıyoruz ama atmosferiniz yalancı bulutlarla kaplı... Gerçek olmayan... Çalışmalar var... Yani sizin metan gazlarınız, sizin çöpleriniz, her şey o arayı kapatıyor... O yüzden

o aradan sızmaya çalışıyoruz... Girmeye çalışıyoruz ama zorlandığımızı söylemek istiyorum.

(Biraz duruyor.)

Türkiye'de neler olacak?

Saadet Ö.: Türkiye'de bir yükseliş var... Sınırlarınızı, topraklarınızı ve doğayı korumak zorundasınız... Tarımı korumak zorundasınız... Çiçeği, her şeyi korumak zorundasınız... Güçlü bir enerji, yeni topraklar ve buradan filizlenecek yeni bir lider...

Bize o lideri anlatır mısın?

Saadet Ö.: Yeni bir lider gelecek.

Tarif eder misin bize?

Saadet Ö.: Onu söyleyemem.

Peki tanınıyor mu şu an? Bilinen birisi mi?

Saadet Ö.: Belki de bir kadın... Onu söyleyemem... Her şey zamanla... Karar verildiğinde olur... Buradan gönderilmiş varlıklarımız değil onlar... Melekler buradalar... Ve bir de gönderdiğimiz diğer boyuttaki ruhlarımız var... O ruhlar kanatsızlar... Yani insan şeklindeler... Işıklar... Daha iyiler... Toprakla uğraşıyorlar... Çiçekle uğraşıyorlar... Bir şeylerle uğraşıyorlar... Ama görevlerinin farkına varamıyorlar... Anlayamıyorlar çünkü... Çocuk ruhlarını kurtarıyoruz... Tek görevim çocuklar değil... Son kalanlar zarar görmesin diye elimizden geleni yapıyoruz.

Dünya'da değişim olacak mı?

Saadet Ö.: Değişim başladı.

Dünyanın geleceğini nasıl görüyorsunuz?

Saadet Ö.: Ölümler olacak... Büyük tufanlar... Büyük depremler.

Dünya sıfırlanacak mı? Yoksa...

Saadet Ö.: Dünya sıfırlanamaz... Yapay zekâ ruhları içine çekiyor... Topraktan ve doğadan kopup öfkelenmiş insan kitleleri

etrafınızı saracak... Bahsettiğiniz şey zombi dediğiniz şey değil... Tükenmiş insanlar... Doğadan kopmuş insanlar... Her şeyden... Yemek yemeyi unutmuş insanlar.

Şehir insanları.

Saadet Ö.: Onlar... Her yerdeler... Hepinizin görevi var... Şu an Türkiye'de sadece 9... 9... 9... Uyandırabildik... Rahatlarının bozulmasından korkmayacak olanları bulmanız lazım... Görevlileriniz daha çok orada... Tam kapının ağzındakilersiniz.

Buradan mezun olanlar nereye gidecekler?

Saadet Ö.: Sizin bildiğiniz gibi değil... Dünya dışı varlıklar arada bir yerdeler... Onlar sadece bir kalkan... Bir de sahte uzaylılar yaratıyorlar... Yani bir istila gibi bir şey yaratacaklar ama istila diye bir şey yok... Biz istila etmeyiz... Biz sadece iyi olan ruhları yanımıza çekeriz... Evrenimize alırız.

Sahte araçlarla mı?

Saadet Ö.: Bir oyun düzenleniyor.

Bir anda gökyüzünde sahte araçlar mı belirecek?

Saadet Ö.: Sahte araçlarla plan yaptılar... Bir türlü olmadı... Olmuyor.

Başaramayacaklar mı?

Saadet Ö.: İnsanların beyni buna inanmaz... Gerçek insanlar gerçek olanı bilirler... Biz gerçek insanların hepsini biliyoruz... Dünya dışı varlıklarla ilgili olan kısım... Onlar çok basit olan taraf... Bunlar böyle arada... Biz başka taraftayız... Yirmi bir boyut var... Düşündüğünüz ve idrak ettiğiniz o bir, iki, üç, dört, beş, altı, yedi değil... Biz iyi olanların ışıklarını görüyoruz... Tek tek hepinizi görüyoruz.

Bahsettiğiniz yer Dünya'da cennet olarak tanımlanan yer mi?

Saadet Ö.: Değil... Çünkü sizin cennet tasviriniz çok farklı.

Evet.

Saadet Ö.: Saadet'e yolladık kazayla birlikte... Ama anını bekledik... Olgunlaştırdık ve o bedene kazayla birlikte yolladık... Yani meleği içine soktuk.

Orada Saadet'in ruhu ayrıldı ve başka bir ruh mu devraldı?

Saadet Ö.: Onun içine harmanladık sadece... Şöyle düşün... Işığının içine sadece meleği kattık... Sizinle konuşurken diğer boyutta da olabiliyor... İnsanlar görmek istediğinde insan formunu görüyorsunuz... Öbür tarafta diğeri... Bakın boyutların içinden geçiyorsunuz... Uykuda bazıları sadece bu boyutta... Ama aynı anda birçok boyut var... Farklı boyutlara gidip gelenler var... Ama o boyutların içinde... Size yıldızımızı söyleyemeyiz... Çünkü biz evrenin kendisiyiz.

Siz idareci misiniz?

Saadet Ö.: Evet.

Peki en tepede ne var?

Saadet Ö.: Çok güzel!... (Sonrası anlaşılamıyor)

Peki Dünya'nın idareci sistemi var mı?

Saadet Ö.: Gezegenin atmosferinin dışından size rahmet yağdırıyoruz... Toprak, su, hava... Hepsinden rahmet gelir.

Sirius'la Dünya'nın bağlantısı nedir?

Saadet Ö.: Sadece bir ara kapı... Başka bir şey değil... Sadece bir kalkan gibi düşünün... Biz sizin gördüğünüz ve inanmak istediğiniz şeyleri etrafa koyduk... Bunlar sadece sizin görüp inanmak istediğiniz şeyler... İnsanların anlayacağı şeyler... Cebrail birçok Cebrail... Anladınız mı?... Gönderiyoruz... Rüyalarınıza gönderiyoruz.

Peki peygamberler?

Saadet Ö.: Onlar da ışık... Yoklukları, kıtlıkları, bir şeyleri gösterebilmek ve onları düzeltebilmek için mucizeler... Ama düşündüğünüz gibi değil... Çok derin... Kitapta okuduğunuz gibi değil.

Ya dinler?

Saadet Ö.: Dinlerde ışıklar var... Sayılarda ışıklar var... Ama kelamlar sizin kelamlarınız, bizim değil... Ama istemeden söylediğiniz şeylerle ışık kapıları açıyorsunuz... O kelamların hepsinin frekansı var ve siz her duanızda istemeden kapılar açıyorsunuz.

Saadet'in daha önce Dünya'da enkarnasyonları var mı?

Saadet Ö.: Şu zamanda çok zaman var... Ben bu anda değilim sadece... Geçmişin de geleceğin de bugünde.

Peki o kazaya gidelim mi?

Saadet Ö.: Oradayım.

Ne gördüğünü anlatır mısın bize? Yanına gelen varlık kimdi? Orada neler oldu?

Saadet Ö.: Mikail'le kendi yerime gittim... Kendi yerime götürdü... Hatırlattı.

Saadet'in bedenine ne oldu? Orada koruma altına mı alındı? Ne oldu?

Saadet Ö.: Saadet'in bedenini arabada bıraktım.

O sırada ölü müydü beden? Yoksa hayatta mı tutuyorlardı?

Saadet Ö.: Saadet'in bedeninin etrafında melek varlıklar vardı.

Onun bedenini hayatta mı tuttular?

Saadet Ö.: Onun bedenini korudular.

Nasıl döndün bedenine?

Saadet Ö.: Işınlandım.

Bedeninden ayrıldığın zaman sana ne söyledi orada yuvanda?

Saadet Ö.: Ben zaten bildiğim yerdeydim... Bir şey söylemelerine gerek yoktu... Anlaşmayı zaten ben yaptım... Zaten onlara, ne kadar üzülürsem üzüleyim, ne olursa olsun kuralı yıkmamaları gerektiğini, oraya gittiğimde tüm ruhları geri toplayalım dediğimde bile beni almamaları gerektiğini, asla bunu yapmamaları gerektiğini defalarca söyledim.

Vazifeyi sen mi talep ettin yoksa sana mı önerdiler?

Saadet Ö.: Bana geldiler... Ben Dünya'ya hiç gelmedim... Dünya'nızla işim yoktu açıkçası... Bana gösterdiler.

Çocukları mı gösterdiler?

Saadet Ö.: Hayır.

Yardım ihtiyacı mı var dendi? Ne oldu?

Saadet Ö.: Hayır... Savaşlarınız... Katliamlarınız... Çuvallara konulan insanlar... Yok edilenler... Kadınlar... Erkekler... Çok acınız vardı... (Ağlıyor...) Çok üzüldük... Şöyle anlatmak istiyorum... Allah sonsuz sevgiyi her evrene atar... Anlatır mı desem?... Sizin kelimenizi bulamıyorum... (Yine bilinmeyen bir dilde konuşmaya başlıyor. Dilek söylenenleri anlıyor ve şöyle açıklıyor: "Yayar ve tohumlarını her ruhun, her zerrenin içerisine, her köşeye bırakır.")

Tamam.

Saadet Ö.: Bize geldiniz... Dualarınız ve istekleriniz bize geldi... Sonra siz bizim derdimiz oldunuz... (Gülerek...) Yani o kadar çok frekans yolluyorsunuz ki, her yerimizi acıtıyorsunuz... Bizden size gelenler yorgun dönüyorlar... Ve onları düzeltip biz öbür tarafa yollayamaz olduk... Çünkü bizim öbür tarafımızda sizden (Dünya'dan) dönenlerin gitme şansı kalmıyor... Gönüllü geliyorlar, perişan dönüyorlar... O yüzden, sizin kötülüğünüz sonucunda, artık bebekleri gönderiyoruz... Onlara cennet bahçesi dediğiniz şeyleri gösterip, onları melek yapıp, eğitip göndermeye başladık.

Bunun bir bedeli olmayacak mı Dünya'da?

Saadet Ö.: Zaten bedel ödüyorsunuz... Hep bedel ödüyorsunuz... Hiçbiriniz mutlu değilsiniz ki... Tam bir mutluluk haliniz yok... Saadet çok yorgun... Bunu söylemeli miyim?

Söyle.

Saadet Ö.: Ayrılmak istiyor... Gitmek istiyor... Mesela sizler için aşı olmak zorunda kaldı... Uçağa binebilmek, insanlara faydalı olabilmek, işini yapabilmek için... İstemeye istemeye bunları vuruldu ve çok acı çekti, damarları acıdı... Onun karşısına bir deniz yosunu çıkarttık... Bunu iç ki vücudunu arındıralım dedik... Çünkü hastalanıyor, yorgun düşüyor... (Gülerek...) Israrla gitmek istiyor ve koruyoruz!

Ama kontratı bozma demişsin.

Saadet Ö.: Çok fazla acı çektiriyorsunuz çocuklara... Hayvanlara.

Evet.

Saadet Ö.: Yani siz bizim kapımıza yapıştınız... Işık tohumları oldunuz... Biz de ışık tohumlarını bırakamayız... Bizim bir üst evrenimiz var... O üst evrene gelebilecek mertebede bir türlü olamıyorsunuz... O üst mertebeye alamıyoruz sizi... Nasıl anlatabilirim ki?

(Dilek Saadet Öğretmen'in artık beden bilincine ve bu boyutun farkındalığına geri dönmesi gerektiğini düşünüyor ve yavaş yavaş seansı sona erdiriyoruz.)

6. BÖLÜM

YAVER

İstanbul'da yaşayan, kırklı yaşların ortasındaki, içmimar Demet D., üç yaşından itibaren evde varlıklar görmeye başlamıştı. Bir keresinde, pencereden aşağıya tehlikeli bir şekilde sarktığında, ona kanatlı, beyaz bir at formunda görünen bir varlık küçük Demet'i içeri itip kurtardı. O yıllarda evde meleksi ışık formları sürekli ortaya çıkıp kayboluyorlardı.

Demet, gördüklerine ailesini bir türlü inandıramadığı için deneyimlerini içinde saklayarak büyüdü.

İlk Dünya dışı araç deneyimini yaşadığında 12 yaşındaydı. Ankara'da oturdukları dönemde, kardeşiyle birlikte 15. kattaki evlerinin balkonunda UFO gözlemi yaptıktan çok kısa bir süre sonra uykusunda kendisini bir Dünya dışı aracın içindeki gri bir ortamda, sedyede uzanırken gördü. Etrafta küçük, ışıklı düğmeler ve kolon gibi dikey bölüntüler vardı. Sedyeden doğrulduğunda yanında üç tane gri varlık duruyordu ve Demet'e sakin olmasını, vefat etmiş babasını görmesi için onu aldıklarını söylediler. Az sonra o kolon benzeri panellerin arkasından çıkıp gelen babası Demet'e sıkıca sarılıp, ona ölümü için kendisini suçlamamasını telkin etti. Babası, iyi olduğunu görmesi için onu aldıklarını, bir gün tekrar beraber olacaklarını ama şimdi dönmesi gerektiğini de söyledi. Demet o deneyiminden sonra kendisini suçlamayı bıraktı.

Lise döneminde psişik yönü psikografiye (yazıcı medyumluk) evrildi. Yıllarca otomatik yazılar yazdı, düzenli olarak Dünya dışı araçlara götürüldü, varlıklardan şifa için yardımlar aldı. Rehberi Demet'e hem enerji şifası hem de bitkisel şifa yöntemleri öğretiyordu.

Demet'in Dünya dışı rehberi bizim seansımızda da yanı başımızdaydı...

Türkiye'de ortaya çıkacak yeni lider ve değişim konusu ise yine tüm gücüyle merkeze oturdu.

Demet D. Seansı
5 Temmuz 2023

(Nefes, gevşeme ve enerji çalışmasının ardından seansa başlıyoruz.)

Demet D.: Grilerle deneyimlerim var ama başka varlıklarla da var... Yanımda olacaklarını söylüyorlar.

Tamam. Tabii ki. Asla yalnız bırakmazlar. Şu anda hissettiğin bir varlık var mı?

Demet D.: Evet var.

Bu varlıkla ilişkilerin nasıl?

Demet D.: Çocukluğumdan beri hep yanımda.

Peki onun seninle ilgili bir görevi mi var?

Demet D.: Bana birçok konuda yardım ediyor...

Neden sana yardım ediyor?

Demet D.: Bilmiyorum.

Bunu sorabilirsin.

Demet D.: Benim insanlara şifa vermemi istiyor.

Şifacılık yeteneğin mi var?

Demet D.: Var... Onlar verdi... Şifa yaparken bazen gözümün önüne bazı şeyler getiriyorlar... Onları yapınca insanlar daha çabuk iyileşiyorlar.

Nasıl?

Demet D.: Yani bitkisel şeyler gösteriyor.

Bitki karışımları mı yaptırıyor sana?

Demet D.: Evet... Bitkisel karışımlar.

Peki neden seni seçmiş böyle bir görev için?

Demet D.: Net söylenmedi ama babam öldükten sonra bağımız kuvvetlendi... O zaman oldu daha çok.

Kim bu varlık?

Demet D.: Bazı seanslar yapıyorum... O zaman devrede oluyor.

Tamam. Hangi varlık bu? Onu soruyorum.

Demet D.: Onun söylediğine göre... Kendi adına "Yaver" dedirtiyor... Senin yaverinim diyor.

Nasıl bir boyut bu?

Demet D.: Melekler bize aracı oluyor dedi... Kapıları onlar açıyor dedi.

Tamam.

Demet D.: Ben başka bir gezegenden geliyorum dedi.

Peki Demet. Şimdi seni ikinci şahıs olarak bırakıp onu biraz devreye alsak? Ona izin versen ve senin ses tellerini kullansa? (Onunla doğrudan iletişim kurmak istiyoruz.) Onun sözcüsü olmanı istiyoruz.

Demet D.: Tamam.

O zaman başlıyoruz. (Nefesle derinleştiriyoruz. Kısa bir sessizlik.) Bize kim olduğunu söyler misin?

Demet D.: Yaver.

Neden kendine yaver diyorsun?

Demet D.: Yardımcı.

Kimin yardımcısı?

Demet D.: Demet.

Neden Demet'le ilgili bir görev aldın?

Demet D.: Bize emanet.

Siz kimsiniz? Nereden geliyorsunuz? Neden size emanet?

Demet D.: Gri... Bize ait.

Geldiğiniz yer neresi?

Demet D.: Yakın gezegen.

Neresi?

Demet D.: Söylemiyor.

Dünya'yla ilgili göreviniz ne?

Demet D.: Yardımcıyız... Bu gezegen için buradayız... Koruyucuyuz.

Kim verdi bu görevi size?

Demet D.: Yaradan.

Yaradan'ın altında başka mekanizmalar var mı?

Demet D.: Var.

Bize anlatır mısın?

Demet D.: Meleklerle ortak çalışıyoruz.

Melekler kim?

Demet D.: Üst boyut.

Aşağıda kimler var?

Demet D.: Bizden varlıklar... Aranızdayız.

İnsan bedeni kullanarak mı?

Demet D.: Evet.

Nasıl yapıyorsunuz bunu?

Demet D.: Bizim için çok kolay.

Anlatır mısınız? Anlamak istiyoruz bunu.

Demet D.: Çok kalmıyoruz ama girip çıkıyoruz... Siz öyle görüyorsunuz.

Yani insanların bedenine mi girip çıkıyorsunuz?

Demet D.: Hayır... Beden yaratıyoruz.

Nasıl? Bir fizik bedeni nasıl yaratıyorsunuz?

Demet D.: Siz öyle algılıyorsunuz.

Yani hologram gibi mi? Anlamaya çalışıyorum.

Demet D.: Daha üst.

Katı fiziksel mi? Nasıl tam olarak?

Demet D.: Bunları size söylemem şu an yasak.

Peki. Bize söyleyebilecekleriniz neler?

Demet D.: Korunmaya ihtiyacınız var.

Kimlerden?

Demet D.: İnsanlardan.

Neler olacak peki?

Demet D.: Sizin sayınız çok az.

Dünya'da bir değişim olacak mı?

Demet D.: Olacak.

Nasıl olacak?

Demet D.: Önce yıkım.

Yıkımı kimler yapıyor?

Demet D.: Kendiniz.

Bilinçlenmiş, iyi ruhlara ne olacak?

Demet D.: İyi ruhlar korunuyor... Onun için buradayız.

Onlar bu yıkım sırasında korunacaklar mı?

Demet D.: Evet.

Peki sonra?

Demet D.: Görevlenecekler.

Dünya'da mı?

Demet D.: Her yerde... Oradaki görevleri bitince burada... Şu an biz sadece yardım ediyoruz. (Bir süre sessizlik...) A!... Benim yazmamı istiyor!

(Demet psikografi medyumu, yani yazıcı medyum olduğu için bilgiyi bu şekilde daha akıcı nakledebilme yeteneğine sahip. Ancak seans koşulları o an sözlü iletişime daha uygun olduğu için bu şekilde devam ediyoruz. Demet bir yandan konuşurken bir yandan da sağ elini, kalemle yazar gibi havada hareket ettiriyor.)

İnsanları bu yüzden mi alıyorsunuz?

Demet D.: Evet.

Neye göre seçiyorsunuz?

Demet D.: Ruhlara göre... Bize daha yakın bilinçler... (Biraz duruyor...) İletişime geçmek isteyince parmaklarımla mesaj veriyorlar.

Genetik çalışmaları neden yapıyorsunuz?

Demet D.: Sizi öğrenmek için... Daha geliştirmek için.

Daha gelişmiş ruhlar enkarne olabilsinler diye mi?

Demet D.: Evet.

Bedenleri mi geliştiriyorsunuz?

Demet D.: Bedenleri de ruhları da geliştiriyoruz.

Melez projesi hakkında ne söyleyebilirsiniz?

Demet D.: Melezler çoğaldı... İnsan görünümünde aranızdalar.

İnsan görünümünde olmayan melezler var mı?

Demet D.: Var ama şu an çok anlamıyorsunuz... Çok fazla bebek var... Bir kısmı burada... Gemide.

Onları üretmenizin amacı ne?

Demet D.: Gelecek.

Ne olacak gelecekte?

Demet D.: Daha bütünsel varlıklar olacağız.

Dünya'da bir bütünsellik mi yaşanacak pozitif anlamda?

Demet D.: Evet.

Ne zaman olacak bu?

Demet D.: Sizdeki zamanla bizdeki çok farklı.

Bu tufan veya yıkımdan sonra mı olacak?

Demet D.: Tufan bu defa daha farklı.

Nasıl?

Demet D.: İnsanlar yaratacak ama daha fazla insan kurtarılacak.

Peki ya Türkiye?

Demet D.: Türkiye bizim için özel.

Neden?

Demet D.: En çok korumamız orada var.

Neden özellikle Türkiye?

Demet D.: Bu sırları paylaşmam yasak.

Türkiye'nin bir vazifesi olacak mı?

Demet D.: Var.

Nedir?

Demet D.: Dünya'yı yönetecek.

Türkiye bir değişim yaşayacak mı?

Demet D.: Çok fazla değişim var.

Nasıl? Biraz anlatabilir misiniz?

Demet D.: Kapılar açıldı... Değişim başladı... Kapı açık.

Nerede kapı?

Demet D.: Bir tepede... Kayalık bir tepe.

Türkiye'nin neresi burası?

Demet D.: Biliyorsun... Biliyorsun.

Teyit almak istiyorum.

Demet D.: Güneydoğu.

Biliyoruz ama teyit almak istiyoruz sizden.

Demet D.: Sekiz çiziyor... (Demet de eliyle havaya çiziyor...) Ya da sonsuzluk işareti... Bilmiyorum.

Türkiye'deki değişim nasıl olacak?

Demet D.: Bir ölümle başlayacak.

Kimin ölümü?

Demet D.: (Bir süre sessizlik...) Yönetim değiştikten sonra her şeyin başlangıcı...

Nasıl?

Demet D.: İki... İki ay gibi hissettim... Size göre.

Bir ölüm mü var?

Demet D.: Evet.

Sonra?

Demet D.: İçeride karışıklık.

Kim çıkartıyor bu karışıklığı?

Demet D.: İçinizdekiler... Biz buradayız... Korumadasınız... İyi ruhlar.

Ne yapmalı bu iyi ruhlar?

Demet D.: Siz düşünce gücüyle korumadasınız.

Peki.

Demet D.: Negatif yok... Sevgi var.

Peki sonra?

Demet D.: Suyla... Suyla gelecek.

Bunun anlamı ne?

Demet D.: Denizden karalara gelecek.

Sular mı kaplayacak karaları?

Demet D.: Biz geleceğiz... Gösterdim bunu Demet'e.

Türkiye'de neler olacak?

Demet D.: Yeni bir lider.

Nasıl biri? Tanıyor muyuz?

Demet D.: Orta yaş.

Fiziği?

Demet D.: Uzun... Geniş omuzlu... Sağlığına önem veriyor... 35-40 yaşlarında... Renkli gözlü.

Peki tanınıyor mu şu an?

Demet D.: Kısmen... Herkes değil... Askeriye odaklı biri.

Şu an Türkiye'de mi?

Demet D.: Görev için çıkıyor.

Nereye gidiyor?

Demet D.: Sınırlarda görev yapıyor.

Yurtdışına mı çıkıyor?

Demet D.: Evet... O gelecek bu aralar.

Bu aralar kendisini mi gösterecek?

Demet D.: Evet.

Vazifesini biliyor mu?

Demet D.: Hazırlanıyor.

Nasıl hazırlanıyor?

Demet D.: Uzun zamandır farkında... Biz ona yardım ediyoruz.

Yani çocukluğundan beri yetiştirilen biri mi?

Demet D.: Evet... Bugünler için yetiştirildi... Halktan yetişti... Baba kaybı yaşadı.

Ya ruhsal kökeni?

Demet D.: Melez.

O zaman müdahale edilmiş.

Demet D.: Evet... Anne babaya müdahale edildi... Anne baba bilmiyor.

Türkiye'de mi yetiştirildi yoksa yurtdışında mı?

Demet D.: Türkiye.

Hep sınır içinde miydi? Sınır dışında da yaşadı mı?

Demet D.: Yaşadı... Hep git-gelli bir hayatı oldu... Toprak seviyor.

Başka bilgi var mı?

Demet D.: O geldiğinde önce kimse inanmayacak... Alaşağı edilmeye çalışılacak.

Sonra?

Demet D.: Ama çok güçlü bir ordu arkasında duracak... Ekip kuruluyor... Tüneller kazılıyor... Toprağın altı hareketli.

Ne tünelleri bunlar?

Demet D.: Labirent gibi... Her yerde var.

Türkiye'nin altında mı?

Demet D.: Evet... Her yerde geçişler var... Çok kapılar açıldı... Bilmediğiniz çok fazla kapı var.

Buralardan kimler geliyor?

Demet D.: (Ses tonu daha sert ve kararlı...) Türkiye'nin kurtuluşu için gerekli tüm geçişler yapılacak!

Tamam.

Demet D.: Ordu... Ordu... Ordu.

Nasıl bir ordu?

Demet D.: Tarafsız... Halk odaklı... Hükümet kalkacak... Hükümet diye bir şey yok... Hepsi yalan.

Ne olacak?

Demet D.: Çemberin içine alındık... Çember çiziliyor... Hepimiz bir olacağız... Türkiye merkez.

Türkiye'nin görevi ne olacak?

Demet D.: Türkiye dünyayı yönetecek... Dünyayı kurtaracak... Bize destek.

Yeni bilgiler gelecek mi Türkiye'ye?

Demet D.: Evet... Şu an önemli olan şeyler önemini kaybedecek.

Bunlar nasıl bilgiler? Kim aktaracak?

Demet D.: Seçilen çok var aktarım için... Hepsi görev yerlerine geçecek... Zamanı gelince.

Zaman nasıl bir zaman? Uzun bir zaman mı?

Demet D.: Hayır... Birkaç ay sonra dönüşüm başlıyor... Geldiklerinde bir anda olmayacak... Beş yıl... Beş yıl içinde büyük değişim var.

Pozitif değişimler mi?

Demet D.: İlkönce yıkım... Ölmesi gerekenler ölecek.

Doğal afetler mi?

Demet D.: Kısmen... Başka şeyler var... Savaşlar var.

Kiminle kim savaşıyor?

Demet D.: Dünya'da savaşlar çoğalacak... Bombalar... Kendinizi koruyun... Nükleer.

Dünya bir sıfırlanma yaşayacak mı?

Demet D.: Sıfırlanma gibi değil ama yakın... Ve negatif olan insanlara yer yok.

Yeni bir devre mi başlayacak?

Demet D.: Yeni bir devre başladı!

İnsan tipi değişecek mi?

Demet D.: Bir süre sonra evet.

Temasların amacı yeni tür bedenleri oluşturmak mı?

Demet D.: Beden değiştirmek mecburiyet... Uyumlama için... Yeni Dünya'da daha korunaklı olmanız için beden değişiyor.

Peki Dünya dışı genler mi ekleniyor insanlara?

Demet D.: Evet... Bizden genler ekliyoruz.

Yeni çocuklar öyle geliyor o zaman?

Demet D.: Evet... Bazıları geldi.

(Burada aniden görüntü değişiyor...)

Mantislerle ilgili bilgin var mı?

Demet D.: Yeşil ırk.

Evet. Neden öyle bir beden kullanıyorlar? Yani peygamberdevesine benzer bir beden?

Demet D.: Onlar için kutsal.

Neden kutsal görüyorlar o bedeni?

Demet D.: Aynı zamanda bulundukları yere uyumlu... Başka bir boyut.

Peki Griler neden böyle bir beden kullanıyorlar?

Demet D.: Biz size daha yakınız... Hep öyle hissettik.

Bizimle olan bağınız nereden kaynaklanıyor?

Demet D.: Siz bizim çocuğumuzsunuz.

Nasıl?

Demet D.: Siz bizdensiniz... Başlangıçta biz vardık.

Sizin gerçek bedeniniz bu mu yoksa Dünya için kullandığınız bir kılıf mı?

Demet D.: Biz çok bedene girebiliyoruz ama aslen kemiksiziz... Geçirgeniz... Işığız.

Ya Reptilianlar?

Demet D.: Onlar aşağıdalar.

Aşağıda derken?

Demet D.: İnsan ırkı gibi düşünün... İyisi ve kötüsü var.

Onlar Dünya'da insan bedenlerini kullanıyorlar mı?

Demet D.: Evet... Hem de hiç beklemediğiniz insanlar.

Onlara etkide mi bulunuyorlar? Nasıl yapıyorlar?

Demet D.: Evet.

Dünya'da neredeler?

Demet D.: Her yerde... İnsanların içinde en kötüler onlar.

Siyasetçileri ele geçiriyorlar mı?

Demet D.: Evet... (Birkaç isim söylüyor.)

Başka?

Demet D.: Bunları söylemem yasak!

Peki. Bunların zamanı bitecek mi?

Demet D.: Bitecek... Onun için buradayız.

Dünya'nın ruhsal mekanizmasından bahseder misiniz?

Demet D.: Tepede... Dev bir gemi... En tepede.

Onlar nereye bağlı?

Demet D.: (Ağlamaya başlıyor...) Sirius!... Sirius çok önemli!...

Fonksiyonu ne?

Demet D.: Merkez... Evrenin idare merkezi.

Bütün sistemler oraya mı bağlı?

Demet D.: Evet... Başka sistemler de var bu işte... Çok zorluyorsun.

Kısaca?

Demet D.: İfşa edemem.

Pekâlâ.

Demet D.: O merkez bir üs gibi... Asıl başka bir yerle bağlantılı ama söyleyemem... Bu Demet'e zarar verir.

Anlıyoruz.

Demet D.: Başka her şeyde yardım edebilirim.

Dünya'da üsleriniz var mı?

Demet D.: Dağlarda... Denizlerde de var... Denizde bir portal açtık.

Türkiye'de?

Demet D.: Türkiye'de denizde bir portal açtık... Akdeniz... Güneydoğu... Şile.

Şile'de nasıl bir yerde?

Demet D.: Dağlık alan... Sizden bilenler var... Askerler var.

(Biraz sessizlik...)

Demet D.: Kurşunlar bile gelemeyecek size... Sizi koruyacağız... Ölmesi gerekenlere üzülmeyin... Güneydoğu... Sınırda bomba... Güneydoğu'da başlayacak... İçeride... İç sıkıntılar... Bombalara dikkat edin... Mayınlanan bir bölge var... Sınıra yakın ama amacı doğru değil... Çok başka şeyler var... Zeytinlik bir alan... Zeytinlik alanın altındaki labirent!... Tüneller!... Bir deprem daha!... Bomba gibi... Of!...

Neresi Demet?

Demet D.: Gediz yazıyor ama anlamıyorum... Neden Gediz yazıyor?... Ve çiziyor... Artı işareti yapıyor.

Ne görüyorsun? Anlat bize.

Demet D.: Çadırlar görüyorum... Çok çadır var... Yoksulluk var... Açlık var... Bir nehir kıyısı sanki.

İzmir gibi.

Demet D.: Şu an bir şey görmüyorum... Bir şey yazmaya çalışıyor ama anlamıyorum.

Bedeninden ektoplazma çıktı mı Demet?

Demet D.: Meditasyon sırasında yaşadığım olay... Ama onun ektoplazma olduğunu bilmiyordum.

Nasıl olduğunu anlatır mısın?

Demet D.: Sizin eğitiminizi dinlerken öğrendim... Fotoğrafları görünce anladım.

Böyle beyaz, sümüksü bir doku muydu?

Demet D.: Evet... Bir varlık beni salladı... Kırmızı gözleri vardı... Uzun boylu bir varlık... Bu şekilde yatıyordum... Beni yatağımla beraber bir orman kenarına aldılar... Sonra beni cenin pozisyonuna soktu... Kendi eksenimde çevirmeye başladı... Sonra sağa sola sarsmaya başladı... Aşırı bir mide bulantısı yaşadım... Ama garip bir şekilde hiç korkmadım... Hâlâ sevgi doluydum varlığa karşı... Beni bıraktığında kusmak istedim... Aşağıda toprak

görünüyordu... Toprağa doğru eğildim... Ağzımdan çıkan şey tıpkı o fotoğraflardaki gibi bir şeydi (ektoplazma). Yani katı değildi ama buhar gibi bir şey de değildi... Anlatamıyorum... Garip.

(Bu arada seans odasındaki kitaplıkta hiçbir ışık kaynağı olmamasına rağmen kırmızı bir ışık parlayıp sönüyor. Bir süre duruyoruz.)

Demet D.: Sonra vücudumda izler oluşmaya başladı... Varlıklar şifa yapıldığını söylediler... Hep laboratuvar gibi ortamlarda görüyorum kendimi... Göğsümün arasında izler çıktı... O varlık beni sallayıp ağzımdan o madde çıktığı zaman, sabah uyandığımda buradaki leke gitmişti (göğüs bölgesini gösteriyor). Ama sonra tekrar çıktı... Burada bir "A" harfi oluştu... Sonra o da gitti.

O maddeyi çıkardığın ana gidelim mi?

Demet D.: Gidelim.

(Demet o anı tekrar yaşıyor. Çok yoğun bir kusma hissi gelince durduruyoruz.)

Tamam, oradan çıkıyoruz. Çık oradan.

(Bir süre nefes çalışması yaptırıyoruz. Demet sakinleşiyor ve seansı bitiriyoruz.)

Seans Sonrası:

Demet'in sağ eli seans sonrasında da hâlâ titriyor ve bir şeyler yazmak istiyordu. Hemen kâğıt ve kalem bulduk ve Demet "Yaver" takma ismiyle kendisini tanıtan varlıktan gelen tesiri yazıya çevirmeye başladı. Önce şiddetli karalamalarla bir süre devam eden yazma süreci gelen tesirin uyumlanmasıyla hızla okunaklı hale geldi...

Demet şunları yazdı:

"Olay olmadan akıllanmayacak insanlar... Bu yüzden bir seferberlik olacak... Hayatlara dokunmaya başladık... İlk temasçılarımız

dahil olacak buna... Kaybettikleriniz kazancınızdan az olacak... Biz buradayız... Siz burada... (Gezegenlerinin Dünya'ya nazaran pozisyonunu çiziyor...) Siz ve Güneş... Sistemler farklı biliniyor... Güneş, gezegen sistemleri farklı işliyor... Evren ve gezegenler, yörüngeler farklı... Ben asıl görevimi o konuda yapacağım ve şifa getireceğim... Beni istediğiniz zaman kullanın... Görevim insanlık için... Şifacılığım aktif... Ama artması size bağlı... Şifacılar yetiştiriliyor ama hepsi bilinçli değil henüz... Doktorlardan bile daha büyük fayda sağlayacaklar... Beni her zaman bulun."

(Enerji çok artıyor. Demet'in kolu buna yetişemiyor.)

Yaver'den rica edelim, tesiri biraz azaltsın.

Demet otomatik yazıya devam ediyor:

Demet: "Geceleri şifaya daha uyumluyum... Beni gece kullanın... Hâkimiyetim ellerinden geçiyor... Bazen uzaktan da yapıyoruz... Geliştirmesine yardım edin... Kendine inanması için yardım edin."

Ne yapabiliriz Demet için?

Demet: "Zaten şu an bile yardım ettiniz ama zaman karşınıza çıkartacak."

Doğru insanlar çıktığında biz onları Demet'e yönlendirelim mi?

Demet: "Evet... Her şey planlandı."

Daha çok kimler olacak bunlar? Ruhsal rahatsızlıklar mı? Fiziksel rahatsızlıklar mı?

Demet: "Hepsi... Ama şifa bizde... Korkmayın... Birleşeceksiniz ve atlatacaksınız."

Anlaşılmıştır. Demet'le otomatik yazı çalışmaları yapalım mı? Onun için faydalı olacak mı?

Demet: "Evet... Onun için burada... Zaman içinde size daha çok bilgi aktaracağım... Ama izinler doğrultusunda."

İzinleri kimden alıyorsunuz?

Demet: "Üst kademeler var burada... Ben ortada bir kademeyim."

O kademeleri bize kısaca anlatmanız mümkün mü?

Demet: "Merkez üssündekiler en büyük olanlarımız kademe olarak."

Merkez üs nedir? Ruhsal boyuttan mı bahsediyoruz?

Demet: "Burayı bir ordu gibi düşünün... Düzeni... Erler ve üstler var... Ben ortalardayım... Ama bazen daha üst komutadan yardım alıyorum... O zaman yalnız gelmiyorum."

Bu bahsettiğiniz yer neresi? Bir sistem mi?

Demet: "Biz genelde gemideyiz ama bağlı olduğumuz gezegen var ve size yakın."

Bizimle aynı boyutta bir gezegen mi?

Demet: "Farklı ama bazen aynı... Bunu nasıl anlatırım size?"

Mesela bizim sistemimizdeki bir gezegenin spatyomu gibi düşünebilir miyiz?

Demet: "Evet."

Bildiğimiz bir gezegenin daha akışkan boyutu gibi mi?

Demet: "Evet."

(Otomatik yazı bağlantısı kesiliyor ve yazı seansını da sona erdiriyoruz.)

7. BÖLÜM

TESLA & ATATÜRK

İstanbul'da ithalat ve ihracat işiyle uğraşan, birçok farklı alanda da iyi bir kariyeri olan başarılı işkadını, 58 yaşındaki Yasemin Karadağ "Griler" ismiyle bilinen Dünya dışı varlıklarla deneyimler yaşıyordu.

Çocukluk yıllarında astral çıkışları oluyor, bahçede, merdivenlerde otururken kendisini başka apartmanların pencerelerinden, aşağıda oturan "kendisine" bakarken buluyordu.

Yıllar bu şekilde geçti.

2022 yılı Temmuz ayında bir toplantı için gittiği Ankara'da çok ilginç bir olay yaşadı. Biri uzun boylu, diğeri ise onu hep ziyaret eden kısa boylu iki varlık sabaha karşı onu uyandırdılar ve telepatiyle seslendiler:

"Kalk... Kendi dinindeki şekilde arın!"

Yasemin şok yaşıyordu. Kalktı ve dediklerini yaptı. Varlıklar Yasemin'den masaya geçip kâğıt kalem almasını istediler ve ona bir sayfa dolusu yazı yazdırdılar. Yaşadıklarına inanamıyordu. Uzun olan sol omzumun yanındaydı. Kısa olan ise o sırada sağında duruyordu.

"Sen sevgi frekansındasın, bunu unutma" dediler.

2021 yaz aylarında daha önceden hiç tanımadığı bir bayan Yasemin'e yeni satın alınmış bir *Novus* kitabını ulaştırdı. *Novus*'u bir solukta okurken, yazılanların neredeyse hepsini

yaşamış olduğunu şaşkınlıkla görmüştü. *Novus*'tan sonra her şey onun için daha farklı olmaya başladı. Temaslar iyice sıklaştı.

2017'de İzmir-Güzelbahçe'deki işyerinde sakin bir şekilde otururken sağ elinin başparmağımdan 3-4 santimetre uzunluğunda mavimsi gri bir ışık çıktığını fark etti. İki saat süren olaya o anda yanında bulunanlar da tanık oldular. Aynı olay daha sonra 2020 yılı Ağustos ayında İzmir-Bodrum arasında arabayla seyahat ederken tekrar etti. Bu kez sağ elinin tüm parmaklarında birden aynı ışık çok hafif şekilde ve ilkinden daha uzun olarak çıkıyordu. Kızı ve damadı da ışığı gördüler.

Hayatı boyunca kabına sığamadığını hissetti, Dünya'ya ait olmadığını düşündü. Gençlik çağlarında yoğun kasık ağrıları yaşadı ve bunun genetik projeler için kendisinden yumurta alınmasıyla bağlantılı olduğunu çok daha sonraları anladı.

Yasemin sebebini bilmeden, sadece içsel bir dürtüyle uzun yıllar tohum topladı. Onlara gözü gibi bakıyor, soranlara "*Yeni hayata geçince kullanacağız*" diyordu.

Yasemin Karadağ'ın seansı çok sürpriz bir girişle başladı, ardından işler vatanımızın ön planda olduğu, bambaşka noktalara uzandı.

Yasemin Karadağ Seansı
6 Temmuz 2023

(Nefes, gevşeme ve enerji çalışmasının ardından Dilek Yasemin'le rezone oluyor ve seans başlıyor.)

O varlıkların gelmelerindeki amaç ne?

Yasemin: En son geçen yaz yirmi taneye yakın çok küçük Griler gördüm... Kapının önüne geldiler... İçeriye bakmaya, içeriye girmeye çalışıyorlardı ve inanılmaz mutlulardı.

(Dilek ona daha önce fiziken, insan formunda yaklaştıklarını görüyor.)

Yasemin: (Devam ediyor...) İnsan formunda karşıma çıktılar... 1990'larda insan formunda uzaktan gördüm... Muhteşem bir insan yanıma geldi... İnsanlar da vardı... Bir sürü insan ama bana doğru geldi ve eğildi "Senin yardımına ihtiyacım var" dedi... Ben de para istiyor zannettim... Para çıkardım verdim... Bir anda kayboldu... Ne sağa gitti ne sola gitti... Hiçbir yere gitmedi... Kayboldu!... Tüylerim şu an diken diken... Ardından arkadaşlarım ne olduğunu sordu... Yardım istedi dedim... Keşke biz de yardım etseydik dediler.

Nerede oldu bu olay?

Yasemin: Tekirdağ Çorlu.

Tamam.

Yasemin: Sonra 2000 yılında Çorlu'dan Yeniçiftlik'e geçerken önüme Nikola Tesla çıktı.

Devam.

Yasemin: Çorlu'dan Yeniçiftlik'e gidiyorum ara yoldan... Tam tarlaların başladığı yolda yüksek bir tırmanışım var ve çok keskin bir sağa dönüşüm var... Tam sağa döndüğüm an çok yaşlı bir adam karşıma çıktı... Tam benim yolumun ortasında arabamın önüne çıktı... Upuzun boyu vardı... Hemen hemen 1,90...[7] Simsiyah bir kıyafeti vardı... Kıyafet çok eski modeldi... İncecik beyaz çizgileri vardı... Avurtları aşırı çöküktü... Tarlaların oradan büyük apartmanlara bakıyordu... "Neredeyim ben!" gibi bir bakışla... Çok şaşkındı... Sonra elinde siyah, kocaman bir torba vardı... Torba inanın balon gibi şişkindi... Ne bulduysa tıkıştırmış içine diye düşündüm... Kesin bu adam evden kaçmış dedim... Sağa çektim ve polisi aradım... "Bir amca var burada... Yolun ortasında duruyor, çok da keskin virajda... Bir araba çarpabilir... Gelin bu amcayı kurtarın" dedim... Öyle bitti.

7. Nikola Tesla 1,88 metre boyundaydı.

Tesla olduğunu nasıl anladın?

Yasemin: Geçenlerde... İki üç ay önce cep telefonumla oynarken onun fotoğrafını gördüm ve "İşte buydu!... Buydu benim karşıma çıkan amca!" dedim ve bir baktım ki Nikola Tesla! Çok ağladım... Çok ağladım... Kendimden geçtim.

Sanki geçmişte deney yaparken bir anda kendisini gelecekte bulmuş gibi.

Yasemin: Çok şaşkın bakıyordu!

Nasıl yapmış bunu acaba?

Yasemin: Bilmeden yapmış.

Nasıl?

Yasemin: (Şimdi görmeye başlıyor...) Sanki küçücük bir yerden çıktı... Karanlık bir odadan geldi... Bilinçsiz geldi.

Bilinçsiz olarak karşına çıkarken ne yapıyormuş orada?

Yasemin: Önünde makine var... Onunla oynuyor... Işığı var... Kırmızı ve sarı ışığı var.

Devam.

Yasemin: Bunu yaparken bir anda kendisini gelecekte buldu... (Yasemin şimdi o anı izliyor...) Biriyle konuşacak ama kiminle konuşacak?

Tamam.

Yasemin: Şu an şaşkın halini görüyorum... Yani "Nasıl gidebilirim, dönebilirim?" gibi bakıyor bana... Çok uzaklara bakıyor.

Tesla nasıl biri?

Yasemin: Fiziken mi?

Hayır. Ruhsal kökenini soruyorum. Nereden gelmiş?

Yasemin: Kalbim çok atıyor!... (Sakinleştiriyoruz...) Sirius!

Neden gelmiş Dünya'ya?

Yasemin: Bilgi... Bilgi yaymak için.

Peki. Sirius'tan başka gelen olmuş mu onun gibi?

Yasemin: Einstein.

Başka?

Yasemin: Atatürk... Başka görmüyorum... Bu üçünü görüyorum.

Biraz duralım.

Yasemin: Çok heyecanlı konuşmalar yapıyorlar... Çok heyecanlı!... Çok hararetli... Çok ateşli!

Kimler konuşuyor?

Yasemin: Tesla'yla Atatürk konuşuyor ama çok hararetli konuşuyorlar!

Nerede konuşuyorlar?

Yasemin: Mağara gibi sanki... Yerin altında gibi.

Dışarıya çık ve oradan bak.

Yasemin: Işık var.

Etrafına bak. Ne görüyorsun?

Yasemin: Etrafımda ağaçlar var... İki tane ağaç var... İki büyük ağaç görüyorum.

Başka birileri var mı?

Yasemin: Başkaları var ama uzaktalar... Postalları var ayaklarında.

Ne konuştuklarını dinler misin?

Yasemin: Adamın elinde sigarası var... O da heyecanlı ama onlara bakmıyor.

Üçüncü bir kişi mi o?

Yasemin: Asker kıyafetli birisi... Uzun çizmeleri var.

Atatürk'ün üzerinde ne var? Kaç yaşlarında?

Yasemin: Onun da asker kıyafeti var üzerinde... Kırklı yaşlarda... Genç görünüyor... Çok hararetli konuşmaları var.

Konuşma neyle ilgili?

Yasemin: Dünya'yla ilgili.

Özelikle konuştukları bir yer var mı?

Yasemin: Türkiye'deler... Türkiye'deler ama şeydeler... Akdeniz'in sonu gibi... Ama yerin altında görüyorum... Yerin altındalar... Çok heyecanlılar!

Ne konuşuyorlar?

Yasemin: Birbirlerinin gözlerinin içine bakıyorlar şu an... Türkiye'nin geleceği hakkında konuşuyorlar.

Ne konuşuyorlar Yasemin? Tesla ne söylüyor? Atatürk ne söylüyor?

Yasemin: Gelecek diyor... Gelecek.

Türkiye'nin geleceği mi?

Yasemin: Hayır... Biri gelecek anlamında.

Kim gelecek?

Yasemin: Atatürk'ün sol elinde sigara var.

Kim gelecek? Nereye gelecek? Niçin gelecek?

Yasemin: Gemiyle gelecek... Tesla gemi diyor.

Kim bu gelecek olan? Anadolu'ya mı, Türkiye'ye mi gelecek?

Yasemin: Akdeniz'in doğusuna... Güneydoğu Anadolu... (Yasemin şaşkınlıkla bir şey fark ediyor...) Gemi yerin altında!... Gemi o!... (Yasemin'in önce mağara zannettiği şeyin gemi olduğu anlaşılıyor.)

Tamam. Bu gelecek kişinin fiziğini tarif eder misin?

Yasemin: İnsan görünümünde olabilir ama insan değil... (Biraz duruyor...) Sol tarafıma metal bir şey batırdılar sanki şu an!... Yani gelecek dediğim kişi onayladı sanki.

Kim o? Ne olarak gelecek?

Yasemin: Yüzü çok fazla insana benzemiyor.

Bir proje mi? İnsan görüntüsünde ama ruhu yukarıya ait bir proje?

Yasemin: Evet... O da çok heyecanlı.

Bu gelecek kişinin vazifesi ne? Ne yapacak?

Yasemin: Kurtuluş!

Ülkenin kurtuluşu mu?

Yasemin: Evet... Kurtuluş!

Tamam.

Yasemin: İkisi de çok heyecanlı şu an!... Çok heyecanlı!... (Atatürk ve Tesla'yı kastediyor.)

Yani yeni bir lider gibi mi anlamamız gerekiyor?

Yasemin: Söylemiyorlar... Ama ikisinin de kalbi çok hızlı atıyor.

Peki Türkiye'de ne olacak?

Yasemin: Söylemiyor.

Verilmesi gereken mesaj verildi sanırım. Zaman olarak ne zaman?

Yasemin: İki görüyorum... İki... Sıfır... İki... Üç.

Şimdi şunu istiyorum. Bu kişinin geleceği zamana gidip Türkiye'ye yukarıdan bakmanı istiyorum. Nasıl bir dönemde geliyor?

Yasemin: Çok ateş var... Bombalar gibi... Çok ateş var... Bomba değil ama sanki atıldığı yerde çok devasa ateşler çıkıyor.

Türkiye saldırıya mı uğruyor?

Yasemin: Evet... Bir sürü... Bir sürü yerde... Şehir şehir kocaman ateşler var.

Dışarıdan bir saldırı mı var?

Yasemin: Görünmüyor... Ama ateşler bomba gibi küçük bir yerde değil... Çok büyük ateşler var... İl il... Ankara var... Ankara'nın altı... Ankara'nın doğuya yakın altı var... Doğuya yakın altı!

Ne var orada?

Yasemin: Ateşler var... Çok büyük ateşler... Isparta gibi... Gökyüzünden gördüğüm bunlar... Çok büyük ateşler.

Bayrak görüyor musun?

Yasemin: Amerikan bayrağı var.

Başka?

Yasemin: Mavi-beyaz bayrak var... Ortasında sarı bir şey var sanki... Adamın elinde var bayrak... Kocaman bir bayrak taşıyor... Adam Türk değil yabancı.

Bunlar Türkiye'yi işgal etmek isteyenler mi?

Yasemin: Türkiye'yi işgal etmek isteyenler evet... Yani başardık, başardık diyor.

Şimdi ileriye saralım biraz. İlerle. Ne oluyor ondan sonra?

Yasemin: Kömür gibi olmuş birçok yer... O alev alev yerler var ya... Onlar kömür gibi olmuş... Sönmüş ama göçük... Üç tane çok büyük göçük var... Kapkaranlık oralar.

Peki sonra? Biraz daha ileriye gidelim. İlerle. Bak bakalım neler oluyor?

Yasemin: Bilinç var... Işık... İnce ışıklar yeryüzüne iniyor... Şeyden... Doğu tarafından batıya doğru görüyorum ışıkları... Batıya doğru ince ince bulutların arasından doğmuş ışık.

Sonra? Aşağıya bak şimdi.

Yasemin: Yeryüzünde hâlâ o büyük göçükleri görüyorum... Kocaman, devasa oyuklar var... Simsiyah olmuş... Bir şehir... İki şehir yok gibi görünüyor...

İleride pozitif bir değişim var mı?

Yasemin: Mutlu insanlar var... Türkler var... Mutlu insanlar var.

Nasıl olmuş o?

Yasemin: Yani onlar var... Zıplıyorlar sanki... Muratlarına ermişler gibi... Çok heyecanlılar... Üstleri altın sarısı hepsinin... Altın sarısı.

Peki o gelecek olan lider orada mı? Onu görüyor musun?

Yasemin: Onun üzerinde kırmızı bir kıyafet var... Belki kırmızıya boyanmış bir kıyafet olabilir... Ama ışıltılı.

Peki. Türkiye'nin bir vazifesi olacak mı ileride?

Yasemin: (Bir süre sessizlik...) İnsanlar şaşkın bakıyorlar birbirlerine.

Gökyüzü nasıl?

Yasemin: Gökyüzü çok güzel... O doğudan yayılan ışıkla beraber... O güneş ışığı olmayabilir... Gelen bir şey olabilir... Gelen bir şeyin ışığı olabilir o... Işık o kırmızı kıyafetli, uzun boylu, biraz yapılı kişinin yüzüne vuruyor.

Biraz beden yapısını tarif eder misin?

Yasemin: Omuzları geniş... Uzun boylu... Biraz yapılı.

Saçlarına ve gözlerine bakmanı rica ediyorum.

Yasemin: Arkası dönük bana... O güneş gibi olan yere bakıyor... Yüzünde mutluluk ya da mutsuzluk ifadesi yok... Sadece o ışığa kenetlenmiş, ışığa bakıyor.

Şimdi sana dönsün. Gözlerine bakmanı istiyorum.

Yasemin: Döndü... Gözleri çakmak çakmak... Mavi.

Saçları?

Yasemin: Sarı... Beyaza da benziyor ama... Sarı-beyaz... Yani yaşı ilerleyip beyaza dönmüş olabilir... Ama yüzünde hâlâ mutluluk ya da mutsuzluk ifadesi yok... Ciddiyet var.

Zaman hissin var mı?

Yasemin: 60 diyor.

O 60 yaşındayken mi acaba? Peki, nasıl olacak ondan sonra Türkiye?

Yasemin: Türkiye bembeyaz görünüyor!... Bembeyaz!... Her yeri beyaz!... Her yeri bembeyaz!... Sol elinin uzun parmağını görüyorum...

O değişimden sonra Türkiye'nin görevi ne olacak?

Yasemin: Türkiye kale ördü!... Bütün Doğu ve Güneydoğu Anadolu'ya kale ördü!... Kale örüyor.

Sınırlara mı?

Yasemin: Evet... Komple... İran'a kadar... Yani taşlardan... Çok yüksek... Şey gibi... Çin Seddi gibi!

Tamam. Ondan sonra? Dünya için bir vazife yapacak mı Türkiye?

Yasemin: Yukarıyı gösteriyor... Rusya'yı gösteriyor... Parmağını Rusya'ya çevirdi... Upuzun parmağı var.

Sor bakalım nedenini?

Yasemin: Yardım yok diyor... Oradan yardım yok diyor... Şimdi aşağıları gösteriyor... Oralarla ilgimizi kestik diyor.

Aşağıda ne var?

Yasemin: İran var... Suriye var... Irak var... Parmağıyla Rusya'nın tepesinden, Karadeniz'den başladı, aşağıya kadar gösteriyor... Oraları kapkaranlık gösteriyor... Oralar bizim için karanlık diyor.

(Bu noktada Yasemin'in vücudu fazlasıyla geriliyor ve artık o alandan çıkması gerektiğine karar veriyoruz.)

Yasemin: (Biraz sessizlikten sonra...) Operasyon odasındayım.

Tamam. Niçin oradasın?

Yasemin: Aşağıdayım... Dışarıda yine Atatürk'ü görüyorum.

(Vermek istediği bir mesaj olduğunu anlıyoruz çünkü Yasemin'in Dünya dışı araç içindeki anılarına gitme çabamız engelleniyor ve sahne yine Atatürk'e dönüyor.)

Şimdi onun yanına gider misin? Mesaj için hazır olduğunu söyler misin?

Yasemin: Kahkahayla gülüyor bana... Elinde sigara var... Çok mutlu... Her şey yolunda diyor... Çok güzel olacak diyor... Gülümsüyor... Dudağının kenarı iyice yukarıya kalkarak gülümsüyor.

Özel bir mesajı var mı?

Yasemin: Çocuklar... Çocuklar... Çocuklar diyor ama bunlar normal çocuklar değil... Başka yerden gelen çocuklar... Evet... Kurtuluş... Çocuklar diyor.

Yani o çocuklar vazife alacak. Doğmuş mu o çocuklar?

Yasemin: Küçücük çocuklar... 6 yaşında yoklar daha... Küçücükler... Çocuklar karşısında... Yanında değil... Önünde duruyorlar... En az 7-8 çocuk var.

Ne yapacak o çocuklar? Görevleri ne?

Yasemin: Türkiye'ye dağılmışlar.

Çok güzel.

Yasemin: Hepsi çalışıyorlar ama çok küçükler... Büyümeleri gerekiyor... Büyümelerine daha var.

Türkiye'de ileride yönetimi onlar mı devralacak?

Yasemin: Evet... Türkiye'nin her yerine dağılmışlar... Özellikle 7-8 yer gösteriyor... İstanbul ve Ege'yi gösteriyor... Kıyıları gösteriyor.

Em çok oralarda mı bu çocuklar?

Yasemin: Evet... İstanbul'da ve Ege'de... İzmir'de varlar.

Ne yapacak bu çocuklar?

Yasemin: Halı süpürür gibi her yeri ışıl ışıl yapacaklar... Yani halı üzerindeki pislikleri süpürüyorlar... Üstü ışıl ışıl oldu... Dağları tepeleri görüyorum... Hepsi ışıl ışıl... İçeriye doğru süpürüyorlar... Yani içeriye doğru dediğim, denizden Konya'ya doğru, Ankara'ya doğru süpüre süpüre geliyorlar.

Çok güzel bir sembolik anlatım var burada.

Yasemin: Halıların üstü ışıl ışıl... Yani o kadar iyi temizliyorlar... Doğuya doğru.

Evet. O zaman daha ruhsal bir Türkiye mi olacak?

Yasemin: Evet.

Daha yüksek bilgiler gelecek mi Türkiye'ye?

Yasemin: Kafasını sallıyor... Size o cevap verdi... Gülümsüyor zaten... (Ağlamaya başlıyor...) Çok güzel yüzü var!... Çok mutlu... Mutlu olduğunu söylüyor.

(Burada ilerideki bazı çalışmalarımıza ilişkin özel nitelikli bir bilgi alışverişi oluyor.)

Yasemin: (Atatürk'e bakarak ve ağlayarak...) Yüzü aydınlık... Daha da aydınlandı... Işıl ışıl... Pırıl pırıl... Gözlerinin içi zaten gülüyor... Sağ elinde küçük bir sigara var... Bitti bitecek sigara... Sadece tek bir lider gelmeyecek... Liderler gelecek diyor... Yetişiyorlar diyor... Onlar hazırlanıyorlar... Hazırlar... Çok az kaldı diyor... Hepsi birlikte hazırlanıyorlar... Aşağıda Antalya taraflarında da var... Hep Antalya'nın ilerisini gösteriyor... Antalya'nın ilerisi ama orası daha karanlık... Ege'den süpürerek geliyorlar ya... Antalya tarafından güneydoğuya doğru gösteriyor.

Bu liderleri ya da lideri tanıyor muyuz şu an?

Yasemin: Bilenler biliyor... Bilenler biliyor... Onların kim olduğunu bilenler biliyor.

Kimler biliyor? Kimler var yanında?

Yasemin: Bir isim veriyor ama...

Koruyucuları mı var?

Yasemin: Evet onlar korunuyor... Üç koldan korunuyor... Üç tane... Önlerinde her birinin yüzüne bakan bir tane büyük var... İki tane yanlarında ileriye bakan var... Sağında solunda... Hepsinde insanlar var ama şey gibiler... İfadesizler... Koruyorlar... O süpürenleri koruyanlar var... Hepsinin yanında bir büyük var... Koruyucu melek gibi... Yüzleri nurlu ama şey yok... İfade yok... Yüzleri çocukların yüzüne dönük... Sırtları doğuya dönük.

Evet.

Yasemin: Gelecekler... Çok az kaldı diyor... Hazırlan diyor.

Yani ortaya çıkacaklar?

Yasemin: Evet... Hazırlan... Hazırlan.

Şu an hepsi Türkiye'de mi?

Yasemin: Hepsi Türkiye'deler... Ege'den süpürmeye başlamışlar zaten... Koruyucularıyla birlikteler hepsi... Temizleyenler küçüklükten yetişenler... Büyük olan koruyucular... (Bir anda duruyor...) Sus dedi... Parmağıyla sus işareti yapıyor.

Tamam.

Yasemin: Mis gibi kokuyor her yer... Çok güzel bir koku var... Çok yoğun bir çiçek kokusu gibi... Her yerde bir ışıltı görüyorum... O karanlıklar gitti.

Evet.

Yasemin: Rusya karanlık... Suriye, İsrail, Lübnan... Oralar hep karanlık... Ama oralarla bağlantımız yok... Orayla bağlantımızı kesiyor... Değişik, koyu renk giymiş insanlar var... İnsan siluetindeler... Onlar kesiyorlar... Ama boyunları çok geniş... Saçları yok... Hiçbirinde saç yok... Kulakları yok... Kulaklarını göremiyorum.

Devam et.

Yasemin: İstanbul daha geç... Ege'den temizlik başlıyor ama İstanbul daha geç olacak.

Nasıl olacak bu temizlik peki?

Yasemin: Temizliği o yetişenler, yetiştirilenler yapacak... İstanbul'da bir tane var... Zayıf kalıyor... Güçlenmesi lazım.

(Uzunca bir sessizlik. Bizi bu alandan çıkartmıyorlar. Sorulması gerektiğini hissettiğimiz birkaç soruyu soruyoruz.)

Atatürk'ün en büyük hayal kırıklığı neydi?

Yasemin: Etrafındakiler... Ona güvenmemişler... Onun sırtını dayadığı insanlardan bazıları yanlış insanlarmış.

Atatürk'ün hâlâ gizli olan bilgileri, defterleri var mı?

Yasemin: Var.

Kimlerin elinde?

Yasemin: Takkeli insanlar var.

Bu bilgiler zamanı geldiğinde çıkacak mı?

Yasemin: Çıkacak.

Peki Atatürk o defterlere neler yazmıştı?

Yasemin: Çok gizli bilgileri var... Kendi elleriyle yazmış... Kendi elleriyle.

Neler yazmış?

Yasemin: Kurtulacak Türkiye diyor... Kurtuluş gösteriyor... Sayfalar dolusu... Çok güzel yazısı var.

Peki başka sırlar var mı?

Yasemin: Var... Var... Yine kapılar var... Sanki geçilince toz bulutu oluyor.

Peki bu takkeliler kim?

Yasemin: İsrailliler olabilir mi?... Beyaz takkeleri var... Siyah giyimliler.

Onlar mı ele geçirmiş?

Yasemin: Evet.

Peki onlara bu defterleri veren kişi Atatürk'ün tanıdığı birisi mi?

Yasemin: Evet.

Kadın mı erkek mi?

Yasemin: Kadın... Uzun saçları var... Yüzünü görmüyorum... Arkadan görüyorum... Sağ kolunda çantası var... Koluna geçirmiş.

Atatürk'e yakın bir kadın mıydı?

Yasemin: Evet... Arkasında duruyor.

Kim?

Yasemin: Latife... Zaten kendisi cevap verdi... Latife vermiş defterleri... Atatürk'ün arkası şu an Latife'ye dönük.

Şu an İsrail'de mi o defterler?

Yasemin: İsraillilerde ama İsrail'de olduğunu söylemiyor... İsrail kapkaranlık diyor.

Peki biz bunları geri alabilecek miyiz?

Yasemin: Geçecek... Geçecek... Ama zamanı var... Şu an karanlık diyor.

Defterde hangi bilgilerin olduğuna bakabilir misin?

Yasemin: Kurtuluş... Kurtuluş diyor.

Neyi tarif ediyor?

Yasemin: Karanlıktan çıkacağız diyor... Ben geleceğim diyor... Beni bekle diyor.

O zaman bugünleri görmüş ve ona ilişkin şeyler mi yazmış?

Yasemin: O kâğıtlar benim elime geçecek diyor... Defter değil kâğıtlar diyor... Kâğıtlar bana gelecek, ben geleceğim diyor.

Şu anda nerede?

Yasemin: Ben kapıdan geçtim diyor... Sirius diyor... Gittim diyor... O kapıyı gösteriyor bana... Yusyuvarlak bir kapı... O kapıdan geçiyorum geri geliyorum, geçiyorum geri geliyorum diyor... Açık renk kıyafet var üzerinde.

Başka bir şeyler görüyor musun? Devamı gelecek mi?

Yasemin: Şu an baktığı yer karanlık... Arkası dönük... Elimde kâğıtlarla geleceğim diyor... Şu an elinde en az 10 sayfa kâğıt var... Büyük kâğıtlar... Normal A4 değil... Daha büyük... Eski Türkçe yazılar var... Kâğıtlar ışıl ışıl.

Türkiye'nin şu anki durumuyla ilgili bir şey söylüyor mu?

Yasemin: Karanlık diyor... Ama sonu gelecek... Ben hep buradayım diyor.

Şimdi soru sormuyorum. Sana bırakıyorum.

(Bir süre sessizlik. O alandan çıkıyoruz.)

Neden seni gemilere aldılar Yasemin?

Yasemin: Gemilere aldılar çünkü çok çocuğum var orada.

Yumurta mı aldılar?

Yasemin: Çok aldılar... Çok aldılar.

Bu çocukları üretmedeki amaç ne?

Yasemin: Çoğaltmak... Tertemiz insanlar getirmek dünyaya... Kurtuluş insanları.

O çocuklar nerede büyüyorlar peki?

Yasemin: Yukarıdalar... Yuvarlak bir alandalar... Oyun oynuyorlar... Çok mutlular... Çok zekiler... Çocuklar eğitiliyorlar... Kurtuluş... Hep kurtuluş kelimesi geliyor.

Yani senden aldıkları yumurtalarla bir aşılama yapıp sonra anne karnına mı yerleştiriyorlar? Dünya'da mı doğmuş bu çocuklar?

Yasemin: Yok hayır... Yukarıdalar.

Onlar nasıl gelecekler peki buraya?

Yasemin: Yükleme bitince.

Yükleme mi yapıyorlar çocuklara?

Yasemin: Evet... Yükleme bitince.

Buraya bırakacaklar mı onları?

Yasemin: Evet... Bırakacaklar.

Melez mi onlar?

Yasemin: Hepsi melez.

Tipleri nasıl?

Yasemin: Gözleri büyük ama çok güzel suratları var... Alınları geniş.

Biz tanışacak mıyız onlarla?

Yasemin: Evet tanışacağız.

Ne zaman?

Yasemin: Yedi.

Yedi?

Yasemin: Sadece yedi.

İleride insanların arasına karışacaklar yani?

Yasemin: Evet... Toplu gelecekler... Teker teker değil, toplu gelecekler.

İnsanlığın bundan bilgisi olacak mı yoksa gizlice mi gelecekler?

Yasemin: Yok insanlar bilecekler... İnsanlar bilecekler... (Duruyor...) Belimden bir şey sokuyorlar sanki... Çok ince bir iğne gibi hissettim.

Sedyede kendini görebiliyor musun gemide?

Yasemin: Hayır... Ben aşağıdan bakıyorum... Ama her şeyi görebiliyorum.

Üzerinde yapılan işlemlere bakar mısın? İyileştirme gibi bir operasyon oldu mu? Yoksa sadece yumurta mı aldılar?

Yasemin: Yaptılar... Birkaç defa geldiler... 14 Temmuz 2014'te... Marmaris'teydim... Kalbimde dayanılmaz bir ağrı... Kalp krizi geçiriyorum zannettim... Çok öksürdüm... Kalbime bir şey yaptılar.

Kalbinde bir rahatsızlık var mıydı peki?

Yasemin: Mitral stenozum vardı benim.

İyileşti mi ondan sonra?

Yasemin: Ondan önce de iyileşmiştim de... Orada bir şeyler yaptılar anlayamadım... Ondan beri bir şeyim yok... Kalbimle ilgili bir şey yok... Boynumun sol tarafına bir şey koydular... Minicik bir şey... Hâlâ sol tarafıma döndüğümde çok başım dönüyor... Görüntü kesildi.

Evet, hiç şaşırmadık. Buraya gelme amacın aslında Atatürk'le ilgili konuydu.

(Seansı bitiriyoruz...)

Seans Sonrası:

Seansın bitiminde Yasemin bize bazı ek bilgiler aktardı:

Yasemin: Ankara'ya toplantı için gittiğimde, uzun boylu, iki metre kadar... O gri uzun varlık bana "Kalk dinin gereği arın" dedi... Kalktım boy abdesti aldım... Beni odaya götürdü... Yaz dedi... Kalem kâğıt al yaz dedi... Adını soyadını yaz dedi... Yazdım... Tarihi at dedi... Tarihe baktım telefondan... 31.07.2022... Geçen sene... Saati yaz dedi... 06.36... Sağımda kısa olan varlık duruyor... Çok heyecanlı... Unutma... Sen sevgi frekansındasın dedi... Ama uzun boylu olanın yüzünde ifade yoktu... Bana dedi ki... Sizin bir araya getirilme sebebiniz...

Kiminle?

Yasemin: Bilmiyorum... Bilmiyorum... Dedi ki... Saf koşulsuz sevgi enerjisinde birleştiğiniz zaman, sizin enerjinizi 1 birim olarak kabul edersek, onun da enerjisini 1 birim olarak kabul edersek, ikinizin saf koşulsuz sevgi enerjisini bir araya getirdiğimiz zaman 36 birime çıkıyor dedi.

Kim vardı o zaman? Var mıydı öyle birisi?

Yasemin: Birisi vardı ama hayatıma girdi ve çıktı... Ondan bahsettiğini sanmıyorum.

Belki de gelecekte olacak bir şeydir.

Yasemin: Size söylemem gereken şey buydu... Dedi ki; saf sevgi enerjisi 36 birime çıktığında sizi hiçbir şey tutamaz... Artık her türlü boyuta geçebilirsiniz... Her türlü şeyi yapabilirsiniz... 36 birim en yüksek frekanstır dedi... Ve sevgi enerjisi birleşimi gerçekleştikten sonra... Buraya çok dikkat edin... Nallıhan'daki tepenin üzerindeki kırmızı ışık sizin kurtuluşunuz olacaktır dedi ve noktayı koydurdu bana.

Nallıhan?

Yasemin: Evet... Ankara Nallıhan... Orayla ilgili hiçbir bilgim yok, alakam da yok... Ama orada bir şey var!... Ve orayla ilgili bir

şeyi size aktarmam gerektiğini söylüyor... Hangi tepe?... Ne zaman?... Bilmiyorum... Bunlar benim kelimelerim değildi... Benim lügatimde olan kelimeler değildi.

İleride anlayacağız.

Yasemin: İkincisi; o yirmi tane küçük gri varlığın geldiği geceden sonra sabah uyandığımda göğsümde kocaman bir işaret oluştu... 20-25 gün kaldı bende... Bir başka gün kalktığımda sağ ayağımda kocaman bir kına vardı... Kopkoyu kına... Bir kez de üç gri varlık sağ ayağımdan kocaman bir çubuk soktular... Acısını hiç hissetmedim.

Evet.

Yasemin: Büyükannem insanları böyle hafifçe dokunarak tedavi edermiş... Şu an ellerim çok karıncalanıyor... Şu an ellerimde çok değişik bir şey var.

Sizde manyetik şifa yeteneği var büyük olasılıkla.

Yasemin: Yıllar önce bana birileri geldi... O zaman Dünya dışı varlık nedir bilmiyorum... Sadece ses... Dedi ki... Sen insanların gözlerini iyileştireceksin dedi... Nasıl dedim... Biz sana öğreteceğiz dedi... (Tekniği anlatıyor.)

(Yasemin ayrılırken göz şifası meselesiyle ilgili olarak kendisine bir sesin sürekli "Novus 307" diye seslendiğini ekledi. İlk *Novus* kitabının[8] o sayfasını açtığımızda karşımıza Nebahat Gümüştekin seansının "Değerlendirmelerim" bölümü çıktı. Okuyucularımız, Nebahat Gümüştekin'in seansı sırasında mucizevi bir göz şifasının yaşandığını anımsayacaklardır. Demek ki Yasemin Karadağ'a da vazifesi bu şekilde hatırlatılmak ve göz şifasına yönlendirilmek isteniyordu.)

8. *Novus*, CBN Yayıncılık, 2018, s. 307

8. BÖLÜM

SİRİUS

İstanbul'da sağlık sektöründe çalışan, 46 yaşındaki Nurhan Bekdamar'ın ilk deneyimleri, tıpkı diğer birçok temasçı gibi çocukken başladı. İki ablası ve bir kız kardeşiyle birlikte aynı odada uyurlarken gece bir anda uyandığında odanın içini yoğun bir beyaz ışığın kapladığını gördü. Kapının önünde boyu iki metreye yakın, beyaz tenli birisi vardı. Nurhan'a korkmaması gerektiğini, onları korumaya geldiğini söyledi.

Yirmili yaşlarındayken, bir gün evde hasta yattığı sırada bir anda gözlerini açtı ve odanın diğer ucunda bir delikanlı gördü. Delikanlı ona kardeşi olduğunu ve korkmaması gerektiğini söyledi. Oysa Nurhan'ın Dünya'da erkek kardeşi yoktu.

Bir defasında, işten çıkıp eve doğru araba ile giderken bir anda tanımadığı birisiyle telepatik bir temas oluşmaya başladı ve iletişime geçti. Telepatik bağlantı kuran kişi ona babası olduğunu söyledi. O kişiyle, o güne değin hiç deneyimlemediği kadar güçlü ve yoğun bir duygu bağı hissetti. İletişim sırasında zaman ve mekân kavramı adeta kaybolmuştu. Arabanın kontrolü dahi kendisinde değildi. Babası olduğunu söyleyen kişi onun önemli bir görevi olduğunu da ekledi.

İleriki yıllarda Nurhan'ın temasları da psişik yetenekleri de giderek arttı, şifa özelliği gelişti.

Rüya olarak hatırladığı ama melez projesiyle bağlantılı olduğu anlaşılan tipik bir temas anısını bize şöyle aktardı:

"Beyaz bir elbise giymişim... Bir anda hamile olduğumu duyuyorum... Sonra aniden karnım büyüyor ve ben çok şaşırıyorum... Beni her tarafı beyaz olan bir ameliyathaneye götürüyorlar... Doğum koltuğuna yatırıyorlar ve bana doğum yaptırıyorlar... Doğum acısını bütün vücudumda hissettim... Doğum sonrası çocuğu kucağıma verdiler... Sonrasında uyandım ama orada yaşadığım acıyı uyandığımda aynı şekilde yaşadım diyebilirim... Buna benzer, bir kez daha aynı şekilde bir rüya gördüm ama onu tam hatırlayamıyorum... Sadece bir çocuk doğurduğumu hatırlıyorum."

Nurhan'ı seansa aldık. Seanstaki yolculuğumuz uzun mesafeler kat etti.

Anadolu'da başladı... Sirius'ta sona erdi.

Nurhan Bekdamar Seansı
8 Temmuz 2023

(Nefes, gevşeme ve enerji çalışması...)

Nasıl hissediyorsun Nurhan?

Nurhan: Ağlama hissi geliyor.

Ağla o zaman. Rahat bırak kendini. Bırak.

Nurhan: (Ağlıyor...) Çok büyük bir özlem duyuyorum!

Nefes alıp verir misin Nurhan?

(Dilek bir çocuk travması algılıyor.)

Geldiğin yer neresi Nurhan?

Nurhan: Çok uzak.

Uzak derken?

Nurhan: Çok uzak... Farklı bir dünya.

Nasıl bir his veriyor sana orası?

Nurhan: Orada çok mutluyum.

Kimler var orada yanında?

Nurhan: Ailem var.

Görebiliyor musun şu an onları? Görüntüye geliyorlar mı?

Nurhan: Sadece his var.

Kaç kişiler?

Nurhan: 3 veya 4 kişi.

Neden buraya geldiğine odaklanmanı istiyorum şimdi.

Nurhan: Bir görevim var.

Nedir?

Nurhan: Aktarmak.

Neyi?

Nurhan: Işığı.

Nasıl yapıyorsun bunu?

Nurhan: Bilinçlendirerek... Merhametle... Sevgiyle.

Buraya ilk nasıl geldiğini söyler misin?

Nurhan: Işık küresiydim... Ben istedim... İhtiyaçları vardı bana.

Peki buradaki anne babanı nasıl seçtin?

Nurhan: Onlar acımasızdı... Onlara sevgiyi vermek istedim.

Seninle birlikte bir değişim geçirdiler mi?

Nurhan: Çok fazla değil... Ben hep yalnızdım.

Oradaki ailen seni ziyaret ediyor mu?

Nurhan: Evet.

Şimdi ona odaklanmanı istiyorum.

Nurhan: Çocuklarım var benim.

Orada doğum nasıl oluyor?

Nurhan: Rahmine bir şey koyuyorlar... Karnın büyüyor... Sonra doğum yaptırıyorlar.

Normal doğum mu?

Nurhan: Evet.

Bedenleriniz nasıl?

Nurhan: Ben maviyim... Tenim mavi... Üç parmağım var.

Karşıdan bedenini görmeni istiyorum.

Nurhan: Ama sanki bedenim farklı... Sarı saçlı... Uzun... İncecik... Gözler kocaman... Masmavi.

Nasıl bir gezegen?

Nurhan: Parçalanmış... Sanki bir kısmı var, bir kısmı yok olmuş gibi.

Bir savaş mı olmuş acaba?

Nurhan: Evet... İnsanlar o yüzden Dünya'ya gelmeye karar vermişler ırk olarak.

Senin gibi kaç kişi var burada?

Nurhan: Çok var.

Oranın bir ismi var mı?

Nurhan: Kaçırdım... "G" ile başlıyor... Galoris gibi bir şey... Aslında o kadar güzelmiş ki her yer... Çok güzel bir şelale varmış.

Dünya'ya mı benziyor?

Nurhan: Dünya'ya benziyor ama cennet gibi... Bir tarafı da yok olmuş... Cehennem gibi... Ateşlerden.

Dünya'ya neden yardım etmek istiyorsunuz?

Nurhan: Dünya yok olmak üzere... Felaket kapıda.

Neler olacak Dünya'da?

Nurhan: Çok büyük bir savaş gözüküyor.

Dünya çapında bir savaş mı?

Nurhan: Evet... İnsan ırkı azalıyor... Bunu durdurmaya çalışıyoruz.

Nerede başlayacak? Kimler çıkartacak?

Nurhan: İsrail'den... Yani... Onlar planlıyorlar gibi... Rusya ve İsrail gibi gösteriliyor... Emin olamıyorum... Ve bunun için üç yıl gibi bir zaman gösteriliyor.

Peki nükleer savaş var mı?

Nurhan: Sineklerle bir virüs yayacaklar... Böcek gibi... Sinek gibi... Ona benzer bir şey.

Nereden yayacaklar bunu? Çıkışı neresi?

Nurhan: Makedonya.

Nerede yetiştiriyorlar sinekleri?

Nurhan: Çok soğuk bir yer... Kuzeyde bir yer... Sibirya gibi sanki.

Türkiye'ye gelmeni istiyorum. Yukarıdan Türkiye'ye bakar mısın?

Nurhan: Şehir yok oluyor.

Hangi şehir?

Nurhan: İç Anadolu'da bir şehir... Yok oluşu var.

Deprem mi?

Nurhan: Değil... Sanki kimyasal bir şey... Ankara'ya saldırı var... Çin'den... Rusya'dan geliyor.

Türkiye'ye bakmaya devam et.

Nurhan: Felaketler var... İnsanlar çığlık çığlığa.

Yakın gelecekte mi?

Nurhan: Çok uzak değil.

Sonra?

Nurhan: Sonra yeniden doğma var.

Nasıl?

Nurhan: İnsanlar uyanıyor... Yardım alıyorlar... Göklerden çok büyük yardımlar geliyor.

Kim yardım ediyor?

Nurhan: Uzay gemileri geliyor.

Yönetim?

Nurhan: Yönetim altüst olacak.

Sonra?

Nurhan: Yeni bir lider doğuyor!... Yeni bir lider geliyor!... Herkesi birlik ve beraberlik içinde toplayacak!... Bu lider doğmuş!

Kaç yaşında?

Nurhan: Şu an 25'lerde.

Nerede?

Nurhan: Saklanıyor... Aslında kendisinin lider olduğunu biliyor!... Ona bu mesajlar verilmiş... İletilmiş.

Türkiye sınırlarında mı?

Nurhan: Evet... Birileri onu koruyor.

Kim koruyor?

Nurhan: İç Anadolu'da bir yerde bu kişi... Hani böyle şey derler... Nasıl anlatsam?... Mevlana'nın mektebi gibi bir yerde şu an... Onu gizli tutuyorlar... Anlatamadım.

Dergâh gibi mi?

Nurhan: Evet... Orada onu yetiştiriyorlar.

Tamam.

Nurhan: (Biraz durduktan sonra şaşkınlıkla...) Bu kişi boyuta gidebiliyor!

Tamam. Orada kal. Boyutu tarif et. Nasıl gidiyor? Ne yapıyor? Nereye gidiyor?

Nurhan: Ruhsal olarak gidiyor.

Uykusunda mı?

Nurhan: Uykusunda da gidiyor, uyanık da gidiyor.

Bilinçli mi yapıyor bunu?

Nurhan: İlk önceleri bilinçli değilmiş... Sonrasında idrak etmeye başlamış.

Devam.

Nurhan: İdrak ettikçe açılıyor... Ama sonrasında şuradaki (eliyle gösteriyor) boyut kapısından geçiyor!

Devam et.

Nurhan: Konya'yı görüyorum... Oradan açılıyor... Giriyor.

Şu an bilinçli gidiyor diyorsun?

Nurhan: Evet... Artık ona anlatılmış... Aktarılmış.

Şimdi boyuta odaklan. Hangi boyuta gidiyor?

Nurhan: Sirius.

Bu kişiyi tarif eder misin bize?

Nurhan: Uzun boylu... Yüz hatları şu şekilde... (Eliyle gösteriyor...) Çenesinde gamzesi var... Saçları koyu renk... Hafif sola tarıyor... Dişleri çok düzgün... Ama gözleri böyle bal elası gibi... Ateş fışkırıyor sanki bakınca!

Tamam.

Nurhan: Ama vücudunda bir doğum lekesi var.

Nerede?

Nurhan: Göğüs bölgesi... Kalp hizasının üzerinde bir lekeyle doğmuş.

Doğum lekesi.

Nurhan: Sanki kurt!... Kurt... Kurda benziyor leke.

Biraz daha bak.

Nurhan: Çok cüsseli birisi değil.

Onun yüzüne baktığında ne hissediyorsun?

Nurhan: Huzur.

Başka ne hissettiriyor?

Nurhan: Atatürk.

O enerjiyi mi taşıyor?

Nurhan: Evet... Daha güçlü bir enerji bu ama... Sanki Atatürk'ten daha güçlü.

Evet.

Nurhan: Sanki Dünya'ya birliği, beraberliği getirecek gibi... Sadece Türkiye'ye değil.

Çok güzel.

Nurhan: Sanki Atatürk'ün soyundan gelmiş gibi... Yani sanki tüm gezegenler tarafından özellikle seçilmiş birisi gibi... O yüzden hem Atatürk'ün soyundan, aynı zamanda güçlü bir ırkın soyundan gibi... Ama bunu çözemiyorum.

Çözebilirsin.

Nurhan: Sirius ve Pleiades.

O zaman bu Türkiye'ye gelecek lider aracılığıyla Dünya'da bir değişim mi olacak?

Nurhan: Kesinlikle olacak... Ama Dünya ırkında bir azalma olacak.

Ama önce savaşlar olacak diyorsun?

Nurhan: Evet.

Bir zaman hissin var mı Nurhan?

Nurhan: Çok uzun bir vade yok... Üç beş yıl gibi.

Peki Türkiye'de herkes bu liderin etrafında mı toplanacak?

Nurhan: İlkönce kabul etmeyecekler ama sonra herkes kabul hissine girecek... İç karışıklıklar gelecek çünkü.

Türkiye'de mi?

Nurhan: Evet... İç karışıklıklar... Yakında... Çok yakında... İki yıl... İki yıl gibi bir süreç var.

Kim çıkartacak?

Nurhan: Dışarıdan müdahaleler var... Dış ülkelerden gelmiş, ülkeye yayılmış kişiler var... Hem de devletin üst kademelerinde... Bir tane böyle sakallı bir adam görüyorum... Gri sakalları var... Esmer... İsmi... Bu kötüye çalışıyor... Ülkeyi karıştırmak için... Savaşın çıkması için çalışan da bu adam.

(Nurhan burada, yurtiçindeki kötü niyetli yabancı uyruklu unsurların da vatanımıza karşı kullanılmaya çalışılacağına dair bilgiler aktarıyor.)

Nereden başlayacak ilk olarak? Türkiye'nin neresinden?

Nurhan: Adana'dan... Sonra Karadeniz... Bir de Van var.

Bu lider tek başına mı çıkacak ortaya?

Nurhan: Hayır... Tek başına çıkmayacak... Onu destekleyen insanlar ve şu an inanan insanlar var... Yavaş yavaş toplanmaya başlamışlar... Şu an onu yavaş yavaş yetiştiriyorlar... Etrafında toplanmaya başlamışlar ama kişinin zarar görmemesi için şu an her şekilde gizli... Varlığını gizli tutuyorlar... Ama arkasında çok ilahi bir güç var.

Burada koruyanlar kim?

Nurhan: Bu kişi Konya'da şu an.

Onun etrafında kimler var?

Nurhan: Bu dergâh dediğim kısımda... Onlar şu an koruyorlar... Oradakiler onun varlığını, görevini, bilincini, her şeyi biliyorlar.

Şu an 25 yaşlarındaysa... Vazifesine kaç yaşında başlayacak?

(Biraz sessizlik...)

(Nurhan'ın daha önce 25 derken aslında onun gençliğini görmüş olduğunu anlıyoruz.)

Nurhan: Şimdi 43 yaşında.

Tamam. Bir parti kurarak mı çıkacak?

Nurhan: Partiye ihtiyacı yok.

Devam et Nurhan. O alandasın çünkü.

Nurhan: Bu kişi evli değil.

Şu an etrafındakilerin dışında kimse tanımıyor onu değil mi?

Nurhan: O dergâhtakilerin dışında onun görevli olduğunu bilen, devletin içinden sanki bir ya da iki kişi gibi görüyorum... Onun dışında bilen kişi yok... Bekle denilmiş ona... Bekle!... Zamanı var!... Çıkacaksın... Varlığını, bilincini herkese yayacaksın... Biz de seni destekleyeceğiz demişler.

Devam et.

Nurhan: Şurada hangi il vardı?... (Türkiye haritasını düşünerek kuzeyi gösteriyor...) Orada bir yok oluş var... Doğu Karadeniz'in en doğusu... En uçtaki... Orada bir yok oluş var... Ateşler... Ama gökten de destek gelecek.

Nasıl?

Nurhan: Birçok uyandırdıkları kişiler aracılığıyla onlar da yardım sağlayacaklar ama göklerden gemilerle de yardımlar gelecek... Gemilerden bir şeyler iniyor... Işıklar iniyor... Böyle ışık huzmesiyle aşağıya iniyor... Orada sanki asker gibi biri var.

Ya çocuklar?

Nurhan: Çocukların çoğunu alıyorlar zaten... Çocukların çoğuyla şu an temas varmış... Onlar gelecek... Geleceği oluşturmak için onlar şu an koruma altındalar... Üstteki nesil, yani yaş grubu daha üstte olanlar temizlenecekmiş... Fosilleşmiş beyinler gidecek.

Bu çocuklar mı devralacak ileride?

Nurhan: Evet.

Türkiye'nin vazifesi ne olacak o zaman Nurhan?

Nurhan: Türkiye çok ileride dünyayı yönetecek.

Peki başka bir ruhsal vazifesi olacak mı?

Nurhan: Bu topraklar zaten her zaman ruhsal olarak görevli... Bu topraklar farklı.

Yeni bilgi gelecek mi Anadolu'ya?

Nurhan: Evet... Aktarımlar zaten çok uzun zamandır varmış.

Kim aktarıyor bunları?

Nurhan: Göklerden... O Konsey gibi... Birçok şeyi de onlar engellemişler... Türkiye'de daha öncesinden kaos yaşanabilirmiş... Ama onlar bir kısmını engellemişler... (Biraz duruyor...) Bir patlama görüyorum... Büyük bir patlama var... Endonezya... Orada büyük bir patlama görüyorum... Sanki bomba mı koymuşlar, lavlar mı?... Öyle bir şey.

Volkanik patlama mı?

Nurhan: Evet.

Yakın zamanda mı?

Nurhan: İçimden geçen... Beş... Beş ay sonrası gibi sanki... Ya da beş yıl içerisinde.

Şimdi sana bir şey soracağım. Sizler gibi bilinçli insanlar, uyanmış insanlar o kaotik zaman içerisinde nerede olacaklar?

Nurhan: Biz çocukları koruyacağız... Biz geleceği koruyacağız... Biz her yerdeyiz.

Sizleri kim koruyacak?

Nurhan: Biz kendimizi koruyabiliyoruz... Bize o bilgiler aktarıldı... Zamanı geldiğinde hatırlatacaklar.

Pekâlâ. Şifacılar?

Nurhan: Şifacılar da çoğalıyor ama sahte şifacılar da çok fazla.

Doğru.

Nurhan: O şifacılar pozitife hizmet ettiklerini zannederken aslında o kadar negatif şeyler yayıyorlar ki... Negatif boyut kapılarından buraya getiriyorlar... Aslında kötü bir şey yaptıklarının farkında değiller... Kabul etmiyorlar... Kötü olduklarını kabul etmiyorlar.

Obsesyon aslında.

Nurhan: Evet.

Siyası duruma bakmanı istiyorum.

Nurhan: Bir tanesine komplo kurulacak... Siyasi liderlerden biri ölecek yakın zamanda.

Anladım.

Nurhan: (Bir süre duruyor...) Türkiye'nin İç Anadolu bölgesinde çok büyük bir boyut kapısı var... Az zamanı kalmış... Bu boyut kapılarının açılmasına çok az kalmış... Bir yeraltı şehri var... Hiç

kimse bunu keşfetmemiş... Kimse bilmiyor... Şu an orada birçok şeyler yapılıyor... Şu an onun çalışması yapılıyor.

Peki fonksiyonu ne olacak bu kapının?

Nurhan: Kötü değil ama...

Tabii.

Nurhan: Kaos olduğu zaman çocukları alıp gidecekler oradan.

Anadolu'da başka bir yerde daha var mı böyle bir kapı?

Nurhan: Bu kadar büyük olan mı? Bu çok büyük ama... Nasıl söyleyeyim... İki üç şehri kapsayacak kadar yüzölçümü bakımından... O derece büyük.

Büyüklüğü önemli değil. Başka nerede var Anadolu'da?

Nurhan: Çorum'u görüyorum.

Göbeklitepe?

Nurhan: Aktif değil... Üç tane boyut kapısı var... Üçünü de kapatmışlar... Bizimkiler bunu kasti yapmışlar... Göbeklitepe'de çok önemli bir şey bulunmuş... Nasıl diyeyim?... Çubuk gibi... Üzerinde semboller var... Sembollerden bir tanesi çok önemli bir boyut kapısının anahtarıymış... Bu alınmış... Artık kim bulduysa bunu alıp ülkeden dışarı çıkmış... Ondan sonra o anahtarın üzerinde işlemler yapılarak boyut kapıları kapatılmış... Üç lokasyonda... Yani üçgen olarak algıladığınız takdirde her bir uçta bir boyut kapısı varmış... Küçük küçük kapılar görüyorum ama onlar bir şey ifade etmiyor... Anlık şeyler onlar... Bir tane ağaç var orada... O üçgenin tam ortasında büyük bir ağaç var... O ağacı merkez alıp üçgen çizdiğiniz zaman boyut kapıları orada... Ağacın gövdesinde kökten hafif bir yarılma var... Ağaç çok belirgin... Yüksek bir yer... Tek başına o ağaç.

(Burada Nurhan'ın Dünya dışı deneyimine geçme gereği hissediyoruz.)

Dünya dışı bir ortamda doğum yaptın mı Nurhan?

Nurhan: Evet.

Nasıl hamile kaldın peki?

Nurhan: Bana bir şey enjekte ettiler... Sonra bir anda karnım şişti... Sonra beni doğum masasına yatırdılar.

Bu Dünya dışı bir aracın içinde mi oldu?

Nurhan: Evet.

Kim vardı peki etrafında?

Nurhan: Beyaz önlükler giymiş, maske takmış insanlar var... Çok uzun ve incecikler.

Senin tanıdığın varlıklar mı bunlar?

Nurhan: Yok hayır.

Bu çocuklar nerede şimdi? Büyüdüler mi?

Nurhan: Bir tanesi... İnsan yüzü gibi değil... Mavi tenli... Gözleri yanlara doğru... Çok geniş... Dudakları yok gibi... Yüzünde beyaz çizgiler var... Doğum yaptıracakları kişileri de sıraya koymuşlar.

Neden yapıyorlar bu operasyonu? Bu çocuklar ne olacak?

Nurhan: Onları kendi istedikleri gibi yetiştirmek istiyorlar... İyi veya kötü... Yeteneklerine göre görevlendirecekler ve Dünya'ya yönlendirecekler.

Nasıl gelecek bu çocuklar Dünya'ya?

Nurhan: Enkarne olarak değil... Doğrudan gelecekler.

Dünya'ya mı bırakılacaklar?

Nurhan: Evet.

Nasıl olacak bu?

Nurhan: Bahsettiğim bu dünya çapındaki savaş var ya... İşte o savaştan sonra gelecekler.

Bu çocuklar melez mi?

Nurhan: Melez.

Peki bedenlerine baktığın zaman insandan farklı mı?

Nurhan: Hepsi farklı farklı ama insan bedeninden ayırt edilemeyecek olanlar da var... Altın saçlı, kocaman gözlü, incecik olanlar var.

Yeni devrenin yeni çocukları yani. Dünya'da değişim böyle mi başlayacak?

Nurhan: Evet.

Peki. Melez projesinin başka bir amacı var mı?

Nurhan: Var.

Nedir?

Nurhan: Pozitife hizmet edecek melezler ayrı... Bir de negatife hizmet edecek, yetiştirecekleri melezler var... Onlar dünyanın yıkımı için hazırlanacaklar.

Savaş için mi?

Nurhan: Evet... Onlar da yıkım için savaşacaklar.

Onları hazırlayan negatif ırklar mı?

Nurhan: Farklı farklı ırklar.

Bu da bir plan dahilinde o zaman?

Nurhan: Aslında bu gizli bir plan gibi... Bir grubun gizli planı.

Aynı elden çıkıyor aslında. Dünyanın gelişimi için bu savaşın olması gerekiyor. Anladım. Bu da o zaman dünyanın idareci mekanizması tarafından organize ediliyor. Dünyanın idareci mekanizmasını anlatır mısın bize?

Nurhan: Ruhsal mekanizma... Büyük bir ışık kütlesi görüyorum.

Tamam. Yaklaş ve o ışık kütlesinin içine gir şimdi.

Nurhan: Burası bir koridor... Sağımda solumda odalar var... Ama burada kadınlar var... Doğum yaptırılmak üzere bekletiliyorlar.

Seni tekrar oraya soktular. Başka yerdesin. Gemidesin.

Nurhan: Sonra koridordan yürüyorum ve o ışığa doğru gidiyorum... Büyük bir saray gibi bir şey görüyorum.

Ne var o sarayda?

Nurhan: Laboratuvar burası... Melezler burada üretiliyor... DNA'lar vs. burada değiştiriliyor... Yüzünün her tarafı kıllı bir varlık var laboratuvarda... Yüzünü çok net göremiyorum... Vücudu, elleri, yüzü insan ama kıllı her tarafı.

Niçin üretilmiş bu varlık?

Nurhan: Bu bahsettiğim varlık üretim değil... Çalışmaları yapıyor... Melez genetiğini yapıyor... Melez genetiğini alıyorlar ve kadınlara bir şey enjekte ediyorlar... Birçok varlıktan topluyorlar... Çok fazla... Yüzlerce.

Birçok ırk katkı veriyor bu projeye o zaman. Öyle anlıyorum.

Nurhan: Evet.

(Bir varlık Nurhan'a yaklaşıyor.)

Nurhan: Bana diyor ki... Kendimi niye açmıyormuşum.

Dinle ve aktar.

Nurhan: Bana diyor ki... Sen kendinden korkuyorsun ama içindeki gücü bilmiyorsun...

(Şimdi bize sesleniyor.)

Nurhan: Türkiye'de yaşanacak olan sıkıntılı günlerde, görevli çocukları koruma altına almanız gerekiyor... Bunların isimleri sizde mevcut diyor... Bu bilgilerin verilmemesi lazım. Sanki bu bilgileri sizden çalmak isteyecekler gibi...

Nasıl koruyabiliriz?

Nurhan: Sizde bulunan listeye sahip çıkmanız ve gizli bir yerde tutmanız gerektiği söyleniyor... Sizinle iletişim kuran çocuklar çok özel, çok önemli çocuklarmış.

Bize söylüyorlar değil mi?

Nurhan: Evet.

Anladım. Çocukları nasıl koruyabiliriz?

Nurhan: Zamanı geldiğinde size aktarılacak.

(Tam bu anda üçümüz birden, aynı anda tepemizde büyük bir gemi vizyonu görüyoruz. Bu görüntüde bizi altındaki açıklıktan yukarıya çekiyor. Birbirimize aynı görüntüyü tarif ediyoruz. Boşluğun içinden giriş yapıyoruz.)

Dev bir salon. Salonda...

Nurhan: Sütunlar var... Dev sütunlar... Bir... İki... Üç... Dört tane sütun görüyorum ben.

(Üçümüz aynı anda...) Salonda sütunlar. Etrafımızda siluetler...

Nurhan: Oluşmaya başladılar... Etrafımızda toplanmaya başladılar.

Toplanıyorlar. Çok kalabalık. Bilgeler heyeti gibi. Bir sürü varlık...

Nurhan: (Aynı anda...) Elinde asası var.

Evet. Çembere alıyorlar.

Nurhan: Sanki koruma kalkanı oluşturdular etrafımızda... Karşımda beyazlar giymiş... Asası var ve asanın ucunda da Ay var.

Bize bir şey aktaracak galiba senin aracılığınla. Dinle onu. Bekliyoruz.

Nurhan: (Aktarmaya başlıyor...) "İnsanlar varoluş sebeplerini unuttular... Niçin geldiklerini unuttular... Azap içerisinde yaşamayı kendileri seçtiler... Yok olmayı kendileri seçtiler... Biz elimizden gelen tüm desteği sunmamıza rağmen onlar yok olmayı tercih ettiler... Birbirlerini yok etmeyi tercih ettiler... İşte asıl savaş burada başladı... Kendi hırslarına yenilerek kendilerini yok ettiler... Ama yeni dünya varoluşu çok uzak değil... Hazırlanmanız gerekiyor... Yeni dünyaya, yeni varoluşa, yeni insanlığa, yeni uygarlığa hazırlanmanız gerekiyor... Herkesin

bilinç seviyesi yükselecek... Zamana ihtiyaç var... Pozitif olanları etrafınıza toplayın... O güçle birlikte hepiniz yeni varoluş sisteminde çok büyük görevlerde bulunacaksınız... Görevlisiniz... Sebepsiz gelmediniz."

Türkiye için bir mesajı var mı?

Nurhan: Bekleyeceksiniz diyor... Liderinizi bekleyeceksiniz diyor.

Kendisinin kimliği?

Nurhan: Sirius-B.

Mustafa Kemal?

Nurhan: Oradan.

Dünya'ya vazifeliler Sirius'tan mı geldi?

Nurhan: Evet... Çoğunluğu... Sirius-B'den... Orası Sirius-A'dan daha ileri bir ruhsal seviye... Örneğin peygamberler Sirius-B'dendir... Sirius-A'dan daha alt seviyedeki vazifeliler gelir.

Sirius A ve B derken bizim gördüğümüz astronomik Sirius sisteminin ötesinde bir boyut mu kastediliyor?

Nurhan: Tabii ki... Hiç görmediğiniz ve bilmediğiniz bir boyut... Aslında bildiğinizi zannettiğiniz veya gördüğünüzü zannettiğiniz ama asla görmediğiniz bir boyut... Sizin hesapladığınız gibi değil... Farklı... Sirius yıldızı değil.

Bunu bize biraz daha açabilirler mi? O yıldızın astronomik konumu bizim için yanıltıcı mı?

Nurhan: Evet... 43, 57, 48 koordinatlar verildi... Ne olduğunu bilmiyorum.

Yani astronomik olarak Sirius'un bulunduğu...

Nurhan: Gerçek hesaplanan konum değil... Sizin hesaplamalarınız yanlış... Sizin düşüncelerinizdeki boyutta değiliz... Sizin araştırmalarınızdaki boyutta değiliz.

Nasıl bir boyut bu?

Nurhan: Sonsuzluk boyutu.

Neden Sirius gibi bir astronomik adres vermek durumunda kalıyorlar?

Nurhan: Kimlik belirtmek gerekiyor.

Onların bulunduğu yerin astronomik Sirius'la bağlantısı nedir?

Nurhan: Çok bağlantısı yok.

Bir idareci merkez mi orası?

Nurhan: Evet.

Nereler bağlı o sisteme?

Nurhan: Tüm evren.

Peki. Ruhsal idare mekanizmasından mı bahsediyoruz?

Nurhan: Evet.

Bu mekanizmayı kısaca anlatabilirler mi bize?

Nurhan: (Bilinmeyen bir dilde konuşuyor.)

Anlamı ne?

Nurhan: Bilmiyorum... Onlar konuştu.

Bizim çözmemizi istiyorlar sanırım.

Nurhan: Evet... Size bir mesajmış.

(Bağlantıyı kesiyorlar ve seansı sona erdiriyoruz.)

9. BÖLÜM

HARİTA

Bir reklam ajansında editör ve tasarımcı olarak çalışan 33 yaşındaki Burcu Aydın, çocukluk çağını geçirdiği Kastamonu'da gözünü gökyüzünden adeta hiç ayırmadan büyüdü.

2019 yılında mavi, ışık bedenli bir varlıkla temas deneyimi oldu.

2020 yılında denizde yüzerken bir Ölüme Yakın Deneyim yaşadı. Bu deneyim onun yaşamında bir kırılma noktası anlamına geliyordu. Daima baskın olan, Dünya'ya ait hissetmeme duygusu güçlendi, rüyaları derinleşti. Sadece kendisinin değil, ailesinin de rüyaları hep gerçekleşiyordu.

Dünya dışı araçlar Burcu'nun rüyalarının her zaman başaktörü oldular.

Ancak seansta konu yine süratle ve engellenemez şekilde Türkiye'ye ve ülkemizin yakın geleceğinde beklenen büyük değişimde çok kritik rol oynayacak "o kişiye" geldi.

Burcu Aydın Seansı
8 Temmuz 2023

(Nefes, gevşeme ve enerji çalışması.)

Nasıl hissediyorsun Burcu?

Burcu: Hafif... Boşluktayım.

Tamam. Çok güzel.

(Bir temas anısı ve Dünya dışı aracın içi görüntüye geliyor.)

Burcu: Ekranda bir şey gösteriyorlar.

İzle bakalım.

Burcu: Orada bir araştırma yapılıyor... Sesler... Araştırma gibi.

Varlıklar mı araştırma yapıyorlar?

Burcu: Evet... Bir tane hayvanı araştırıyorlar... Sesini duyuyorum.

Dünya'dan hayvan mı almışlar oraya?

Burcu: Nereden aldıklarını bilmiyorum.

Neyi araştırıyorlar Burcu?

Burcu: Karakteristik özelliklerini.

Orada ne var?

Burcu: Tam göremiyorum.

Etrafına bak Burcu.

Burcu: Bir su var... Yerde bir su var... Etraf böyle... Ekranlar... Koyu renk.

Ekranlarda ne var?

Burcu: Analiz yapıyorlar... Hiç bilmediğim bir şeyler yazıyor... Yeşil.

Yazılar mı geçiyor?

Burcu: Evet... Haritalar var.

(Bizi yine yavaş yavaş Türkiye'ye doğru çekiyorlar.)

Haritalarda ne var? Nereye bakıyorsun?

Burcu: Orada veriler var.

Dünya'yla ilgili veriler mi?

Burcu: Evet.

Peki Türkiye var mı orada?

Burcu: Hepsi var... Dünya'nın her yeri var.

Şimdi üzerinde Türkiye'nin olduğu ekrana doğru gitmeni istiyorum senden. Türkiye'ye yukarıdan bak. Ona bakıp bize anlatmanı istiyorum.

Burcu: Geldim oraya.

Anlat.

Burcu: Sayılar var... Haritanın kenarında.

Devam.

Burcu: Az kalmış... Üç tane dolum var... İki tanesi olmuş... Bir tanesi kalmış... (Ekranda sanki bir gösterge, bir veri ölçeği gibi üç tane çubuk görüyor. Sanki belli konularda ölçüm yapıyorlar ve o durum gerçekleşince o veri çubuğu dolu görünüyor.)

Nedir o?

Burcu: Üç tanesi de dolunca bir şey olacak... İki tanesi dolmuş... Bir tanesi yarısında... O da dolunca bir şey olacak.

Ne olacak?

Burcu: Değişiyor her şey... Harita değişiyor.

Ne olacak Türkiye'de?

Burcu: Su var her yerde... Yani kıyıların haritası değişik... Üçe bölmüşler Türkiye'yi.

İyice yaklaş ekrana.

Burcu: Çok kargaşa var... Bir taraf güllük gülistanlık, bir taraf...

Ne olmuş peki?

Burcu: Sistem değişmiş.

Devam et. Kim değiştirmiş? Nasıl değişmiş?

Burcu: Bir tane beyaz kafalı... Beyaz.

Kim o?

Burcu: Tanımıyorum... Yüzünü hiç görmedim.

O mu değiştirmiş?

Burcu: Evet.

Nasıl bir his veriyor sana?

Burcu: Atatürk hissiyatı geldi... Yani öyle güçlü biri.

Fiziği nasıl?

Burcu: İnce, upuzun.

Vücuduna bak.

Burcu: Kır saçlı... İnce dudaklı... Omuzları geniş.

Gözleri?

Burcu: Kahverengi mi?... Mavi mi?... Maviye daha yakın gibi... Ela da olabilir.

Evet.

Burcu: Yüksekten bakıyor her şeye.

Yüksek bir varlık mı?

Burcu: Evet... Çok yüksek bir varlık... Kurt enerjisi olabilir o adamda.

Nerede o adam şimdi?

Burcu: Yukarıda... Türkiye'de değil şimdi... Doğrudan gelecek bence.

Kim o peki? Vazifesi ne?

Burcu: Alanları yönetmek.

Alanları yönetmek? Ne demek bu Burcu?

Burcu: Devleti yönetecek.

O mu başa geçecek?

Burcu: Hep başta görüyorum... Yüksekte görüyorum.

O çıkmadan önce ne olacak Türkiye'de?

Burcu: Çok büyük bir değişim var... Göçler var... Kaçış var ondan sonra.

Kimler kaçıyor?

Burcu: İnsanlar kaçıyor... Toplanıyor, kaçıyorlar... Kaçanlar var, gelenler var... Çok karışık... Kaçanlar hep esmer esmer... Esmer tipliler... Kısa boylu, uzun boylu.

Tamam. Peki bu kurt enerjisi olan adam?

Burcu: Çok güçlü... Sert... Herkes korkuyor ondan... Yani görüntüsüyle bile etkiliyor... Hiçbir şey demeden bile.

İnsanları etkileyecek mi?

Burcu: Evet.

Nasıl?

Burcu: Herkes biat edecek ona.

Atatürk enerjisi var dedin değil mi?

Burcu: Evet... Şu an karışık yani... Tek o değil.

Başkaları da mı var?

Burcu: Sert tarafı da var.

Ne demek istediğini anladım. Sert tarafını da kullanması gerekecek çünkü.

Burcu: Evet.

Onu koruyanlar var mı?

Burcu: Onu uzaktan koruyorlar.

Şimdi onun nerede olduğuna tekrar odaklanmanı istiyorum.

Burcu: Masa başında.

Anadolu'da mı?

Burcu: Şu an Anadolu'da hissetmiyorum... Şu an izliyor... Plan yapıyor, gözlemliyor.

Ya Dünya? Şimdi Dünya ekranına git.

Burcu: Üst tarafta bir kırmızılık var.

Neresi?

Burcu: Amerika ve Kanada'nın olduğu bölge... Alarm gibi.

Dünya haritasını göz önüne getir.

Burcu: Numaralar vermişler... Bir şeyin yol haritası var... Oradan başlıyor ama... Yukarıdan başlıyor... Aşağıya doğru... Navigasyon gibi... Bu kişi de bu planların hepsini biliyor.

Bütün planları biliyor mu bu kişi?

Burcu: Evet... Öyle biri gelecek yani Türkiye'nin başına.

Evet.

Burcu: Bir kritik nokta var... Tam yarısına geldiğinde... O noktadan sonra o gelecek!

Süreç başlamış mı?

Burcu: Başlamış.

Peki bir işaret olacak mı? Geleceğini nasıl anlayacağız?

Burcu: Tam o kritik noktada ortaya çıkacak.

Türkiye zor bir durumda mı olacak o noktada?

Burcu: Her yer öyle olacak... Dünya zor durumdayken.

Bu kişinin vücuduna bakmanı istiyorum. Bir işaret var mı?

Burcu: Elleri çok uzun... Beyaz tenli.

Vücudunda bir işaret var mı?

Burcu: Üçgen gibi bir şey ama neresinde göremiyorum... Ama var olduğunu biliyorum.

İyi bak Burcu.

Burcu: Yıldız gibi... Şurasında sanki... (Eliyle bel bölgesini gösteriyor.)

Doğum lekesi var mı?

Burcu: Var... Böyle... Kahve lekesi gibi.

Herhangi bir şeye benziyor mu?

Burcu: Sanki iki şeyin birleşimi gibi... Özellikle yapılmış gibi... Hatırlatma gibi.

Şimdi o şekle dikkatli bakmanı istiyorum.

Burcu: (Biraz duruyor...) Dört bacaklı bir şey... Köpek şekli gibi... Sağ tarafında... Sağ kaşının üzerinde de küçük bir beni var.

Bütün katılımcılardan neden aynı mesaj geliyor?

(Burcu'nun bu soruyu neden sorduğumuz hakkında aslında en ufak bir bilgisi yok. Çünkü katılımcı süjelerin hiçbiri

diğerlerini tanımadığı gibi, seanslarda ne anlatıldığını da hiçbir şekilde bilmiyorlar.)

Burcu: Bilinsin istiyorlar.

Bilinsin istiyorlar, anladım.

Burcu: Ama benim de bilmem lazım... Görevliyim ben.

Bizim açıklamamız mı gerekiyor?

Burcu: Evet... Evet... Herkesin her şeyi bilmesi lazım artık... Az bir süre kalmış.

Ne kadar?

Burcu: 22 mi desem?... Bilemiyorum.

Söylemiyorlar sana bence.

Burcu: Çok az kalmış.

Sürelere takılmayalım zaten.

Burcu: Her şey çok hızlı gelişecek.

Ne isteniyor bizden Burcu?

Burcu: Küme küme birleşmemiz, toplanmamız.

Peki çocuklar?

Burcu: Onları da güvenli bir alanda toplamamız... Bilgilendirmemiz lazımmış onları da... Onların da bilmesi lazım.

Sizin gibi bilinçli, pozitif insanlar ne yapacak peki bu süreçte?

Burcu: İnsanları bilgilendireceğiz.

Siz koruyacaklar mı?

Burcu: Evet.

Belli yerlerde toplanacak mısınız?

Burcu: Evet.

Nerelerde?

Burcu: Toprak... Açık alanlarda... Sonra da kapalı alanlarda.

Anadolu'ya tepeden baktığında ne görüyorsun?

Burcu: Yıldız yıldız... Parlıyor... Türk bayrağını görüyorum... Güzel görüyorum.

Güzel olacak.

Burcu: Evet.

İçeride sıkıntılı durumlar var mı?

Burcu: Bölüm bölüm var.

Bölgesel mi olacak?

Burcu: Evet.

Nereler?

Burcu: Kıyılar... Çok giremeyecekler içeriye.

Güneydoğuya bakmanı istiyorum şimdi.

Burcu: Boşluk var orada... Bir şey olmuş.

(Seansın başından beri gözümüzün önüne Galata Kulesi vizyonu geliyor. Bununla ilgili bir soru sorma gereğini şiddetle hissediyoruz.)

Galata Kulesi ile ilgili bir bağlantı var mı? Ya da orayla ilgili bir anın?

Burcu: Hayır.

Oraya odaklanır mısın Burcu?

Burcu: (Bir süre sonra...) Hımmm... Oranın altından bir yerlere gidiliyor... Mahzenler var... Oranın altından yeraltına açılıyorsun... Yukarısında birileri var... Esmer birileri... Ayasofya'yı gösteriyor bir tanesi eliyle... Önce burası, sonra burası, sonra burası gibi... Plan yapıyorlar.

İyi hisler mi yoksa kötü hisler mi alıyorsun?

Burcu: Pek iyi hissetmiyorum... İyi hissetmiyorum.

Yani bazı yerlerle ilgili planlar var. Galata Kulesi var, Ayasofya var. Başka?

Burcu: Haliç.

Kim bu planları yapanlar?

Burcu: Amerikan Başkanı geliyor gözümün önüne.

Başka?

Burcu: Hindistan.

Hindistan mı? Yoksa Hintliye benzer mi?

Burcu: Hintliye benzer.

Bir bayrak görüyor musun?

Burcu: İki bayrak daha var.

(Burada biraz ara veriyoruz. Burcu'nun iletmesi gereken bir şeylerin daha olduğu hissiyatımız var.)

Bir mesaj vermek istesen mesajın ne olurdu Burcu?

Burcu: Çok hızlanmalıyız.

Devam et.

Burcu: Sizi bir yere götürebilirler... Beklenmedik şekilde bir yere gidebilirsiniz.

Fiziksel mi?

Burcu: Evet... Böyle alınma gibi olacak... Hiç beklemediğiniz bir anda alıp götürecekler.

Niçin peki? Bu işlerle uğraşmamızı mı istemeyecekler?

Burcu: Tam tersi.

Destek için.

Burcu: Artık ciddi destekler alacaksınız.

Türk Devleti mi bu?

Burcu: Ben çok devlet gibi hissetmiyorum... Yukarıdan gibi... Türkiye'yle ilgili.

Ama aşağıdan birileri mi?

Burcu: Ama yukarıyla bağlantısı olan aşağıdan birileri.

Bizden bir şey mi istenecek?

Burcu: Evet.

Peki yeni gelecek liderin bununla bağlantısı var mı?

Burcu: Evet.

(Burada, şimdilik paylaşmanın sakıncalı olabileceği bazı özel bilgiler aktarıyor ve seansı bitiriyoruz.)

10. BÖLÜM

KURT

İstanbul'da yaşayan, 38 yaşındaki resim öğretmeni Belgin A., *Novus*'un birinci kitabında da yer alan temasçılardandı.

Aradan geçen zaman içinde Belgin'in uyanık zihinle gördüğü vizyonları daha da artmış ve farklılaşmıştı. Rüyaları da aynı şekilde bilgiyle doluydu. Onunla zaman zaman yaptığımız özel çalışmalarda aktardıklarının yıllar içinde gerçekleştiğini görüyorduk.

En çok güvendiğimiz süjeler listemizin daima en başlarında yer alan Belgin, *Novus*'un ikinci kitabı için yaptığımız çalışmada da bizi yanıltmadı.

Belgin A. Seansı
9 Temmuz 2023

(Nefes, gevşeme ve enerji çalışması.)

(Seansa başlamadan önce Dilek bana Belgin'de Dünya ve Türkiye ile ilgili bilgiler olduğunu güçlü şekilde hissettiğini söylüyor. Buradan ilerlemeye ve sıcak çalışma yapmaya karar veriyoruz.)

Dünya'ya ve Türkiye'ye bakar mısın Belgin?

Belgin A.: Dünya'nın altında, yerkürenin altında bir ateş gibi...

Nasıl bir ateş Belgin?

Belgin A.: Volkan da var... Ama sanki ağacı dibinden tutuşturursun ya... Yansın diye.

Ateş derken mecazi anlamda mı kullanıyorsun?

Belgin A.: Evet.

Sanki bir olaylar zinciri başlayacak diye anlıyoruz.

Belgin A.: Aynen... Aynen... Sanki böyle ateşi yakmışlar... Körüklenmesini bekliyorlar.

Anladım. Süreci hazırlıyorlar. Peki bu dünya genelinde olacak bir şey mi?

Belgin A.: Evet.

Ne olacak? Gezegene yukarıdan bak.

Belgin A.: Gökyüzü sararmış... Toz... Sanki yukarıdan bir şeyler... Böyle taş düşer ya... İnsanlar kaçışıyor.

Neler oluyor? Savaş mı?

Belgin A.: Savaştan ziyade... Gökyüzündeki o şeyleri kullanıyorlar gibi... İklimle alakalı... Karıştırmaya çalışıyorlar... Taş yağmuru gibi... Ağaçlar fırtınadan uçuyor.

İnsanlar mı bozmuş iklimi? Yoksa doğal olaylar mı?

Belgin A.: İnsan gibi ama kötü.

Türkiye?

Belgin A.: Türkiye de sapsarı... Hiç yeşillik kalmamış gibi.

Türkiye'yi yakın gelecekte neler bekliyor?

(Belgin önce negatif tesir altındaki bazı siyasi figürlerle ilgili bilgiler aktarıyor.)

Neler olacak Türkiye'de?

Belgin A.: O doğu deprem bölgeleri var ya... Sanki zift gibi... Karanlık çekilmiş gibi oraya sanki gökyüzünden... Oraya zift çekmişler.

Karanlıktan nasıl çıkacağız?

Belgin A.: O karanlık yüzler geliyor ama yayılamıyor... O aslında Türkiye'nin tamamına yayılmaya çalışıyor... Orada engelliyorlar.

Ne geliyor Güneydoğu'dan?

Belgin A.: Sanki gök kubbenin üzerinde böyle... Orayı kapatmışlar... Orada mağara delikleri gibi yerler var... Tam sınırda... Oralardan geliyor... Orada bir enerji var... Orada ne yapıyorlarsa, onunla sanki harekete geçiyor... O kısmı sanki delikler gibi görüyorum.

Nerelerde bunlar?

Belgin A.: Tam deprem bölgeleri var ya... Ama Türkiye haritasının Güneydoğu kısmından itibaren... Komple... Urfa, Maraş, Mardin, Hatay, Diyarbakır... Oralardan o enerjiyi yayıyorlar.

Kötü bir enerji mi bu?

Belgin A.: Evet... Onu deniyorlar ama Batı Anadolu tarafından başka bir enerji geliyor ve onu engelliyor... O yayılmaya çalışıyor... İkisi çarpışıyor ama kötü enerji yayılamıyor... Engelliyorlar.

Kim o kötü enerjiyi yayan?

Belgin A.: Sanki onun da ilerisinde böyle balçık gibi... Türkiye'nin daha da doğusuna doğru gidiyor.

Nasıl bir enerji engelliyor? Yani pozitif olan ve Türkiye'nin batısından gelen enerjinin kaynağı ne?

Belgin A.: O kadar güçlü ki o!... Sanki böyle güneş doğmuş!... Türkiye'nin bir kalbi var sanki!... Oradan bir ışık!... Bir güneş!... Ama o gelen negatif enerjiden çok daha güçlü.

Şimdi o güneşe odaklanmanı istiyorum. Nasıl bir güneş?

Belgin A.: Bir girdap oluşmuş... Döndükçe o enerjiyi yayıyor.

Bir değişim mi yaşıyor ülke?

Belgin A.: Evet... Değişim başlıyor.

Nasıl olacak bu değişim?

Belgin A.: O doğu bölgelerini gördüm yine... Karanlık insanlar var... Onlar bu tarafa doğru gelmeye çalışıyorlar ama onları da engelliyor... Sanki böyle siyah elbiseli insanlar Anadolu'ya doğru girmeye çalışıyor... Ama engelleniyor... Öyle bir karışıklık.

Şimdi onu engelleyen güce odaklan. O güneşe.

Belgin A.: Anıtkabir'i görüyorum!... (Belgin çok yoğun bir duyguyla ağlamaya başlıyor.)

(Sessizce bekliyoruz...)

Belgin A.: Ata'mı gördüm!... (Ağlayarak...) Sandalye gibi, koltuk gibi bir şeyde oturuyor... Elinde baston ya da asa gibi bir şey var... Onu böyle tutmuş... Onun olduğu tarafa yaklaşamıyorlar... Ankara'ya kadar o enerji gelemiyor... Sanki bir duvar örülmüş orada!... Sanki o pozitif vorteksi o açtırmış!... Anıtkabir sütunları var ya... Tam onun önünde oturuyor... Arkada upuzun ışıklar... Muhafızlar gibi... Bekliyorlar... Ama çok rahat Atatürk... O kadar kendinden emin ki... Kolunu böyle koltuğa koymuş... Çok emin kendinden... Yaklaşamıyorlar.

Onun vazifelileri var mı burada?

Belgin A.: Var.

Onlara bir bak bakalım şimdi. Neler olacak?

Belgin A.: Genç bir çocuk var... Orta boy... Hafif yuvarlak yüzlü... Beyaz tenli ama saçlar koyu gibi... Çok açık renkli değil saçları.

Kim o?

Belgin A.: Şu an bilinen biri olarak görmüyorum.

Devam. Gözlerine bak.

Belgin A.: Sanki o çocuk biliyor bunu ama söylemiyor!... Çocuk da çok kudretli... Çok güçlü... Onu ofiste görüyorum... Bir devlet dairesi gibi... Böyle eli cebinde dolaşıyor... Planları var...

Düşünceleri var... Lacivert takım elbisesi var üzerinde... O kadar planları var ama saklıyor kendisini... Ama o kudreti biliyor... O enerjiden sanki onda da var!

Atatürk enerjisi mi?

Belgin A.: Evet... Biliyor gibi... Çok değişik... Hazırlanıyor gibi.

Nerede şimdi o çocuk?

Belgin A.: Anadolu'da gibi sanki.

Kaç yaşında?

Belgin A.: Yirmi beş.

(Belgin aslında onun gençliğini görüyor. Dilek ve ben 25 yaşın onun uyanış yaşı olduğunu biliyoruz.)

Şu an nerede?

Belgin A.: Biraz bozkır bir yerde... Anadolu'da bir yerde... İç Anadolu... Sarı topraklar... Köy mü, kasaba mı?... Küçük, beyaz bir bina... Kaymakamlık gibi.

Etrafında insanlar var mı?

Belgin A.: Başka insanlar da var.

Ona yakın, onun vazifesini bilen insanlar var mı?

Belgin A.: Annesi... Annesi biliyor... Korkuyor gibi.

Gelecekte ne yapacak bu genç?

Belgin A.: Komutan gibi olmuş... Bir ordunun başında gibi... Karar veriyor... Temizliyor sanki... Ülkeyi temizlemeye çalışıyor... Dünya'daki liderlere kızıyor.

Ülkenin başına mı gelmiş? Nasıl geliyor? Bir partiden mi? Yoksa...

Belgin A.: Aslında bir partinin başında değil ama onlarla beraber çıkıyor... Yani birilerinin yanında oluyor... Sonra dikkat çekiyor.

Tamam. Şimdi onun gözlerine bakmanı istiyorum.

Belgin A.: Gözbebeği çok büyük.

Ne renk gözleri?

Belgin A.: Kahverengi ama koyu bir renk.

Nasıl bir enerji alıyorsun?

Belgin A.: Atatürk'le bağlantılı... Çok güçlü... Sirius... Doğrudan "Sirius" geldi.

Ülkenin başına kaç yaşındayken gelecek?

Belgin A.: Kırk iki.

Ne kadar zaman var?

Belgin A.: Şu an çok sabırsız... Böyle dönüyor odada... Ama bekletiyorlar onu... Beklemesi gerekiyor... Uygun olduğu zaman onu çıkaracaklar.

Kim bekletiyor? Kim çıkaracak?

Belgin A.: Yukarıdan.

Kendi vazifesini biliyor.

Belgin A.: Evet... Çok sabırsız ama... Şu an olmaması gerekiyor.

Ona yardım edenler var mı?

Belgin A.: Var... Onu koruyanlar var.

Kim onlar?

Belgin A.: O onları memur gibi düşünüyor... Yanında takım elbiseli, bıyıklı bir adam var... Aslında o yukarıyla bağlantılı... Ama bu genç bunu bilmiyor... Onu sıradan birisi zannediyor... Zaten ona her şeyi söylemiyorlar daha.

Atatürk'ü ve bu Türkiye'nin başına gelecek olan genci düşündüğünde ne söylersin?

Belgin A.: Sanki Atatürk'ün bazı enerjileri ona aktarılmış gibi... Onu güçlendirmişler... Güçlendiriyorlar.

Kimler yapıyor bu işlemleri?

Belgin A.: Aracılar var yukarıda... Onu uyumluyorlar.

Alıyorlar mı onu?

Belgin A.: O bilmiyor... Sadece şey olarak biliyor... Kudret hissediyor... O cesareti hissediyor... Ama o süreçleri çok bilmiyor... Onu düzenli olarak uyumluyorlar.

Nasıl bir ortamda gelecek o başa?

Belgin A.: Askerler gördüm... Karışıklık var... Halk toplanmış... Siyasiler... Propaganda yapılıyor... Karışık... Yabancı uyruklular da var... Onlarla sanki bir karışıklık oluşuyor ama çok büyük bir karışıklık değil... O olayın önünü kesiyorlar.

Bir olayı mı engelliyorlar pozitif olanlar?

Belgin A.: Evet... Aynen.

Bir iç karışıklık mı yaşayacak Türkiye?

Belgin A.: Çok büyük değil.

Sınırlı mı?

Belgin A.: Evet... Yani ülkemize karşı kötü niyetli yabancı uyruklularla karşılıklı bir şey var ama çok büyük değil... Sanki hepsi üst üste binmiş... İnsanların üzerine gönderiyorlar gibi... Ama halk sanki duvar örmüş... İzin verilmiyor... İzin vermiyorlar.

Anladım.

Belgin A.: Yeraltı... Yeraltını gördüm.

Tamam seni bırakıyorum. Gördüklerini aktar.

Belgin A.: Bir yerde bir delik açılmış... Bir duman çıkıyor... Gaz gibi... Bir şey bulunuyor sanki... Bir yerde bir çukur açılıyor, oradan bir şey buluyorlar... Maden olabilir... Değişik... Kaya gibi... Kıymetli taşlar... Ama sonu yok... İnsanlar toplanmış buraya... Siyah giyimli adamlar var... Kapatılmaya çalışılıyor orası ama insanlar gördüğü için kapatamıyorlar.

Türkiye'ye bir dış saldırı ihtimali var mı?

Belgin A.: Uçaklar var.

Hangi ülkeler? Bayrak görüyor musun?

Belgin A.: Amerika var... İngiltere... Yunanistan var.

Az önceki konuya dönelim. Bu kişi ortaya çıktığı zaman hemen insanlar inanacak mı? Biraz oraya gidebilir miyiz?

Belgin A.: Bir azınlık var... Onu hissedecek... Önce insanlar yine inanmayacak... Ama o azınlık hissedecek onu... Sonra yayılıyor... O kadar hızlı yayılıyor ki... Sanki domino taşı gibi... Herkes etrafında toplanıyor... Ama önce çok az insan.

Sonra Türkiye'de bir değişim mi olacak?

Belgin A.: Sanki Türkiye'nin sınırlarının hepsini çevirdi... Kapattı... Kapı gibi.

Hangi sınırları?

Belgin A.: Önce batıdan başladı... Batıyı kapattı... Aşağıya indi... Akdeniz... Doğu... Saat gibi çizdi... Sonra Karadeniz... Kapıyı kapattı.

Nasıl görüyorsun Türkiye'yi o kapatmalardan sonra?

Belgin A.: Hepsinden ışıklar yükseldi... Sanki güneş tam tepeye çıktı... Bütün kapılardan oraya örümcek ağı gibi ördü.

O zaman Türkiye'yi çok pozitif bir gelecek mi bekliyor?

Belgin A.: Aynen öyle... O güneş sanki dönüyor... Yine o vorteks... O böyle döndü döndü... Her yer sararmıştı ya... Sonra yeşilleniyor yavaş yavaş.

Peki Türkiye'nin vazifesi ne olacak?

Belgin A.: Doğrudan Sirius geldi yine.

Tamam. Devam et.

Belgin A.: Oraya bağlandı Türkiye... Güneş oradan bağlandı gökyüzüne... Sonra oradan verilen kararlar var... Dünya'ya reçete gibi sanki... Oradaki talimat... Sanki şey... Şimdi bunlar, bunlar, bunlar yapılmalı... Mühürlendi sanki orası... Türkiye... Orayla bağlantılı oldu... Oranın bilgileri geliyor... Sanki Dünya bunu kabul etmek zorunda gibi... O bilgiler Dünya'ya Türkiye'den dağılıyor... Sanki uygulanması gereken prosedürler var... Dünya

bunu yapmak zorunda... Çok güçlü bu enerji... Diğer ülkeler korkuyor... Metafiziksel şeyler var... Hepsi böyle sindi.

Çünkü merkez biz oluyoruz.

Belgin A.: Evet... O güneş hâlâ dönüyor... Orayla bağlantılı.

Bizler nasıl yayacağız bu bilgileri?

Belgin A.: Nüfus biraz azalmış gibi ama olması gereken olmuş... İnsanların hepsi o vortekse doğru hareket ediyor... Güneşe doğru... Ortaya... Türkiye'nin kalbine... Oradan bilgileri alıyorlar, yayıyorlar.

Türkiye'deki vazifeliler uyanmış artık.

Belgin A.: Evet... Herkes o merkeze gidiyor.

Dünya'ya ışık Türkiye'den mi yayılıyor?

Belgin A.: Evet... Bütün güç burada.

(Burada bizimle ilgili bazı özel bilgiler paylaşılıyor.)

Belgin A.: Gemiler gördüm... Yunanistan sınırında gibi... Deniz kenarında... Kıyılarda... Ne karada ne denizde... Yukarıda duruyorlar... İnsanlar korktuğu için açıklamalar yapacaksınız... "Bu süreci biliyorduk... Bu süreç olacaktı" şeklinde insanları sakinleştirmeye çalışıyorsunuz... Ama sizi engellemeye çalışan siyah takım elbiseli insanlar var... Ama bu sefer çok tedirginler... Sadece izliyorlar... Hep çevrenizdeler ama hiç yaklaşamıyorlar... Sadece izleyip haber götürüyorlar... Şu an yaptığınız her şey izleniyor... Sanki haber bekliyorlar.

Biliyoruz.

(Burada yine bazı özel bilgiler paylaşılıyor.)

Belgin A.: Başka insanlar da var... Onlar da biliniyor... Her tarafta planlı bir şekilde aslında yerleşmeye başlamışlar... Onlar da onun etrafına bir ağ örmüşler onu korumak için... Enerji anlamında da... Onu bir küre içine almışlar gibi... (Yeni ortaya çıkacak liderden söz ediyor.)

Yeni çocuklar?

Belgin A.: Çok güzel hissediyorum... Gülüyorlar... Şu an habersiz gibiler ama aslında her şeyden haberleri var gibi... (Ağlamaya başlıyor...) Hatırlayacaklar ama şu an sadece oynuyorlar... Gülüyorlar... Ama sonra her şeyi hatırlayacak onlar... Çok güçlü enerjileri var... Sanki el ele tutuşmuşlar... Kocaman bir halka yapmışlar... Enerji çemberi gibi... Herkesi içine almışlar... Çok güzel!... (Ağlıyor.)

Çok güzel. Onların vazifesi ne olacak büyüyünce?

Belgin A.: Çok güçlü ve çok akıllılar... Kötü hiçbir şeye geçit vermiyorlar... Asla... Duruşları dimdik... Kuralları var... Eskiyle alakalı tüm kötü şeyler bitiyor sanki... Bir duvar olmuş bedenleri... Geçit vermiyorlar... Çok sevecenler ama çok da sertler.

Büyüdüklerinde ne yapacaklar?

Belgin A.: Çok teknolojik bir dünya... Çok güzel... Tertemiz... Kimse kimseyi ezmiyor.

İleride yönetimi bu çocuklar mı devralacak?

Belgin A.: Eski Göktürk yazısı görüyorum... Göktürkçe bir şey yazıyor.

Nerede görüyorsun bu yazıyı?

Belgin A.: O buzdan gibi binalar... Çok teknolojik... Orada görüyorum... Yüzüklerin Efendisi'ndeki yapılar gibi... Hem teknolojik hem görkemli.

Yeni Dünya?

Belgin A.: Evet.

Yeni Dünya'da yönetim nasıl olacak?

Belgin A.: Bir kişi yönetmiyor... Herkesin bir görevi var... Herkes görevini yapıyor ama uyumlu... Herkes tertemiz, mutlu... Ama çok profesyonel herkes... Negatif hiçbir şeye izin verilmiyor... Sanki kapatmışlar Dünya'yı... Negatif hiçbir şey yaklaşamıyor bile.

İnsanların bedenleri değişiyor mu peki?

Belgin A.: Uzun... Kolları, bacakları... Vücut uzun ve ince.

Melez gibi mi?

Belgin A.: Evet... Arada normaller de oluyor ama genel olarak uzun, ince... Keskin yüz hatları var.

Gözler?

Belgin A.: Daha iri... Çoğunun renkli ama yine çok kahverengiler de var.

Dünya'da enerjiler de değişmiş demek ki.

Belgin A.: Evet.

Kılık kıyafet?

Belgin A.: Bizim kıyafetlerimiz gibi değil... Daha gösterişsiz... Daha sade... Sanki bedeniyle bir gibi... Değişik... Ama aksesuvarları var sadece.

Şimdi ben soru sormayacağım Belgin. Gelen bir bilgi ya da iletilecek bir mesaj olursa aktar bize.

Belgin A.: Dikkatli olun... Ama güzel olacak... Güçlü olun... Korkmayın... Mesajlar doğru.

Son bir şey soracağım. Şimdi tekrar o yeni gelecek liderin bedenine bakar mısın?

Belgin A.: Üst tarafı biraz daha geniş... Geniş omuzlu... Bacakları biraz daha ince.

Bedeninde biz iz, bir leke var mı?

Belgin A.: (Biraz sessizlik...) Göğsünün... Kalbinin sanki üzerinde... Kırmızı... Spiral gibi döndü böyle... Hilal gibi. Orada bir işaret.

Neye benziyor?

Belgin A.: Böyle... Üçgen gibi... Değişik bir sembol... Doğum lekesi.

İyi bak.

Belgin A.: Işıklı gibi üçgenler... Ters... Düz... Kahverengili... Buluta benziyor... Kıvrımlı kıvrımlı... Göğsünün tam yan tarafında... İçe doğru... Göğüskafesine doğru... Orada işte bir yıldız... Kurt gibi bir şey oldu!... Kurt!

Tamam.

Belgin A.: Arada aynadan bakıyor... Elini istemsizce oraya atıyor... Sonra çekiyor... Bir şeylerin farkında ama tam değil.

Çok güzel.

Belgin A.: Lacivert giyiyor... Hep devletle alakalı bir görev istiyor... Yaşından çok daha olgun... Ciddi... İdealist... Yönetme gücü var... Çok net.

Başka söylemek istediğin bir şey var mı?

Belgin A.: Yok.

(Seans sona eriyor.)

11. BÖLÜM

VASİYET

İzmir'de yaşayan, 39 yaşındaki müzisyen Ece A., uzun yıllardır temas deneyimleri yaşıyor, geleceğe yönelik, oldukça ayrıntılı vizyonlar görüyordu. Ece'nin uyanıkken gördüğü vizyonların gerçekleştiğine son birkaç yıl içinde defalarca tanık olmuştuk ve onun duru görü yeteneğine güvenimiz çok üst seviyedeydi.

Ece'nin ayrıca melez üretimine dair puslu anıları da vardı.

Ece ile yaptığımız seans, tıpkı diğerleri gibi, yine Atatürk'e ve Türkiye'nin misyonuna doğru karşı konulamaz şekilde yön alarak bizi son derece sarsıcı bilgilerle yüz yüze getirdi.

Ece A. Seansı
9 Temmuz 2023

(Nefes, gevşeme ve enerji çalışması.)

Ece A.: Enseme bir ağrı girdi.

Şifa akışı oluyor şu anda.

(İlk görüler gelmeye başlıyor.)

Ece A.: Dünyanın geleceği... Karışık.

Nasıl bir karışıklık?

Ece A.: Ülkeler arasında... Bir masada konuşmalar.

Karışıklık dediğin şey ne?

Ece A.: Biraz zor bir araya gelecekler... Onun öncesinde biraz karışıklık olacak.

Nerelerde?

Ece A.: Kuzeyde başlayacak... Karların olduğu... Çok soğuk bir yerde.

Neresi orası?

Ece A.: Çok soğuk bir yer... İnsanlar yaşamıyor.

Dünya'ya bakar mısın?

Ece A.: Hâlâ kuzeyi görüyorum şu anda... Oradan başlayacak bir olay var... Bir şey görüyorum... Bir araç olabilir.

Dünya dışı bir araç mı?

Ece A.: Sanırım öyle.

Türkiye'ye bakmanı istiyorum şimdi.

Ece A.: Türkiye'yi bir karışıklık bekliyor.

Nasıl bir karışıklık?

Ece A.: Suikast... Ama Türkiye'de değil... Biri öldürülecek, sonra karışacak.

Neresi karışacak?

Ece A.: Türkiye'yle bağlantısı var ama yabancı... Yabancı bir lider.

Türkiye'nin geleceğine bak.

Ece A.: Değişecek.

Nasıl bir değişim?

Ece A.: 2024'ün sonlarına doğru.

Sonra?

Ece A.: Gözlüklü birisi geliyor.

Seçim mi oluyor?

Ece A.: Bilmiyorum ama geliyor.

Gelecek kişiye odaklan.

Ece A.: Çok doğru bir kişi... İyi biri... Engelleyecekler ama gelecek... (İdarede bir değişim olacağını ve şu an siyasi lider olmayan ama tanınan bir figürün "asıl lider" ortaya çıkıncaya kadar, geçici bir süreyle yönetime geleceğini görüyor.)

Devam et. İlerle zamanda.

Ece A.: İstemeyecekler... Olay çıkartacaklar... Ama çok hızlı bir değişim olacak... Çok güzel olacak ama bir şey var beni rahatsız eden... Bir olay var... Çok karışık.

Yukarıdan izle.

Ece A.: İstanbul... İstanbul'da... Gizli bir yapılanma var... Gizli yapılanma değişim olmasını istemiyor.

Kim bunlar?

Ece A.: Tarikat gibi tipler... Bunlar Arap ülkelerinden... Dışarıdan başka ülkelerin Türkiye'ye soktuğu insanlar var... Karıştıran onlar.

Onlar iç karışıklık mı çıkartacaklar?

Ece A.: Evet... Ama bir şey olmayacak... Yapamayacaklar... Değişim olacak... Temizlenecek.

Kim temizleyecek?

Ece A.: Biri var.

Ona odaklanır mısın?

Ece A.: Beyaz tenli... Uzun boylu... Geniş omuzlu... 1,80 boylarında... Kumral saçları sanki... Şu an şey yapamıyorum ama... Bir dakika!... O geliyor!

Onun enerjisinde kalır mısın? Biraz tarif eder misin?

Ece A.: Çok güzel bir enerjisi var.

Nasıl bir enerji?

Ece A.: Genç... 40'lı yaşlarda... 45 gibi en fazla.

Peki o tanınan biri mi şu an?

Ece A.: Hayır.

Gözlerine bak. Nasıl bir enerji alıyorsun?

Ece A.: Özel yetiştirmişler bunu... Devleti koruyanlar.

Devleti koruyanlar kim?

Ece A.: Başka bir yapı var Türkiye'de... Devleti, ülkeyi koruyan şeyler var... Her şeyi biliyorlar... Her şey planlı... Seçimler de planlıydı... Her şey planlıydı... Her şey değişecek... Zamanını bekliyorlar.

Devam et.

Ece A.: Özel yetiştirdikleri o kişi var... Onun için uğraşıyorlar... Zamanını bekliyorlar... Bunlar Atatürk'e bağlı insanlar.

Bunlar mı yetiştirmiş o kişiyi?

Ece A.: Evet... Çok uzun süredir yetiştiriyorlar.

Nerede yetiştirmişler?

Ece A.: Yurtdışında yaşamış bir dönem.

Nerede?

Ece A.: Yakın yerlerde... Türkiye'ye yakın... Öyle hissediyorum.

Sınırlara yakın yerlerde mi?

Ece A.: Evet... Şey olabilir... Göçmen kökeni olabilir... Selanik'ten göç edenler gibi... İlginç bir şekilde Atatürk'ün enerjisini hissediyorum onda şu an... Çok benziyor enerjileri.

Onun vazifesi ne?

Ece A.: Her şeyi baştan düzeltecek.

Neler yapacak?

Ece A.: Hepsini temizleyecek... Zararlı insanların hepsini yok ediyor... Yavaş yavaş yapacak.

O gelmeden önce nasıl Türkiye?

Ece A.: İç karışıklık çıkartamayacaklar... Yapamayacaklar... Olaylar küçük çaplı olacak.

Nerede başlayacak?

Ece A.: İstanbul'da... Taksim Meydanı'nda bir grup var... Kalabalık yürüyecekler... Sakallı... Ellerinde bir şeyler var... Pankartlar... Onların yürümesiyle bir şeyler başlayacak.

Zaman hissin var mı?

Ece A.: 2024... Taşlar atıyorlar... Bir şeyler atıyorlar.

Bu yeni lider ne zaman başa gelecek?

Ece A.: 2024'ün son dönemi ya da 2025.

Bedenine bakar mısın şimdi? Bir işaret var mı?

Ece A.: Saat var sağ kolunda... Solak olabilir.

Bedenine bak.

Ece A.: Sadece bir "M" harfi gözümün önüne geldi... Bu da sembolik gibi... (Sessizlik...) Şu anda onu koruyorlar... Onu görüyorum sadece.

Kimler koruyor?

Ece A.: Devletin yararına çalışanlar... Her şeyi takipteler.

Başka koruyanlar var mı?

Ece A.: Sadece sayılı kişiler biliyor... İzliyorlar... Özel olarak yetiştirilen birisi.

Ne kadar zamandır yetiştiriliyor?

Ece A.: Çok erken yaşlarda başladı.

Küçük yaşta mı?

Ece A.: Evet... Askeri eğitim var.

Hangi yaşlarındayken?

Ece A.: 15 yaşlarında.

Kendi vazifesinin bilincinde mi?

Ece A.: Bilincinde evet... Ama bir taraftan da o yanındaki adamlar onun ne kadar büyük bir yük altında olduğunu çok hissettirmiyorlar.

Yavaş yavaş galiba.

Ece A.: 2030 görüyorum şimdi... Masada bir kâğıt görüyorum... 2030 yazıyor... Başka bir şey bu ama.

Nedir?

Ece A.: Gemiler... 2030'larda bir şey olacak.

Nasıl bir şey?

Ece A.: Güneydoğu'da antik bir yer var... O antik bölgede çalışma var.

Nasıl bir çalışma?

Ece A.: (Ağlamaya başlıyor...) Çok yoruldum!... Burada çok yoruldum!

Buraya neden geldin? Nereden geldin?

Ece A.: Düzeltmek için... (Ağlıyor.)

Şu an seni duygulandıran şey ne?

Ece A.: Özledim!

Aileni mi?

Ece A.: O Güneydoğu'daki yerde bir şeyler hatırladım... Koydukları bir şey var oraya... Toprağın altında.

Neresi?

Ece A.: Antik... Manastırlar var çevresinde... Oraya yakın... Onun açılması gerekiyor!

Ne var orada?

Ece A.: Birisinin açması gerekiyor!

Açınca ne bulacaklar?

Ece A.: Bilgileri bulacaklar.

Neler var onun içinde?

Ece A.: Bütün bilgiler var... Bunu bilenler vardı eskiden... Onlar biliyorlardı o bilgileri... Dünyanın bütün sistemini biliyorlardı... Ama şu an insanlar zarar veriyorlar her yere, her şeye.

Onu kim koymuş oraya?

Ece A.: Koruyucular... Onların hepsi koruyor... Onlar burada değiller... Başka yerdeler ama sürekli burada gibiler.

Nasıl bilgiler var orada? Kitap gibi bir şey mi?

Ece A.: Hayır... Değil... Notlar.

(Biraz duruyor.)

Ece A.: "M" harfi gördüğüm lider... Türkiye'de başa gelecek olan... Rus bir lider suikast yaşayacak... Ondan sonra olacak.

Ölecek mi Rus lider?

Ece A.: Yaralandığını görüyorum sadece.

Putin mi?

Ece A.: Bilmiyorum... Biraz zaman var daha.

Bu şehir hangi şehir? Altında notlar olan.

Ece A.: Manastırların olduğu yer.

Tahmin edebiliyorum.

Ece A.: Mardin ve çevresi.

Evet. Değerli notlar mı bunlar?

Ece A.: Açmıyorlar onu özellikle... Devletin bildiği bir şey bu... Başka bir yerde yapılmış bir şey var.

Ne gibi bilgiler var bu notlarda?

Ece A.: Bütün dünyanın bilgileri var ama insanların eline ulaşırsa bunu kötüye kullanabilecek olanlar var... Kötüye kullanılmaması için sadece bilenlerin açması gerekiyor.

Nasıl bir bilgi peki bu? Dinlerle mi ilgili?

Ece A.: Değil.

Teknolojik bilgi mi?

Ece A.: Sistem... Matematik... Bütün her şey var.

Çıkacak mı o bilgi?

Ece A.: Çıkacak... Hepsi çıkacak... Çok vakit var ama.

Yeni liderden sonra Türkiye nasıl olacak?

Ece A.: Değişim hemen olmayacak... Yani biraz zorlanacak başta... Ama sonra çok şey değişecek.

Neler değişecek?

Ece A.: Bu çok büyük bir lider... Ben Atatürk'ün enerjisini hissediyorum sadece onda... Masaya oturuyor... Hükmediyor gibi herkese... Çok güçlü.

Neleri değiştiriyor? Neler yapıyor?

Ece A.: Gelmesinden korkanlar var... Engellemek istiyorlar ama yapamayacaklar.

Bilenler de var demek ki.

Ece A.: Bilen birileri var... O yüzden onu koruyorlar.

Kimliği saklanıyor. Şu an bulunduğu yeri görebiliyor musun?

(Ece ağlamaya başlıyor.)

Seni şu an ağlatan şey ne Ece?

Ece A.: (Ağlayarak...) Burası çok önemli bir yer olduğu için buradayım!... Yoruldum!... İzlemekten yoruldum!... Sürekli izliyorum çünkü... Burayı korumaya çalışıyor bazıları ama... Bütün dünyanın gözü burada!

Neden?

Ece A.: Çok önemli şeyler var burada çünkü!... Her şey burada!... Her şey burada başladı!... Artık çok zorlanıyor herkes... (Ağlıyor...) En zorlayıcı kısma geldi artık!... Sona doğru yaklaştı artık... En zor kısım bu... Bu sene!

Evet. 2023.

Ece A.: 2023'ün sonuna kadar... 2024 de dahil... Sonuna kadar uğraşacaklar yok etmek için ama yapamayacaklar... Çok fazla zararlı yapı var... Türkiye'nin her bölgesine dağılmış durumda... Her yerdeler!... Her yerdeler!... Buna izin vermemek için çok uğraşanlar var... Bir yer var... Burası başka bir ülkede bir yer... Orada böyle devlet adamları var... Sürekli bu konuyla ilgili konuşanlar

var... Belki 10-15 kişi... Bunlar çok güçlü yapıda adamlar... Sürekli Türkiye ile ilgili konuşanlar var... Zarar verici... İstemiyorlar... Çünkü onların bütün her şeyi (planları) bozulacak... Buranın karışması onların işine gelecek... Burayı ele geçirmek isteyenler de var.

Kim bunlar?

Ece A.: Onlar çok karanlık adamlar.

Bayrak görüyor musun?

Ece A.: Kilise gördüm.

Türkiye'nin vazifesi ileride, değişimden sonra ne olacak?

Ece A.: Vazifesi aslında sadece iyilik üzerine ama bu bozuldu... (Bir süre sessizlik...) Evet... Şimdi görüyorum.

Söyle.

Ece A.: Birleştirmek... Bütün dünyayı toparlayıcı rolü var... Düzenlemek zorunda... Bulunduğu yerden dolayı.

Başka?

Ece A.: Burası merkez çünkü... Merkezin olduğu bir yer var... Bütün her şeyi birleştirici.

Birleştiricilik vazifesi mi var Türkiye'nin?

Ece A.: Evet... Dünyanın yararı için... Bunu yapmak zorunda.

Peki bilgi anlamında vazifesi var mı?

Ece A.: Burada kaynaklar var... Kaynakların olduğu yerler var... Bunu bilen kişiler var ama bilgileri vermek istemiyorlar.

Evet.

Ece A.: Türkiye'de teknolojik şeylerin üretildiği bir bölge var.

Nerede?

Ece A.: İç Anadolu'da... Kurak bir yer var... Dümdüz bir yer... Orada şey... Mekanik aletler var... Yapılıyor... Türkler çalışıyor... Mühendisler... Kimse bilmiyor orayı... Ankara'nın çevresinde... Dışında... Haritadan bakıldığında Ankara'nın sol tarafında kalı-

yor... Orada çok büyük bir teknoloji var ve bunu kimse bilmiyor... Dünya bilmiyor... Çok gizli.

Dünya dışı bir teknoloji mi?

Ece A.: Her şey yapılıyor... Bütün aletler... Bu bilgileri biliyorlar.

Bu bilgilerin kaynağı ne?

Ece A.: Türkiye'de buldukları bir bilgi bu.

Nerede bulundu?

Ece A.: Doğu Anadolu ya da Güneydoğu Anadolu... A!... Mağarada bulunmuş sanki... Kapalı bir şeyin içinde bulundu bu bilgi... Şeye de benziyor... Lahde benziyor... Çok eski... Oradan çıktı bu bilgi ve bunu birisi elden ele ulaştırdı... Sadece Türkler biliyor ve Dünya'da kimse bilmiyor... Ama bu bilgiyi araştırıyorlar.

Ne bilgisi bu?

Ece A.: Matematiksel hesaplamalar var ama diğeri gibi değil... Dünyanın sistemiyle ilgili değil... Bir şey üretiliyor... Çizimler var üzerinde... Çizimler yapılmış... Hesaplar var... Makine çizimleri var... Gemi çizimleri var.

UFO gibi mi?

Ece A.: Her şey... Farklı farklı gemiler var... Formüller var... Bunların bilen Türk mühendisler sadece... Üzerinde çalışıyorlar... Geliştiriyorlar... Orayı bilen çok az insan var.

Mağaradan mı çıkmış? Dikkatli bakmanı istiyorum.

Ece A.: Kapalı bir alan... Karanlık... Mağara olabilir... Yeraltında bir yer de olabilir.

Tamam.

Ece A.: Bu bilgi çok önceden bulunuyor aslında... Birinin elindeymiş bu bilgi... Uzun yıllar saklamış.

Sonra devlete mi teslim etmiş?

Ece A.: Evet... İletişim halinde olan birileri var... Gemiler ve bu teknolojiler... Sadece gemi değil başka şeyler de yapılıyor orada... Çok yüksek teknolojide şeyler yapılıyor.

Neler?

Ece A.: Türkiye hazırlanıyor... Çünkü başka şeyler olursa bu ülkeyi kurtarabilecek bir teknoloji var... Çok güçlü silahlar ve aletler var... Ama bunu hiç kimse bilmiyor.

Bir işgal girişimine karşı mı?

Ece A.: Her şey için... Yolculuk planı yapmak isteyenler var... Deneme uçuşu yapıyorlar arada... O araçları kullanıyorlar.

UFO mu?

Ece A.: UFO'ya tam benzemiyor... Daha değişik şekilli... Bunlar o bölgeye şey yapmışlar... Alanı çevrelemişler... Oraya kimse gitmiyor... Çünkü çok büyük bir tesis burası... Haritada bulamazsınız.

Devletimizin kontrolünde. Askerler mi var?

Ece A.: Askere benzemiyor... Başka... Kendine güveniyor bu konuda Türkiye... Oranın hâkimiyeti başka birinin elinde... Başka bir şey için hazırlıyorlar... Yetişen, çalışan mühendisler görüyorum... Yerin altına inen bir bölüm var... Çalışmalar var... İletişim var!

Dünya dışı mı?

Ece A.: Evet.

Kimlerle?

Ece A.: Oradan birileri biliyor...

Tamam.

Ece A.: (Başka bir görüntüye geçiyor...) Deneyler!... (Ağlıyor...) Başka bir yerdeyim... Başka bir ülke... Deneyler yapıyorlar yakaladıkları varlıklarla... Çok kötü.

Dünya dışı varlıklarla mı?

Ece A.: Evet... Canlarını yakıyorlar çok.

Neresi orası? Hangi ülke?

Ece A.: Amerika ve İngiltere.

Peki nasıl yakalamışlar bu varlıkları? Neden kaçamıyorlar?

Ece A.: Bilmiyorum... Çok kötü durumdalar... Çıkamıyorlar... Her şeyleri alınmış... Bir sürü operasyonlar yapılıyor onlara... Onlar acı çekiyor!... Yardım istiyorlar!... Klonlama için kullanmaya çalışanlar var... Burası kesilmiş!... (Karın bölgesini gösteriyor...) Aşağıya doğru kesilmiş.

Nasıl varlıklar bunlar?

Ece A.: Karnı biraz şiş... Parmakları uzun... Bağırıyorlar.

Tamam. Ayrıl oradan. Az önce anlattığın Türkiye'deki tesise dönelim. Kimin hâkimiyetinde?

Ece A.: Türkler... Üç kişi... Bunlar çok sağlam insanlar... Bilgileri koruyanlar bunlar... Çok gizli yapı... O tesislere aldıkları mühendisler de özel yetiştirilmiş... Kimseyi almıyorlar oraya... Çalıştırmak için sadece özel yetişen insanları seçiyorlar... Bunun için çocukluklarından beri yetiştirdikleri kişiler var... Çünkü bu bilgiler çok eskiden geçmiş birisinin eline... 10 yıldır çok yoğun şekilde çalışıyorlar orada.

Kim kurmuş bu yapıyı?

Ece A.: O adam... Orta boylu.

Kadim Türk Devleti ile ilgili bir yapı mı?

Ece A.: Bu çok eski bir bilgi... Elden ele gitmiş... Saklamışlar bunu.

Ne kadar eski sence?

Ece A.: Babil'e kadar neredeyse... Ama tam söyleyemiyorum ismini.

Türkiye'de ne zaman çıkarılmış bu bilgi?

Ece A.: 1800'lerde olan bir şey... Bunu anlamamışlar... Birisi almış.

Tarsus değil o zaman.

Ece A.: Tarsus değil... Bu başka bir şey... Tarsus'tan bilgi çıkmadı... Bunun gibi bir bilgi yok... Başka bir şey var orada... Tarsus'tan çıkan şeyi kötüye kullandılar... Yurtdışına gitti... Önemli bir kısmını bir şeyin... Şu an göremiyorum... Bir kısmı Türkiye'de... Devlet el koydu ama başka şeyler var gibi... Çok anlayamıyorum o kısmını... Anlayamıyorum... Çıkamıyorum... Çok karışık orası... Buradaki... Türkiye'deki... Kurtuluş... Orası... O teknolojinin olduğu diğer yer... Tarsus değil.

Kim bunların sahipleri?

Ece A.: O üç kişi... Kimse tanımıyor onları.

İsimlerini sormuyorum aslında. Yapı olarak, organizasyon olarak soruyorum. Atatürk'le bir bağlantıları var mı?

Ece A.: Var... O bilgiyi Atatürk biliyordu zaten.

Onun kurduğu bir yapı mı var?

Ece A.: Onun vasiyeti bu.

Şimdi Atatürk'ün vasiyetine gelelim.

Ece A.: O biliyordu zaten... Çünkü 1800'lerde bulundu o bilgi... Ona ulaştı.

Onu korumak için bir yapı mı kurdu Atatürk?

Ece A.: Evet... O dönem bunun altyapıları hazırlandı ama çalışmalar için çok uzun süre uğraştılar.

O zaman olmadı demek ki.

Ece A.: O zaman başlanmıştı... Sadece çok uzadı çalışmalar... Devam ediyor.

O bölgede mi? Yani Atatürk zamanında mı kuruldu orası?

Ece A.: Atatürk yapıyı oluşturdu ama erken olduğu için yetişmedi... Çok uğraştı... Bunu vasiyet etti.

Atatürk'ün gizli vasiyetine odaklanmanı istiyorum senden. Başka bir şey sormayacağım.

Ece A.: Sadece Türkiye değil, dünyanın yararına... Ama önce Türkiye ve sonra dünya için, bunun korunması, geliştirilmesi ve çalıştırılması için çok yakın birine bir vasiyette bulundu... Ölürken de söyledi bunu.

Peki yazılı bir vasiyet bıraktı mı?

Ece A.: Evet... Bunlar Atatürkçüler... Orayı devam ettirenler... Onlar onun vasiyetini yerine getirmek için çalışıyorlar... O üç kişiden birinde bir vasiyeti var.

Defteri, notları var mı peki?

Ece A.: Evet... Onlar da saklanıyor... Kapalı bir yer... Karanlık... Göremiyorum... Taş görüyorum sadece... Atatürk'ün... Onun bildiği çok özel bilgiler var... Hepsi duruyor orada... Buranın korunması için... Buraya verilmiş bir görev olduğunu düşünüyor... Buranın bir görevi var.

Türkiye'nin mi?

Ece A.: Evet... Kökenler... Çok eskiden beri... Bu coğrafyanın dünyanın kaderini belirleyecek bir şeyi var.

Nedir o görev?

Ece A.: Buraya geldiklerini görüyorum ben.

Kim geliyor?

Ece A.: Dünya dışı... Gelecek.

Bu mu Türkiye'nin görevi?

Ece A.: Sadece bu değil.

Başka?

Ece A.: Evrenle ilgili bir şey var... Sanki o şeyin korunması gerekiyormuş... Bu dünyanın evrene zarar vermemesi için Türkiye'nin buradaki bir şeyi koruması gibi... Çok karışık... Çok büyük, çok önemli bir şey var ama tarif edemiyorum ben bunu.

Dünya dışı varlıklar realitesi ilk olarak Türkiye'den mi yayılacak? Öyle bir şey mi?

Ece A.: İlk olarak kuzeye gelecekler zaten... Ama 2030'larda burada, Türkiye'de başlayacak olan bir şeyin görüntüsü var... Dünyada ilk kez... Televizyonlarda görüyorum ben... İlk kez Türkiye'de... İşte o yüzden Doğu... Güneydoğu... Oralarda bir yerde gerçekleşecek olan bir görüntü var... İlk kez bütün dünya görecek gerçek şeyi.

Gerçek araçları mı?

Ece A.: Bunlar gerçek.

Bu çok önemli.

Ece A.: Atatürk her şeyi biliyordu.

Nasıl?

Ece A.: Çünkü bunu öğrendi... Gitti... Gitti ve bir yerlerden bir şeyler öğrendi.

(Bir süre bizimle ilgili bazı özel bilgiler paylaşılıyor ve ardından seansı bitiriyoruz.)

12. BÖLÜM

KİTAP

İstanbul'da bir sağlık kuruluşunda hemşire olarak görev yapan, 30 yaşındaki Sibel Ş. çocukluk dönemini şu ifadelerle anlatıyordu:

"Kendimi hiçbir zaman bu Dünya'dan hissetmedim... Çoğunlukla buraya düşürüldüğümü düşünüp hep depresif ve mutsuz halde gökyüzünü izliyor, yıldızlarla konuşuyordum... Geceleri uyuyamıyordum çünkü akşamları belli bir saatten sonra tepeden tırnağa siyah giyinmiş varlıkların eve gelip hareketsiz şekilde bizi izlediğini görüyordum... Annemi her gece uyandırır, uyumaması için yalvarırdım... Onlardan korkardım... Onlar sadece durup izlerlerdi... Üç kişi oluyorlardı genelde ve yüzleri ya da ayakları olmuyordu... Uzun süre bu şekilde devam etti."

Sibel daha sonraları, ilkokul ve ortaokul yıllarında insanların akıllarından geçenleri okumaya başladı. Birisinin yüzüne baktığında, o kişinin aklından geçirdiklerini onun sesi ile duyuyordu.

Bütün bu durumlar ve geceleri gelen karabasanlar onu haddinden fazla etkiliyordu. En yakınlarının ya da herkesin çok sevip saygı duyduğu insanların içlerinden neler geçirdiklerini bilmek Sibel için büyük bir yüktü. Bazen dayanamayıp söylediğinde insanlar ondan korkuyor, *"Sen müneccim misin?"* diyorlardı.

Lise yıllarında açık rüyalar görmeye başladı. O dönemde en yakın arkadaşına tüm rüyalarını anlatıyor, bütün rüyaları arkadaşının gözü önünde gerçekleşiyordu.

Yine o dönemlerde duru görü yeteneği iyice gelişmeye başlamıştı. İnsanların yüzüne bakınca film izler gibi tüm yaşamlarını izliyordu.

Daha sonraki yıllarda bilmediği birçok şey ile ilgili bilgiler almaya başladı. Yıllardır çözülemeyen bir matematik problemi, depremler, seller, bir makinenin çalışma şekli, motor mekaniği, evrenin işleyişi gibi, aslında bir kısmı hiç ilgi alanında olmayan bazı konularda eğitimler alıyor, bilgiler zihnine akıyordu. Araba sürmeyi dahi rüyasında öğrenmiş, kursa gittiğinde arabaya biner binmez yıllardır sürüyormuş gibi ustalıkla kullanmıştı. Sürüş hocasını bu duruma bir türlü inandıramadı.

Rüyalarında sürekli uçuyor, başka boyutlara ve gezegenlere gidip bilgiler alıyordu. Bu ruhsal yolculukları sırasında yüksek boyuttan varlıklarla tanıştığını da söylüyordu. Sibel adeta iki ayrı hayat yaşıyordu. Geceleri başka bir boyutta bir asker gibi savaşıp psişik görevler yerine getiriyor, gündüzleri ise hastaneye gidip hemşirelik yapıyordu. Bazıları simülasyon ya da eğitim niteliğindeydi. Bazıları ise gerçek görev gibi hissettiriliyordu.

Bir gece yakın arkadaşıyla aynı odada yatarken yükseldiğini hissetti. Gözünü açtığında havadaydı ve arkadaşı ona bakıyordu. Çığlık atarak yatağa düştü. O odada daha önce varlıklar gördüğünü hatırlıyordu.

Bazı geceler yatağından alınıyor ve gemilerde geziyordu. Ona bilgiler veren varlıklar vardı. Sibel'e, uyandığında bunları unutacağını söylüyorlardı.

Sibel'le yaptığımız seans pek çok heyecan verici bilgiyi açığa çıkardığı gibi Türkiye'nin geleceğiyle ilgili bilgileri de yeni verilerle takviye etti.

Sibel Ş. Seansı
10 Temmuz 2023

(Nefes, gevşeme ve enerji çalışmasından sonra Sibel'i temas anılarına götürmek istiyoruz ancak bu görüntüler bloke ediliyor ve Sibel diğer süjeler gibi Dünya'nın geleceğiyle ilgili görüntülere doğru ilerletiliyor.)

Ne görüyorsun Sibel?

Sibel Ş.: Dünya haritasının sağ tarafı... Patlamalar görüyorum... Kuzey Kutbu'na yakın yerde... Patlamalar.

Neresi orası Sibel? Haritanın sağı olduğuna göre Asya mı?

Sibel Ş.: Olabilir... Kuzey Kutbu'na yakın ve sağ tarafta... Büyük bir delik açılacak.

Hangi ülkenin toprakları orası?

Sibel Ş.: Şu an önüme kocaman bir kuş geldi ve göremiyorum.

Göstermiyorlar.

Sibel Ş.: "J" ve "A" harfleri.

O delik nasıl oluşmuş?

Sibel Ş.: Dışarıdan bir basınçla... Yuvarlak.

Gökten bir şey mi gelmiş? Yoksa...

Sibel Ş.: Evet... Yuvarlak bir şey çarpıyor.

Öyle mi başlıyor olaylar Dünya'da?

Sibel Ş.: Evet... İlkel oluşumlar... Solucanlar gibi hareket eden bir şeyler var.

Dünya haritasına biraz geriden bakar mısın? Uzaktan. Bütün dünya haritasına bak bakalım. Başka nerelerde hareket görüyorsun?

Sibel Ş.: Ben şey görüyorum... Hem de hissediyorum aynı anda... Birçok yerde büyük bir kaos var... Büyük bir yıkım.

Nedir sebebi?

Sibel Ş.: Dışarıdan bir etki olacak.

Ne gibi bir etki? Görüntüde kal.

Sibel Ş.: Böyle... Şey gibi... Dünyanın olağan dönüşü içerisinde beklenen bir şey ama çok hızlı gerçekleşiyor... Hiç beklenmedik bir anda.

Gökyüzüne bir bak bakalım.

Sibel Ş.: Araçlar var... Yuvarlak... Çok büyük.

Büyük araçlar mı gelmiş?

Sibel Ş.: Evet.

Ne hissediyorsun onların niyetleri hakkında?

Sibel Ş.: Kötü hissetmiyorum... Sanki yardıma gelmişler gibi hissediyorum.

Aşağıda karmaşa var, yukarıda araçlar var. Öyle mi?

Sibel Ş.: Ama her şey çok kaos içinde.

Aşağıda ne var? Doğa hareketi mi? Savaş mı? Salgın mı? Bilemiyorum. Ne olabilir? Aşağıdaki karmaşanın kaynağına bakar mısın? Nasıl başlamış?

Sibel Ş.: Patlama gibi bir şey olmuş... Asfaltlar çökmüş... Herkes koşuşturuyor... Kaçıyor... Bir yandan da başka şeyler oluyor sanki.

Şu an görüntü geliyor mu? Vizyonun içinde misin?

Sibel Ş.: Şu anda araç görüyorum dışarıdan.

Tamam. Araçlar ne yapıyorlar? Bekliyorlar mı?

Sibel Ş.: Evet... Gökyüzünde duruyorlar... Şu an bir tanesini görüyorum çok yakından.

Nasıl bir araç bu? Tarif eder misin?

Sibel Ş.: Yuvarlak... Metalik... Mavi ışıkları var.

Nasıl yardım edecekler insanlara?

Sibel Ş.: Sanki onlar da endişelenmiş ve gözlem yapıyorlar... Olanı izliyorlar.

Bir zaman hissin var mı? Yakın, orta, uzak gibi.

Sibel Ş.: Çok yakın bir zaman değil ama çok da uzak bir zaman değil.

Şimdi dünya haritasının karşısındasın. Türkiye'ye bakmanı istiyorum senden. Türkiye'de neler oluyor?

Sibel Ş.: Akdeniz'e yakın taraflarda ama daha içeriye doğru kırmızı yanıp sönüyor... Bir alarm durumu var.

Neresi tam olarak?

Sibel Ş.: Kıyıdan birkaç şehir içeride.

Türkiye'nin neresi oluyor bölge olarak?

Sibel Ş.: İç Anadolu'ya yakın ama kıyıya da yakın.

Neyin alarmı acaba? Bak bakalım. Yakala o görüntüyü.

Sibel Ş.: Sıcak... Ateş.

İyice yakınlaş. Yakından görelim.

Sibel Ş.: Toplumsal bir şey yaşanacak... Ama çok az kişi kaçabiliyor gibi.

Bir değişim var mı Türkiye'de?

Sibel Ş.: Yeniden doğmak için önce büyük bir yıkımın olması gerekiyor.

Anladım. Nasıl bir yıkım?

Sibel Ş.: İnsanlar kendi felaketlerini getiriyor zaten.

Tüm gördüklerini anlat.

Sibel Ş.: Pankartlar falan görüyorum... Siyasi bir karışıklık var gibi... Ondan sonra... Bir yandan da böyle birkaç yangın olayı.

Bu yeniden doğum nasıl olacak peki?

Sibel Ş.: Yeniden doğum olduğunda Türkiye'de Türkler dışında kimsenin kalmamış olması gerekiyor... Çok az insan kalmış.

Nasıl oluyor peki bu süreç? Nasıl başlıyor?

Sibel Ş.: Atatürk büstü görüyorum!

Devam.

Sibel Ş.: Şey gibi hissediyorum!... Tüylerim diken diken oldu!

Ne hissediyorsun?

Sibel Ş.: Sanki onun ruhu birçok bedene yayılmış ve onların hepsi birdenbire tek bir bilinç haline gelip bir şeyler yapıyorlar gibi!... (Ağlıyor.)

Neler oluyor? Çok önemli bir yerdesin şu an.

Sibel Ş.: Bir yerlere bayrak dikiyor insanlar!... Türk bayrağı!... Sanki yeniden ele geçiriliyormuş gibi!... Yeniden kazanılmış gibi!

Evet.

Sibel Ş.: Ama böyle çok az insanla çok şey yapılmış gibi... Tarihin tekerrürü gibi.

Nasıl?

Sibel Ş.: Çok az insan var... İmkânlar çok kısıtlı ama o kadar kolay yapılıyor ki... Gidip böyle burası da, burası da, burası da gibi geri kazanıyoruz.

İşgal mi edilmiş peki ülke?

Sibel Ş.: İşgal gibi değil ama görünmez bir kaybetmişlik... Geri kazanılıyor... Ama böyle toplu tüfekli bir savaş ortamı gibi bir şey yok.

Anladım. Nasıl başarılıyor?

Sibel Ş.: Şöyle bir cümle geliyor sürekli... Sanki birisi şu cümleyle başlatıyor: "Ben bu topraklara sadık bir köpeğim!" gibi bir cümle...

Kim o?

Sibel Ş.: Birisi söylüyor ve sanki bütün enerji o zaman açığa çıkıp her şey başlıyormuş gibi.

Kim o kişi Sibel?

Sibel Ş.: Adını göremiyorum... Genç bir enerji hissediyorum ama.

Kaç yaşında?

Sibel Ş.: Yani böyle 28-32 arası.

Şu an kaç yaşında o kişi?

Sibel Ş.: 17-18... O yaşlarda... 17.

O kişi ne yapıyor şu anda?

Sibel Ş.: O kişi amacını yeni hissetmeye başlıyor.

Bir vazifesi mi var?

Sibel Ş.: Evet... İçine yeni yeni o ateş düşmeye başlıyor.

Şu an ne yapıyor?

Sibel Ş.: Elinde bir defterle görüyorum... Bir masada oturuyor.

Nasıl biri? Tipini tarif eder misin?

Sibel Ş.: Boyu 1,80'e yakın... Zayıf... Fit.

Devam.

Sibel Ş.: Siyah saçlı, beyaz tenli, koyu kahverengi gözleri var.

Gözlerine bakar mısın? Göz göze gelin.

Sibel Ş.: Çok düşünceli... Kafası çok dolu... Bir şeylerin yanlış gittiğini biliyor... Ve şu an yapması gereken şeylerin hiçbiri umurunda değil... Yani böyle dayatılan şeyler vardır ya... İşe git, okula git gibi şeyler.

Baktın mı gözlerine?

Sibel Ş.: Tutku ve öfke var.

Enerjisi nasıl?

Sibel Ş.: Çok güçlü... Hani böyle bir yumruğuyla masayı ikiye ayıracak kadar bir enerji birikmiş sanki içinde.

Ne yapacak bu kişi? Nasıl bir misyonu var?

Sibel Ş.: Onun etrafında zaten kendiliğinden onun gibi insanlar yavaş yavaş toplanmaya başlayacaklar... O hiç çaba sarf etmeyecek... Her şey aslında kendiliğinden olmaya başlayacak... Sadece onun başlaması gerekiyor.

Peki etrafında birileri var mı şu anda?

Sibel Ş.: Yok... Şu anda yalnız... Bir iki kişi belki.

Kendi vazifesinin farkında mı?

Sibel Ş.: Şu an değil ama yeni yeni fark etmeye başlıyor sanki... Ama fark etmesine daha çok var.

Türkiye'de nasıl bir rol üstlenecek?

Sibel Ş.: Karar verdiği an sanki bütün kapılar onu bekliyor açılmak için... Kapılar açılacak ve hızla ilerleyecek.

Evet.

Sibel Ş.: Aslında sadece bir kişi olarak değil... Zaten yaparken "Ben yaptım" gibi bir egosu yok... Sanki bir bütünün parçalara ayrılmış hali gibi.

Başkaları da var.

Sibel Ş.: Evet.

Peki bu desteği, gücü, enerjisini nereden alıyor?

Sibel Ş.: Mesela şu an içinde bir şeyler başlamasının sebebi öfkesinden kaynaklanıyor... Bir şeye çok öfkeli... Öfkelenince içinde bir ateş yanıyor ve o ateşle her şeyi yapabilecek güçte oluyor.

Ruhsal bağlantı olarak?

Sibel Ş.: Evet... O izleniyor ama hislerinin çok kuvvetli olduğunu zannediyor... Aslında izleniyor.

Evet.

Sibel Ş.: Osmanlı tarihine meraklı sanki... Şu an onu araştırıyor... Fatih Sultan Mehmet'e özel bir ilgisi var.

(Bir süre sessizlikten sonra yeni görüler gelmeye başlıyor.)

Sibel Ş.: A!... Bu kişiye bilgiler gelecek!... Elinde kitap var demiştim ya... Elindeki kitap şu anda bembeyaz parlıyor... İçinde bir şeyler yazıyor ama ne yazdığını göremiyorum... Heyecanla onları okuyor ve çok şaşırıyor... Çünkü normalde o kitapta yazılan şeyler değil... Sanki bir anda yazılar değişip ona o bilgiler geliyor.

Biraz okumaya çalışır mısın?

Sibel Ş.: Okumaya çalışınca önüme siyah bir gölge geldi... Okuyamıyorum... Şu an kapandı tamamen.

Okutmuyorlar.

Sibel Ş.: Ama çok şaşırıyor... (Bir süre sessizlik...) Yok o farkında izlendiğinin... Gayet farkında... İçinden kendiyle konuşuyormuş gibi yapıp aslında bir başkasıyla konuştuğunu bilerek konuşuyor... Bir rehberi var... Kitap tamamen kapandı şu an.

Rehberi kim?

Sibel Ş.: Bilmiyorum... Mavi ve beyaz enerjisi olan bir şey... Gözleri mi mavi, enerjisi mi?... Yoğun bir mavi ve beyaz enerjisi alıyorum sadece... Aydınlık... Elindeki bilgileri çok güzel kullanacak... Orada yazılanları çok güzel değerlendirecek.

Evet.

Sibel Ş.: Kedi görüyorum... Sanki kedi suretinde bir şey önünde duruyormuş gibi.

Peki Türkiye'nin misyonu ne olacak?

Sibel Ş.: Türkiye'nin ortasında kalp gibi atan bir enerji var... Bir insanın kalbi gibi atıyor... Kocaman... Sanki böyle şey gibi... Dünyadaki bütün spiritüel insanlar o kalbe doğru mıknatıs gibi çekiliyor.

Çok güzel. Bu tarz spiritüel bilgiler mi yayılıyor acaba?

Sibel Ş.: Burada geçiş kapısı var!... Kara delik gibi bir şey görüyorum.

Nerede? Yukarıdan bak bakalım Türkiye'ye. Nerede görüyorsun?

Sibel Ş.: Tam orta noktada... En orta noktada... Güçlü bir şey var... Ve orası şu an biliniyor... Bulunmuş orası.

Kim bulmuş?

Sibel Ş.: Bilmiyorum ama sadece iki kişinin oradan geçtiğini gördüm.

Nereye geçiliyor oradan?

Sibel Ş.: Başka bir boyuta ama o geçilen boyut Dünya üzerinde bir boyut değil... Başka bir evren... Orada her şey çok farklı gibi... Sadece delikten görebiliyorum... Böyle lacivert bir yer.

Neresi orası Sibel?

Sibel Ş.: Ters Dünya.

Ters Dünya? Ne demek istedin?

Sibel Ş.: Canlılar farklı... Orada yaşayan her şey çok farklı... İnsan yok.

Evet.

Sibel Ş.: (Tekrar dünya haritasına dönüyor...) Şey görüyorum... Haritaya baktığımda insanları görüyorum ve insanların bazıları normal şekilde burada oluşmuş gibi... Ama çoğunluk... Aslında ben de şaşırıyorum... Bu kadar çok olduğunu bilmiyordum... Böyle yıldız parçaları gibi parlayan birçok insan var.

Dünya dışından gelip buraya doğanlar mı?

Sibel Ş.: Evet...

Peki çocuklar? Çocuklara bakar mısın?

Sibel Ş.: Çocuklar çok fazla.

Nerelerden geliyor bu çocuklar daha çok?

Sibel Ş.: Tek bir yer yok.

Ya sen? Sana yardım eden birileri var mı?

Sibel Ş.: Evet.

Kim onlar?

Sibel Ş.: Ailem.

Dünya'daki ailen mi?

Sibel Ş.: Burada değiller.

Neredeler? Nasıl bir yer?

Sibel Ş.: Suların daha mavi olduğu... Toprak yok... Gökyüzü çok farklı.

Oradan mı geldin?

Sibel Ş.: Evet.

Çocukluğunda ailen seni ziyaret ediyor muydu?

Sibel Ş.: (Ağlayarak...) Hep ediyorlardı.

Uykunda mı? Uyanıkken mi?

Sibel Ş.: Her zaman.

Neden buradasın Sibel?

Sibel Ş.: Ben gelmek istemiyordum buraya!

İkna mı ettiler seni?

Sibel Ş.: Öyle gerektiği için... (Ağlıyor.)

Neden buradasın?

Sibel Ş.: Neden burada olduğumu bilmiyorum ama şu an burada olmam gerekiyor.

Şimdi sana bir süre soru sormayacağım. Geleni aktar.

Sibel Ş.: Yunan mitolojisindeki değişik varlıklar var ya... Kanatlı insan formu... O tarz şeyler görüyorum... Öyle bir şeyler ortaya çıkacak sanki.

Melez varlıklar mı acaba?

Sibel Ş.: Evet... Onlar zaten var sanki ve saklandıkları yerden çıkacaklar... Çünkü Dünya çok boşalacak ve o boşluktan faydalanacaklar... İnsan kalabalığı gittiği için... Çok uzak bir gelecek değil ama bu.

Ne olacak peki Dünya'da?

Sibel Ş.: Sanki bütün her şey bekliyor gibi.

Boyut değişimi gibi mi?

Sibel Ş.: Ama çok ağırlıklar var... Bundan kurtulmak gerekiyor... Bu şekilde olmaz... O yüzden yakın gelecekte değil... Çok güçlü bir varlık görüyorum şu anda... Yerden böyle toprakla beraber yükseliyor ve kollarını açmış... Bembeyaz... Yerden yükselecek.

Sen melez üretimini gördün mü Sibel?

Sibel Ş.: Evet... Tüplerde insanlar vardı... Bebekler vardı... Ameliyata aldıkları insanlar vardı... O an zihnim çok açık oluyor ve kendimi ameliyathane ortamında görünce kaçmak istiyorum.

Şimdi tekrar oraya gitmeni istiyorum. Güvendesin. Orada mısın?

Sibel Ş.: Evet.

Etrafında bir varlık var mı? Bakar mısın?

Sibel Ş.: Evet... Şey yapmıyorlar... Sadece kaçarsam diye yanımda duruyor.

Şimdi sormanı istiyorum. Neden bu bebekleri üretiyorsunuz?

Sibel Ş.: Sizin için.

Nedir bu bebeklerin fonksiyonu? Bize nasıl yardım edecekler?

Sibel Ş.: Bir üst boyuta taşıyacak.

Aramıza karışacaklar mı?

Sibel Ş.: Bazıları.

Nasıl? Doğum yoluyla mı? Doğrudan mı?

Sibel Ş.: Çoğu doğrudan.

Nasıl yapacaklar bunu?

Sibel Ş.: Cevap vermiyor.

Bize söylemek istediği bir şey var mı?

Sibel Ş.: O bebeklere ışık yüklüyoruz diyor.

Bunu biraz daha açabilir mi?

Sibel Ş.: Ana kaynaktan gelen ışıktan yüklüyoruz.

O zaman Dünya'nın frekansını mı yükseltecek bu çocuklar?

Sibel Ş.: Evet.

Tamam.

Sibel Ş.: Hasta olmak zorunda değilsiniz... Savaşmak zorunda değilsiniz... Aslında her şeyin çok kolay olacağını gösterecekler.

(Kısa bir sessizlik.)

Sibel Ş.: Bana ne yaptıklarını sorabilir miyim?

Tabii sor.

Sibel Ş.: (Ağlıyor.)

Güvendesin.

Sibel Ş.: (Varlığın yanıtını aktarıyor...) Hatırlaman gerekenleri veriyoruz... Sana da yükleme yapıyoruz.

Neden?

Sibel Ş.: Hatırla!... Hatırla diyor sadece.

Hatırlıyor musun?

Sibel Ş.: Hayır.

Elinde veya ayağında kına benzeri izler oldu mu Sibel?

Sibel Ş.: Elimde olmuştu.

Şimdi onu sormanı istiyorum o varlığa. Bu nasıl oluşuyor?

Sibel Ş.: Aldıklarında işlem yaparken kullandıkları bir şey olduğunu söylüyor.

Neden el ve ayaklar?

Sibel Ş.: Geçiş oralardan daha kolay oluyormuş.

Nereye geçiş?

Sibel Ş.: Avuç içi ve ayak altındaki bazı kanallar açık olduğu için oradan çabuk aktarım yapılıyormuş.

Ne tür bir aktarım bu?

Sibel Ş.: Bazen şifa...

Bunu bir cihaz mı yapıyor o zaman?

Sibel Ş.: Cihaz kullanılmadan önce kendileri bir şey sürüyor... (Biraz durup izliyor...) Yani sürmek gibi de değil... Şu an gösteriyor nasıl yaptığını... Ama tam anlatamıyorum.

Anlatmaya çalış.

Sibel Ş.: Dokunmak yok... Dokunmadan yapıyor.

Enerjiyle mi?

Sibel Ş.: Evet onun gibi... Ama elini falan da tutmuyor... Düşünüyor sadece galiba... O orada oluşuyor... Sonra saniyeler içinde yapmaları gerekenleri yapıyorlar.

O frekans demek ki bir iz oluşturuyor orada. Bize söylemek istediği bir şey var mı o varlığın?

Sibel Ş.: Çok büyük bir sevgiyle gülümsüyor şu anda... Her şey yolunda.

Seninle ilgili söylemek istediği bir şey var mı?

Sibel Ş.: Seninle ilgileniyoruz diyor.

Birkaç dakika seni serbest bırakacağım. Bir vizyon gelirse söyle sadece.

Sibel Ş.: Erkek bebek görüyorum... Sarışın.

Kimin o bebek?

Sibel Ş.: Şu an orada... Onların yanında... Bana verecekler.

Senin mi bebek?

Sibel Ş.: Evet... (Ağlıyor.)

O bebeğe karşı ne hissediyorsun?

Sibel Ş.: Sarılmak istiyorum!... (Ağlıyor...) Gidemiyorum yanına!

Tamam Sibel.

(Sibel'i ağır bir duygusal bir travmadan korumak için onu dünyasal bir alana çekiyoruz ve seansı bitiriyoruz.)

13. BÖLÜM

SIFIRLANMA

Ellili yaşların başındaki arkeolog S. Kosovalı'nın gece uykuda deneyimlediği birtakım temasların ve gerçekleşen rüyalarının dışında tamamen bilinçli yaşadığı, son derece sarsıcı bir fiziksel vakalar zinciri vardı.

Kosovalı bu olayı şöyle anlatıyordu:

"2014 yılında bir kafede arkadaşlarımla otururken, çok uzun boylu birisi yanıma yaklaştı ve doğrudan adımla ve soyadımla hitap ederek, 'Arkeolog olduğunuzu öğrendim... Size sormam gereken birkaç şey var' dedi... Buyurun dedim ama adımı ve soyadımı nereden bildiğini anlayamamıştım... İlk sorduğu soru 'Temas kurdunuz mu? İletişim kurdunuz mu? Görüşüyor musunuz?' oldu... 'Ne sorduğunuzu anlamadım' diye cevap verdim ama ısrarla, bana farklı kanallardan ya da boyutlardan varlıklarla iletişim kurup kurmadığımı soruyordu... Tedirgin olmuştum... 'Sizin aradığınız cevabı veremem... Siz başka birisine sorun... Aradığınız kişi ben değilim' dedim... Paniklemiştim.

Birkaç gün geçtikten sonra, o gün masada yanımda olan arkadaşım aradı... Birisinin benimle acil olarak görüşmek istediğini söyledi... Tamam dedim, merak ettim, gittim ve buluştuk.

Karşımdaki kişi çok ilginç, değişik bir kişiydi... Benimle konuşurken, hakkımda kimsenin bilmediği birkaç bilgiyi söyledi ve 'Seni korkutmak istemiyorduk... Zamanın gelmesini bekliyorduk... Hazır olmanı bekliyorduk direkt temas kurmak için...

Ben şu anda bu bedeni kanal olarak kullanıyorum... Bu beden üzerinden seninle iletişime geçtim... Bunu yaparken de bazı kurallara karşı geldim... Bir ceza ödemem de gerekecek bizim boyutumuzda fakat mecburduk... Seninle konuşmamız gerekiyordu... Seni bulmuşlar' dedi.

Ardından öyle enteresan şeyler anlattı ki!... Dünya'daki düzeni... Sisteme nasıl müdahale ettiklerini... Nerede devreye girdiklerini... Neden burada olduklarını... Dünya zamanından farklı bir zaman diliminde yaşadıklarını... Bizim katı fiziksel beden kullandığımız için hareket alanımızın kısıtlı olduğunu fakat kendilerinin çok özgür olduklarını anlattı... Işık hızından bahsetti... Hepsini çok ayrıntılı bir şekilde anlattı... Ben bunları, gerçek olamayacağını düşünerek dinledim... 'Yardıma ihtiyacın olduğu zaman bu bedendeki kişiyi ara... Biz zaten onun üzerinden seninle iletişim kurarız' dedi... Uzun bir süre sonra vedalaşıp ayrıldık.

Ben yine bunların hiçbirisine inanmak istemedim... Aradan epeyce uzun bir zaman geçti.

Bir gün Taksim'de aracımla ara sokaklardan geçerek bir görüşmeye yetişmeye çalışıyordum... Navigasyon beni yol diye merdivenlere sokmuş... Tabii ben hızlı gittiğim için o anda fark edemedim ve birden merdivenlerden aşağıya doğru araç kaymaya başladı... Güçlükle merdivenlerin sonunda durabildim... Bulunduğum yer çok sapa bir sokaktı ve çevrede de mülteciler vardı... Bir anda etrafımı sardılar... Aracımı oradan kurtaramıyordum... Yüksek kaldırımdan da inemiyordum... Çekici araç çağırdım... Taksim olduğu için iki saatten önce gelemeyiz dediler... Polisi aradım... Onlar da gelemeyeceklerini söylediler... Ne yapacağımı bilemediğim, çaresiz bir durumdaydım.

Panikle, bir anda o kişinin bana söyledikleri aklıma geldi... Onu aradım ve dedim ki: 'Şu an kiminle görüşüyorum bilmiyorum ama yardımlarına ihtiyacım var... Bana yardım etsinler.'

Telefondaki kişi, 'Şimdi birazdan iki kişi gönderiyoruz... Seni oradan çıkaracaklar... Hiç soru sorma... Oradan çıkardıklarında devam et, evine dön' dediler... Gerçekten birkaç dakika sonra iki kişi geldi... Mültecilerle kendi dillerinde konuşarak talimatlar verdiler, aracın oradan kolaylıkla inmesi için kaldırımın altına bir şeyler yığdırdılar ve ben oradan kolaylıkla indim... Çıktım ve oradan ayrıldım... Tabii o esnada onların gelmiş olmasına inanamadım.

Ardından daha çok şeyler yaşandı... Bir de yanıma geldiklerinde kokudan anlıyorum... Farklı, çok değişik, güzel bir koku yayılıyor ansızın[9]... Anlıyorum yakınımda olduklarını...

Bu kadın figüründeki ve farklı bir ses tonuyla konuşan varlık bana pek çok şey anlattı... Biz Dünya'yı hiçbir zaman sahipsiz bırakmadık dedi... Hatta çok enteresan bir bilgi verdi... Fatih Sultan Mehmet de bizdik... Alparslan da bizdik... Atatürk de bizdik dedi... Özellikle Anadolu'yu hiç sahipsiz bırakmadıklarını söyledi... Dünya var olduğu sürece Türk milleti var olacaktır dedi... Bu bir ırktır dedi... Bu ırkın görevini şey olarak söyledi... Düzen koruyucular dedi... Onlar var olacaklar ki düzen korunsun dedi... Onlar içeride biz dışarıda, hep bağlantılı şekilde sürdürdük dedi.

Anadolu'da Kadim Devlet çok arandı, Ergenekon çok arandı, Aksakallılar çok arandı dedi ve gülerek 'Daha çok ararlar bizi' dedi... Belki o an bir simitçinin üzerindeyiz dedi... Biz görevimizi yapmak istediğimizde gerekirse bir işadamını kontrol altına alırız... Belli bir süre onun içine girer, yapılması gerekeni yapar, atılması gereken insanları atar, olayları çözer ve çıkarız dedi... Biz bu yetkiye sahibiz dedi... Senin gözünü açıp kapattığın sürede ben Dünya'yı dört kez turlarım dedi... Sizin zamanınızla bizimki çok farklı dedi... Kalabalık bir aileyiz dedi...

---

9. Bu eterik, enerjetik bir kokudur.

Benimle konuştuklarında Türkçe isimler kullanıyorlar... Ahmet, Mehmet gibi... Bana bu bilgileri aktaran 'Şu an Ahmet'le konuşuyorsun' dedi... Ahmet lafını ne zaman duyarsan bil ki biz oradayız ve temizlik yapıyoruz dedi... Dört erkek komutanın Dünya'dan sorumlu olduğunu, bir tanesinin geri planda kaldığını, bir tanesinin diğer boyutta olduğunu, iki tanesinin Dünya'da olduğunu söyledi... Asla bulunamayacaklarını, asla hiç kimsenin onlara ulaşamayacağını, sadece onlar isterse görüşülebileceğini söyledi... Anadolu'yu korumakla görevliyiz dedi... Mahşerin dört atlısı gibi değerlendirin, doğunun, batının, kuzeyin, güneyin koruyucularıyız dedi... Önlem alınmazsa Anadolu'ya bir işgal girişimi olacağını ama dirilişin ondan sonra başlayacağını söyledi... İçeriden gelebilecek darbelere dikkat edilmesi gerektiğini söyledi... Şu an halkın bir uyku içinde olduğu bildirildi..."

Seansta S. Kosovalı'nın naklettiği mesajlar, çoğunluğu hâlâ derin bir uykudaki insanlar için tam anlamıyla "kırmızı alarm" niteliğindeydi.

S. Kosovalı Seansı
10 Temmuz 2023

(Nefes, gevşeme ve enerji çalışması.)

Nasıl hissediyorsun?

S. Kosovalı: Denizin üstünde.

Hafif ve şeffaf mı?

S. Kosovalı: Evet.

Birtakım blokajların var burada.

(Dilek bir işlem yapıyor.)

S. Kosovalı: Metalik bir yer... Sonsuz, sınırsızmış gibi ama sınırlar da var... Asansörle çıkarılıyor gibiyim.

Tamam devam et.

S. Kosovalı: Yuvarlak bir ışık huzmesi çekiyor.

Yanında varlıklar var mı?

S. Kosovalı: Sanki ben korunmak için yukarıya doğru çekiliyorum.

Tamam.

S. Kosovalı: Beyaz ışığın olduğu bir yer... Başka bir boyut.

Orada mısın hâlâ?

S. Kosovalı: Durdu.

Tamam. Çık oradan. Neredesin şu anda? Etrafına bakar mısın?

S. Kosovalı: Geniş bir boşluk... Gri.

Pencereler var mı?

S. Kosovalı: Yok... Işıklar var ama nereden geldiğini göremiyorum.

Tamam. O ışıkların olduğu yere gider misin?

S. Kosovalı: Kalabalıklar.

Ne var orada?

S. Kosovalı: Konuşan ışık huzmeleri var.

Tamam. O ışıkların içine girelim.

S. Kosovalı: Kendi aralarında telaşla konuşuyorlar.

Şimdi o konuşmalara kulak verin.

S. Kosovalı: Kelime yok... Zihin akışı.

Neyin telaşındalar?

S. Kosovalı: Karar vermeye çalışıyorlar.

Neyle ilgili?

S. Kosovalı: Bunlar sanki bir üst yönetimin altındakiler gibi... Üst yönetimin verdiği kararın doğru olup olmadığını tartışıyorlar sanki... İtirazlar var... Kabul edenler var.

Üst yönetim kim?

S. Kosovalı: Başka bir yer.

Nasıl bir yer? Farklı bir boyut gibi mi?

S. Kosovalı: Sanki gemi gibi düşünün... Geminin altında bunlar var... Sanki bir üst kat ya da üst tabaka gibi... Orasının verdiği kararı tartışıyorlar.

Karar neyle ilgili?

S. Kosovalı: Dünya'yı görüyorum.

Ne görüyorsun Dünya'da?

S. Kosovalı: Fırtına var.

Bütün Dünya'da mı?

S. Kosovalı: Belli bir bölgeden sanki Dünya'yı kasıp kavuracak gibi.

Nereden kaynaklanıyor bu?

S. Kosovalı: Sanki Dünya'yı bir şey içine çekmek üzere.

Kaotik bir olay mı?

S. Kosovalı: Evet ama dışarıda... Uzayda.

Uzaydan Dünya'ya gelen bir şey mi?

S. Kosovalı: Müdahale edebilirler... Ama bir kısmı etmek istemiyor... Bir kısmı istiyor.

Nedir bu?

S. Kosovalı: Sanki böyle kuyruklu bir şey yaklaşıyor... Ama öncüleri var... Nasıl diyeyim?... Kayalar, taşlar, bir şeyler var önden... Ama arkası geliyor... Dünya'nın nasıl korunacağı ile ilgili tartışmadalar.

Anladım.

S. Kosovalı: Üst yönetim müdahale etmek istemiyor.

Kim bunlar? Nasıl varlıklar?

S. Kosovalı: Beden siluetleri var fakat şekil yok... Işıl ışıl... Çok farklı bir ışık... Dünya'nın sıfırlanmasını istiyorlar.

Üst yönetim?

S. Kosovalı: Evet... Başaramadık... İnsanlar başaramadı.

Zaman hissin var mı? Kısa, orta ya da uzun vade?

S. Kosovalı: Gelmek üzere olan henüz karanlıkta ve daha yaklaşmadı... Sanki göktaşları düşmeye başladıktan sonra süreç başlayacak.

İlk nereye düşecek? Nasıl anlayacağız?

S. Kosovalı: Amerika'nın üstü.

Üstü derken kuzeyi mi?

S. Kosovalı: Evet... Kutba doğru.

Bu uzak bir gelecekte mi olacak?

S. Kosovalı: Çok uzak değil.

Peki Dünya'nın o süreçten sonraki haline odaklanır mısın?

S. Kosovalı: Volkanik patlamalar... Çukurlar... Yanmış.

En büyük volkanik patlamayı nerede görüyorsun?

S. Kosovalı: Amerika'nın kuzeyi.

İnsanlar ne durumda?

S. Kosovalı: Düştüğü yerde hiç kimse yok.

Issız bir bölge mi?

S. Kosovalı: Derin... Karanlık... Cehennem çukuru burası... Çok büyük bir çukur... Alt tarafta kalanlar koşturuyorlar... Şaşkınlar... Kaos.

Türkiye'ye bakmanı istiyorum.

S. Kosovalı: Türkiye kurtuluyor.

Yakın gelecekte neler olacak Türkiye'de?

S. Kosovalı: Çok büyük bir kargaşa var.

Nereden kaynaklanacak bu?

S. Kosovalı: Sanki Rusya'nın da üstlerinden gelen bir kargaşa.

Bunu anlayamadım.

S. Kosovalı: Rusya... Onun üstlerinden aşağıya akın akın inen bir kargaşa... Önce hiçbir şeyin farkında değiliz... Her şey ansızın gelecek.

Neler olacak Türkiye'de?

S. Kosovalı: Beşik gibi sallanıyoruz... Kıyılar çok sallanıyor... İstanbul... Üstten gelecek Türkiye'ye gelecek olan zarar sanki... Kısmen.

Yukarıdan mı gelecek?

S. Kosovalı: Yukarıdan... Rusya üzerinden... Ama çok büyük bir hasar değil... Deprem gibi... Sanki suya taş attığınızda onun dalgaları gelir ya... Yayılır, yayılır, yayılır... O dalga vuracak bizi... Şöyle bir dalgalanma geliyor... (Eliyle dalga hareketi yapıyor...) Bütün kayalar yerinden oynayıp sonra yerine oturuyor... Sanki kıta yerinden oynayıp oturuyor gibi.

Sonra?

S. Kosovalı: Sessizlik.

Nasıl bir sessizlik?

S. Kosovalı: Birisi var yönetimi alacak Türkiye'de... Genç birisi.

Nasıl birisi? Tarif eder misin?

S. Kosovalı: Çok güçlü... Çok güçlü bir karakter.

Evet.

S. Kosovalı: Ama bu görevli... Dünya'ya yerleştirilmiş... Süreci geçirmesi için... Atlatması için.

Nereden görevlendirilmiş?

S. Kosovalı: Yukarıdaki gemide tartışanlar... Onlardan biri... Amaç Dünya'yı kurtarmak değil zaten... Kalanlarla yeniden başlamak.

O zaman dünya çapında bir görevi mi olacak bu kişinin?

S. Kosovalı: Ama Türkiye'den başlatıyor.

O kişiye odaklan. Fiziğini anlatır mısın bize?

S. Kosovalı: Çok güçlü... Genç... Uzun... Fit... Omuzlar geniş... İnsanlar sadece bakarken dahi güven duyuyorlar.

Gözlerine bakar mısın?

S. Kosovalı: Dünya'da olacakları hatırlamış... Biliyor... Yetiştirilmiş.

Ne zamandan beri yetiştirilmiş?

S. Kosovalı: Doğduğu andan beri.

Kimler yetiştirmiş onu?

S. Kosovalı: O süreci geçirmesi için gemide tartışanlar... Altta tartışanlar değil... Üsttekiler... Biliyorlar... "Bizden biri orada... Atlatılacak" diyorlar.

Nereyle bağlantılı bunlar?

S. Kosovalı: Başka bir gezegen... Farklı bir yer... "S" harfi var... Farklı seslendiriyorlar... Anlamıyorum.

Belki bize bir sembol gösterirler, anlarız.

S. Kosovalı: Evet... Bir sembol var.

Nedir sembol?

S. Kosovalı: Nasıl tarif edebilirim?... Üç tane oval halkanın iç içe geçmiş hali... Üçü birbirine kenetlenmiş ve bir üçgen oluşturmuş sanki... Şurada taşıyorlar hepsi ... (Sol göğsünü gösteriyor...) Ama görünmüyor.

Bizim anlayacağımız bir sembol var mı?

S. Kosovalı: Dünya'ya hiçbir şekilde bilgi aktarmamışlar... Kapalı... Sadece izliyorlar.

Bunlar idareci varlıklar mı?

S. Kosovalı: Evet... Sanki kendi haline bırakıp ne yöne gideceğimizi görmek istemişler gibi... Sanki burası bir deney laboratuvarı gibi... Ve insanlık kaybetti.

Tekrar bu uzun boylu gence dönelim mi? Ondan nasıl bir enerji alıyorsun?

S. Kosovalı: Kalanları koruma derdinde... Sanki bir miras... Yok edilmemesi gereken... Dünya'da değil bütün kâinatta yok edilmeye karşı bu grup... Bu gemi... Mutlaka devam etmeliler... Soylar yok edilmemeli... Türler yok edilmemeli... Kalan en iyileri koruyup onların tekrar çoğaltılması gerektiğini düşünüyorlar... Türlerin yok edilmesine karşılar... Sorun çıktığında azaltılabilir ama yok edilemez... Puzzle'ı tamamlayanlarız... Bütün varlıklar.

Burayı bitirenler olacak mı? Mezun olanlar?

S. Kosovalı: Çoğu düştü.

Nasıl?

S. Kosovalı: Bir alt tabakaya düştüler... Dünya'nın bir altı... Çıkacaklarını bilenler çok rahat.

O çıkacak olanlara ne olacak?

S. Kosovalı: Kabuk değiştirir gibi... Şekil değişiyor.

Beden mi değişiyor?

S. Kosovalı: Beden değişiyor... Fakat çok minicik bir ışık şeklindeki öz devam ediyor... Yukarıya böyle ağustosböceklerinin ışıkları gibi çekiliyorlar... Şey gibi bu... Bir düğmeye basarsınız hepsi ölür ama onların içinden minik ışıklar yukarıya doğru yükselirler... Görev bitti deyip devam ediyorlar yeni göreve.

Nereye gidecek onlar peki?

S. Kosovalı: Geminin üst tabakası onların hepsini yanlarına alıyor... Aslında hiç kimse buraya (Dünya'ya) gelmek istemiyor... Çok zor bir görev burası... Çok zor bir yer.

Nedir Dünya'nın asıl fonksiyonu?

S. Kosovalı: Burası deney yeri.

Neyin deneyi yapılıyor burada?

S. Kosovalı: Gelişim... Ne kadar gelişilebileceğine bakılıyor... Ama Dünya'dakiler hiç gelişemiyorlar... Tekrar sıfırlanıyor...

Yeniden başlıyorlar... Tekrar sıfırlanıyor... Tekrar başlıyorlar... Büyük bir mücadeleyle başaracaklarına inanıyorlar... Araya kendilerinden görevlileri yerleştiriyorlar... Onlar katkı sağlasın diye... Fakat başaramıyor burası hiç... Hiç başaramıyor... Gelişemiyorlar.

Neden?

S. Kosovalı: Çok alt bir katman... Çok büyük bir kandırmaca var Dünya'da... İnsanlar önce uyandıklarında çok olağanüstü, çok güzel bir yerde olduklarını zannediyorlar... Çok ağır tabakalar var insanlar arasında da... Basamak basamak... Ve altlar hep uyuyor... Hepsi uyuyorlar.

Uyanamayacaklar mı onlar?

S. Kosovalı: Uyanamıyorlar... Uyanamadıkları için izin verilecek sıfırlanmasına... Ve yeniden başlatacaklar.

Ne kadarlık bir kitle uyanabilecek sence?

S. Kosovalı: Şöyle tarif edeyim... Şöyle yuvarlak bir şeyin üzerinde milyonlarca varlık var... Sadece Dünya'nın kalbi gibi bir yerden bir avuç yukarıya çıkacak... Geri kalan hepsi bomboş.

Onu gösteriyorlar mı sana şu an?

S. Kosovalı: Evet.

Anladım. Onlara ne olacak peki? Elenenler.

S. Kosovalı: Çok üzücü... Farkında bile değiller elendiklerinin... Çok ilginçler... Hiç farkında değiller.

Ne yapacak onlar devre kapandığında?

S. Kosovalı: Tamamen yok oluyorlar... Toprakla birleşiyorlar.

Ruhlarını soruyorum.

S. Kosovalı: Bekletiliyor.

Ne için bekletiliyor?

S. Kosovalı: Başarıp başaramayacakları... Tekrar denenip denenmemesi... Dünya üzerinde üçüncü ya da dördüncü deneme... Her seferinde başarısız oluyor... Bu tartışılıyor yukarıda.

O zaman başaramayanlar yeni devrede Dünya'da doğup tekrar mı ediyorlar devreyi?

S. Kosovalı: Bir sonraki devreyle ilgili farklı düşünceleri var... Bu kez müdahale etmeye karar vermişler.

Nasıl bir müdahale?

S. Kosovalı: Zoraki bir uyandırma.

Biraz zorlayacaklar, anladım. Daha büyük yardımlar mı gelecek acaba?

S. Kosovalı: Kontrol artırılacak... Kontrol artırıldıkça, sıkıştırıldıkça uyanacaklar... Fakat bu birkaç sefer devam edecek... Tek seferde değil... Çok uzun bir süreç var.

Dünya'nın sıfırlanması için bir zaman hissiyatın var mı?

S. Kosovalı: İlk göktaşları küçük düşecek... Ardından çok daha büyüğü ve ondan sonra karanlık... Dünya'ya yukarıdan vuruyor... Dünya yerinden oynuyor aşağıya doğru... Büyük bir yalpalama var.

O göktaşlarını buraya yönlendiren güç ne?

S. Kosovalı: Aslında hiçbir şey yok... Düzen... Kendi yolunda ve rotasında olan bir şey var... Rotasına geçecek... Sadece geçerken bizi savuruyor... Bizi savuracağını biliyorlar.

Rotasından geçen ne?

S. Kosovalı: Çok büyük bir medeniyet var orada... Dünya'ya bu taşların düşmesine sebep olacak olan... Çok büyük bir medeniyet burası!

Bir gezegen mi?

S. Kosovalı: Çok farklı... Yakınımızdan geçiyor sanki... Çok farklı!... Tarif edemiyorum... Işığı farklı... Farklı bir madde... Çok farklı... Yaşam çok farklı... Fazlasıyla farklı... Şu an gördüğümü tarif edebileceğim bir kelime yok... Büyük... 7-8 Dünya kadar... Yuvarlak değil... Uzun bir sopaya benzer gibi... Yamuk... Nasıl

anlatayım?... Altı ve üstü yamuk... Uzun... Ağaç dalı gibi düşünün... Eni daha geniş olanı... Farklı bir ışığı var... Farklı bir parlaklığı var... Deniz yok.

Yapay bir şey mi acaba?

S. Kosovalı: Onu çözemiyorum... Metal ağırlıklı... Metalik... Metalin kıvamının farklı olduğu yerleri var... Farklı bir metal bu... Geçtikleri yerleri izleyerek geçiyorlar... Sıfırlanan hiçbir yerden rahatsız değiller... Yeniden başlatma hazırlığı yapıyorlar.

Nasıl başlatacaklar?

S. Kosovalı: Dünya'dalar.

Yeni bedenler mi?

S. Kosovalı: Bedenlere dokunmayacaklar... Aynı form devam edecek... Bu formun Dünya'ya uyumlu olduğunu kabul etmişler...

İlkel bir yaşamdan mı başlayacak Dünya tekrar?

S. Kosovalı: Hayır... Sanki şey yapacaklar... Çocuklar gider bir yere çadır kurarlar... Hemen orada yaşam oluşturulur... Bir şey aktarılacak sanki... Çocuğa öğretir gibi... Çocuklarına öğretir gibi... Teselliyle beraber... Süreci hep biliyorlar... Sürecin hep başlayıp bittiğini biliyorlar.

Ne kadar sürüyor bu devreler? Belli bir süresi var mı?

S. Kosovalı: Bizim için çok uzun... Onlar için değil... Dünya'da bir kıtanın yanında bir kıta yükselecek... Çok dik kayalıklar var... Çok keskin kayalıklar... Burada şekil değişti... Fırtınalar var üzerinde... Değişik... Simsiyah bir kıta... Avustralya kurtuluyor.

Anadolu?

S. Kosovalı: Kurtuluyor... Çok hafif şekil değişiklikleri var.

O zaman Yeni Dünya'yı Anadolu mu kuruyor?

S. Kosovalı: Sanki kalp orada atıyor gibi... Bir kalp atışı var orada... Sanki hasta birisi var da geri dönecek gibi... Kalp atışı var orada... Bir titreşim var.

Buradan Anadolu'nun vazifesine geçelim o zaman. Türkiye'nin vazifesine.

S. Kosovalı: Dünya'nın çekirdeğine doğru üçgenimsi bir şey iniyor... Zemini çok sağlam bir üçgen... Sanki Dünya'nın dengesini de burası sağlıyor gibi... Savrulduğunda rotasına geri çekecek... Gerçekten denge mekanizması burası sanki... Nasıl anlatayım?... Buraya bir şey koymuşlar... Buraya bir müdahale yapılmış... Önceki geçişte yapılmış... Şöyle anlatayım... Kayık fırtınada alabora olduğunda bir şey çakarlar ya... Hani alabora olurken o çakılı yer tutar... Savrulur, savrulur fakat durduğunda çakılı olduğu yer nedeniyle çok gidemez... Savrulamaz... Sanki Türkiye'nin altındaki o sivri, saplantı, üçgen yer Dünya'nın savrulmasını durduran denge gibi... Orada bir denge var... Orada bir şey var... Dengeliyor... O savrulmayı durdurup dengeleyecek nokta orası... Buraya bir müdahale yapılmış... Daha önceki geçişte yapılmış bu... Denge oluşturmuşlar orada.

Bu toprakların ruhsal vazifesi nedir?

S. Kosovalı: Buradakiler zeki... Gemidekiler buraya çok indirilmiş.

Kimler gelmiş mesela?

S. Kosovalı: Şeffaf, ışık bedenliler indirilmiş... Yeşil görünümlüler var... Farklı... İndirilmiş... Hep burada olmuşlar.

Şimdi Türkiye'de yönetimi devralacak gence döner misin?

S. Kosovalı: Çok cesur... Cesur olması kendisinin kim olduğunu hatırlamasından.

Kim o?

S. Kosovalı: Yukarıdan... Işık bedenlilerden birisi... Şu an öfkeli... Fazlasıyla öfkeli.

Nerede şu an?

S. Kosovalı: Türkiye'de değil.

Türkiye dışında bir yerde mi?

S. Kosovalı: Evet.

Nasıl bir yer?

S. Kosovalı: Güneşli bir yer.

Türkiye'ye yakın bir yer mi? Deniz var mı?

S. Kosovalı: Yakın... Sanki geziyor gibi.

Kaç yaşında?

S. Kosovalı: Sanki 19-20... Çok genç... Ayağa kalktığında omuzlarındaki yük nedeniyle omuzları öne eğilmiş... Şu an 40'lı yaşlarında görüyorum... Fakat insanlar hiç itiraz etmiyorlar... "Evet bu... Bu görevliydi" diyorlar... Farkındalar... Konuşmuyorlar... Telaffuz edilmiyor bu... Herkes çok kabul etmiş onun liderliğini.

Gözleri ne renk?

S. Kosovalı: Koyu.

Saçları?

S. Kosovalı: Dalgalanıyor böyle... Yumuşak... Enerjisi genç... Sanki talimat veriyor.

Hep yukarıda mı yetiştirmişler?

S. Kosovalı: Dünya'da.

Dünya'da kim yetiştirmiş?

S. Kosovalı: Gelmişler sürekli... Sürekli gelmişler.

Devam.

S. Kosovalı: Büyüdüğü süreçte hep yanında olmuşlar... Fakat çok ortaya çıkmasını istemiyorlar... Hatta nasıl söyleyeyim?... Bu da olmazsa, yani onunla da başarılamazsa Dünya'yı komple bile sıfırlayabilirler... Bu genç son bir şans gibi... Dünya için son şans... İnsanlar bunu değerlendirecek mi, değerlendiremeyecek mi?... Bunu görmek istiyorlar... Birçok kişi aslında süreci biliyor da... Nasıl söyleyeyim?... O genç ortaya çıktığı zaman, harekete geçtiği zaman etrafındaki her insan "Aslında biz bu kişinin

o olabileceğini biliyorduk" diyecekler... Ama şu an bilinmemesi gerekiyor... Çocukta öyle bir enerji var ki, otomatikman biat ediyorsunuz... Son derece modern bir aileden çıkacak ama Anadolu kültürüyle yetişmiş... Şu anki halini bile görseniz, "Evet, eğer biri olacaksa bu olmalı" dersiniz... Bütün yaşıtlarının çok üzerinde, çok donanımlı ama farkında değil... Sınavları hızlandırılmış... Şu an çok hızlı sınavlardan geçiriliyor... Yaşıtlarının çok üzerinde şeyler yaşıyor şu an... Güçlü bir karakter.

Bir şey yazıyor... Kurallar kitabı gibi bir şey yazıyor... Anayasa kitabı gibi... Sanki geçişten sonra insanlığın bir arada yaşamasının kurallarını aktarıyor gibi... Hani "Bunu uygulamak zorundasınız... Bunu uygularsanız devam edebilirsiniz... Uygulamazsanız her şey sonlanıyor" gibi bir şey hazırlıyor... İnsanlar içten içe onda Dünya dışı bir etki olduğunun farkındalar ama bunu telaffuz edemiyorlar...

Siz de şahit tutulacaksınız onun gelişine... Şey hazırlığı yaptırıyorlar size... Bunlar okunacak ve o kişi geldiğinde kabulü daha kolay sağlanacak... Göreviniz bu... Daha kolay kabul edilebilmesi için bir hazırlık yapılıyor.

Anladım. Peki vücudunda belli bir iz ya da işaret var mı?

S. Kosovalı: (O an S. Kosovalı'ya bize hitaben bir mesaj ulaşıyor. Bir başka varlığın mesajını iletmeye başlıyor ve sesi değişiyor...) "Bunu karıştırmayın... Vakti geldiğinde seyredeceksiniz!"

Peki. Seyredeceğiz. Tamam.

S. Kosovalı: "Onu korumak zorundayız... Sizin iyiliğiniz için..."

O yüzden mi onunla ilgili farklı tanımlar ve farklı fiziksel tarifler geliyor?

S. Kosovalı: Evet.

Onun vazifesi ne zaman başlayacak?

S. Kosovalı: "Vaktimiz var... Sizin kaderiniz ona bağlı... Herkes onu arıyor."

Biz de onu korumaya çalışıyoruz ama insanların bilgilendirilme zamanı geldi.

S. Kosovalı: "Vakit geldiğinde o çocuğun aslında nasıl yetiştirildiğini hepiniz anlayacaksınız!... Sizler şu an şahit tutuluyorsunuz... O çocuğun kim olduğunu vakit geldiğinde siz de açıklayacaksınız... Evet... Çok yakınınızda ama bir o kadar da uzağınızda... Bu bir oyun değil... Çıkış noktanız!"

Şu an kiminle konuşuyoruz?

S. Kosovalı: "Sizin anlayabileceğiniz bir ismimiz yok... Rakamlar... Rakamları birleştirebilirseniz ismimize ulaşırsınız... Dünya'yı sadece bu sınavı geçmeleri için uyandırın... Geçemeyenler için hiçbir şey yapamayız... Ruhların tekâmülünde bütüne ulaşmak için hepinizin geçmesi lazım... Geri kalanlar yüzünden biz de ilerleyemiyoruz... Gerçekten geri kalıyorsunuz... Sabrımızı çok zorluyorsunuz... Yardım kabul etmiyorsunuz... Artık uyanın!... İçinizde gözcülerimiz var... Bizim için Dünya'ya inip çıkmak çok yorucu... Vakit kaybetmek!... Buna vaktimiz yok... Gözcülerden bilgileri alıyoruz... İyiye gitmiyorsunuz... Sürekli geriliyorsunuz... Gözcülerimiz çok yoruldu... Hepsi geri gelmek istiyor... Tutunamıyorlar Dünya'da... Nasıl böyle bir dünya yarattınız kendinize!... Oysa bütün yolları gösterdik... Daha iyi olmanız için her türlü desteği verdik... Sürekli veriyoruz... Sürekli veriyoruz... Ve biz verdikçe geri gidiyorsunuz... Sürekli geri gidiyorsunuz... Neden ilerleyemediğinizi anlamıyoruz... Sizi ne geriye çekiyor?... Bir şeyler var... Onu çözmeye çalışıyoruz... Hep izledik... Sadece Dünya yok... Başka yerler de var... Hepinizin kontrolünü sağlıyoruz... Fakat Dünya bir türlü ilerleyemiyor... Diğerleri aydınlıktalar... Dünya çıkamıyor!"

Dünya benzeri başka okullar var mı bu boyutta?

S. Kosovalı: Var.

Onlar başardılar mı?

(Yanıt gelmiyor.)

Bize iletmek istediğiniz bir mesajınız var mı?

S. Kosovalı: "Çocukları koruyun!... Çocuklar geleceğiniz... Enseden yaklaşan karanlık bir şey... Hepinizi esir aldı hastalık... Hastalık gibi bir şey... Bir duygu durumu."

Melezlerle ilgili çalışmalar?

S. Kosovalı: "Dünya üzerine birkaç tane ırk bırakıldı... Hepsi kendi ırklarının gelişimini görmek istedi... Bir iki ırk başardı... Gelişimini tamamladı... Dünya'nın üst tarafına doğru... Soğuk bölgede olanlar kısmen başardı... Sıcak bölgede olanlar başaramadı... Bozuldu... İnsanlar bozuldu... Bir hastalık giriyor... Sanki bedenleriyle birlikte, düşüncelerini, algılarını, her şeylerini kaybettiler... Ve bunlar Dünya'ya bir virüs gibi saldırıyorlar... Gittikleri yeri kendi karanlıklarına çekiyorlar... O yüzden Dünya'nın kurtarılıp kurtarılmamasına karar vermeye çalışıyoruz."

Ama net bir karar verilmedi. Bu değişebilir mi?

S. Kosovalı: "Bir bölge gidecek... Sadece olması gerektiği için... Koruyucu perdelerimizi korunması gerekenlerin üzerine koyacağız... Siz göremeyeceksiniz... Koyarsak diğer tarafları kurtarabiliriz... Sizin anlayamayacağınız bir fanus... Sizin anlayamayacağınız bir kalkan olacak... Buna karar vermedik."

Yani tekâmülde ilerlemiş olanları mı koruyacaksınız?

S. Kosovalı: "Evet."

Ve biz bunu anlayamayacağız.

S. Kosovalı: "Evet çünkü izin yok... Sizler anlarsanız kurallar bozulur."

Onlar Yeni Dünya'ya mı alınacak? Başka bir plan mı var?

S. Kosovalı: "Sizin anlayacağınız dilde ışınlanma diye tarif edeyim... Yani ışığınızı buradan alacağız, buraya koyacağız... Siz onu anlayamazsınız."

Başka bir boyut mu? Anlayacağımız şekilde anlatır mısınız?

S. Kosovalı: "S. Kosovalı'yı nasıl aldık biliyor musunuz?... Yatağında yatıyordu... Onu yatak odasının perdesinin içinden geçirerek aldık."

Bunu nasıl yapıyorsunuz?

S. Kosovalı: "Bunu size nasıl anlatabiliriz?... Milyonda bire kadar küçültüp alırız... Siz göremezsiniz... Size nasıl müdahale ediyoruz biliyor musunuz?... Geliyoruz... Geçici bir süre zihninize yerleşiyoruz... Virajdan geçiriyoruz... Sonra tekrar sizi bırakıyoruz... Siz devam ediyorsunuz."

Kimleri alıyorsunuz?

S. Kosovalı: "Hazır olanları."

Fizik bedenleriyle mi alıyorsunuz hepsini?

S. Kosovalı: "Hayır... Işıklarıyla."

Işık?

S. Kosovalı: "Bu büyüklükteki bir insan küçülüyor... Ve ruh ışığını alıp devam edebiliyor... Burada istediği formu alabiliyor."

Geminin içinde titreşimsel olarak daha hızlı bir boyut mu var?

S. Kosovalı: "Evet... Çok hızlı."

İnsanlar orada nasıl bulunabiliyorlar?

S. Kosovalı: "Fizik beden alınırsa koruyucu bir alan içinde tutuyoruz."

Evet.

S. Kosovalı: "Bazen müdahale ettiklerimiz var... Sorduğunuz o gence bu şekilde müdahale edildi."

Genetiği mi değiştirildi?

S. Kosovalı: "Evet."

Yani o bir melez diyebilir miyiz?

S. Kosovalı: "Bizden."

Ya Atatürk?

S. Kosovalı: "Bizden."

İnsanlardan sperm veya yumurta neden alıyorsunuz?

S. Kosovalı: "Bizim sperm veya yumurtaya ihtiyacımız yok."

Peki bunu yapanlar kim?

S. Kosovalı: "Sizi deneye tabi tutanlar var... Kendi soylarını kontrole gelenler var... Burada çoğalmak isteyenler var... Kendi türlerini melezleştirmek isteyenler var... Onları bir süre izliyoruz."

Onlara izin veriliyor mu?

S. Kosovalı: "Bir süre... Ne yapmak istediklerini çözdüğümüzde müdahale başlıyor."

Yani olumsuz bir niyete müsaade edilmiyor.

S. Kosovalı: "Asla... Ancak hiçbir türün gelişimi durdurulamaz."

Onun için izin veriliyor ama bunu kötüye kullananlar olursa müdahale ediliyor. Böyle mi anlamalıyız?

S. Kosovalı: "Kesinlikle... Hiçbir tür asla yok edilemez."

Bir yardımlaşma var.

S. Kosovalı: "Evet... Seviyeler var... Katman katman düşünün... Dünya'nın pozisyonu -sizin anlayacağınız tabirle- ortada... Onun altında da var.

Dünya'dan daha altta neler var?

S. Kosovalı: "Daha karanlık... Daha ilkel... Daha zor... Orayı görseniz zaten gelişmek için yukarı çıkmak isterdiniz... Buraya gelen türler en vahşi, en ilkel türler... Onlara da müdahale ediliyor... Fakat orası da olması gerekli... Dünyanız ortada... Dünyanız ortada olduğu için laboratuvar görevi görüyor... Çok fazla deneye maruz kalıyorsunuz... Düşecek mi, çıkacak mı?...

Bazen alt tabakada varlıkların sayısı azalıyor... Dünya'dan oraya gönderilenler oluyor... Dünya'ya gelenlerin bir kısmı başaramayıp tekrar iniyor... Bazıları özellikle başarsın diye Dünya'ya konuluyor... Fakat Dünya'ya çok kötü bir etki bıraktıkları görülünce tekrar eski yerlerine gönderiliyorlar... Burası ortada bir durak."

Dünya'ya gelenlerin çoğunluğunu kimler oluşturuyor? Alt katmanlardan gelenler mi? Beşer-altı seviye mi?

S. Kosovalı: Bütün gezegenlerin yok olma ihtimalleri var... Yok olma ihtimallerini bildikleri için kendi türlerini birçok tabakaya serpiştiriyorlar ki, burası yok olursa türleri yok olmasın diye... Fakat sizin dünyanızda birkaç tür var... Melezler... Alttan gelenler... Üstten gelenler... Burası karışık."

Onun için bu kadar zor bir okul.

S. Kosovalı: "Evet... Alttan gelenler çok fazla bozuyor fakat biz burada üstten gelenlerin neden bozulduğunu anlamaya çalıştık."

Üstten gelenler de burada dejenerasyona mı uğruyor?

S. Kosovalı: "Evet... Bir kısmı kaybetti... Birçok zekiler kaybettiklerinde çok daha tehlikeli olabiliyorlar... Çok daha fazla bilgiye sahip oldukları için... Size nasıl anlatayım?... Kırmızı Taraf-Beyaz Taraf diye anlatayım... Kırmızı Taraf çoğalırsa Beyaz Taraf yok olur... O zaman her şey kontrolden çıkar... O yüzden Beyaz Taraf'ın daha çok olmasını sağlamak zorundayız... Lideri soruyorsunuz... Onlar da soruyor... Öğrenirlerse sisteme müdahale ederler... Bizim için her şey çok zor olur."

Negatif tesirlere hizmet edenler?

S. Kosovalı: "Siz negatif diyorsunuz... Biz kendilerine hizmet edenler diyoruz... Vahşileşiyorlar... Vahşiliğin verdiği bir haz var... O haz onları çok mutlu ediyor... Geçici bir hastalık gibi değerlendirin... Buna müsaade etmiyoruz."

Griler?

S. Kosovalı: "Griler öğrendiler... Başarmaları gerektiğini... Yükselmeleri gerektiğini... Öğrendiler... Sonra sınavdan geçtiler... Çok sorun çıkarmıyorlar artık... Onlarla çok uğraşmıyoruz."

Neden onları temas vakalarında daha çok görüyoruz?

S. Kosovalı: "Kendilerini çoğaltmak istediler... Büyük bir güç olmak için... Büyük bir güç olduğunuzda tehlike de o kadar büyür... Bunu fark ettiler."

Son olarak söylemek istediğiniz bir şey var mı?

S. Kosovalı: "Dünya yaşaması gereken süreçten kurtulamayacak... O süreci mutlaka yaşaması gerekecek."

Tekâmülü için mi?

S. Kosovalı: "Evet... Bu sizin anlayacağınız şekilde mekanik, olması gereken bir şey... Rota... Rota bu şekilde... Çünkü rotadan saptırırsak diğerleri zarar görür... Destek gelecek... Buradayız ama bu bizim için de bir avantaj... Yeniden başlatırız ve insanların gelişimini yeniden seyrederiz."

(Bağlantı sona eriyor ve seansı bitiriyoruz.)

14. BÖLÜM

DOĞU

38 yaşındaki deneyimli reklamcı Emine B. çocukluk yıllarında başlayan ve sonraları artık iyice kabullenip yaşamına entegre ettiği sıra dışı deneyimler yaşıyordu. Farklı enerjilerdeki varlıklar Emine'yi çocukluk çağlarından itibaren ziyaret ediyorlardı.

Yedi yıl önce açık rüyalar görmeye başlamıştı. Aynı dönemde istem dışı astral çıkışları oluyor, etrafında varlıklar hissediyordu. Ayrıca, insanlarla, hayvanlarla, bitkilerle, doğayla ve herhangi bir enerjetik varlıkla güçlü bir empati ve iletişim kurabiliyor, dillerini zaman zaman algılayabiliyordu.

Götürüldüğü ameliyathane benzeri ortamları hatırlıyor, farklı formlarda varlıklarla temas kuruyordu.

Emine'nin, kendisini hiç yanıltmayan, gelişkin bir duru görü yeteneği de vardı. Kitlesel kayıplara yol açan büyük olayları da önceden sezinliyor, ardından o olaylarda yaşamlarını yitirenlerle iletişime giriyordu.

Emine B. seansında yeni çocuklar konusu hayli ağırlıktaydı.

Ancak bu ışıl ışıl çocuklar yine Atatürk ve yeni lider konusuyla bağlantılı şekilde karşımızdaydı...

Emine B. Seansı

11 Temmuz 2023

(Nefes, gevşeme ve enerji çalışması.)

Nasıl hissediyorsun Emine? Aynı zamanda uyumlanma ve şifa da oluyor.

Emine B.: Çok iyi.

Tamam.

Emine B.: Görüntü var.

Ne geliyor gözünün önüne?

Emine B.: Yılan.

Devam et.

Emine B.: Çok büyük yılanlar... İletişim kurabilen yılanlar... Kafaları daha öncekiler gibi değil... Uzun... İnsan boyutlarında... Asker olabilirler.

İki ayak üzerinde mi duruyorlar?

Emine B.: Evet.

Yüzleri nasıl?

Emine B.: Yüzleri yılan.

Gözleri?

Emine B.: İnsan gözü gibi.

Nasıl bir his alıyorsun onlardan?

Emine B.: Çok iyi değil... Negatife yakın... İlk defa görüyorum bu türü.

Kim bunlar? Ne yapmaya çalışıyorlar? Fonksiyonları ne?

(Bir süre sessizlik.)

Onların gözünden Dünya'ya bakar mısın? Ne görüyorsun?

Emine B.: Patlamalar var.

Nerelerde? Dünya'ya yukarıdan bakmanı istiyorum şimdi.

Emine B.: Birçok yerde ama kutuplarda da var.

Nasıl bir patlama? Sebebi ne?

Emine B.: Atom bombası gibi... Turuncu bulutlar... Çok büyük patlamalar.

Kuzey Kutbu'nda mı yoksa Güney Kutbu'nda mı?

Emine B.: Kuzeyde.

Bunun sebebi ne olabilir? Emin misin nükleer patlama olduğundan?

Emine B.: Daha önceden yerleştirilen bir şeyler.

Neden oralarda patlıyor?

Emine B.: Sanki Dünya'daki yöneticilerle bir bağlantıları var gibi.

Ne var orada?

Emine B.: Hiçbir şey yok Kuzey Kutbu'nda... Bomboş... Beyazlığın ortasında sadece çok büyük patlamalar görüyorum ve dışarıdan atılan bir şey değil... İçeriden patlayan bir şey... Volkanik patlamalar gibi.

Başka yerde var mı volkanik patlama?

Emine B.: Var... Yukarıdan baktığımda sol ortalara doğru... Ekvator... Tam lokasyon, ülke bilmiyorum ama merkez noktalarında patlamalar var.

Bu esnada Türkiye ne durumda?

Emine B.: Karışıklık var sadece... Bizde patlama yok... Karışıklık var... İnsanlar savruluyorlar... Yani bir oraya bir buraya... Ne yapacağını bilmeden koşan insanlar.

Neden savruluyor insanlar?

Emine B.: Fiziki bir savrulmadan ziyade mental, zihinsel bir savrulma... Sanki merkez noktalarındaki patlamalar dünya düzenini etkiliyor... Biz de etkilenenlerdeniz ama bizde patlama yok.

Kaygı ve şaşkınlık mı var?

Emine B.: Evet... Kaygı... Ne yapacağını bilememe... Savunma... Birbirlerini kucaklama... Saklamaya çalışma... Çocuklar korunmaya çalışılıyor... Anneler çocuklarını korumaya çalışıyor.

Zaman hissiyatın var mı? Kısa, orta, uzun vade şeklinde?

Emine B.: Kırsal kesimlerde görüyorum çocukları... Zaman olarak yakın değil bence... Daha doğu tarafında... O taraf çok

karışık... Olduğu gibi Türkiye'nin yarısı... Doğu... Hep çocuklar korunmaya çalışılıyor.

Neler olmuş Türkiye'de peki?

Emine B.: Tam ortadan ikiye bölünmüş gibi... Sağ ve sol... Tam ortadan... Sağ taraf... Doğu tarafı çok karışık... Sol tarafta hiçbir şey yok gibi... Kaçanlar var ama çok az... Çok zor kaçmak... Zaten sağ yarım bölgede oluyor ne oluyorsa... Solda hiçbir şey yok.

Sebep ne?

Emine B.: Yeraltıyla alakalı bir şey... Bir kaynak... Galiba topluyorlar... Nerede ne kaynak varsa onu toplamaya gelecekler gibi... Kendilerinin ihtiyacı olan bir enerji kaynağı olabilir... Hayatta kalmaları için ihtiyaçları olan bir şey... Çok göz var çünkü... Ve beklemişler olgunlaşmasını... Çok veri toplamışlar.

Yakın gelecekte ne görüyorsun Türkiye'de?

Emine B.: Birkaç sene bir şey görmüyorum... Her şey olduğu gibi devam edecek gibi görünüyor... Ama birkaç sene sonra bir karışıklık var... Sonra bir müdahale görüyorum... İstanbul'a bir müdahale gelecek... Türkiye çok büyük bir çıkmaza giriyor ve İstanbul'a müdahale ettiriliyor... Ama bu doğa olayı olmayacak... Öyle gibi görünecek... Çok fazla altın görüyorum... Altın küreler... İstanbul'da... Yani bu altın kürelerin peşinde de olabilir müdahale edenler... Dünya'dan veya Dünya dışından... Zaten hepsi aynı... İhtiyaçları var.

Değişim görüyor musun?

Emine B.: Görüyorum.

Nasıl bir değişim?

Emine B.: Çok güzel... Herkes mutlu... Çok paraları yok ama mutlular... Sanki 1970'ler, 60'lar gibi... Bakkala ekmek almaya giden çocuklar... Bakkallar var... Mutlular... Selamlaşıyorlar... Sokakta top oynayan çocuklar var... Mutlular... Yokluk var ama mutlular.

Nasıl olmuş bu?

Emine B.: Bir şey değişmiş gibi... Bir şey başa dönmüş gibi.

Orada kal ve nasıl olduğunu gör şimdi.

Emine B.: Birisi öldürülüyor.

Kim?

Emine B.: Bir siyasi lider... Ondan sonra karışıyor... Ondan sonrası güzel... Birbirlerine giriyorlar... Sonra başa dönüyor her şey ve güzel oluyor... Çok para yok... Altınlar da yok... Ama mutlu insanlar var... Huzurlu insanlar var.

Devam.

Emine B.: Şişman bir adam görüyorum... O da çok iyi biri değil ama her şey daha iyi... Ama çok büyük bir yıkım var... Bunların hepsi ondan sonra olmaya başlayacak.

Nasıl bir yıkım bu?

Emine B.: Çok mu abartıyorum acaba?... Önce füze gibi bir şey İstanbul'a... Sonra bir deprem... Ama aslında deprem değil o... Doğal afet diyecekler... Değil.

Yapay bir şey mi?

Emine B.: Yapay... İstanbul'da evet... Çok büyük... Büyük kulelere... Denizaşırı gelen bir füze.

Türkiye'ye bir saldırı mı var?

Emine B.: Bir füze var... Doğuya değil... Büyük kulelere füze... Sonra karışıyor.

İstanbul'daki kulelere mi?

Emine B.: Evet... Amerika'daki ikiz kuleler gibi bunlar... Ama İstanbul... Mermi gibi büyük bir füze geliyor denizaşırı... Karadeniz üzerinden... Ondan sonra yönetim sarsılmaya başlıyor... Sonra sarsıntı, deprem... Adı neyse... Doğal afet diyecekler... Denizden gelen bir tehlike görmüyorum... Denizin üzerinden ve altından gelen bir tehlike var... Ama deniz taşmıyor.

Türkiye çıkacak mı bu süreçten?

Emine B.: Evet ama çok fakir çıkacak... Daha huzurlu ama parası olmayan insanlar... Değeri olmayan bir şehir... Doğu daha değerli... Doğudaki çocuklar çok değerli... Bilmiyorum... Buradaki çocuklar çok değerli... Anneleri çok üzgün... Çok yorgun... Çok akıllılar... Çok yetenekliler... Alıp götürmek isteyecekleri kadar yetenekliler.

Yeni çocuklar mı bunlar?

Emine B.: Evet... Yeni çocuklar doğuyor... Uzun bir süreç bu.

Neden o bölgeye doğuyor o çocuklar?

Emine B.: Çaresizlik var çünkü.

Bir yardım gibi mi?

Emine B.: Evet... Çaresizlik var... Çözüm gerekiyor... Batılı çözüm bulamaz... İmkân var çünkü... O çocuklar bulacak... İmkânsızlık içinde çözümler bulacaklar... Ama götürmek isteyecekler o çocukları.

Nerede yetiştirilmişler?

Emine B.: Bilerek geliyorlar... Her şeyi biliyorlar... Her şeyi biliyorlar... Çok iyi niyetliler... Çok yetenekliler... Her şeyi biliyorlar... Topraktan çıkıyor gibiler... O toprakları biliyorlar... Anneler bunun farkında... Vermek istemiyorlar çocukları.

Dünya dışı bağlantıları var mı bu çocukların?

Emine B.: Var... Ve engel olabilirler.

Doğuda bilinç yükselmesi için sanki...

Emine B.: Aşılanmış gibiler... Toprağa ekilmiş gibiler... Çok acayip... Çok güçlüler ayrıca!... Ordu gibiler!... Küçük küçük ordular gibiler... Bu çocuklar çok acayip!... Her şeye karşı koyacak güçleri var.

Nedir asıl misyonları?

Emine B.: Doğuyu kurtarmak... Batı bitecek çünkü... Batıyı da onlar savunacak... Ankara olduğu gibi duruyor... Karmaşalarda Ankara'ya hiçbir şey olmayacak.

Ankara'ya odaklanır mısın?

Emine B.: Yeni bir bayrak var orada... Kıpkırmızı üçgen bir bayrak... Dalgalanıyor.

Neyi sembolize ediyor?

Emine B.: Meclis duruyor... Anıtkabir duruyor... Atakule duruyor... Atatürk duruyor... (Ağlıyor.)

Orada kal. Ne görüyorsun şu anda?

Emine B.: (Ağlayarak...) Atatürk!... Kalkmaya çalışıyor!... Tertemiz ışık saçıyor!... Çok güzel görünüyor!...

Gözlerine bak. Atatürk'te kal.

Emine B.: Saldırılar var... Her şeyi göğüslüyor ve gülümsüyor... Görev veriyor!

Ne görevi veriyor?

Emine B.: Çocuklarla ilgili görev veriyor... Çocuklardan birkaçını almak istiyorum ben... Doğudaki çocuklar.

Ne olacak?

Emine B.: Hiç kolay olmayacak... Çocuklar bizim için geldi... O çocukları almamız lazım... Öğreneceğimiz şeyler var o çocuklardan... O çocukları korumamız lazım... Onlar da bizi koruyacak... Büyütmemiz lazım... Yetiştirmemiz lazım... Hiç kolay olmayacak ama güzel olacak.

Nasıl?

Emine B.: Fiziki savaşa karşı bilinç yükseltmemiz lazım... Çünkü bir yerde kaynaklar tükenecek... Bu çocukları yetiştirmek lazım... Çocuklara sahip çıkılması lazım... Koruyucu ailelik yapılması lazım... Nerede olurlarsa olsunlar bu çocukların alınıp büyütülmesi, eğitilmesi, hazırlanması lazım... Çünkü savaş bittiğinde o çocukların zekâsına ihtiyacımız olacak... Aynı Atatürk'ün yaptığı gibi.

Savaş bittikten sonra ne olacak Türkiye'de Emine?

Emine B.: İşte o zaman başa dönüyor... İşte o zaman kaynaklar tükeniyor... Daha fazla fiziki saldırı olmuyor... Çünkü olamıyor... Kaynak yok.

Sonra?

Emine B.: Yeni biri...

Nasıl biri?

Emine B.: Daha genç... Fiziki olarak iyi... Fit... Mavi gözlü, kumral, uzun saçları var... Uzun elleri ve ayakları var.

Enerjisi nasıl?

Emine B.: Tertemiz.

Kaç yaşında tahminen?

Emine B.: 50'nin üzerinde değil... 40'larında... Çok özel biri... Temiz bir enerjisi var... Ama yeterli mi onu bilemiyorum.

Nasıl özel? Ne anlamda?

Emine B.: Şu an eğitiliyor gibi zaten... Bir süredir eğitiliyor, öğretiliyor.

Kim eğitiyor?

Emine B.: Birçok yerden alıyor eğitimi... Kendi çevresinden alıyor... Ailesinden bile eğitim alıyor... Dünya dışından da eğitiliyor... Özel biri.

Etrafında birileri var mı?

Emine B.: Yalnız... Yalnız bir karakter.

Türkiye'de mi şu anda?

Emine B.: Evet.

Ne hissediyorsun?

Emine B.: Atatürk geliyor gözümün önüne... Gülümsüyor... Çok güzel ışık saçıyor... Mavi beyaz ışık saçıyor... Kadının da mavi ışığı var.

Kadın mı bu kişi?

Emine B.: Evet.

Emin misin?

Emine B.: Hayır... İlkönce erkek diyecektim... Sonradan kadın hissi geldi.

Nasıl bir enerjisi var?

Emine B.: Atatürk'ün soyundan.

Vazifesi ne?

Emine B.: Geçiş dönemini iyi yönetmek... Hafifletmek... Sanki o kurtuluş denen şey bir yöneticinin eşliğinde olmayacak... Biz yapacağız onu... O çocuklar yapacak... Biri gelip Atatürk'ün yaptığı gibi bizi kurtarmayacak... Çocuklar yapacak... O çocukları sahiplenecek, alıp yetiştirecek çok insan var... Bu çocuklar sanki Atatürk'ün soyundan gibi... Bu geçiş sürecini yönetecek olan karakter de onun soyundan... Birbiriyle bağlantılılar.

Tanınıyor mu o kişi?

Emine B.: Yok... Henüz tanımıyorlar... Bence o da henüz farkında değil.

Sonra Türkiye'nin bir vazifesi olacak mı?

Emine B.: Bu çocukların bir misyonu var... Vazifesi var... Sanki doğu tarafı yönetecek ve yön verecek gibi... Dünya dışı temaslarda da doğu tarafının rolü olacak.

O kişide bir işaret görüyor musun?

Emine B.: Yıldız.

Tamam.

Emine B.: Gücünü enerjisinden alıyor... Ruhen güçlü bir varlık... Çok güçlü bir sağaltım yeteneği var.

Şifa.

Emine B.: Evet... Şifa... Arabulucu gibi aynı zamanda.

Herkese eşit mesafede gibi.

Emine B.: Evet.

Dünya'yla ilgili vazifesi var mı?

Emine B.: O geçiş dönemini hafifletecek... Aradaki iletişimi, bağlantıları sağlayacak... Yani bence bir yöneticiden çok, aradaki o iletişimi sağaltacak, şifalandıracak, negatif enerjileri temizleyecek, iyileştirecek birisi gibi... Dengeye getirecek gibi... Daha hafif atlatalım diye... (Bir anda duruyor...) Yine Atatürk geldi!... Hep gülümsüyor!... Çok iyi görünüyor!

Dinle bakalım onu. Kalbinle dinle.

Emine B.: Korkmayın diyor.

Devam.

Emine B.: Bu geçici bir süreç... Korkmayın... Sizde bunu yapacak güç var, korkmayın diyor... Ben buradayım, hiçbir yere gitmiyorum diyor... Başarırsınız diyor... Ben sizi bugünler için yetiştirdim diyor... Çocuklara iyi bakın diyor.

Çocuklar Atatürk'ü neden rüyalarında görüyorlar?

Emine B.: Eğitiyor... Konuşuyor... Güç veriyor.

Evet.

Emine B.: Hatay...

Orayı mı gösteriyor?

Emine B.: Evet... Hatay'da atıyor Türkiye'nin kalbi gibi... Toprağın kalbi atıyor... Orası çok önemli... Orada sanki bütün Dünya'ya yarayacak bir şey var... Yeni bir enerji kaynağı sanki... Daha önce oraya yerleştirilen bir şey değil... Yeni keşfedilecek bir şey gibi... Dış dünyadaki varlıkların da bir kısmının gözü orada... Orası önemli... Orada bir şey var... Sanki Dünya'nın devamlılığını sağlayacak yeni bir maden gibi bir şey... Dünya için daha az zararlı, daha ekolojik bir şey gibi... Ama altınlar da var... Değerli şeyler de var... Henüz çıkmamış... Hâlâ orada... Çok büyük bir bölge... Yani koca bir bölgeyi kazsalar... Orada.

Sana şimdi soru sormayacağım. Gelen vizyonları aktar.

Emine B.: Başından beri gözümün önüne gelen bir kapı var... Bir kardeşlik kapısı gibi... Dünya dışı... Dünya içi... Kötü değil...

Güvenli bir yer... Dünya'nın merkezine giden bir kapı... Dünya dışı ırklar.

Dünya içindeki varlık sistemlerine mi ulaşıyor o kapı acaba?

Emine B.: Evet... Onlar zaten... Dünya'nın içindeki kardeşlerimiz gibi onlar... Henüz fark edilmemişler... Güvendeler o yüzden... Dünya'nın içindeler ama tertemizler... Parlaklar... Genel olarak da kadınlar ve kız çocukları... Ben gemiye de alındım ama bunları ilk defa görüyorum... Gemidekiler başka... Onlar deney yapıyorlar... Çok uzun boylular... Çok büyük kafalılar... Eller ve ayaklar çok uzun... Babam da görmüştü.

Senden yumurta alındı mı Emine?

Emine B.: Beni iyileştirdiklerini biliyorum... Daha uzun yaşamamı istiyorlar... Bazı şeyleri iyileştirdiler bende... Biliyorum... Çünkü doktora gittiğimde onlar da şaşırmışlardı... Kanımın değiştirildiğini biliyorum... Doktorlar çok şaşırmıştı.

Neden sen?

Emine B.: (Biraz duruyor...) Benden çocuk mu yapıyor bunlar!

Görüyor musun?

Emine B.: Yani o anı görmüyorum ama çocuklarım varmış gibi hissediyorum... Beş altı tane... Ameliyathaneye giriş anımı hatırlıyorum... Ameliyathanede yan yana yatan ve derisi kaldırılmış insanlar hatırlıyorum... Bütün derileri kaldırılmıştı... Tutturulmuştu.

Ne yapıyorlardı?

Emine B.: İnceliyorlar... İnsan vücudunu inceliyorlar... O görüntüyü gördükten sonrasını hatırlamıyorum zaten... Bileğimde bir iz var... Sol bileğimde... Ne zaman gidip dönsem leke oluyor parmaklarımda... Avucumun içinde leke görüyorum... Kına lekesi gibi... Elim yanıyor çünkü.

Nasıl oluşuyor o leke? Gör onu.

Emine B.: Elim yanıyor... Alet gibi bir şeylere dokunduğum için... Bir şeyden kurtulmaya çalışıyormuşum gibi.

Nasıl bir alet bu?

Emine B.: Bir şey enjekte ediyorlar... Onu çıkarmaya çalışıyormuşum gibi... Sanki derinin altına, damar yoluna bir şey enjekte ediyorlar... Kelebek gibi... Ben de onu tutup çıkarmaya çalışıyormuşum... Sıcak değil... Sıcak değil ama vücudumla uyumlu değil... Dokunduğumda yakıyor... Deriyi yakıyor ama ısısı yok... İki üç gün kalıyor o iz sadece.

Bir enerji.

Emine B.: Evet... Galiba bütün kanımı... Çok abartılı ama...

Devam et.

Emine B.: Bütün kanımı değiştirdiler galiba onunla!

Kanında problem var mıydı daha önce?

Emine B.: Daha önce problem yoktu kanımda... Kanımı değiştirmeden önce apandisit ameliyatı oldum... "0 Rh Negatif" idi kanım... Sonra, çok yoğun iletişimde olduğum dönemde bir gün uyandım... Yemyeşil oldum... Annem de gördü... Başım döndü... Anne ben iyi değilim dedim... Onlar da paniklediler benim sarı-yeşil halimi görünce... Sonra kan testi yaptırmaya gittiğimde kanım "B Rh Pozitif" olmuştum... Defalarca test yaptırdım... Hepsi "B Rh Pozitif" gösteriyordu... Babamın kanıydım... Şimdi annemin kanıyım... Babamı da alıp götürüyorlardı.

Varlıklara nasıl bir katkın var senin? Nasıl bir proje?

Emine B.: Üreme... Üreme bakımından... Annem ve anne tarafım bu açıdan çok müsait... Teyzem 60 yaşında doğum yaptı... Baba tarafında bütün kadınların yumurtalıklarında hep hasar var... Ama anne tarafı üremeye fazla müsait.

(Bazı kişiye özel paylaşımların ardından seansı sona erdiriyoruz.)

15. BÖLÜM

TÜRKİYE

Özel bir şirkette yönetici asistanlığı yapan, 46 yaşındaki Seda D.'nin yaşamında her şey daha üç yaşındayken başladı.

Seda yaşadıklarını şöyle anlattı:

"Annem bir gece yarısı benim çığlığımla uyanmış... Odaya girdiğinde burnumdan kan geliyormuş ve sadece 'Korkuyorum... Korkuyorum!' diye sayıklıyormuşum... O an annemi babamı tanımamışım... Boş gözlerle bakıyormuşum... Beni gece yarısı acile götürmüşler... Doktorun söylediği tek şey 'Siz bu çocuğa ne yaptınız? Büyük bir şok geçiriyor!' olmuş... O yaşta bana rüya görmemem için ilaçlar verilmiş.

6-7 yaşlarındayken evde görünmeyen arkadaşlarım vardı... Sürekli gökyüzünü izlerdim... Sabah akşam hep camın önündeydim... Evin dışında mavi-beyaz ışıklar görürdüm... Hatta evin içine de girerlerdi.

Küçüklüğümden beri hislerim çok kuvvetliydi... Olacakları söylerdim ama pek dikkate alınmazdım.

13-14 yaşlarında Mısır'a gitmem lazım demeye başladım... Orada yaşayacağım bir şey var, orada olmalıyım diyordum... Ailemi o zamanlar hiç ailem gibi hissetmiyordum... Sanki ailem başkaydı... Öyle bir hissim vardı.

16-17 yaşlarında rüyalarım aktifleşmeye başladı... Hiç gitmediğim yerlere götürülüyor, gezdiriliyor gibiydim... Gözümün

önünde ekranlar açılıyordu... Bu bazen rüyada bazen de gündüzleri uyanıkken oluyordu... Geleceği gördüğüm rüyalarım vardı.

17 yaşındayken bir gece, yatağa yatmamın üzerinden yaklaşık 15 dakika geçmişti ki, yatağım deli gibi sarsılmaya başladı... Önce deprem oluyor sandım... Sonra yavaşça gözlerimi açtığımda yatakta kendimi yatarken görmem ve bedenime düşmem bir oldu... O olay sonrasında ruhum bedenimden ayrılıyor gibi olmaya başladı... Bedenimden ayrılıp, arkadaşlarımın evine gidiyor, şunu yapıyorsun, elinde bunu tutuyorsun gibi, hepsi yüzde yüz doğru olan şeyler söylüyordum.

20'li yaşlarımda sanırım bir tür kanallık durumu ortaya çıktı... Durup dururken yazmaya başlıyordum... Farkındalık, birlik, sevgide kalmak, kancalardan kurtulmak, özgürleşmek gibi bir sürü bilgiler veriliyordu... O dönemde şifa yetileri de gelişmeye başladı ama hiçbirini bilinçli yapmıyordum... Vücudumda 3 noktalı üçgen gibi bir işaret belirdi, sonrasında üçgenlere, geometrik şekillere hep bir ilgi... Rüyalarımda hiç bilmediğim dinlerden, inançlardan bahsediliyor, 'Onu oku, bunu oku' deniliyordu.

25 yaşında, bir gece her şeyin iplikçik gibi enerjilerle birbiriyle olan bağını izledim... O vizyon sonrası o gece gemiye alındığımı da gördüm... Başımda Griler vardı... Sedye gibi bir şeyin üzerinde yatıyordum.

Dilek Hoca'yla yolumun kesişmesi öncesi ise çok zorlu bir süreç geçirdim... Metafiziksel saldırılara maruz kaldığım (özellikle deprem zamanı), rüyamda farklı birçok ırktan mesajlar aldığım, ellerimde tuhaf hislerin, kolumda işaretlerin oluştuğu bir dönemdi... Gözümün önüne sürekli Dilek Hoca'yı getiriyorlardı... Nereye baksam onu görüyordum, ki ömrümde hiç görmemiştim... Beni ona yönlendirdiler..."

Seda'nın kişisel öyküsü bu şekildeydi.

Onun seansta gördükleri ise vatanımız için ışık ve umut doluydu...

Seda D. Seansı

17 Temmuz 2023

(Nefes, gevşeme ve enerji çalışması.)

Seda D.: Ellerim açık... Çömelmişim dizlerimin üzerine... Kafam geride... Alnımın ortasından ve avuçlarımın içinden bir şey akıyor.

Tamam. O akım sana ne hissettiriyor?

Seda D.: Yükleme gibi... Enerji aktarıyorlar gibi.

Orada kal ve devam et. Aktarsınlar.

Seda D.: Bir kapı açılacak gibi.

Tamam. İzin ver açılmasına.

Seda D.: Oradan başka bir yere geçiliyor.

Çok güzel.

Seda D.: Daha başındayım... Bana yükledikleri enerjiyle kanal gibi oluyorum ve ben yapmıyorum, onlar yapıyor aslında.

Biliyorum.

Seda D.: Başka bir boyut!

Geç oraya.

Seda D.: Geçtim... Korkma diyorlar.

Geç oradan. Korkma.

Seda D.: Her şey çok farklı!

Ne var orada Seda?

Seda D.: Çok berrak bir gökyüzü var... Bulut yok gibi ama.

Başka?

Seda D.: Çok hafif... Ağırlığı yok... Havanın ağırlığı yok... Çok hafif.

Peki yalnız mısın orada?

Seda D.: Biri karşıladı beni... Kadın... Çok güzel!

Tarif eder misin?

Seda D.: Uzun bir şey giyiyor... Böyle pelerin gibi... Işıl ışıl bir şey giyiyor.

Kendine bakar mısın? Üzerinde ne var?

Seda D.: Bende de öyle bir şey var.

Ellerine, kollarına, ayaklarına bir bak.

Seda D.: Saydam gibi!... Dört parmağım var!... Enerji beden gibi!... Saydam ama iç hissiyatım hep yeşil diyor.

Tamam.

Seda D.: Dolaştırıyor beni... Botanik bahçeleri var... Sera gibi ama açıklık da var.

Etrafına bakar mısın? Başkaları da var mı?

Seda D.: Var... Şehir gibi... Pırıl pırıl... Tertemiz... Sevgi dolu!

Kadın yanında mı hâlâ?

Seda D.: Evet.

Onun gözlerine odaklanır mısın?

Seda D.: Beni sevdiğini, hep yanımda olduğunu, koruduğunu söylüyor... Annem o benim!

Devam.

Seda D.: Bana sarılan o muydu acaba?... Zaten hep içimdeymiş... Orayı tanıtmak istiyor... Korkma gel diyor.

(Dilek bunun sadece bir giriş olduğunu ve tıpkı diğer vakalarda olduğu gibi Seda'yı başka bir yere götürüp mesaj vereceklerini algılıyor. Nitekim az sonra Seda kendisini yine bir gemiden Dünya'ya ve ardından Türkiye'ye bakarken buluyor.)

(Uzunca bir sessizlik...) Neredesin şu anda?

Seda D.: Gemideyim... Camlar görüyorum... Dünya'yı görüyorum.

Dünya'yı izler misin? Ne görüyorsun?

Seda D.: Türkiye!

Ne görüyorsun Türkiye'de?

Seda D.: Bir enerji alanı var... Çok yüksek... Çepeçevre, dört bir tarafından sarıyor ülkeyi... Ve yukarıya yükselen bir enerji alanı var... Çok yüksek... Bunu delmeye çalışıyorlar.

Kim delmeye çalışıyor?

Seda D.: Negatif... Yükseliş oradan olacağı için!

Nereden? Türkiye'nin neresinden?

Seda D.: Türkiye'nin bütünü çepeçevre bir kanal gibi... Nasıl söylesem?... O yüzden buraya geliyorlar... O yükselişte burada olmak için geliyorlar... Bir de onu delmeye çalışan bir taraf var... Yükselmesinler diye... Çıkış olmasın diye... Kendi bir gemi gibi geliyor... Çok acayip!... Nasıl bir şey bu!... A!... Çok acayip!... O yüzden her yerde bir şey var... Saklı şeyler var... Hepsi aynı anda, aynı şekilde başladığı zaman hepsi bütünü oluşturacak... Çok acayip!... (Ağlıyor...) Olağanüstü!... Çok olağanüstü!... Belli bölgelerde, yeraltında gizli gemiler var... Hepsi birbirine bağlı aslında!... O yüzden açığa çıkmıyor!

O bölgelere odaklanır mısın?

Seda D.: Dağların altında.

Üsler mi var?

Seda D.: Çok ama çok!... Bir iki değil ki!... Yukarıdan bakıyorum... Sanki tek bir şey hepsini harekete geçirecek gibi... Birbirleriyle öyle koordineli ki!... Hepsi birbirini harekete geçirecek... Hepsi birbiriyle iletişim halinde.

Beklenen bir hareket mi var?

Seda D.: Onun bir başlangıç noktası var!

Türkiye'yi neler bekliyor?

Seda D.: Kaos var ama kaos olmak zorunda.

Nasıl bir kaos?

Seda D.: Biraz karmaşa var... İnsanların sokağa çıkması var... Kaotik bir ortam var... Ama niye böyle peki o zaman?

Biraz ilerler misin? Nasıl sona erecek?

Seda D.: Bir kişi düğmeye basacak!

Ne olacak peki ondan sonra?

Seda D.: Onlar (gemiler) harekete geçecek... Hepsi birden... Yukarıdan da yardım var... Aslında zaten ona gerek bile olmayacak şekilde bir şeyler içeride var.

İçeriye odaklan o zaman biraz.

Seda D.: Açığa çıkacak şeyler var!... Gemiler var!... Orada üsler var!... Zaten dışarıda değiller ki!... İçerideler!

Tamam.

Seda D.: Dışarıda gözcüler var... Gerek olursa.

Bunlar müdahale mi edecek?

Seda D.: Enerjetik bir boyut atlayacak.

Sonra? Türkiye'nin geleceği nasıl?

Seda D.: Sanki... Ülke olarak bir boyut değiştiriyor gibi... Başka bir gerçeklikte gibi... Ondan sonrası çok güzel!... (Ağlıyor.)

Güzel olan kısma bak. Ne olacak? Nasıl olacak?

Seda D.: Aslında olması gereken olacak... Bir "Birlik" gibi bir şey olacak... Türkiye o birliğin içinde olacak... Sanki Türkiye'de kurulacak... Başka bir gerçeklikte gibiyiz... O organizasyonun içinde insanlar da var... Işık varlıklar da var gibi... Ortak... Karma.

O yapının içinde Türkiye'nin temsilcisi kim?

Seda D.: Genç bir adam var!

Tamam. Onu tarif eder misin?

Seda D.: Aslında o da ışık!... Uzun boylu... Beyaz tenli... Renkli gözlü... Saçları açık kumral gibi... Geniş omuzlu... Işığı o kadar güzel ki!... İnsan suretinde ama ışığı çok güzel!

Nereden kaynaklanıyor bu ışığı?

Seda D.: Yukarıdan!... Çok çok yukarıdan!

Enerjisi?

Seda D.: Atatürk'ü hatırlatıyor!... O da öyleydi çünkü... Aynı frekansta!... Sanki onun gençliği gibi!... Yeniden bedenlenmiş gibi!... Güneş gibi... Hep Sirius diyorlar ama Sirius'un çok ötesi bir şey bu!

Bu kişi Dünya'da mı peki şu anda Seda?

Seda D.: Dünya'da ama daha tam o geçiş olmadı... Akıyor... Akış var ama o da henüz ne olacağının tam farkında değil... Tam anlamlandıramıyor... Gideceği yeri henüz bilmiyor.

Tamam.

Seda D.: Şu an akışla yavaş yavaş, alıştıra alıştıra enerjisini dönüştürüyorlar... Yavaş yavaş yapılıyor.

Şu an nerede?

Seda D.: Türkiye'de.

Nasıl bir yerde?

Seda D.: O kadar saklı bir yerde ki... Çok insanın olduğu bir yerde gibi değil... Dağlar var... Doğal bir ortam var... Çok büyük bir yer değil... Kendisini geliştiriyor... Enerjisi o kadar tanıdık ki!... (Ağlıyor...) O kadar ışık ki!

Bu olaylar olduğunda o kişi kaç yaşlarında olacak?

Seda D.: 35-40 arası... Genç duruyor ama 20 değil... Yaşını göstermeyen birisi... Enerjisi o kadar parlak ki!... Gittiği her yeri aydınlatıyor... Ülke ışıl ışıl... Herkesin söz hakkı var!...

Yenilikler getirecek ve yukarıyla bağlantısı var. Öyle anlıyoruz. Doğru mu?

Seda D.: Evet... Şu anki Türkiye'yle uzaktan yakından alakası yok... Çok farklı... Bambaşka bir enerji yayılmış... Çok güçlü... İnsanların da enerjisi öyle olacağı için dönüşemeyenler elenmek zorunda kalacaklar... Yoksa bu oluşamaz... Kaos da bu yüzden gerekiyor.

O zaman kaostan sonra yönetime Atatürk enerjisi taşıyan birisi gelecek.

Seda D.: Siz bu insanı koruyacaksınız.

Kim?

Seda D.: Sizler koruyacaksınız... Çünkü onun korunması gerekecek.

(Burada bize bazı özel bilgiler aktarılıyor.)

Seda D.: Bir akış var... Bir akış görüyorum.

Sana mı?

Seda D.: Evet.

Nasıl bir akış peki?

Seda D.: İzin veriyorlar... Görmeme de izin veriyorlar... Nasıl oluyor bu?... Aslında onu çok koruyorlar... Herkesin görmesine izin yok... İzin çıkarsa görebiliyorsun... Ama yüzünü net göstermiyorlar bana da... Perdenin arkasından gibi.

Gelecek olan kişi mi bu?

Seda D.: Evet... Yine dağlar, bayırlar... Öyle bir yerde gösteriyorlar... Bulunduğu yerde bir tepe var... Şehrin merkezi değil, dışı.

Evet.

Seda D.: Her gece eğitimde!... Bir şeye hazırlandığını biliyor ama ne olduğunu bilmiyor... O bağı kuracaklar... Gözlerden uzakta ayarlanacak iletişim... Niye ben onu hep tek görüyorum?... İzole.

Demek ki öyle şu an. İnsanlardan uzak tutuluyor olabilir.

Seda D.: (Bir süre sessizlik...) Zamanı gelince göreceksin dediler... İzin istedim ama... Zamanı gelince... (Yine bir süre duruyor...) "Frekansın uyumlu" ne demek?

Sor.

Seda D.: Onu görmeye, ulaşmaya da...

Başka önemli gördüğün ya da iletmek istediğin bir sahne var mı?

Seda D.: Sormam gerekiyor galiba... Çünkü onun iki yanında iki varlık var... Onlar benimle konuşuyor... Onlar izin verirse görüyorum.

Tamam o zaman. Soru sorabilirsin. Nereden bu varlıklar?

Seda D.: Pleiades geliyor... Niye?

Olabilir.

Seda D.: Zamanı gelince bilgi vereceklermiş kendileri hakkında da... Daha fazla bilgi vermek istemiyorlar... Başka bir dilde konuşuyor varlık... Sanki biliyorum ama hatırlamıyorum... Biliyorum... Hatırlayacağım.

Başka bilmemiz gereken bir şey var mı?

Seda D.: "Hazırlanın" diyor.

Kişinin gelişine mi?

Seda D.: Evet.

Başka?

Seda D.: Peki ne yapmamız gerekiyor diyorum... Hızlanacakmış bir şeyler.

Bizim ne yapmamız gerekiyor o sürede?

Seda D.: Şu an bir şey söylemiyor... Bilgi gelecek... Yol doğru... Frekansı bozmayın.

Genel olarak sen bir şey söylemek ister misin?

Seda D.: Her şey olması gerektiği gibi oluyor... Karşı koymak isteseniz de koyamazsınız... Saat işliyor.

Neye karşı koyamayız?

Seda D.: Sürece... Kabul... Kabul... Kabulleniş... Süreç böyle işleyecek... Bu akışta... Zamanı gelince bilgi verilecek... Zaten yapmanız gerekenleri yapıyorsunuz... Her şey kontrol altında... Bekleyin... (Biraz sessizlik...) Şimdilik bu kadar diyor.

Tamam.

Seda D.: Çok yakında... Çok uzak değil... Seneye yaza bir şey olacak... Ne olacak bilmiyorum... Sanki onun ilk tohumları gibi... Bu karşılaşmanın ilk tohumları... Seneye... Bahar, yaz ayları... Yolculuk var ama... Keşif gibi.

(Bazı kişiye özel bilgiler aktarılıyor.)

Seda D.: Son bir kez soracağım... Bir şey söylemek isteyip istemediklerini sordum... Zaten bilgi gelecek diyor... Bu kadar.

Peki.

Seda D.: Gözlerime bakıyor.

Kim?

Seda D.: Onun yanında gördüğüm varlık... Yükleme yapıyor gibi... Çünkü görmem de gerekiyor... Duymam ve görmem de gerekiyor. O yüzden her şeyi gösterdiler... Onlar gibi görmem lazım... Benim için de zaman başlamış... Bunun ne olacağını da söylemişler... Şu an bir şey görmüyorum, sadece akıyor... Bu işlem bir iki defa daha olacakmış.

Devam etmek ister misin?

Seda D.: Zaten bir şey yapıyorlar... Durduramam.

Durdurma.

Bu noktada seans sona erdi ama Seda üzerinde yapılan işlem devam etti. Seda yapılan işleme dair hissettiklerini bize şöyle aktardı:

"Seansın sonuna doğru gözlerime bir şeyler yapıldı... Sanırım bir yükleme yapıldı... Bilmediğim bir dil konuşuldu ve yakında o konuda sanki bir inisiyasyon yapılacak gibi hissettim... Artık çok fazla silmeler, unutmalar olmayacağı söylendi."

İKİNCİ KISIM

DEĞERLENDİRME

Değerli okuyucularımız:

Mesaj – Novus II doğrudan doğruya hedefe yönelik bir bilgilendirme kitabıdır.

Dünya gezegeninin ve ülkemizin ufkunda belirmekte olan yeni bir realiteye dair bazı özel bilgi ve veriler barındırmaktadır. Bilgilerin geniş bir bölümü birbiriyle örtüşmekle birlikte, bir kısmı ve bazı detayları farklılıklar göstermektedir. Bunun olası sebepleri aşağıda, ilgili başlıkta açıklanmıştır.

Genel görüş, Dünya'da ve Türkiye'de mevcut durumun çok uzun süreyle bu şekilde devam edemeyecek oluşudur.

Zaten böyle ağır bir dejenerasyonun sürüp gitmesi tekâmül yasalarına da bütünüyle aykırıdır. Dünya gezegeni, ya üzerindeki insan topluluklarıyla birlikte rejenere olarak bir üst realiteye tırmanacak ya da tamamen dağılarak yerini yeni bir tekâmül sınıfının yepyeni öğrencilerine bırakacaktır.

Seçim insanlığın bütününe aittir. Karar, ruhsal sistemin üst katmanlarıyla birlikte alınacak kolektif bir nitelikte olacaktır.

Mesaj – Novus II tıpkı birinci kitapta olduğu gibi, bu sürece dair önemli ipuçları vermektedir.

Kitap, ülkemiz bağlamında çok önemli bir mesajı merkezine almıştır. Bu merkeze alma meselesi kendiliğinden meydana gelmiştir.

Türkiye'de ortaya çıkacak ve Atatürk'ün bağlı bulunduğu ruhsal planın enerjisini taşıyan yeni lider meselesi, yaklaşan değişim ve bu bilinci taşıyan yeni çocuklar konuları tüm süjeler tarafından ortak olarak dillendirilmiştir.

Bu çalışmanın sarsıcı tarafı, seansa davet edilen 16 kişiden 15'inin kitapta yer almasıdır. Sadece bir kişinin seansı –çok önemli deneyimleri olmasına karşın– bazı ağır duygusal yükleri sebebiyle kısa kesilmiş, ileriye ertelenmiştir. Burada ifade etmek istediğimiz kritik nokta şudur:

Çok sayıda süjeyle seans yapılıp da, sadece Türkiye'nin yakın geleceğiyle ilgili içeriği olan seanslar seçilip kitaba konmuş *değildir*. Davet edilen hemen herkes, mesajı zihinlerinde sanki bir posta taşır gibi taşıyarak gelmişler ve benzer mesajları bırakıp ayrılmışlardır. Davet edilecek süjelerin seçimi de zaten bizler için şaşırtıcı şekilde olağandışı eşzamanlılıklarla gerçekleşmiştir.

Mesaj - Novus II, araştırma içerikli klasik bir kitap çalışmasının dışına çıkarak, Anadolu halkına bir mesaj, bir haber haline dönüşmüş, adeta "yukarıda" her detayıyla hazırlanmış olan bir süreç yaşanmıştır.

Okuyacağınız bu İkinci Kısım'da, kitap içeriğinde baskın olarak yer alan olay ve kavramların bir analizi, sizlerin zihninde oluşabilecek sorular temel alınarak yapılmıştır.

Aşağıda yer alan sorular ve yanıtlar kendi araştırma, bilgi ve deneyimlerimize dayanarak hazırlanmış, seanslarda geçen ifadelerle desteklenmiştir.

Ancak şunu da önemle belirtmek isteriz ki özellikle ülkemizin yakın geleceğine dair bilgilere ilişkin dağarcığımız sadece bu kitaptaki seanslara dayalı olarak oluşmamıştır. Kişisel olarak bizlere ulaşan bilgiler de aşağıda okuyacağınız yanıtların içeriğinde yer almaktadır.

Seanslarda bahsedilen lider bir "kurtarıcı" mıdır? Bu kişinin nasıl bir vazifesi ve fonksiyonu olacaktır?

Hayır. Bir kurtarıcı değildir ve bir kurtarıcı beklenmemelidir.

Beklenmesi gereken kişi, ülkenin potansiyel ruhsal ve fiziksel enerjisini bir merkez etrafında toplayabilecek, bir araya getirebilecek, odaklayabilecek, kitleleri pozitif yönde ve ülkemizin tekâmül rotası doğrultusunda harekete geçirebilecek kudrete sahip bir kişidir.

Bu kişi vatanımızın üzerine çöreklenmiş negatif unsurları elimine ederek, Anadolu'nun asli vazifesine başlayabilmesi için zemini düzleyebilecek, zemindeki taşları, ayrıkotlarını, çöpleri temizleyebilecek bir güce, idealizme ve yaşam programına sahip bir kişidir.

(4. Bölüm) Ezgi: "İleri görüşlü... Melez o... Çok yüksek enerjisi... Onu televizyonda görünce insanlar bakakalacak... Onu görünce böyle enerjisine kilitleneceksiniz... Baktığımızda Atatürk enerjisi verecek... Temizlik yapacak... İstifalar olacak arka arkaya... Melez ve vazifesini biliyor... Bazı siyasilerin açıklarını biliyor... Sürekli bilgilendiriliyor, eğitiliyor."

(11. Bölüm) Ece A.: "Hepsini temizleyecek... Zararlı insanların hepsini yok ediyor... Yavaş yavaş yapacak."

Bu kişi bir "kurtarıcı" değil ateşleyicidir.

Anadolu'nun kadim geçmişinden getirdiği, muazzam zenginliğe sahip kolektif bilinç alanına birçok şuurlu ve vazifeli varlık enkarne olmuştur. Bu vazifeliler halihazırda, kendi yaşam misyonlarının farkında olmaksızın ülkenin dört bir tarafına dağılmış, yorgun, bitkin, umutsuz durumdadırlar. Bu halkın ortak bir hedef doğrultusunda tekrar toparlanması, bir merkezin etki alanı içinde birleşmesi ve ataletten harekete, umutsuzluktan umuda geçmesi gerekmektedir.

Bireyler ne kadar aksiyon alma, harekete geçme/geçirme, değiştirme, dönüştürme isteği duyarlarsa duysunlar, bu çabalar dağınık, zayıf ve verimsiz kalmaktadır. Bu bakımdan, toplumun kolektif bir hedef doğrultusunda yön alabilmesi için, şarj edici, kuvvetlendirici, hedef gösterici ve motive edici bir *Merkez*'e şiddetle ihtiyaç duyulmaktadır.

Böyle bir *Merkez* karakter; bireylerin düzensiz, dağınık, verimsiz çabalarını tek bir havuzda toplayan dev bir harekete dönüştürecektir.

(12. Bölüm) Sibel Ş.: "Onun etrafında zaten kendiliğinden onun gibi insanlar yavaş yavaş toplanmaya başlayacaklar... O hiç çaba sarf etmeyecek... Her şey aslında kendiliğinden olmaya başlayacak... Sadece onun başlaması gerekiyor."

Ne var ki; toplum pasif bir bekleyiş içinde hareketsiz kalırken bir liderin gelip kurtarıcı rolünü üstlenmesi söz konusu olamaz. Bu, birlikte başarılacak bir süreçtir. Araba tüm sistemleriyle, mekanizmalarıyla, iç ve dış aksamıyla hazır olabilir. Ancak motorun çalışmasını sağlayacak bir ateşleme sistemi olmaksızın aracın park halindeki varlığının hiçbir değeri ve fonksiyonu yoktur.

Bu tarz, lider nitelikli vazifelilerin iki büyük özelliği vardır:

Birincisi, birleştirici varlık olmalarıdır. Onların bir ruhsal tesir alanı mevcuttur ve bu alan içerisine giren varlıklar süratle bu vazifenin içine çekilirler. O tesirin kaynağı da kendi bağlı bulundukları o ruhsal organizatör plandır.

(1. Bölüm) Aylin: "Herkese eşit mesafede... Her görüşe aynı mesafede... Birleştirici olacak... Sevilecek... Sevilecek."

Bu tür varlıklar moral olarak yıkık kitleleri, kendi tesir alanlarının oluşturduğu çember içerisinde bir araya getirirler, onların maneviyatının bu alandan beslenmesini sağlarlar. Mensup bulundukları ruhsal planın enerjisini paratoner gibi çekerler, dağıtırlar ve bu enerjetik saha içerisine dahil olan varlıklarda

tekrar yüksek bir moral gücü meydana getirirler. Bu işler herkesin harcı değildir. Bunlar büyük yollar aşmış varlıkların işidir. Büyük yollar aşmak o varlığa bir liyakat, yüksek seviyeli ruhsal güç ve himayeyi kullanabilme yetkisi verir. Ruhsal ve uzaysal mekanizmaların desteği daima arkalarındadır.

İkincisi; lokomotif varlık olmalarıdır. Bireylerde oluşan yüksek moral gücünü toparlayıp, büyük bir ortak alanda birleştirip, aksiyon haline dönüştürürler. Arkalarındaki yüklü ama harekete geçemeyen vagonları çekip götürürler. Ülkenin maddi ve manevi, fiziksel ve ruhsal bütün değerlerini, topyekûn ve eşzamanlı olarak ayağa kaldırarak, kitlesel bir hareket meydana getirirler. Halkta ne kadar güçlü bir ayağa kalkma isteği olursa olsun, vazifeli bir lokomotif gelmeden bu istek bir aksiyona dönüşmez. Bu daima böyle olmuştur. Önümüzdeki süreçte de böyle olacaktır.

Bu kişi –tıpkı Mustafa Kemal Atatürk'ün– İstiklal Savaşımız öncesinde ve sonrasında gerçekleştirdiği gibi, Anadolu halkının ruhsal potansiyelini harekete geçirecek, Anadolu'ya inen ruhsal tesirin bir *Merkez* bünyesinde odaklanarak sirküle edilmesini sağlayacak ve bu tesirin dış halkalara da dalga dalga yayılmasını temin ederek, ülke içindeki vazifelilerin de aktivasyonunu hızlandıracaktır.

Varlık topluluklarının devreler içinde tekâmül yürüyüşleri, ayrı ayrı, kitlesel, toplumsal tekâmül programları vardır. O gidiş artık aşağıya doğru olmaya başladığında, mevcut siyasal ve toplumsal yapı içerisinde daha fazla tekâmül imkânı kalmadığında, o topluluk, o halk atalet içine, durağanlık içine girer. Üstelik geçmişte, o durağanlığın sonucu olarak bu topraklar düşman işgaline uğramıştır. Aynı tehlike –içeriden ya da dışarıdan olmak üzere– bugün için de söz konusudur.

Anadolu son derece değerli bir tekâmül sahasıdır. Bir tekâmül sahası, dejenerasyona uğrayıp, artık daha ileri tekâmül fırsatları

yaratamıyorsa, tekâmüle hizmet edemeyecek hale gelmişse, bir kısırdöngüye, bir kapalı-devre sistem içine girmişse, ruhsal mekanizma o tekâmül sahasına müdahale eder ve kendi bünyesi içinden yüksek seviyeli bir varlığı o dejenere olmuş, tekâmülü durmuş olan sahada ıslahat yapmak üzere vazifeli kılar.

Yani o ruhsal planın, bir "ruhsal görevlisi" Dünya'da yapacağı işlere yüksek ruhsal ve uzaysal mekanizmaların yardımlarıyla hazırlanır ve bu vazifeli vasıtasıyla, o enkarnasyon alanının tekâmül hattında makas değiştirilir. Çünkü trenin gittiği istikamette raylar sona ermektedir. Geçmişte Mustafa Kemal Atatürk Anadolu tekâmül sahasına gelmiş, gerekeni yapmış, yönü, Anadolu'nun yeni vazifesine uygun şekilde değiştirmiştir. Belli noktalarda makas değiştirilmezse toplumlar dağılır giderler.

Türkiye, bu şekilde, tıkanmış durumda bulunan tekâmül hattının tekrar akışa geçişini deneyimleyecektir. Ülkemiz kendi gelişim planında, çok öncelerden üstlendiği büyük vazifesini layıkıyla yerine getirmek üzere, daha yüksek bir tekâmül basamağına tırmanmak, ruhsal misyonunda artık yeni bir aşamaya geçmek durumundadır. Çok zaman kaybedilmiştir. Kaybedilen zaman süratle geri kazanılacaktır.

Ülke tüm bireysel ve kitlesel varlıklarıyla, toprak altı ve toprak üstü değerleriyle toparlanacak, rayına girecek ve vazifesine tazelenmiş bir güç ve bilinçle, hız kazanarak devam edecektir.

Neden bu kişi için seanslarda farkı fiziksel tanımlamalar yapılmıştır?

İlkönce, süjelerin bu kişiyi seanslarda nasıl gördüğünü ya da bir başka deyişle, seansta gördükleri vizyonların kaynağını anlamamız gerekmektedir.

Süjelerin neredeyse tamamında zaten gelişkin bazı psişik özelliklerin mevcut bulunduğunu, çocukluk çağlarından itibaren Dünya dışı temaslar deneyimlediklerini, duru görü ve prekognisyon yetenekleri de sergilediklerini biliyoruz.

Burada birkaç olasılık karşımıza çıkmaktadır:

Birincisi; kişiyi duru görü yeteneğiyle görmüş olmalarıdır. Ancak duru görü yeteneği de kişinin psişik kapasitesine paralel şekilde, çok ayrıntılı ve açık vizyonlardan puslu ve kaba imajlara kadar geniş bir yelpaze içindedir. Seanslarda ana vizyon değişmese de, kişinin fizik bedenine ait detaylar, yaşı, şu anda bulunduğu yer vb. gibi bazı bilgiler şahsi algıya göre çeşitli farklılıklar gösterebilmektedir.

İkinci olasılık; süjelerin seans sırasında görüntüleri bir dış kaynaktan veya kendi ruhsal rehberlerinden almış olmalarıdır. Bu durumda, sözü edilen "lider" vasıflı kişinin vazifesinin hassasiyeti ve kişisel güvenliğinin sağlanması bakımından, kimliğinin, fiziksel özelliklerinin ve şu an bulunduğu yerin, vizyonu nakleden varlıklar tarafından kasıtlı olarak saklanmış ve "hedef şaşırtma" yönteminin kullanılmış olmasıdır -ki doğrusunu söylemek gerekirse- bu, seanslarda bize en güçlü olasılık gibi görünmüştür.

(13. Bölüm): S. Kosovalı: "Onu korumak zorundayız... Sizin iyiliğiniz için..."

O yüzden mi onunla ilgili farklı tanımlar ve farklı fiziksel tarifler geliyor?

S. Kosovalı: "Evet."

Keza birçok süje o kişinin yüzünü çok da net görememiş ya da tam görecekleri anda görüntü karartılmıştır. Hatta süjelerin çoğunluğu "erkek" olarak ifade etse de, bazı süjeler bu potansiyel lideri kadın olarak algılamıştır.

Seanslarda su yüzüne çıkan vizyon ve bilgiler, katılımcıların önceden yaşadıkları bir temas deneyimi sırasında kendilerine

gösterilmiş bulunan ve daha sonra dünyasal bilinçle hatırlamadıkları bilgi ve görüntüler de olabilir. Bu olasılıkta da yine ana mesaj değişmemekle birlikte, bazı detaylarda kasıtlı bir gizleme işlemi yapılmış olabileceği akla gelmektedir. Nitekim son dönemde bize ulaşan bazı temasçılar benzer bilgilerin kendilerine aktarıldığını ifade etmekte ve ayrıntıları dünyasal bilinçleriyle, seansa gerek kalmadan hatırlayabilmektedirler.

Üçüncü olasılık; sadece bir kişinin değil, birden fazla kişinin aynı anda bu vazife için yetiştiriliyor olmasıdır. Gerektiğinde ya da planda bir aksilik olduğunda birbirlerinin yerini alabilecek, alternatifli bir kadronun yetiştiriliyor olması da bir olasılık olarak düşünülebilir.

Bu "lider" böyle bir vazifeyi tek başına mı yerine getirecektir?

Hayır. Bu türden vazifeler büyük bir *kadro* işidir.

Bu vazifelerin bir ucu fizikötesi sahada bulunurken, diğer ucu fizik sahaya uzanır. Bunlar, aynı ruhsal plana mensup ya da aynı ruhsal plandan tesir alan varlıkların koordinasyon içinde çalışmalarını gerektiren işlerdir.

Aslında tek bir kişinin değil, koca bir *sistemin* enkarnasyonunu düşününüz. Bunun anlamı bir ruhsal organizatör sistemin kendi tesirini, tıpkı güneş ışığının mercekten geçirilip odaklanması gibi, Dünya fizik planında enkarne durumda bulunan vazifelileri aracılığıyla odaklamasıdır. Tesirin belli bir hedef doğrultusunda yoğunlaştırılması, ruhsal planın aşağıya uzanan uçları aracılığıyla sağlanır ve vazife yerine getirilir.

(7. Bölüm) Yasemin: "Sadece tek bir lider gelmeyecek... Liderler gelecek diyor... Yetişiyorlar diyor... Onlar hazırlanıyorlar... Hazırlar... Çok az kaldı diyor... Hepsi birlikte hazırlanıyorlar..."

(8. Bölüm) "Bu lider tek başına mı çıkacak ortaya?"

Nurhan: "Hayır... Tek başına çıkmayacak... Onu destekleyen insanlar ve şu an inanan insanlar var... Yavaş yavaş toplanmaya başlamışlar... Şu an onu yavaş yavaş yetiştiriyorlar... Etrafında toplanmaya başlamışlar ama kişinin zarar görmemesi için şu an her şekilde gizli... Varlığını gizli tutuyorlar... Ama arkasında çok ilahi bir güç var."

(12. Bölüm) Sibel Ş.: "Aslında sadece bir kişi olarak değil... Zaten yaparken 'Ben yaptım' gibi bir egosu yok... Sanki bir bütünün parçalara ayrılmış hali gibi."

İlahi mekanizma, çeşitli tekâmül sahalarında hızlanma meydana getirmek, o sahayı durağanlıktan çıkarmak için orada bir tesir odağı meydana getirir. Yani oraya inecek yüksek bir değiştirici/dönüştürücü/aksiyon meydana getirici tesiri alabilecek ve bu tesirle bir hareket başlatabilecek şuurlu bir varlığın ya da bir vazifeli grubun aşağıda bulunması gerekir. Siz bir yayın yapıyorsunuz ama bu yayını alabilecek güçte bir alıcınız yoksa o yayının bir anlamı yoktur. İşte bu fonksiyoner varlık ya da varlık grupları aracılığıyla yeryüzünde bir enerji odağı meydana getirilir. Onlar da anten gibi o enerjiyi çekip dağıtırlar.

Yani o vazifeli grup, o ruhsal mekanizmanın gözü ve kulağı olmak üzere inmiştir. Tesirin alınıp nakledilmesi o planın, o dünyasal kimlikleri taşıyan görevlileri üzerinden gerçekleşir.

Bunun üzerinde iyi düşünmek gerekir.

(12. Bölüm) Sibel Ş.: "Sanki onun ruhu birçok bedene yayılmış ve onların hepsi birdenbire tek bir bilinç haline gelip bir şeyler yapıyorlar gibi!..."

İşte bir asırdan fazla bir süre önce, Atatürk'ün mensubu bulunduğu ruhsal vazife planı buraya o görünümde uzanmıştır. Bu plansal bir uzantıdır. O gün, o plan Atatürk bedeninde görünür, başka bir zamanda başka bir fizik kimlikte tezahür eder. Beşeri

kimlikler önemli değildir. Hepsi aynı planın farklı tezahürleridir. Onu tek başına bir varlık olarak düşünmemek gerekir. Bir varlık grubunun, bir ortak şuurun, bir kompoze şuurun temsilcisi, bir uzantısı olarak düşünmek daha doğru olacaktır. O şekilde tanımlayabileceğimiz bir kuvvettir. O, Anadolu tekâmül programını sevk ve idare eden, bizim sorumluluğumuzu üstlenmiş bir ruhsal sistemin dünyasal kimliğidir. O ruhsal planın tesiriyle, işgal altındaki Anadolu'nun bitkin düşmüş, yorulmuş bütün unsurları mıknatısın üzerinde toplanan iğneler gibi toplanmıştır.

Anadolu asla yalnız bırakılmamıştır, bırakılmayacaktır.

Şimdi gelinen noktada, benzer bir operasyonun bu topraklarda bir kez daha gerçekleştirileceği anlaşılmaktadır.

Ruhsal plan ne demektir?

Ruhsal plan, hizmet ve vazife bakımından aynı hedefleri seçen, aynı hedefe yönelen varlıkların ortak şuur alanı demektir. Benzer bir hedefe yönelmiş olan varlıklar bir ruhsal plan meydana getirirler. Bilinçlerinde bir ortak alan oluşturmuş, hepsi birbirine şuursal bakımdan entegre olmuş varlıklar bütününe "plan" adını veriyoruz. Planlar, ruhsal ortak alan organizasyonlarıdır. Dünyanın ruhsal idareci sistemi içerisinde katman katman, küme küme vazifelenmiş mekanizmalardır.

Yeryüzündeki insan topluluklarının, milletlerin de bağlı oldukları ruhsal planlar vardır. O ruhsal planlar milletleri kitlesel tekâmül hedeflerine ve toplumsal karmalarına uygun şekilde sevk ederler, onların gelişimleri için mizansenler, olaylar, sınavlar hazırlarlar.

Her milletin, her insan topluluğunun bağlı olduğu bir ruhsal sistem vardır. O ruhsal mekanizma, o ülkenin tekâmülünü sevk ve idare eder.

Üst planın alt plana inişi, aşağıya doğru uzanması hem o ülkenin hem de dünyanın gelişim programına yardım ve hizmet içindir. Biz bu uzantılara "vazifeliler" diyoruz. Bu vazifeliler gün olur peygamberler, gün olur filozoflar, gün olur bilim insanları olarak görünürler, üst planlardan buraya uzanarak, alttaki varlıkları yukarı çekme vazifesini yerine getirirler.

Anadolu'nun ruhsal vazifesi nedir?

Dünyanın, içinde bulunduğumuz eğitim devresinin son bölümüne ait tekâmül programı temel olarak iki ana koldan yürütülmüştür.

Bir tarafta katı bir rasyonalizm, diğer tarafta ise Doğu mistisizmi, ruhsal ve manevi akımlar ve büyük inanç sistemleri yer almıştır.

Yani bir tarafta, bilginin doğuştan gelen akıl ve aklın bir fonksiyonu olan düşünme gücü ile elde edilebileceğini benimseyen ve doğru bilginin kaynağını duyularda değil, sadece akıl ve zihinde arayan bir felsefe varken, diğer tarafta ise bilgi kaynağı için doğaüstü ve duyular-dışı bir modelleme yapan, maneviyata dayalı bir felsefe egemen olmuştur.

Tekâmül programının bu şekilde iki ana kola ayrılması, ruhsal sistemin, devrenin son dilimi için tasarladığı bir proje çalışmasıdır.

İnsan topluluklarının göçleri, birbirlerine karışmaları, coğrafi keşifler döneminin başlaması, siyasal değişimler, maddeci felsefi akımlar, endüstri devrimi gibi etkenler Batı'yı ruhsallıktan iyice uzaklaştırmış ve "materyalizm", "rasyonalizm" ve "bireycilik" tatbikatı yapma noktasına getirmiştir. Bu plana uygun olarak, özellikle 17. yüzyılda Batı'da ardı ardına "akılcılık" prensiplerini savunan varlıklar enkarne olmuşlardır.

Ayrıca bu ruhsal plan doğrultusunda Batı dünyası, tekâmül imkânlarının artması için teknolojik gelişimin hızlandırılması görevini de üstlenmiştir. Bu sayede, teknolojinin çok ilerlediği bu yüzyılda insana deneyim yapabilmesi için her türlü olanak sağlanmıştır.

Örneğin internetin devreye sokulması bilginin süratle yayılmasını sağlamıştır. Dünyanın her köşesinde yaşanan birçok olayın tüm insanlık tarafından anında izlenebilmesi çeşitli duygu hallerinin süratle yaşanmasına imkân vermektedir. Gözlem olanağı artmıştır. Bunun anlamı bireyler ve kitleler arasındaki bilgi ve tesir alışverişinin hızlanmasıdır.

İnsanların farklı tekâmül aksiyonlarına girebilmeleri için teknolojik imkânlar genişletilmiştir. Yani işin teknik kısmını Batı üstlenmiştir. Bu teknolojiler her ne kadar zaman zaman insanlığın aleyhine, negatif amaçlar için kullanılıyor olsa da, görünmeyen kısımda aslında enformasyonun hızla sirküle edilmesini sağlamıştır.

Ardından buna uygun kurumlar oluşmuş, olağanüstü icatlar yapan varlıklar özellikle son 200 yıl içinde Batı'da ardı ardına doğmuşlardır. Bunlar asla tesadüfi işler değildir. Bu varlıklar, ruhsal sistemin, "bilginin ve tesir alışverişinin" insanlar arasında yayılmasının hızlanması ve dünyanın yeni ve süratlenmiş bir tekâmül programına geçişi planının uygulanması için dünya sahnesinde ortaya çıkmışlardır.

Avrupa'nın doğusuna doğru geldiğimizde ise, Anadolu topraklarından başlamak üzere, Asya, Arabistan Yarımadası ve Uzakdoğu yönünde daima maneviyat ve ruhsallık temelli bir sosyolojik ve kültürel yapının ağır basmış olduğunu görüyoruz.

Aslında bunların hepsi Yukarı'nın projesidir. Birer deneysel çalışmasıdır. Yeni bir fikrin, yeni bir felsefi sistemin Dünya Tekâmül Okulu'nda nasıl bir etkisi olacağına, nasıl bir sonuç

vereceğine bakılır. Önce bu yeni düşünce akımını yayacak varlıklar dünyaya doğarlar ve onların vasıtasıyla bir tesir alanı, bir tesir şebekesi meydana getirilir. Ardından farklı realitelerin testleri yapılır. Bu, Dünya Okulu'nun eğitim sistemidir.

İçinde bulunduğumuz bu devrede farklı felsefelerin nasıl harmanlanacağı test edilmektedir. Bir başka ifadeyle, bir tarafta rasyonalizm ve materyalizm, diğer tarafta ruhsallık ve maneviyat varken bunların optimal şekilde nasıl sentezleneceğine bakılmaktadır. Bir uçta sert, katı bir bireyselcilik, diğer uçta ise gözle görülmeyen fizikötesi yüce değerler, birlik-bütünsellik anlayışı vardır. Burası fiziksel bir boyut olduğundan her ikisine de gereksinim duyulmaktadır. Bu iki zıt ucun en uygun ölçülerde nasıl bir araya getirilebileceğinin deneyi yapılmaktadır.

İşte Anadolu bu büyük proje için bir laboratuvar, bir merkez ve kavşak noktası olarak seçilmiştir.

Neden Anadolu bu görevi üstlenmiştir?

Her şeyden önce; Anadolu coğrafi olarak, maddeci ve bireyci akımların hüküm sürdüğü Batı sınırlarıyla ruhsallığın ön plana çıkmaya başladığı dev bir Ortadoğu, Asya ve Uzakdoğu coğrafyasının tam ortasında, merkezi bir konumda bulunmaktadır. Bir koluyla Batı'ya, diğer koluyla Doğu'ya uzanmış bir denge merkezidir.

Zaten saf ruhsallığa dayalı dev bir ana uygarlık olan Mu genetik mirasını taşıyan Türklerin Anadolu'ya göçleri de, bu toprakların hâkimiyet altında tutulması ve hâkimiyetin genişletilmesi de yine bu plan gereğidir.

(13. Bölüm) S. Kosovalı: "Bu kadın figüründeki ve farklı bir ses tonuyla konuşan varlık bana pek çok şey anlattı... Biz Dünya'yı hiçbir zaman sahipsiz bırakmadık dedi... Hatta çok enteresan bir bilgi verdi... Fatih Sultan Mehmet de bizdik... Alparslan da bizdik... Atatürk de bizdik dedi... Özellikle Anadolu'yu hiç sahipsiz

bırakmadıklarını söyledi... Dünya var olduğu sürece Türk milleti var olacaktır dedi... Bu bir ırktır dedi... Bu ırkın görevini şey olarak söyledi... Düzen koruyucular dedi... Onlar var olacaklar ki düzen korunsun dedi... Onlar içeride biz dışarıda, hep bağlantılı şekilde sürdürdük dedi."

Türk ulusunun Orta Asya'dan Anadolu'ya çıkıp gelmesinin, bu konuda vazifelendirilmesinin asıl sebebi, görünmeyen sebebi budur. Batı'yla Doğu arasında bir ruhsal kavşak noktası oluşturma deneyi içindir. Asıl mesele Doğu'yla Batı arasında coğrafi bir köprü olma meselesi değildir. Burada bir ruhsal operasyon vardır. Bu köprü her şeyden önce ruhsal bir köprüdür. Bir ruhsal bilgi köprüsüdür. Bu da, kozmik devrenin kapanış diliminde tatbikata konan büyük projeyle doğrudan ilintili bir durumdur.

İkincisi; bu toprakların, her türden felsefi akımı, sayısız farklı uygarlığı, sayısız farklı kültürü barındırmış olan tarihiyle muhteşem bir kolektif şuur sahası vardır. Böyle bir kolektif şuur sahası dünyanın hiçbir coğrafyasında mevcut değildir.

Bu projenin başlangıcı, tarihin çok eski dönemlerine dayanmaktadır.

Anadolu tekâmül sahasının geçmişinde büyük kehanet merkezleri, inisiyasyon odakları vardır. Kitabi dinlerin en yüksek felsefi ve kültürel izlerine, ayrıca en ileri yorumlarına da –her ne kadar içinde bulunduğumuz dönemde bu konuda ağır bir dejenerasyon yaşanmakta olsa da– bu topraklar ev sahipliği yapmıştır.

Anadolu muazzam zenginlikte bir kolektif-enerjetik şuur sahasıdır. Bu derece yüksek seviyeli bir kolektif şuur sahasının benzeri bu gezegende yoktur.

İşte Anadolu bu sebeple, böyle büyük bir çalışmaya zemin oluşturmak üzere, birçok farklı düşünce akımının bir arada

nasıl bir sonuç vereceğine dair proje için ruhsal sistem tarafından merkez noktası olarak seçilmiştir.

Anadolu'nun çok önemli bir vazifesi, maneviyattan kopmuş Batı ile, akılcılıktan kopmuş bir Doğu âlemi arasında bir denge oluşturmaktır. Bu harmanlamanın tasarımı ruhsal planda yapılmıştır.

(11. Bölüm) "Türkiye'nin vazifesi ileride, değişimden sonra ne olacak?"

Ece A.: "Birleştirmek... Bütün dünyayı toparlayıcı rolü var... Düzenlemek zorunda... Bulunduğu yerden dolayı."

"Başka?"

Ece A.: "Burası merkez çünkü... Merkezin olduğu bir yer var... Bütün her şeyi birleştirici."

"Birleştiricilik vazifesi mi var Türkiye'nin?"

Ece A.: "Evet... Dünyanın yararı için... Bunu yapmak zorunda."

Vazife tam anlamıyla başladığında, bu nitelikleriyle Anadolu gelecekte bir denge merkezi olacaktır.

(13. Bölüm) S. Kosovalı: "Dünya'nın çekirdeğine doğru üçgenimsi bir şey iniyor... Zemini çok sağlam bir üçgen... Sanki Dünya'nın dengesini de burası sağlıyor gibi... Savrulduğunda rotasına geri çekecek... Gerçekten denge mekanizması burası sanki... Nasıl anlatayım?... Buraya bir şey koymuşlar... Buraya bir müdahale yapılmış... Önceki geçişte yapılmış... Şöyle anlatayım... Kayık fırtınada alabora olduğunda bir şey çakarlar ya... Hani alabora olurken o çakılı yer tutar... Savrulur, savrulur fakat durduğunda çakılı olduğu yer nedeniyle çok gidemez... Savrulamaz... Sanki Türkiye'nin altındaki o sivri, saplantı, üçgen yer Dünya'nın savrulmasını durduran denge gibi... Orada bir denge var... Orada bir şey var... Dengeliyor... O savrulmayı durdurup dengeleyecek nokta orası... Buraya bir müdahale yapılmış... Daha önceki geçişte yapılmış bu... Denge oluşturmuşlar orada."

Mustafa Kemal Atatürk, bu harmanlama çalışması kapsamında, geniş çeşitlilikte yaşam tarzlarının yaşanması için zemin hazırlamıştır. Çünkü o dönemde artık buraya, bu projenin ilerletilmesi için daha farklı bilinçteki varlıkların doğması mukadder olmuştu. Yani hem Batı akılcılığını, rasyonalizmini, hem de Anadolu bilgeliğini ve maneviyatını bir arada yaşamak, dengelemek isteyen varlıkların gelmesi gerekiyordu. O varlıklar ardı ardına bu topraklara doğmaya başlamışlardı.

Atatürk'ün dünyasal anlamda da kabiliyeti yüksekti. Çünkü Anadolu'da maddesel boyuttaki birtakım düzenlemeleri de yapmak zorundaydı. Bunu gerçekleştirmek için gerektiğinde sert tesirleri de kullanmıştır.

Mustafa Kemal, zemin düzlenirken, eski, sert ve köhne kayalarla karşılaşılmıştır. O kayalar kırılıp atılmıştır. Devrin koşulları ve yapılacak vazifenin önemi bunu gerektirmiştir. Anadolu'da zemin böyle düzlenmiştir.

Bu ruhsal proje için, Batı benzeri ama Türk motifli, Türk adaptasyonlu kurumların oluşması gerekiyordu. Birleştirici ve farklı tekâmül planlarını harmanlayıcı bir Türk kimliğine ihtiyaç duyuluyordu. Ardı ardına yapılan reformlar da bu tekâmül planının bir parçası olarak hayata geçirilmiştir.

Bu reformlarla, bu toprakların insanlarına tek tip değil, birçok farklı varyasyonda tekâmül imkânları sağlanmıştır. Bu nokta çok önemlidir... Halk durağanlıktan çıkarılmıştır. Halkın önüne çok yönlü bir tekâmül planı konulmuştur.

Atatürk bu reformları yüksek bir sezgiyle, derin bir içgörüyle yapmıştır.

Mustafa Kemal bu reformlarla Anadolu'nun "mental" gelişimini sağlamak istemiştir. Mental gelişim realitesi duygu realitesinin bir üzerindeki realitedir. Bunun anlamı, bilgiye dayalı bir duyarlılık, şuurluluk ve yüksek akıldır.

Yani maneviyatın, ruhsallığın yanı sıra, bilgi, şuurluluk ve muhakeme gücünün, yüksek seviyeli düşüncenin de bu topraklarda yeşermesini istemiştir. Bir başka ifadeyle, maneviyatla akılcılığın paralel ilerlemesini hedeflemiştir.

Ruhsal bilgiler açısından baktığımızda, mental gelişim, verimsiz duygusallığın kontrol altına alındığı, yüksek akıldan süzülmüş, ileri bir ruhsal seviyedir.

Anadolu insanı duygusal bakımdan çok gelişmiştir. Duygu çeşitliliği çok fazladır. Dünya ortalamasının hayli üzerindedir. Yüksek duyguları derinliğine yaşayan bir halktır. Ancak aşırı duygusallık ruhsal gelişimde ciddi bir handikaptır. Akılla desteklenmeyen bir duygusallık ilerlemeye engeldir. Artık Anadolu'da mental seviyede de bir devrim yapılması gerekmiştir ve buna yönelik atılımlar yapılmıştır.

Ancak Anadolu'nun vazifesi gereği, bir orta yolun bulunması, ruh ve madde dengesinin, yani duygusal ve mental gelişim dengesinin sağlanması koşulu vardır. Bunun için de Anadolu halkının, kendi duygusal ve manevi gelişimine, zihinsel gelişimi de eklemesi gerekmektedir. Birçok reform da bu bakımdan yapılmıştır. Böylelikle, akılcılıkla desteklenen bir maneviyat tatbikatı başlatılmıştır.

İşin dünyasal tarafında bunları görebilmek mümkün değildir. Ancak arka planda bunlar vardır.

Atatürk'ün gerçekleştirdiği reformlar Türkiye'de devrim niteliğindeki ruhsal araştırmaların başlaması için de zemin hazırlamıştır. Böylelikle çok yüksek seviyeli bilgilerin alınması sağlanmıştır.

Cumhuriyet'in yarattığı o daha serbest inançsal iklim sayesinde, Batı'da gelişen deneysel metapsişik çalışmalar takip edilmeye başlanmıştır. Böylece Atatürk'ün dünya vazifesini tamamlamaya hazırlandığı yıllarda ilk ruhsal tebliğler alınmaya, arkasından, büyük bilgiler ardı ardına inmeye başlamıştır.

Kısacası; Atatürk Anadolu'nun tesir planını değiştirmiştir. Anadolu daha yüksek tesirlere hazır hale gelmiştir. Bu bilgiler bu şekilde inmiştir. Atatürk ülkeyi dar banttan geniş bant yayınına çekmiştir. Veri akımı artmıştır. İşte Mustafa Kemal bu zemini hazırlayıcı bir vazifeyle dünyaya gelmiş bir varlıktır.

Anadolu, asli vazifesinin hazırlık çalışmalarına o dönemlerden itibaren başlamıştır. Bu vazifenin hakkıyla yerine getirilebilmesi ve ruhsallığın Batı dünyasına aktarılabilmesi için, Batı'ya ait buluşların ve teknolojilerin de kullanılması ve kısmen Batı'ya da entegre olunması gerekiyordu. Çünkü o kısmi entegrasyon olmazsa, Anadolu'ya aktarılan yüksek ruhsal bilgileri, o enerjiyi, o tesiri nakledebilmek mümkün olamayacaktır. Anadolu, ileride daha da netleşecek olan "bilgi köprüsü", "bilgi nakil merkezi" vazifesini hakkıyla yerine getirebilmek için bir tarafıyla Batı ile de adaptasyon içinde olmak zorundadır.

Seanslarda yer alan temasçıların önemli bir kısmının Anadolu'nun ortasında bir "kalp" görmeleri son derece kritik bir değerdedir. Gezegenin kalbi adeta burada atmaktadır. Kalp sembolizmi Anadolu'nun Dünya için ruhsal enerji üreten bir "jeneratör" vazifesini üstlendiği anlamına gelmektedir.

(10. Bölüm) Belgin A.: "Nüfus biraz azalmış gibi ama olması gereken olmuş... İnsanların hepsi o vortekse doğru hareket ediyor... Güneşe doğru... Ortaya... Türkiye'nin kalbine... Oradan bilgileri alıyorlar, yayıyorlar."

(12. Bölüm) Sibel Ş.: "Türkiye'nin ortasında kalp gibi atan bir enerji var... Bir insanın kalbi gibi atıyor... Kocaman... Sanki böyle şey gibi... Dünya'daki bütün spiritüel insanlar o kalbe doğru mıknatıs gibi çekiliyor."

(13. Bölüm) S. Kosovalı: "Sadece Dünya'nın kalbi gibi bir yerden bir avuç yukarıya çıkacak... Geri kalan hepsi bomboş."

(13. Bölüm) S. Kosovalı: "Sanki kalp orada atıyor gibi... Bir kalp atışı var orada... Sanki hasta birisi var da geri dönecek gibi... Kalp atışı var orada... Bir titreşim var."

Bu toprakların, Doğu ile Batı arasında, dev bir kartal gibi kanatlarını açıp, zıt gelişim gösteren iki yüksek medeniyeti birleştirmesi gerekecektir. Çok yüksek seviyeli ruhsal bilgiye odak teşkil edip, o bilgiyi alıp, hem Doğu'ya hem Batı'ya adapte etme, nakletme işi hâlâ Anadolu'nun üzerindedir.

Neden Anadolu ve Atatürk söz konusu olduğu noktada hep Sirius Sistemi'ne atıfta bulunulmaktadır?

Her şeyden önce, Sirius'u bir astronomik sistem olarak değil, bir yüksek boyut, bir vazife odağı, muazzam bir tekâmül kültürünün hazırlayıcısı, yayıcısı ve sahibi bir ruhsal plan olarak düşünmek gerekmektedir. Sirius bir tekâmül seviyesini temsil etmektedir ve bu büyük evrensel vazife merkezinin tasarladığı tekâmül planı bizim fizik evrenimizin ana öğretim sistemini oluşturmaktadır.

Sirius'u astronomik konumuyla değil, daha akışkan, süptil boyutuyla değerlendirmek doğru olacaktır. Örneğin süptil varlığıyla dev bir grup bilinci, bir ruhsal plan olan Güneş'i biz fizik âlemimizde sadece bir gaz kütlesi olarak görürüz.

Her biri evrendeki bir yıldız sistemiyle ve o sisteme bağlı gezegenlerle bağlantılı olan birçok ruh âlemi vardır. Çeşitli ruh âlemleri titreşimsel olarak birbirleriyle hizalanmıştır ancak gezegenlerin farklı konumlarıyla bir ölçüde ayırt edilebilir durumdadır. Ruhsal varlıklar bir ruh âleminden diğerine geçebilir ve ilgili gezegenlerin herhangi birinde enkarne olmayı seçebilirler.

Sirius adıyla anılan bu ruhsal vazife merkezinden Dünya'ya enkarne olmuş vazifeliler, Siriusyen tekâmül kültürünü Dünya'da çeşitli anlayış düzeylerine adapte ederek, dinler, felsefeler ve ruhsal öğretiler şeklinde uygulamaya koymuşlardır.

Devrenin kapanışından önce, Sirius bilgilerinin alınarak hazmedilmesi ve Dünya'ya nakledilmesi vazifesi Anadolu'nun üzerindedir. Atatürk 100 yıl önce bunun ilk zeminini hazırlamıştır. Şimdi daha yüksek seviyeli bilgilerin alınması ve bunların ileri uygulamalarının yapılması için Türkiye'de sahanın temizlenerek hazır hale getirilmesi beklenmektedir. Tüm çabalar bu yöndedir. Anadolu'nun asli vazifesi bundan sonra başlayacaktır. Yeni bir liderin ortaya çıkışı da doğrudan bu planla bağlantılıdır.

(1. Bölüm) Aylin: "Sirius... Anadolu'nun vazifesi Sirius'la bağlantılı... Sirius bilgileri Anadolu'dan aktarılacak ve insanların bilinçlerine göre anlatılacak... Türkiye'ye büyük bilgiler verilecek... Anadolu Sirius'tan görevli."

(10. Bölüm) Belgin A.: "Doğrudan Sirius geldi yine... Oraya bağlandı Türkiye... Güneş oradan bağlandı gökyüzüne... Sonra oradan verilen kararlar var... Dünyaya reçete gibi sanki... Oradaki talimat... Sanki şey... Şimdi bunlar, bunlar, bunlar yapılmalı... Mühürlendi sanki orası... Türkiye... Orayla bağlantılı oldu... Oranın bilgileri geliyor... Sanki dünya bunu kabul etmek zorunda gibi... O bilgiler dünyaya Türkiye'den dağılıyor... Sanki uygulanması gereken prosedürler var... Dünya bunu yapmak zorunda."

Eldeki veriler ve yaptığımız çalışmalar, Dünya dışı temas realitesine ait ilk somut bilgilerin de bu topraklardan yayılacağına işaret etmektedir. Anadolu'nun bir vazifesi de bu olacak gibi görünmektedir.

Yeni çocukların değişimde nasıl bir rolü olacaktır?

Değişim stabil ve sabit bir süreç değildir. Değişim dinamik bir süreçtir. Yani başladıktan sonra hızlanarak ve katlanarak devam ettirilmesi gerekmektedir. Bu rolü de şimdi yetişmekte olan yeni çocuklar üstleneceklerdir. Böylece, başlatılan değişim hareketinin rotası korunacaktır.

(8. Bölüm) Nurhan: "Çocukların çoğunu alıyorlar zaten... Çocukların çoğuyla şu an temas varmış... Onlar gelecek... Geleceği oluşturmak için onlar şu an koruma altındalar... Üstteki nesil, yani yaş grubu daha üstte olanlar temizlenecekmiş... Fosilleşmiş beyinler gidecek."

"Bu çocuklar mı devralacak ileride?"

Nurhan: "Evet."

Kimdir bu çocuklar?

Yeni donanımlarıyla Dünya'ya doğmakta olan, ileri bir tekâmül seviyesindeki bazı ruhlar iki kaynaktan buraya gelerek enkarne olmaktadırlar.

Birincisi; Dünya Tekâmül Okulu'ndan mezun olup, artık öğretmen seviyesine ulaşmış varlıklar.

Bu tür varlıklar daha önce bu okuldan yetiştikleri için buraya enerjetik adaptasyonları daha kolay gerçekleşmektedir. Bu fiziksel boyuta enkarne olma zorunlulukları ortadan kalkmış olmakla birlikte, burayla kurdukları karmik bağlar ve Dünya'ya karşı hissettikleri görev sorumluluğu onları tekrar bu sahaya çekmekte, bu kez tekâmüle yardımcı olmak ve değişimde ön alıcı vazifeleri yüklenmek üzere doğmaktadırlar. Onların genetik yapıları ve biyolojik ebeveynleri bu plan doğrultusunda belirlenmekte, yaşam planları da aynı paralelde tasarlanmaktadır.

İkincisi; Dünya dışı sistemlerde tekâmül etmiş olup, yine devre sonu sürecinde beşer varlıklarına yardım etmek ve ruhsal evrimi tetiklemek üzere Dünya'ya doğan varlıklar.

Bunların ciddi bir kısmı, Dünya Okulu'nun sertliği ve ağırlığı karşısında hayli zorlanmakta, kaba madde yapısına ve yoğun nefsaniyet barındıran yaşama uyum sağlayamamakta, buraya gelmeden önce bulundukları Dünya dışı ortamlarına ve ruhsal ailelerine karşı çok derin bir özlem duymaktadırlar. Bununla birlikte, "Evrensel Yardımlaşma Yasası" uyarınca, bu varlıklar Dünya'ya enkarnasyon yoluyla gelmeye devam etmektedirler. Yapılan birçok bilinçaltı çalışması -hepsi olmasa da en azından bir bölümünün- Dünya'nın bu geçiş döneminde vazifelenmek için bir şekilde ikna edilmiş olduklarına işaret etmektedir.

(5. Bölüm) Saadet Ö.: "Dünya'daki bedenimi istemiyorum!... Burada kalmak istiyorum!... İstemiyorum Dünya'ya gitmek!... Dünya'yı istemiyorum!... Bu anlaşmanın kararını ben verdim ama istemiyorum!... İstemiyorum!... Kararı ben verdim ama istemiyorum!"

(12. Bölüm) Sibel Ş.: "Neden burada olduğumu bilmiyorum ama şu an burada olmam gerekiyor."

(13. Bölüm) S. Kosovalı: "Geminin üst tabakası onların hepsini yanlarına alıyor... Aslında hiç kimse buraya (Dünya'ya) gelmek istemiyor... Çok zor bir görev burası... Çok zor bir yer."

Bir kısmı çeşitli genetik operasyonlar sonucunda, daha anne karnında bazı Dünya dışı genlere sahip olan bu çocuklar, yüksek psişik seviyeleri, geniş muhakeme güçleri, empatileri ve kozmik bilince yatkınlıklarıyla, yetişkinlik çağlarında kademe kademe, gerek Dünya'da gerekse Türkiye'de önemli pozisyonlara yerleşecekler, kritik makam ve mevkileri ellerinde tutarak, ülkelerin idarelerini devralacaklardır.

(14. Bölüm) Emine B.: "Aşılanmış gibiler... Toprağa ekilmiş gibiler... Çok acayip... Çok güçlüler ayrıca!... Ordu gibiler!... Küçük küçük ordular gibiler... Bu çocuklar çok acayip!... Her şeye karşı koyacak güçleri var."

Bu çocuklara, Dünya'da üstlendikleri vazifelere ve yaşam planlarına göre, Dünya dışı ortam içerisinde çeşitli bilgi yüklemeleri yapılmaktadır. Bu bilgi yüklemeleri onların ilerideki mesleklerini de belirlemektedir. Hedef, siyaset, bilim, teknoloji, tıp, kültür, sanat vb. tüm alanlarda bu çocukların değişim yaratmaları ve öncülük etmeleridir. Çocuklar bu bakımdan özel olarak yetiştirilmekte ve enkarne edilmektedirler. Büyük bölümü düzenli temas yaşayan yeni çocuklar, gerek fiziksel gerekse mental sağlıkları bakımından da sürekli kontrol altında tutulmaktadırlar.

Devrenin fiziksel kapanışı, yani maddesel kıyameti ertelenip de Dünya gezegeni devre sonundan önce yepyeni ve çok ileri bir realiteyi yaşayacak ise bu ruhsal çağ, ileride tamamen bu çocukların yönetiminde yaşanacaktır.

Eğer Dünya gezegeninde bir sıfırlanma gereği ortaya çıkacaksa, o noktaya kadar olan kapanış sürecini de onlar yönlendireceklerdir.

Türkiye'ye baktığımızda bu çocukların giderek kendilerini belli etmeye başladıklarını görüyoruz. Bu çocukların çoğu rüyalarında Atatürk'le konuştuklarını, hatta onun tarafından eğitildiklerini anlatıyorlar. Çocuklar aslında Anadolu'yu himaye eden ruhsal idareci plan ve onun uzantısı olan bazı Dünya dışı varlıklarca eğitime tabi tutuluyorlar ve onların tesirlerini alıyorlar.

(10. Bölüm) Belgin A.: "Çok güçlü ve çok akıllılar... Kötü hiçbir şeye geçit vermiyorlar... Asla... Duruşları dimdik... Kuralları var... Eskiyle alakalı tüm kötü şeyler bitiyor sanki... Bir duvar

olmuş bedenleri... Geçit vermiyorlar... Çok sevecenler ama çok da sertler."

3. Bölüm'deki Hakan S. seansında, Hakan'ın oğlunun daha 2,5 yaşındayken *"Beyaz bir ışık kapısından geçerek Sirius'tan geldim... Ben Atatürk olacağım"* demesi onun Atatürk'ün yeni bir bedenlenmesi olduğu anlamına gelmemektedir. Bu ifadelerden, o bilinci, o tesiri alacak ve yayacak birçok çocuğun yakın dönemlerde doğduğu anlaşılmaktadır.

Bu, aynı yüksek bilincin adeta dallara ve kollara ayrılarak onlarda tezahür etmesi olarak düşünülmelidir.

Bu çocuklar Batı'dan Doğu'ya tüm Türkiye'yi değiştireceklerdir.

Felaket senaryolarının gerçekleşme olasılığı nedir?

Seansların içeriğinde, özellikle Dünya'da gerçekleşeceği söylenen birçok doğa olayına ilişkin ortak vizyonlar yer almaktadır.

Bu vizyonlar kolektif rüyalarla da desteklenmektedir.

Dünya gezegeninin de, tıpkı üzerinde yaşayan insan toplulukları gibi, bir kadersel planı vardır. Aslında bu kadersel plan, belli bir devrede o gezegende tekâmül eden, öğrenim gören varlıkların genel kader planıyla bir bütünlük, bir paralellik içindedir. Bir başka deyişle, Dünya Okulu'nda eğitim gören varlıkların tekâmül ihtiyaçları Dünya gezegenindeki birçok şiddetli doğa olayına uyumlanmış, doğal felaketlerin zamanlamalarıyla senkronize edilmiştir.

Bundaki temel amaç:

1) İnsan topluluklarının yavaşlamış olan gelişim seyirlerine doğa olaylarıyla hız kazandırılması.

2) Bu şekilde katılaşmış, körelmiş vicdanların uyandırılması ve yardımlaşma niteliklerinin geliştirilerek nefsaniyetlerinin törpülenmesi.
3) Gelişimlerini sürdürme imkânı kalmamış kitlelerin, daha farklı tekâmül sahalarına nakledilmek üzere, bireysel ya da kitlesel olarak dezenkarne edilmesi.

Bu süreç içindeki yaşanacak bazı doğa olaylarının zamanlaması, şiddeti ve coğrafi etki alanı, ruhsal sistemin tesirleriyle ve bazı ileri Dünya dışı varlık sistemlerinin teknolojik imkânları kullanılmak suretiyle değiştirilebilmektedir.

Bu olayların şiddet, zaman ve etki alanlarının belirlenmesini sağlayan temel unsur ise, genel olarak insanlığın veya gezegen üzerindeki belli insan topluluklarının Dünya'nın orijinal tekâmül planına ne derece uygun hareket edebildikleridir. Yani, insanlığın gelişim hedeflerine ulaşmadaki yavaşlığı veya sürati, yaşanacak olayların da şiddetini tayin etmektedir.

Bazı olaylar, ruhsal idareci sistemin onayıyla ertelenebilir, şiddeti azaltılıp çoğaltılabilir, iptal edilebilir veya zamanı hızlandırılabilir.

Bu bakımdan, kolektif olarak algılanan, rüyalarda görülen veya bizim seanslarımızda yer aldığı gibi, temasçılara bilgi ya da vizyon şeklinde aktarılan olaylara dair verilerin aynen görüldüğü şekilde gerçekleşip gerçekleşmeyeceği konusunda yüzde yüz kesinlikte hükümler vermek imkânı bulunmamaktadır.

Bu konuda bazı mesajlar ileten ya da temasçılara uyarılarda bulunan Dünya dışı varlık sistemlerinin de olacakları önceden bildirme yeteneklerinin sınırsız olmadığını söyleyebiliriz. Yaptıkları şey, elde edebildikleri kadar çok veri toplamak, bunları deneyimlerinin ışığında analiz etmek ve en olası

olaylar dizisinin ne olduğunu keşfetmek için geleceğe doğru projeksiyon yapmaktır. Sebep-sonuç ilişkilerine ait zinciri bize göre çok daha geniş bir perspektiften görebilmektedirler. Bu varlıklar gerektiğinde Bütünsel Şuur'dan da bilgi çekerler. Bu evrensel, kolektif bir şuur sahasıdır. Bu nedenle, analizlerinin gerçekleşme olasılığı genellikle çok yüksektir. Fakat yine de her şey onların öngördüğü gibi olmayabilmektedir. Bunun nedeni Seçme Özgürlüğü Yasası'dır.

Bu meselenin bir başka boyutu da insanoğlunun kendi eliyle yaratmakta olduğu doğal felaketlerdir. Bu da kitlesel olarak hepimizin bir sınavıdır.

Haklı olarak şöyle bir soru gelecektir:

Bizler doğaya karşı son derece hassas bir tutum içindeyiz. Bitkileri, hayvanları, kısacası tüm canlıları korumak için elimizden geleni yapıyoruz. Doğayı katleden kurum, yapı ve şahısların bu karanlık tutumlarından neden hep birlikte sorumlu olalım?

Doğayı acımasızca katledenler kendi bireysel sınavlarını kaybetmektedirler ve bunun elbette bir bedeli olacaktır.

Tüm canlılara karşı koruyucu ve şefkatli bir tutum içinde bulunanların sınavı ise her türlü olumsuzluğa karşı bu tutumlarından taviz vermeden devam edebilme iradesini göstermeleridir. Tekâmülünde mesafe kaydetmiş ve Dünya'daki vazifesi devam edecek olan bu "iyi ruhların" olası bir sıkıntılı olaylar süreci içinde özellikle himaye edileceği bilgisi zaten sürekli şekilde aktarılmaktadır.

(13. Bölüm) S. Kosovalı: "Koruyucu perdelerimizi korunması gerekenlerin üzerine koyacağız... Siz göremeyeceksiniz... Koyarsak diğer tarafları kurtarabiliriz... Sizin anlayamayacağınız bir fanus... Sizin anlayamayacağınız bir kalkan olacak... Buna karar vermedik."

"Yani tekâmülde ilerlemiş olanları mı koruyacaksınız?"

S. Kosovalı: "Evet."

Her ne olursa olsun, nihayetinde her olay varlıkların gelişimine hız kazandırmak için yaşanacaktır. Ruhsal ve onların bir uzantısı olan uzaysal mekanizmalar gerektiğinde şok tesirleri kullanarak insanlığı uyandırmaya çalışırlar.

Bu olaylarla devreler açılır, devreler kapanır.

Sıfırlanma nedir? Buna gerek var mı?

"Sıfırlanma" her bir kozmik devrenin sonunda, Dünya gezegeninin, eksen kayması vb. etmenlerle topyekûn bir coğrafi değişiklik yaşaması, uygarlığın tamamen sona ermesi, dejenerasyona uğramış beden yapılarının ortadan kaldırılması ve o devrenin Dünya nüfusunu oluşturan öğrencilerin topyekûn bir ayıklanmaya tabi tutulmasıdır.

Dünya'da artık daha üst bir realitenin yaşanma imkânı kalmıyorsa, Dünya Okulu'ndan mezun olma liyakatine ulaşmış varlıklar daha yüksek bir tekâmül sahasına nakledilir, kalanlar devreyi tekrar eder veya benzer bir tekâmül alanına çekilirler.

(13. Bölüm) S. Kosovalı: "Uyanamıyorlar... Uyanamadıkları için izin verilecek sıfırlanmasına... Ve yeniden başlatacaklar."

(13. Bölüm) "Dünyanın sıfırlanması için bir zaman hissiyatın var mı?"

S. Kosovalı: "İlk göktaşları küçük düşecek... Ardından çok daha büyüğü ve ondan sonra karanlık... Dünya'ya yukarıdan vuruyor... Dünya yerinden oynuyor aşağıya doğru... Büyük bir yalpalama var."

Bu şekilde bir kapanış gerçekleştiği takdirde, Dünya gezegeninin yeni tekâmül devresindeki kadrosunu:

- Beşer-altı gezegenlerde tekâmül ederek beşer seviyesine yeni ulaşmış varlıklar.[10]
- Önceki devrede Dünya Tekâmül Okulu'ndan mezun olmayı başaramamış ve bu devrenin başında ya da ilerleyen dönemlerinde telafi için enkarne olan varlıklar oluşturacaktır.

Dünya yeni devreye, yepyeni bir tekâmül programıyla, yepyeni kıtalarla, yeni coğrafi düzeniyle, sıfırdan başlar. Eksen kaymaları ve gezegenin eğim açısının değişmesi, Dünya'nın kozmik/astronomik tesirleri alma kapasitesini de değiştirir. Eğitim programı da buna göre düzenlenir.

13. Bölüm'de, S. Kosovalı seansında yeni devrenin programıyla ilgili önemli bir bilgiyle karşılaştık. Bu, daha önce yaptığımız bir çalışmada ifade edilen bir bilginin teyidi oldu.

S. Kosovalı seansta şu ifadeleri kullanmıştı:

"Bir sonraki devreyle ilgili farklı düşünceleri var... Bu kez müdahale etmeye karar vermişler... Zoraki bir uyandırma... Kontrol artırılacak... Kontrol artırıldıkça, sıkıştırıldıkça uyanacaklar..."

Bu bilgi şu anlama gelmektedir:

Dünya'nın bir sonraki devresinde mezun olacakların sayısının artırılması ve devrenin öğretim sisteminden en yüksek verimin alınabilmesi için rehberlik sistemi yardımları çoğaltılacaktır. Buna göre, belki de çok daha fazla sayıda yüksek varlık doğum yoluyla gelerek, yeni devrede Dünya Okulu'nda eğitim gören beşer varlıklarının arasında yaşayacaktır.

İçinde bulunduğumuz devrede rehberlik mekanizmasının yardımları daha çok endirekt yoldan, yani rüyalar, sezgiler vb.

10. Bunlar, şu anki Dünya kadrosunda bulunan bizler gibi beşer-üstü düzeyine ulaşma dersleri için Dünya Temel Tekâmül Okulu'nda bedenlenecek olanlardır.

kanallardan yapılmaktadır. Bunun yanı sıra, medyonomik çalışmalarla alınan tebliğ tarzı bilgi akışlarıyla da insanlık daima desteklenmiştir. Negatif tesir planına ise ilahi mekanizmanın onayıyla devre kapanışına kadar serbestlik tanınmıştır.

Eğer yeni devrede insanlığın daha ileri düzeyde ve doğrudan müdahale yöntemiyle desteklenmesi planlanıyorsa, negatif tesirlerin biraz daha azaltılarak direkt temaslarla yardım yönteminin yürürlüğe konması söz konusu olabilir.

Diğer taraftan, devre sonlarında Dünya dışı faaliyetlerin artışı da, bu varlık sistemlerinin -Dünya idareci mekanizmasının onayıyla- mümkün olduğu kadar çok bilgi ve veri toplama çabalarından kaynaklanmaktadır. Mu ve Atlantis devresinin kapanışında olduğu gibi, uygarlıkların sonu geldikten sonra bu bilgiler bekletilmekte, yeni devrede uygarlıklar yükselmeye başladıktan sonra, belli bir gelişim noktasına gelindiğinde, bu bilgiler insanlara (bilim insanlarına, araştırmacılara, spiritüel gruplara vb.) yavaş yavaş aktarılarak gelişim hızlandırılmaktadır. Şu anda temasçılara yeni devrenin ön bilgileri de nakledilmektedir.

Sıfırlanmaların bir diğer fonksiyonu da, artık dejenere olmuş ve ruhsal tesirlere iyice kapalı hale gelmiş eski beden tiplerinin ortadan kaldırılması gereğidir.

Sıfırlanmalarda ayrıca topyekûn bir fiziksel ve enerjetik temizlik operasyonuyla Dünya astralindeki tüm negatif birikimler nötralize edilir, böylelikle Dünya yeni devreye temiz bir astral saha ile başlar.

Negatif sistemin ilahi mekanizmadaki rolü nedir?

Negatif tesir planı, ilahi sistem tarafından, bireylerin gelişimi için zıt yönde kuvvet uygulayarak tekâmül aksiyonları meydana

getirmek, nefsaniyeti besleyerek varlıkları çeşitli olaylar ve sınavlar içine sokmak, bu şekilde ayrıştırma ve ayıklanmanın meydana gelmesini sağlamak üzere düzenlenmiş bir geri tesir şebekesidir.

Bu sistemin de bedenli ve bedensiz vazifelileri vardır. Bunlar da bir tekâmül okulunda köstekleyici, saptırıcı, geriletici ters aksiyonlarla tekâmül hareketlerini hızlandırma rolünü üstlenirler.

Bu tesir şebekesi ve buna hizmet eden varlıklar daima üst planların denetimi altındadırlar ve eylemlerine belli ölçülere kadar müsaade edilir.

8. Bölüm'deki Nurhan Bekdamar seansında geçen aşağıdaki ifadeler bu mekanizmanın çalışma şekline çok kritik bir örnek oluşturmaktadır:

Nurhan: "Pozitife hizmet edecek melezler ayrı... Bir de negatife hizmet edecek, yetiştirecekleri melezler var... Onlar dünyanın yıkımı için hazırlanacaklar."

"Savaş için mi?"

Nurhan: "Evet... Onlar da yıkım için savaşacaklar."

"Onları hazırlayan negatif ırklar mı?"

Nurhan: "Farklı farklı ırklar."

"Bu da bir plan dahilinde o zaman."

Nurhan: "Aslında bu gizli bir plan gibi... Bir grubun gizli planı."

"Aynı elden çıkıyor aslında. Dünyanın gelişimi için bu savaşın olması gerekiyor. Anladım. Bu da o zaman dünyanın idareci mekanizması tarafından organize ediliyor."

Yukarıdaki ifadelerde çok önemli bir bilgi görüyoruz. Yeni çocukların tamamı pozitif yönde yetiştirilmiyor. Bazıları Dünya'da tekâmülü tetikleyici aksiyonlar yaratmaları için vazifelendiriliyor. Çünkü "gelişim" ve "ayıklanma" ancak bu şekilde meydana getirilebiliyor. Pozitif varlıklar barışçı ve sevgi odaklı

yapıları sebebiyle bu türden hareketleri başlatamadıkları için, zaman zaman negatif yöndeki tesirleri kullanabilen ruhların da Dünya'da bedenlenmesi sağlanıyor. Her şey "Yukarı"nın, yani ilahi sistemin planına göre tanzim ediliyor.

Bir diğer kritik ifadeyi 1. Bölüm'deki Aylin Aygün seansında görüyoruz:

"Konsey neden bu yılan gibi varlıkların bu kişileri kontrol altına almasına izin veriyor?"

Aylin: "Ayrıştırmak için... Çünkü insanlara seçim hakkı veriyorlar... Negatifte mi kalıyorsun yoksa pozitifte mi kalıyorsun?... Çünkü aynı şeyi bize de yapıyorlar... Negatifte misin? Pozitifte misin? Pozitifteysen seni seçiyorlar zaten."

3. Bölüm'deki Hakan S. seansında geçen ifadeler de bu negatif tesir planının "mühlet verilmişlerden" olduğu bilgisini destekliyor.[11]

"Peki ruhsal sistem onlara neden müsaade ediyor?"

Hakan: "Zamanları var."

"Zaman mı verilmiş onlara?"

Hakan: "Evet."

Bizler pozitif-negatif değerlendirmesini yaparken daima iki zıt kutbun aslında aynı tekâmül çubuğunun iki ucu ya da aynı kumaşın ön ve arka yüzleri olduğunu aklımızda tutmalıyız.

Yüce Yaradan'ın ve O'nun oluşturduğu ilahi sistemin mevcudiyetinin; aslında her şeyin varlığın gelişimine ve dolayısıyla pozitife hizmet etmesinin en büyük garantisi olduğunu unutmayalım.

---

11. Kuran-ı Kerim, Araf: 14-15: *İblis, "Bana insanların yeniden diriltilecekleri güne kadar mühlet ver" dedi. Allah, "Haydi, sen mühlet verilenlerdensin" buyurdu.*
Bu ayetlerde son derece önemli bir sembolik anlatım vardır. Negatif tesir üreten ruhsal jeneratörün (İblis olarak isimlendirilmiş bir sistemdir) tekâmül aksiyonları yaratmak ve ayıklanmayı sağlamak üzere, devre sonuna kadar saptırıcı tesirleri kullanmasına İlahi Sistem tarafından müsaade edilmesini anlatan ayetlerdir.

Dünya dışı varlıkların ruhsal sistem içindeki yeri nedir? Bu varlıkları nerede konumlandırabiliriz?

Dünya dışı olarak adlandırdığımız varlıklar; henüz çok yüksek seviyeli vazife planlarına geçmemiş ama bu planların sistematiği ve organizasyonel yapısı içinde yaşayan, çok ileri seviyedeki, çok süptil, çok akışkan bir ruhsal sahayla fizik âlemimiz arasında "ortada" bir noktada bulunan ve bu şekilde fizik sahalara da yaklaşabilen, fizik dünyalarda da faaliyet gösterebilen varlık sistemleridir.

Bu varlık sistemlerini genel olarak ruhsal idareci sistemle fizik boyutumuz arasındaki titreşimsel sahalarda konumlandırabiliriz. Bu sahalar da tıpkı bizim fizik evrenimiz gibi, daha akışkan, daha gelişkin madde cevherlerinden oluşmuş astronomik sistemlere sahiptirler. Bir Dünya dışı varlık örneğin "x" gezegeninden geldiğini söylüyorsa, bu gezegeni zihnimizde bizim fiziksel titreşim oktavımız içinde bir konuma yerleştirmemiz doğru olmayacaktır. O gezegen büyük olasılıkla farklı bir titreşimsel saha ya da boyutta yer almaktadır.

Dünya dışı varlık sistemleri bizlerle aynı fiziksel yoğunluk, titreşim ve vibrasyonel değerleri paylaşmayan ve bizimkiyle aynı moleküler titreşimdeki bedenlere enkarne olmayan varlıklardır. Bu varlıklar diledikleri zaman düalizm-ötesi birleşik alan evreni içerisinde boyutlar arası operasyonlar düzenleyebilecek bir evrim seviyesine ulaşmışlardır.

Dünya dışı varlıklar, kendi tekâmül düzeylerine göre, bizim sistemimize ait üst spatyom sahaları, hatta spatyom vibrasyonlarının ötesindeki sahalarla irtibat kurabilmekte, rehberlerimizle bir koordinasyon içinde temaslar gerçekleştirebilmektedirler. (Bizler fiziksel ölümü takiben enerji bedenimizin titreşimine uygun bir spatyom yoğunluğunda otomatikman kendimizi

buluruz. Biz daha üst katmanlara ancak Dünya Okulu'nu bitirdikten sonra geçebiliyoruz.)

Ancak şunu da ifade edelim ki, Dünya'ya giriş için Dünya İdareci Planı'ndan izin almaları gerekmektedir.

Gözlediğimiz, gözleyemediğimiz her gezegen, her uzaysal obje, spatyomuyla birlikte bir plansal yapının, bir plansal organizasyonun maddesel tabanıdır. Bu plansal yapı bir koni şeklindedir ve bir gezegenin fizik sahası o koninin tabanını teşkil eder. Dünya'nın ve her gezegenin üzerine enkarne vaziyette bir ruhsal organizasyon mevcuttur. Bu hiyerarşik organizasyonun tabanı biziz, tepe noktası da o gezegenin idarecisidir. Bu yapı o gezegenin Ruhsal İdareci Mekanizması'dır. Kâinat çapındaki, devasa bir mekanizmanın dünyaya ait bölümüdür.

Bu bakımdan bu varlıklar yukarıda da ifade ettiğimiz gibi çok daha yüksek titreşimli varlık sistemleriyle dünya insanlığı arasında bir köprü gibidirler. Bizden daha farklı bir boyutta olmalarına karşın titreşimsel olarak bize yakın olduklarından, ilahi sistemin dünyayla ilintili operasyonlarında bu varlıklar kullanılmakta, ruhsal sistemin daha üst kademelerinin bir uzantısı gibi hareket etmektedirler.

Farklı varlık sistemleri, bilim, teknoloji veya ileri şifa sistemleri gibi konularda hayli ileri bir noktadadırlar. Bu varlıklar, gelişmişlik seviyeleri ve uzmanlıklarına göre, daha alt sistemlerin tekâmülünde vazifelenirler. Bir başka şekilde ifade edersek, bu varlıklar Dünya beşeriyetinin ruhsal evrimine yardımcı olmak ve bu amaçla hazırlanan projeleri yürütmek için daha yüksek düzeyli ruhların denetim ve idaresi altında çalışmaktadırlar.

Evreni, bizim algı sınırlarımız içinde bulunan tek bir fiziksel katmandan ibaret olarak düşünürsek, Dünya dışı varlıklar meselesinin altından kalkamayız. Temas vakalarında

gördüğümüz karakteristikler bize, bu varlıkların farklı bir vibrasyonel sahadan geldiklerini ve bildiğimiz doğa yasalarının, fizik yasalarının üzerinde birtakım yasaları da kullandıklarını göstermektedir.

Eterik gezegenler vardır, ayrıca halen gaz halinde bulunan ve katılaşma sürecinde olan gezegenler vardır. Bunların ilk oluşumu, ilk kaynağı astral âlemdir. Dünyamıza gelen bir kısım varlıklar, duyularımızla ve cihazlarımızla algılayamadığınız eterik gezegenlerden gelmektedirler.

Bu "eterik" kavramını, bizim maddesel vibrasyonumuzun hemen üzerindeki bir varoluş katmanı olarak düşünebiliriz.

Bu varlıklar Dünya'da fizik bedenle tezahür edebilirler. Güneş Sistemi'mizin herhangi bir gezegeninden gelebilirler. Bir gezegenden başka bir gezegene kolayca geçebilirler. Bir varlık bizim Güneş Sistemi'mizdeki bir gezegenden geldiğinden söz ediyorsa, biliniz ki kastettiği şey o gezegenin fizik sahası değildir. Her gezegenin bir spatyomu ve eterik sahaları vardır. Bu sahalardaki varlıklar o gezegenin hiyerarşik şekilde sıralanmış idarecileridir. Gezegenler, astral/eterik ikizlerinde yerleşik varlık sistemlerinin kontrolü altındadır. Bunlar ruhsal vazife gruplarıdır.

Planlar, boyutlar, spatyom vb. kavramları sabit birer sınırı olan mekânlar olarak düşünmek yanlış olur. Bunlar vibrasyonel sahalardır ama hepsinden ötede, aslında birer şuur halidir.

Tüm planlar (vibrasyonel katmanlar) gerçekte birdir. Sadece "fiziksel", "eterik" ve "astral" yoluyla giderek yükselen, sürekli artan bir titreşim frekansı vardır. Varlıklar, şuur sahalarının, enerji bedenlerinin titreşimsel durumuna göre, "Uyum Yasası" uyarınca, kendi durumlarına uygun ölçekteki vibrasyonel sahalara çekilirler. Bu katmanların nerede başlayıp nerede bittiğini söyleyebilmek mümkün değildir.

Bir örnek verelim:

Örneğin bir varlık Venüs'ten gelmiş olduğunu söylediğinde aslında bu genel bir adrestir. Astronomik açıdan çok anlamlı değildir. Bir varlık Venüs'ten geliyorum dediğinde, bizim fizik algılarımız içine giren, oraya gönderdiğimiz uzay araçları ile araştırılabilen, tespit edilebilen, Venüs'ün fizik sahasında yaşadığı anlamına gelmez. Bir varlık sistemi, kendi enerji bedenleri o gezegenin spatyomuyla adaptasyon sağladığı takdirde, bir gezegenin eterik sahasına yerleşebilir. Bu bizler için ancak genel bir adres anlamını taşır. Bu, ben Doğu Anadolu'dan geliyorum demek gibi bir durumdur. Genel bir adrestir. Net lokasyonu anlamak imkânımız yoktur. Biz Venüs'ün spatyomunun yerini tarif edebilir miyiz? Dünya'nın spatyomunu da fizik koordinatlarla tarif edemeyiz. Bu şekilde düşünmek doğru olacaktır.

Tüm planlardaki varlıklar, bir zamanlar muhtemelen şu veya bu gezegenin fiziksel katmanında enkarne olmuşlardır. Ya çok uzak bir geçmişte ya da nispeten daha yakın geçmişte muhakkak bu fiziksel katılığı, yoğunluğu deneyimlemiş ve enerji bedenlerini geliştirerek, akışkanlaştırarak, daha süptil gezegen sistemlerinde enkarne olma niteliğini kazanmışlardır. Bu nedenle, katı teknik anlamda, belki bir bölümünün Dünya'da, bir bölümünün de Dünya benzeri, Dünya kategorisindeki gezegenlerde tekâmül etmiş olduklarını düşünebiliriz.

Bizim evrenimizin tekâmül yasalarına, katı fiziksellikten akışkanlığa doğru giden yükseliş skalasına baktığımızda bunu öne sürebiliriz. Titreşim ölçeğinde ne kadar yükselirse, onları dünyevi veya fiziksel unsurlara bağlayan ip o kadar incelir. Sonunda, fiziksel olanla tüm bağlantılarının koptuğu bir noktaya ulaşırlar. Artık şuurları ve titreşim seviyeleri tamamen farklı bir durumda, farklı bir çizgidedir ve bizimki gibi bir fizik bedene dönmek

ancak bir vazifenin yerine getirilmesi maksadıyla olabilir. Varlık isterse, özel bir amaçla, özel bir hedefle bizim fizik katmanımıza geri dönmemesi için bir sebep yoktur. Yardımlaşma ve Dayanışma Yasası'nın tatbikatını yapmak için buralara gelebilir. Ruh varlığı gözü pektir, gözü karadır.

Dünya insanının muhatap olduğu, karşı karşıya bulunduğu varlık sistemlerinin vazife ve nitelikleri bakımından, temel olarak şu ilkeleri sıralayabiliriz:

- Kâinatta çeşitli titreşim hızlarına sahip sonsuz vibrasyonel sahalar, sonsuz maddi mekânlar ve o mekânlara gerek enerji bedenleriyle gerekse biyolojik bedenleriyle uyum sağlamış varlıklar vardır. Bunların hepsi, bir hiyerarşik yapı içerisinde bir bütün oluştururlar. Dünya dışı olarak isimlendirilen varlık sistemleri bunlardır.
- Zamanın kronolojik akışı bizim boyutumuza ait bir durumdur. Zaman, hakkında çok az şey bildiğimiz bir tür enerjidir. Zaman enerjisinin farklı yoğunluk ve hızları vardır. Zaman enerjisi kâinata homojen şekilde dağılmamıştır. Zaman enerjisini kontrol edebilen varlıklar mevcuttur. Farklı varlık sistemleri zaman enerjisinin farklı yoğunluklarda işlev gördüğü tekâmül sahalarında yer almaktadırlar. Varlık sistemleri arasındaki zaman algısı bu bakımdan geniş bir skala içinde değişiklikler göstermektedir.
- Bu varlık sistemlerinin birçoğu bizlere göre oldukça akışkan (süptil) ortamlar içindedirler.
- Tekâmül hiyerarşisinde birçok bakımdan bizlerden daha ileri varlık sistemleri söz konusudur.
- Uygarlıklarını büyük ölçüde ruhsal esaslar üzerine kurmuş varlık sistemleri mevcut olduğu gibi, negatif

tesirleri çeşitli düzeylerde kullanan varlık sistemleri de bulunmaktadır.

- İleri bir evrim düzeyine ulaşmış varlıklar adeta fizik bedende ruhsal bir yaşam sürdürmektedirler. Bu Dünya insanlığı için de varılması gereken bir hedeftir.
- Bazı Dünya dışı varlık sistemleri, yeni oluşan gezegenlere, o gezegenin idareci sistemi tarafından enkarne edilen varlıkların eğitimlerinde gözetmen pozisyonu ve vazifesi üstlenirler. (Bu görevler, vazife planının içinde yer alan bir kademe sayılabilir.)
- Dünya dışı varlık sistemleri seviye, uzmanlık, liyakat ve bilgi düzeylerine uygun şekilde, evrensel idareci mekanizmanın fizik ortamlarındaki eli ayağı olarak bazı uygulamaları fiilen gerçekleştirirler.
- Çok yüksek tekâmül seviyesindeki Dünya dışı varlık sistemleri, fizik boyuttaki gezegen, güneş sistemi ve galaksilerin ruhsal idarelerini üstlenen yüksek ruhsal planlarla işbirliği halinde birçok genetik, teknolojik, şuursal gelişim operasyonlarını gerçekleştirirler.
- Şimdi bizlere öğretmenlik yapan varlıkların en azından bir bölümü daha önceki Mu ve Atlantis devresinde Dünya Tekâmül Okulu'nu tamamlamış, mezun olmuş ve buradan daha ileri seviyedeki gezegenlerde bedenlenme liyakati kazanmış varlıklardır. Yani bu varlıkların bir bölümünün Dünya ile çok öncelere dayanan bir yakınlık, bir sempatizasyon durumu vardır.
- Bazı varlık sistemleri ise Dünya'da beşer bedeninin meydana getirilmesi ve sonrasında sürekli genetik müdahaleler ve aşılamalar yapılması operasyonunda vazifelendikleri için, bu aksiyonlarının takibini yapmak durumunda olanlardır. Bu bir çeşit karmik sorumluluktur.

Bunu kabaca, bir bahçedeki ekosistemi, biyolojik yaşamı meydana getiren bir bahçıvanın bahçesine ara ara gelip, bitkilerin gelişimini kontrol etmesi gibi düşünmek uygun olacaktır.

Belirli kozmik yasalar kapsamındaki yükümlülüklerinin yanı sıra, bazıları genetik prodüksiyon sürecini yürüttükleri için Âdem ırklarına karşı özellikle sorumludurlar. Bu vazifeli varlık sistemleri, buradaki tekâmülün hız kazanabilmesi için seçici üreme ve melezleme yoluyla mümkün olduğu ölçüde buraya adapte olmuş bir fiziksel beden geliştirmişlerdir. Bu süreç içinde yapılan bazı hatalar da bu varlıklara karmik bir borç yüklemektedir.

Dünya dışı varlıklardan bazıları "gönüllü olarak" insan bedeninin fiziksel ve zihinsel gelişimine yardımcı olmak için enkarne olurlar. İşte "düşmüş melekler" bunlardır. Fiziksel bedene enkarne olanların sayısı, toplamla karşılaştırıldığında çok azdır ve bu tür enkarnasyonlar için herhangi bir kişisel tercihten ziyade bir zorunluluk duygusuyla gönüllü olurlar. Bundaki amaç, ilk başta gezegenimizin yeni oluşan Âdem ırklarının gelişim ve adaptasyonuna yardım etmek olmuştur. Şu an içinde bulunduğumuz devre sonu döneminde ise bu süreci kolaylaştırma, uykuda olanları uyandırma ve uyanmış olanları negatif etkilerden koruma amacı gütmektedirler.

Dünya'nın bir laboratuvar ya da deney yeri olmasının anlamı nedir? Bizler kobay mıyız?

Yukarıda, tekâmül hiyerarşisinde birçok bakımdan bizlerden daha ileri varlık sistemlerinin mevcut olduğundan söz etmiştik. Bu varlık sistemleri en kabadan en akışkana doğru giden bir boyutsal dizi halinde sıralanmaktadır.

Çok gelişkin bir maddesel boyut olmasa da, kaba maddesel fizik âlemin en alt basamağında da bulunmayan, daha çok süptil âlemlerin hemen sınırında konumlandırabileceğimiz gezegenimiz bu niteliğiyle bir temel gelişim tekâmül okulu kimliğindedir.

Bu orta-alt seviye kimlik, gerek Dünya'ya gerekse bu boyuttaki Dünya benzeri tekâmül okullarına, üst âlemlerdeki idareci varlıkların ve onların uzantıları olan varlık sistemlerinin bazı deneysel çalışmaları için bir laboratuvar teşkil etme vazifesi yüklemektedir. Bu "kobay" olmak anlamına gelmemektedir. Bu durum Dünya'nın tekâmül seviyesine uygun bir görev olup, Dünya ve benzeri gezegenler evrende varoluşun devamına bu şekilde katkıda bulunmaktadırlar. Evrende yaşam bu çalışmalar sayesinde gelişmekte, yayılmakta ve ara ara ıslah edilmektedir.

Bugün bu çalışmalara bu tarzda katkı veren Dünya insanlığı, ileride daha yüksek varoluş sahalarına geçtiğinde bu deneylerin sonuçlarından faydalanacağı gibi, bu kez "deneyci" sıfatıyla bizzat çalışmalara katılacaktır.

Dünya dışı genetik çalışmaların amaç ve hedefi nedir?

Bizim de bulunduğumuz fizik evrende farklı tekâmül okulları meydana getirilmesi, buralarda yaşamın tohumlanması, yeni beden tiplerinin birbirleriyle karıştırılarak, yeni oluşturulan gezegen biyosferlerine uygun bedenler üretilmesi temel hedeftir.

Çok uzun zamandır farklı galaksilerde, farklı sistemlerin farklı gezegenlerinde, bu varlık grupları tarafından, oraların koşullarına uygun "Âdem ve Havva"lar tohumlanmaktadır.

Bu işler ruhsal idareci sistemin işlerinin fizik planda yürütülmesi operasyonlarıdır.

İnsanlık bu gezegeni bir şekilde yaşanmaz hale getirirse bu İlahi Tekâmül Planı'nın uygulanması bakımından bir aksaklığa yol açmaz çünkü Dünya'daki gibi yaşam olanakları birçok kürede tohumlanmış ve bu çalışmalarla yedeklenmiştir.

Neden buradan genetik örnekler topluyorlar?

İnsan türünün optimal versiyonunu oluşturmak için, ruhsal sistemin eli ayağı olan gelişmiş varlık grupları tarafından genetik çalışmalar yürütülmektedir.

Dünya bir genetik laboratuvardır. Sadece Dünya beşeri değil, evrendeki tüm varlık türleri, ilahi sistemin izniyle yürütülen genetik mühendislik çalışmalarının ürünüdür. Her varlıkta evrensel DNA'lar vardır. Dünya'daki tüm hayvan türlerinin evrende gelişmiş karşılıkları vardır.

Evrende genetik mühendislik çok yaygın durumda olduğundan hiçbir tür birbirine tüm detaylarıyla benzemez. Yeni bir gezegen kolonize edilmek istenirse, o gezegenin biyosferi içinde hayatta kalabilecek, oraya uyum için ön çalışmaları yapılmış bir tür meydana getirilir. İhtiyaç duyulan genetik materyal de Dünya'dan ve Dünya gibi birçok gezegenden toplanır.

Her varlık sisteminin kendi türünü geliştirmek, ıslah etmek için evrenin her yerinden genetik materyal toplama hakkı vardır. Bu bir varoluş hakkıdır. Hiçbir türün yok olması arzu edilmez. Ancak bu genetik materyal toplama sürecinde, kendilerinden gen örnekleri alınan kişilerin bireysel hakları ihlal ediliyorsa, daha yukarıdaki varlık sistemleri derhal müdahale ederler.

(13. Bölüm) S. Kosovalı: "Sizi deneye tabi tutanlar var... Kendi soylarını kontrole gelenler var... Burada çoğalmak isteyenler var... Kendi türlerini melezleştirmek isteyenler var... Onları bir süre izliyoruz."

"Onlara izin veriliyor mu?"

S. Kosovalı: "Bir süre... Ne yapmak istediklerini çözdüğümüzde müdahale başlıyor."

"Yani olumsuz bir niyete müsaade edilmiyor."

S. Kosovalı: "Asla... Ancak hiçbir türün gelişimi durdurulamaz."

"Onun için izin veriliyor ama bunu kötüye kullananlar olursa müdahale ediliyor. Böyle mi anlamalıyız?"

S. Kosovalı: "Kesinlikle... Hiçbir tür asla yok edilemez."

Dünya'nın tekâmül planı gereğince, burada birçok ırkın genetiğinin karıştırılması deneyi de yapılmaktadır. Bunların birlik haline bakılmakta, pozitif ve negatif eğilimli ırkların hangi ölçüye kadar birlik oluşturabileceği de test edilmektedir. Bizler yüksek ırkların daha aşağı boyuttaki karşılıklarıyız.

Temasların temel amacı nedir?

• Evren bütünüyle bir tesirler sistemidir ve Dünya beşeriyeti de ruhsal idareci sistemlerin tesirlerine sürekli şekilde muhatap olmaktadır. Ancak insanlar yüksek nefsaniyet, maddesel değerlere bağımlılık derecesinde aşırı odaklanma gibi sebeplerle bu yüksek tesirleri istenen şekilde alamamaktadır. Beşer varlığı Dünya ötesi tesirlere kapalı hale gelmiştir.

Bu durumda ruhsal sistem bize doğrudan etki edebilecek, doğrudan ulaşabilecek birtakım varlık sistemlerini devreye sokmaktadır.

Şuna benzetebiliriz:

Ruhsal sistem, rehberlik sistemi bize adeta telsiz sinyaliyle mesaj gönderiyor. Ancak cihazlarımız yetersiz olduğu için bu sinyalleri alamıyoruz. Durum böyle olunca sistem, aracı varlık

sistemlerini vasıta kılıyor ve mesajı elden getiriyorlar. Postacı gelip kapıya vuruyor.

- Daha ileri ve yüksek realitelerin bilgileri daima ruhsal idareci mekanizma tarafından verilir. Yani insanlık bilgiyi alabilecek hale geldikten sonra bilgi bir üst plandan verilir. Dolayısıyla bilgi bir üst kaynaktan verilmedikçe elde edilemez. İşte Dünya dışı varlıkların bu noktadaki fonksiyonu, insanlığın daha üst bir bilgiyi ruhsal sistemden alabilmesi için zemin yaratmaktır. İnsanlarda bir yeni bilgi arayışını, isteğini tetiklemektir. Daha üst bir realitenin, daha üst bir tekâmül seviyesinin tesirlerini alabilme arzusu meydana getirmektir. Yüksek varoluş sahalarına, daha ileri tekâmül realitelerine dikkat çekmektir. Temasların en temel işlevlerinden bir tanesi budur.

- Bu varlıkların bu kadar sık görünmeleri, Dünya çapında bu kadar çok kişiyle etkileşim içine girmeleri de bu yeni realite tesirlerine dahildir. Yani insanları "eski realitelerinde rahatsız etmek" fonksiyonunu yerine getirmektedirler. Zira insanlık mevcut realitesinde rahatsız olmadan yeni ve daha ileri bir realitenin arayışı içine girmemektedir. Eski realiteler mutlak surette dejenere olmak zorundadır.

Şimdiye kadar bilginin alınışı yeryüzündeki varlıkların isteğinin karşılığı olmak üzere, ruhsal mekanizmanın yardım ve rehberliği altında, dinler, inisiyatik öğretiler ve doğrudan ruhsal tebliğler tarzında gerçekleşmiştir. Yukarısı, rehberliğini, aşağının gidişine göre yapmıştır. Dünya dışı varlık sistemlerinin faaliyetlerinde artış varsa bunun sebebi yine insanlığın kolektif şuurunun talebidir.

- Temasların bir diğer önemli işlevi de, temasçıda "ben" tanımını değiştirmesidir. Kişiyi daha geniş bir "ben" tanımına ve dolayısıyla bütünselliğe yaklaştırır. "Ben" tanımını evrendeki tüm bilinçli yaşama genişlettiğiniz zaman davranışlarınız da değişmeye başlar. Birine zarar vermek kendi kolunuzu kesmekle eşdeğer hale gelir. Temasın dönüştürücü etkisini yakalayabilen, bunu bilincine bir artı değer olarak katabilen kişi için artık "varlıklar" yoktur, "varlık" vardır.

- Temasların ciddi bir bölümü, bu varlıkların kendi sistemlerinden Dünya'ya biyolojik doğum, yani bedenlenme yoluyla gelmiş olan türdeşlerini kontrol etme ve Dünya maceralarında onları destekleme çabalarından kaynaklanmaktadır.

Tekâmüle doğrudan müdahale etmeme yasası gereği birçok Dünya dışı varlık Dünya'ya, en doğrudan yöntem olan enkarnasyon yoluyla gelmektedir. Bir bilgiye göre bu oran yüzde 10 ile yüzde 20 arasındadır.

Temaslarda alınanların çoğunluğunu bu bireyler oluşturmaktadır. İyileştirilen, yeni Dünya dışı kökenli enkarnasyonlar olabilmesi için hamile bırakılıp bebekleri alınan, eğitime sokulan, implant takılan, düzenli kontrol edilen temasçıların büyük bir bölümünü bu kitle meydana getirmektedir.

Son olarak şunu ifade etmek gerekir ki, temasçıların hemen hepsi Dünya dışı varlıklarla birtakım projeler içinde görev almaktadırlar. Temasların temel amaçlarından bir tanesi de bu projelerin devam ettirilmesidir.

2. Bölüm'de, Gül seansında şöyle ifadeler geçiyor:

"Peki iyileştirdikleri insanlar, temasçılar bu projelerin içinde olanlar mı?"

Gül: "Bir kısmı evet, bir kısmı hayır."

"Diğerlerini neden iyileştiriyorlar?"

Gül: "Onlar farklı projelerdeler."

"Hepsi görevli mi?"

Gül: "Evet... Bir de yaptıkları deneyler var... Dünya'da bazı hastalıklara hızlı bir şekilde çözüm gelsin diye mecburen insan bedenine enjekte ettikleri sıvılar geliştiriyorlar... Bunları böyle insanlarda denemek zorundalar... Kendilerinde zaten öyle bir şeye ihtiyaçları yok... İnsanlar için yapılıyor bu."

Yine aynı bölümde, yürütülen çalışmalardan önemli bir örnek yer almaktadır:

"İnsan duygularının fiziksel bedene olumsuz yansımasının engellenmesi üzerine bir çalışma yürütülüyor. İnsanlar duyguları aracılığıyla kaslarını, hücrelerini, bölgesel alanlarını yorup kilitleyebiliyorlar ve o alanda bozulmalar meydana gelebiliyor. Bu böyle olmak zorunda değil. Duygular ile fiziki beden artık birbirinden ayrılabilir. Duyguları insan sadece his olarak yaşayabilir. Fizik bedenini duygu tesiri altında bırakmaktan kurtulabilir."

Yukarıdaki ifadede çok kritik bir bilgi vardır. Biliyoruz ki, henüz duygu realitesinde bulunan beşeriyet, kontrolsüz duyguların beden üzerinde yarattığı tahribatın sonuçlarını ciddi hastalıklar olarak deneyimlemektedir. Bu ifadelerden, varlıkların, duyguların fizik bedene hasar vermesini engelleyecek, duyguları biyolojik sistemden izole edecek bir şifa tekniği üzerinde çalıştıkları anlaşılmaktadır.

Aynı seansta yer alan aşağıdaki ifade de temasların ana hedeflerinden bir tanesine ışık tutmaktadır:

Gül: "Sağlık konularında ileride çözümler sunacaklar ama şu an bunların hepsi çok gizli bilgiler... O yüzden insanlara ihtiyaçları oluyor... Hazır olan insanlarla çalışıyorlar."

Temaslarda ruhsal kontrat olgusu mutlak bir koşul mudur?

Temasların çoğunluğunda, "gönüllülük" esasına dayalı, enkarnasyon öncesi anlaşmaların geçerli olduğunu söyleyebilmek mümkündür.

Bununla birlikte, yaşam süresi içinde temas için uygun bir şuursal seviyeye ulaşmış kişilerle de temas kurulabilmektedir.

Ancak, enkarnasyon öncesi ruhsal bir anlaşması olduğu halde Dünya yaşamında belirli bir bilinç düzeyine gelemeyenlerin temas programları iptal edilmektedir.

3. Bölüm'deki Gül seansında bunu destekleyen ifadelere rastlıyoruz:

"Sizin gibilerin bu varlıklarla doğmadan önce bir anlaşması oluyor mu? Bir anlaşmaya göre mi seçiyorlar? Yani izin verenleri mi alıyorlar?"

Gül: "İki konu var... Birincisi izin verenler, ikincisi Dünya'da belli bir seviyeye geldikten sonra bir anlaşma olabiliyor."

"Temasçının kendisi Dünya'da ama yine de ruhsal boyutta mı yapıyor anlaşmayı?"

Gül: "Evet ruhsal boyutta yapıyor. Fakat doğmadan önce anlaşmayı yapıp Dünya yaşamında o noktaya gelememiş çok insan var diyorlar."

Temasların büyük kısmı enkarnasyon öncesinde planlanmış durumdadır. Varlıklar bu bakımdan bizlerin kullandığı "temas" ifadesi yerine "randevu" ifadesini kullanıyorlar.

Şunu da belirtmek gerekir ki, bazı insanlara, istisnai de olsa, enkarnasyon öncesi ya da sonrası herhangi bir onayı olmaksızın müdahale edilmektedir. Böyle bir müdahale, ani gelişen ve kişinin yaşamını olması gereken süreden önce bitirebilecek bir hastalık durumunda yapılabilmektedir.

(3. Bölüm) "Özgür iradeye aykırı alınmalar oluyor mu?"

Hakan: "Bazen mecbur kalıyoruz... Hakan'ı da öyle aldık... Onu bağlamak zorunda kaldık... Yoksa kendisine zarar verecekti... Hatırlamaması gerekiyordu ama birden uyandı."

Bu durumu şu örnek çerçevesinde düşünmek doğru olacaktır:

Trafik kazası geçirmiş ve ağır yaralı şekilde yerde baygın yatan bir kazazede var. Bu kazazede için ambulans çağırmak üzere ondan izin almayı beklemek gerekir mi?

Yanıt elbette "hayır" olacaktır.

Kına benzeri izlerin sebebi nedir?

Çok tartışılan ve çok sorulan kına benzeri izler meselesine ilişkin olarak seanslarda değerli veriler elde ettik.

Öncelikle şunu ifade edelim:

Dünya dışı bir aracın içindeki titreşim ortamı ile Dünya boyutundaki titreşim ortamı arasında hatırı sayılır bir fark vardır. Boyutları rakamsal sıralamalar ile betimlemeyi çok doğru bulmasak da, anlaşılabilmesi bakımından, Dünya 3. boyut ise, Dünya dışı bir aracın iç titreşiminin 5. boyuta karşılık geldiğini söyleyebiliriz.

13. Bölüm'deki S. Kosovalı seansında geçen ifade önemlidir:

"Geminin içinde titreşimsel olarak daha hızlı bir boyut mu var?"

S. Kosovalı: "Evet... Çok hızlı."

"İnsanlar orada nasıl bulunabiliyorlar?"

S. Kosovalı: "Fizik beden alınırsa koruyucu bir alan içinde tutuyoruz."

Buna bağlı olarak:

1. Araç içindeki cihazların da aynı titreşimsel düzeyde olduğunu düşünebiliriz. Dolayısıyla bu cihazlarla yapılan bir temas frekans düzeyinde bir yanma meydana getirmektedir. Bu, Dünya'daki gibi ısı kaynaklı bir yanma değildir.
2. Ellerimiz ve ayaklarımız başlıca enerji giriş ve çıkış noktalarıdır. Varlıklar çeşitli sebeplerle enerji aktarımları yaparlarken, yine frekans yüksekliği sebebiyle aynı izler oluşmaktadır.

(4. Bölüm) Ezgi: "Onlar insanların vücuduna el ve ayaklardan enerji verdikleri için, onların enerjisinin temasçının enerjisiyle uyumlanması sırasında iz meydana geliyormuş... Uyumlanırken oluşan yoğun enerjiden kaynaklanıyormuş... Onların bedeninden akış temasçının bedenine geçerken oluyor... Bu işlem cihazla da yapılıyor."

"Eller ve ayaklardan mı yapılıyor hep?"

Ezgi: "Eller ve ayaklar çok önemliymiş... Enerjinin insan vücudunda en kolay geçtiği yerler eller ve ayaklar... O yüzden."

(12. Bölüm) Sibel Ş.: "Avuç içi ve ayak altındaki bazı kanallar açık olduğu için oradan çabuk aktarım yapılıyormuş."

(14. Bölüm) "Nasıl oluşuyor o leke?"

Emine B.: "Elim yanıyor... Alet gibi bir şeylere dokunduğum için... Bir şeyden kurtulmaya çalışıyormuşum gibi."

"Nasıl bir alet bu?"

Emine B.: "Bir şey enjekte ediyorlar... Onu çıkarmaya çalışıyormuşum gibi... Sanki derinin altına, damar yoluna bir şey enjekte ediyorlar... Kelebek gibi... Ben de onu tutup çıkarmaya çalışıyormuşum... Sıcak değil... Sıcak değil ama vücudumla uyumlu değil... Dokunduğumda yakıyor... Deriyi yakıyor ama ısısı yok... İki üç gün kalıyor o iz sadece."

Ülkemizde ve dünyada mevcut durum nedir?

Ülkedeki genel duruma ve insan manzarasına baktığımızda, artan bir cehalet, artan bir bağnazlık, artan bir dejenerasyon ama hepsinden önemlisi, ne yazık ki, giderek artan ve neredeyse patolojik bir hale gelmeye başlayan bir umutsuzluk görüyoruz...

Ancak şu anki durum Türkiye'nin ne gerçek potansiyelini ne de bu toprakların gelecekteki durumunu yansıtmaktadır. Şu an gözlemlediklerimiz yanıltıcıdır. Arka planda işler bambaşka bir yöne doğru ilerlemektedir.

Önce şunu ifade edelim:

Ruhsal sistem tüm dünyada yozlaşmayı bizzat körüklemektedir.

Bugün insanlık ağır bir boşluk, kaybolmuşluk, yön bulamama hali içinde kıvranmaktadır. Ağır ekonomik krizlerle, savaşlarla, bilginin yozlaşmasıyla vs. bu boşluk hali giderek arttırılmakta ve şiddetlendirilmektedir. Bu, ruhsal sistem tarafından özellikle yapılmaktadır. Çünkü değişim için eskinin dejenere olması ve halkın bu dejenerasyonu gözlemlemesi gerekmektedir.

Bu boşluk halinin ana sebebi yeni bir realiteye uyum, eskiyi bırakma sürecidir. Eski realitesindeki dengeyi kaybetmektir. Dengeyi daha yüksek bir realitede bulmamız gerekmekte, bu bakımdan mevcut realitemizden, mevcut halimizden bıkmamız, yeniyi talep etmemiz istenmektedir. Zira insanlık başka türlü konfor alanından çıkamayacaktır.

İçinde bulunduğumuz kozmik devrenin kapanışına hızla yaklaşıyoruz. Devrenin kapanışından sorumlu ruhsal mekanizma, varlıklara, olumsuz yönlerinin, egolarının yüzeye çıkması için büyük baskı yapmaktadır. Ayıklanma için nefsaniyeti de

yukarısı körüklemektedir. Yani çevremizdeki aşırı nefsani davranışlar bu ağır baskının sonucudur.

Basınç arttıkça bazılarında egolar daha çok kabarmaktadır çünkü ağır basınca ruhsal olgunluk bakımından hazır olmayan bireyler buna ancak yüksek bir ego zırhıyla karşı koyabilmektedirler. Enerjiler ağır gelince bireyler nefsaniyet zırhıyla kendilerini korumaya almaktadırlar. Enerjinin şiddetine dayanamayan fertler ve halklar ağır sarsıntılar içindedir. Bunun daha da artacağı kesindir. Olumlu olumsuzdan ayrılmaktadır. İşte şu an böyle bir süreç yaşanmaktadır.

Yozlaşmadan sıyrılabilmeleri ve yüksek pozitif değerlere yönelebilmeleri için insanlığın önüne her imkân konmaktadır. İnsanlığın odağını aşağıdan yukarıya çevirebilmesini sağlamak üzere içsel ve dışsal sarsıntılar, şok tarzındaki olaylar artırılmaktadır. Bu da aynı yüksek tesirin kitlesel tekâmülü hızlandırma sürecinden kaynaklanmaktadır.

Ülke olarak yaşamakta olduğumuz şey de budur.

Ülkemizdeki dejenerasyonun, düzensizliğin, karmaşa halinin artışı "yeni" olanın gelişinin ön hazırlığıdır. Her değer, her kurum, her kavram süratle yozlaşmakta ve halkın gözünde değer kaybetmektedir. Beklentimiz ve bilgimiz odur ki, bu süreç, değerlerin, kurumların ve kavramların çok daha yüksek bir anlayış çerçevesinde, bütünüyle yenilenmesiyle sonuçlanacaktır.

Anadolu, Dünya'yı devre sonuna taşıyacak bilgi yükünü sırtlanacak ve hedefe mutlaka ulaştıracaktır.

Ne kaygıya ne de korkuya yer vardır.

Bu iş halledilecektir.

Birlikle...

Beraberlikle...

"Bir ulus, sımsıkı birbirine bağlı olmayı bildikçe yeryüzünde onu dağıtabilecek bir güç düşünülemez."

– Gazi Mustafa Kemal Atatürk

ERHAN KOLBAŞI
GALAKTİK
DİPLOMASİ

ERHAN KOLBAŞI
KOZMİK
DOKUNUŞ
In Vitro
ALIKONMA OLAYLARININ ARDINDAKİ GÖRKEMLİ
KOZMİK OPERASYON ve TÜRKİYE ALIKONMA
VAKALARI

ERHAN KOLBAŞI
77
YETMİŞ
YEDİ
RUHUN ve
VAROLUŞUN
BÜYÜK YASALARI